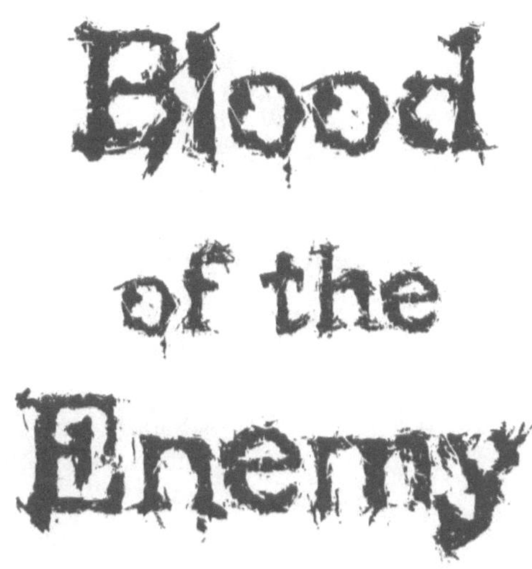

CHRONICLES OF AVILÉSOR
- WAR OF THE REALMS -
BOOK III

Cover font: Black Asylum by Kevin Christopher // KC Fonts
Used by Permission.

Cover design and print layout by Sara A. Noë
E-book layout by Polgarus Studio

Dedicated to my grandparents,
Rosalie & Gordon

Thank you for your everlasting love and support.

AVILÉSOR

Sara A. N...
N.T.S.
KUZIN RIVER
RAZORBACK MOUNTAINS
KAVÓLT
LAKE MULZON
JEMET RIVER
GLACIES ISLAND
QUOTAL
DRAEDE
THE GREAT EYE
SOLARIS
LUMEN
MT. BOREAS
JETHRO
XYLAS
MT. ACURE
SHOLL
TH
IZAN
FORMENDEST
ARAS
SYLVER
SEA
OAST
FELKATOR
AVAKREE
KUZIN RIVER
VEL
SZION
ZYLSIN RIVER
NAGEM
CATALINE
FOREST
CLEPSYDRA ISLE
ADELEF
RONASIN
ELYSIAN.
VESTIGE
TYME
RIVER
LAKE SOROR
ZORIAN
GOSTIN
MOTÓLITH
STYXX
SELKIE
ISLE
LAKE CASIDE
DELKOA
UNDERLIN
MT. VERN
ONYM
WILOWAY
RUBY LAKE
EVERMIS
ARSTENYA FOREST
HELVAS
BLOOD RIVER
SICLE RIVER

THE GHOST REALM

ELEMENTAL GUILDS

 AIR

 DARKNESS

 EARTH

 FIRE

 ICE

 LIGHT

 LIGHTNING

 METAL

 SAND

 STONE

 VAPOR

 VEGETATION

 WATER

 WEATHER

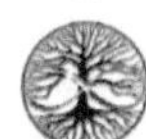 WOOD

PHANTOM HEIGHTS

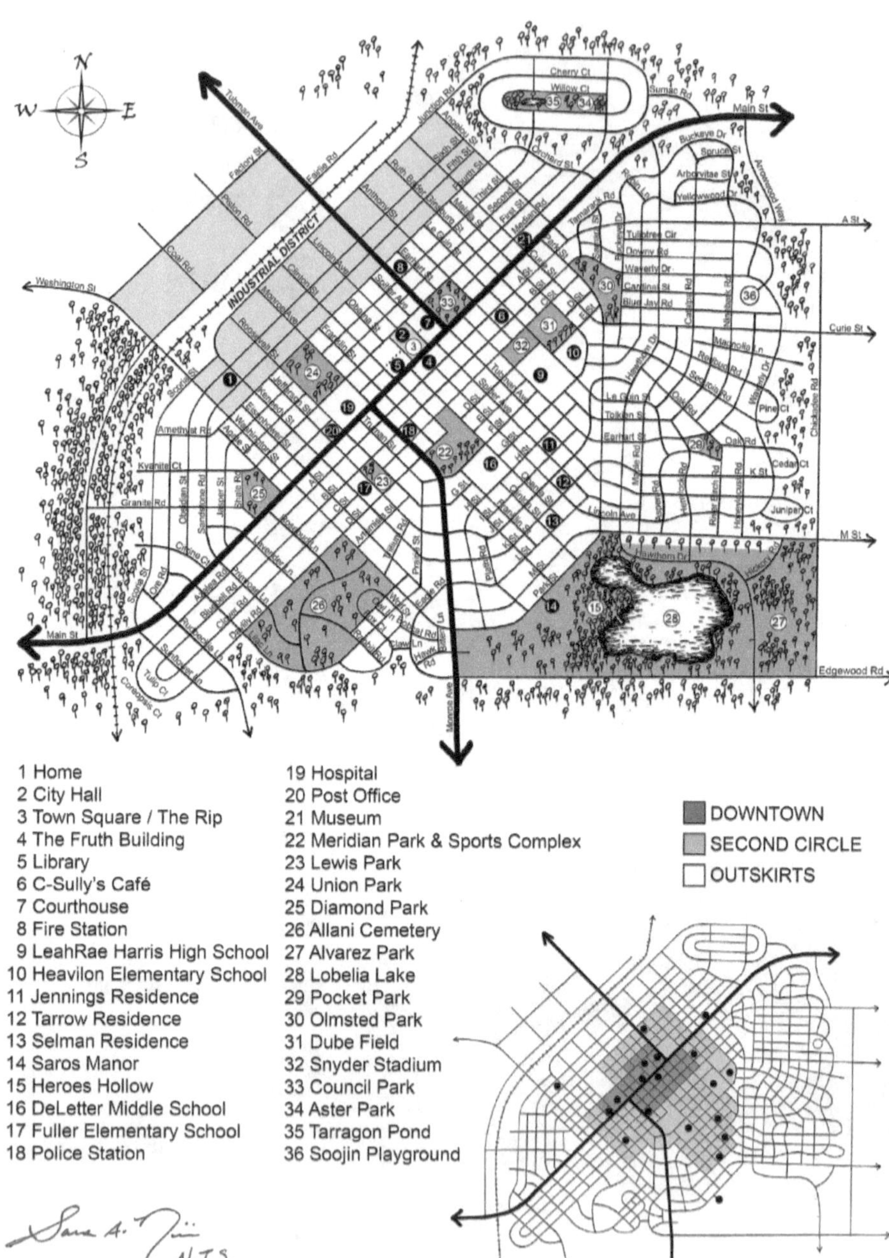

1 Home
2 City Hall
3 Town Square / The Rip
4 The Fruth Building
5 Library
6 C-Sully's Café
7 Courthouse
8 Fire Station
9 LeahRae Harris High School
10 Heavilon Elementary School
11 Jennings Residence
12 Tarrow Residence
13 Selman Residence
14 Saros Manor
15 Heroes Hollow
16 DeLetter Middle School
17 Fuller Elementary School
18 Police Station
19 Hospital
20 Post Office
21 Museum
22 Meridian Park & Sports Complex
23 Lewis Park
24 Union Park
25 Diamond Park
26 Allani Cemetery
27 Alvarez Park
28 Lobelia Lake
29 Pocket Park
30 Olmsted Park
31 Dube Field
32 Snyder Stadium
33 Council Park
34 Aster Park
35 Tarragon Pond
36 Soojin Playground

DOWNTOWN
SECOND CIRCLE
OUTSKIRTS

SAROS MANOR

SECOND FLOOR
THIRD FLOOR
GROUND LEVEL

Spiral Staircase
Walkway
Bath room
Laundry
Closet
Gallery
Gym
Ground Floor
Game Room
Balcony
Guest Bedroom
Guest Bedroom
Closet
Closet
Guest Bathroom
Closet
Guest Bedroom
Stairs to Third Floor
Stairs to First Floor
Closet
Study

Balcony
Living Room
Bathroom
Stairs to Second Floor
Sleeping Quarters
Closet

Lawn
Seating Wall
Firepit
Patio
Pool House
Wooden Arbor over Bluestone Path
Sunroom
Closet
Guest Bedroom
Pool
Hot Tub
Herb Garden
Porch
Great Room
Guest Bath
Privacy Hedge
Spiral Staircase
Fireplace
Master Bath
Fountain
Lawn
Kitchen
Library
Den
Bar
Flower Garden
Pantry
Staircase
Closet
Bathroom
Master Bedroom
Patio
Privacy Fence
Mud Room
Dining Room
Foyer
Parlor
Closet
3-Car Garage
Porch

Driveway
Lawn
Lawn
Front Walk (Allée)
N.T.S.
2   1   3

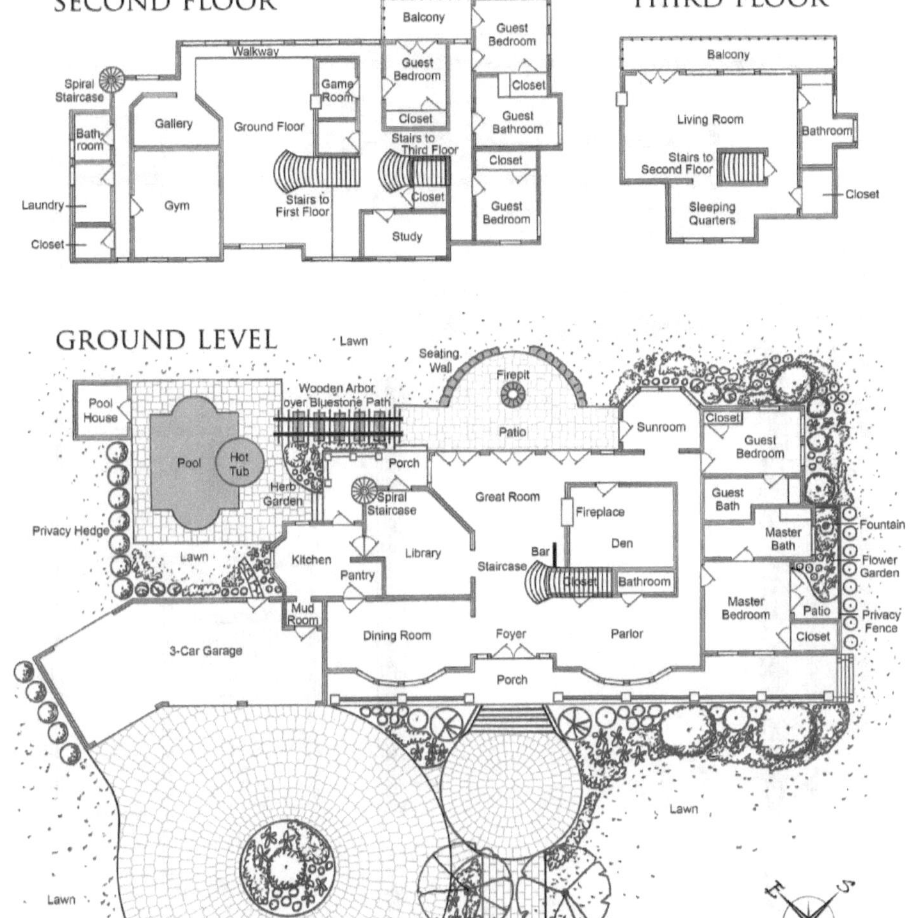

PROJECT ALPHA

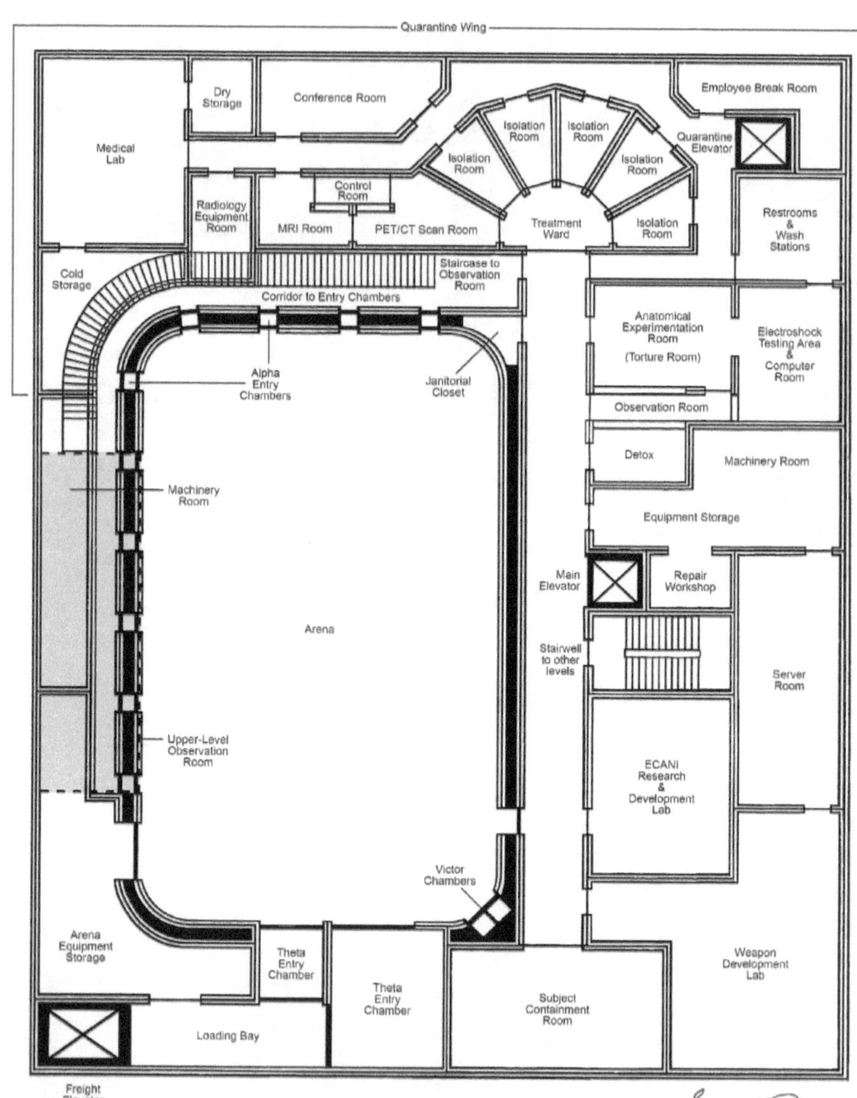

AIR
EARTH
WOOD
FIRE
WATER

*Purest of demons,
child of beast,
harbinger of light,
blinded who sees,
blood of the enemy,
son without wings,
slaves who will rise
to one day be kings.*

*Seven to bring the Seventh,
but Eight are the key.
They must decide
what the fate of the Realms
shall be.*

Sara A. Noë

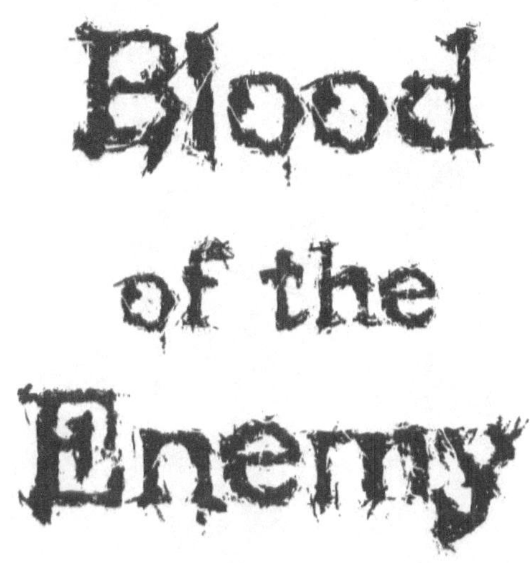

Blood of the Enemy

Chronicles of Avilésor
- War of the Realms -
Book III

— Prologue —

Voices.

That was how this nightmare began.

Voices whispering all around me.

Hundreds of eyes.

It's happening all over again.

I stood in a sea of blood and bones and bodies, surrounded by twisted, mangled faces staring up at me, their mouths still open in silent screams. Some died by the teeth of a werewolf, others by a quick, clean slice of blades from a silver disk, and some by my own hand with shards of glistening ice.

But most were slaughtered by Axel.

He didn't mean to do it. He couldn't help himself. All the dead were Shadow Guards, but honestly, that was lucky happenstance. Axel couldn't differentiate between allies and enemies when the bonds on his self-control snapped. He could have killed Ash while she lay unconscious at his feet—could have killed any of us. And it could happen again, except it might be humans in his path instead of ghosts. Axel was created to be a weapon of mass destruction, and he was, except he was a weapon that couldn't be controlled, couldn't even be pointed in the right direction. Anything with warm blood and a heartbeat became a target.

If the people of Phantom Heights knew that, they'd call for his immediate banishment or execution. Mine, too. Maybe I deserved to be executed. Downtown was in ruins because of me. If there was ever any question as to whether mixing bloodlines was a good idea, Axel and I were living proof that it wasn't.

But what happened minutes ago didn't matter, and neither did the pending consequences. All I cared about was right now. This moment frozen in time while I stood as still as my statue in the suspended snow, listening to the final echoes of a woman's voice calling my name.

A few seconds ago, if anyone had asked me my name, I would have chosen from what seemed to be a growing list. Seph, A7, 5292, maybe even Phantom. Or Cato.

Just Cato.

I stared at my mother cowering on the ground before me. Her face was bloody and bruised, but it was familiar. Beyond the constraints of the photograph's edge, I could see it in my memories—the first face in my vision after the Flash. And when my eyes locked with hers, a memory that had been lost resurfaced with startling clarity.

I was standing at the bottom of a dark stairwell. In front of me, a strange green light leaked around the edges of a door. It was surreal, mesmerizing—frightening, even—but curiosity overruled my caution. I reached out and set my open hand on the wood, which creaked under the weight of my palm.

The door swung open. The light grew brighter and brighter, like a green sun. I gasped and threw my arm over my eyes, stumbling back, blind. The light was all around me. It enveloped me until the staircase and door were gone, replaced by green light. The world didn't exist anymore. Just light. It penetrated my skin, my cells, until I was light, too.

And then it was gone. The blackness in its absence felt so abysmally empty, both hot and cold, and somehow neither. My entire body tingled and burned as if I were being electrocuted with a low voltage. I couldn't see, couldn't move.

"Cato? Cato! Can you hear me?"

Footsteps.

A girl's breathless voice: "Mom, what's going on? The whole house just shook and . . . Oh my gosh! What happened? Is Cato okay?"

"I don't know! I thought you were both in the kitchen. My sample was unstable, and it just . . . I turned around, and . . . he was lying on the floor . . ."

"Shouldn't we take him to the hospital?"

I tried to shift my body. Although the prickling sensation still had me in its throes, I was able to stir and moan. I wasn't paralyzed, but my muscles weren't working right.

"He's coming to," the softer of the two female voices whispered.

My eyes opened, but I couldn't focus. A hand turned my face up so my eyes could find a woman kneeling over me in concern. A teenage girl peered over her shoulder. They blurred out of focus and then sharpened to such crisp lines that my eyes hurt, as if I were looking through optometry lenses spinning to extremes.

"He's freezing," the woman said. "Cato? Can you speak?"

Vertigo. I opened my mouth and gagged as my abdominal muscles contracted. The woman hauled me into a sitting position and propped me up so when I retched, I was facing the floor and didn't choke. "He was exposed to a high level of unstable ectoplasm," she said. "He's having a negative reaction. I don't think taking him to the hospital will do much good. It's best to keep him here, where I have all of my equipment. Unless he gets worse . . ."

"Worse? Mom, he looks awful."

"I'll see if Doc will make a house call under the circumstances."

I was chilled and burning at the same time, shivering so violently that my teeth chattered. The woman dragged me across the concrete floor so I was out of the doorway and away from the vomit. "Get some blankets," she ordered. "And a pillow and bucket. We'll set him up on the cot down here for now."

My body still tingled, as if I were being stabbed with a million tiny needles over every inch of my skin. The girl was gone, and the woman left me all alone on the cold floor. I tried to call out for her, but the sound that croaked out of my throat was an incomprehensible sob.

"Shhh, I'm here," she said, reappearing in my vision. "You're okay. I've got you." She worked her arms underneath my deadweight body to reposition me, then clutched me tightly and rose with a strained groan, lifting me up and transferring me onto the cot.

I stared straight up, sick and terrified. Although I wasn't blind, I still couldn't see. The world was a blur of light and shadows and shapes I couldn't bring into focus.

The woman looked down on me, talking to me in a gentle voice, stroking my face, telling me I was going to be all right, that she was going to take care of me and not to be scared. I gazed up at her. Set in her kind face was a pair of intense emerald eyes—the only objects in focus.

Everything before that was a blur, everything after broken into fragments. I'd been hiding and lying and running ever since, and I was *so* tired.

But I did it.

I cracked the ghost hunter's armor wide open to reveal my mother inside. She was a surprisingly weak thing—a trembling, sniveling creature at my feet. Once again, her eyes were what I zeroed in on. Intense emerald, bright, the same hue as Before . . . but wearier. Older. There were wrinkles around the edges I didn't remember from Before. They were the same, and yet different. When she had looked at me then, it had been with love. She'd thought I was still human when she lifted me up off the cold concrete floor.

Now, she looked in horror upon the mutated half-breed she'd created.

I couldn't let go, and I couldn't run anymore. The names I took and forsook, the clothes I wore, the company I kept, the masks I hid behind . . . none of that could change who I was.

Because whether she would claim me or not, I was and would always be the half-ghost son of a ghost hunter.

— Chapter One —

Gathering Darkness

Rayven stirred on his perch, the dry rustle of his feathers the only sound in the otherwise-silent room. Neither Cisco nor Hassing dared to make a noise without Azar's permission, and Lieutenant Inalli was a silent figure beside her captain.

Azar surveyed his subordinates. Hassing's jet-black hair, usually tied neatly into a short ponytail, was windswept and unkempt, a twig still tangled in his locks. Cisco was in worse condition with his cloak torn and his uniform wrinkled, ripped, and stained with the blood of his comrades.

Inalli's fresh appearance was a stark contrast to the bedraggled captain and bloody Shadow Guard lieutenant. She was the only Guard who didn't wear a traditional uniform, instead garbed in her usual knee-length charcoal dress with a deep slit up each thigh to reveal skintight violet shorts underneath. Although all the other Guards wore boots, Inalli had always favored a pair of sandals strapped around her bare feet and ankles. A belt of interlocking metal links hung low over her hips. The hood was up on her full cloak, which was such a deep purple it looked almost black. A long brown braid snaked over her shoulder like a serpent emerging from a cave, and her violet eyes gleamed in the shadows.

Azar had never seen her without the hood on. He wasn't even sure what her face looked like. On her chest, she wore a small round mirror that could be detached with a quick twist. The shield on her back was also a perfect mirror, always shined without a single smudge. Not exactly common accessories, but then again, Inalli was no commoner. That was why Azar had chosen her to be the lieutenant of the Prison

Guard with a rank equal to Cisco beneath Captain Hassing.

The Warden wouldn't make eye contact with any of them. He stood at one of the windows overlooking Szion, so grand once with its tall arches and elegant spires stabbing the ever-present cloud cover. Eroded by age and war, the City seemed to be fading before his eyes, but perhaps that was just the haze drifting in. Despite it being midafternoon, Szion was almost as dark as night. The veins of lumenite crystals embedded in the stone walls of Azar's office, normally capable of fully lighting the room, gave off a weak, eerie glow, unable to compete with the wrath driving his Divinity.

"How many?" he asked.

The captain's reflection shifted in the window. When Hassing didn't respond, Cisco reluctantly answered, "Thirty-two dead. Nineteen being treated by Leah."

"Before Leah heals them all, I want you there to assess their injuries. Every scratch, Cisco. I want to know exactly how five kids took down half of the First Branch."

"Yes, sir."

"Wait."

Cisco, who had already turned toward the door to escape, completed a full circle to face the Warden again. "Yes, sir?"

"What can you tell me about them?"

The lieutenant swallowed. He took his time to review the details before reporting, "There was a girl. Pyrokinetic, but only Level 2. Unusually weak for an Elemental."

Azar finally turned, but he still wouldn't look at his subordinates. Instead, he leaned over the Census open on his desk, sending the shadows away from the yellowed pages so he could read the text. "The only two Pyrokinetics listed are both male," he muttered as his finger trailed to the last name. "She must not be registered."

"A boy," Cisco said quickly. "Telekinetic, Level 4."

Again, Azar skimmed the list. "Hmm. Well, now. Three listed here. One female, two male, and one of these boys was reported as a runaway. What else?"

"A Blinker. Level 2."

Azar didn't bat an eye at the knowledge that one of the extinct Tri-ad Divinities had resurfaced in the gene pool. He muttered, "Jay, no doubt."

"There was another boy, Level 4. He . . . well, I don't understand it, but he had two Divinities."

Azar lowered himself into the chair. "There's only one kálos in history who's ever had two Divinities. I believe you've had an encounter with the Demikan."

Cisco inclined his head. "And then there's the last boy who slaughtered so many . . ."

"Yes, he's the one I'm most interested in. What is his Divinity?"

Cisco scratched the back of his head. "He didn't have one. Sir," he added after briefly meeting Azar's gaze and no doubt seeing a dangerous flicker.

"Really," said the Warden. He flipped through the pages of the Census. "How curious."

Hassing shifted his weight again. "Do you think the humans have figured out how to strip us of our Divinities? Is that the Agents' secret weapon?"

"I don't like guesses, Hassing. Incorrect assumptions just get in the way when you're trying to uncover the truth. I believe, after counting the twins, there's one more from Project Alpha, am I right?"

Cisco replied, "Absent from the battle, so I can't personally confirm, but other Shadow Guards have reported a feline Amínyte."

Azar rubbed his chin, his gaze wandering to his Amínyte slave watching from the perch in the corner. "So, Rayven was correct after all. What an odd assortment of Divinities for our enemies to group together in Project Alpha. Well. I hope you're both as humiliated by this defeat as I am."

Inalli remained an impassive statue. Cisco's shoulders slumped. Hassing bowed his head and glared at his boots.

Azar drummed his fingers on the desk. "Let's play a little game called 'analyze your failure.' Go."

Cisco and Hassing both hesitated. The lieutenant was the first to speak up. "Well . . . Ero the Telepath was there."

"*Ero*." Azar all but spat the name. He stood again, too restless to remain sitting. "I shouldn't be surprised that he's involved. I knew the twins were Mind-Readers; of course he got to them already." Azar gripped the bridge of his nose. "That complicates the situation."

Cisco said, "I'm confident our extraction would have been successful if Ero hadn't interfered. My Shadow Guards all had the delusion that they couldn't use their Divinities. When I questioned them afterward, they weren't able to explain why."

"Which forced you into close combat conditions, where a group of children bested you."

Cisco's mouth hung open for a few seconds before he recovered enough to mutter, "W-we train our Guards to utilize the strengths of their Divinities in combat, not—"

"Then I think we just exposed a paralyzing weakness in our training methods, didn't we, Lieutenant?"

"Yes, sir. I suppose you're right."

"Hmm. Then tell me, do you solely blame Ero for your failure?"

Cisco glanced helplessly at Hassing as if hoping for guidance, but the captain maintained a steady glower and simply inclined his head, signaling the lieutenant to answer.

Cisco admitted, "We were wearing our targets down. The Pyro and Telekinetic had been incapacitated with shock rods. Given time, we would have overpowered the others, if only with sheer numbers. But . . . we weren't prepared for A6."

Azar glanced at the Census once more. "You weren't able to identify his bloodlines?"

"No, sir. All I know is that he was well above Level 5, more than double anyone I've ever sensed. I . . . Frankly, I've never felt a power level like his before."

"And yet, no Divinity. He just gets more and more interesting." Azar turned to gaze out the window again. "Inalli?"

She replied, "The Prison Guard is prepared to receive the new Prisoners." Although she remained motionless, her violet eyes shifted to deliver a frigid sidelong glare to Cisco. "If the Shadow Guard could get its act together and contain them."

"Enough," Hassing scolded before an argument could erupt between his two lieutenants.

Azar ignored the remark. "What do we know about the Demikan?"

"The abomination?" Hassing blurted.

Azar turned and raised an eyebrow. "I was hoping for an unbiased report."

Lieutenant Cisco answered, "He's the son of that ghost hunter in Phantom Heights. We know he's a Cryokinetic who was born as a human in Cröendor. Rumor had it he also possessed a second Divinity, but that was just speculation."

"Until now," said Azar.

Cisco inclined his head. "Until now," he agreed. "I verified the boy is also a Sonic. Some say his transformation was an accident; others think his mother experimented on him and intentionally crossed bloodlines."

Hassing grumbled, "However he came to be, he was a small-scale nuisance about three years ago. He never stepped foot on our side of the Rip, so there was no need for the Shadow Guard to engage him. He was mostly just a thorn in the sides of Traders."

Cisco added, "From all accounts, he wasn't very powerful then. Level 2 at most. But I sensed him today, and he was definitely mid-Level 4, no question about it."

"Level 4?" Azar frowned. "That can't be right. Not if he was a Level 2 just a few years ago. Nobody's power grows that much in such a short amount of time."

Hassing asked, "Do you think the Agents—?" Azar silenced him with a stern glare. "Sorry."

Cisco shrugged. "At any rate, even if he was a Level 4 back then, witnesses testified that his ectoplasm usage consistently reflected Level 2, and his cryokinesis was crude at best."

Azar asked, "Any idea how a lowly Level 2 half-human managed to earn such a reputation?"

Hassing scoffed. "Yeah. His success had nothing to do with his physical prowess. Kálos were calling him Phantom before the humans were. The kid was a master at stealth since he can assume a human form and bypass our sensing ability. By the time he called upon his power, he was right on top of his target and already attacking. There was no time to react."

Cisco added, "If memory serves, Phantom's strength was in his defense. He developed a talent for utilizing conservative ice armor to take direct hits instead of avoiding them with intangibility like most kálos would, which saved his power reserves. He'd wait for an opportunity, then go on the offensive using his cryokinesis. Obviously, the best way to avoid an ice weapon is to counter with intangibility, so Phantom used a small amount of power himself while letting his opponent deplete their reserves with a much more taxing strategy."

"It's a ghost hunter's tactic," Hassing said, his nose wrinkled in disgust, "baiting your opponent to a near burnout. And speaking of ghost hunters, if Phantom knew he was outmatched in a fight, he had an annoying habit of luring his opponent toward his mommy. Once they were close enough, he'd vanish, leaving her to finish his fight after he'd already weakened his opponent. No doubt he watched from his hiding place to offer a helpful shot in the back or jump back in if she was in trouble. As far as fighting skills, Phantom was reportedly rather clumsy."

"Obviously, he isn't so clumsy anymore," said Azar. "I thought I'd heard that he died in the Agents' custody."

"I'd heard that rumor, too," said Hassing.

"As did I," added Cisco. Inalli inclined her head.

Azar rubbed the back of his neck. "Well, the Demikan might not have had my attention before, but he certainly has it now. I'm rather fascinated by the idea of power reserves increasing two levels in just a couple of years. I think I'd like to interrogate anyone who claims to have faced Phantom, see what they remember about him. I want to unravel the myths from the facts."

He glanced down at the open book on his desk again. "According to the Census, the runaway Telekinetic's family was last reported to live in Erumyn. Cisco, why don't you send someone to visit them? I'd like to know why our young friend RC decided to run away from home and get himself captured. Inalli, you're dismissed."

"Yes, sir," their voices rang in harmony. Azar listened to their footsteps and waited until the door opened, then closed. He rounded on Hassing. "And where in King's name were *you* during that embarrassing defeat?" he thundered.

Hassing tried to stand up straighter, but he couldn't stop his foot from moving back as if to flee. He cast a bitter glare at Rayven, who peered back at him with beady black eyes. Hassing and Rayven were always vying for Azar's attention, although Hassing's cost of failure was a demotion from the position he'd spent most of his life clawing to reach, whereas Rayven's punishment was a sound beating and weeks locked away in the dark. Still, Azar could acknowledge how humiliating it must be to have a lowly Amínyte slave as a rival. But it was a good incentive to tell the truth since Rayven had returned first from the battlefield and delivered his report.

"Titon bolted on me, sir." Quailing under Azar's wrath that caused the room to darken even more, he gulped and rambled, "That's never happened, sir, not ever. Titon has flown straight at a dragon without flinching. I don't understand—one minute he was fine, and then the Alphas showed up, and the next thing I knew—"

"Stop talking."

Hassing closed his mouth so quickly his teeth clicked together. Azar rubbed his eyes. "That was a grave miscalculation," he said, glaring at the chessboard on his desk.

The black king and a knight stood erect in the back row. Clustered in a nearby corner were the corresponding queen, bishops, rooks, and knight. The white pawns weren't even on the board anymore; they lay scattered across the floor.

The remaining white pieces were upright in the center of the board, surrounded by a circle of black pawns all lying on their sides. The white king was isolated in the farthest corner.

"It would seem," said the Warden, nudging the horsehead carving beside the black king, "that I've been going about this the wrong way." Hassing's gaze was fixed on the figurine at Azar's fingertip; he knew that was his piece and was likely praying it wasn't about to join the white ones on the floor.

To Hassing's visible relief, Azar's finger left the knight to rest on one of the black bishops in the corner. "I've offered my help, and they turned me down. I've tried deals and blackmail and force. I think it's time for something a little more subtle." He slid the bishop a few spaces over to join the black king and knight. "Rayven," he called. The bird glided from his perch and alighted on his master's shoulder. "You remember that discussion we had earlier, don't you? I'd like you to track down that Trader for me."

Rayven spread his wings and launched himself through the open window. Hassing frowned as he watched the bird soar beneath a sky bridge and out of sight. "If I may ask, sir, where did you send Rayven?"

"That's between him and me, at least for now."

"I see," said Hassing, unable to mask the injured note in his tone. "Then, about the Telekinetic . . . Do you plan to use his family as leverage?"

Azar, much calmer now that he was studying his game board, nudged the pieces marginally to adjust their placement. "Oh, we'll see," he murmured absently. "It's too soon to tell. They'll be either pawns or players, and I won't know which until I have a little more information."

Azar seated himself again and leaned back casually in the chair. "RC and Axel are the only names I've found in the Census. The others, there's nothing. No names, no history, no records anywhere. I barely know a thing about them. Well . . . except the Demikan." He pondered for a moment, then asked, "Tell me, what do you think about the idea of a half-breed?"

"It's not natural," said the captain without a second's hesitation. "Crossing lower bloodlines with our noble race . . . It makes me sick just thinking about it."

Azar nodded. "And yet," he murmured, "I'm intrigued. Is that so wrong of me?"

Hassing knew better than to answer a rhetorical question; silence was always safer than the wrong answer.

Azar whispered, "Seven to bring the Seventh . . . but Eight are the key . . ."

Hassing cleared his throat and nervously inquired, "Sir?"

Azar raised his head. "The Sixth Dynasty is about to end, which means my empire is going to change. I have to ensure the shift goes in the direction I want. Can I count on you?"

Hassing adjusted his posture to militant perfection. "I will always stand beside you, sir. You've sent Rayven and Cisco on missions. What would you like me to do now?"

"Nothing."

"N-nothing?" Hassing echoed.

The Warden spun his chair to face the window. In the reflection, he saw the captain's whole body slump with defeat, only to stiffen again when Azar lifted his hand with one finger extended. "On second thought, I do have a task for you. In light of today, I have an old friend I'd like you to contact on my behalf." He let his hand fall. "I think I'd like to call in a favor he owes me. You'll be briefed by the end of the day. *Now* you're dismissed."

Azar waited until the captain had closed the door before he rose and circled the chair to lean over the desk once more. He gazed down at the game board and all the pieces so carefully arranged. This game wasn't over yet.

Not even close.

Chapter Two

Blood-Family

"You're supposed to be dead."

Madison's weak voice drifted above the murmurs. I stared at her mouth moving. On some level, I understood the words, but they reverberated in confusing undulations as if they were foreign.

"I . . . don't understand. Are . . . are you a Shifter? No, you can't be. Your eyes . . ."

"What's the matter, *Mom*?" I snarled, spitting out the final word as a mockery. It hung before me, a cloud in the wintery air, and the words broke my paralysis. "You don't look happy to see me."

"Are you a clone?" she whispered. "Or . . . a moorlin? Is that even possible? What are you?"

My powers continued to roil, hot at the core and cold at my extremities. Another scream was building, tearing my lungs apart, and while it frightened me, I had the guilty desire to give in to it, to let the raw power consume me again as a physical manifestation of the hatred and pain I'd been carrying for so long. All that kept me from doing just that was the terror of losing myself again, so I tried to smother my scream in the cold, as if I could freeze the pressure to weigh it down and keep it contained inside.

I said, "I'm not a Shifter. Or a clone, or a moorlin. I'm your *son*. You can't keep pretending I no longer exist."

"Please," she begged. She gripped her arms, shivering. Strands of her dark hair had pulled free from her ponytail and matted into bloody cuts coagulating on her bruised face. "C-Cato? You don't understand. I—"

"Understand?" Hot tears froze on my cheeks as soon as they rolled free of my eyelashes. The snow swirled around me, stirring my cloak. "You abandoned me," I whispered, my voice strained. "I waited, and you never came. I didn't even get a phone call or a letter! You just left me! What is there to understand? How could you do that to me?" I swung my arms in an arc, freezing the snowflakes together into a storm of ice shards directed at my mother.

They embedded around her in what remained of the wall. She flinched and squeezed her eyes shut even though none struck her. I lowered my voice to a cutting snarl. "And the worst part is, you didn't have the nerve to look me in the eye and explain to me *why*. Your stupid ghost-hunting career was more important to you than I was."

She reached her hand out toward me. "Cato, please, you have to listen to me."

"Why? I don't owe you *anything*!"

Almost . . . That scream almost escaped. *My ear itches.* I touched it with my fingertips, surprised to discover warm stickiness. My fingers were red.

I curled them back into a fist. I had to hold it together, but I felt as if I were coming apart at the seams. Judging by the expression on her face, I must have been a terrifying sight to behold. Green tendrils of ectoplasm whipped around my arms. Ice coated my gloves and gauntlets, broken at the joints. Half of my face was covered with a crust of ice creeping across my skin and clinging to my hair. Behind me lay a horrifying backdrop of destruction.

When she looked at me, she didn't see her long-lost son, the boy she'd held in her arms on the basement floor. No, she saw a powerful Alpha ghost. She saw the monster *He* had always promised I'd become.

I strode forward and seized the front of her jacket in my fists. Madison didn't resist. The ice encroached from my fingers to the fabric. With a growl, I slammed her against the wall, *hard*, evoking a grunt of pain and a blubber of nonsense. The fearsome ghost hunter was nothing now, and I wasn't sure why I had feared her before.

I pounded my metal-studded knuckles into the wall mere inches to the left of her face. There was so much I needed to say, but I could barely put words together into tangible sentences anymore. "You . . . sold me out, you . . . sold me, like a piece of property . . . or a research experiment. Is that all I am to you? Research? Was I some kind of twisted experiment?"

"What? No! I swear, Cato, I thought you were dead! Don't you get it? I buried you! You are *dead*!"

"Yeah, I know I'm dead to you! I figured that out when you abandoned me. I still deserve to know *why*. I want to hear you say the words!"

"I buried your ashes," she whispered. Tears rolled down her cheeks. "We had a funeral."

"Why are you lying to me?"

"I'm not!"

"I want the truth, Madison! *NOW*!"

A groaning, creaking sound splintered the frigid air—wood and stone cracking. I heard a distant, roaring crash of an unstable structure collapsing a few blocks away. Madison winced, cowering away from me again. I should have burned out by now—the blood dripping from my ear was a warning sign—but I felt stronger than ever. The anger and hatred were intense enough to sustain me far past my normal limits.

My mother started to scold, "Cato Jax—"

"Don't you *dare* call me that!"

"It's your name."

I stepped away from her. "You don't get to decide when it's convenient to claim me. You disowned me."

"I did not!"

"I saw the paperwork with *your* signature on it! Don't lie to me!"

"Cato, I have no idea what you're talking about."

I wanted to scream again. The power was clawing at my lungs, climbing up my throat. I clenched my teeth so hard my jaw hurt.

I didn't want to hear her lies. What I wanted was for her to admit what she'd done and then explain why. I wanted to hear her reasons for betraying me.

I had to wait a few seconds to control my power before I could say,

"You sold me! Ten thousand, right? That's what I'm worth? Ten thousand dollars!"

My mother's eyes widened in shock. "What?"

"Your signature was on the custody transfer!"

"But I didn't sign anything!"

"Then it was a damn good forgery!"

"Of course it was! I don't know what's going on, but I swear to you, Cato, I *swear*, I did *not* sell you!"

If I opened my mouth again, this power would consume me. All I could do was hold my breath and stare at her. She rose to her knees, sobbing. "Please, listen to me. They took you away. I called every single day, demanding you back. I offered everything—money, weapons, research—*everything*! I wrote letters to our governor and congressmen. I went on the news, begging for help from someone, anyone. I contacted the White House. But . . . a few weeks after Kovak took you, he said you'd committed suicide."

I shook my head. "Liar."

She stumbled to her feet and insisted, "It's the truth!"

"*Stop it*!" I yelled, on the brink of screaming the words at her. "No more lies! I am so *sick* of hearing your lies!" I clenched my fists and let the cold fill my hands until I was holding solid icicles. In a low, deadly voice, I said, "All I wanted from you was the truth. Since you won't give me that, I'm done with you."

I took a menacing step toward her. Every time I'd stabbed a Scout in the Arena, I had channeled my rage from Madison to its body. No more surrogates; this time I'd get to hear her pain instead.

Revenge was a disease devouring my sanity. Perhaps later I'd regret this, but now, my pulse was flying with anticipation. I wasn't human anymore. Ghosts kill—it was second nature, written into their DNA.

And my ghost half was wide awake.

She pressed her back against the wall, drawing another gun from her belt. Her finger was on the trigger, but the gun was pointed at the ground. "Please don't make me shoot you."

I raised my icy blade.

A young woman slid to a stop between us.

I ordered, "Vivian, get out of my way."

"No," she said.

"I don't want to hurt you. *Move*."

She jerked her head back and forth and stood her ground. My vengeance was meant for Madison, not her. I lingered in indecision.

Madison gripped her daughter's shoulder. "Don't get in the middle of this. I don't want you to get hurt."

Of course our mother would protect her favorite child—her human child.

"But that's my brother," Vivian said in a daze. Her voice wavered. "Isn't it?"

"I don't know," was Madison's unexpected answer.

Vivian stared at me. Why was she so uncertain? Was I really so terrifying that I was unrecognizable to her? "Vivian," I croaked in sorrow.

She took a step back, away from me. Toward Madison. "Who are you?" she asked.

"Vivi . . ."

Her lower lip quivered. "Seph, if this is a joke, it's not funny!"

"It's me."

"Prove it. I gave my real brother something right before he was taken away. What was it?"

I stared at her for several long heartbeats. Slowly, the buzzing in my ears receded, and my head began to clear. The ice in my hand melted.

I reached into the pouch on my right thigh and withdrew the crumpled, torn photograph she'd given me on Lastday with her parting words: *"Don't forget."*

Her eyes flooded when I unfolded it and held it up. She pressed her hand over her mouth to trap a gasp as she stared at the photograph. "Ca-to-Cay?"

Madison stepped forward. "That's impossible," she whispered. The disbelief returned to denial. "I . . . you, your file, there was a number in the file Kovak sent me. If it's really you, the identification number on your arm should match."

I phased away my left gauntlet. Beneath the lacy veil of crystals on my pale skin, dark numbers were tattooed into my forearm. "5292," I said, holding up my fist. "Or A7, whichever you prefer."

Horrified, she backed away, her face pasty white. "No," she whispered. "No, it can't be . . . If—if that's really you, then that means . . . I . . . Oh no. Oh no, no, no . . ." She dropped the gun and buried her face in her hands, sobbing uncontrollably. In the midst of her blubbering, I caught the words, "What have I done?"

"You abandoned me in that hellhole."

"No." Her head jerked up, her hands still pressed to her mouth. "You have to believe me. I thought you were dead. You were. Your body was lying on the autopsy table. I touched you, and . . . you were cold and stiff. Your heart wasn't beating. And afterward . . . I wanted to give you a proper funeral, but Agent Kovak said you were being dissected. When they were done—I didn't want them to, but they cremated you against my wishes, and we made a statue in your honor. We buried your ashes in front of it."

I glared at her, wanting so desperately to believe but afraid of being ensnared in her lies. What she was saying didn't make sense. I had seen the document myself.

I searched her eyes for a hint of the truth—her body language, the pleading way she stared at me—but I couldn't read people like Axel could. When I closed my eyes, I could still see her signature. *Madison Ann Tarrow*, scrawled neatly at the bottom of the document that transferred custody of me to the Agency of Ghost Control for the sum of ten thousand dollars. That was a fact, concrete and provable. And yet . . . could it have been a forgery as she claimed?

I shook my head and backed away from my mother. What should I believe? The words from her mouth, or what I'd seen with my own eyes?

"Cato," she begged.

I shuddered. That was the first time she'd said my name with loving tenderness. Not shock, not anger, not pleading. I almost forgave her in that very instant, but I wasn't going to let her lull me into submission so easily. I continued to shake my head as I took another step back. "No."

"It's the truth. I don't know how else to convince you." She paused, brows knitting together as she looked away from me to search for someone in the crowd. "I have a memory I want to share with him. Can you do that?"

I reluctantly peeled my attention away from her to follow her gaze. Once I spotted Ero, I was taken aback by how ill he looked. I couldn't imagine how much power he must have exerted to fully eclipse three people at once during the battle while also manipulating the minds of dozens of Shadow Guards trying to disable us with their active Divinities. A trail of blood had painted a red line from his nose down to his chin. He said, "I can. If you are both willing."

Madison stared intently at me, and although I met her gaze, I still couldn't find my voice. A memory . . . I was still secretly afraid of Ero's Divinity, but maybe reliving her memory would finally give me the answers I needed for closure.

I didn't vocalize my permission. Ero didn't need me to.

I closed my eyes.

— Chapter Three —
Project Omega

The darkness blurred into hues like a watercolor painting blossoming on a wet canvas, the fuzzy edges becoming crisper and clearer.

I recognized the place from my nightmares. He was standing in front of a set of closed doors. We were inside an elevator.

My first instinct was to shy away and run, but my body wouldn't move. I felt like a passenger inside a vessel preprogrammed to move on its own. I looked at the buttons to see which one was lit. A Greek symbol: Ω.

My stomach dropped. Omega. The worst but final hell a prisoner had to endure before sweet escape. It was the Project everyone dreaded where, rumor had it, ghosts were dissected alive.

Vivian was standing next to me, and after a moment, I understood that I was experiencing this memory from my mother's perspective. He said, "Are you sure you want to do this?"

"Yes," I replied in Madison's voice. "I need to see him."

He nodded, but He was unusually solemn. This wasn't how I remembered Him. I knew Him to be cold and heartless, yet in this memory, He seemed almost sympathetic. The doors slid open. "Right this way, then," He said.

Viv took my hand as we followed Him into Project Omega. My eyes darted with curiosity and dread. Omega was one long hallway with doors lining either side. Madison didn't know it, but this hallway was different from Alpha. There weren't as many doors on the Alpha level, and they weren't spaced evenly as they were here in Omega. This hallway smelled different, too—formaldehyde and alcohol and synthetic lemons. And death.

My mouth was so dry I couldn't swallow. I squeezed Vivian's hand for support. She gave me a feeble squeeze in return.

She wasn't real. This wasn't real. But her grip was soothing nonetheless.

He halted in front of one of the doors and pushed a button; the door slid open. He strode in, but Vivian and I hesitated at the threshold. We exchanged uneasy glances before we stepped inside.

In the center of the small room was a single metal table covered by a white sheet. A bright fluorescent light was positioned directly over it, surrounded by ominous machines on the ceiling with long picks, prongs, needles, blades, and scopes. Three walls were lined with cabinets above and below a metal counter that held trays of surgical tools, a computer monitor, and a deep sink.

He was standing beside the white sheet draped over the form of a body on the table. "Are you ready?"

Numb, I simply nodded.

"We've already started the autopsy, so I recommend you don't move the sheet any further." He folded it back to reveal the head of a person underneath.

It was me.

Vivian let out a cry of anguish and collapsed on top of my body, sobbing hysterically. I gasped and pressed my hand over my mouth. My doppelgänger's eyes were closed, the skin sunken around his eye sockets and cheekbones. Gauze had been wound around his head as if to bandage an injury, but I knew it was really to cover the NMS ports that had been embedded in my skull.

I was seeing all of this through Madison's eyes. Tears jarred my vision. "How could you let this happen?" I shouted in her voice. I seized the front of His lab coat in my—her—hands. "He was in your care! You were responsible for him!"

He calmly detached my grip. "Maddie, I understand how upset you must be. Believe me, this was a terrible accident. Your son was a scientific breakthrough. The last thing I wanted was to see him dead. I know you don't want to hear this, but you need to know the truth: he did it to himself. Suicide by hunger strike."

"No."

"I'm afraid so."

"Why didn't you stop him?" I asked, turning to watch Vivian sob over my body.

He let out a heavy and convincing sigh. "It's normal for new test subjects to lose weight when they first adjust to the diet here. We didn't notice anything was wrong until he became lethargic. We tried our best to save him. Look."

He directed me to the computer monitor on the counter, which He activated with a remote. The screen illuminated to reveal footage from a security camera showing two men standing in a white room. He was easy to recognize. My mother didn't know the other man in this memory, but I did. Dr. Anders.

A pair of handlers entered the frame, dragging a fifth person—me. They lifted me onto the padded table, and one supported me since I didn't have the strength to sit up on my own.

Anders grumbled, "Is there a particular reason you brought a subject for an unscheduled trip into Quarantine without my clearance?"

He added, "And interrupted me in the middle of a meeting with the Board of Directors?"

One of the handlers cleared his throat and said, "We wouldn't waste your time or break protocol if it weren't of the utmost importance. A7 hasn't touched his food or water from last night, sir. Agent Enzo had yesterday's feeding shift, and he reported that A7 didn't eat or drink then, either."

The other sheepishly added, "The test subject is lethargic and unresponsive. We decided it was necessary to invoke emergency Quarantine removal."

Anders approached the sink and filled a plastic cup with water. The handlers held me tight when he stepped forward and pressed the edge to my lips. "Drink," he commanded.

I refused.

He set the cup down, then gripped my chin and forced me to look at him as he held up a tube and a catheter. "It's your choice. Either you start eating and drinking, or this needle is going into your vein and this tube is going down your throat. You remember the last time that happened, don't you? It wasn't fun. You want to do it again?"

When I still didn't respond, He *muttered, "The hard way it is, then."*

"Fine," said Dr. Anders. "Strap him down."

The assistants pulled me back onto the table and fixed restraints around my wrists and ankles. Dr. Anders inserted the needle into the back of my hand. He loomed over me, tube in hand as he gripped my jaw again and forced the tube down my throat. My counterpart on the screen started squirming weakly until the scene froze.

He *set the remote down. "As you saw, we tried to revive him. But cryokinesis is a water-based elemental power. I'm afraid the dehydration had a more severe effect on his body than we anticipated. We did all we could, but we were too late. We couldn't save him, Maddie. He died a few hours later. I'm truly very sorry for your loss."*

I gazed vacantly at the frozen image on the screen—the black-haired teenager restrained on the padded table with a feeding tube in his mouth and an IV in his hand. Slowly, I turned and stared at the same boy lying dead on the metal table. In a trance, I drifted toward the corpse.

Vivian sniffed and backed away to give me space. He *cleared* His *throat and awkwardly handed her a brown paper bag. "Here are his personal belongings." I couldn't tear my eyes away from the boy on the metal table, but in my peripheral, I saw Vivian open the bag and pull out Phantom's folded uniform.*

She searched all the contents of the bag with increasingly frantic movements, frowning, then peered up at Him. *"Where's the picture?"*

He *returned her stare. "Picture?"*

Vivian nodded. "I gave him a photograph. Can I have it back?"

He *narrowed* His *eyes. When* He *spoke,* His *voice transformed to an even, dangerous tone that was harrowingly familiar to me. "I'm afraid we never recovered one. That's everything he had on him when we brought him to the AGC. It must have fallen out on the trip here."*

"Oh," she said, hanging her head.

He picked up a scalpel and inspected it, tilting it slowly so it reflected the light from above. "In retrospect, Maddie, I suppose I should have asked if you were interested in the autopsy. We've only just started cutting. Would you like to oversee the procedure on him?"

He was mocking me—her. It took everything I had to keep my voice steady when I said, "No. Do whatever you need to, but I don't want to see it. Just the results. I'm only interested in the file when you're done."

I tried, so very hard, to stay strong beneath His scorn, but when I stared down at the body, only fifteen, so unfairly young lying dead on a metal table, I felt my spirit break.

A rush of tears filled my eyes, and I leaned over the corpse, setting my hand against the back of my dead version's head and pressing my forehead against his. The skin was cold and stiff. I entwined my fingers in the coal-black hair and cried, "Why did you do it? I was coming for you, Cato. Didn't you know that? I was coming for you . . ."

— Chapter Four —

Deceived

I didn't exit the memory as easily as I'd slipped in.

The scene jerked, jagged and sharp, then out of focus. I felt myself falling.

"Ero?" someone called. "Are you okay?"

I opened my eyes again, but my vision was blurred through a film of tears.

Ero had fallen to his knees. Finn and Reese were kneeling on either side of him in concern. Reese reached out to touch his teacher's hand, but midair, he second-guessed himself and sheepishly folded his hands in his own lap instead.

"I will be fine," the Telepath assured with a forced smile. He coughed blood into his hand.

I swallowed once, hard, to clear my throat, but it didn't help. I still couldn't breathe. She *had* come for me after all, and I'd never known. I felt as if I were in a free fall again.

Madison said, "Your skin was cold. Your heart wasn't beating, and you weren't breathing. You were dead. I don't understand how you can be standing right in front of me."

I shook my head with no explanation. My gaze found Finn and Reese again, and like Ero, they didn't need me to put my thoughts into words for them. Ero said, "My apologies, but they do not have an answer for you."

"That couldn't have been me on the table," I finally managed to say. ". . . could it?"

Ero looked at Wes and said, "In Avilésor, a false death could be fabricated with vidon venom or a Witch's brew. Would I be incorrect to hypothesize that the right combination of human drugs could achieve the same effect?"

"It's possible," Wes concurred with a rather nonchalant one-shouldered shrug. "Factor in Cato's naturally low body temperature due to his cryokinesis, and I wouldn't question Agent Kovak's creativity to put him in a comatose state and slow his heart down to an imperceptible crawl."

Everything was illuminated with such clarity that it hurt. I'd been driving myself into the throes of insanity trying to understand what had changed in the short amount of time between when Madison had fought to keep *Them* from taking me and when she'd disowned me. Her actions hadn't been logical. Why would she say she loved me and she was going to rescue me, then turn around and sell me?

Because she never did.

"Cato," she said, "if I'd known you were still alive . . ."

I just stood there, shaking my head. "*They* told me you didn't want me anymore."

"How could you believe that?"

"Because I lied to you. I ruined your reputation as a ghost hunter."

"But—"

"*They* showed me the custody transfer with your signature," I spilled before she could interrupt. "I didn't believe *Them* at first, but you never came to see me. I did try to kill myself—that wasn't a lie. I stopped eating and drinking. But *They* wouldn't let me die. *They* . . . forced a tube down my throat and . . ." I closed my eyes and took a deep breath, then whispered, "It was all a lie. Bloody Scout, I'm such an idiot."

His voice whispered on the wings of a memory: *"I told you I'd break you . . ."*

"Cato."

I opened my eyes. Madison slowly approached, silent tears still streaming down her face. Vivian stayed behind to give her the courtesy of being with me first, just as she had given her space to let her mourn over my body in Project Omega. The townspeople surrounding us

27

whispered white noise that took me back to Lastday again.

My mother halted in front of me. "I never stopped loving you. There hasn't been a day that's gone by when I haven't been thinking about you."

She reached for me, but I flinched away. Human hands always brought pain, and she was a ghost hunter. Her hands would be no different.

She hesitated. "Sweetheart, I'm not going to hurt you."

I wanted to believe her. I really did. But years of pain had conditioned me to fear the human touch. When she reached out again, I had to force myself to hold still. My body twitched with the instinct to shy away; I stiffened and clenched my fists. She threw her arms around me.

My hands remained at my sides. Eyes wide, I gazed over her shoulder on the verge of panic. I remembered her hugs being warm and comforting, a cocoon of protection. Now, rather than feeling safe in her arms, I felt at least two guns digging into my ribs, and I was acutely aware that each and every weapon in her belt was designed to hunt creatures like me.

I didn't move a single muscle, not even when her arms tightened and she whispered in my ear, "You're really here." She squeezed me even tighter, constricting to the point of suffocation. "I'm so sorry, Cato. I let you down when you needed me. I am *so* sorry."

I closed my eyes but still didn't return the embrace. "So, you don't hate me, then?"

"Never. I could never hate you."

"But I lied to you. And you're a ghost hunter, and I'm half-ghost, and—"

"None of that matters." Madison held onto me for a full minute. I squirmed, a subtle hint to let go, but she clutched me tighter, inadvertently digging her weapons deeper into my ribs. Finally, I couldn't take it anymore, and I sought my power to become intangible.

Madison's arms passed through me as I stepped back to escape her grasp. She was surprised at first, as if she'd forgotten I had the ability to do that, but she quickly recovered as she studied me intently. I must have changed since she last saw me; her gaze eagerly roved across my face, drinking in my features. She frowned and started to raise her hand, but then hesitated and drew it back. "Cato . . . your face," she said in concern.

I touched my cheek, startled to discover a crusty layer. I looked at my hand. Segments of ice coated my glove and bare fingers, forming a strange exoskeleton that extended up my forearm. It was in my hair too, but only on the right side of my head.

I set my open hand over my right eye, drawing upon my power to melt the ice. If Ero's theory was right, my blue eye was where my cryokinesis manifested itself. Water dripped from my hair as the crystals melted. I lowered my hand.

Madison's eyes were still fixed on me. "Let me look at you," she said. "You've grown so much. I think you're taller than me now. You're almost the spitting image of your father, you know. Oh, if Jaxon could see you. And your clothes! And your eyes . . ." I tilted my head, studying her and causing her to pause. "What?"

"You look different too," I said. "Older."

She chuckled with an air of bitterness. "A couple years of grief and stress gave me some gray hairs and put a few extra wrinkles on my face, huh?"

I noticed the darkening bruises on her skin. Her lip was cut and starting to swell, and now I felt guilty for what I'd done to her. I hung my head. "Sorry for hurting you."

Madison scoffed and replied, "I think you deserved to give me a few free punches after what I put you through." Her carefree reassurance didn't ease my guilt, and I made a fist, channeling the cold power into my hand. I wordlessly extended my offering. She seemed surprised, as if once again she'd already forgotten I was half-ghost. Once the shock dissipated, she accepted the ice and pressed it against an unseen knot on the back of her head with a wince.

"Thank you." She reached out.

All I saw was her hand coming toward my face. I batted it away and leapt back, ready to defend myself. "Don't touch my head!" Ectoplasm escaped in loose tendrils around my hands again.

My mother gazed at me in terror, as if she no longer recognized me. "Okay, Cato. Okay. I'm sorry. I . . . didn't know. I won't touch your head. I promise." I slowly straightened, watching her warily. "What happened to you?"

I clenched my jaw.

She forced an uncomfortable smile and said, "That's okay. You don't have to tell me right now. I don't want to fight with you. I'm just . . . so *happy* . . ."

She almost started crying again, but she sobered when she gazed past me at Jay and the others, who stood nearby watching our reunion with neutral expressions.

Vivian crept forward and stopped a few feet away. "Hi," she said awkwardly.

"Hi," I echoed.

"I really missed you."

"Missed you, too." I reached into my pouch and withdrew the broken bracelet, then held it out to her. Once she realized what I was holding, her eyes widened. "Um, this is yours, right? I found it."

Gingerly, she took the bracelet in her trembling fingers. "I've been looking everywhere for this."

"Sorry."

She jerked her head up. "No, don't be sorry." She handed it back to me and held out her hand. "Will you please tie it for me?"

I took the braided cords in my fingers and clumsily tied the frayed ends into a knot around her wrist. "Seph," she said, chuckling. "I think part of me knew it was you. My heart did, anyway, even though I knew it was impossible. Why didn't you tell me who you were?"

I shifted, conscious of the crowd watching every move and hanging onto every word. "I wanted to, Viv. I really did."

She looked as though she wanted to hug me, but after her multiple encounters with Jay and the way I'd reacted when Madison had thrown her arms around me, she must have realized how sensitive I was about being touched. Instead, she held her arms out in the hopes that I would come to her.

I couldn't do it. I did trust Vivian, but Madison had practically suffocated me, and I didn't think I could handle another embrace right now. My blood-sister dropped her arms and laughed nervously to alleviate the tension. "So, you're the one who kidnapped me."

"No, but it was my idea. I carried you, though. I kept you safe. Sorry for scaring you."

"I should have recognized your voice. I mean, I guess I thought, or . . . hoped, but . . ."

Our mother was glaring at the Telepath leaning on Wes's shoulder for balance. "You knew Cato was here," she accused.

"Yes," Ero answered casually.

"And you knew he was my son."

"Correct."

"And you didn't tell me?"

Ero forced a faint smile. "Forgive me. It was not my place to tell."

Kit sullenly crept toward me on silent bare feet. She gave Madison and Vivian a wide berth, eyeing them suspiciously. I reached out to welcome her, and she slipped her small hand into mine as she peered up at me with her innocent golden eyes. "Cato?" she asked shyly. "Do we have to go back to the bad place now?"

I stroked her hair, surprised by her question. "Why would you ask that?"

Her fingers tightened inside mine. "Because you said if Mrs. Tarrow found out who you were, we'd have to leave. But I really like it here."

I knelt and pulled Kit into a tight embrace. She closed her eyes, leaning into me. "We can stay. Madison isn't going to make us leave."

I felt my blood-family watching me, observing how I held Kit so lovingly after I'd rejected Vivian's hug and hadn't returned Madison's embrace.

My mother said, "You thought I was going to send you back to the AGC?"

I released my lab-sister and straightened to meet Madison's

wounded gaze. Kit, still afraid of the ghost hunter, pressed against me for protection.

Clearly uncomfortable, Madison said, "You're not going back to the AGC. You can come home. Your room is ready for you."

Home. I'd lost count of how many times I had dreamed of hearing her say those words. And yet, I hesitated. Madison noticed and frowned. "What's wrong?"

I turned to find my lab-family. They returned my solemn stare. Ash gripped her staff, head bowed so her dark-red hair drifted down over one eye like a curtain. RC stared blankly at the ground. Finn and Reese tilted their heads as they read my mind. Jay wouldn't look at me, as if I'd already betrayed him.

I glanced down at Kit, whose face fell as her silky black ears flattened. She reached out with her other hand to clutch mine in both of hers, gazing up at me with a pleading expression.

I redirected my stare to Vivian, who watched me hopefully, and my mother, who was visibly perplexed by my indecision. She'd expected me to agree without a second thought and resume my old life as if nothing had changed. As if I'd never left. As if I'd never met Finn, Reese, Jay, RC, Ash, Axel, and Kit. As if that whole nightmare had never happened.

I shook my head. "I can't."

"Why not?"

I peered down at Kit again. "You're my family, but so are they. And . . . I'm sorry, but they need me more than you do."

Kit wrapped her arms around my waist, resting her head on my hip. For a moment, my mother looked hurt by my statement. Her voice rose, panicky, as she cried, "How can you say that? You have no idea how much I need you!"

Jay informed her in a dangerous tone, "Cato made his decision."

"Stop!" I begged. "This isn't fair. You can't expect me to choose between you."

Madison gazed at my lab-family, then back at me. She sighed. "Okay. You're right. I . . . understand that a lot has changed. And . . . if they're your family, then . . . I guess that makes them our family too, right?"

The relief almost manifested in the form of laughter. *Everything is going to be okay.* I could keep both families. The laughter bubbled up my throat but came out in a coughing fit instead. I tried to keep it trapped behind my lips, but it burst out, and I covered my mouth with both hands to contain the deep, wet hacking. Kit let go of me and stepped back as I fell onto my knees.

My hands were shaking when I lowered them. I stared at my fingers drifting in and out of focus. More blood.

"Cato?" Kit asked softly. She set her hand on my leg, her velvety ears pinned back and her golden eyes wide with worry.

Madison knelt to one knee so we were on the same level. "Are you okay? Did I hurt you? Do you need a doctor?"

I coughed again and spat a mouthful of blood on the cobblestones. "No," I mumbled, wiping my mouth with the back of my glove. "I just . . . I pushed myself too hard . . . used too much power." Now that the adrenaline was wearing off, I was crashing. *Hard.* My untethered rage had pushed me far beyond my normal limits, and now the overexertion was catching up.

Madison settled back on her heels with a concerned frown. She surveyed the damaged buildings, the snowdrifts, the lethal spikes of icicles perpendicular to the ground, and the shivering crowd, as if noticing our surroundings for the first time.

"Jay," I called weakly, holding out my hand. "Help me up."

He approached and clasped my hand. I felt unusually light when he hauled me up with his good arm; I was pretty sure RC had lent assistance with telekinesis. "I'll Blink you Home," said Jay.

"No." I wrenched my hand free and took an unsteady step away from him. "You'll burn out, too."

He didn't argue, just hung his head in weary acceptance of the truth. He might be strong enough to reach Saros Manor on his own, but not with a passenger.

"You need to stay here," Madison insisted as she rose. "Let Doc help you."

I shook my head. Darkness was encroaching on the edges of my vision. I was going to pass out, and I didn't want to do it here, in the open, surrounded by humans, vulnerable. "I want to go Home."

"Okay. Your room is ready. We'll—"

"No. *Home*. Saros Manor."

A spasm of pain twitched Madison's brow when she realized that I no longer viewed her house as my home. "Are you sure you can make it that far?"

I bobbed my head. "I can make it," I mumbled.

Jay said, "We'll take him."

Madison stared at me, and then her attention shifted to something in the distance over my shoulder, although I didn't turn to look. Her expression hardened. "Vivian, go with them."

"But Mom—"

"I want you all to go. Right now. You'll be safe there. I have to take care of something."

She marched between RC and Ash without looking back. Something had ensnared her attention, although I couldn't tell what her destination was as she strode into the crowd.

I hung my head in exhaustion, feeling rather like a dog that had just been ordered into its kennel. But I would obey her, because her voice was the voice of all-knowing reason from my childhood, and although I shouldn't, part of me still trusted that voice.

— Chapter Five —

Saving the Damned

So much destruction.

Buildings had become piles of bricks, shingles, beams, and siding. Trees had snapped like toothpicks. Shards of glass lent a shimmering, jagged surface to the ground plane. Streetlights were down; cars had been flipped; columns from hydrants that had spewed high-pressure water jets into the sky were frozen solid; icicles thicker than me defied gravity by hanging like sideways stalactites away from City Hall, the epicenter of my fury.

"You told me you never met Cato."

Vivian's voice jolted me. I'd been concentrating so hard on putting one foot in front of the other while keeping my balance that I'd forgotten she was here, scrambling over a rafter beside my lab-family. When I turned toward the sound of her voice, I found her eyes trained on Jay, and mine followed. "You did?" I said in surprise. It wasn't like Jay to tell an outright lie.

My lab-brother raised one eyebrow at my blood-sister. "If I remember correctly, I said I never met any ghosts outside of Project Alpha. I never actually denied knowing Cato."

Vivian nodded, as if she wasn't surprised. "I *knew* you weren't going to hurt me."

Jay nodded solemnly while RC used telekinesis to clear a path for us. "You were never in any danger when we kidnapped you. Sorry about the inconvenience—that wasn't a great first impression."

They're getting along. That's good.

I wanted to feel relieved, maybe even happy. But I couldn't. Not when facing the horror I'd unleashed upon this town.

I did this. I stared at my trembling hands, wondering if Axel, wherever he was right now, was staring at his hands too and thinking the same. Strangely enough, I craved his company. He would understand. He knew what it felt like to lose control.

The faint, persistent ringing that had been nagging in my ears ever since my last sonic scream suddenly swelled into a deafening crescendo. I stumbled, momentarily off balance, then fell to my knees. I bowed my head with a grimace. After a moment, the ringing faded back into the distance, although it hadn't completely left.

"Ice melts," I mumbled, reaching out to seize a splintered chunk of wood that might at one time have been the corner of a doorframe. "But I can't rebuild all of this."

RC crouched down beside me. "I can help." He waved his hand, and the debris drifted away from my fingers as another piece rose. A screw levitated and drove through the two pieces of wood to bind them together.

I held my palm beneath RC's creation. When he released his power, gravity dropped it into my hand. I clenched it tightly as I coughed again, then doubled over and spewed more blood across the snow and debris. The retching reduced back to a cough again before the fit settled, and I groaned in pain. Every single part of my body, right down to my hair follicles, hurt. Breathing in the cold air felt like inhaling needles; breathing out felt as if my chest cavity were collapsing.

"Are you okay?" Vivian asked from far away.

My vision swam out of focus. I blinked a few times to correct it. "Cato?"

I lifted my head to meet her worried gaze. "Huh?"

"I asked if you're okay."

"Yeah. Just let me rest for a minute."

Kit's thin arms circled my torso from behind, and she rested her cheek on my shoulder. I patted her hand in reassurance. "I'm fine, Kit-Kat," I whispered hoarsely. "Just a burnout." She nuzzled against my back.

I set the wood down, placed my hands on the asphalt, and leaned forward, freeing myself from Kit's embrace. Although I took my time in rising, the blood still seemed to rush from my head. I swayed, side-stepping into Ash, who held me upright despite her own injuries.

Jay had been silent for a while. He was standing a few paces away by Finn and Reese, holding his injured arm, staring down the street.

"What's wrong?" I asked.

"I'm worried about Axel."

Ash asked, "Any idea where he went?"

Jay didn't answer; he just shook his head and continued to stare into space.

Once the spell of shock broke, a flurry of activity stirred town square like a beehive.

The people of Phantom Heights were well-versed in the art of survival. Already, paramedics were setting up stations to treat minor injuries while Doc, Lily, and Shay made rounds through the bloody, snow-covered rubble.

Madison, are you all right? You must be so happy! My apartment! It's gone! Where am I supposed to live? Is Phantom okay? Who's going to be responsible for all the damages? Madison, where are you going? Madison! Madison!

She ignored the voices and shoved her way through the mob. Madison had eyes for only one person—a woman striding down the pedestrian road toward the church's magnificent steeple. "Holly!" she called, stymied by bodies blocking her path.

The councilwoman glanced briefly over her shoulder but then turned forward again, her stride quickening.

Mayor Correll called, "Everybody, calm down. Everything's under control. If you're injured, stay where you are and wait for the paramedics to come to you. Anyone who's not, let's get some cleanup crews assembled. I'm sure Madison can deactivate the shield around City Hall and reroute electricity to the town again in no time, right? Madison?"

She pushed between bodies, muttering, "Excuse me, sorry, I need to get through, *move!*"

Finally, she broke free and pounded down the pedestrian road of herringbone pavers that connected town square to the church and court-house. Mayor Correll's voice called after her, "Madison!"

Holly's black pump was settling on the first step when Madison seized her wrist. "Wait!"

The councilwoman yanked her arm free and whirled. "I have nothing to say to you." Her green eyes sparkled with sorrow otherwise masked behind the wrinkles of her scowl.

The church was still intact, but its beautiful stained-glass windows now lay broken in a coat of many colors at their feet. When Madison retreated, her step was punctuated with a sharp *crunch*. "What are you planning to do?"

Holly's laugh possessed a cold, cruel edge. "What's the matter? Afraid I'm on my way to call Agent Kovak?"

"Please don't do anything rash. I'm begging you. I'll do anything. I . . . I'll look for your son, if that's what you want."

"It's a little late for that, don't you think?" Holly seethed. "Do you remember what you told me when I came to you for help?"

"I . . ." Madison wavered beneath Holly's stubborn glare. "I don't," she admitted.

"No? Your exact words were, 'It's too late. He's probably already dead. There's no point in even trying.'"

"I—"

"All you could think about was your own son! And now look— you've got yours back, and mine is still gone! Because of *you*!"

"I'm sorry. I know that doesn't bring him or anyone else back, but—"

"You failed at your job, Madison. You failed to protect this town and the people in it while you were on your hopeless, single-minded crusade against the AGC."

"So Cato has to suffer the consequences of my mistake?"

Holly huffed. "Oh please, do you really think I'm that shallow?"

Madison stepped closer and pleaded, "Convince city council to continue protecting the Alpha ghosts."

Holly backed away. "My priority has always been the safety and well-being of the *humans* of Phantom Heights."

"This was an accident."

"An *accident*? Look around! This place is in ruins! All those bodies in town square!"

"Not human bodies," Madison said.

"Not this time," Holly retorted without missing a beat. She exhaled and pinched the bridge of her nose to calm herself. "Look, Madison, you're a good ghost hunter when you're focused on the mission—you really are. But you're biased. Your son isn't human anymore. He's dangerous, and you can't seem to see that even though everyone else can. Look at the damage he caused."

"I can keep him under control." At Holly's skeptical look, she continued, "Listen, if you report him to the Agents and he has to run, I'm going with him. And if Kovak catches him, I'm not going to stop until I get him back. Either way, I won't be focused on ghost hunting. So, take away Cato, the Alpha ghosts, me, and probably Trey too, and where does that leave Phantom Heights? What happened to your family would probably happen to a lot of others."

"Are you threatening me with the deaths of human children?"

"Of course not! I'm just asking you to think of the bigger picture before you make your decision. Yes, Phantom Heights suffered a lot of damage today, but we just fought off an invasion without losing a single human life! Doesn't that count for something?"

"You forget the only reason that army came through the Rip in the first place was because of the Alpha ghosts. They have targets on their backs. They attract trouble."

Madison clasped her hands together. "Holly, *please*. I will get on my knees in this glass if I have to. There are a lot of angry people out there. All it will take is one person to call the AGC, and then it's all over. I can't lose my son again. *Please*. This kind of situation is your specialty."

Holly crossed her arms and glared down the pedestrian road at the crowd in town square. "You're right—people are angry and confused. And I can't blame them. They have a few moments of joy to see their long-lost hero return, and then what does he do? He destroys their homes and almost buries them all beneath the rubble. I can only guess at what they're saying, can't you? Is Phantom a hero anymore?"

"He's still a kid. That's a lot of pressure to put on anybody, especially someone who's been tortured for two years and then hunted like an animal."

"Don't make excuses for him. He's not a kid; he's more than old enough to know that knocking down buildings is a no-no. The fact that he even can makes him a monst—"

"Don't you even say it! I don't care what you and Kovak think; Cato has a human heart. He's still one of us."

Holly looked as if she had sour candy in her mouth. "That's your opinion, and it's not a popular one."

"What do you want, Holly? Money?"

"I don't need your money." She considered for a moment, absently stirring the rainbow shards of glass with the toe of her shoe. Finally, she said, "Mayor Correll should be making a statement asking people to wait for city council to reach a consensus. We'll make a public announcement soon."

"*And*?" Madison pressed.

Holly smirked. "And you and Cato are both going to be in my debt if I decide to take him under my wing, aren't you?"

―――――――――――――――――――――

Finn was already pulling out a chair for me as I crossed the threshold into the dining room. Reese emerged from the kitchen with a glass of ice water in hand.

I sank into the chair. *Thank you*, I thought, too tired to speak it aloud. Sometimes it was nice not having to tell someone what I wanted or needed. Bloody Scout, I hadn't even realized what I needed; they must have tapped into my subconscious thoughts.

They didn't answer me—not with a human in our presence. I accepted the glass of water, and in an instant, the brief feeling of gratitude was swept away in an abyss of heartache and anger when I looked at Reese. *You knew*, I realized. *You betrayed me.*

The twins winced and shrank away from me, as if repulsed by the aura of anguish that engulfed me in darkness. I glared at them until they bowed their heads and stared at their feet in shame. My head was spinning. I didn't even want to look at my lab-brothers.

I needed both hands to hold the glass steady as I lifted it to my lips. Vivian, seemingly bitter that she hadn't thought of bringing me a chair or water, quietly asked, "Is there anything else I can get you, Cato?"

I drained the glass, then popped an ice cube into my mouth and sucked on it. "No," I told her. "I just need to rest."

She nodded, but she looked uncomfortable and eyed my lab-family with a peculiar expression. I'd swear she was mentally analyzing and cataloging them. Jay—our cunning leader with a silver tongue to match his eyes. RC—stern, quiet, and withdrawn, always on guard and ready to activate his deadly Divinity of telekinesis. Finn and Reese—brilliant Mind-Readers with a conjoined mind but no personality to the untrained eye. Ash—a beautiful warrior with confidence on the battlefield but a shy demeanor in social situations. Kit—outwardly the epitome of innocence but secretly an intel expert and thief.

Vivian shifted her weight, as if engaged in a silent debate with herself, and then she crossed in front of Ash, who had to yield a step to let her pass. Head high, Vivian sat down in the chair next to me.

Ash stared at her for a few seconds, then took a couple of steps to stand right behind me. She set her hand on my shoulder. "It's going to be all right, Cay."

Vivian glared at her and said, "Of course it will." She leveled her gaze at me. "Mom will take care of everything."

RC scoffed, but when Vivian whirled on him, he stared pointedly across the room. "What?" Vivian challenged.

I crunched the ice cube and said, "Look, Viv, uh . . . no offense, but . . . we've been on our own for a long time."

"So?" she said, rounding on me. "Don't you trust Mom to protect you?"

I gazed at her, weary and sorrowful, until her frigid scowl melted. "Cato?" she asked, her voice suddenly meek.

"I learned how to protect myself."

"But . . . you don't have to anymore. You know that, right? We can take care of you." She turned to face Jay, RC, Ash, Kit, and the twins. "All of you."

Ash's grip tightened on my shoulder. Even if I shared faith with Vivian, I could never expect my lab-family to give that same trust. Not to an Outsider, and definitely not to a ghost hunter.

"Yeah, right," RC grumbled. He stormed away toward the staircase.

Kit's ears fell as she watched him leave. She peered at us, then at the doorway, then back at us. Jay suggested, "Why don't you go keep him company?" Even with his blessing, she lingered in indecision, her golden gaze settling uncertainly on Vivian. Finally, she followed RC, although she still glanced back at us over her shoulder. Jay cleared his throat and looked at the twins, wordlessly giving them the same instructions. They obeyed without hesitation, although they both cast a brief glance at me.

The silence in their wake was suffocating. Ash was staring Vivian down over my shoulder, but Vivian's attention was on me, and Jay's cloudy eyes told me his thoughts weren't even with us.

My lab-sister broke the quiet with her soft voice: "You need to sleep, Cato. You burned out."

I stared at the empty glass on the table in front of me. She was right. I had to remind myself to blink when my eyes became too dry because all I felt like doing was staring into the space between wakefulness and sleep. I'd swear my body wasn't made of flesh anymore. It was too heavy to move. A statue, just like Phantom, while my mind drifted on another plane.

I didn't notice Ash half lifting, half dragging me out of the chair until I was leaning on her shoulder and her warm arm was wrapped around my middle. Jay woke from his trance and went to my other side to help support my weight.

Vivian stood. "I can help."

"We got him," Ash said quickly.

My blood-sister shifted, then glanced at the front doors. "I know Mom wants us to stay here and wait, but I'm going out to check on her. I'll be right back, Cato. I promise."

I was having a difficult time focusing on her. *Blink. I need to blink.*

She backed away, unwilling to peel her gaze away from me. Jay waited until the door shut behind her before he Blinked us into our room on the third story.

Ash lowered me onto the sofa. I was half-addled in a sleepy fog of exhaustion, relief, and crashing adrenaline, but not too oblivious to notice who was sitting naked by the French doors, his knees drawn up to his chest as his clothes dried on the balcony railing.

The sunlight made Axel's irises shine like rubies, his porcelain skin radiant, his raven hair glossy. With the fabric of RC's uniform smoothing the angles of his muscles and the cloak further making his figure amorphous, I'd almost forgotten just how *strong* Axel looked. Every muscle in his body was carved to perfection. I always knew he could break me in half; it was just sobering to realize how easy it would actually be.

His eyes, which had been so dilated they were almost black, now glowed vibrant red with constricted pupils. Usually that would put me at ease because he should be in an amiable mood. This time, his good health alarmed me. There used to be a severe difference between when Axel left us every week, gaunt and restless, and when he'd return, lucid and healthy. But he'd been steadily deteriorating, and the last few times, he'd returned from his mysterious trips already looking ill. I truly believed he was dying.

Now . . . he was practically glowing in the sunlight. He hadn't been this healthy since our escape, and while his improvement should have been heartening, it wasn't, because it proved what Axel and all of us had been trying to deny—that he had to kill to survive in the Outside.

Just as he wouldn't speak, he wouldn't look at us either, not in his shame. Still, his mere presence brought me relief. We were all together and safe inside Proto.

RC, Ash, Kit, Finn, and Reese gathered around Jay. All I wanted to do was curl up in a ball and close my eyes, but I propped myself up and willed myself to stay awake just a little longer.

"Is anybody seriously hurt?" Jay asked. Either my hearing was failing, or his words were starting to slur with exhaustion. RC and Ash, too drained to respond aloud, shook their heads.

"I'm okay," Kit said, crawling into Jay's lap and snuggling in his arms.

He kissed the top of her forehead. "Good. I think it's safe for us to rest. I can't imagine the Shadow Guard will be launching another coordinated attack anytime soon."

Kit tipped her head back to gaze up at Jay. "We really don't have to leave? You promise?"

He nodded. "Cato's blood-family isn't our enemy anymore."

RC folded his arms and glared past Axel out the French doors. Kit's ears flicked back. "So, we have to do everything Mrs. Tarrow says now?" she asked.

"Of course not," I mumbled drowsily.

Jay glanced at me, as if surprised that I was still conscious. "Cato's right. But I want everyone to show her respect." He shot a meaningful glare at Axel. "That includes you."

The hybrid growled softly. "She's a human and a ghost hunter. I don't like her."

"Can you at least try to be civil? For Cato?"

Axel rolled his eyes until his gaze landed on me. "If she doesn't cross me, I won't cross her, but that's all I can promise."

Ash plopped down in front of the sofa. "I know she's your mother, but . . . Axel's right—she's a ghost hunter. I'm sorry, but I don't trust her."

"I understand," I said. "I don't completely trust her myself."

"Things are going to be different now, aren't they?" she asked.

I nodded, my eyelids finally too heavy to resist gravity anymore. I'd dreamed of this for a long time, and it was really happening. I had *both* of my families now. I felt complete. The real question was . . . could they coexist symbiotically with each other? Considering my mother's lifelong dedication to hunting ghosts and my lab-family's merited distrust of humans, these two important pieces of my life didn't seem compatible.

I sighed, one last thought threading its way through my mind just before the rejuvenating deep sleep of a burnout claimed me—things were going to be very different indeed.

— Chapter Six —

Red

"He won't stop screaming," said Leah.

The Healer had blood caked on her fingernails. She wrung her hands together and peered through the window at her patient. "I already healed his wound. I don't know what else to do."

Lieutenant Cisco followed her gaze. He didn't know much about the victim, only that he had recently been promoted to the First Branch, he was a Level 4 Dendrokinetic, and his name was Salem. The man thrashed on the floor, his eyes squeezed shut, his mouth stretched wide open to release the most agonizing wails Cisco had ever heard. Even the torture master's victims didn't scream this much.

"Tell me about his wound."

Leah shrugged. "It was nothing special. Looked like something bit him. Something with very sharp teeth. Easy to heal—took only a few seconds. His pain should have stopped." Leah whispered, more to herself than Cisco, "Last thing I could get out of him before he lost his mind was that his blood was on fire."

"His power is fading," Cisco realized aloud as he watched Salem writhe. "He's already dropped a full level." He turned away from the grisly sight. "What's your diagnosis?"

"Officially? I have no idea what's wrong with him."

"Unofficially?"

Leah used her thumbnail to scrape flecks of blood off her fingernails. Her narrow, almond-shaped eyes glimmered with tears. She bit her lower lip, reluctant to answer. "I've never treated one before, but . . . if I had to guess . . . this looks like a bite from a fiend."

"Impossible. In broad daylight in Cröendor?"

Leah shifted and peered at her flailing patient again. "Could've been a ghoul, maybe. You said he's losing power. I don't know what else would cause symptoms like this." She bowed her head. "I'm sorry, Lieutenant. Whether it's fiend venom or something else, there's nothing more I can do." She heaved a melancholy sigh and muttered, "I've never lost a patient before."

"He's the last one?" Cisco asked.

"Yes. All the others have been healed."

Cisco nodded. "You may leave."

Leah jerked her head up. "What are you going to do?"

"What has to be done." Cisco opened the door, and Salem's screams reverberated through his bones. He closed the door before Leah could follow, then lingered over his fallen soldier. Salem had been screaming for so long that his voice was hoarse, and still, he continued to howl in agony. His muscles twitched with spasms. The pain made him blind and deaf to everything else.

Cisco sighed and drew a knife from his boot. He knelt beside the Shadow Guard and laid his hand across the man's forehead. Salem, oblivious to Cisco's touch or even his presence, wailed and twisted. His skin was hot and fevered, and his soaked hair was plastered to his drenched face. "You fought well," Cisco murmured. "Rest now. May you find peace in Afterlife before you choose your next path."

He pressed the tip of the knife into Salem's neck to pierce the carotid artery. Salem didn't even register the wound. Blood spurted, then slowed to a steady flow, pooling around his head.

Cisco leaned back. Salem's struggles slowed and his screams weakened to whimpers, but the pain never left his eyes, not even when the life finally faded from them.

Cisco waited until the last spasm had passed and Salem exhaled his final breath before he reached out and closed the soldier's eyes. Cisco started to withdraw, then paused. He shifted his hand from Salem's eyes to his mouth. Gingerly, Cisco pushed back Salem's lip. The canines and lateral incisors had lengthened and sharpened.

Whatever Salem had been in the process of transforming into, Cisco could only guess, but he didn't regret his decision to put the faithful Shadow Guard out of his misery and stop whatever monster would have emerged in Salem's place.

***

Holly sat alone in the middle of the pew.

Usually the church was quiet, as if sealed away from all the noise of the impure world outside, but with the windows shattered, she could hear the drone of voices all the way from town square.

Slowly, she turned a piece of red glass between her thumb and forefinger, watching the light catch the smooth face.

She took a deep breath. Held it. Let it out.

So, Cato was back. And, as long as none of the kálos in Phantom Heights with the annoying ability to read minds delved into her private thoughts, nobody would ever have to know that Agent Kovak had confided in Holly more than two years ago. Or that she'd known, even while standing solemnly in Alvarez Park during the funeral service on a warm, sunny afternoon, that Cato's suicide attempt had been a failure and the ashes laid to rest in Hero's Hollow did not belong to the ghost hunter's son.

Holly continued to turn the piece of glass in her fingers. She still cursed Kovak for pulling her into that mess of lies without any warning. She didn't need to know the truth—hadn't even asked for it—but that bastard had told her anyway. The guilt had eaten away at her for months afterward, every time she had to look at Madison, until Holly had finally been able to almost forget her sin.

That was, until Cato's unforeseen escape shoved the lies right down her throat again. Madison deserved better, but what else was there to do? Admitting that Holly had allowed Cato's torture and Madison's grief to continue unnecessarily for two whole years was out of the question. Holly wouldn't have lost only her political standing; the townspeople would have exiled her for turning her back on their hero.

And yet, if given a chance to go back and do it all over again, she wouldn't have changed her decision. Cato's sacrifice, tragic as it was, had been the only salvation that kept Phantom Heights from total annihilation. Although Holly's silence had been cruel, it had been necessary, and that eased her guilt . . . even if only slightly.

Yes, Madison had mourned after Cato's "passing," but then she'd moved forward. She had made the entoplasm shield operational around City Hall. She had manufactured a cache of ectoplasm guns and other weapons that the raiders would come to rely upon for scavenging. She had channeled her pain and rage into something more productive—defending the town she was supposed to protect.

All because Holly and Agent Kovak had steered her in the right direction with a lie that saved Phantom Heights and gave the world a chance to develop the weapon that would spare them from an invasion.

Holly knew she would never be thanked. Such was the life of a politician—the general public didn't understand difficult sacrifices made for the greater good. Cato's fabricated death was one more secret Holly had intended to take to the grave.

But finally, that miserable existence was over. She could stop worrying about the past and focus on the future. Now that the potential disaster had been averted, she would be a fool to waste the opportunity that had just dropped into her lap.

Phantom had come home, and Holly's reputation remained unscathed. What better marketing strategy for her political campaign than a long-lost hero? Of course, setting up that play would require investment first. Cato did, after all, nearly blow the whole town to smithereens.

Holly swirled her thumb in circles across the smooth glass. It almost wasn't fair to manipulate him—not after she'd remained silent and allowed Kovak to torture the poor kid with cruel experiments.

But then again, Holly hadn't made it this far in life by playing fair.

— Chapter Seven —
White Cat

Madison hummed a cheery rendition of "You Are My Sunshine" as she unpacked folded clothes from boxes.

As irritating and pompous as Wesly Cooper could be sometimes, he'd graciously offered for her and Vivian to have the guest bedroom on the second floor. Right under Cato. The silly grin on her face refused to fade.

Her son was alive. Never in her entire life had she been this elated. She might just float away. But keeping him safe . . . That wasn't going to be easy. Poor Cato, still being hunted by the Agents and the Shadow Guard. He must be so tired of running and hiding and fighting on his own for so long. And where had she been to protect him? He was a fugitive because of her. Stirring beneath the joy lurked a current of worry, but even that couldn't dampen her high spirits.

Still humming, she turned but then stumbled back with a startled yelp to retreat from the figure standing in the doorway. Madison quickly turned away, hiding her face in the crook of her arm in embarrassment while setting her hand over her pounding heart. "Axel, I think you just gave me a heart attack. Where are your clothes?"

"I had to wash them again. I didn't get all the blood out the first time."

"Could you at least cover yourself with a towel or something?"

"Why?"

"Because this is very inappropriate."

"Why?" he said again, as if puzzled.

Madison, her eyes still squeezed shut, heaved a deep sigh and pried her arm away from her face. She held up her left hand to shield Axel's pelvis from view before she could bear to look at him. And then a new wave of embarrassment swept over her because Axel was . . . not what she'd expected.

Madison had never seen him out of uniform before. Despite the recent battle, not a single scratch, scar, mole, bruise, or imperfection marked his smooth porcelain skin. He wasn't bulky, but his whole body was cut, every single muscle chiseled. Except for his eyes and fangs, she'd always thought he was close in physique to a human. But humans had flaws, and Axel didn't. He looked more like a youthful Greek warrior god sculpted from marble. What bloodlines could the Agents have possibly combined to achieve this creature?

Axel was shameless in his nudity, but Madison was so humiliated she wanted to crawl under the bed. All she could do was look away and mutter, "How long have you been standing there?"

"You hurt Cato."

The happiness deflated. She tensed, her bright mood immediately plummeting to guilt and regret. "I didn't mean to."

Axel stared coldly at her, displaying no sympathy. Madison took a nervous step away from him. He didn't look threatening. Despite his inhuman perfection, he was, after all, just a fourteen-year-old kid. But something was wrong with the air—it was thick and charged with an ominous, pulsing energy—and Madison remembered all too vividly the image burned into her retinas of Axel standing in a sea of corpses, the blood of his victims dripping from every part of his body. She hadn't actually witnessed him kill anyone, but the horror of seeing men and women with their throats ripped out, ribs scattering the red cobblestones, hearts pulled from their open chests, silent screams frozen on their faces forever . . . What had Axel turned into? Surely he must have transformed into a demon, because this kid didn't seem capable of such a monstrosity.

He snapped, "Doesn't matter; the point is you did. More than you'll ever know. If you hurt him again, you're going to have to deal with me."

Madison paused, taken aback by his open hostility. Her mind

flashed back to the massacre again, and her body went cold. She smiled uneasily and said, "You don't mince words, do you?" The lines in his brow carved even deeper. "Axel, I, uh . . . Is it true, what you said before?" she blurted in a panic when she couldn't find the words to say what she really wanted. "That the Agents cut your finger off?"

Why had she said that? She must have caught a glimpse of his partial finger—his only visible flaw—while her mind desperately sought a distraction to buy some time. Axel sneered and held up both fists with his pinkies extended. "Actually, *They* cut both off." He held his left hand higher. "This one, *They* taped back on to see if it would heal." He dropped that hand so only his right remained up. "This one, *They* didn't. *They* wanted to see if the new part would grow back."

What he was saying was disturbing enough, but the way he said it while watching her almost gleefully made her realize that, even if this past trauma was upsetting to him, Axel was more interested in coaxing a reaction out of Madison.

But he was lying. His intact left pinky didn't have a scar. He was just playing with her.

"I really wish you'd put some pants on."

"Am I making you uncomfortable?" He stepped into the room, and Madison stumbled back.

She cupped one hand to the side of her face like a blinder. "Very."

"Why? You're a scientist, right? I'm sure you must be curious about the very first hybrid with kálos powers."

He was coming closer. She backed away, almost tripping over a box. *He's testing me*, she realized.

"If you think I'm like Agent Kovak, you're wrong. I mostly study ectoplasm. If I do study kálos, it's in the f-field. I don't experiment on people." She ran into the bedpost. Axel halted and folded his arms, smirking.

Madison took a deep breath and shifted her hand to cover his pelvis from view again. "Listen, I know you don't like me. And I haven't made much of an effort to get along with you, either. So," she said, keeping her left hand up and holding out her right hand, "why don't we start fresh? Truce?"

Axel glared at her extended hand for a moment, exposed his sharp fangs in a bitter sneer, and replied, "I don't care if you're Cato's mother. I'll rip you to pieces if you harm my family."

Madison forced her smile to stay in place. "I don't want to be your enemy, Axel."

"No, you don't," the half-breed agreed with the air of an open threat. She blinked, and Axel was gone. A breeze rustled a stack of papers in the wake of his incredible speed. Madison sighed and sat down on the bed, ignoring the sheets of paper that fluttered to the floor in front of her.

That was definitely a test, all right, although she couldn't decide if he'd been probing to see if her scientific nature was similar to the Agents' or gauging whether she was afraid of him. She felt confident that she'd passed the first test but failed the second. Miserably.

Despite his motives, Axel was right. Whether she had intended to or not, she'd hurt her son in innumerable ways, and the realization made her heart ache. Because of her ignorance, Cato had endured two long years of torture, and she didn't have the courage to ask for his forgiveness because she knew she didn't deserve it.

A great weight seemed to press her down into the mattress. No wonder Finn and Reese had looked at her with such fear in their eyes when they'd awakened from death's grasp in City Hall and found her leaning over them. Or why Kit had hidden behind Jay at their first meeting, too frightened to even say her name aloud. As far as the Alpha ghosts knew, Madison was the embodiment of evil, a backstabbing traitor waiting for an opportune moment to betray them. That was going to be a difficult perception to break. The very thought of that uphill battle already had her feeling overwhelmed.

The bed creaked when she rose. She surveyed the stacks of boxes; the open closet slowly filling with shirts and jackets on hangers; the dresser with the bottom drawer agape, waiting for clothes; the pull-out couch near the French doors leading onto a balcony; the single bed with an ornate cherrywood headboard. She sighed. This place didn't feel like home yet, but it would.

Axel's visit still weighed heavily on her mind. *I suppose I deserve a break,* she told herself.

She wandered into the hallway but paused at the grand staircase. Her head tilted back so she could gaze up at the closed door on the third floor. She debated going up to check on Cato again, but every time she had, the Alpha ghost on duty had given her the same answer—"He's still sleeping"—and what if Axel opened the door this time? Her ego wasn't strong enough for another face-to-face encounter with him quite yet. Since he was hanging around the manor, that probably meant that he was taking a turn watching over Cato and the twins while the others were downtown helping the cleanup crews.

Madison glanced at her watch. Cato had been asleep for more than twenty hours. Was that normal? She had spent decades studying how to fight and kill ghosts—how to quickly identify a divine power, how to strategize an attack based on the Divinity's correlating weakness, how to use ectoplasm to combat intangibility, how to be patient enough to wait for the right opportunity for a kill shot with a bullet—but how to care for a ghost? That, she felt woefully unprepared for.

Ero or Wes would probably know how long it should take to recover from a burnout, she realized. She descended the staircase but paused in the foyer to stare at the antique mirror on the wall. Slowly, she took a few steps forward, then trailed her fingertips down a long crack branching across her reflection. Even Saros Manor, on the southern fringe of Phantom Heights, hadn't completely escaped Cato's wrath, although it had certainly fared better than the buildings downtown in the immediate blast radius. If Cato ever wanted to obliterate the town . . .

Madison let her hand fall. She didn't want to think about that.

She crossed the great room, then turned right down the hallway and strode toward the Telepath's abode next to the sunroom. She stopped outside his closed door and rapped her knuckles lightly on the wood. "Ero?" she called after a few seconds of silence. She pressed her ear to the door. No answer.

Madison let her hand slide down the mullion. Ero had awakened a few hours ago, and by now he was likely out helping the cleanup crews, or maybe in the kitchen for lunch. Cato would no doubt be hungry when he woke up, anyway. She could make him a sandwich as a first and admittedly pathetic peace offering, but at least it was something he would appreciate.

She returned to the great room and passed through the library to enter the kitchen. "Oh, Wes!" she greeted upon spotting the werewolf staring out the window behind the sink.

"Shhhhh-shh-shh!" he hissed without turning. He gestured her over. "Maddie, come here."

She couldn't help but roll her eyes at the annoying nickname as she crossed the tiled floor. "What?" she whispered.

He pointed. "Look."

Madison peered outside. Beyond the empty hot tub and inground pool, the overgrown herb garden, and the wisteria-laden wooden arbor leading to the patio, a lush green backdrop of the Alvarez Park woods stretched across the viridian lawn.

It was a gorgeous view, but . . . "What am I looking at?"

Wes was so close to the window that his nose was pressed against the glass. "There, on the porch step. Do you see it?"

Madison's focus shifted to the foreground. On the porch step, a fluffy white cat was sprawled in the sunshine, dozing contentedly.

"The cat?"

"Yeah." Wes's breath fogged the window for a moment before the glass cleared again. "Does it look suspicious to you?"

"What?" Madison studied it for a few seconds. Except for a lazy tail flick, it didn't move. "Um, no. Why?"

He finally leaned away from the window, although his intense stare didn't leave the furry interloper napping on his step. "The thing about Amínytes is, they have a telltale marking. Their right front foot—paw, wing, whatever—is always white. Which makes it easy to identify certain species—I mean, you don't usually see foxes or squirrels with a white paw—but cats and dogs are harder to spot."

"Oh," Madison said, finally grasping his bizarre reaction. "You think that's Kit?"

"I don't know. It hasn't moved in twenty minutes."

Madison turned away and started opening cupboards. "Well, Kit probably has better things to do than sleep all day in your backyard, so I'm going to take a wild guess that it isn't her. And you're going to drive yourself insane if you're suspicious of every single cat with a white paw in Phantom Heights. Where are your plates?"

"Left of the sink. But, even if it's not Kit, it might be spying on me."

Madison set a plate on the counter and muttered, "Then why don't you go ask it what it wants?"

Wes shot her a cold look from the corner of his eye. "You're not taking this seriously, are you?"

"Of course not. You're being ridiculous and paranoid. Peanut butter?"

"Pantry."

She nodded in acknowledgment and rounded the island, pausing at the fridge to hunt for a jar of preserves before continuing to the pantry. "Hey, Wes?" Madison asked as she skimmed the shelves. "How long does it usually take to recover from a burnout?" She finally spotted the jar and returned to the counter. "Wes?"

"I said I don't know," he growled, eyes still fixed on the white cat outside.

"I didn't hear you."

"Well, I shrugged. Not my fault you weren't paying attention."

Madison closed her eyes and exhaled to keep her patience in check. *He's worse than my kids were when they were little.* "I'm concerned that Cato hasn't woken up yet."

"Don't be. He should have burned out way before he actually did. I can't believe how long he managed to stay on his feet."

"But Ero burned out too, and he's been up and about for several hours now. He seems to have recovered already."

"Ero pushed himself close to his limit. Cato pushed himself well past his. Give him more time." At the sound of drawers sliding open and shut, he added, "Silverware is all the way to the right."

"Thanks." Madison returned with a butter knife and unscrewed the lid of the peanut butter jar. "What Cato did was . . . something I've never seen before in all my years of ghost hunting. That seemed like Level 5 power. Am I wrong?" she asked as she slathered the peanut butter on a slice of wheat bread.

Wes finally stepped away from the window, although his gaze kept darting back to the cat every few seconds. "Probably not. Adrenaline and emotional distress can cause a kálos to expel power beyond their normal limits. And that results in a harder crash from the burnout, which is why I don't think you have anything to be worried about. Don't look at it as he won't wake up. Think of it more like his battery hit zero and now he's recharging."

"I'll admit, you know more about kálos than I do. I'm not . . . well, um . . . I'm a little out of my comfort zone."

"Why? Because you have to take care of a kálos instead of kill one?"

He'd clearly meant it to be a joke, but she admitted, "Yeah."

"You're knowledgeable about kálos, though, and that's a much bigger head start than anyone else would have in your position. Just, you know, don't use that knowledge to kill them. That's not really any different from regular parenting, right?"

Madison couldn't help it; she chuckled. "I suppose you're right."

Wes finally turned his back to the window and leaned against the counter. "That isn't Kit."

"How did you reach that conclusion?"

"Kit's ears are black."

"A cat with black ears and a white paw. Should be easy to spot," Madison muttered sarcastically. "Shouldn't you be downtown helping with cleanup?"

"Hey, I pulled an all-nighter," Wes shot back. "I'm taking a well-deserved break. What's your excuse?"

"I was working all morning and then moving boxes for several hours."

Wes made a big show of yawning and stretching his arms high above his head. "And here I thought you'd be downtown all day kissing up to Cato's new pals he brought home from the AGC."

Madison didn't lift her head or respond. Wes folded his arms with a smirk. "Ah. Did I hit a nerve? Are you avoiding them?"

She shrugged. "They hated me before they ever met me, and for good reason. I can't blame them for that. We have a lot of issues to work out, and I thought, you know, it would be better to wait so Cato can be a mediator between us."

The silence dragged on while Madison waited for Wes to call her a coward, but the word never came, although she was certain that he was thinking it. "Suit yourself," he finally said. "Anyway, here's the deal, Maddie."

"*Madison*," she corrected with wavering patience.

"I'll be honest with you—parenthood is not my thing. Never interested me. I had *no* idea what I was getting myself into when I offered to share my house with dangerous fugitives that turned out to be a bunch of kids. So, since you'll be staying here sometimes, and since you're already a mom, how about I turn that job over to you? I'll be an open resource at your disposal for whatever you need. I'm not really cut out to be father material; I'm more like the fun uncle who gives advice and presents."

Under her breath, she muttered, "They'll be better off with a responsible guardian, anyway."

"I heard that," he retorted. "But . . . you're not wrong. I admit that. I'm not good at stuff like setting rules and disciplining."

She nodded slowly. "Cato is already my responsibility, and he didn't return from the AGC alone. I feel responsible for the others, too." The image of Axel's cold and heartless stare while he told her he had to wash the blood out of his uniform made her shiver. "But you're not completely off the hook. We're in this together."

"Sure, sure. Whatever you say. But I'm content to let you take the lead. I'm just here for backup."

"Let me make sure we're clear—I'm not a nanny, and I'm not a maid."

"Of course not! I know that. You're a guest here at Saros Manor, just like Ero."

Madison sliced the sandwich diagonally. First Jaxon, then Cato . . . Her family had been shrinking no matter how hard she tried to preserve it. Now, she had just added Cato, seven kálos kids, and a werewolf to the roster. Her family seemed to be swelling out of control, and the pressure was already making her short of breath with anxiety.

One step at a time, she reminded herself. And that first step was a peanut butter and jelly sandwich.

— Chapter Eight —

The Accused

I kept my eyes closed as my other senses sluggishly awakened from the deep and groggy murk of unconsciousness.

Quiet. The sound of a ceiling fan above me coincided with the touch of a faint breeze across my skin. Softness beneath my heavy body. I thought I remembered falling asleep on a sofa. Was I lying on a mattress now?

"You're awake."

I recognized the synchronized pair of voices and cleared my scratchy throat before thinking, *I am.*

I cracked my eyelids open halfway. Slowly, my fingertips came into focus, curled at rest. I bent each finger one at a time, testing them, regaining blood circulation. A fresh bandage was wound around my arm. I stared at the dark ink tattooed into my soft, pale flesh. A7. Why was my Mark visible? Where was my wrist gauntlet? My hand was naked, too. My glove was missing, and so was my elbow pad. I could see the darkened veins in the crook of my arm.

I ran my sandpaper tongue over my dry lips and stirred. My body felt as if every drop of blood had been replaced with concrete. Each tiny movement, whether it was blinking my eyes or moving my foot, required intense concentration and a frustrating delay between my brain and my muscles.

My guess had been correct—I was indeed lying on a mattress. Someone had not only moved me off the sofa and into the sleeping quarters but also removed my clothes, washed the blood and filth off my skin, and bandaged my wounds. I was naked, which only made me feel even more vulnerable in this sorry and defenseless state.

Finn and Reese were the only ones keeping me company. Despite the verbal acknowledgment of my return to the world of consciousness, they were both reading thick hardcover books and didn't seem to be paying any attention to me. Stacks of books surrounded them in a semicircle.

I closed my fingers into a fist, rather alarmed by the lack of grip strength and the way my hand was shaking. *How long have I been sleeping?*

"Twenty-two hours and seventeen minutes," said Reese, turning the page.

"There's food and water for you," Finn added.

"And your clothes have been washed." Neither graced me with a glance.

My blank gaze wandered until settling on my Arena uniform folded neatly beside a glass of water and a sandwich on a plate. I drew my arms under my body with a long groan and hauled myself up just enough to crawl a few feet across the mattress. I seized the water first and lifted it to my lips, so desperate and thirsty that I wasted some of it by drinking too fast and allowing it to dribble down my chin.

The sandwich had a pungent and familiar nutty fragrance when I took a bite. I chewed . . . and chewed . . . but the thick brown sauce adhered the bread to the roof of my mouth. I shouldn't have taken such a big bite. I remembered eating this as a kid. *PB&J.* That was an acronym for something, wasn't it?

I mustered every energy reserve to push my barely functioning body up into a sitting position. *What happened?* I asked my lab-brothers as I chewed.

Finn closed his book, set it on a stack, and then reached for another. "You burned out," he said, opening the new book and skimming the print at an impossible pace.

I know that. I meant what happened while I was sleeping?

"Cleanup downtown, mostly. That's where Jay, RC, Ash, Kit, and Ero are."

And Axel?

They both shrugged. No surprise—Axel wasn't likely to help clean up my mess or tell anyone where he was going. He was probably trying to distance himself from the humans. A gruesome, bloody afterimage of the carnage in town square made me shudder.

Despite knowing that I should eat in smaller portions, I couldn't stop myself from taking another ravenous bite. *My blood-family?*

Reese casually replied, "Mrs. Tarrow is in the room below us."

"What?" I blurted through my mouthful.

Finn said, "Mr. Cooper cleaned out a room on the second floor for your blood-family to stay in Saros Manor whenever they want."

"Your mother has been worried about you," Reese added. "She brought the food and water."

"She wanted Dr. Crawford to give you medical treatment."

"But Jay refused to let us deactivate Proto." Reese shook his head in disapproval at Jay's apparent rebellion against human orders. In their mind, he'd broken the Rules.

I forced the gooey wad down my throat and stared at the rest of the sandwich in my hands. Madison made it for me. No wonder it tasted so familiar.

She's below me. Right now.

My stomach knotted with anxiety. I sucked the sauce from my finger and resumed eating, my mind doing its best to replay the foggy memories from before I fell asleep. It all felt like a dream.

"You're angry with us," one of the twins—I wasn't paying attention to which one—said.

He wasn't wrong; the blame and betrayal were starting to fester again as my wits returned. *You lied to me. You let me believe my blood-family didn't want me.*

Reese's gaze flitted up to me and then back to the page again. As if sensing that I'd interpreted that as a sign of guilt, he said, "We didn't lie."

You had to have known the truth. Not telling me is just as bad as lying.

Finn let out a long sigh and lowered his open book until it settled in his lap. Reese solemnly closed his novel and held it up. "Reading minds is not as simple as reading a book. Thoughts are not usually clearly and coherently organized."

"Some people do think in terms of narrated internal dialogue," Finn explained.

"Some envision the words as if they are printed inside their head."

"Many think abstractly. Feelings, emotions, colors, images, desires."

"Most people's thoughts are a combination with layers of different elements."

Reese held the book in both hands and stared at it. "Some people, like Dr. Anders, have organized and analytical thoughts. Easy to follow, easy to understand and obey. His mind rarely wanders. Your mother's thought process is similar to his when she's focused."

I bristled at the comparison but kept quiet and took another bite. Finn continued, "Master Kovak's line of thought is not so linear. If he isn't focusing on a specific command for us, his thoughts are nuanced shades of emotions, concepts, images, and words."

Are you seriously trying to convince me that you didn't know? Because I don't believe you.

They both gazed down at their books to avoid my accusatory stare. "We've been thinking," Reese muttered.

"A lot," his twin added.

"But we're having trouble remembering."

Finn sheepishly glanced up at me. "Our schedule was abnormal for several weeks, starting right around the time Mrs. Tarrow allegedly signed the contract. During that period, we were not assisting Masters Kovak and Byrn, or Dr. Anders."

I frowned as I chewed. *Why?*

Reese replied, "We were instructed to do a complete overhaul on ECANI's main operating system."

"The handlers locked us in a small room. We were mostly in isolation."

"We weren't allowed to take breaks. We barely ate or slept."

"The handlers took us back to our cages in the middle of Lightsout and then brought us back to resume working before Lightson, so we hardly had any contact with you."

"Which was fine," Reese admitted, "because . . ." He gripped his shirt in a tight fist over his heart. "Your pain . . ."

"It was unbearable," Finn said, closing his eyes in a grimace as if reliving it. "You wanted to die."

"We wanted to die."

My chewing slowed, then stopped. I swallowed, but this time, I didn't take another bite. "I'm sorry. I didn't realize I'd forced you to feel that pain with me."

They shrugged off my apology. "The heavy workload continued even after the update was completed and we resumed normal duties," Finn said. "We were exhausted. We're having difficulty recalling details from that time. But . . . in retrospect, that's likely the result Master Kovak desired."

I said, "You think *He* wanted you so sleep deprived and overworked that you wouldn't pay close attention to *His* thoughts in case they wandered to what *He*'d done?" I took a bite as they nodded.

"That's the logical conclusion we reached," Reese said.

That seems like a lot of unnecessary effort, I thought since my mouth was full again. *Why didn't* He *just order you to lie? Didn't* He *trust you to obey a direct command?*

The twins shifted, as if uneasy about the insinuation that their master might have doubted their loyalty. Finn said, "It was an elaborate charade."

Reese added, "Master Kovak wanted to make you believe that your mother had disowned you. He wouldn't have wanted to risk an accidental slipup from anyone—the handlers, medical staff . . . or us—to cast even the tiniest bit of doubt on the story. He was probably worried that we wouldn't be convincing if you ever started asking questions and we were expected to supply information we knew to be false."

"Master Kovak had to mitigate the risk in every way possible."

Reese set the book on the floor and started picking at a fingernail.

"And we had no reason to suspect. Everyone at the AGC, including you, accepted the premise that Mrs. Tarrow had relinquished her custody rights in exchange for money. It wasn't unusual; ghost hunters sell their bounties all the time."

"The intern believed the documents were genuine when she gave them to us for filing," said Finn.

Reese added, "The handlers and medical assistants liked to gossip about whether disowning you would allow Mrs. Tarrow to salvage her reputation in the ghost-hunting community."

"And your memory of seeing the signed paperwork aligned perfectly with the memories from Jay, RC, and Ash," Finn said. "There was no inconsistency in the information, so there was no reason to question its validity."

The anger slowly abated as I considered the massive scope of *His* deceit to break the bonds between my blood-family and me. Fooling me was easy enough, but the lengths *He* had gone to fool Mind-Readers was unnerving.

"What about the money?" I asked. "Wasn't that a red flag?"

"In what respect?" Reese inquired with a quizzical tilt of his head.

"There was supposedly a transaction for ten thousand dollars, but no money was ever paid. Just a signature on a custody transfer."

The twins exchanged puzzled looks. "But Cato," Reese began.

"There *was* a transaction in the sum of ten thousand dollars," Finn finished. "It was wired to a bank account."

I stared at them, completely brain-locked. "What? That doesn't make any sense. Madison really did get ten thousand dollars for me?"

Reese calmly stood up, walked to ECANI sitting on the dresser, opened the drawer, and pulled out the gloves. None of us made a sound as he activated the holograms and navigated through financial records.

"Here," he said, pointing. "Ten thousand dollars, routed to this bank account, coinciding with the day Master Kovak presented the custody transfer to you."

I felt as if I were falling. A strange roar, like that of distant waves, echoed in my ears. "But Madison thought I was dead. What was the money for? A sorry-I-killed-your-son payment? And why didn't she mention it?"

He shrugged. "No internal notes. Just the transfer."

"And you're positive that's Madison's bank account?"

Reese frowned and started tapping at holograms to investigate. After a painfully long minute, he said, "No. This bank account belongs to Holly Jennings."

I stared at him, my brain struggling to process. "But . . . why?"

Reese shrugged and shut ECANI off. Finn offered, "Not sure. It could have been an unrelated business transaction that Master Kovak timed for the specific date to cover his tracks."

I nodded at the explanation, but I was sick to my stomach. Something about this didn't feel right. "*He* really never thought about what *He*'d done? Ever?"

The twins hesitated. They glanced at each other, eyes flashing as they conferred and shared memories. "Well . . ." Finn began. "There were brief moments of . . ."

"Discrepancy," Reese finished after a pause while they sought the most appropriate word. "Master Kovak usually chose his words with great care, but every once in a while, there was an underlying feeling of conflict when he mentioned Mrs. Tarrow."

"We do remember one specific moment when his thoughts didn't feel right. He was trying to make you angry so you would use your sonokinesis, and it felt as if . . ."

"There was a sublayer of contradiction beneath the words on the surface," Reese tried to explain.

Finn nodded. "Almost as if Master Kovak had convinced himself that a lie was the truth, but deep down, he still subconsciously knew it was a lie." He held up the open book so the tiny lines of print were facing me. "In most cases, reading someone's mind is more like putting together a puzzle than it is like reading a book."

Reese said, "Master Kovak's thoughts are often difficult to decipher unless he consciously focuses on giving us specific instructions. A Telepath like Ero would have been able to delve deeper and see the truth below the surface. We were not. And we're sorry."

Finn laid the book across his lap again. "You can be angry with us for not seeing through the deception. But we did not lie or intentionally relay false information to you."

You did lie, I thought as I finished chewing another bite.

"We did not," they disputed.

I swallowed and snapped, "You told Ero that Madison would have taken me back if *He* could make me human again. That wasn't true."

"You told Ero that," Reese corrected.

Oh, yeah. I guess I did. "Okay, fine, but you didn't correct me. Why did you let me keep believing that lie?"

Finn answered, "For the same reason Axel didn't identify it as a lie."

"We're not omnipotent, Cato," Reese said. "You believed it was a true statement, so we accepted that it was."

The bitter resentment was gone now, leaving me feeling cold and empty. "I'm sorry. I'm just . . . I'm confused, and I'm still trying to wrap my head around everything. I shouldn't have blamed you."

"Master Kovak calculated for every foreseeable contingency," said Finn rather proudly.

I shoved the last bite into my mouth and stared at the crumbs on the plate. "Why doesn't Axel remember Madison being in that place?"

"July eighth," they chorused.

I waited for more, but they didn't continue. "Okay, you keep saying that like it explains everything, but it doesn't."

"July eighth," Finn said slowly, as if I hadn't been able to grasp the concept of those two words the first time.

Reese elaborated, "Axel was scheduled for a feeding on that day." As if I were supposed to have memorized Axel's feeding schedule.

"Was that a coincidence?"

"Master Kovak doesn't believe in coincidences," said Finn.

"Then what was the point? *He* doesn't know Axel can talk, so *He* couldn't have been worried about Axel telling me the truth."

"Correct," said Reese. "But Axel did openly communicate through body language. Master Kovak likely removed Axel out of an abundance of caution during major phases of the plan just in case he acted out and made anyone suspicious that something was wrong."

My eyes drifted out of focus as I recollected. "You're right. I don't think Axel was there when *He* showed me the signed custody transfer, either. Axel would have known that it was a lie."

I hung my head in defeat. "*He* had everything planned, didn't *He*? The second my blood-family stepped through the doors, I was comatose in Project Omega, Axel was sedated with a tube down his throat for a feeding, and you two were updating ECANI so you wouldn't be around to read anyone's mind and there wouldn't be any security footage. Just a signature on a sign-in sheet."

They chanted, "Never underestimate Master," in such creepy synchronicity that I succumbed to chills. As if choreographed, their heads tilted slightly as they chimed in unison, "Are you still angry with us?"

"No." I wanted to be angry at someone, but why blame my lab-brothers when my hatred should be directed at *Him*? Finn and Reese had been manipulated, just as I had been.

I stared vacantly at the folded pile of clothes. "Were you reading my mind in town square? Did you see Madison's memory?"

"Yes," they said.

"Was it . . . real? I mean, it must have been, right? Is there any chance it could have been falsified?"

"Yes," Finn said at the same time Reese said, "No."

I groaned and dragged my hands down my face. "You guys can't do that to me—my head hurts. And I didn't think you were capable of disagreeing with each other."

"But you asked two questions," Reese replied. "Was it a genuine memory?"

"Yes," Finn answered. "Could the memory have been falsified?"

"No," said Reese. "Not that memory, anyway. A Telepath does have the ability to create detailed, believable false memories, but that takes time and a lot of power. Ero was close to burning out when he projected Mrs. Tarrow's memory into your mind. Even if he were at full strength with time to spare, he wouldn't have been able to accurately recreate Project Omega to that precise level of detail, not unless he'd been there himself or had thoroughly examined our memories of the Project to reconstruct the setting."

Finn continued, "Humans are able to block out memories sometimes, but when they try to rewrite the details, there are noticeable discrepancies. Gaps in time and logic, missing pieces, a lack of sensory information."

"The memory you experienced was genuine."

A haunted look passed over their faces. "That was Project Omega," Finn muttered.

"No question," Reese added under his breath.

I asked, "You've been there before?"

They stared at me with blank expressions. They didn't answer, but I didn't need them to. Finn and Reese had served *Them* in a variety of duties that spanned across multiple Projects; if Dr. Anders had required their assistance in Project Omega, they'd no doubt spent more than their fair share of time surrounded by the remains of expired test subjects.

I remained silent, reflecting on the haunting residual image of my corpse on an autopsy table with a sheet covering most of my body. *He* had told my mother not to move the sheet because *They* had already begun the dissection. I trailed my finger down the ridge of scar tissue in the center of my chest. That wasn't technically a lie. *He* had just failed to mention that I was alive when *They*'d cut into me and I had already been sewn back up.

"She wants to see you," Reese said.

I hesitated. "Are you sure?"

Finn rubbed his knuckles into his eyes and muttered, "We can hear her thoughts."

The food in my stomach suddenly seemed to harden, as if I'd swallowed a stone. It wasn't that I didn't want to see her. I did, but . . . I felt uncomfortable around my blood-family, and I wasn't sure how to approach Madison and Vivian. "Any advice?" I mumbled.

Reese raised one eyebrow at me. "On how to converse with humans?"

I smirked and huffed through my nose. Had I been feeling stronger, I would have chuckled. "Never mind; I guess that was a stupid question. But you can still hear her thoughts, right? Is she mad at me for fighting with her and . . . um, wrecking most of the town?"

"We haven't sensed any anger," said Finn.

Reese added, "She's been sad. And concerned that you won't wake up."

"Mmm." I stared at the pile of clothing but didn't move. Just the thought of getting dressed and then standing up and going downstairs was exhausting. I seized my shirt between fingers that still felt numb and could barely grip. The fabric was clean and soft. I pressed it to my face and inhaled the fresh fragrance.

I took my time in dressing, using the simple task to reawaken my sluggish body limb by limb. My fingers were clumsy with the finer touches like the laces on my wrist gauntlets and boots, but the motion and concentration seemed to aid in the return of dexterity.

When I was finally dressed and had managed to haul myself up onto my feet with the grace of an awkward toddler, my stiff muscles and joints protested every movement. Finn and Reese were engrossed in their books again, probably trying to drown out the memories of Project Omega and all the other terrors of that place in a tsunami of literature after my insensitive prying.

I stretched my arms above my head with a quiet moan, then said, "I'm sorry I jumped to conclusions before hearing what you had to say. That wasn't fair." They briefly glanced at me and then returned to their books without a verbal reply.

I guess I'll assume that means "apology accepted."

I turned away from the twins and headed toward the door. My first few steps were unsteady, but my body found its balance as it relearned how to function.

I didn't trust myself to make it down the stairs without a firm grip on the balustrade. My mind whirled all the way down the staircase to the floor below, but no matter how slowly I descended, I still couldn't come up with a plan. What was I going to do? Just casually walk in and ask Madison if she needed help? Would she expect me to hug her? I *really* didn't want to be suffocated again. And should I address her as Madison or Mom? It would be weird to call her Mom—I hadn't thought of her as my mom in a long time.

I rubbed my pounding head and leaned against the end post of the balustrade to catch my breath and settle my racing heart. There was no need to guess which room Wes had bequeathed to her—the door was wide open and boxes were stacked in the hallway, waiting to be carried in.

I approached and lingered in the hallway, then took a deep breath and lifted the top box. After a moment of stressful indecision about how to greet my mother, I rounded the doorframe.

— Chapter Nine —

Pieces

Something wasn't right.

It was subtle, so nondescript that I couldn't even identify exactly what it was that caused the hairs to rise on the back of my neck.

I shuddered, but not because I'd sensed a ghost. Heat blossomed in my core—my Divinities ready to activate the second I identified the threat. I felt sick.

The room was filled with more boxes, and at first, I failed to find Madison in the mess. Then, I spotted her. My mother was sitting on the bed, her head bowed. She wasn't in peril, and she wasn't reacting to any external threat. Why did I feel so petrified? Nothing was wrong. Was it her I was so scared of?

I cleared my throat. "Where do you want this?" I asked.

She lifted her head but otherwise remained motionless. "Cato," she croaked with a faint smile. "You're finally awake. I was so worried about you."

I'd assumed she was tired from packing and hauling boxes around, but now I saw the light sparkling on tears pooled in her bloodshot eyes and glistening on fresh trails down her cheeks. "What's wrong?"

"I'm selfish," she whispered in a strained voice. I set the box down and observed her from a distance, making no move to come closer. "When Agent Kovak told me you died, I . . ." She sniffed and wiped her nose on her sleeve. "I'd hoped your spirit wouldn't be able to move on to whatever world is beyond this one. I wanted you to stay here, even if you were a ghost. A real one, I mean, not . . ." She awkwardly gestured at me. "Sometimes when I was missing you, I imagined that you were a moorlin sitting beside me. I couldn't let you move on to a better place, even if you were trapped here in a painful, terrible state of existence. I couldn't let you go. I'm a selfish mother."

I shifted. I had no idea how to comfort her, and to be honest, I resented her for putting me in this awkward situation in the first place. I looked away, surveying the room and all the hiding places among the piles of boxes. I still felt my adrenaline dialed up high as if I were in danger, and I knew better than to disregard my instincts.

Quietly, I answered, "It doesn't matter, right? I'm not dead."

Madison wiped the tears from her cheeks, nodded, and smiled. "Right. You're right. You're okay, and you're back, and that's all that matters." She made an odd sound that was a mix of a laugh and a sob. "Why am I crying? I should be happy."

Brushing off her sad mood as if it were a distant memory, she sniffed and rose, then began rummaging through the box nearest to the bed. "I know these past couple of years, I haven't been there for you," she said, lifting a picture frame out of the box and gingerly setting it on the shelf above the headboard. "I'm going to make that up to you."

"You don't have to," I muttered, my voice devoid of any emotion.

"Yes, I do. I don't care if you're not human anymore. You're my son, and I love you. That will never change, no matter what you are. I want you to know that."

I scooted a stack of boxes closer to the bed to make room for more from the hall. This felt too surreal—how strange to hear her say that after I'd spent so long believing *His* lie that she was ashamed enough to disown me. "So . . . are you going to be staying here all the time?"

"Not all the time, no," she said, her back to me. She hesitated, then turned to glance at me over one shoulder. "But I was thinking a few times a week . . . if that's okay with you."

"Yeah," I croaked, then cleared my throat to revive my voice. "Sure." *Why is my heart racing?*

"How are you feeling?"

I stared at my hands. The sandwich and water had quieted the tremors, although I still wasn't feeling up to full strength. "Better. A little weak, I guess, and sore, but okay."

"Here, I can make space for you on the bed if you need to sit—"

"No. Thanks. I'm fine."

She paused, then nodded, the movement just as strained and jerky as my words. "Okay. I wanted to stay with you, to make sure you were all right, but Jay said you were sleeping and shouldn't be disturbed. Did you eat the sandwich I left for you?"

"Yes. Thank you."

"Good. And you're welcome." She set another picture frame on the shelf. "Cato? I, uh . . . I have to ask, for my own peace of mind . . . Why didn't you ever tell me what really happened to you after the accident?"

"I don't know."

"You didn't trust me?"

I rubbed my eyes with my thumb and forefinger. "You're a ghost hunter."

"And your mom. What, did you actually think I was going to experiment on you or turn you over to the AGC?"

I shuddered, memories of being strapped to a metal table briefly taking me out of the present. "I don't know," I mumbled. The table. The restraints on the metal table. I could almost feel them around my wrists, my ankles, across my chest . . . I couldn't breathe. My discomfort jolted up to a prickling new level. I'd swear I could smell that place.

"Would you mind bringing that box over to the bed?" Madison asked. "I'd like to unpack that one next."

Without a word, I seized the box and carried it closer to her. I froze. "What is that?" I whispered.

"What's what?"

I dropped the box. "Careful!" Madison chastised. Upon noticing my expression, she frowned. "What's wrong?"

The smell. It was stronger. I backed away, my hands and feet turning cold, my eyes probably blue. "Dr. Anders," I whispered, eyes darting. As irrational as it might be, I expected him to jump out from behind a box and grab me.

Madison held her hands out. "Please talk to me. Tell me what's wrong so I can help."

"I smell him."

That scent. It still riddled my nightmares, that razor-sharp peppermint, sometimes piercing by itself, other times mingling with the nauseating odor of disinfectant.

"Dr. Anders?" Madison asked.

Something hard and cold was growing inside my fists. I bumped into the corner of a box and flinched away from it, poised to stab with a lethal ice blade.

Still keeping her voice steady with patience, Madison said, "What does he smell like?"

"Peppermint," I whispered so quietly I didn't think she could even hear me.

For some reason, Madison relaxed. "It's me, Cato." She reached into her pocket and pulled out a small canister. "It's just a breath mint." I stared at it. She extended the pack toward me, but I didn't move. "I'm sorry. I had no idea it would bother you. Here, see? I'm throwing it away now." She made a big show of lobbing it into the trash can in the corner.

The essence still wafted throughout the room. It was lodged deep into my nose, enhanced by torturous memories. I melted my icicles and let the water slip between my fingers and drip onto the floor. Madison reached out to me, but I turned away. "I can go see if Vivian has any boxes to bring over."

Her arm fell back to her side. "I'll drive you."

"I want to walk."

"Are you sure you're up to it?"

"Yes."

She sighed with reluctance. "Please don't strain yourself carrying anything too heavy, and don't take too long. Wes and I are serving dinner at six."

I paused. "Dinner?"

"Yes," she said, drawing out the word for a full second. "At six.

Make sure to tell your friends. I'd like everybody to be there."

"They're not my friends. They're my family."

Madison failed to hide the disapproval that I would dare hold anybody on the same level as her and Vivian. "Fine. Six o'clock."

"Fine," I echoed as I walked out of the room.

"I love you, Cato."

I stopped in my tracks. Slowly, I turned around to face my mother again. I opened my mouth but no sound came out. It was easy. *I love you, too.* Four simple words, one syllable each. All I had to do was say them out loud.

But I just stood there with my mouth open.

I couldn't do it. After years of being cramped in my tiny cage, nursing my hatred of Madison Tarrow, I couldn't utter those four words. I closed my mouth and cleared my throat, avoiding her expectant gaze. "Um . . . yeah . . . you too," I mumbled.

I'd cheated. One look at my mother, and I knew she hadn't missed my evasiveness. She tried to mask the hurt that swept across her face, but I saw it. Damage control was out of the question, so all there was left for me to do was walk away.

I ran my fingers through my tangled hair as I criticized myself over and over again. My hope was that the walk from Wes's house to Madison's would clear my head, but instead, my mind was whirring with more thoughts and worries than ever. After so much time desiring my mother's love again, why was I now uncomfortable in her presence? *I love you, too*—why couldn't I tell her that?

I came to a sudden stop to avoid tripping over the small body in my path. I forced a fake smile as I looked down at Kit.

But it wasn't Kit.

Startled out of my reverie, I stepped back. A little girl with a springy mop of hair framing her thin, dark face gazed up at me with adoring eyes. "Hi, Phantom," she said. She held out her hand, reaching for mine.

I retreated another step. "Um . . . hi there."

An embarrassed woman pulled her away with a stern, "You know better than to run off, Aliyah." To me, she said, "I'm sorry."

Aliyah giggled and peered shyly at me around her mother's hip. Only now did I realize how many people had been watching me. Time seemed to have frozen them in place. Some had paused while pushing wheelbarrows, others holding lumber or brooms or shovels. One man even had his arm cocked back, ready to swing a hammer down on a nail halfway embedded into a wooden plank, but he just stood still, staring, his task momentarily interrupted. The humans whispered and openly pointed at me. Some glares were hostile, but most were as awestruck as Aliyah's.

The girl's mother gazed at me as if stunned that she'd suddenly found herself in such close proximity. I couldn't quite read her expression. Wonderstruck, perhaps, but also nervous. Her hand rose to touch her lips. "It's, uh, I mean, it's good to see you, Cato. Welcome back," she said, brushing away a coiled ringlet of black hair that had drifted too close to her eye.

Should I know her? A wall of panic knocked me back another two steps. Nothing about her or Aliyah was remotely familiar. I suddenly found myself at a major disadvantage—everybody knew who I was, which would make it so much harder for me to remember who I was supposed to know on a personal basis.

Aliyah bounced on the balls of her feet and sang, "Phantom's back! Phantom's back! Phantom's back!"

"Yeah," I whispered, backing away. The street was deathly silent, just the little girl singing her praises, the drip of ice still melting, and the quiet rush of water trickling through grates and flowing in the storm drains below while everybody continued to stare at me. Self-conscious, I pulled the hood over my head and hurried away with a nod of farewell to my young fan.

The hood was a moot measure, I quickly realized. There was no hiding anymore. My bicolor eyes gave me away, and even if I were strong enough to focus one of my Divinities and turn them either blue or green, it didn't matter. None of my lab-siblings had green eyes, and I was obviously not Finn or Reese.

Desperate to find cover from the unending parade of watching eyes amid the widespread devastation that turned my stomach with guilt, I lengthened my hurried step into a full run until I was trotting up the steps to the front door of my old home. I knocked and then waited anxiously, rubbing my nose while shifting my weight from foot to foot. I couldn't get the peppermint smell out of my nasal cavity.

The door swung open to reveal Vivian standing in the doorway.

"Cato," she said in surprise. "You don't have to knock. This is your house."

My eyebrows shot up. *It is?* She stepped aside so I could enter. Vivian flashed me a genuine and dazzling smile, much more at ease without the competition of my lab-family. "I'm so happy to see you! You look like you're feeling better."

"Yeah. Anything I can take to Wes's?"

"I've got some boxes packed upstairs. You can help me carry them down so we can load them into the car."

I trailed up the staircase after her, automatically skipping the creaky fourth step. She disappeared into her room, and I hesitated at the threshold before stepping inside after her.

Vivian had been busy packing clothes into boxes. I couldn't see her, but I could hear her rummaging in the closet. I stooped to lift the nearest stack, then paused. Curious, I pushed the boxes aside to get a closer look at something very out of place in Vivian's room.

Part of a large stone with engraved text was leaning against the wall. I knelt down in front of it. "What is this?"

Vivian poked her head out from the closet. "Oh," she said softly. "That . . . um . . . that was your gravestone."

"Gravestone?" I repeated.

She stepped back into the room, hugging an armful of jackets as if to comfort herself. "Your death destroyed us, Cato. Mom told Agent Kovak she wanted your body back so we could give you a proper funeral, but a few weeks later, he sent your ashes in a box with a note that said it was procedure to cremate all expired test subjects and your body wasn't intact enough to deliver after the autopsy anyway. Mom was devastated. She said we'd still bury you, and the two of us picked out a nice jade urn for your final resting place."

I continued to stare at my gravestone to avoid Vivian's intense gaze, which I could feel drilling into the back of my head. She went on, "You were going to be buried in the cemetery. But people were mad and upset and sort of lost their minds, and there was a petition to bury you in the park so there could be a public memorial. People actually protested outside our house. Mom didn't have the heart to argue, so we buried you in Alvarez Park in front of the statue Wes commissioned."

"Wes paid for my statue?"

"Yeah. It was his 'contribution to your ultimate sacrifice,' he said, or something like that." She paused, then mused, "I wonder whose ashes we buried, if they weren't yours."

"Some poor soul from Project Omega, I'm sure," I muttered. I traced my fingertips over the letters engraved in the smooth surface. "Why isn't my name on my stone?"

"What do you mean?"

"It doesn't say *Cato*."

"Oh. No, it did. I mean, it used to. That isn't the whole stone. It was vandalized when we were living in City Hall. I searched everywhere for the missing pieces but never found them. The gravestone used to say, *Cato Jaxon Tarrow: A beloved friend, son, brother, and hero. He will never be forgotten*."

The floorboards creaked when she shifted her weight. "I'm really sorry I couldn't find the other pieces. I promise I wasn't going to leave your grave unmarked. I was planning to replace your headstone."

"Why are you sorry?" I asked, frowning, although I kept my gaze trained on the broken gravestone and didn't turn to face my blood-sister.

"I don't know," she said hoarsely. "I guess . . . I was upset that your resting place had been disrespected. I couldn't protect you when you were alive, and I couldn't protect your grave when you were dead."

"But it wasn't my grave."

She didn't answer. The floorboards creaked again, and I heard the faint rustle of clothing landing on the bed. "Cato?" came Vivian's timid voice. I kept my head down but glanced up at her. She gripped her wrist, eyes shining. "I would really like to hug you. Is that okay?"

Briefly, in the wave of dread, I felt a tiny glimmer of gratitude that she respected my boundaries enough to ask rather than rush me. I tried to convince myself her embrace would be fine. She wasn't going to hurt me. She didn't have any weapons. She was less likely to smother me than Madison.

Slowly, I straightened, then turned to face Vivian. She hesitantly approached me. *Don't move, don't move, don't move*, I reminded my-self as she came closer.

She slid her arms around my sides and pressed her cheek against my chest. I held still. Her fingers clutched my cloak, and then she was sobbing, holding me tightly. "I . . . can hear . . . your heart," she cried, and then a fresh wave of sorrow rendered her incoherent.

If that was true, at least she hadn't noticed it was racing out of con-trol. I closed my eyes, once again seeing the memory of Vivian mourn-ing over me in Project Omega. The last time she'd held me, my heart-beat had been so faint that she hadn't been able to find it.

"Please hug me back," she begged.

I hesitated, then reluctantly wrapped my arms around her and gave a gentle squeeze. She tightened her grip on me, still sobbing. "I don't like it when you cry," I said.

"I'm . . . sor-ry," came her muffled reply. She gave me another firm squeeze, then let go and stepped back, hiccupping and wiping her eyes. "I'm fine. I'm sorry. I . . . thought I could hold it together."

I let my arms fall. She smiled sadly, but I saw another flood about to break free, and she hastened to turn away and start shoving jackets into a box to hide her tears. "I wish you'd come to visit me after you escaped," she said.

"I did."

Her head jerked up. "When?"

"A few times, in the middle of the night. You woke up once and saw me standing there. You called my name. You don't remember?"

She gazed at me, a single tear slowly trickling down her cheek. She shook her head. "So, you've been watching over me all this time."

I nodded. "Hey, question."

"Answer," she said automatically in the moment when I took my breath.

Startled by the interruption, I stared at her for a few seconds before I could recompose my thoughts. "Um, in town square, you called me Cato-Cay. Why?"

"Don't you remember?"

"Should I?" I asked, immediately horrified. *Did I forget something important?*

"No," she said, thumbing away the tear before it reached the corner of her mouth. "I called you Cato-Cay for the same reason you used to call me Vivi. Those were our childhood nicknames for each other." She picked up a frame from her dresser and passed it to me.

I stared at the faces of two children. One was a little boy with green eyes and a mess of black hair, the other a girl with her dark-brown locks braided in pink ribbons and a familiar teddy bear clenched in her hand. "Is this us?"

"Yep. When you were little, you had a hard time with the letter *n*. You couldn't say my whole name no matter how hard you tried, so you called me Vivi. And when you were a baby, Mom and Dad called you Cato, but then sometimes they called you Cay for short. I got confused and didn't know which name to use, so I sort of mashed them both together and called you Cato-Cay. I haven't called you that in years. I . . . also hadn't heard Vivi in a long time."

I wasn't sure why I suddenly felt so self-conscious in Vivian's presence. I gazed at the youthful faces behind the panel of glass so I didn't have to meet her piercing stare. "I don't know why I called you Vivi. It just . . . I don't know. It slipped out." I glanced up at her. "Where's our father?"

She stared at me in absolute shock for several long, uncomfortable seconds. "What do you mean?"

"He wasn't in the photo you gave me."

"No. He died before that picture was taken. I mean, you were really little, but . . . how could you forget that?"

I set the frame back on the dresser and lied, "I remember. I just wanted to make sure, since it was so long ago." I didn't feel any grief. Perhaps I should have, but I couldn't remember him at all. Vivian's news was no more jolting than if she'd told me a stranger had passed away.

She turned a slow circle, scanning the organized mess. "I know I have a photo album somewhere. When I find it, I'll let you borrow it so you can look at the old family pictures."

A headache was starting to pound at my temples. I felt as if my brain were starting to overload. With a weary sigh, I picked up a stack of boxes.

"Wait, what's wrong?" Vivian asked.

"Nothing," I mumbled as I turned to step through the doorway.

Vivian looked as though she might start crying again. "Did I say something wrong? Are you upset?"

Of course I was upset; I had to learn about my life from someone else because my memory had been shattered into a million pieces, and just as Vivian had fruitlessly hunted for the rest of my gravestone, I had been equally unsuccessful at reclaiming my memories.

Everything was happening too fast. Just yesterday—was it yesterday?—I almost killed my mother because she had sold me to *Them*. And now . . . now she and Vivian said they loved me, and they were moving into Saros Manor, and I had no idea how well my lab-family could coexist in the same space as my blood-family, and I had the sinking feeling that Madison and Vivian wanted me to step back into my old life, but I couldn't do that because I didn't know how that person used to act or who he even was, and I wouldn't be able to bear the look on my mother's face when she realized that I couldn't be the son she remembered from Before . . .

The Spasm swallowed me so fast I barely had time to gasp. The boxes fell from my hands. I hit the ground, screaming and thrashing, isolated from the real world by a wall of unbearable agony that blinded me behind my eyelids and deafened me inside the echoes of my own screams.

"Cato! Oh my gosh, Cato, are you okay?"

Hands were shaking me when I finally went limp. I instinctively flinched away, pulling my limbs inward to protect my body as I sheltered my head behind my arms. The hands retreated. "I won't hurt you," Vivian soothed in response to my reaction.

I peeked through the crook in my arm to find her worried green eyes trained on me. I coughed and swiped at the tears itching my cheeks.

I tried to tell her I was all right, but my throat was sore, my thick tongue next to useless. "'M okay," I mumbled.

"No, you're not—you were just screaming bloody murder."

As I hauled myself up into a seated position, my hand brushed small, hard pieces that clinked. I looked down in confusion to realize that when I had dropped the boxes, something inside had been made of china. I seized a shard and held it up. "I'm sorry."

Viv barely even glanced at whatever I'd broken. "Don't be. I don't care about it. I'm worried about *you*."

"Don't be," I echoed, staggering to my feet. "That wasn't my first Spasm, and it won't be my last."

"What causes them? I know it's an aftereffect of some experiment, but why do you have them?"

"Some sort of withdrawal, I think," I muttered vaguely. I didn't want to relive that torture any more than I already had to in my nightmares.

"Withdrawal from what?" Vivian pressed.

"None of your business," I snapped irritably. My head still hurt, and I had too much to deal with to add the horrors of the neural monitoring system to the list. I pressed my palms to my temples, willing the throbbing to recede.

"Maybe Doc can diagnose what's wrong and come up with a treatment to make them stop."

"There is no treatment. They'll become less frequent over time, but there's nothing anyone can do. I just have to suffer through them until they pass."

"But Cato—"

"Drop it, Vivian. I don't want to talk about it."

She hung her head. "Okay. I'm sorry. I'm just worried about you, that's all." I scowled and restacked the boxes, then hoisted them up in my arms. "Cay, it's almost six. We can get these after dinner."

I set them back down. "Oh, I forgot. I was supposed to tell my lab-family." Vivian winced, as if affronted that I had another family now. I cupped my hands around my mouth and called, "Axel!"

We waited for a few moments. Viv whispered, "Can he really hear you?"

I nodded and raised my hands to my face again, taking another deep breath. Something hit my legs hard and fast from behind. I was fairly certain I did a full flip through the air, too startled to even cry out until I landed hard on my back with a grunt. Axel's voice snarled, "I ain't a dog, and I don't appreciate being summoned like one."

"Oh, bloody Scout, Ax," I grumbled, rubbing my bruised tailbone. "Was that really necessary?"

Dressed once again in RC's spare uniform, he was perched on Vivian's bedpost, his clairvoyant red eyes glaring down at me. "What do you want?"

Vivian scowled at him in blatant disapproval. I sat up, rather bitter myself. "Madison wants us all to have dinner together. Could you tell the others?" He glowered at me. "*Please*?" I added in annoyance. Axel rolled his eyes and vanished.

Vivian offered a hand up. I hesitated, then accepted and let her pull me to my feet. "He's charming," she muttered.

"He's not so bad once you get to know him."

"If you say so." She walked away but then lingered in the doorway to wait for me. "Coming?"

I nodded and followed her out of the room, my gaze lingering on the broken gravestone haunting the corner before I left it behind.

— Chapter Ten —

The First Supper

Wes took his place at the head of the table.

At his right side were two empty chairs meant for my blood-sister and mother, then me, then Ash and Axel. Seated at Wes's left were Jay, Kit, RC, Finn, and Reese. Ero was positioned at the opposite end of the table. He seemed older, both in appearance and in the way he sat slouched in the chair as if his body were too heavy. Dark circles shadowed the bags under his eyes.

My lab-family didn't look much better—Jay, RC, and Ash had glazed, vacant stares of exhaustion and sported battle wounds ranging from healing cuts to yellowing bruises. Jay didn't have his arm in the sling, but he favored it with his stiff movements. Kit's ears weren't as perky as usual, and try as she might to remain attentive, she kept blinking sleepily. I probably didn't look any better than the rest of them. Finn, Reese, and Axel were the only three who looked well-rested and unscathed.

Madison and Vivian circled the table and set heaping plates in front of us, causing my mouth to instantly water. Ash, Jay, RC, Kit, and I didn't hesitate; we seized handfuls of food and shoved it into our mouths.

They used to play a cruel game with us when *They* were bored—if we weren't quick enough to take our food, *They*'d snatch it back and we weren't allowed to eat. The Game had no purpose other than amusing the handlers. Needless to say, we'd learned not to hesitate long enough for a human to take food away.

"Hey, *hey!*" my mother cried. "I'm glad you like my cooking so much, but please use the silverware, not your hands."

Silverware? I barely broke stride as I grabbed the fork beside my plate and shoveled the food into my mouth. I didn't even bother to analyze what exactly I was eating; it was so rich, so *good*, and I was starving.

"Whoa, Cato, slow down!"

A hand was coming toward me in my peripheral.

I dropped the fork, seized Madison's wrist, and slammed her hand onto the tabletop, digging my thumb into a pressure point for good measure. She cried out, but I maintained my grip. In my other hand, I formed an icicle with a sharp point, poised to stab.

Everyone froze. My lab-family, with the exceptions of Axel and the twins, drew their plates closer so their food was easier to guard.

My mother's eyes were wide as she gawked at the icicle ready to impale her. "I won't take your food away. I just don't want you to eat too fast and get sick."

This was good food in front of me, a hundred times better than the kind I'd had to battle my lab-family for in the Arena. "You promise?" I demanded, squeezing harder.

"Yes! Yes, I promise—*argh*—Cato, you're hurting me!"

Reluctantly, I released my hold. She drew her hand back and held it to her chest while I remained hunched protectively over my plate, glaring at Madison until she backed away. Not until she sat down did I finally relax, just a little.

Everyone dropped their gazes and continued eating, though with more reservation now that everyone was seated and there didn't appear to be an immediate threat. Axel, Finn, and Reese were the only ones who hadn't touched their food.

"Aren't you hungry?" Vivian asked.

Through a mouthful, Jay told the twins, "You don't have to wait for permission."

Finn and Reese looked at him with their bright blue eyes, then turned and watched Madison, hopeful, waiting, practically squirming in their chairs. Apparently, they'd deemed her the highest-ranking authority figure, outclassing Wes and Ero with her pureblood human status.

She frowned, assessing the situation. "You can eat."

I chewed my roll as I watched them pick up their forks in sync. Every movement they made was perfectly coordinated; at the exact moment Finn brought his fork to his mouth, so did Reese.

"What about you?" Madison said, twisting her head and leaning forward to peer down the long table at Axel, who regarded her coldly with his arms folded across his chest. "Are you also waiting for permission?"

"I don't need permission from *you* for anything. I ain't eating this garbage."

I closed my eyes in a brief wince. My mother stared at Axel for a moment, visibly taken aback by the hostility, and then her eyes narrowed. I could practically feel the tension spark between the two. *Please*, I silently begged Madison, *don't push Axel right now. He's still upset.* If only she could read minds like my lab-brothers.

"If you aren't eating now, you don't get to eat later," she warned.

Axel glared back at her. "Fine."

"I mean it."

"If it tastes like shit now, it'll still taste like shit later."

Jay let out a breath as if debating a reprimand, but he decided to keep quiet and let Madison handle Axel herself.

"All right then," she said, "since you don't like tonight's meal, any suggestions for what I should cook tomorrow?"

"No." He glared at his plate.

"If you won't eat my cooking, I guess you'll go hungry."

"Guess so," he dismissed without even the slightest hint of regret.

"I think everything is delicious, Mrs. Tarrow," Ash said.

"Thank you," Madison replied pointedly, shooting Axel another glare.

He glowered back at her and set the soles of his boots on the edge of the table, leaning back and rocking on the hind legs of his chair.

Madison's voice was sweet but strained when she calmly requested, "Axel, will you please take your feet off the table?"

He took a moment to yawn—which really irritated me because he never yawned; it was something he'd seen humans do when they were bored, and he knew it was a sign of rudeness—before he rolled his eyes and grudgingly did as Madison had requested. The front chair legs slammed back onto the ground. He fell into a brooding silence, but the tension still hung like fog in the air.

"So," Madison said solemnly as she gazed around the table. "This is our first time . . . you know. Being all together in a normal setting like this. I, uh . . . I know our relationship didn't exactly start out on the best terms. You must have thought so little of me for abandoning Cato."

"*Disowning* Cato," Axel growled. "There's a difference."

She nodded. "You're right. But since I didn't actually disown him, that difference is irrelevant, don't you think?" Axel folded his arms.

Madison set her fork down and continued, "Look, I know it's not easy breaking a stigma after such a terrible first impression. And I've been hard on you ever since you arrived in Phantom Heights."

Her uncomfortable speech was met with silent, wary stares. She cleared her throat, inadvertently causing Finn and Reese to sit at attention and activate their Divinities to read her mind.

"I just wanted to say that I'm sorry for how I've treated you. Our initial perceptions of one another were based on lies and deceit . . . on both sides. Agent Kovak didn't paint you in the best light either when he came here and asked us to help hunt you down. I hope you'll give me the chance to start over and get to know who you really are since you're, um, you're Cato's . . ."

She trailed off. She couldn't say it. She couldn't say *family*, because in her eyes, they weren't.

Madison sighed and awkwardly redirected, "How are you all feeling?"

When she didn't receive an answer, she pried, "Cato?"

"Tired," I muttered.

She waited a few seconds, as if hoping I would say more and contribute to the conversation so she wouldn't be the one doing all the talking. I took a drink to make it clear that I had nothing else to add. She moved on: "And you, Ash?"

"Sore," Ash admitted, and I suspected she wasn't referring to the bruise and gash on her cheek. She'd been hit with multiple shock rods during the battle; that had to hurt. One shock alone was enough to down a victim.

My mother's gaze settled on Jay in a wordless inquiry. He shifted and said, "My arm hurts. But I'm all right."

"Would you consider letting me look at it after dinner to see how it's healing since you refuse to let Doc examine you?"

He glared at her across the table. "No."

RC rubbed his collarbone and quietly said, "Ero? Can I ask you something about Lieutenant Cisco?"

The Telepath inclined his head. "Certainly."

"He . . . did something to me. I don't know what. He struck me in the chest, and then my power failed."

"Ah," said Ero. "He must have hit your killswitch."

Wes shook his head. "You made the mistake of letting Cisco get that close to you?"

RC asked, "What's a killswitch?"

Ero hesitated and cast a sidelong glance at my mother. Her eyebrows rose. "Wait . . . do you not want to tell because I'm a ghost hunter? Is it a universal weakness among kálos?" She leaned forward with a new sense of alertness. "Hold on. Is it like an actual kill switch?"

"You are familiar with the term?" Ero asked.

"Sure. A kill switch is an emergency shutoff for a machine or computer."

"Huh," he said, genuinely surprised. "I did not realize the etymology was Cröendorian."

Wes countered, "Or the humans of this Realm borrowed the term from Avilésor."

Ero shrugged and said, "I suppose there is no harm in telling you. It is common knowledge in Avilésor, and knowing about the killswitch certainly would not give you an upper hand in battle."

He focused on RC again and explained, "Think of the way your power originates here—" he pressed his fist to his heart "—and flows through your body. It is not unlike your circulatory system. All kálos have what is known as a killswitch, which is a cluster of nerves located just beneath this bone." He ran his thumb along his clavicle to demonstrate. "It is a very small cluster, about the size of your fingertip, and it is located on your dominant side. If struck precisely with enough force, it . . . How would you describe it, Wes?"

The werewolf swallowed his mouthful and said, "It breaks the circuit of the power flow, causing a momentary shutdown."

Ero nodded. "As I am sure RC can attest, losing your power for even a few seconds can be detrimental in the middle of battle."

Vivian chimed in, "Why did you say knowing about the killswitch wouldn't give ghost hunters an upper hand? That seems like a huge advantage."

Ero replied, "The nerve cluster is such a small target that unless you knew precisely where to strike, you would never hit it by pure chance. Lieutenant Cisco is a Sensor. He is able to immediately identify your Divinity and power level, and he knows exactly where your killswitch is." Ero paused and glanced at Axel. "I am curious, Axel . . . Are you also able to sense it?"

My lab-brother narrowed his eyes and tilted his head as he studied Ero. "Yeah. I didn't realize what it was, though."

"Interesting. Well, should any of you encounter Lieutenant Cisco again, I highly recommend you stay out of arm's reach. There is a reason he was promoted to such a high rank despite having a passive Divinity. He is a master strategist who excels at exploiting weaknesses."

I chewed slowly, digesting this new information. I was right-handed, which meant my killswitch must be on my right side, just under my collarbone somewhere between my sternum and shoulder. I'd seen Cisco strike RC's killswitch and cut off his telekinesis with a single blow. If I ever had to fight the lieutenant myself, I'd have to remember to protect that vulnerability with ice.

Wes took a sip and set his glass down. "Form-changing kálos also have a susceptible nerve right where the neck meets the shoulder.

Squeezing that nerve forces them to change. Shifters. Beasts. Amínytes." He glanced at Kit, who pinned her ears and sank lower into her chair. He picked up his fork and knife and started cutting the meat on his plate. Noticing our hostile glares, he muttered defensively, "What? It's not like I would ever force Kit to change forms. I'm just pointing out that the possibility exists."

Madison gently said, "I don't suppose I can convince all of you to take it easy for the next few days so you can properly recover?"

She was answered with resolute silence. Madison took a deep breath and continued, "I, uh, I don't know much about any of you . . . but I'd like to. Maybe you could tell me a little about yourselves? Where you lived, about your families . . ." As soon as the words left her mouth, the tension returned and thickened to the point of suffocation.

"Jay?" she pressured, looking across the table at him. She probably hoped that getting the leader to start would inspire the others to follow suit.

His silver eyes flicked up at her, then back down to his plate. Madison shouldn't have brought up this touchy subject. Most of my lab-siblings didn't like talking about their pasts—or at least, what they remembered.

"Are you absolutely sure you don't have families in the Ghost Realm who miss you?"

"Yes," Jay answered dryly.

"But how can you know that beyond the shadow of a doubt? Yesterday, Cato thought I didn't want him. Isn't it possible that your families miss you?"

"That's about as probable as a Delta in Gamma," RC muttered. We all scoffed and snickered at the dark joke. Even Axel smirked as he imagined his feral venom-brothers in Project Gamma. Ero tilted his head with a polite grin, understanding the comic remark only because he could read our minds.

"I don't get it," Vivian admitted.

"Oh," I explained, "see, Gamma is where ghosts are bred, but Deltas don't reproduce by giving birth, so . . ." I trailed off at her uncomprehending stare.

"Isn't Axel originally from Delta?" she asked. When I nodded, she only looked more puzzled by RC's joke.

"And Gamma," Madison murmured. "Where have I heard Gamma before?"

"Finn and Reese were born in Gamma," Ash offered quietly.

The twins kept their attention focused on their plates, making no reply or acknowledgment. "Yes," Madison said slowly, "that must be it. I knew I'd heard something to do with Gamma before." She hesitated, as if she wanted to ask the twins something, but she wisely chose not to push the subject. Instead, she told them, "It feels like it's been a long time since you two were so sick in City Hall with us. I still haven't heard your voices. Ero says you're very smart, and I'd love to have a conversation with you."

Madison waited patiently, but when it became clear they weren't going to answer, she added, "Talking isn't against the rules, you know." I took another drink of water, glancing between my mother and the twins. She was wasting her time. Finn and Reese avoided eye contact and continued to eat in silence.

Vivian asked me, "Will they ever talk?"

I set my glass down. "They do talk. Just not around humans unless you issue the right command."

"But you're human."

"Half. And they wouldn't speak to me at first, either. It took a while before they were comfortable talking to me."

Madison, her attention still fixated on the twins, said, "So, theoretically, I could order them to speak." Her voice had adopted a dark, detached tone, as if she was weighing the option from the mindset of a scientist contemplating how to test a hypothesis.

Finn and Reese glanced up at her briefly, then dropped their gazes again.

I coldly replied, "Yes. But they wouldn't really be speaking by their own free will so much as reciting whatever information you command from them."

She nodded, as if my answer didn't surprise her. "I'm not going to do that," she said, her tone transforming back to a warmer octave. "I want them to talk when they feel comfortable."

The conversation died like an Omega—slowly and painfully—and an awkward silence settled over the table again, broken only by the clinking of silverware. I wasn't sure what to make of my mother's interactions with my lab-family so far. She seemed to be toeing a fine line between authoritative sternness and an awkward attempt at compassion to connect with them on a more intimate, motherly level.

I chewed slowly, frowning as I analyzed her behavior. Was that how I remembered her from Before, or was she acting out of character? The inability to find clear, specific memories frustrated me. What had Madison been like as a mom? What did I remember about her prior to the dark period of my life when any mention of her made me sick with hatred?

I remembered taking shelter in her bed when I was little and a thunderstorm had awakened me. I remembered Vivian cooking dinner often because Madison was locked in her lab in the middle of important research and couldn't be disturbed. I remembered being afraid to tell Madison that I had failed another math test, but I also remembered her hugging me when I brought home a good grade after hours and hours of studying before the exam. I remembered her laying me on the cot after the Flash, covering me with a blanket, wiping the sweat from my brow, and kissing my forehead as she promised that I was going to be okay. And I remembered her trying to shoot me when she faced off against Phantom.

Madison Tarrow, I was pretty sure, had been a good, kind, loving mom, but she'd possessed a rigidness and aura of supreme authority that had caused my peers to fall silent in respectful awe when she was in their presence. My mother wasn't like most others. But yes, now that I had gathered a handful of partial memories, I was fairly certain in my conclusion that she was acting true to nature, at times frightening and strict, but also soft and caring.

An ear-shattering screech broke the silence and lifted me to my feet. I immediately assumed a defensive crouch. Jay, Ash, and RC were up too, ready for a fight.

I straightened in confusion when I realized that Kit was the one screaming even though nothing appeared to be wrong and she wasn't suffering the usual symptoms of a Spasm. Vivian pressed her hand over her heart as Wes, who had risen halfway out of his chair, lowered himself back down. Ash slowly replaced her weapon. My mother said, "Kit, sweetheart, what's the matter?"

Tears streamed down the girl's face. "I'm bro-ken!" she sobbed.

"What is she talking about?" Vivian asked, but I didn't have the slightest idea. Ero subtly put his hand over his mouth to conceal a grin.

Jay knelt down beside Kit, who was practically hysterical now. "Hey," he murmured. "Kit-Kat, what's wrong?"

"I'm broken!" she cried again, holding out her fist. Frowning, Jay opened her clenched hand and pinched a small object between his thumb and forefinger, then held up a tiny pointed tooth.

Ash, RC, and I sat down. "Kit," Madison said, smiling and leaning forward, "everybody loses their baby teeth, and then big strong grown-up teeth grow in to replace them. You aren't broken."

The Amínyte hiccupped and whimpered, gazing at my mother with her sparkling golden eyes. Jay gently wiped the tears away. He set his hand under her chin and tilted her head up. "Let's see it."

Kit opened her mouth to reveal a new gap where the small tooth used to be next to her top right fang. "Oh yeah," Jay said, closing one eye and cocking his head a little to one side. "I think I can see the new one already."

Axel scoffed through his nose—the only hint that I'd just heard Jay tell his second lie that I knew of to date.

Kit sniffed, her eyes still flooded with tears. "R-really?"

"Uh-huh. You know what that means, right?" She wiped her nose with the back of her arm. With another big sniffle, she shook her head. "It means you're growing up. Soon you'll be as tall and strong as Ash."

Kit blushed, positively melting under the comparison, while Ash's face turned vermillion. As Jay rose and reseated himself, Wes gestured at Kit's plate with his fork and said, "If you want that new tooth to grow, you better eat all your vegetables."

True enough, all of the plates were now empty except Axel's and Kit's. The little girl glared moodily at the broccoli and made a disgusted face, shaking her head.

"Kit," Madison said, her voice soft and motherly but possessing that hint of sternness again, "Wes is right. We have to get you on a healthy, balanced diet, which means you need to eat vegetables."

Kit eyed her plate, then pinched the green vegetable in her fingers and popped it into her mouth. After a moment, she grimaced and spat it back onto her plate, pinning her ears back in distaste as she stuck out her tongue.

"Okay," my mother said, standing up. She walked behind Wes and circled the table. Kit shrank into her chair and threw her arm up to protect her head, expecting punishment. Madison hesitated. Jay, RC, Ash, and I stiffened, ready to defend Kit if Madison tried to strike her.

"I just want your plate," Madison said. Kit gazed up at her, every muscle in her small body locked with tension. My mother lowered herself down to one knee so she could meet Kit's fearful stare at eye level. "Kit, sweetheart, I will never ever hit you. I promise."

The Amínyte timidly lowered her arm, but she remained completely rigid. Madison slowly and carefully slid the plate away from Kit before she rose. "I'll be back in a minute," she called brightly over her shoulder, disappearing into the kitchen with the plate of broccoli.

We all exchanged confused glances but said nothing. I exhaled and let my shoulders fall as the tension seeped out of my muscles. Madison hadn't even raised her voice at Kit; I should have known she wouldn't hit my lab-sister.

When she returned and set the plate in front of Kit again, the green broccoli had been covered by a yellow blanket of gooey, melted cheese. Kit speared the vegetable onto her fork to take an experimental bite. Her ears pricked forward, and she started eating zealously. Madison smiled. "Vivian didn't like vegetables when she was little, either."

"Clever," Ero praised.

My blood-family began to collect the empty dishes from the table, and Ero stood to assist. Wes made no move to help.

I yawned and slumped against the back of my chair, feeling full, content, and sleepy again.

Madison said, "I'm glad *most* of you—" she paused to send Axel a special glare "—enjoyed your dinner. I'm going to the store tomorrow. Do you have any favorite meals you'd like me to make?" We answered with quiet mutterings of "no" and assurances that anything she cooked would taste good. She made eye contact with Axel again and said, "Axel? Are you sure there's nothing I can cook for you?"

"I already told you I'm not eating any garbage you set in front of me."

Finally losing her temper, she snapped back, "Well, maybe I'll fix a fillet of Shadow Guard since you seem to have acquired a taste for that."

Dangerous, potent tendrils of Grade G ectoplasm erupted in a red glow around the half-breed. Axel, forgetting his strength, brought his fists down on the table with a furious, "*Fuck* you!"

The beautiful mahogany wood splintered under his might as the legs on his end of the table buckled. All the dishes that hadn't yet been collected slid down the slope—plates, bowls, glasses, and silverware clinking as the china slid and shattered into a sharp pile at Axel's feet. He stood and whipped his chair at the wall on his way out, effectively smashing the chair, putting an impressive hole in the wall, and causing a few of the landscape paintings to fall.

Kit's fork was still suspended, her mouth open and ears back as she stared at the cheesy broccoli among the ruins of dinner. Ash's hand flew to her lips in horror. Finn and Reese cowered and backed away from the table as if afraid they would be punished for Axel's misconduct. The rest of us were frozen in place. We all turned to look at Madison, but she seemed to be shell-shocked.

Wes sighed and rubbed his eyes with his thumb and forefinger. "Not like that was an antique or anything," he mumbled, although the bitterness in his voice told me it was, indeed, antique. He dragged his hand down his face and added heavily, "Oh well. I guess an upgrade is overdue."

"I'm so sorry," said Jay.

Madison still hadn't found the sense to close her mouth. Ash bent down and picked up a shard, but my mother raised her hand and said wearily, "No, I'll clean it up."

Nobody moved. Frustrated, Madison snapped, "Go. It's fine."

Like zombies, my lab-family and I wandered toward the foyer in a daze. I paused to glance over my shoulder at my blood-family before I left them in the disastrous dining room to clean up yet another mess. At least this one wasn't my fault.

— Chapter Eleven —

Evolution

Madison rinsed a soapy plate and set it on the stack. No sooner had she released it than a pair of hands picked it up and began to dry it with a towel.

Startled, Madison raised her head to find Ero beside her. "Oh. This is a pleasant surprise."

The Telepath smiled. "You did all the work cooking; I figured the least I could do was help clean up."

"But you should be resting."

Ero responded by offering his hand until Madison handed him the clean glass she was holding. "I don't understand why you and Wes are friends. You're complete opposites." The lazy werewolf was lounging in one of the cushy recliners in the den.

Ero chuckled and wiped the inside of the glass. "It is a complicated friendship, I suppose. I met Wes the first time he came into Avilésor through a Tear, and I suppose I was intrigued about a lunos from Cröendor with no pack. He wanted to pay me for a tour of the village."

Ero smiled and shook his head as he set the glass down and accepted another. "By your standards, I think he offered me a hefty sum. It was paper money, good for nothing except kindling. I declined, and Wes's last resort was to offer the few coins he had in his pocket. Again, most were worthless, but he had the human equivalent of an æz."

"A what?"

"Copper."

"A penny?"

"Next to worthless here, but valuable in Avilésor. So, I accepted his offer and gave him a tour of Avakree."

"Huh." Madison turned on the faucet and rinsed the suds off a plate before passing it to Ero. "Well, that explains how Wes made his fortune in the Ghost Realm."

"His ascent up the social ladder is an impressive feat."

Madison scoffed. Ero gave her a sidelong look and added, "Weir are treated as barely a step above the scarbacks when in human form, and they face fear and discrimination when in animal form. I have to commend Wes for his determination to establish a reputation for himself."

"What, by collecting the lowest-value currency here? That's not remarkable."

"Wealth alone would not be enough to elevate the status of a lunos. How much do you know about his form-shifting abilities? Have you seen him in limbo?"

"Yes, I have. Many times."

"Then you are aware, at least on some level, how difficult it is to be in limbo. His body tries to complete the transformation one way or the other; it is not meant to remain so unstable halfway in transition. But Wes, through an admirable amount of training, has conditioned himself to trigger the early spark of power and hold it without advancing the shift."

"Meaning?"

"Meaning he can make his eyes glow for an extended period of time without any other physical change. With his glowing eyes and a wardrobe change, Wes can pass as a kálos if one does not pay too close attention to him. Of course, he has limited windows to time his trips into Avilésor. It must be near enough to the full moon for the power to be easily drawn upon, but not so close that the wolf risks awakening, and not so far away that the strain is too great. It is a fine balance that has required intense training to master."

"Maybe he's 'admirable' in your Realm, but here, he's a conman and a thief. He says he made his fortune investing in stocks, but I know his initial investments were made with stolen money. I can't prove it, but I'd bet my life savings he used some of those pennies in your

Realm to charter ghost heists in this one. That, and he'll stab you in the back to save his own skin."

Ero admitted, "The trust I have placed in Wes is the result of being able to read his mind. I can see why you are not able to give him that courtesy."

"Pennies," Madison muttered, shaking her head. "He claims to be such a brilliant businessman, but he cheated."

"Perhaps. But the system he cheated was rigged against him."

Madison, increasingly conscious that the Telepath could sense her true distress about the dinner catastrophe, bit her lip to keep it from trembling. She tried to joke, "Well, at least there aren't too many dishes to wash tonight."

Ero didn't speak for a moment, and when he did, his voice was solemn. "I do not think you need to be warned about Axel's temper."

Madison clenched her teeth and angrily threw a handful of silverware into the sink. She took a deep breath to calm down.

"I urge you to remember that Axel is still adjusting to his body. Have a little patience with him. Although he has had his enhanced abilities for seven years, he has had only months outside of a cage to learn how to control his strength and resist temptations an animal would normally give in to. All factors considered, he has adapted much better than I would have expected, given his bloodlines."

"What is he?"

"I cannot say."

"But Ero—"

"I apologize, but his secret is not mine to tell. If you want to know, you will have to get the answer from Axel himself. I can promise you this: Axel does not *want* to kill. Despite his threats, you do not have to worry about convincing him to spare lives."

"I don't know if I can believe that after what he did to those Shadow Guards." Ero's silent acknowledgment of the tragedy was no consolation. Madison stared blankly at the stream of water. Her throat tightened.

Gently, Ero said, "You did not ask for my opinion, but if I may offer it regardless?"

She swallowed and nodded.

"You put too much pressure on yourself tonight." Madison blinked away the excess moisture blurring her vision and glanced at Ero, who smiled at her. "Your desire to host a perfect dinner and make a good, shall we say, second first impression was admirable."

Madison sighed and turned her gaze back to the sink. "I'd already screwed up any chance to make a good first impression before they even arrived in Phantom Heights." She picked up a bowl and started cleaning it more forcefully than necessary. "Their first impression of me was a heartless ghost hunter who disowned her son and sold him to the government. And even if you don't count that, my first face-to-face impression with them was at the festival. I didn't exactly give them the most warmhearted welcome, did I?"

"Amends do not have to come in one dinner."

Her movements slowed. "I was too much of a coward to try to talk to the others until Cato was awake. I thought he would be able to lessen the tension." She felt her shoulders sag. "Tonight didn't go the way I'd hoped."

Ero gently took the bowl from her hands. "First impressions rarely do, and tonight was, indeed, a first impression even though it was not your first introduction. You should not blame yourself."

"I suppose you're right." Madison scrubbed at a cheesy plate and felt an involuntary grin tug at her lips. "Kit is such a sweetheart, isn't she? Once I realized what she meant when she said she was broken, it was all I could do not to laugh."

"Madison," Ero said seriously, "you should tread lightly with Kit."

"Why? Do you think she's dangerous?"

"Dangerous? No. Excluding the twins, Kit is the least dangerous of the group. Amínytes have weak, Level 1 passive powers. But they are also very low in the social order in Avilésor, below the weir even, and the chances of a domestic like Kit not being exploited on the Black Market are slim. I do not think she was at the AGC very long, and yet she still shies away and cowers as if she expects to be abused, which leads me to believe that she may be a scarback."

"A what?"

"A slave," Ero rephrased.

"Oh." Madison shook most of the droplets from a plate before handing it to Ero. "But she's so little."

"The younger the better," he answered dryly as he took the plate. "Masters like to train their slaves to be obedient from an early age. I cannot know for a fact that she was sold on the Market without searching her memories, and I will not invade her privacy like that. But if she was not, then she was most certainly hunted by Traders her entire life. The life of a domestic Amínyte is not easy."

"The Black Market *and* tortured by the Agents . . . poor baby." She shook her head. "And I don't have a clue how to connect with Finn and Reese."

"I wish I could offer advice, but I have also struggled to connect with them, although I have made some headway."

Madison passed him a bowl. "I know Finn and Reese served the Agents. But Amínytes aren't powerful, and Kit is too young to fight like the others do. She doesn't seem to fit into the equation. Why do you think she was in Project Alpha?"

"I cannot say for sure, but I would wager a guess that Sorrin's Theory might be a plausible explanation."

"What is that?"

"A theory about the evolution of our Divinities. Sorrin himself is long dead, but during his time, he was a deep thinker, which can be rather dangerous in Avilésor."

"Really? Why?"

Ero set the bowl on the stack of clean dishes. "Well, in our Realm, it does not matter what you look like, or what color your skin is, or where you were born. All that matters is your power. Those born with it are blessed and do not question their gift, while those born without it are simply trying to survive. Sorrin spent his lifetime studying the evolution of our powers. He deduced that every Divinity was connected and could ultimately be traced back to a single common ancestor. According to Sorrin's Theory, the very first kálos was an Amínyte. It was the original Divinity from which all others evolved. My guess, to answer your question, is that the Agents have reached a similar conclusion from their research and therefore saw value in placing Kit in Project Alpha to study her divine power as the potential founder of all Divinities."

"Interesting," said Madison as she dunked a plate into the suds. "Is Sorrin's Theory credible?"

"That depends on who you ask. Most kálos discredit it, but not because the logic is unsound. Rather, accepting it would disrupt the social order. Amínytes are either feral or scarbacks in present society, disregarded as a lower class either way. No one wants to admit that the Amínytes' ancient ancestor might have founded our noble race. But, when looking at the theory from an unbiased perspective, there is no question that their power is certainly unique. With the sole exception of Cato, they are the only kálos who can assume a non-kálos form undetectable to our sensing abilities. Also, the pendant an Amínyte is born holding is enchanted. It transforms in tandem with the Amínyte, taking a shape that is useful for its owner to carry in animal form. Amínytes are a mystery, but one that kálos have refused to unravel for fear that it might upset the current balance of power in our society."

"It sounds like you agree with Sorrin's Theory."

Ero shrugged as he accepted the plate from Madison. "Sorrin did not come to his conclusion lightly. Theorizing the evolution of Divinities was his life's work."

"Hmm. Well, I'd say your theory is sound, too. If Kovak thinks an Amínyte was the common ancestor from which all Divinities evolved, I can see why he would show interest in Kit."

"Yes. Even if he does not agree with or even know of Sorrin's Theory, there is no denying that Amínytes are different from all other kálos, even from Beasts and Shifters. I would imagine that he is astute enough to notice that, at the very least."

Madison frowned as she scrubbed a pan. "Well, that bastard can't hurt her anymore. But is it really true that none of the others from Project Alpha have families who care about them? I can't believe that."

Ero nodded. "Sadly, that does seem to be the case. I believe Axel had a good life until right before his incarceration. As for the others, I know very little about their early lives."

Madison rinsed her hands as the whirlpool of water drained in the sink. "I'm going to give them all a new life," she declared.

Ero raised an eyebrow as he carried a stack of clean plates to a cabinet. "They have a natural distrust of humans, especially ghost hunters. The odds of gaining their trust are not in your favor."

"Then give me advice."

The Telepath chuckled. "Madison, you are a parent already. You have raised two children by yourself. You do not need advice."

"But these aren't regular kids," Madison replied, drying her hands on a towel. "I don't know how to raise kálos, especially ones who were tortured and treated like animals instead of people. Please. You've connected with them. I would really appreciate any advice you might have."

Ero closed the cabinet and turned to face her. He remained silent for a moment, then nodded toward the breakfast nook and said, "Perhaps we should sit."

"Why do I feel like you're about to give me bad news?" she asked with a nervous smile. She realized her hands were shaking when she struggled to drape the towel across the rod. Ero politely gestured toward the table.

Heart pounding, she obliged and timidly perched on the edge of the seat, palms pressed together and sandwiched between her knees to keep them still so she wouldn't fidget.

Ero slowly lowered himself into a chair across the table with the vigor of an old man. Madison kept forgetting that he had burned out yesterday.

"Madison," he murmured, eyes closed. She held her breath. Slowly, his eyes opened, and he gazed at her tiredly for a few seconds, only the *tick* of a clock making any sound in the kitchen. "I sincerely do admire your desire to be a mother to these children."

"I sense a 'but' coming," she replied.

He nodded. "That 'but' is particularly in regard to Finn and Reese. I want to impress upon you how important it is that a child develops a loving and trusting relationship with an adult in early development. It is a survival method imprinted into our young as well as yours; they must rely on a caregiver if they are to have any hope of surviving when they are so small and helpless. But in the case of Finn and Reese, that bond never formed. They were immediately taken from their mother and deprived of any semblance of a healthy relationship with an adult. Without that critical connection early in life, certain neurological pathways cannot develop. In most cases, children in those situations are incapable of ever experiencing meaningful relationships in their lifetime."

"I don't fully understand what you're saying."

Again, Ero nodded, although this time it seemed to be with a great weight bearing down on him. "Sadly, the clock cannot be turned back to undo that damage and form those missing connections. Your natural inclination is to overcompensate and offer them the love and affection they never had, but that is beyond their comprehension and would likely do more damage than good. They would be overwhelmed and confused, likely to retreat even further from you. My advice to you is this: rather than try to show that you love them, it is much more important to impress upon them that this is a safe place and you will not harm them. They cannot see you as a loving mother, through no fault of your own. Instead, you must strive to make them see you as a guardian and caregiver instead. Those roles are within the realm of possibility."

Madison's jaw clenched as she stared blankly at the tabletop. Her stomach churned. "Just as an intermediate step though, right? I want them to know what it feels like to be loved. I want to see them laugh and play games and act like normal kids someday. Are you saying that's not possible?"

"I do not know that answer. Finn and Reese grew up with minimal physical contact as infants. They were fed from a bottle secured in place in the crib instead of being cradled in someone's arms. Nobody ever sang to them or rocked them to sleep. No one soothed them when they cried or when they were in pain or afraid. They never made the connection that an adult, or even another living being, could do anything to help them, only to cause them harm. Try to imagine that unbearable loneliness in a small child who does not understand why he is suffering all alone in a cage and enduring painful experiments."

Ero sighed. "If the twins had remained in Project Gamma, I fear they would have been irreparably damaged and unable to experience compassion in any sense of the word. Project Alpha was, in a way, salvation for them when they bonded with their lab-family. Jay most certainly deserves the credit for that; he was the first person to ever care about Finn and Reese. But there is so much damage from their formative years. They do not comprehend selfless love. They do, however, understand loyalty. That is where you must begin, and then you can potentially build from there."

Too sick to open her mouth and answer, Madison simply nodded.

Ero rubbed his eyes and continued, "Please do not be too discouraged. I think the ability to read minds will prove to be advantageous in their continual development over time. Other children in their position would face the world terrified, confused, and suspicious, always trying to analyze the actions of the people around them to ascertain true intentions. Finn and Reese are better equipped to identify someone's intentions and then, hopefully, begin to process emotional levels and learn to trust what they are perceiving. As for their lab-siblings, I recommend a similar course of action. Their trust for Outsiders has been destroyed, and that is not something that can be rebuilt in a single dinner. You will be walking a razor-thin line. You must prove to them that you are strong enough to protect them but also compassionate enough for them to see you as a caregiver they can trust."

"That's a tall order."

"It is," Ero agreed. "But I have faith you will be up to the task." He forced a faint grin. "Believe it or not, I think your battle with Cato in town square worked to your advantage."

"How in the world can you say that?"

"You were strong and held your ground in what came very close to a fight to the death. Now, your task is to become a protector instead of an adversary."

"I don't suppose you have any advice on how to deal with Axel, do you?"

"Axel is someone who greatly values and respects strength."

"Oh, perfect. I could challenge him to an arm-wrestling match."

The Telepath humored her with a faint smile. "Strength comes in many different forms."

"Come on, Ero. Don't you have any more advice for me?"

Ero stared up at the ceiling, lips pursed, head lilting slightly from side to side as he contemplated. "I think honesty and perseverance are your best tools."

He leveled his gaze across the table. "Axel can sense deception with perfect accuracy—he knows a lie is coming before you even take a breath to speak, and he has no tolerance for wasting time on dishonesty. He is, without a doubt, going to test your limits to see how far he can push you. I recommend staying calm, keeping your emotions in check, and being as straightforward as you possibly can. Set boundaries. Make your rules and expectations clear. You know you will never be able to physically force him to do anything, as does he, and that is part of the game. But I do think he may come to respect your authority as long as you remain firm and do not bend too far under his pressure. That will not be an easy feat. Humans have caused Axel immeasurable pain. I sense so much sadness, rage, and self-loathing in him, and I doubt you will ever be able to make peace with him on your terms. It will have to be on his."

Ero set his hands on the table and pushed himself up slowly, his body so stiff that Madison was surprised she didn't hear creaks and cracks. "Just remember to be patient. They will not open up to you overnight." He yawned. "I think I must call it an early night."

"I understand. Thank you, Ero. I appreciate your advice. And your help with the dishes."

He smiled and inclined his head, then shuffled away to bed.

Madison sat alone at the table for a long time, replaying their conversation.

In a daze, she stood and finished cleaning the kitchen and dining room, all the while reciting his advice: *Tell them this is a safe place. Let them know that I won't harm them. I'm a protector and a caregiver. Be patient. They won't open up to me overnight. Be patient . . .*

And patient she was. She maintained her steadfast patience as she waited in the parlor for Cato and the others to return from their scouting expedition . . . patient at ten, eleven o'clock, midnight . . . and then her patience began to waver. Her gaze drifted frequently to her wristwatch. Cato never used to stay out so late. Maybe they'd come in through one of the back doors rather than the front and she'd missed them.

Finally, at 12:31, Madison walked up the staircase to the third story and knocked on the door. She shifted, trying to plan what she would say, but the words jumbled inside her head. She knew absolutely nothing about her own son now. Would he be embarrassed if she told him good night under the scrutiny of his friends? She wouldn't tuck him in like she used to—that would be too awkward—but a simple good night was acceptable . . . wasn't it?

Lost in her thoughts, Madison hadn't even noticed that she'd been standing outside the closed door for several minutes now. She frowned and knocked again, louder this time. A bolt slid back from the other side of the door.

Madison smiled as the door opened a crack and a single blue eye peered sleepily up at her. The boy was wearing a well-worn hat flipped backward over his brown hair. "Hi there . . . Reese?" His brow wrinkled marginally. "Sorry," she said quickly. "*Finn.* I was wondering if I could say good night to Cato. Is he here?"

Finn shook his head. Madison raised one eyebrow and glanced down at her watch for the hundredth time. "Are you sure? It's after midnight." Finn blinked at her and yawned.

Frustrated with trying to obtain information from someone who wouldn't speak, Madison peered past him, but all she could see was the wall behind Finn. No view inside the dark room.

"Is there anyone here I can talk to?" she asked. Since Finn had been the one to answer the door despite clearly being roused from sleep, she had to conclude that the twins were the only ones here. "Okay . . . then maybe I could come in and wait for Cato?"

She didn't want to exploit him, but she knew he would yield to her. And maybe a little one-on-one time would help her start to connect with the twins. Madison reached out to push the door open farther, but her hand collided with a solid barrier.

She froze in surprise, unable to comprehend. There was no visible obstruction to block her passage, but her palm was pressed against a flat, solid surface as if an invisible wall stood between Finn and her. "It's . . . a shield," she realized aloud. "You have a shield protecting your room?"

Madison withdrew her hand and stared at Finn. "It repels humans instead of ghosts?" she asked.

The boy tilted his head to the side. Realizing she could coax no answers out of the mute twins, Madison relented. "Never mind. Could you please send Cato to my room when he comes back?" Finn nodded. "Okay. Thank you. And . . . good night. I hope you sleep well. I'll see you tomorrow, okay?" She smiled warmly at him as he closed the door.

Madison turned away, her smile collapsing into a perplexed frown. An invisible shield that repelled humans? The scientist in her was intrigued, although it was eclipsed by a mother's worry. The thought of her son being out after midnight was troublesome enough, but knowing he was either fighting a creature from another Realm or looking for one to fight was almost unbearable.

What if Azar had caught him? What if he'd been injured and he was bleeding to death in an alley? What if . . . ?

When Vivian asked how Cato was, Madison lied and told her he was already asleep. No need to worry her. Vivian accepted that with a bright smile, happy to know that her little brother was alive and safe in bed just one floor above. She settled into the pull-out couch and fell asleep almost immediately.

Madison sat down on the bed, her knees drawn to her chest, her vacant gaze on the door as her mind played out scenarios of Cato in trouble. Her head nodded with exhaustion, then jerked back up as she battled to stay awake. She stared into the darkness, worrying, waiting, hoping to see a shadow in the hallway going upstairs.

The grandfather clock in the foyer was tolling two in the morning when I closed the front door.

Ash yawned and stretched, holding her staff high above her head in both hands for a few seconds before sheathing it in the harness across her back. "I'm *done*," she said softly in the otherwise-silent manor. "I'm so exhausted I can barely think straight. What do you think the chances are that we'll be able to sleep without nightmares tonight?"

The two of us tread quietly up the stairs in the dark house. "If we're lucky," I said through a yawn of my own as my hand slid along the balustrade, just in case I lost my balance. At the top of the staircase, we became intangible and strode through the locked door of our room.

Jay and RC had just beaten us back and were removing their cloaks and boots. The twins were fast asleep with Kit curled up in her fur and nestled in the crook of Reese's neck.

As I unclasped my cloak, Finn stirred and opened his eyes. "Cato?"

"Yeah?" I whispered back.

He closed his eyes again and mumbled, "Mrs. Tarrow came to see you. She wants you to go to her room."

I hesitated at the unwelcome news. "I'm sure she's asleep by now."

"That's what she told us," Finn slurred, slipping back into slumber. I exhaled in indecision, then turned toward the door. Jay and RC were settling onto the mattresses. Ash watched me leave as she pulled off her boots.

I slunk down the stairs and turned down the second-floor hallway, then lingered outside the bedroom where Madison and Vivian slept. The door wasn't closed all the way. I crept into the room, straining to see in the darkness. Stacks of boxes formed pillars silhouetted in the faint light seeping in through the sheers over the French doors. I could barely make out one dark form lying on the pull-out couch near the doors and another on the far side of the bed.

"Madison?" I whispered uncertainly. I navigated the maze of box towers and approached the bed, hesitating as I drew near. What if she slept with a gun under her pillow? What if she'd jolt awake, see my glowing eyes, and shoot me?

I sucked in a nervous breath and touched her shoulder. "Madison?"

She stirred. I yanked my hand back and automatically assumed a defensive stance, ready for anything.

"Cato?" she called, her voice thick with sleep. "What time is it?"

I let my breath out. "Late. Or early, I guess, depending on how you look at it."

"Why are you home so late . . . early . . . whatever?" she asked drowsily, sitting up and rubbing her eyes.

I shrugged. "We always train at night. Then we wake up before dawn and have another training session before we leave to scout the town."

"Haven't you heard of this custom called *sleeping*? I don't like you being out so late. And you're still recuperating. You need to take it easy, Cay."

I scowled. *Great, she's already trying to mother me like I'm a little kid again.* "What did you want to tell me?" I asked curtly to change the subject.

"I just wanted to tell you good night," she said, her voice gentler and less condescending. "And that I love you."

There it was again. I licked my lips, grateful that the darkness concealed my facial expressions but annoyed that my eyes still glowed so she could tell that I was avoiding looking at her. "Um . . . good night," I answered.

Madison was silent as she stared at me until I began to feel uncomfortable. "What's the matter?" she asked.

"I don't know. It's just . . . I don't know. I used to imagine coming back home for so long, but now . . ." I shook my head. "I don't know. Everything has changed so much, and . . . it doesn't feel like I thought it would. Even you . . . I'm sorry. You feel like a stranger," I admitted.

"Or . . . maybe I'm the stranger now."

"No," Madison said firmly. "Things are different, but you are right where you belong. You just need time to readjust. You've been through so much trauma, but the hardships are over now, and I'm here for you. I promise. Okay?"

Despite her reassurance, I rubbed my right arm where the neutralizer used to be. Maybe everything hadn't changed after all. Maybe I was the only one who had changed, and I just couldn't fit in with the Outside world anymore.

Madison's dark form leaned back against the pillow. "I love you," she said again. "But you don't have to say it back to me if it makes you uncomfortable."

I nodded half-heartedly. "Okay," I whispered, turning away. "Good night, Madison."

"Cato . . . you can call me Mom. I *am* still your mom—that hasn't changed."

I didn't face her, and I didn't answer.

She sighed and said, "Good night, sweetheart. We can talk some more tomorrow, figure things out. And I want you to come with me to meet somebody in the morning."

I immediately cringed and sifted through excuses in my head. "I'll be busy scouting with Ash."

"Please? I really need you to do this for me."

With great reluctance, I conceded. But I had to admit that I resented Madison a little for guilting me into the commitment.

Chapter Twelve

Latrophobia

My instincts told me this was not a safe place.

Superficially, I couldn't find anything wrong. Madison was talking to a woman seated behind a desk. The receptionist seemed nice; she smiled as she tapped at a keyboard, all the while nodding and listening to my mother, occasionally saying a few words in return. According to the tag on her blouse, her name was Blythe.

Glass doors and wide windows let in a generous amount of sunlight, although after my sonic scream in town square, every panel had transformed into an intricate spiderweb of cracks. Framed paintings of abstract art decorated the walls. A tall, dark form lurking in the corner made me stiffen, but I realized it was only a potted plant.

I couldn't find anything wrong with this place. There was no logical reason to be afraid.

But I was.

My body was in fight-or-flight mode, my power fluttering subconsciously, my gaze incapable of settling in one place for more than a second. It must have been the smell that was making me uneasy. It was too sterile, too nauseatingly clean, too much like the place from my nightmares.

This building did not feel safe. But Madison had brought me here. I should trust her.

"Cato," she called. I jumped. Madison gestured down a hallway that Blythe had indicated. Warily, I trailed after my mother.

"What is this place?" I asked.

"The hospital."

The carpet ended at linoleum. I froze at the edge. Carpet and tile, good and bad, safe and dangerous—I felt as if this was the border. The floors and walls were white now; the smell was stronger. "I don't like it here." I took a shaky step back. "I want to leave."

Madison paused. "It's all right, Cato. I'm here with you. Come on, we're just going to that room a few doors down. See?" She pointed toward our destination.

I tried to swallow the lump in my throat. *Madison wouldn't hurt me*, I told myself again. Against my better judgment, I followed her.

When we entered the room, my panic shot up another notch. No one was here—just a chair in the corner and a sink built into the white countertop with cabinets above and below. A padded table covered in crisp white paper dominated the center of the room. Posters of the human skeletal, muscular, circulatory, and nervous systems were odd and uncomfortable decorations on the walls.

Madison started to close the door, but I couldn't stand the thought of being trapped in here. "No, don't close it!"

She looked at me, then shrugged and sat in the chair, crossing her legs as if perfectly at ease. "Why don't you have a seat up there?" she suggested with a nod at the table.

"Why is there paper on it?" My stomach was churning; I was afraid I might throw up.

"To keep it sanitary."

"Why are we here?"

"Because I'm worried about you. I want to make sure you're okay."

I stiffened when a familiar woman entered the room. The wrinkles creasing her umber skin told me that she was older than my mother. Her naturally crimped, graying hair was pulled back with a colorful headband, but the stark white lab coat was all I could focus on.

In the midst of flipping through pages on a clipboard, she said, "Sorry I'm late—I'm terribly busy. I've had people coming in nonstop with frostbite and ringing ears and . . ." She trailed off when she noticed the look of absolute horror on my face. Embarrassed, the woman cleared her throat and set the clipboard down on the counter. "I'm sorry. If it's any consolation, I haven't diagnosed any permanent damage.

Only minor injuries."

A man stuck his head through the doorway and held out a thin stack of folders. "Here are those files you needed, Doc. And the Parker kid's test results are in. I put them on your desk."

"Great, thanks," she said, accepting the folders. "Could you please let my ten o'clock appointment know that I'm running a bit behind and will be there shortly?"

"Yes, and your ten-fifteen is here early. He's waiting in exam room three." The man walked away.

"Lord, I miss my private office," Doc muttered as she skimmed through the files. "It was so much quieter and more peaceful." She set the folders down on the counter and gave Madison an exhausted smile. "Didn't make sense, though. Not with all the medical equipment here at the hospital and staff at a barely functioning all-time low. I can't be in two places at once. It made more sense to set up shop here."

She reached for the door to shut it. I opened my mouth, although I wasn't sure if I'd be able to get any words out. Before I could try, Madison said, "Would you mind keeping the door open? It would make Cato more comfortable."

I closed my mouth, but I was too petrified to feel any relief. The woman looked at me and smiled. "Of course. Whatever I can do to make this comfortable for you. Do you remember me, Cato?"

Voice hoarse, I managed to choke out, "You saved Finn and Reese."

"Yes, but do you remember me from before that?"

I shook my head. I couldn't even look at her face. All I saw was the pristine white lab coat, and it turned my entire body numb with fear.

"That's okay. I usually saw you once a year for your physical. You can call me Doc. I'm going to give you a quick checkup and run a few tests to make sure you're okay after your recent ordeals. I promise I'll make this as quick and easy as possible. Would you like to take a seat on the table there for me?"

"No," I said, curling my fingers into fists.

Doc appraised me for a moment, then picked up the clipboard. "All right. If you're more comfortable standing, that's fine." She glanced at my mother briefly before flipping through the pages on the clipboard. "I pulled Cato's medical record. No allergies reported, no serious injuries other than a sprained ankle when he was eleven, no severe illness except for a couple of nasty bouts with the flu when he was five and six."

She pulled a stool out from under the counter and perched herself on the edge. "I'd like to be thorough and draw enough to run a few different panels, if that's okay."

Madison nodded. "Yes, that's fine. I'd like copies of the results. Could you also draw a separate sample for me to study as well?"

"Sure." Doc scribbled a quick note and then peered up at me, and I felt my stomach drop. "So, how are you feeling today, Cato?"

I swallowed. My hands were shaking no matter how tightly I clenched my fists. "Fine." The word cracked on its way out.

Doc set the clipboard on her lap and folded her hands on top of it. "Anything you'd like to tell me? Any injuries? Pain or soreness? Fatigue?"

I shook my head. Yes, just about every part of my body still ached, but no, I didn't want to admit that. She lifted her eyebrows and tilted her head in a way that made me suspect she knew I was lying. "Are you sure?" she pressed. I nodded.

"Okay." She set the clipboard down and rose, then turned away to wash and dry her hands before pulling a pair of latex gloves out of a box sitting in the corner by the sink. "I'm going to give you a checkup now. It'll be nice and easy—no need to stress. I'm going to check your blood pressure, listen to your heart and lungs, take your temperature, do a brief exam to make sure there's no serious damage, and then run a few tests. Like I said, nice and easy."

I couldn't breathe. She snapped on the gloves, and I winced at the sound of latex slapping skin. My ears were ringing. Below the rising buzz, I heard her ask, "Is there anything specific I should be on the lookout for?"

"Can you check for internal damage?" my mother replied. "He was vomiting blood and bleeding from his ear before he collapsed, and then he slept for more than twenty-two hours straight. I can't imagine how much strain he put on his body when he burned out, but the bleeding especially concerned me."

"Let's see what his vitals are and go from there."

My vision clicked into painfully sharp focus as the doctor approached me. I backed away. Doc was between me and the door, and I was painfully conscious that I didn't have much room before I was backed into a corner.

Madison rose from the chair. "It's all right. You don't have to be afraid, Cato. I promise Doc isn't going to harm you."

I no longer saw a doctor approaching me, but one of *Them*. "Stay away from me," I warned, my knees bending to lower my body into a defensive crouch. One opponent. Didn't look very spry or strong. I seemed to hold the advantage unless she had a trick to subdue me, which she probably did. I couldn't let my guard down.

The doctor hesitated. Confused, she looked at Madison for direction.

My mother took a step toward me. "Cato, you're not in any danger. This is a safe place. Doc is here to help you."

I shook my head but didn't dare take my eyes off the doctor. "I recovered from my burnout. I'm not hurt, and I'm not sick."

"And we're going to make sure, that's all. Just a few tests to make sure you're healthy. Everything is fine. I need you to trust me."

I was shivering so hard I couldn't see straight anymore. "I don't believe you."

Doc held her hands up in surrender. "Okay. Let's just settle down now, all right? I didn't mean to make you uncomfortable, Cato." She retreated, sidestepping toward Madison and granting me a bit more space, although not enough to relax. Doc spoke softly in my mother's ear so I couldn't hear what she said. Madison, still watching me, relented with a subtle but reluctant nod.

Doc drew a small electronic device from her pocket. Her attention seemed to be on it rather than me, but I backed up another step. "I want to leave."

"We can't. Not yet," said Madison.

I stiffened again when two more people appeared in the doorway—a man and a woman dressed in scrubs. "Got your page, Doc," the man said.

The doctor nodded at me. She kept her voice low, but I heard her murmur, "I need your help sedating him. Please, be as gentle as possible, but be careful. I don't want anyone to get hurt."

The nurses inclined their heads in understanding and advanced toward me. They both had fake, wide smiles carved into their deceitful faces. "Hey, Cato," the man said, holding out his hand as if to give me a handshake. "I don't think we've ever had the pleasure of meeting face-to-face. My name is Shay. I was always a big fan of Phantom."

"And my name is Lily," the woman said sweetly. "It's an honor to meet you."

My lungs seemed to shrivel up in my chest as my abnormally loud heartbeat throbbed in my ears. This room was too small, and there were too many people in here, and they were closing in on me, and I didn't have much more room to retreat. I backed up. "Madison?" I croaked in terror.

"Please, just hold still, Cato," she begged. "I promise, it'll be okay in a minute."

It's not okay.

I took another step back and hit the wall. I was trapped in a corner. What should I do? Fight? Madison didn't want that. Phase through the wall and run? Would that even work? In that other place, intangibility wasn't an option. Only fighting. What were my options? My brain didn't seem to be processing.

The two nurses were almost in range to grab me. "Easy," the woman soothed. "We're not going to hurt you."

I needed to act, but still, I was locked in hesitation. I didn't know what was on the other side of the wall. There could be more enemies lying in wait.

"We just want to give you something to calm you down," the man assured. "You don't need to be scared."

Now or never. I'm out of time.

Just as I started to reach for my center, my gaze flicked over their shoulders in time to see Doc draw an object from a drawer. To my absolute horror, she turned to face me with a syringe in her hand. My attention was fixated on the needle, delaying my reaction when the nurses rushed forward and seized my arms.

The faces all blurred out of focus. I no longer saw two nurses holding me. I couldn't hear my mother's voice.

I was back at that place. The hand squeezing my biceps felt like the neutralizer's constricting grasp. *They* were pulling me toward the table, preparing to restrain me for Dr. Anders to resume his torture. *No!*

I recoiled, then whirled with all my strength. It was all *They* could do to maintain *Their* grip.

Fights with the handlers were completely different from battles with my lab-family in the Arena. At least in the Arena, I had my powers, and I faced opponents who fought with honor and grace. The handlers always cheated. *They* stripped me of my powers first, used drugs and stun guns and physical strength to subdue me, tied me up so I couldn't defend myself. Those fights were the wild, flailing struggles of an animal desperate to escape the pain that would befall it the second it was rendered helpless.

And I was going to be the most savage animal *They*'d ever had the misfortune of handling.

The ghost hunter in the corner scrambled out of the way as our scuffle lurched away from the wall and into the middle of the room. "Wait!" she cried.

Why does her voice sound so familiar?

"Please don't hurt him!"

We crashed into the counter, knocking objects from the shelves in the cabinets above. I didn't even feel the edge of the countertop bruise my hip.

But the man was strong with a height and weight advantage on me—he wrenched me away and threw his body to the side to force me off balance. I landed on top of the paper-covered table. The handlers labored to hold me down. "Wow, he's strong," the female said through clenched teeth.

"Doc, could you hurry? We can't hold him!" the male cried.

The doctor loomed over me—I saw the needle in her hand, the white lab coat, the latex gloves; I registered the sharp, sterilized smell; the hands that held me down hurt. My ears were buzzing.

"You won't feel more than a quick pinch. I promise," the doctor said. The needle was near my arm, but she was having a hard time positioning it as I continued to thrash like a beast caught in a trap. "Can you keep him still? I just need a second."

"We're trying," the man said through gritted teeth.

Her arm came down like a viper's strike, but I didn't even feel the needle pierce me. I didn't feel anything except cold. Cold and hard. Ice. I had my ice? I had ice! My powers weren't neutralized!

"Damn it," she muttered, pulling back after jabbing the improvised armor instead of skin.

"Get away from me!" I shouted.

I brought my feet up and kicked out, the soles of my boots sinking deep into the doctor's stomach. She gasped and doubled over. The syringe fell to the floor.

I didn't even notice the green light growing around me. Finally, the dam broke. A domed shield of swirling green ectoplasm engulfed me, separating me from my attackers.

"Stop! This has gone way too far!" the ghost hunter said, stepping forward. Her mouth was still moving, but I couldn't hear her. I was *not* going to be stuck with a needle and drugged again.

The power continued to build. My shield glowed brighter and brighter until it finally exploded in brilliant green light.

My assailants reeled back. The male handler hit the wall beside the door. The doctor and ghost hunter smashed into the counter on the other side of the room, bottles and utensils falling from the open cabinets above and raining down on them. The female handler had ducked just before the explosion, and she cowered on the floor with her arms over her head.

I rolled off the table and landed on all fours, then jumped to my feet before anyone else had a chance to recover.

"Cato!" the ghost hunter called as she pushed herself up on her hands and knees, but I dashed past her, leaping over her outstretched arm as she tried to grab my cloak. I whipped around the edge of the doorway and crashed into someone. Small metal objects scattered all over the hallway as we both landed on the linoleum floor.

I raised my head to see a stunned woman in a white lab coat gazing at me. I scrambled back, sharp metal instruments clattering around me, increasing my panic to the point of hyperventilation. The ringing in my ears crescendoed to an unbearable pitch. My brain seemed to be operating on autopilot; I felt like a passenger disconnected from what my eyes saw, what my ears heard. My sense of touch had faded away altogether. I was acting and reacting on survival instincts now.

I scrambled to my feet. I had to get out of here, but I couldn't think straight. I couldn't remember the way out.

In a panic, I dashed away from the woman. I was back at that place, running down the sterilized white hallway of Project Alpha, knowing *They* were right behind me and there was no way out.

No way out. No escape.

I pounded down a strange corridor I knew I hadn't seen before. Two men walked out of a room ahead of me, and I slid to a stop as they turned and noticed me. Lab coats. *They* were coming for me.

I sprinted back the way I'd come. *There's no way out of this place.* Every fiber of my being knew that was an undisputable fact.

I didn't know where I was. Everywhere I turned, I saw humans in lab coats and scrubs. White floors, no windows leading to the Outside, just doors to other rooms, and the sterilized smell, and I couldn't catch my breath but still kept running, even though I knew there was no way out . . .

A man stepped through a doorway right in front of me, and I tackled him without breaking stride. Before he'd even registered what hit him, I had already thrown him to the ground and straddled him.

He started to struggle, but his movements ceased when I conjured a long icicle in my hand and pressed the cold point against his exposed neck. "The way out," I snarled, a hint of insanity darkening my voice. "Tell me the way out, or I'll kill you."

Trembling, he pointed. "D-down that hallway and turn left."

I released him, on my feet immediately. His instructions guided me back to the carpeted lobby with the woman seated behind the desk. As soon as I was in sight, she rose in concern. "Mr. Tarrow?"

The doors were right there! Sunlight! I could see the Outside again!

I sprinted past her, my gaze on the doors, but she reached beneath her desk and hit a switch. They wouldn't open.

I raised both fists above my head, and with a short, feral scream, I pounded hard on the fractured glass. A sonic shock wave exploded from my voice, and the glass shattered beneath my fists.

The receptionist dove under her desk as objects exploded into lethal shards—the windows, the vase filled with flowers on her desk, the glass in the frames on the wall, the ceramic pot holding the large plant in the corner.

The floor sparkled with the remains of the automatic sliding doors and wide windows. I leapt through the metal frame and into the sunlight, and I kept running, and I wouldn't stop until the hospital was far behind me and my muscles couldn't carry me anymore.

***

Madison stood in the doorway, staring down the hallway where her son had disappeared. A technician was on her hands and knees gathering spilled surgical instruments and placing them on a tray.

Madison turned and hurried over to Doc. ". . . too old for this," the doctor was complaining as she pulled herself into a sitting position.

"I'm *so* sorry," Madison said. "Are you okay? Is anyone hurt? That look in his eyes . . . I didn't even recognize him. I'm not sure he recognized us, either."

"It was my fault," Doc admitted. She pushed back her headband, which had slipped down her face. "Agent Anders was wearing a lab coat when he came to Phantom Heights. I was the thoughtless fool who came at Cato dressed like this and holding a syringe in my hand."

Lily stood up on the other side of the padded table, her lip cut and bleeding, her hair sticking out in every direction. Shay sat up with a groan, a bruise already starting to blossom beneath his eye.

Madison snapped, "I conceded to letting you sedate him. I didn't know you were going to hold him down like that."

Doc rubbed her chin. "I'm sorry. I underestimated his reaction. Finn and Reese didn't like the exams or treatments, but they never fought me like that. Cato seems to have developed a severe case of latrophobia and trypanophobia, much worse than anything I was expecting."

"What?" Madison asked.

"A fear of doctors and needles," Doc clarified. "Given these phobias on top of PTSD, I have no idea how to evaluate Cato or any of the others, let alone take blood samples if they won't even let me touch them. Isn't there anything you can do?"

"They barely trust me enough to stay in the same room with me. As it is, Cato probably won't ever trust me again after I brought him here."

Lily helped Shay to his feet. "Doc," she said, "even without his powers, I think you need at least four big guys to hold him down. He's strong."

Doc turned to her nurses. "Go clean yourselves up. There's nothing more you can do here."

"Don't you need help?" Lily asked, glancing around at the items from the shelves that lay scattered on the floor.

"No. It's fine. I'll handle this mess." The nurses exchanged looks, then shrugged and walked away. Doc stared at the syringe by her feet. "How would you feel about slipping a sedative into their drinks?"

Madison shook her head. "With two Mind-Readers and Axel? Not a chance I'd get away with it. And besides, they're very touchy when it comes to meals. It's like they're on the brink of starvation and ready to fight to the death if anyone tries to take their food away. I don't want to risk it. If they don't trust me to prepare their meals, I can't make sure they're at least eating a healthy diet."

"I understand. What about telepathy? Ero could force them to hold still and cooperate. At the very least, he could keep them calm long enough for me to sedate them."

"Ero won't agree to that."

"He might if we convince him how important it is. I really need to run blood panels and see what kinds of antibodies they have, and I'm going to guess they also have some major nutrient deficiencies. But I can't start a treatment plan until I'm able to run the tests and make a diagnosis."

Madison was silent, thinking. Finally, she said, "Give it one more shot before I go to Ero. We'll try examining Cato again, but next time don't dress in a lab coat, and we'll meet him in a familiar setting. Let's take it slow and see if we can reason with him before going to extreme measures."

Doc nodded in understanding. "We should wait a few days and give Cato time to calm down. I think it's safe to say this experience traumatized him. Trying to restrain him was the wrong move." She shook her head in disappointment. "If I just could have gotten that sedative into him, everything would have been fine."

Madison promised, "I'll work with Cato. Thank you for trying, Doc. And again, I'm sorry about the way he behaved. Next time will be better."

— Chapter Thirteen —

Emerald Fire

Leaves filtered sunlight into dappled patches of light and shadow beneath a shrub in Meridian Park.

I inhaled the scent of earth and tried to ground myself, to drive away the memory of the sterilized smell that wouldn't leave my nose. I hugged my legs tighter against my chest, shivering so violently my teeth chattered.

Why would my mother take me to a place like that? I had told her I wanted to leave. I'd asked for her when I was afraid. And then she stood there and let those people grab me and try to stab a needle into my body. *"You don't have to be afraid,"* she'd told me. *"Please, just hold still."*

Hold still? She *wanted* them to hurt me?

Boots appeared beneath the leafy branches. "Cato?" a soft voice asked. I didn't answer, but the figure seemed to know I was there. Even though I hadn't been able to discern the telltale shiver down my spine amongst all the trembling, she had no doubt sensed me. In the distance, I could hear the rhythmic, twangy *pop*s of a tennis ball from the courts on the north side of the park.

She knelt to peer at me through the leaves with smoldering orange-red eyes. "You okay?"

"I want to be alone."

Ash settled down in the dirt. "I can wait."

I should have been angry that she refused to respect my wish for solitude, but her presence was secretly comforting. "How did you find me?"

"Axel," she said matter-of-factly.

Of course. I took a deep breath, exhaled, then crawled out from my hiding place.

"Did something happen with your mother?" Ash asked as she rose with me.

"I don't want to talk about it."

I halfway expected Ash to repeat, "I can wait," but she didn't. She studied me intently. "You used your sonokinesis," she said. "We all felt it. Were you attacked?"

I rubbed my face with both hands and started walking farther away from the fields and courts. Ash followed. "Yes. No. I don't know. It all happened so fast."

"Where's Mrs. Tarrow?"

"Bloody Scout, Ash, I don't know, okay?" I shouted, the burning green power rising to the surface again. Her face fell when she saw my eyes change. "Look, I just, I need to sort my thoughts out."

"Right, sure. I understand." She scuffed the toe of her boot against a rock. "It's almost my turn to check on Finn and Reese anyway, so . . . I'll just go now and spend a little extra time with them." She took a few steps, then hesitated. "I'll see you in a bit. If you change your mind and want some company, come find me."

I nodded. After she left, I lingered in the shade of a tree, halfway considering crawling back under my shrub again. But I didn't want to hide; I was restless now. I wandered through the park, not sure where to go.

I didn't want to go to Saros Manor, where Finn and Reese could read my mind and Madison was probably waiting to ambush me. Vivian. She was the one I wanted to talk to. Maybe she could put our mother's betrayal in perspective.

I altered my course for the Tarrow house. Even though Viv had told me I didn't need to knock, I did. I paced the porch, my frustration rising as the seconds dragged on. Maybe she was upstairs and couldn't hear me.

I stopped pacing and stared at the doorknob. *It's my house. I'm allowed to go inside. I'm not an intruder.*

Then why did I feel so guilty when I became intangible and walked through the wall? As soon as I solidified in the living room, I froze. My heart was beating so fast it was humming. The lump in my throat prevented me from swallowing.

I crept up the stairs to Vivian's room, hoping that her blessing of my presence here would ease my guilt for breaking in. Upon finding her room empty, I felt my stress level skyrocket through the roof. I was alone in the house, which made me feel even more like an interloper. I had to get out of here.

I rushed down the stairs, subconsciously skipping the creaky fourth step. The back was less conspicuous—I'd sneak out that way. I was halfway through the sunlit kitchen when the doorknob turned.

The back door burst open, and I jumped in fright. "Cato! I've been looking everywhere for you!"

I grimaced at the sound of my mother's breathless voice. Of course she had been—I'd attacked multiple humans, caused more property damage, and run away from her. We hadn't even been living in the same house for more than a day, and I was already in a world of trouble.

Slowly, Madison closed the door behind her. "Please don't run," she said.

I didn't trust that sickeningly sweet tone. I backed up a step, contemplating making a mad dash for the front door and calculating if I could outrun her . . . although I wouldn't be able to outrun a shot of ectoplasm in the back, nor would I have a chance to dodge it at such close range.

Madison's expression crumpled at my reaction, as if I had slapped her across the face. I watched her warily, judging her expression, uncertain if she was about to yell or cry.

She seemed more sad than angry as she cleared her throat and hung her head. "I'm sorry about what happened this morning. I didn't stop and think about the similarities between the hospital and the AGC. Please understand—with the exception of my last trip, whenever I've been to the AGC, I'm always in lobbies, and meeting rooms, and offices, and . . . the version of that place in my head must be very, very different from yours. I didn't think about that. I understand how scared you must have been, and I apologize for putting you in that position."

She paused, watching me for a response, but I remained stone-faced. She was apologizing? I wasn't in trouble?

"I trusted you," was all I was able to force out.

"I know. I know, and I am *so* sorry. I had no idea how badly it would frighten you. I just . . . I wanted Doc to make sure you're healthy after your burnout and the trauma you've been through over the last two years. It was supposed to be a basic checkup, that's all. I just need to know that you're okay. I'm worried about you. Please forgive me."

I stared at my feet, keeping her in my peripheral. How could I trust her again after she misled me? My instincts had warned me not to enter that hospital, but I'd allowed my mother to override my better judgment.

I had no answer for her, so I simply lifted my head and maintained my stony glare.

Madison sighed, but she nodded. "I guess I deserve that. I'm going to have to work really hard to earn your trust back, aren't I?"

I said nothing. I wouldn't even nod.

She wrung her hands together. "How about this to start—I'll make you whatever you want for dinner tonight. Just tell me what you're hungry for, and I'll cook it."

I stared blankly at her. "I don't know."

"Anything at all," she pressed.

"I don't care," I rephrased.

"You used to like cheeseburgers. Do you still like them?"

My eyes lost focus as I sifted through pieces of memories. "I'm not sure," I admitted. I wanted to ask her what a cheeseburger was, but that would be suspicious. I was supposed to know that basic information.

"I bet Wes would grill some for us, and we'll see if you still like them. How about that?"

"Okay." I covered my face with both hands. "I really screwed up again, didn't I?"

"You mean your sonic scream?"

I nodded. "People are afraid of me, and if I can't control my power, maybe they should be." I sensed Madison shift, and I immediately lowered my hands so I could keep her in sight. I admitted, "I don't like disappointing you."

"And I don't like scaring you. We both have some adjustments to make, okay? I promise I'll try to be more mindful about your limits and not push you outside of your comfort zone like that again, if you promise you'll let me know when something is wrong. I'm not a Mind-Reader."

"I told you I wanted to leave," I snapped. Madison blinked in surprise, but I suspected it had less to do with my cutting tone and more to do with my eyes briefly flashing green.

She nodded. "Yes, you did. I didn't listen, and I'm sorry. But Cay, I need you to *talk* to me next time. Tell me how you're feeling. Don't just tell me you want to leave; I need to know exactly what's scaring you or bothering you so we can have a discussion and work it out together. Does that make sense?"

"Yeah. Okay." I hunched my shoulders as I shuffled toward the closed basement door. "Hey, Madison?" I said, resting my palm against the wood.

"Mom," she corrected.

"Mm-hmm."

"Cato, please?"

I sighed. "*Mom*. Um . . . what do you do down there? In your lab?"

I turned to watch her answer. She shifted, glancing between me and the door. "Nothing like what you saw at the AGC. I design weapons. I experiment with samples—ectoplasm mostly, sometimes blood and tissue samples that I collect from the scene after a fight. Not people."

"Execpt me," I muttered.

"You were an accident. Not an experiment."

We were both silent for a long minute. My gaze settled on the weapon belt around her waist, where one gun in particular kept catching my eye. I took a breath. This was it; I had to confront her. "Question—"

"Answer," she said, then smiled at me, as if we'd just shared an inside joke I didn't understand.

Her immediate reply before I could even pose my inquiry flummoxed me for a second. I stepped toward her, and she raised her arms, as if expecting me to embrace her. Instead, I reached out and drew the silver, double-barrel gun from her belt. She let her arms fall as I held it up. The Zeta symbol was clearly imprinted on the base of the weapon. Although I'd expected to find it, I had hoped that I wouldn't. "Where did you get this?"

"It's not what you think."

Frustrated by her indirect answer, I asked louder, "Where did you get a weapon from Project Zeta?"

"From Trey." That wasn't the answer I'd anticipated, so I shot her a dubious look. She explained, "Part of the deal we made with you was that we would find a way to remove the neutralizer bands. Trey went to the AGC and came back with two prototype ectoguns as a gift from Agent Kovak. That's it."

I stared at the weapon in my hands, unsure whether I believed her. "Finn and Reese said you used to work for *Them*."

"Okay. Sit down, Cato. I have no secrets from you." I observed her for a few seconds, assessing her sincerity, then walked to the table and pulled out a chair. Madison smiled faintly and said, "That's the chair you always used to sit in." She seated herself across from me. "What did Finn and Reese tell you about my work?"

"They said you were an independent researcher."

"That's right. I was free to research whatever I chose, and if I made any discoveries, I sold the information. Usually, Agent Kovak purchased my data and prototypes, but occasionally, the private sector outbid him. I wasn't contractually bound to the AGC. I had contact with the Agents only once or twice a year at most. You actually met Agent Kovak a few weeks before the accident. Do you remember that?"

"No," I said in surprise.

"You don't? Well, it was just a brief introduction. He came here to see my lab."

I pressed my tongue against the inside of my cheek in thought. "Do you still work for *Them*?"

"No," she replied with conviction. "I never worked *for* them, and I cut off all contact after they gave me your—well, what I thought were your remains. Until they showed up here in Phantom Heights asking for help to capture the eight of you, I hadn't spoken to Kovak in two years."

I absently traced the Zeta symbol with my thumb. "Any more questions?" Madison asked.

"Yes." I exhaled, knowing this was the most important question yet and hoping I wouldn't be disappointed with her answer. "Do you know what the Origin is?"

I narrowed my eyes, scrutinizing her face to detect even the slightest trace of a lie. All I registered was surprise as she stared back at me, her eyes blank. "The origin of what?"

Relief drew some of the tension out of my stiff posture. I wasn't the best lie detector, but I was pretty sure no one could fake such genuine confusion. But still . . .

"I heard you have my file. Is that true?"

Madison stood up. "I do. Would you like to see it? It's down in the lab." She took a few strides, then opened the door and trotted down the stairs.

I was much slower in following. I rose from the chair and lingered in place, staring at the doorway. The staircase went down into the depths of the underground shadows.

One timid step at a time, I approached. My perception and fear stretched the staircase to make it appear longer than it actually was. Once my eyes adjusted, I spotted Madison at the end of the stairs at another closed door. She called up, "Come on, Cato."

My knees were shaking again. I swallowed, shook my head, and retreated a step. At my hesitation, Madison asked, "What's wrong?"

"I'm not going down there."

My mother faltered. She gazed up at me, then over her shoulder at the door she was about to open. "You've been in my lab hundreds of times."

"I'm not going down there," I repeated firmly.

"Okay. All right, that's fine; you don't have to. You just wait up there, and I'll be right back." She twisted the knob and vanished into the dark lab.

I was an unblinking statue at the top of the stairs. A light turned on down below, but from my vantage point, I couldn't see more than a few feet into the lab. After several painfully long seconds, the light turned off again and Madison reappeared from the darkness with a folder tucked under her arm. "Got it," she announced cheerily. She closed the door and ascended the stairs, smiling to reassure me as she held it up.

I backed away to let her reach the top and close the door. As soon as the latch clicked into place, I relaxed a little.

Madison sat down at the kitchen table, crossed her legs, and set the folder in her lap. "We promised we were going to talk to each other, remember? Are you afraid to go into my lab?"

I cast an uneasy glance at the closed door, then reluctantly nodded.

"Because of the accident?"

I pondered for a moment, then shook my head. I barely remembered the Flash—certainly not enough to warrant that deep, mind-numbing fear that filled me when standing at the threshold of the basement steps.

She looked down at the folder. "Are you afraid of my lab because of the AGC?"

My throat immediately clenched. I didn't even need to nod; she correctly interpreted the look of terror on my face.

"Cato, my lab is nothing like the AGC. You know that. None of the equipment I have down there is used to experiment on kálos, alive or deceased. I have a high-powered microscope and a few machines to analyze and manipulate ectoplasm, and then most of what's down there is dismantled machine parts and failed inventions that either didn't work or were never finished. Now, to be fair, I haven't been in Project Alpha or any part of the AGC except the main level and the autopsy room, but I feel confident that my lab is very, very different from the part of the AGC you're familiar with."

"It's underground," I barely managed to whisper. I looked out the window, appreciating the precious sunlight on a deep, emotional level Outsiders couldn't understand.

She nodded ever so slightly. "Okay. Thank you for helping me understand what's bothering you. I want to make sure you know that I'm not hiding anything or performing any unethical experiments in my lab. If you ever want to go down and see for yourself, you're allowed to. I'll give you a tour and explain the functions of the different machines."

Mute again at the mere thought of venturing back into an underground laboratory, I inclined my head in acknowledgment even though I had no intention of ever going down there. I'd have to take my mother's word that her work was ethical.

Madison set the folder on the table. "This is everything Kovak gave me."

In a trance, I crossed the kitchen and lowered myself back into the chair. I stared at the folder for several seconds before I took a deep breath and dared to brush my shaking fingers across the folder with the printed words:

```
Subject: 5292
Project: Classified
```

This was it. All the tests Dr. Anders had conducted on me—well, probably not all of them, since I was sure he hadn't shared *everything* with my mother—but some of them were here. Maybe I could find out what happened to me.

Before opening it, I asked, "Why do you have this?"

Madison cast a forlorn look at the folder beneath my hand. "I thought you were dead . . . and I never knew what I'd done to you. The last time I went to the AGC to see your body before it was cremated, Kovak promised he'd send the results of the tests and the autopsy. But he never did. It wasn't until recently that I was able to ask him for the file. Since I never had the opportunity to run any tests of my own, all I could do was study his and try to understand what happened that day."

I opened the folder. "Do you?"

"I wish I could give you some answers. But . . . no. Your DNA isn't human anymore, but it's not exactly kálos, either. It's very strange, and I'm going to need a lot more time studying it."

"Do you still have the sample of ectoplasm that turned me?"

"No. I had the original control sample for a while, but the variant that I'd manipulated was destroyed in the explosion. Agent Kovak confiscated all of my notes. All that's left from that day is . . . you."

My elation at getting my hands on my secret file was quickly dissipating as it became clear that these results were far beyond my comprehension. I flipped through the papers and gleaned nothing new. Charts, analyses, DNA tests, medical summaries with so much technical jargon that they didn't even look like English . . .

With a sigh, I closed the folder again. Madison scowled at it and said, "When I first received that in the mail, I didn't think anything was abnormal because Kovak had you for only a few weeks. Now that I know he actually had you for two years, it's way too thin. There's a lot missing."

In a dead voice, I informed her, "Even with my complete file, *He* doesn't know what happened to me." I hesitated, then asked, "What if I could get you the whole file? Would that help?"

"Maybe. But how would you pull that off?"

"Finn and Reese have access to it. But since Alpha's classified and you're not authorized, I'm not sure if I'll be able to convince them to breach security." I scoffed and shook my head, the idea already flitting away into hopelessness. Who was I kidding? Showing classified files to an Outsider would no doubt be a serious Rule infraction.

"Never mind," I said. "But do you know why I have two Divinities instead of one? I mean . . . that's not normal. Ero told me it's never happened before."

She picked at a chip in one of her fingernails and muttered, "It's just a working theory."

"Okay," I said, sitting up straighter to give her my undivided attention.

She studied me for a moment before explaining, "Well, from what I understand, only one Divinity manifests in an individual. In most cases, children inherit one of their parents' powers, although it's possible to carry the genes of an ancestor's Divinity down the bloodline until the conditions are right for it to become dominant again. My guess is the ghost whose ectoplasm I was manipulating was the offspring of a Cryokinetic and a Sonic, so both active Divinities had a strong presence. But I had degraded the ectoplasm to an unnatural state, and you were a vessel that wasn't genetically coded to differentiate between a dominant and recessive Divinity, so . . . when you were exposed to the mutated ectoplasm, both Divinities manifested."

I pondered her answer. My mother remained quiet, waiting for me to ask another question. I traced the words on the front of the folder with one finger. "Madison—"

"Mom."

"Right, sorry."

"Cato . . . are you still mad at me? Is that why you keep calling me Madison instead of Mom?"

I shrugged and shook my head. "I don't know. It just became a habit, I guess. I spent a long time believing you didn't want me anymore, so I had to stop thinking of you as Mom. It made the situation a little easier."

She took a breath, but I quickly added, "I know it wasn't your fault. But I can't erase those feelings as if they never happened. I promise I'm working on it. But I was wondering . . . what were you working on when the Flash happened?"

"I suppose we never did get the chance to talk about what happened like we should have." She twisted a jade ring on her finger to avoid meeting my solemn gaze. "Part of that is my fault. I didn't make you feel like you could trust me."

Silence hung between us. She didn't say that it was mostly my fault for lying and hiding my secret. She didn't have to.

In my resolute silence, she continued, "I was working on the first prototype for the entoplasm shield. It . . . well, it's actually very complicated, so I'll simplify it as best as I can. The shield repels ectoplasm, but to make that happen, I had to study the molecular structure of Grade A ectoplasm. The shield itself was originally a fairly accurate replica of what kálos create, and then I had to break down its structure and rebuild it from that ectoplasmic base. I was trying to isolate a certain property in a small sample, but it became too unstable. *Kaboom.* Next thing I knew, I was on my back staring up at the ceiling. I thought you and Viv were still in the kitchen working on homework, so I got up to check on you, and that's when I saw you lying in the doorway at the base of the stairs."

Now she was looking at me, and I was the one who couldn't meet her eyes. I traced my number on the folder for the seventh time. "So . . . the Dome was manufactured from the same ectoplasm that's inside me?"

Madison raised her shoulders while tilting her head. "Sort of. It came from the same original supply."

Only now did I notice the increasing blush in her cheeks. She said, "Cato, I . . . uh, I-I was wondering if . . . You don't have to if you don't want to . . ."

"What?"

Madison took a quivering breath before letting the words fall in a rush: "I was wondering if you'd be willing to let me examine a sample of your ectoplasm."

I stared at her. She quickly added, "Like I said, it's completely voluntary. I won't force you. And if you're not comfortable with it, I don't want to pressure you at all. You can tell me no."

I was admittedly uneasy about her request. "What are you going to do with it?"

"I'd like to see if it's normal compared to other samples I've studied over the years or if it's, well . . ."

"Mutated?"

She answered with a reluctant nod. I rubbed my right arm where the neutralizer used to leech my power. I didn't like the idea of labs and experiments, but it would be nice to have some real answers. Madison, unlike *Him*, would share her findings with me. Besides, it would be painless and noninvasive, and my decision. That last part floored me. *My* decision. I could say no.

I nodded my consent. Madison gave me a nervous smile and fumbled to remove a vial from her belt. She set it on the table and withdrew, leaving it between us.

Right, my choice. I could do it when I was ready. That was still almost beyond fathoming after all *They* had put me through.

I tapped a finger on the file, staring at the waiting vessel, and then I reached out and picked up the vial. It seemed to be made of glass, but I suspected it was actually something else—something stronger. Madison watched me with uncomfortable intensity as I uncapped it and held the end up to my fingers. Summoning such a small amount of ectoplasm was easy, barely any concentration or effort, and the green energy sparked from my fingertips to be caught in the vial.

Madison extended her hand, eager to take it, but after I sealed the vial, I held it in my palm, making no move to relinquish it. This ectoplasm was a part of me. It was so bright, moving and twisting in glowing tendrils within the tube, as if I were looking at a living piece of my own soul.

I didn't know why I felt attached to it. I'd fired ectoplasm at enemies without a second thought, used it as a light source in the dark, created shields, domes, and orbs—but seeing it trapped in a vial to be manipulated and tested in a laboratory made it seem more sentient. That was stupid, of course. It was energy. It wasn't alive, and it couldn't feel pain.

Madison's hand was hovering in wait. I started to pass the vial to her, then paused. "Can I change my mind later?"

"Of course," she said patiently. "I hope you don't, but if you decide later that you want this back or you want me to destroy it, I will."

I handed it over. Madison drew the vial close to her face. It pulsed like emerald fire in its container, painting her cheeks with shifting swathes of dancing light. "It's beautiful," she whispered.

I gazed at the glowing ectoplasm and then glanced up at her face. She was still entranced by the vial in her hand, her face illuminated in green light that made her eyes sparkle even more brilliantly than usual. I'd heard *Them* describe ectoplasm in many ways. Potent. Powerful. Sustainable. Never *beautiful*.

"Thank you, Cato," she said as she slipped the vial into a pouch on her belt.

A sickening pit of dread was condensing in my stomach. Maybe it wasn't such a good idea to give her permission to experiment on my ectoplasm. This time it was just a tiny sample, but what would happen when she started asking for more of me? Hair, saliva, and if it got worse? Blood, muscle, bone marrow, spinal fluid . . . I couldn't go through that hell again.

"You'll tell me what you find, right?"

"Of course. The second I learn anything, you'll be the first to know. If you don't mind my curiosity, what are the highest and lowest grades of ectoplasm you can produce?"

"Grades B and F, but only for a few seconds, and only if I'm at full power and concentrating really hard."

She nodded. "That's . . . wow. That's impressive. Would, uh . . . would you maybe let me study your Grade B shield sometime? I think it could help me with a project."

"What kind of project?" I asked suspiciously.

She leaned forward, grinning with excitement. I leaned away from her. "I want to recreate it," she said breathlessly. "Forming solid ectoplasm shields would be a huge asset for ghost hunters. I want to create a portable shield generator that's small enough to be worn on the arm and activated to form a disk of ectoplasm, but if I can't concentrate it to a low-enough grade, the shield would be useless. So . . . what do you say? Will you let me study your Grade B shield and try to recreate it?"

I shrugged. "I guess so."

She smiled at me. I tried to return it, but she must have noticed how forced it was because hers faltered. I blurted, "Finn and Reese would be able to help you more than I could."

"Really? Why do you say that?"

"They're brilliant inventors. Really gifted with technology. Their mother was a Technopath, I think."

"Is that so," she said, although it wasn't a question. "And that's something they enjoy doing? Maybe an opportunity to find common ground?"

"Yeah, I guess. They seem to like inventing and upgrading things."

She settled back into her chair, her fist pressed loosely to her lips in deliberation. "There's a shield protecting your room on the third floor."

I narrowed my eyes. "How did you know that?"

"I wanted to say good night to you last night. Can you tell me about the shield?"

"Not really. Finn and Reese made it. I don't know how it works. Something about DNA and cell membranes . . . I don't know. You'd have to ask them."

"Will they talk to me?"

"Probably not."

I jumped at the sound of the front door shutting in the living room. Pleasant humming carried a melody into the house, and then Vivian strolled through the doorway. Upon spotting us seated at the kitchen table, she hesitated. "Oh, I didn't know you were here." Our expressions must have betrayed the seriousness of our topic, because her grin faded. "Am I interrupting? I'm sorry."

She started to retreat back into the living room, but Madison stood up. "No, you're fine." She clapped her hands together and proclaimed, "I have an idea."

Still skittish from this morning's terror, I flinched at the sound of her palms slapping. Yes, she noticed, and yes, she looked hurt again. "Let's go out to lunch."

I felt my lips turn down immediately while Vivian's curled up with an exuberant grin. "I'm in," she said. "Where do you want to go?"

"I was thinking Joe's Bar & Grill."

Should I recognize that place? I didn't. Viv closed one eye and tilted her head, scrunching her face up as if in thoughtful disapproval. "What about C-Sully's so we can sit outside? It's a nice day." Vivian turned to me and said, "How 'bout it, Cay? You can choose."

I didn't recognize that place, either. Should I confess that? Play along? I didn't want to go. Actually, I didn't usually eat lunch—just breakfast and dinner. But if I had to endure this outing with my blood-family and pick a place to eat, I'd rather be outdoors where I could easily fight or flee than indoors where it would be easier to fall prey to an ambush. I wasn't sure if my mother had an ulterior motive for suggesting lunch or if it truly was the peace offering it appeared to be at face value. I shrugged and said, "That second place sounds fine."

My innards squirmed with guilt and unease. I should be meeting Ash for scouting duty, not wasting time eating lunch with my blood-family. And I still didn't trust Madison, especially not after this morning's assault, but hopefully, being outdoors in a public place would bring a degree of safety. She wouldn't want to make a scene. Still, I'd have to be on guard, just in case.

I let my breath escape through my teeth. *It's just lunch with my blood-family. What could go wrong?*

— Chapter Fourteen —

Autograph

Madison's condition for going out to lunch: I had to change out of, as she put it, "that disintegrating uniform."

Granted, my clothing was ripped, bloodstained, and threadbare. But it was mine—the only thing I was allowed to have at that place. I crossed my arms defiantly and said, "I'm comfortable in my uniform."

"You've been wearing it for months."

"So? It's clean."

She rationalized, "Maybe you'll feel more like your old self in your normal clothes." She handed me a bundle of blue jeans, a T-shirt, boxers, socks, and sneakers. "I'll see if I can patch your uniform up for you. Deal?"

Reluctantly, I retreated to my old bedroom and stripped off my Arena uniform to don the old clothes, but I didn't feel more like myself. I felt naked. These shoes gave me no support; the pants were loose at the waist and short at the ankles; the shirt hung listlessly off my frame. Nothing to protect my knees and elbows. I'd become so accustomed to the weight of a cloak on my shoulders that I felt too light, as if I might float away with nothing anchoring me. I opted to keep the wrist gauntlets to conceal my Marks.

I tromped downstairs and opened my mouth to complain that I felt ridiculous wearing these clothes, but as soon as Madison and Vivian saw me, they both gasped. Madison's eyes sparkled with tears. She covered her mouth with her hands while Vivian beamed and said, "Hey, there's the little brother I remember!"

The words died in my throat. I closed my mouth and stood still as they circled me and made comparisons. Madison prattled off a list:

"You need a haircut, that's for sure, and you've outgrown your jeans, and you're practically drowning in that shirt, Cay—we need to put some meat back on your bones."

She probably would have gone on like that for an hour if Vivian hadn't declared, "Speaking of that, I'm starving. Can we go now?"

Madison cheerily led the way. Behind her back, I caught Viv's eye, but I didn't even have to say thank you because she winked and smiled. Somehow, despite everything we'd each been through, we still shared some level of sibling intuition.

The Tarrow house was several blocks south of downtown, so we walked to this C-Sully's place. Unfortunately, I still had celebrity status, and walking with my blood-family meant I couldn't keep to the shadows to avoid the attention.

I wasn't the only VIP, though—everybody knew Madison Tarrow, the fearless leader of the raid team when Phantom Heights had been on the brink of disaster. People called out greetings to her, all the while purposely trying to make eye contact with me, which I resolutely avoided.

A group of girls giggled and blushed as we passed, calling, "Hey, Phantom! Hi! How are you?" Then they cowered away, cheeks pink, snickering at their brashness. I inclined my head to acknowledge that I'd heard but otherwise didn't pay them any attention.

"Quite the ladies' man now, aren't you?" Vivian teased. I shrugged one shoulder, ignoring another girl who was shyly waving from across the street. "Come on, you could probably date any girl in town now. Has anybody caught your eye? Anyone cute?"

I looked over my shoulder to skim the girls we'd just passed. Since they were all watching me, they gasped and turned away, or smiled, or twitched a hand in a small wave when our eyes met for a sliver of a second.

Again, I shrugged. "Not really."

"Well, I guess none of them compare with Ash, do they?"

I couldn't tell if she was teasing me or vocalizing bitterness, and before I could ask, Madison absentmindedly said, "You know, kálos are incapable of reproduction until they're about a century old, so it wouldn't surprise me if your body isn't producing androgens at the same level it was before the accident."

Heat traveled up my neck and scorched my cheeks. "Madison!" I whispered in a sharp hiss.

"Mom," she corrected.

"*Whatever*! Bloody Scout, do you have to scientifically analyze me like that?"

"Hmm? Oh, I'm sorry," she said, finally noticing the humiliation on my face.

Vivian said, "What does that expression mean, anyway? *Bloody Scout*. I've heard you say it before."

I monotonously recited, "A Sacrificial Creature Originating Under Theta." At their uncomprehending stares, I muttered, "Never mind; it's not really important."

C-Sully's was a modest little sidewalk café with small lights strung overhead on a wooden arbor. I'd stolen food out of the dumpster here before. I wasn't going to mention that, though.

A hostess seated us immediately, although I'd barely taken my seat when a little boy appeared beside me. "Hi, Phantom," he said sheepishly. His gaze flitted away in shyness and then returned to my face as if he were hypnotized. "May I please have your autograph?"

He reached up and pushed a napkin and pen across the tabletop. Puzzled, I stared at them, then turned to Madison and Vivian, wordlessly asking them what to do. My mother nodded at the objects and said, "He wants you to sign your name. Or Phantom's name, actually."

Sign my name? I couldn't remember the last time I had to write anything. I picked up the pen with my clumsy fingers, hoping my hand would remember how to hold it. I thought I was gripping it correctly, but when I pressed the tip to the napkin, it didn't make a mark. I pressed harder—still nothing. It should be so simple. *What am I doing wrong?*

"Click the top," Vivian gently advised.

Oh, there was a button. I did as she suggested. Slowly, with painstaking care, I scratched out *Phantom* letter by shaky letter, lips moving as I sounded out the word and reminded the muscles in my hand how to work a pen. By the time I crossed the *t*, I was confident enough to loop out the *o* and *m* a little quicker.

From the corner of my eye, I noticed that Vivian was purposely looking out across the street to avoid putting additional pressure on me. But Madison was scrutinizing every movement I made, studying me. *She knows something is wrong.* Thank a bloody Scout my body barely produced sweat anymore, but my hands were starting to shake with nerves.

When I handed the signed napkin to the little boy, Madison reached out, snagged a waiter walking past, and pulled him down to speak quietly to him. He glanced at me, nodded vigorously, and then hurried away. My mother straightened with a smile and said, "No one else is going to bother us while we eat."

As if to contradict her statement, a young woman approached and stood right next to our table. "H-hi. How're we doing today?" she stammered. Without giving us a second to answer, she continued, "M-my name is Harmony, and I'll be your server. Can I grab, uh, get—b-bring you something to drink?"

"Iced tea," said Madison.

Vivian ordered something called root beer, then asked, "You want pop too, Cay?"

I blinked at her. I must have misheard. "What?"

"Pop." At my blank stare, she hesitated, then added, "Soda?" I was still totally clueless, and Vivian seemed perplexed by my confusion. "C'mon, Cato. Soda pop. You know, flavored, carbonated sugar water."

"I just want regular water," I said, still befuddled.

Harmony said in a rush, "I'll get that for you right away," before she whirled and hurried off.

I tapped my finger anxiously against the tabletop. *This isn't going well. I should have known how to activate the pen. I should have signed the napkin faster. I shouldn't have been confused by a drink order. They're going to figure out that I lost my memories.* Now that we were in a casual setting where these little situations should have been second nature, I was struggling to play off my ignorance.

Madison unrolled a paper napkin to reveal silverware inside, so I decided my safest course of action was to copy her.

The waitress reappeared with a breathless, "Here you go." Her hands were shaking so badly that the glasses rattled on her tray. She set two glasses down, each containing dark liquid. Harmony reached up to grab my glass of water, but she was so busy smiling nervously at me that she bumped the glass off the tray.

I didn't even think; I just reacted. My cold Divinity awakened, and then a beautiful, abstract splash of ice encased the glass suspended in the air, frozen as a levitating sculpture before it had a chance to hit the table and shatter. "Oh god," Harmony whispered. "Oh, I'm such a klutz. I am so, *so* sorry. It-it was an accident! I'm *so* sorry—"

"No harm done," I interrupted before she could continue with the lengthy and repetitive apology.

"I'm so sorry," she said again.

"It's fine." I seized the glass, turned it right side up, and set it on the table. With a wave of my hand, I melted the ice back into water without a single drop wasted from its container.

Harmony's jaw dropped. "Wow. You're amazing. I-I mean, um, that. *That* was amazing."

She was staring at me, eyes wide and wonderstruck, and I offered her an uncomfortable grin in return. Madison said curtly, "I need another minute to decide what I want."

"Oh." Harmony jolted, as if she'd forgotten her job. "Yes. Okay. I'll, uh, I'll give you a few minutes." She backed away, her heel colliding with a chair leg and almost sending her sprawling backward over the table behind her. Red-faced, she let out a nervous chuckle and left us again.

Vivian asked, "How does it feel to be a celebrity?"

I shook my head and reached for my water. "I think I know why I had a secret identity," I muttered. I eyed Harmony talking animatedly with two other servers by the bar. She kept stealing glances at me. I couldn't tell if her nerves were because she was starstruck that I used to be Phantom or because she was petrified of my abilities and thought maybe I'd freeze her in a block of ice if she upset me.

The glass was almost to my lips when I froze. What if it was drugged? What if Madison told the staff to put something in my drink when she pulled that waiter aside?

Slowly, I lowered the glass back to the table, watching my mother closely to see if she'd react. She and Vivian each grabbed a laminated paper and started reading, seemingly oblivious.

"Don't you want to look at a menu?" Viv asked, offering me one of my own.

There was no point. It would take me too long to actually read it, and I wouldn't recognize most of the food anyway, so I said, "I'll just have the same as you."

Apparently, that was the wrong thing to say because Vivian set down her menu and scowled at me. "But my favorite has peppers, and you hate peppers. You always used to get the BLT."

"Okay, yeah, I'll get that, then."

Madison didn't question my sudden change of mind, but Vivian was still staring at me, her brow wrinkled in suspicion, which only deepened when Harmony returned to take our order and I made the mistake of saying, "I'll have the B . . ." I couldn't remember what Vivian had called it. "Um, the BMV."

Harmony gave me a funny look and said, "The . . . BLT?"

"Uh-huh, that one." My cheeks burned with humiliation. I wanted to crawl under the table and hide. The clock tower chimed noon, which meant it was RC's turn to check on the twins.

"Cato?" I jerked my head up to face Madison. "I asked you a question."

"Erm, sorry, what?"

"I asked if you'd like to do anything this afternoon. I'm going to be busy at the town meeting, but you and Viv could do something fun, maybe go to the park, or—"

"I need to meet up with Ash."

Vivian's nostrils flared as she clenched her jaw. She was fuming, but what could I do? I still had a job, and it wasn't fair to leave Ash on patrol and cleanup duty all by herself. I mumbled, "Maybe Ash and I will go to the town meeting."

"You absolutely will not."

Startled by my mother's sudden hostility, I blinked and asked, "Why?"

"Because people are upset, and I don't want you anywhere near town square."

"What," I joked, "are you expecting an angry mob?"

Madison didn't answer. Vivian asked, "Mom?"

"Just stay away from town square, all right?"

"Yeah," I muttered. "Okay, sure."

I was relieved when our food arrived because it was an excuse to stuff my mouth and not be obligated to speak, but again, the paranoid worry of being drugged threaded its way through my thoughts. I stared at the toasted sandwich on my plate. My mouth was watering.

"Aren't you hungry?" Vivian asked as she twirled her fork into a nest of pasta.

"Yeah," I whispered miserably. I didn't know what to do.

A sudden shiver worked its way up my spine; I stiffened and gripped the edge of the table, gasping when a voice whispered in my ear, "It's fine."

"What's wrong?" Madison asked, frowning.

"Fine. I mean, nothing." I forced an uneasy grin. "Just got a sudden chill is all."

Her hand immediately went to her hip. "You didn't sense a ghost, did you?"

"Nope. Everything's fine." She and Vivian were studying me suspiciously. I lifted half of the sandwich in front of my mouth as if about to take a bite.

Barely moving my lips, I whispered under my breath, "Are you absolutely sure?"

"I told you it's fine," came Axel's nearly imperceptible voice in my ear. "There's nothing wrong with the food or water."

"Thank you," I murmured in relief.

Vivian shuddered and rubbed her arms. "Weird. I feel it, too. Must be a chill in the breeze."

Axel snorted in my ear and whispered, "What the hell are you wearing?"

"You can leave now," I shot back under my breath right before I took a bite, chewed three times to make the flavors burst, then closed my eyes and savored it. *Delicious.* I actually sighed in ecstasy. I needed to remember what this food was called so I could ask for it again.

The tension in the air dissipated, signaling that Axel was gone again, although I suspected he was still dutifully keeping an eye on me after the hospital incident.

I was hungrier than I'd realized. Even after the delay, I was almost done when my blood-family's plates were still half-full. Just as I shoved the last morsel into my mouth, I noticed a woman from the corner of my eye heading straight toward our table.

"Ma'am," a waiter intervened, reaching out to stop her, but then he hesitated. "Oh, um, Councilwoman. I'm sorry, but they've requested not to be disturbed."

"Just a few minutes for me to welcome the hero of Phantom Heights back?"

The waiter reluctantly yielded a step. He didn't retreat, but he didn't stop the woman from approaching, either. Madison stood, throwing out her arm in front of me. Her entire body was coiled with protectiveness. Unsure what I might need protection from, I pushed my chair out and rose partway out of my seat.

The woman chuckled at my mother's reaction. "Oh, relax, Madison. Honestly, you act like I'm here to execute him."

"What do you want, Holly?" The acidity in Madison's tone indicated that something was wrong. I wasn't sure how to prepare myself. Were we about to be attacked? Based on Madison's stance, it was a very real possibility, and yet this human didn't have any visible weapons and her body language told me she wasn't a fighter.

The stranger—Holly, my mother had called her—ignored Madison and forced a cold smile in my direction. "Hello, Cato. No need to worry; you can sit back down. I didn't mean to disturb your lunch. Maybe I could buy you dessert?"

I looked from Holly to Madison, then back to Holly. I detected hostility but no actual threat at the moment, so I grudgingly lowered myself back into my chair. "Uh, no. I mean, thank you, but no."

"Are you sure?"

"He said no," Madison snapped.

Vivian subtly slid a napkin across the table until the corner touched my wrist. I frowned at it. She'd printed three letters on the white square—*SOS*.

Shoot-On-Sight.

My stomach knotted. Practicing Vivian's subtlety, I covered the napkin with my arm and stared at Holly. She had pinched eyes and thin eyebrows to match her thin, tight lips, as if she'd been scowling for so much of her life that even when she smiled, her face was still partially frozen in a frown. There was something ominous about her, especially with those three letters resonating through every thought now.

She tried to take a step closer to me, but my mother blocked her. Holly gave Madison a meaningful look but forced another smile that might break her taut face. "You're so *lucky*, Madison," she said. "To have your son return from the dead . . . I can't even imagine. Lucky, lucky you." Bitterness and jealousy struck a displeasing note in her level voice, but she fixed her dark-green eyes on me and shot me a smaller, less painful but no less fake grin. "And you're lucky to be here, aren't you?"

I swallowed, beyond uncomfortable now.

Still kept at bay by Madison, Holly adjusted a bobby pin in her dark hair and continued, "If you didn't know, I'm a member of the city council. People really look up to you, Cato—or should I say, Phantom. I encourage you to attend some of our meetings and give us your input, and I was thinking you'd be a great spokesperson. You could dress in your costume and—"

"Oh, no," Madison cut in, taking a step so her body was squarely between Holly and me now. "He is not going to get sucked into your political agendas."

The smile vanished in an instant. Tension like what Axel naturally expels thickened the air as the ghost hunter and councilwoman stared each other down. Holly's voice transformed to something cold, slimy, and dangerous. "Careful now, Madison. I think, considering the circumstances, having a political ally would be in Cato's best interest. We need to make sure he stays a secret so Kovak doesn't find out about him, right?"

"Is that a threat?" My mother took a step forward so the two women were practically nose-to-nose.

Holly smirked and took a casual step back. "Of course not. Just a friendly warning. Like you said, all it takes is one person to betray him, and game over. I mean, he *did* destroy half the town."

Heat dusted my cheeks with warmth, but Madison didn't wait a second before defending me. "It was an accident."

"Yes, well, accident or not, people lost their homes and businesses, and I'm sure there's more than a handful upset about that. I can help protect him. All I'd ask for in return is his public support."

"That isn't what I had in mind, Holly. His service to the town is payment enough. If you're going to use him as your political puppet, then maybe we don't need your help after all."

Holly inspected her pristine fingernails. "Don't burn any bridges now. Remember who signs your paycheck."

Madison snorted. "You're only one in a council of seven. I'm not afraid of you."

"Maybe you should be," seethed Holly in a lethal undertone so her voice didn't carry to any of the other patrons. "The council votes the way I want it to, which means I can be your greatest ally or most dangerous enemy. I suggest you don't forget that."

Although my mother's expression didn't change, her voice was quieter and more subdued when she said, "Cato has enough trouble without adding your problems to his list."

Holly glanced at me, then Viv, then innocently raised her hands. "I'm just saying—"

"No, you're just *leaving*," Madison warned.

A cool smile cut across the woman's face. "Have it your way. Cato, I hope I'll be seeing you around." She pivoted on her heel and, under the scrutiny of everyone sitting on the patio, strode away without a look back.

My mother didn't sit until Holly had turned the corner. I moved my arm and stared at the letters printed on the napkin. Questions stirred, but I didn't even know where to start.

"*That*," Madison grumbled quietly as she lowered herself back into her chair, "was Holly Jennings, the most outspoken anti-kálos council member who drafted the S-O-S Doctrine and has a personal vendetta against ghosts. I want you to stay as far away from her as possible, got it?"

Although I did find it ironic that a ghost hunter was telling me to keep my distance from a comparably much less threatening politician, I had no intention of getting close enough to have another conversation with the woman who had decided the best solution to the ghost-human conflict was to station a firing squad at the Rip.

A pit was sinking into my stomach. "Holly . . . Jennings?" I repeated. The woman who had received ten thousand dollars from *Him* on the same day I'd learned that my mother had disowned me. That couldn't have been a coincidence.

"Why does she hate ghosts so much?" I asked.

Madison stared at me as if I'd asked the most profound question. She glanced over her shoulder to make sure Holly was gone before she sighed and faced me again. "Holly used to have a son named Greyson. He was eight or nine years old. Sweet kid. Anyway, after your funeral, I . . ."

She bowed her head. "I didn't take your death very well. I didn't leave the house much, and with you gone and me distracted, ghosts were getting bolder and attacking humans more frequently. Greyson was taken, and Holly blames me for letting it happen." Madison played with the napkin in her lap for a moment, her eyes downcast. "I'm sure Greyson died the day he was abducted, or if not then, soon after. But no one ever recovered his body. You, on the other hand . . ." She swallowed. "I buried you. If there was ever any hope of one of you coming back . . ."

"It was Greyson," I finished when she trailed off again. "Not me."

She nodded. "In Holly's eyes, I have what she's lost. I'm just afraid she's going to take her frustration out on you. But you listen to me, Cato. I didn't protect you before like I should have, but this time will be different."

We were interrupted by our waitress setting a small plate in front of me. "Our famous berry cheesecake. It's on the house," she said.

I stared at the dessert, so surprised that it took me a few seconds to stammer, "Oh, uh, thank you." Harmony backed away from us while I poked the cheesecake with my fork. It was a weird texture, but Madison and Vivian were watching me, expecting me to taste it, so I tried a bite. It wasn't at all what I was expecting; I made a face and cringed.

"You don't like it?" Viv asked.

I forced myself to swallow. "It's good, um, it's just, it's really . . ."

"Sweet?"

I nodded. "I'm not used to it."

Vivian was all too happy to say, "I'll help you," as she held up her fork and smiled. I pushed the plate across the table.

While Vivian dug into the cheesecake, Madison anxiously picked at the edge of her napkin until it started to tear. "I don't want you fighting ghosts anymore," she blurted.

Viv, as if she'd known this topic would arise sooner or later and had been hoping she wouldn't be present for it, dropped her head to focus completely on her dessert. I stayed quiet for a moment, rolling the tines of my fork across the edge of my plate. I answered solemnly, "We've already had this discussion."

"No, we haven't. I was talking to Seph, not *you*." My entire focus was on the fork; I wouldn't look up at her, but in my peripheral, I saw her rest her forearms on the tabletop and lean forward. "Cato," she said gently, "I want . . . I mean, you *need* to relax and spend some time getting readjusted. You had a very traumatic experience, and it's going to take time for things to feel normal again. I want you to feel safe. That isn't going to happen as long as you're fighting."

I set the fork down and raised my head. "We both know I'm always going to be a fugitive whether I fight or not. I have to keep my skills sharp. And fighting . . . it's important to me."

"Why?"

"It's complicated."

"No, it isn't. Explain it to me and I'll understand. You promised you would talk to me."

I nudged the fork with my fingertip. "When I was in the Arena . . ." I took a deep breath to clear my head before I restarted. "When I fought in the Arena, that was the only time I was ever able to move freely. I wasn't in a cage or restrained or strapped to a table. At first, I hated the fights because I lost every time. But after a while, I realized fighting was the only tiny bit of freedom I could have at that place."

Vivian raised her head just enough to give me the most pitiful look from the corner of her eye. Madison said, "Why did the Agents make you fight in the Arena?"

"Mom, don't ask him that," Viv begged.

But Madison waved her hand in dismissal. "I'm not going to pretend nothing happened. I want to know."

I curled my fingers into my palms, painfully conscious of the Marks tattooed into my skin beneath the wrist gauntlets. I wished Madison would just let it go. It was easier to pretend it never happened.

But she insisted. I drew in a shaky breath and said, "This is a whisper, okay?"

"What?"

"A *whisper*. It means what I tell you is confidential between us, and you can't tell anyone else."

She nodded, looking sick already. I felt sick, too. My only hope was that by getting this over with, I wouldn't have to deal with Madison pestering me about that place anymore. "It was never about the fighting."

"But then why did . . . ?" She trailed off at my severe look. "Sorry."

I stared down at my hands. "I'll tell you, but please don't interrupt." Was that my voice? It sounded so old, so weary. A dull ache started to pound behind my eyes. "*They* were studying our powers. The usual way was to force us to use them by . . . electrocution."

I heard Madison gasp. In a deadened monotone, I continued, "A shock at the right voltage targeted at the right part of the brain would trigger our powers. But some of the equipment was too sensitive to handle the electricity. *They* needed us to use our abilities without being forced, so . . . *Their* solution was to put sensors in us and make us fight."

Only now did I glance up. My mother looked like a real ghost. I'd never seen her skin so pasty before, her eyes so wide. "*In* you?" she whispered.

"I meant 'on.'"

Dazed, she jerked her head back and forth. "No, you didn't." I stared down at my hands. "In your head, right? That's why you have those implants?"

Vivian couldn't take any more. Without a word, she stood up and walked away. I watched her dark-brown hair recede as she navigated a path between the tables. "To record the connection between brainwave activity and power exertion," I informed Madison robotically.

"And that's why you have Spasms?"

I nodded. "Spasms are probably some sort of withdrawal. They'll get less frequent over time. Finn and Reese go months between Spasms now, and mine have decreased from several a day to a couple per week."

Madison was slowly recovering from the shocking truth I'd just dumped on her. "Thank you for telling me."

She wasn't grateful. Not really. That was just a courtesy to make me believe I could tell her anything, which I couldn't. She subtly wiped her eye and suggested, "Why don't you go find Viv while I pay? Try to calm her down. I'll see you at dinner tonight, okay?"

I pushed my chair back and rose, then turned away without a word and marched between the tables, ignoring the humans who greeted me in the hopes that I'd acknowledge them. Behind me, I heard Madison ask for the check. Harmony's voice answered, "It's already been covered."

"By whom?" Madison demanded.

"Councilwoman Jennings."

Vivian was already out of sight. I rounded the corner in pursuit, only to find my path blocked by a smiling face and a sickeningly sweet, "Hello, Cato."

I opened my mouth to answer but had no time to make a sound as Holly Jennings gripped my shirt and steered me into the recessed doorway of an antique shop. "I was hoping you would pass by this way."

Intangibility freed me from her grip. I stepped back, and, sensing I was about to run—which I was—Holly said, "I just need to speak with you for a few minutes, that's all."

She kept talking even though I was craning my neck to look down the street. No sign of Viv.

Frustrated, I tuned back in to the councilwoman, who was saying, "After all, I did promise Madison I'd try to help you."

"Wait, what?"

Holly barely contained her exasperation that I hadn't been paying attention. "I wasn't sure if you'd heard, but there's going to be a public meeting this afternoon."

"Yeah," I muttered, annoyed and despondent. "Madison forbade me to go."

"Why?"

The sharp, direct question finally caught my attention. "Um . . ." I swallowed and stammered, "I don't know. I guess she's afraid it might not go well."

Holly analyzed me carefully. "Is that so? Well, no offense to Madison, but I think that would be a grave mistake." Before I could ask, she leaned closer and said, "It's crucial that you be there. I want you to speak in front of the town."

"I, uh—"

"People are confused and scared right now. Try to understand—they see all the damage you caused. We need to remind them that you are Phantom and you're here to protect them, not harm them."

This is wrong. I can't trust her. She's somehow involved with Them.

I edged away from her. "Before I agree to anything, I want to know about the ten thousand dollars."

Her face instantly went sheet white, and a nervous giggle escaped. "I'm afraid I don't know what you mean," she said with a stiff smile.

"The money that was wired to your bank account the same day I saw the forged custody transfer," I seethed.

"Okay—shhhhh," she begged, holding up both hands and glancing around guiltily in search of eavesdroppers. "All right. But this has to stay between us."

She dropped her voice to a barely audible whisper: "The AGC funded the final phase of your mom's entoplasm shield. But Agent Kovak knew she wouldn't accept the money directly from him, so he sent it to me instead. Madison thinks I'm the one who made a personal contribution to get the shield operational around City Hall. You can *not* tell her the truth. She'll be furious if she finds out that he was involved."

I studied her closely, my eyes narrowed with suspicion. I couldn't tell if she was lying. Maybe Finn and Reese had been right—maybe this deal had already been in the works, and the precise timing was just part of *His* elaborate lie to make sure the records showed a monetary transaction coinciding with Madison's alleged relinquishment of custody. Maybe *He*'d even felt a tiny shred of guilt, which was why *He* had ensured the money still went indirectly to my mother.

"Okay," I said with great reluctance.

Holly let out a shaky sigh of relief. "Good. We're on the same page now. Let's get back to business—I really need you to give this speech. I promise it'll be quick. If you don't do it, the consequences could be terrible. I'm afraid somebody is going to call the Agents and report you."

I stared at my feet to avoid meeting Holly's gaze as I deliberated. Madison had explicitly told me not to go to the town meeting. But she was my mother; she was overprotective. She didn't want me fighting anymore either, and that was a mistake. If I did what Holly wanted, I'd be protecting my lab-family. That was what Jay would do.

Holly smiled at me with as much warmth as an ice sculpture. "You and I have never been enemies, Cato. In fact, I met with Phantom once to discuss how we could implement safety classes in the schools in case of a ghost attack. You came to my office, and we strategized over a cup of tea. You remember that, don't you?"

She was staring at me with electrifying intensity. I swallowed. Why did this feel like a test? She was looking at me as if . . . as if she suspected most of my memories were gone. But there was no way. Not even Madison or Vivian knew. I forced a stiff grin and answered, "I remember," although my gaze flitted to the side to escape Holly's gaze when I lied.

Her smile became more of a smirk. "Of course you do. We had similar goals before, and I hope we can work together again like we used to."

I wasn't paying as close attention to her speech as I should have been. I was too busy straining to remember having tea with her. She hadn't known I was Phantom back then . . . had she? How had I drunk tea without taking off my mask and revealing my face? Did I even like tea? This didn't feel right.

". . . you'd been in favor of S-O-S when I first proposed it to you."

"I was?" I blurted.

She raised her eyebrows, as if silently challenging, *Don't you remember?*

"I, uh, I mean . . . my stance has changed."

"Hmm. That's a pity. Maybe I'll be able to sway you back to the side of reason, but for now, my goal is to help you. It's nice and easy. All you have to do is read the speech I've written for you. That's not too complicated, is it? Just put on your costume and remind the people of Phantom Heights who you used to be. That's all you have to do for now."

I nodded, but my stomach churned with unease. Holly seemed to be an ally. Madison was wrong . . . right?

Was I making the right decision?

— Chapter Fifteen —

Resurrecting Phantom

Phantom's uniform was a slight improvement over the clothes Madison had given me.

It was nothing fancy by any stretch of the imagination—a sleeveless black shirt, black running pants, combat boots, and gloves. I had needed a minimal uniform so I could wear it under my normal clothes. Although it offered less support than my Alpha uniform, it did have much more flexibility for combat than the T-shirt and blue jeans I was all too happy to discard.

I tried to tweak the uniform by adding my cloak, but Holly insisted that I remove it. "You have to look exactly like Phantom," she told me.

"Why?"

"Because that's the only way this is going to work. Ideally, we'd give you a haircut, but there's no time. Take those armbands off."

"No. Those stay," I said firmly. I didn't want my Marks on display to remind me or anyone else where I'd been. Holly would have to wrestle the wrist gauntlets off me.

She shook her head in irritation but relented, although it was with great reluctance.

We were standing in one of the shops facing town square. City Hall's portico was supported by scaffolding, giving it a rather haunted skeletal appearance. The building was in better shape than it had been when I'd left it half-buried in rubble, but it wasn't stable enough yet to serve as the usual grand stage for a public speaker. Instead, a simple wooden stage with a podium had been erected in front of City Hall at the base of the steps.

The people in town square were restless. I leaned to the side to peer around Holly and watch out the window. "Madison is speaking?"

"Yes." She handed me the neoprene mask. "Put this on."

"I didn't know Madison was giving a speech."

"Yes, Madison is speaking, now *please*, Cato, pay attention. It's imperative that you do this right."

I listened to my mother's speech as I fastened the mask over my face. She was talking about me, how I had selflessly protected this town as Phantom at great personal risk and sacrifice.

Holly had to snap her fingers in front of my face to regain my attention. "Okay, here's what you have to do. You stand there, you make eye contact with as many people as possible, and you read exactly what's printed on these note cards. You're Phantom, got it? If nothing else goes right today, that's your goal. Convince every single person out there that you're Phantom."

"But I'm not anymore."

"It doesn't matter. Those people want you to be their hero, but they're scared. They don't know what to think of you."

"What do you mean?"

"I mean, you seemed a lot more human before when you were first outed as Phantom. People were ready to rally and defend you. But now, they see you as a powerful and dangerous kálos whose allegiance is uncertain. That makes people uneasy. My job is to convince them that having more power will make you a more effective guardian. *Your* job is to remind them of the hero they used to love and trust. There's no room for error. We have to sway every single person out there, because if even one calls Agent Kovak, it's all over."

Betraying a hint of nervousness for the first time, Holly glanced out at the crowd. So quietly I at first thought she was speaking to herself, she added, "Axel complicates this. He slaughtered half an army in a matter of minutes. People are afraid that he'll do it again, only next time it won't be kálos blood on his hands."

"How do we address that?"

Her piercing gaze flicked back to me. "We start by making them trust *you* again. They need Phantom to tell them everything is all right.

Can you do that?"

I nodded, the nerves starting to pool in my gut as the seconds ticked closer to my presentation. It wasn't just stage fright, either; Madison was going to be livid when I not only disobey her by being here, but also give a speech in front of the whole town. I was *not* looking forward to the inevitable confrontation with my mother afterward.

Holly flattened a crinkle in her blouse. "Okay. I'm going to go out there to talk for a few minutes. You wait here, and then when I introduce you, come out and read your speech. Be confident, try to make eye contact with the audience, speak clearly, and *ugh*, fix your hair—"

"Don't touch me," I snapped, batting her hand away.

She rolled her eyes. "Don't screw this up." She opened the door, raised her chin, and strolled confidently toward Madison standing at the podium.

My mother finished her speech with, "We have difficult times ahead. We might have won the last battle, but we're a long way from winning the war. I'm here to lead you as I always have, and my son has returned with powerful allies. Cato and I are going to work very closely to plan our strategies with the police and other Alpha ghosts."

I made a face and leaned against the doorframe. *Hypocrite. Talk about a change of heart from her request an hour ago for me to stop fighting.*

"And now, I'll turn it over to Councilwoman Jennings," Madison finished as Holly stood beside her. "Thank you."

A blonde woman at the front of the crowd called, "Madison, can you elaborate on the strategies you mentioned?"

"No comment," my mother replied.

"What about Phantom? What are his thoughts on—?"

"No comment," she repeated, stepping away from the microphone.

People immediately shouted dissent and questions, but Holly cleared her throat to recapture their attention as Madison stepped off the stage. "Good afternoon, everyone. As I'm sure you've guessed, I'm also here to discuss the return of our young hero. Madison, thank you for that moving speech."

My mother, who lingered in the front row, inclined her head in acknowledgment. Holly set both hands on the podium. "Our town has seen better days, hasn't it? I understand that you're scared. I know."

She gestured at the resurrected ruins of City Hall forming an ominous backdrop behind her. "I look at the destruction, and I'm a bit frightened myself. But then I remind myself that the force responsible for all of this is here to protect us. The Agents took our hero, who was an inexperienced boy just learning how to use his newfound abilities, and they turned him into a great and powerful warrior. Our enemies may be strong, but as you can see, so are our allies."

A woman interrupted, "My house was destroyed!" Others shouted similar complaints.

Holly calmly replied, "Houses can be rebuilt."

A man retorted, "What happens when my family is inside when the roof caves in?"

Immediately, a flood of concerns: "I can't afford to fix the damages! How does city council plan to keep Cato in check? And what about A6? What will we do when an even bigger army comes through the Rip looking for the Alpha ghosts?"

"All excellent points," Holly acknowledged with a smile that somehow showed every perfect white tooth. "That being said, I'd like to turn the floor over to someone more capable of answering those questions than I am." She turned to me and gestured.

The crowd stirred with confusion; apparently it was out of character for Holly to willingly pass the spotlight to someone else. I gulped and approached the stage.

Voices. So many they sounded like leaves in a summer breeze just before a storm—the sound I awoke to the very first time I slept Outside, tucked in the damp roots of the giant tree by the creek. I didn't look at Madison, although I could feel the holes her eyes were drilling through me. Holly backed away so I could have the microphone at the podium. The whispers ceased.

My knees were shaking so badly my legs were about to buckle. I surveyed the crowd, the lump in my throat choking me as a pit of nerves twisted into a tight knot in my stomach. Town square was death-ly quiet. Eerie, suffocating silence.

I swallowed and squinted down at the note cards. "Um, hi. Hello. I'm . . . I'm Cato, but you know me better as Phantom."

I couldn't do this. These cards were handwritten, and the writing was too small. I was going to sound like an illiterate idiot if I tried to stumble my way through this speech. I released a shaky breath and set the cards on the podium. "I, uh, I was supposed to read you a speech today. But, see, I'm really not a good speaker, and . . . what's the point of me speaking if they aren't my words, right?"

Councilwoman Jennings was shaking her head and gesturing at the podium for me to pick up the cards again, but I ignored her. An inap-propriate nervous chuckle escaped. "I guess I never really did this Be-fore, did I? Speak publicly to you, I mean. I, um . . . well, I'll be honest with you—I had no idea what I was doing back then."

Granted, I had no idea what I was doing now, and since I didn't remember much about being Phantom, it was safe to assume that I'd been just as clueless Before. Phantom's reputation outlived his memory. People shifted at my admission, as if they'd taken for granted that I had been an expert superhero straight out of a comic book.

I coughed to clear my throat before explaining, "You trusted me to protect you once, but the truth is, I was just a kid trying to learn how to control these new powers and not fail high school. Now . . . I'm strong-er. I'm more powerful. I-I know it doesn't seem like it after what hap-pened here, and I'm really sorry about that, but I have more control over my abilities than I ever did when I was Phantom."

On a whim, I held my arms out and reached for my center to sum-mon the blue Divinity. Crude ice armor formed on my arms and torso. This was the power they needed to see—not my sonokinesis, which they rightfully feared.

I formed a blade in my right hand and stabbed it down on the po-dium, where it embedded in the wood and remained erect after I let go. I decreed, "I'm not alone anymore, either. I have a team now, and we work really well together, and if you let us, we want to protect you even better than Phantom could. The thing is . . ."

I stared down at the cards, then remembered Holly's advice to make eye contact and jerked my head back up to face the spectators. "When I was Phantom, I never asked for anything in return. I protected people because it was the right thing to do. But things are different now. My lab-family and I are still fugitives, which means if we're going to protect Phantom Heights, I need your help. I'm not really asking you *for* anything, though. I'm just asking you to not let us down. Not send us back . . . to that place. That's all. Do that, and we'll continue to put our lives on the line and defend you to our last breaths."

My final plea was met with steady silence. Madison was fuming, but when the person next to her started clapping, her scowl softened just a little. Soon, she was looking over her shoulder in surprise as applause arose from the sea of moving hands. I smiled behind my mask.

As the noise diminished, the blonde woman I'd noticed at the end of Madison's speech lifted a hand and said, "Caslynn Swan with the local news. I have a question." A weak nod was all I could muster. "You stated that you can protect us. Can you protect us from A6?"

The immediate silence was a javelin in my lungs. The crowd stared at me, waiting, and I stared back. "Axel isn't your enemy," I finally managed to say.

Caslynn raised her eyebrows. "You're evading the question. All I need is a yes-or-no answer. Can you or can you not protect us from him?"

I weighed her seemingly simple inquiry. Axel was faster than me, stronger, more powerful in every way despite our difference in age. And yet, he wasn't invincible. His weakness hung around Jay's neck, plus I had a weapon of my own that his sensitive ears couldn't handle. The only problem was that Phantom Heights would be damaged if I used it again.

"Yes," I said. People murmured in response, prompting me to add in desperation, "But Axel is my lab-brother. I understand there's concern about his, uh, bloodlines, but . . . but he's my ally. That should mean something."

The reporter was quick to fire back, "*Your* ally. Not ours. He's already made that very clear."

To that, I had no rebuttal. These people wanted to mold me into their hero and conform Axel to be my rival, but he wasn't. I didn't even think I could claim the title of *hero* anymore. I felt like an imposter wearing a fallen hero's mask, as if Phantom had been an entirely different entity who died in battle and pretending to be him was the ultimate dishonor.

Caslynn interrupted my thoughts: "Could you tell us what happened to you in the two years you spent at the AGC?"

The horror and immediate defensive response made my power prickle. "No." My knees were trembling again. "No," I repeated louder, shaking my head. "I didn't come here to talk about that."

"Then perhaps you could elaborate on this secret weapon being developed in Project Alpha."

"I can't tell you that, either."

"Why are you protecting Agent Kovak?"

Thoroughly flustered, I gazed helplessly at my increasingly restless audience that wanted answers I was never prepared to give. "I-I'm not."

"Then why won't you answer the question? Do you have some kind of agreement with him?"

"No. I, uh . . ." I turned to Holly. What did she want me to say?

She gave me no insight. No nod, no shake of the head, no response at all. Her expression was neutral as she watched me flounder under Caslynn's onslaught.

The reporter changed tactics again and caught me off guard when she asked, "Cato, do you still consider yourself human?"

What kind of question is that? I found my mother, who raised her eyebrows and nodded at me to answer while turning her palms up in expectation. I stammered, "Yes. And no. I guess, sort of, but . . . not really. I mean, I used to be—"

Caslynn interrupted, "You can turn your powers off, right?"

"In a sense . . . yeah. I guess you could put it that—"

"Then let me ask you this: if the community decides that you've become too dangerous, would you be willing to shut your powers off for good and live as a human?"

I gawked at her, mouth open, too stunned to answer. My ears were ringing. People were murmuring amongst themselves, but I couldn't hear the words issuing from their moving lips. Caslynn was watching, waiting. I couldn't even consider such a possibility. I didn't know how long I could suppress my power. Maybe indefinitely, but I didn't know, and I felt as if a part of me was missing whenever I did. Become human for good?

A body was now between me and the microphone, and Madison was saying, "I think that's enough. No more comments."

Holly strolled past me, so calm and collected that I couldn't tell if this nightmare went according to her plans or if I'd just left her a bigger mess to clean up. Madison yielded the microphone to her, as if Holly's very aura pushed her back.

The councilwoman cleared her throat with an innocent *ah-hem* that immediately snared the attentive silence of the crowd. She chuckled and said, "Not the most eloquent speech, but you have to admire Phantom's blunt honesty."

I thought that was supposed to be a joke, but nobody laughed.

Holly seamlessly moved on: "Really, though, we can't blame Cato for giving us that less-than-vague answer about whether or not he's still human. After all, our own government decreed that he is not. But then again, he wasn't human when Phantom was keeping watch over this town, was he? That didn't diminish his loyalty. I have faith in him."

She smiled at me. I gazed back at her, my mind blank. Madison forced a smile of her own, but she was gently pushing me away.

Holly didn't try to stop us from leaving. She faced the crowd again and proclaimed, "You should know that city council intends to work closely with Phantom and his allies. I'm sure many of you, like me, are still a little concerned about having ghosts protect us. You have my promise that city council is going to keep a close eye on our new heroes. If we have any reason to believe they will turn against us to join their own kind, rest assured the police will be trained to handle such a situation and protect you."

She paused to fold her hands on the podium and survey the crowd, making eye contact with as many as possible. "In the meantime, though, I must remind you that in order for them to protect us, they in turn need the protection of every single one of you. Our federal government left us here to die. If we give them the chance to do it again, they will. To them, we are collateral damage. Don't trust the AGC; trust your city council. We've fought, foraged, and survived beside you. We will lead a town that is better and stronger than it ever was before. Of course, by protecting Phantom, technically you are all committing a felony."

Holly held up her hands dramatically and spoke over the current of murmurs: "But the law didn't protect us in our time of need. Kovak promised us aid and never delivered. In my eyes, now we're even. He unknowingly sent us a team of powerful weapons as payment for his earlier neglect. I urge you all to remember that, remember what he's done to us, remember how our lives were before the Alpha ghosts came. I . . . well, I can't even imagine what might befall anyone who decides to betray this whole town and contact the AGC."

Her sweet threat hung over the crowd. She masterfully paused to let her words sink in, then finished, "I ask that no one does anything rash and irresponsible. If the time comes that we will be best served by allowing Agent Kovak to come and collect his fugitives, let it be by city council's majority vote. We serve you, the people. Please, come to us with your concerns instead of going straight to the AGC. I promise we will listen to you and base our decision on what is best for this community."

Madison, as if afraid the audience was about to transform into an angry mob at any second, steered me toward the street. "I told you not to come here! What were you thinking?"

Still numbed by the experience, I pulled free and muttered, "I didn't know it was going to be like that."

"I also told you to stay away from Holly Jennings. I don't think I could have been any clearer about that."

"She said she wanted to help us."

"Don't you get it, Cato? She's using you."

"So what?" I fired back, fed up with being criticized. "Did it occur to you that I actually know what I'm doing? It's a political game. She wants the humans of Phantom Heights to support me—us—so we have the same end goal."

Madison pinched the bridge of her nose and shook her head. "She's clever and manipulative, and she always gets her way. It might seem like you're on the same side right now, but the deeper you get in this political mess, the more control she'll have over you. If you aren't careful, you're going to turn into her puppet, and then if you don't do exactly what she wants, she will call Agent Kovak herself and report you."

"She just told everyone not to trust *Him*."

"Yes, and Kovak is the one who got her elected in the first place. Did you know that?"

I blinked. "What?"

"You can't trust her, Cato. The Agents funneled a lot of money into her campaign when she ran for city council. Kovak wanted somebody in office who would start pushing anti-kálos laws through the system so there would be a precedent for the courts when he's ready to apply those laws to the federal level. She owes him her political career. She may claim that her loyalty is to Phantom Heights, but I don't know how deep any residual trust she might have for Agent Kovak goes."

I hung my head. This was why—as if I needed to be reminded again—Jay had always been the leader of the team, not me. I thought in the moment while Jay calculated and planned ahead. I should have listened to my mother.

Madison said, "I want you to stay out of sight for a while, okay? Go back to Saros Manor. I'm going to talk to Holly."

"What are you going to say?"

"I don't know yet." We paused at the street corner. Before we parted ways, she added, "You don't have to fight all your battles alone anymore. I'm here to help you, Cay. Let me protect you."

I didn't agree, but I nodded anyway. Madison tried to reassure me with a smile before she turned and marched back toward City Hall. I stood still, watching until she left my sight, and then I faced the direction of Wes's house.

After a lingering moment of debate, I turned and walked in the opposite direction.

***

Madison knocked on the front door of the Jennings residence. The door opened almost immediately.

"Mrs. Tarrow," Shannon said politely, opening the door wider. "My mom said you would probably be coming. She's in her study." She stepped aside and gestured toward an open door by the entryway.

Madison clenched her teeth, too irked to bother with etiquette and thank Shannon as she should have. She strode inside.

Holly was sitting behind a desk in a modest sunlit study. Bookshelves lined the wall behind her, but there were no other chairs; apparently she didn't usually entertain guests here. Madison had always met with the councilwoman in her office on the second story of City Hall, but until the building was deemed structurally sound again, this must be where Holly intended to conduct her business.

The councilwoman didn't bat an eye at Madison's arrival. "I was expecting you."

"What the hell was that?" Madison demanded as she closed the door.

In the corner of the room, a yellow canary was startled onto its perch in a frenzied flapping of wings. Holly stirred the steaming liquid in her teacup with a delicate silver spoon. "I took the liberty of pouring you tea," she said, nodding at a second cup on the desk.

"No thanks."

"Are you sure? It's Earl Grey."

"I am."

Holly shrugged and blew away the curling fingers of steam grasping at the air from her china teacup. "Cato wasn't nearly as compelling as I'd hoped he'd be."

"I told you not to involve him."

"Yes, well, it was necessary. I've been interviewing a lot of people, and unfortunately, many are afraid that Cato isn't really one of us anymore."

"But he—"

Holly raised a hand. "Did you know that being interrupted is one of my worst pet peeves?" She waited for Madison to close her mouth and look away in angry shame before continuing, "I can't say I share that concern. If you ask me, the biggest threat Cato poses is his lack of control. The one who concerns me is Axel. Ms. Swan made an excellent point today, don't you think?"

"That doesn't mean he's an enemy," countered Madison half-heartedly. "Cato trusts him."

"Hmm." Holly blew on her tea again and took a dainty sip. "Well, despite what Cato says, in my opinion, it's only a matter of time before another incident occurs. We've had a glimpse of what Axel is capable of. People are saying that you created a powerful hero, but the Agents made an even more powerful villain. What do you think, Madison? Is your creation strong enough to stand against Kovak's?"

Stunned, Madison stared at the corner of Holly's desk. She'd always thought of Kovak as her business partner, not her competition. Now, though, her pricking ego made her wonder if what Holly said might be true. Although Cato's transformation had been an accident and Axel's had been carefully engineered, would people compare Level 4 Phantom to Level 9 A6 and whisper that her hybrid was the lesser creation?

"It's not fair to compare them. They're . . . very different."

"Yes, they are. One born human and given the power to protect us all, the other born an enemy and then transformed into a monster. The question is, which one is stronger? I'm sorry, but I just don't have faith that Phantom is powerful enough to stand against the demon Kovak made."

"It doesn't matter. Axel would never turn against Cato."

"And who would Cato choose, then?"

Madison scowled. Her gaze wandered back to the large cage in the corner where the canary ruffled its feathers and started singing a cheerful tune.

Holly rocked a little in her chair and said, "Did you know that canaries are astonishingly perceptive when it comes to detecting invisible ghosts? Kálos or moorlin—doesn't matter. If there's an unseen intruder, they'll chirp a warning until the coast is clear. I bought that little guy as soon as I moved back into my house. He makes me feel safer. I do love hearing him sing, but his true purpose is serving me as an alarm system."

"What's your endgame?"

Holly observed her over the teacup as she took another sip. "I'm afraid I don't know what you're talking about."

"You threw my son out in front of that piranha crowd with Caslynn at the forefront like Cato was live bait. Are you going to protect him, or are you waiting for the right moment to call Kovak?"

Holly, thoroughly bemused by the question, leaned back in her chair. "You still think I owe something to Kovak." She took another sip. "I have no loyalty to him. That being said, I'm not opposed to seeking his help if Phantom can't do his job."

"You don't need to worry about that," Madison snapped, turning on her heel. Holly wasn't going to answer any of her questions, so there was no point in continuing this annoying little game.

"You know," Holly called to her back, "Agent Kovak might be willing to grant Cato his human rights back."

Madison halted in her tracks. As much as she didn't want to turn around, she couldn't help herself. "What?"

"Don't you remember?" Holly teased her with a sly smile. "When Kovak came here to ask for help, he stressed that he'd do just about *anything* to get A1 and A2 back, no matter what the cost. Didn't you find that specification a bit odd, or was I the only one who noticed?"

Madison suddenly couldn't breathe. "You think he was covertly saying that he'd be willing to sell Cato's immunity in exchange for Finn and Reese? Just in case we were harboring them?"

Holly casually sipped her tea before she continued, "Cato really doesn't have much of a future, does he? He can't go to college, can't get a real job, can't get any government-issued licenses, can't leave Phantom Heights, really. He'll have to hide forever, always hunted . . . unless you trade the others for his freedom. Kovak wants Finn, Reese, and Axel so desperately that I think he's willing to bargain. Throw in the other four as a bonus, and Cato's freedom is all but guaranteed."

Finally, Madison choked out, "I . . . I couldn't do that. Cato cares about them. And they—"

"Save the morality speech, Madison. I don't care. Whatever you feel you have to do for your son's future, I won't judge you. I just want to ensure that you're aware of all your options."

Option? Is it even an option?

Madison slowly backed away from Holly, her mind reeling. She bumped into the door and fumbled behind her back for the handle, angry that Holly would suggest such treachery and disgusted at herself for thinking, in the darkest part in the back corner of her mind, how easy it could be to save her son from a lifetime of danger.

One phone call. That was all it would take.

The window was still broken.

I hopped onto the sill and lowered myself down into the abandoned office. It still looked exactly the same. The old oak desk; the dented filing cabinets with open, vacant drawers; the chair with a broken wheel. I dragged my finger through the dust as I passed the desk. The door leading to the main storage area of the warehouse was agape.

I lingered in the doorframe. Industrial drums had been positioned under the holes in the ceiling to gather rainwater. The walls were nicked from metal disks ricocheting, and that dark spot on the floor showed where a woodless fire had burned hot. Unexpected sentimentality swelled in my chest. I shivered. I'd actually missed this place. It was the very first Home we had. Proto was born here. I had felt safe here for the first time since our escape.

A cloaked figure in the corner kicked at the pile of filthy, thread-bare blankets Finn and Reese had almost died in. "Been a while since we were here, huh?" he said. He turned his head so his red eyes gleamed at me. "Great speech, by the way. You really fucked up that interview."

"You heard it?"

Axel rolled his eyes up toward the ceiling. *Right, of course he did.*

"Hey, Cato. A piece of advice—just because somebody says, 'Don't you remember?' at the end of a statement doesn't make it any less of a lie."

I hung my head. I was already feeling the sting of being played; I didn't need him to rub salt into the wound. "Yeah. Got it. I was just . . . I was trying to remind them that I'm still part human."

He tilted his head. "Why?"

"Because I thought that would help us."

"Why?"

I opened my mouth, but silence was my only answer. It had made sense when Councilwoman Jennings explained it, but now, standing before my lab-brother who despised humankind with every cell in his body, I realized that any explanation I could conjure would be stupid against his condescension.

Sensing that I was tongue-tied, he shrugged and said, "Whatever."

I cleared my throat. "Hey, Ax, um, can we talk?"

He didn't answer, but he waited, his impatience prominent while I struggled to arrange my thoughts into sentences. "Spit it out already."

I bobbed my head, flustered as I cleared my throat again. "I wanted to talk to you . . . about when we fought the Shadow Guard."

"Are you serious?" He turned away.

"Wait!" I pleaded. "Not you. I mean, this is about . . . me." He paused and glanced over his shoulder in time to see me whisper, "What I did."

Axel smirked and faced me again. "What, you mean almost level the whole town?"

My fingers compressed into tight fists, and I clenched my teeth to contain the frustrated scream Axel was coaxing to life. I couldn't lose control again. "I thought you of all people would understand." I squeezed my eyes shut so Axel couldn't see that they were glowing green, even though I was sure he knew. "I don't know what happened," I croaked weakly. "It just . . . did."

I was under control again, and I raised my gaze to face my lab-brother. He didn't give me the sympathy I'd hoped for, but at least his expression had softened. "Yeah."

Acknowledgment that he knew exactly what I was talking about—that tipping point, the moment you lose control of yourself and you're swept away by the force living inside of you, just a bystander in your own body as the world around you is destroyed.

"It scared me," I admitted. "I'm still scared."

He didn't answer, just stared into space, his crimson eyes dancing in thought. Why wouldn't he speak? He was the only one who could give me the solace I craved. I was annoyed that he'd reduced me to doing this, but I begged, "Ax, please talk to me."

"There's nothing to say," he answered gruffly. "It happened. You can't change it, and you can't guarantee it won't happen again."

"So, what?" I demanded, angry again. "I just give up? I have to live in fear of losing control all my life?"

"I didn't say that."

"Bloody Scout, you're no help at all." He watched me storm away, even though I wished he'd call me back or chase after me.

We weren't the same, not even close. Human, nydæa, one race powerless but power hungry and the other driven by feral instincts. And yet, we did share something I was realizing was our curse—the curse of the half-breeds. It didn't matter that our blood was diluted by non-kálos creatures. We were too powerful for our own good, and when we lost control of ourselves, there was no stopping the monsters that were unleashed.

I shoved my hands under my armpits to make them stop shaking. When I thought back to that day, my whole body turned cold with horror as I remembered that single moment of clarity in the echoes of a devastating, anguished scream . . . when I had opened my eyes and watched the world around me being torn asunder, and I'd realized why humans had caged me in a hell with no sunlight.

I tried to remind myself that I wasn't the only Sonic. Sonokinesis was a power that others had mastered already, and I could master it, too. But that rage . . . that was something else. A normal Sonic would have burned out after that one long scream. I'd still been leaking ectoplasm in the vortex of a blizzard. Even by ghost standards, that wasn't normal.

— Chapter Sixteen —
Family Reunion

The next day, something didn't feel quite right.

I couldn't put my finger on what it was. My lab-family and I woke before dawn as usual to train. Instead of scouting, we spent the day assisting with downtown's reconstruction, which mostly meant clearing rubble and hauling building materials for the construction crews. Ghost activity had been pretty much nonexistent since we'd decimated the Shadow Guard's forces, so this way we could be useful while staying near the Rip in case of trouble.

I noticed the first clue that something was off when I went to Saros Manor for my shift to spend time with Finn and Reese. To my surprise, I walked through the front door to find my mother pulling sheets off the furniture in the front parlor.

"Hey, Cato!" she greeted cheerily.

"What are you doing?"

"Oh, just a bit of cleaning," she said, setting her hands on her hips and arching her back to crack it. "This is such a great space, so I thought I'd make it usable again. Did you come for lunch? Would you like me to make you something?"

"No," I replied as I backed toward the staircase. "Just came to check on Finn and Reese."

"Okay. Well, if you change your mind, let me know. I can make lunch for them, too. Oh! Before I forget, Ero and I have a surprise for you. I mean, not just you—all of you. Could you please come home early today so we can give it to you before dinner?"

I stopped in my tracks with my foot on the first step and my hand on the balustrade. "What kind of surprise?" I asked suspiciously.

"Wouldn't be much of a surprise if I told you, now would it?"

Still, I couldn't help but hesitate. "Is it a surprise we're going to like?"

"I hope so," she said with a mysterious smile.

The second clue wasn't anything I'd thought twice about at the time. As requested, we returned to the manor an hour before we normally would have for dinner. Ero warmly invited us into his bedroom, where neatly folded bundles of fabric had been arranged on his bed.

"Come closer," Ero encouraged. "No need to be shy."

Jay, RC, Ash, Kit, and I approached the Telepath's bed. Axel, making a point to let everyone know he was bored, sulked in the corner by Finn and Reese while Madison lingered in the doorway with a smile on her face.

Ero explained, "I took a trip to Szion this morning. I hope you do not mind, but I did a bit of shopping on your behalf to find suitable replacements for your uniforms, which I know have served you well. But they are overdue to be replaced, and they are also human-made replicas. I think you will appreciate the higher quality of authentic Avilésian clothing. I did my best to find the right style for each of you. Shall we start with the fearless leader?"

Jay seemed more inquisitive than excited, and he maintained his composure as Ero showed off a chocolate-brown cloak. It was a regular full style, the same as the black ones we'd always worn, and Ero had paired the cloak with dark pants and an olive shirt with three-quarter sleeves.

For RC, a full wine-colored cloak with a dark-gray shirt and black pants, both trimmed in gold.

For Ash, a forest-green halter top that complemented her burgundy hair. The snug, lightweight shirt was cut short to reveal her midriff, similar to her current uniform. Accompanying it was a pair of black pants slit and laced in a crisscross pattern all the way down the outsides of the legs. A hunter-green, front-cut full cloak completed Ash's ensemble.

Madison had new sweatpants and T-shirts from the Human Realm for Finn and Reese since that was all they had ever worn. She also had a simple but pretty azure dress for Kit, whose cheeks flushed with pleasure when she took it in her hands and bashfully mumbled, "Thank you."

Ero added, "I also have something for you, Kit." He handed her navy leg wraps and arm sleeves, then lifted a beautiful sea-green cloak with a flourish and set it over the girl's shoulders. Kit craned her neck to watch him fix the clasp, and then he stepped back to admire it. Her cloak, Ero explained, was a layered style, which meant it had a striking extra piece of deeper blue-green fabric draped over the shoulders like a shawl that had been sewn on at the clasp. It was still hooded and full length, tailored to settle just above her ankles so Kit finally had a child-sized cloak that fit.

She cried, "I *love* it!" before throwing her arms around Ero's waist.

He chuckled at her reaction. "I thought you would," he said with a pat on her head. "And, one more accessory." He handed her a leather belt that was filled with small compartments. A larger pouch hung on each hip. "For any treasures you find while scavenging," he explained as Kit cinched the belt and admired all of her new pockets. "Axel, I brought you something, too."

The half-breed grunted and snatched his new clothes from Ero without a word of thanks. From the glimpse I'd seen, Ero had wisely stuck with an all-black ensemble for Axel.

"And finally, Cato," Madison said. She smiled at me and placed a folded pile of clothes on the bed—clothes that were very different from those Ash, Jay, RC, Kit, and Axel had been gifted. They were human clothes.

I stared at them in disappointment, reluctant to part with the Alpha uniform I'd grown so accustomed to wearing. It was like my armor; I felt safer wearing it.

Ero cleared his throat, causing Madison to glance at him. They shared knowing looks that made me suspect they'd taken part in a private conversation earlier. My mother exhaled in submission and added, "But I can't deny that you're half-kálos now." Under Ero's scrutiny, she laid a second set of clothes on the bed. "It's your choice."

As I stared at my two options, I could feel all eyes trained on me. Despite my mother's claim of impartiality, her hand lingered near the human outfit, trailing over the fabric as she backed away to let me approach.

I touched the clothing on my right, much to my mother's obvious relief and pleasure. A pair of blue jeans and a T-shirt with a logo that meant absolutely nothing to me—a skeleton in a black robe holding a scythe, the words *LeahRae Harris High Reapers* emblazoned around the logo in bold white text. This would have been what I used to wear Before, and yet my eyes were magnetically drawn to the next set of clothing. I moved my hand to touch the charcoal-gray cloak. Madison's lips pressed together in subtle disapproval.

Ero smiled and said, "Let me tell you about the clothing I chose for you. I took your Divinity of cryokinesis into account. It is important for you to be able to move freely and have some protection in battle, but not become overheated. The cloak is lightweight but durable. The pants are similar to the pair you are wearing now. The shirt is ribbed with extra padding to protect your torso, but to keep you cool, it is sleeveless and the fabric is breathable."

My attention was now laser focused on the foreign clothes. I held up the gray cloak to admire it. The full-length, hooded garment was a muted gray, and its hue seemed to shift in my fingers based on how the light caught the threads. This would be perfect for slipping in and out of the shadows. The shirt was a dark gray that had silver stitched into simple patterns around the edges of the extra padding.

I cast a fleeting glance at the human clothing and knew immediately which set I wanted. I'd been raised human but had adjusted to dressing like a ghost. My Arena uniform, even though it hadn't been authentic kálos clothing, made me feel more secure. "I choose these," I said, still gazing lustfully at the cloak in my hands.

Madison's shoulders slumped, but she said nothing. No doubt she had wanted me to maintain my human roots. But the thought of exchanging my reliable attire for such inferior human clothes made me feel vulnerable again, like when I'd been in a metal cage wearing nothing but sweatpants. The clothes Ero had brought were genuine from the Ghost Realm, sure to be even better than the human imitations from the Arena. Despite my mother's clear disappointment, I was itching to try the new clothes on.

The Telepath smiled. "An excellent choice. I am sure these clothes will suit you well."

"Thank you," I told him. I tried to convey the depth of my sincerity in my voice, but I knew he could feel it in my thoughts. He gave me a friendly wink.

Ash dropped her cloak, and Jay had already removed his cloak and shirt. I started to undo my clasp, but Madison held up her hands and cried, "Whoa, whoa—whoa! Stop!"

"Are we not supposed to wear these yet?" I asked in confusion.

"Well, yes, but don't take your clothes off here. Go upstairs to change."

"Why?"

"Because I said so." She pointed at the door. "Okay, new house rule—everybody has to be dressed in public spaces. If you're not in your room, you need to have clothes on. That means pants at a *bare minimum*, and Ash, that includes a bra for you. Am I clear?"

Although we exchanged puzzled looks, we nodded that we understood Madison's rule.

Kit hugged her new clothes to her chest and meekly asked, "What about when I'm in my fur? Do I have to put on clothes then?"

Ero grinned. With an amused smile, Madison said, "No, sweetheart." She faced all of us and finished, "Turning into an animal is an exception to the rule, which means *only* Kit and Wes get that free pass. Got it?" She ended with a stern glare at Axel, who returned the look with a sneer.

And now, here we were, wearing our new clothes and sitting in the newly cleaned parlor, which had the faint scent of synthetic lemon and wood polish. That foreboding feeling from earlier was settling into an unpleasant pit in my stomach as I scrutinized my mother. She was still smiling, but it looked forced now, and she kept casting anxious glances toward the front doors.

"Good news," she said, her voice a little too high pitched and chipper. "Wes, Ero, Trey, and Emerton have volunteered to take over scouting for tonight with extra patrols, which means you have the night off."

The mood instantly darkened even though her smile stayed in place. Axel folded his arms, glaring at Madison. Ash, RC, and I turned uncertainly to Jay, who scowled and said, "We didn't ask for the night off."

"No, I know," she said, wringing her hands together. "This is, um . . . a personal request. I'm really sorry to spring this on you, but . . . Cato . . . uh . . ."

"We're having guests tonight," Vivian chimed in. "The family wants to see you, Cay."

Madison nodded and gave me an apologetic smile. I stared blankly at my blood-family, struggling to process the news. I could feel the inquisitive stares of my lab-siblings on me. "What?"

My mother glanced at the front doors again before she faced me and said, "Well, I called them this morning. I mean, I had to let them know what happened—that you're here. Alive. And . . . when I told them, they insisted on driving here to see you. You know how stubborn they are—they wouldn't take no for an answer. The last time we saw them was at your funeral. But, uh . . . well, actually, they wanted to come stay here for a few days to spend time with you."

"What?" I barely managed to force out again.

Madison quickly held up her hands and said, "Before you get overwhelmed, I told them I didn't think that was a good idea. They were willing to compromise. But they do want to see you, and meet your friends, and see us, too, since it's been more than two years now. I promise, they're just here for dinner and a quick visit, and then they'll drive back home tonight. Is . . . that okay? Do you think you can handle one dinner with the whole family?"

My head was reeling with this unexpected development. I had other family besides Madison and Vivian? I guess it made sense. Madison must have parents, right? And maybe blood-siblings of her own. But I was drawing a total blank.

"They really want to see you, Cato," my mother added softly, misinterpreting the baffled look on my face. "They've missed you."

My lab-family was watching me, waiting to hear my verdict. I swallowed and dragged my hand through my hair. "Just one dinner?"

"Just one dinner," she promised with a nod. "A few hours, that's all."

"What if I say no?"

Madison hesitated. "Well . . . they'll be here very soon, but if you don't want to see them, you don't have to. Vivian and I will have dinner with them. But I really wish you would stay. They're mostly coming to see *you*."

I turned to Jay for guidance, but he deferred, "It's your call."

I rubbed my forehead in indecision. "Why didn't you give me more time to think?"

"I'm sorry," said Madison. She shifted with guilt. "I wanted this to be a casual dinner, not a big event you would stress about all day. I thought it would be a pleasant surprise. I . . . well, I thought you'd be happy to see the family."

Before I had time to decide, a knock on the front door made us all jump. "They're here," Madison said, turning toward the door. She hesitated. "Are . . . you staying?"

I dropped my hand and sighed in reluctant surrender.

"Thank you. I want everybody to be on their best behavior. *Please* try to make a good impression. The family . . . understands the situation, but . . . they're not used to being around ghosts. Just be yourselves, and I'm sure they'll like you."

We exchanged confused glances as she stepped into the foyer and opened the door.

"Aunt Madison!" came a gleeful cry as a girl rushed forward and wrapped her arms around my mother in a tight hug.

"Whoa-ho, who is this young lady?" Madison teased. "You're sprouting up like a weed!"

The girl detached herself as a couple entered the foyer behind her. "Tell me about it," said a tall, thin woman. "Please tell her to slow down on the growth spurt because her poor old parents can't take it."

Madison smiled and embraced the woman. The girl said, "Hey, Viv!" and gave my blood-sister a hug.

"Come in, come in!" Madison said, ushering the group inside. "Looks like it's starting to rain."

"We just beat the storm," said an elderly, white-haired woman as an old man closed the door behind them.

"It's *so* good to see you," Madison said, continuing her round of hugs.

The big man who had accompanied the girl and middle-aged woman tilted his head back to stare up at the crystal chandelier hanging from the dizzyingly high ceiling above the foyer. He let out a low whistle in appreciation. "Some place."

"Yes, we'll have to give you a tour. Here, Mom, let me take your coat. The parlor's right in here."

I backed away from the doorway to let the strangers enter. Kit, Ash, Jay, and RC were on their feet, already in defense mode and gauging my response to determine how they should respond. The twins remained on the couch, watching warily, and Axel didn't move from his position in the corner; he didn't even raise his head. I tensed as the newcomers' eyes immediately locked onto me.

"Hey, there's my favorite nephew!" exclaimed the middle-aged man.

The thin woman next to him turned to my mother. "My word, speaking of growth spurts—you weren't kidding, Mad. He does look like the spitting image of a young Jaxon." The group of strangers advanced on me. I retreated deeper into the room.

The old man shuffled toward me, his gait uneven and aided by a cane. "Hiya, sport! You have no idea how good it is to see you!" He reached out toward me. I shied away from his hand and backed into the wall.

The man paused. "What's the matter, Cato? Don't you know who I am?"

He was staring at me, waiting for my recognition. Everybody was. But I didn't know him. Eyes wide, I shook my head no.

The man's face fell. "Oh." He glanced back at Madison, who looked as if she were in pain. The man turned to me again. "I'm your grandpa. I know it's been a while, and a lot has happened, but we used to come visit every Thanksgiving and Christmas. You always called me Pop-Pop. Do you remember now?"

Memories stirred, but they were murky and just out of reach. In desperation, I looked to Vivian for help. She shook her head sadly, watching me. Madison stepped forward and tried to salvage the awkward situation: "Of course he does. You remember everyone, Cato. Gram and Pop-Pop, Uncle Segan, Aunt Mara, and your cousin Terra. They're your family."

I studied my blood-relatives. My grandparents seemed to have an interesting juxtaposition of fragility yet assertiveness, as if old age hadn't yet succeeded in damping down their spirits or dulling their minds even though it was steadily wearing down their bodies. Uncle Segan was a big man—not obese, just a large, hefty frame. His skin was much darker than I'd expected. I had, apparently incorrectly, assumed everyone would look the same as Madison, Vivian, and me.

Aunt Mara was tall and thin with pale, creamy skin that looked as though it didn't often see sunlight. Her hair was a lighter shade of brown than my mother's, and unlike Madison, she had a smattering of freckles across her cheeks. But her green eyes and the shape of her mouth looked the same.

Terra bore strong features from both of her parents. She looked to be about fifteen, if I had to guess, and her light-brown skin was perfectly balanced between the spectrum of Uncle Segan and Aunt Mara. Her hair was tied back into a half-ponytail on the top while the bottom portion of her springy hair was loose over her shoulders. Although she had her mother's small frame, her round face was a bit on the pudgy side—she was clearly well fed and didn't have to worry about ever be-ing hungry.

So, this was my family. My family that I didn't know. I wasn't sure who to turn to, so I glanced at the people I knew best—my lab-siblings. They were watching, still waiting to determine whether or not these new humans were a threat.

Okay, I can do this. I just have to keep it together for a few hours, and then these people will leave. But I could tell from the looks on Madison's and Vivian's faces that they knew something was very wrong. I should have recognized the other members of my blood-family. But how could I? They weren't in my photograph, so I hadn't been able to memorize their faces. Bloody Scout, how was I going to pull off pretending everything was normal?

My mother cleared her throat, accidentally triggering Finn and Reese to jump to their feet and stand at attention, eyes glowing, ready to serve if she issued a silent command. "All right, introductions," she said in an unnaturally bright tone. "These are my parents, Rosalie and Gordon. Over there is Mara, my sister. This is her husband, Segan, and their daughter, Terra. And then we have—" she pointed at each of my lab-siblings as she listed their names "—Axel, Finn, Reese, Kit, RC, Ash, and Jay. They . . . came here with Cato."

"From the Agency of Ghost Control," Aunt Mara murmured, fold-ing her arms as she surveyed my lab-family. Her expression was hard and judgmental but not necessarily hateful. "And you're all . . . ?"

"Ghosts," Jay calmly finished for her after a few seconds of tense silence with only the sound of the steady rain outside. "Yes."

"Which is *so* cool!" Terra exclaimed, her smile so wide she looked as if she were about to burst at the seams. "That means you all have powers, right? Can you show us?"

"Terra," Uncle Segan said sternly.

Her face immediately fell. "Oh, I mean, um, you don't have to. If you don't want to."

Aunt Mara coldly added, "Please don't be offended; we don't ex-pect you to perform for us."

Uncle Segan stepped toward Jay and jabbed his hand out for a handshake as he said, "It's very nice to meet you."

Jay leapt back in alarm as my uncle towered over him. Madison quickly touched Uncle Segan's extended arm and intervened, "You must be starving after your long drive." She gently pulled him back to give us a little more space. "My original plan was to eat out on the patio and let Segan show off his grill-master skills, but the weather had other plans. So, I decided to keep it simple and get pizza instead."

Terra gasped dramatically and said, "Oh, did you get it from that *amazing* place we had before? That little pizzeria downtown? Is it still open, after . . . ?"

"It is, and I did," Madison said with a smile.

Ash leaned toward me and quietly asked, "What is pizza?"

Terra must have overheard because she ogled us with wide eyes and said, "Wait . . . have you never had pizza before?" Ash hesitated, embarrassed, then shook her head. "Oh. My. God. You haven't *lived* yet!" Terra exclaimed. "Pizza is, like, the best food on the planet!"

Madison said, "Plates, napkins, pizza, and drinks are in the kitchen, and there's plenty for everyone." She looked at us and added, "I'll get them started so everyone isn't crammed in the kitchen at once. Viv, why don't you give the family a quick tour and then bring them through the library to the kitchen?"

My lab-family and I nervously skirted the newcomers to enter the foyer, all except Axel, who looked as miserable as I felt. He was pale and sweating as he stared moodily beyond the commotion into nothing, grinding his teeth in irritation. Without a word, he peeled out of the corner and stormed away through the back of the parlor toward the main-floor bedrooms where Wes and Ero slept. "Is something wrong, Axel?" Madison called after him.

Axel grumbled a certain four-letter word that made Jay call out a reproach, and then he muttered, "Headache. Too many people." He disappeared around the corner.

I wished I could escape so easily. And yet, even in my bewilderment, I felt worry gnaw my insides. Axel wasn't sick—not this time.

His eyes were still bright, his pupils small.

As we entered the dining room, I heard my grandfather say, "She isn't serving the guests first? I know I taught her better manners."

Vivian softly replied, "I know, Pop-Pop. Under normal circumstances, she would, but . . . they're a little touchy when it comes to food. The Agents starved them. It's better to let them get their food first so they know there's enough."

"Poor dears," my grandmother said just before the swinging door between the dining room and kitchen closed behind me.

I inhaled the robust aroma of garlic, herbs, cheese, bread, and marinara sauce, and my mouth instantly started to water. Boxes had been arranged in two rows, filling the center island.

My mother stood between us and the food. "Before you dive in, I promise there's more than enough for everybody. You can take as many pieces as you want. *Please* try to show a little restraint when you eat. Nobody is going to take your food away; we're all just here to enjoy the meal, and if you're still hungry after you've finished your first plate, you can come back and get more."

She pointed toward the far end of the island. "Plates and napkins are over there, and then for pizza toppings, we have five cheese, pepperoni, sausage and mushroom, meat lover's, and veggie supreme. I also have cheesy garlic breadsticks and cinnamon bread knots. Marinara and garlic dipping sauces are here on the end. Take whatever looks good to you."

Kit raised herself up onto her tiptoes but was still too short to see the top of the counter. "Deep-dish?" she asked with an eager smile that showed off her fangs and missing tooth.

I didn't understand her question, but it made Madison pause and stare at her in surprise. "Oh. Um, no. Sorry, I didn't get deep-dish. But the cheese pizza is stuffed crust. Go ahead and dig in. Like I said, take whatever you want and put it on your plate, and then we'll go into the dining room to eat. There are glasses of ice water already on the table, but if you want pop, there's a cooler with drinks in it," she said, gesturing toward a plastic container on the counter.

We converged to see "the best food on the planet," according to Terra. When I saw the round cheese-covered pies sitting inside the square boxes, I knew I'd definitely eaten pizza Before. It all looked so good—I took one of each kind so I could sample everything.

"Cay, I don't think you'll like the veggie supreme," Madison warned. "It has peppers on it, and they're hard to pick off."

I hesitated and studied the last piece I'd set on my plate. "Oh. Right. Thanks," I said with an uncertain grin. I didn't remember what peppers tasted like, but Vivian had pointed out my former aversion to them at the café.

"Here, set it on my plate rather than putting it back in the box. I'll eat it." As I surrendered the slice, my mother glanced down at Kit and kindly said, "That counter's pretty tall, huh, sweetheart? Would you like me to fill your plate for you? Just tell me what you'd like. I can repeat the toppings if you need me to."

Kit handed Madison her plate and recited, "One piece of cheese pizza, one piece of meat lover's pizza, one breadstick, and one cinnamon knot, please."

Madison filled Kit's plate. "You've had pizza before, haven't you?" she said.

Kit nodded. "Can we get deep-dish next time?" she asked as she accepted her plate.

"We absolutely can. When was the last time you had pizza?"

"In the city with the sky towers and the loud metras," Kit replied just before she stuffed the breadstick into her mouth and ripped off a huge bite with her sharp teeth, closing her eyes in ecstasy. She padded away after Jay and RC toward the dining room.

"The sky towers and loud metras," Madison murmured, her brow furrowing as she pondered Kit's riddle. "Hold on . . . is she talking about the Metra train? Was Kit in Chicago?"

I shrugged. "No idea," I said as I added a cinnamon bread knot onto my pizza stack. "Could have been. I don't know where Kit was when *They* caught her." I also wasn't sure where Chicago was or if I'd ever been there before, but at least my ignorance of Kit's past spared me from having to admit that.

Ash was waiting for me by the door, and I could hear voices approaching from the library, so I retreated with my lab-sister before my blood-family entered the kitchen. Finn and Reese trailed after us. Madison called, "Have everyone sit on the far end of the table by the foyer."

As I looked at the dining room table, I understood her request—by having us sit on the far side, Madison had ensured that nobody would have to walk behind us to get to an empty seat, which meant no one would have any valid reason to get too close to our food unless they wanted to try and take it away.

I sat down and immediately started wolfing down my meal. I'd already devoured one piece of pizza when Vivian entered the dining room. She set a beverage can and a plate in front of the vacant chair next to me, then circled the table and did the same in front of the empty chair beside Reese.

I swallowed my mouthful and asked, "Aren't you hungry?"

"Sure," she said brightly. "I'll get my meal after everyone else has been served. I'm just claiming these seats for Mom and me." She glanced at the twins and said, "You don't have to wait for us; you have permission to eat." With a human's blessing, Finn and Reese took their first bites.

I get it—Madison and Viv are a buffer so none of us have to sit right next to my other family members, I realized as my blood-sister returned to the kitchen. That was a slight relief.

As I bit into the cheesy garlic breadstick and relished the explosion of flavor in my mouth, the kitchen door swung open again, and my grandfather limped out with his cane. "I'm not so old and decrepit that I need my food carried for me," he grumbled. "Not yet, anyway."

"I know, Pop-Pop," Vivian said as she followed behind carrying two plates. "I'm just trying to help." She set his plate down at the head of the table, then positioned the other plate at the seat next to his.

Vivian ducked around my grandmother backing through the swinging door with a red can in each hand. "Here you are, dear," she said, setting a can next to each plate. My grandfather circled around behind her and pulled her chair out from the table. "Always the gentleman," she said with a smile as she sat. He returned to his seat at the head of the table, rested his cane on the back of the chair, and sat down.

Terra strolled out next with a plate of pizza in one hand, a can of pop in the other, and a bottle of white dressing tucked under her arm. Aunt Mara and Uncle Segan were right behind her, with Vivian and Madison bringing up the rear.

My mother sat down next to me. Vivian, after doing a quick head count, shifted her seat over one to leave an empty chair between her and Reese. I realized that with Wes and Ero absent, three extra chairs had been brought to the table to accommodate the five new guests, but Axel hadn't joined us, leaving one seat unoccupied.

Terra drizzled white sauce over her pizza slices, then passed the bottle to Vivian. "Okay, you *have* to try ranch dressing on your pizza," she said, grinning down the table at us. "I know it sounds weird, but hear me out. It's like a Midwest tradition, and ranch on pizza is seriously like the best combo ever. Trust me—you'll love it."

Vivian squirted the dressing in a blob on her plate so she could dip her pizza, then passed the bottle along for us to try. When it reached me, I copied Vivian's method instead of Terra's so my pizza wouldn't be ruined if I ended up not liking ranch. I passed the bottle to Madison, who apparently wasn't as keen on the "tradition" and set it in the middle of the table in case anyone else wanted to use it.

I watched Vivian dip her breadstick into the ranch. I copied her, although Madison's scrutinizing sidelong gaze alerted me that after my miserable failure to properly greet the family, I was now under surveillance and every move was going to be carefully analyzed. *Great.*

To my surprise, Terra was right—the sauce completely changed the taste of the pizza, adding an extra layer of flavor. I reached for my water, then paused, noticing that RC hadn't touched his glass of water yet even though he'd consumed more than half of his meal. I surveyed the glasses of water spaced around the table and realized that each one had four ice cubes.

Without a word, I reached for my center and harnessed my cold

Divinity to form a fifth ice cube in my glass, then slid it into the center of the table. "Trade you," I offered.

Still chewing, he glanced up, studied my water glass for a split second, noticed that it contained an odd number of ice cubes, and then waved his hand, sending his glass scooting across the table to settle next to my plate. He seized his new glass and gratefully started guzzling the cold water to wash down his meal.

I picked up his glass and took a drink, feeling slightly perturbed. I hadn't expected a heartfelt thank-you or anything, but minimal eye contact would have been nice. He hadn't even looked at me.

"Whoa," Terra breathed. "How did you do that?"

RC set down the glass and replied, "Telekinesis."

"No. Way. For real? You have telekinesis? That's amazing!"

My uncle smiled. "Telekinesis, huh? Hey, can you pass me the ranch?"

RC glanced at the bottle. His left eye glowed as he flicked his hand, sending the bottle sliding across the table until it came to a stop next to Uncle Segan's plate. My uncle laughed—a pleasant, booming sound that seemed to reverberate in my rib cage. "Very impressive, young man."

RC shot me a quizzical look, unsure how to respond to the compliment. Moving such a small object across such a short distance had hardly been any effort at all to him—a toddler could have performed such a simple feat—so the praise seemed unwarranted. I just shrugged one shoulder and took a big bite, hoping that keeping my mouth full would prevent me from having to talk.

Terra leaned forward, her meal now forgotten. "What else can you guys do?"

She and her dad seemed to be the only ones impressed and excited by our otherworldly abilities. Aunt Mara remained stoic. My grandfather was frowning, and my grandmother looked uncomfortable.

When no one volunteered an answer, Terra turned to me and said, "You have an ice power, right, Cato?"

I nodded and swallowed my mouthful. "And a sonic scream. I have two Divinities."

"And you're Phantom! Which makes you officially the coolest cousin *ever*. No offense, Viv."

My blood-sister held up her hands with an understanding smile. "No, no, I get it. I can't compete with Phantom."

"The rest of you must have incredible powers too," Terra tried again.

My lab-family exchanged uncertain looks, but every stare eventually fell on Jay. Revealing a Divinity often meant revealing one's weakness by association, so they turned to the leader for direction. He reluctantly admitted, "Teleportation."

Ash bowed her head and followed his lead: "I'm a Pyrokinetic."

Finn and Reese continued to eat without a word, and Kit shyly kept her gaze trained on her plate. "The twins are Mind-Readers," Vivian said in their silence. "And Kit can turn into an animal—we think a cat, but she hasn't shown us yet."

"Way freaking cool," Terra said. I wished she could turn down her nonstop enthusiasm, just a notch or two. "Hey, okay, so, I'm thinking of a number. What is it?"

Reese solemnly held up three fingers without looking at Terra.

"Right! Okay, now what number am I thinking of?"

He set his pizza down and held up all ten fingers as Finn held up two, totaling twelve.

"Now—"

"So," my aunt interrupted before Terra could continue quizzing Finn and Reese. "This is a beautiful house." Her gaze lingered on the chandelier overhead before roaming across the huge dining room. "You . . . um . . . you're renting it?"

"Not exactly," Madison said. "Vivian and I are going to be staying here a few nights a week. Our other house is comfortable enough for three or four people, but not ten. Cato didn't want to leave his friends, so they all live up on the third floor, and Wes offered us a guest bedroom whenever we want to stay over."

"And Wes is . . . a werewolf?" my grandmother asked. Her attempt to keep her voice casual failed miserably; she clearly didn't approve.

My grandfather grumbled, "And I thought an ectologist was bad news."

Madison snapped, "Dad, it's for Cato. Besides that, your daughter also hunts ghosts."

"Well, I was never happy about that either," he muttered under his breath.

"Yes, I know. You've never been shy about reminding me."

Aunt Mara quietly said, "I don't think we need to start that tired old argument again. It's safe to say Madison isn't planning to make a career change after all these years, especially now. So, these, ah, *ghosts* are part of the family now?"

Madison nodded. "We've sort of . . . unofficially adopted them."

RC scowled and glared at his plate. Everyone else's attention traveled up to the chandelier, which had spontaneously started trembling with a chime-like tinkling sound. Only after every crystal piece stilled did Uncle Segan break the awkward silence: "A ghost hunter moving in to live with a werewolf so she can raise her half-ghost son and foster six ghost kids. Sounds like the plot of a sitcom."

"Seven, actually," Madison replied. "Axel isn't feeling well, so he couldn't join us. And believe me, we'd be starring in a drama, not a sitcom."

"Well, I think it's awesome," Terra proclaimed.

"You've been quiet, Cato," my grandfather said. "Cat got your tongue?"

I blinked, staring at him uncomprehendingly. "What cat?" I asked. *Is he talking about Kit?*

"He's just a big teaser," Aunt Mara said with a quiet chuckle, playfully slapping her dad on the arm.

"Well," he said, "we came all this way to see Cato. We thought you were dead, sport. Couldn't believe the news when your mom called—Gram started crying, and I thought your mom was pulling my leg. We wanted to come right away and see you. But you've barely said a word."

Pulling on his leg? How could she do that through the phone? And why would she want to pull on his leg in the first place? My grandfather spoke English, and yet I couldn't seem to comprehend what he was saying. I swallowed uncertainly and muttered, "I don't know what you want me to say, Mr. Tarrow."

My blood-relatives stared at me in blatant shock. "No, no, darling," my grandmother gently corrected with an uncertain smile. "First of all, Tarrow was your father's last name. Ours is Hays."

"Second," my grandfather finished, "you are not to call me Mr. Hays. It's Pop-Pop." To my lab-family, he said, "That goes for all of you. If you're going to be a part of this family now, I want you to address me as Pop-Pop."

"*Dad*," Madison said sternly. "Don't push them. I don't force them to call me Mom."

Every painting on the wall suddenly fell to the floor, making us all jump. I shot a glare at RC, who was still resolutely keeping his head down. Terra muttered, "That was weird."

"House must be haunted," my grandfather said. "Good thing we know a ghost hunter."

I thought that was meant to be a joke, but Madison's scowl was anything but amused. Uncle Segan said, "Hey, now. No need for everyone to be so serious. We have a lot of catching up to do in a short amount of time." He chuckled. "Hey, Cato, we were talking on the drive up here—do you remember that Thanksgiving when you were carrying the bowl of cranberries and you tripped? Red juice everywhere—I thought your mom was going to have a conniption! You even managed to put a stain on the ceiling!"

Madison smiled and added, "I spent an hour on the ladder until my neck and arms were numb. The stain is still there if you look hard enough."

My blood-family burst into uproarious laughter. I sat immobile in my chair, smiling unconvincingly. To avoid anyone's gaze, I focused on my food as I swept my crust through the ranch. Ash briefly made eye contact and offered me a sympathetic smile.

I was hoping my relatives would leave right after dinner, but everybody migrated back into the parlor to continue chatting. Terra talked about her high-school choir going to nationals. Uncle Segan described his new job, and then the stories resumed. Apparently, I used to climb trees a lot when I was a kid, and I had a tendency to get stuck. Madison was in the middle of describing the time I'd made it down to the last branch before I fell on my head, and then Terra interrupted, "Well, that explains a lot!"

The laughter was so loud I actually winced. I didn't understand why it was funny; falling on my head must have hurt. After another fifteen minutes of forcing a grimace that was supposed to pass as a smile, I couldn't take it anymore. "I need to use the bathroom," I muttered.

All of my lab-siblings glanced at me in concern; they knew when something was wrong with my voice. My blood-family, on the other hand, accepted my excuse easily, and they didn't question why I slipped out of the room when there was a guest bathroom accessible directly from the parlor.

I ascended the grand staircase and stopped at the second floor, where I sat down on the top step, closed my eyes, and buried my face in my hands. This was a nightmare. These people—my family—were total strangers, and I didn't know what to do.

I pressed the heels of my palms against my eyelids, listening to Uncle Segan's booming laugh and trying to find a memory to match the sound to. I focused on my aunt's voice, my grandmother's soft chuckle, my cousin's high-pitched giggle, but none of the pieces of memories I had left fit with the sounds.

Gone. All gone. I had nothing left of them.

— Chapter Seventeen —

Gamble

I stayed at the top of the stairs, listening to my blood-family. I didn't want to go back into the parlor and face them again. It was easier to hide and avoid the situation altogether.

After a while, I heard Terra ask where I was. Someone answered that I'd left for the bathroom a while ago, and then Vivian volunteered to see if I was all right. I draped my arms around my shins and rested my chin on my knees, waiting for her to find me.

She appeared at the foot of the stairs and spotted me. "What are you doing up there?"

Rather than call down to her, I sat in silence, and as expected, she trotted up the steps to join me. "Viv," I said quietly, trying to convey just how desperate I was feeling, "I don't know what they want me to say, how they want me to act."

My blood-sister sat down a couple of steps below me. "Nobody expects anything from you. They're just happy to see you again, that's all."

I hung my head; her words didn't reassure me. Vivian smiled and rose. "Come on. They're family. They love you no matter what, so just be yourself. Don't think about it too much."

Be myself. That was good advice, except I didn't know who I was anymore. I descended the staircase with her, but then I paused when we reached the foyer. "I'll be there in a minute," I promised. "I want to get some water." Hopefully, it would help to clear my head a little.

Vivian nodded and returned to the parlor while I ventured into the library. Just before I set my hand on the door to the kitchen, I paused. I could hear voices on the other side.

"I'll take a full glass," Aunt Mara was saying. "Segan's driving."

Over the sound of liquid being poured, Madison said, "I'm sorry you have such a long drive for such a short visit."

"No, don't be silly. We agreed to it. We still wanted to come. Although . . . I'll admit, I expected a warmer reception from Cato. He doesn't seem like he wants us here."

"I think he's a little overwhelmed," Madison said. "It's a lot to handle, and he hasn't really been himself. After what he endured, this is all a huge adjustment."

"To be honest, his glowing eyes freak me out. And why do you let him dress like that?"

"What do you mean?"

"Come on, Mad. He's dressed like . . . a ghost."

"Mar, I haven't picked out Cato's clothes for him since he was in kindergarten. I'm not going to dictate what he wears."

"But don't you think you should encourage him to dress more like a human? This isn't the Ghost Realm."

"No, it's not. I get what you're saying. Of course I want Cato to maintain his human roots, but . . . I can't force him. The Agents certainly didn't treat him like a human, and he formed a close bond with the other Alpha ghosts while they were all held in captivity. If he wants to experiment with other customs and dress like a ghost, I'm not going to tell him no."

"It's your decision, not mine," Aunt Mara said dryly. "I'm just saying, I think you should put your foot down a little harder is all."

Part of me wanted to retreat so they wouldn't know I'd eavesdropped. But part of me was also seething. I reached for my center and summoned the power of intangibility, then stepped silently through the door.

My mother and aunt were leaning against the counter with a bottle of wine. Madison was saying, "I just think it's best that— Cato!" They both froze when they spotted me standing in front of the door with my arms folded. Madison smiled. "Hi, sweetheart. Where did you wander off to?"

I fixed my creepy glowing eyes directly on Aunt Mara, whose face was quickly turning red. "If my eyes freak you out, I bet walking through doors is really unnerving," I said in a low voice. I uncrossed my arms and walked toward the sink without looking at them.

In my peripheral, I saw Aunt Mara cover her mouth with one hand. "Oh my gosh. Cato, I'm so sorry."

Normally I'd open the cabinet to get a clean glass, but this time, I used intangibility to reach through the cabinet door, just to make a point. "Sorry for what you said, or sorry I heard it?" I asked, flipping the faucet on and filling my glass.

"Both," she meekly admitted. "You deserve better than that. Please accept my apology."

I turned the water off and took a drink, glaring at them both over the rim. I made them sweat in silence while I drained the full glass, then set it on the counter and looked my aunt in the eye. "For the record, I didn't ask you to come. I didn't get a say in the matter. So I'm sorry if my reception wasn't warm enough for you, but then again—" I summoned my cold Divinity and let ice crystals frost my clothes and hair "—I'm a Cryokinetic, so being warm isn't exactly my specialty."

Even though my gaze was locked on Aunt Mara, my mother was the one whose guilty stare fell to her wineglass.

Aunt Mara looked as if she was about to start crying. "Cato, I'm sorry. This is all just . . . a lot to process. I realize my perspective pales in comparison to what you've gone through, but . . . I really don't want to leave town with you being angry at me. I was speaking candidly to your mom, and I shouldn't have. It's not my place to pass judgment when I don't know even a fraction of all the details. Will you please forgive me?"

I melted the frost and crossed the kitchen with a purposeful stride. "If it'll make the rest of the evening more bearable until you leave, fine," I snapped, shoving the swinging door open and entering the dining room.

As the door swung behind me, I heard Aunt Mara sigh and mutter, "Oh, I really screwed up, didn't I?"

I didn't linger to hear Madison's answer.

"Cato," Uncle Segan greeted amiably when I returned to the parlor. "Up for a game of euchre? C'mon, you and me against Viv and Ter." He was sitting cross-legged on the floor, shuffling a deck of cards with practiced hands on top of the low coffee table. Kit's golden eyes watched the cards with intensity, but I stared at them with dread.

Euchre. The word meant absolutely nothing to me. Did I once know how to play euchre? I must have, or he wouldn't have invited me to play.

I swallowed and opened my mouth, but no sound came out. Everyone was watching me, waiting, but I just stood there. As the discomfort started to become unbearable, Vivian said, "Actually, I'm not really in the mood for euchre right now."

"Me either," I finally croaked.

My uncle's busy hands slowed as he stopped shuffling and straightened the stack. "Next time, then," he said.

I took a shaky breath and let it out in a sigh of relief. My grandmother patted the sofa and said, "Why don't you come sit by us, Cato?"

I just couldn't escape these awkward encounters, one right after another. Reluctantly, I approached, but rather than sit on the cushion within my grandmother's reach, I perched myself on the arm of the sofa, keeping one foot on the floor.

Kit hesitantly asked, "Can I play a game?"

Uncle Segan smiled at her. "Sure! What would you like to play, kiddo? Go fish?"

"Can we play Omaha?"

My blood-family stared at her as if she'd sprouted a second head. Uncle Segan chuckled and said, "Hun, that's poker. You know how to play poker?"

Kit nodded, her ears perked in excitement. "I wanna play Omaha."

He grinned in amusement and said, "Okay. It's your call, so Omaha it is."

"Deal me in too, Dad," Terra said.

Kit knelt on the floor across from Uncle Segan as he resumed shuffling the deck. She sat on her knees, squirming with excitement.

I crossed my arms and leaned back to watch. I didn't know how to play the game, but Uncle Segan started by dealing four cards facedown to Terra, Kit, and then himself. The three players picked up their cards. Finn and Reese crept closer to watch, their eyes glowing as they gleaned the rules of the game from the minds of the players.

"I call," said Terra.

Kit set her cards facedown again and rifled through a pouch on her belt, then placed a silver ring with a red stone on the table and slid it forward. "What's that?" Terra asked.

"My bet," Kit replied sweetly.

Again, my relatives stared at her in shock. "Your bet?" Uncle Segan laughed with his deep, booming voice. "Uh-oh, I'm in trouble! Didn't realize we were betting. All right, then." He dug his wallet out of his back pocket.

"Segan," Madison said sternly. I turned to see her and Aunt Mara watching from the doorway. "Tell me you're not encouraging a little girl to gamble."

"It's all in good fun," he replied, then lowered his voice and promised, "I'll let her keep her stuff at the end of the game." He winked and set a one-dollar bill on the table.

Kit pinned her ears and scowled indignantly. "My ring is worth more than a dollar."

Uncle Segan laughed again. "You are absolutely right, my dear. My apologies." He swapped the one-dollar bill for a ten-dollar bill to start the bet.

My mother and aunt, both still holding wineglasses, settled into two vacant armchairs. "Kit," Madison said in a gentle voice that harbored a touch of firmness, "where did you get that ring?"

"I found it," she said defensively. "I find a lot of pretty treasures."

My mother reluctantly let it go, and I kept quiet. Kit did indeed have a talent for finding "pretty treasures," especially when we'd first arrived in Phantom Heights and she had a whole abandoned town to explore. The problem was, I couldn't guarantee all of her treasures fell under the "finders, keepers" rule. Some of them might have been collected directly from their owners without their knowledge.

Terra leaned over and muttered, "Dad? Can I borrow ten dollars?"

His smile never faltering, he drew another ten to cover Terra's initial bet. He counted out extra bills and handed them to her. "There's a hundred. Bet wisely, because that's all I'm lending you. All right, everybody satisfied with their first bet?"

Kit's ears pricked forward again as she focused on the game. Uncle Segan laid three cards faceup in the middle of the table. The players studied their hands again. Terra set ten dollars on the table. Kit once again set her cards down, reached for her belt, and this time produced an ornate dagger with a jewel in the hilt.

"Madison," my grandmother scolded. "You let her carry a knife around?"

"I . . ." My mother shrugged helplessly. "I didn't know she had that. Jay?"

His shrug was more nonchalant. "She collects things. Probably took that from Traders. I haven't seen it before."

The judgmental tension was cut short by Uncle Segan's deep laugh. "Looks like we've got a serious contender! All right, little lady." He set a twenty-dollar bill into the pool, which was likely not a fair match compared to the dagger, but Kit didn't object this time.

"Segan," Madison reprimanded.

"Hey, she raised the stakes," he said innocently. "I'm just playing the game."

Terra studied her cards again, then matched her dad's bet. Uncle Segan set another card faceup next to the other three.

My cousin's faint scowl told me that she wasn't pleased with her cards. "Check."

Kit responded by adding a sunflower locket to the pot. Uncle Segan placed another ten-dollar bill on the table. "I see your bet, and I raise it," he said, laying down a second bill.

Terra shook her head and set her cards on the table. "I fold."

Kit gave my uncle a sly smile and dropped a bejeweled dragonfly brooch into the collection of money and treasures. He drew another card and laid it faceup on the table, and then they each added another bet to the hoard. "All right, Miss Kit, let's see what you've got."

He and Kit both spread their cards out on the table and studied the results. Uncle Segan's confident grin faltered, then vanished.

"Did Kit win?" I asked, hopelessly confused as I stared at the cards.

She shot me a sweet smile, leaned over the table, and dragged the pile of bets over to her side, then expertly sorted her money into a neat stack next to the pile of treasure.

My grandfather laughed heartily. "Serves you right for being cocky, Segan! Somehow, I don't think Kit is in the mood to extend the same courtesy and let you keep your money."

Uncle Segan leaned back, his fist pressed to his lips as he appraised my lab-sister. "A bet's a bet," he replied. "And I lost, fair and square."

Smiling good-naturedly, Terra asked, "Another round?"

He grinned at Kit. "Up for it?"

She nodded enthusiastically.

I welcomed the card game and silently thanked Kit for taking the attention off me, at least for a little while. She didn't win every round, but by the end, she'd managed to win back all of the treasures and still hoard an impressive sum of money.

My grandmother kindly asked, "What are you going to buy with so much money?"

"Nothing," Kit replied as she folded her wad of cash and slipped it into one of the leather pouches on her belt. "I'll keep it safe in my collection."

For some reason, her answer made my grandmother chuckle. "Well, she's fiscally responsible, I'll give her that," she teased as she glanced at Madison.

Although Uncle Segan pretended to be in a good mood, I suspected he was secretly bitter about losing most of his cash to a little girl in a card game. Aunt Mara said, "Kit, where did you learn how to play poker so well?"

"Oh, Rory taught me!" Kit chimed brightly. "I brought Rory money and shiny things I found, and he gave me food."

"Oh," Aunt Mara said, her smile wavering. "And, um . . . is Rory a friend?"

Kit's ears fell slightly, and her forehead creased with thoughtful wrinkles as she considered the question. She shook her head. "Not any-more. I have this family now," she said, beaming and leaping unexpect-edly into my arms. I caught her in surprise and stroked her hair as she lovingly gripped my cloak and nuzzled her head against my chest.

With the card game finished, the rest of the evening passed with my blood-relatives laughing at jokes I didn't understand, commenting on celebrities I didn't know, and reliving stories that were apparently told every time they visited but I didn't remember.

With each passing minute, I felt more isolated and ruined. Every-one seemed to expect the same old "warm" Cato who laughed with them and chimed in with his own versions of the tales. But even I real-ized that I was nothing more than a shadow of my former self, and no matter how hard any of them tried to bring me back, they just couldn't mend what was broken beyond repair.

". . . right, Cato?" My aunt laughed.

I hadn't been listening, so I just nodded and said, "Uh-huh."

Madison was watching me, frowning, and she almost looked re-lieved when Uncle Segan glanced at his watch and announced, "Whoa, look at the time! Mara, Terabyte, we gotta get going."

"*Terra*, Dad," my cousin corrected with an exasperated sigh.

He ignored her protest and rose, stretching his arms high above his head with a strained groan. "Madison, thank you for dinner. And Cato . . . well, we're happy you're back." He turned to my lab-family and added, "It was nice to meet all of you, too. Kit, I hope you'll be up for a rematch next time!"

Kit smiled, showing off her fangs. She nodded in eager acceptance of Uncle Segan's challenge.

Terra stood up, as did Mara, Madison, and Vivian. Was it proper etiquette to stand up when someone was leaving? I rose too, just in case. As Aunt Mara hugged my grandparents goodbye, Terra said, "It was seriously so great to meet all of you. I can't wait to see you again!" She turned and hugged my mother. "I'll miss you, Aunt Madison!"

"We'll miss you, too. See you in a few months."

When the round of hugs had finished, the three departing guests turned to me, and I realized that Before, I would have been in the foyer hugging them, too. My aunt held out her arms in an open invitation and said, "Goodbye, Cato."

I folded my arms to make it clear that I wasn't going to embrace her. "Bye."

She slowly let her arms fall. "We love you very much. I'm sorry if we overwhelmed you tonight. Seeing you again is . . . truly a miracle," she said, her voice cracking with emotion. "And it was lovely to meet the rest of you," she added.

I inclined my head but didn't answer. Madison set her hand on her sister's shoulder and said, "Safe travels back, and we'll see you for Thanksgiving."

Aunt Mara nodded, although her gaze was on me again. She trailed after Terra and Uncle Segan.

Jay leaned toward me and whispered, "What's a thanks giving?"

I shrugged. He frowned, puzzled, and straightened again when I couldn't provide an answer.

The front door closed. I settled into the corner of the sofa and wrapped my arms around my stomach. I wished I could curl into a little ball and disappear into the cushions.

Madison took a ridiculously deep breath and set her hands on her hips as she expelled it. "Well, I should probably get started on cleaning up the kitchen," she said.

My grandmother rose. "I'll help you." Her husband didn't move, which earned him a glare. "Come on. You'll help, too."

He was watching me, but I stared at my feet to avoid his gaze. "Ah-herm, yes, of course, dear." I lifted my gaze to watch the three humans retreat to the kitchen.

Jay waited until they were gone before he announced, "Let's go."

Vivian immediately tensed. "You have the night off, remember?"

"From patrol," he said, fixing her with his steely, determined gaze. "We can still train."

"But it's raining."

"So?"

She backed off, but when I stood, she ordered, "Stay." I hesitated, glancing between her and Jay. Gentler, Vivian requested, "At least until Gram and Pop-Pop leave. Okay?"

I lowered myself back onto the edge of the cushion and mumbled, "I'll catch up with you later."

Ash gave me a pitying look over her shoulder as they left me alone with my blood-sister. In the foyer, Finn and Reese turned right to go upstairs while Jay, Ash, and RC turned left toward the front doors. Kit lingered uncertainly in the middle.

Jay opened the door but glanced back at her. "You don't have to come out in the rain with us. Why don't you go with Finn and Reese and keep them company?" She gratefully padded after the twins as the other three stepped out onto the porch. Jay shot me a sympathetic glance as he closed the door.

I scowled and slumped against the back of the sofa.

Madison seized the wine bottle and sloshed dark-red liquid into a glass. Her parents lingered in the kitchen, watching as she gulped down the wine in an attempt to relieve the pent-up stress. As she started to pour a second glass, her father said, "Are you sure that's really Cato?"

"Of course I'm sure," Madison snapped, setting the bottle down. "Why?"

"Because whoever that boy was, he sure didn't act like my grandson."

"What did you expect?" Madison whispered miserably. She drained the glass a second time. "He was tortured for two years."

"If that's even him." He folded his arms. "Think about it—you saw

Cato's dead body. What if *this* Cato is actually some kind of replica?"

"Dad, please."

"No one knows what goes on in that laboratory, Madison. The AGC keeps a lot of secrets. You don't think they could make a clone? Or some kind of shape-shifting monster posing as Cato?"

"That's ridiculous." Madison reached for the bottle again, but her mom grabbed it and pulled it away.

"We're worried about you, sweetheart."

"That's right," Gordon said. "You're living with a *werewolf* and eight demons."

"Eight counts Cato," Madison seethed with a hostile glare.

"Well, I'm still not convinced that's really him. And sure, they look like kids, and they seem innocent enough, but we heard what the Agents said about them on the news."

"The Agents," Madison replied wearily, "lied to me about Cato's death. You know better than to believe the PSA they had running on the news networks right after the accident. They wanted people to be afraid and report the 'dangerous fugitives' back to the AGC without knowing the facts. Do those kids out there really seem like demons to you?"

"Looks can be deceiving," her dad warned. "Especially when it comes to ghosts."

"Right," Madison scoffed. "One look at Kit and you can tell she's a killer waiting to slit your throat. And did you see the way Finn and Reese were watching everybody, ready to strike as soon as you turned your back?" She tried to reclaim the wine bottle, but her mom held it out of her reach.

"What's wrong?" Rosalie asked.

Madison rubbed her hands down her face. "Tonight didn't go as planned. Actually, it's probably for the best that Axel didn't join us. 'Unruly' is a polite description . . . I don't think I could have handled him on top of everything else."

"So?" Gordon retorted. "You can't be afraid to be strict if you have to."

"It's not that simple, Dad," Madison shot back.

Rosalie sympathized, "I thought tonight went pretty well, all things considered."

"Cato didn't recognize you. I know he's been a bit out of sorts, but he still should have known who you were."

Her parents exchanged wounded looks. Madison seized the bottle of wine from her mom's hand and poured a third glass. "He'll come around," her dad assured half-heartedly as she drank.

"I'm not so sure," Madison admitted as she stared at the wine in her glass. "I don't know what the Agents did to him. To any of them, actually."

Her mom took her hand and squeezed it. "Just be patient. That's all you can do."

A tear broke free and trickled down Madison's cheek. She watched it land in her wineglass, briefly disrupting the dark surface. "He doesn't call me Mom anymore."

"What do you mean?"

"I mean exactly what I said. I failed him so completely that he doesn't see me as his mom anymore."

"Well, that's just ridiculous," her dad replied. "Of course you're his mom. He knows that."

"Biologically, yes." Another tear was about to escape. "But not on the level that counts. He needed me, and I wasn't there. He waited for me, and I never came. And now, he's—" she waved her hand in the direction of the parlor "—whoever that boy is. He's a completely different person I barely recognize. He looks at me like he's afraid I'm going to draw a gun and shoot him on the spot."

She set the glass down on the counter and tipped her head back, letting the second tear roll down her face as she shook her head. "I completely failed as a mom."

"Oh, honey," Rosalie murmured, wrapping her arms around Madison and pulling her into an embrace. Madison buried her face into her mom's shoulder and cried. "You haven't failed, and Cato isn't a lost cause. You both have a second chance now."

Her dad shifted uncomfortably. "Madison . . . would you consider coming back to Michigan with us?"

She pulled free from the embrace. "What? I can't do that. I'm needed here in Phantom Heights."

"Yes, I know, but . . . is this the best place for Cato?"

"What would we do in Michigan, Dad? People there probably haven't even seen a kálos before. You think Cato and the others would be safe? Nobody would notice their glowing eyes? Nobody would report them to the AGC?"

"Well, just . . . hear me out. The others could go back into the Ghost Realm. That's where their kind belongs, anyway—surely they must have friends, relatives, acquaintances, someone who could take them in. That responsibility shouldn't have to fall on your shoulders. And Cato was able to hide his abilities and pretend to be a human before; he could do it again. I just think some peace and quiet and a sense of normalcy would be good for him."

Madison rolled her eyes and turned away.

"It was just a thought," her mom said quietly.

"And how exactly would this plan work?" Madison snapped. "Are you going to put the three of us into some kind of witness protection program and give us new identities? Is that your idea of a quiet, normal life for Cato? Separating him from the people he bonded with at the AGC, giving him a new name, moving him to a new home away from anything familiar, expecting him to suppress his powers and pretend to be something he isn't while living on a hope and a prayer that the Agents don't track us down?"

Her parents were solemn and silent until her dad muttered, "Actually, I was thinking more along the lines of a cabin secluded in the woods."

"Oh, I see. Completely cut off from society and any human interaction outside of the family."

"And far away from the chaos and violence here," he snapped. "Stop twisting this to make it sound like I'm ashamed of Cato and want to hide him away somewhere or change who he is. I didn't think through all the details—it was just a suggestion to let Cato have a little peace and quiet so he can physically, mentally, and emotionally recover after his traumatic experience. That's all. I don't think Phantom Heights is a healthy environment. Not for him, or you, or Vivian."

Madison leaned against the counter and rested her forehead in her hand as she rubbed her temples with her thumb and middle finger. "I think Phantom Heights is our only option right now. I know it's not the most peaceful place, but the mayhem is a blessing in disguise. Cato doesn't have to hide here, Dad. He can walk down the street without being afraid that someone is going to recognize him and report him to the AGC. This town has more or less accepted him and the others, and they're allowed to use their powers and be themselves. It's not perfect, but it's better than relocating and telling them they can't go outside because someone might see them."

"And that's important, of course," her mom said quickly, stepping in to mediate. "We know that. We trust your judgment and have faith that you'll make the best decisions you can for Cato."

Her dad let out a quiet *harrumph*, which was about as close to a submission as Madison could hope for.

Rosalie smiled sadly. "I wish we could stay longer, but we do have a long drive ahead of us. Tell Cato we said goodbye, okay? We don't want to stress him out any more than we already have."

"No. I think you need to tell him goodbye. That's not fair to duck out the back door without letting him know that you're leaving."

Her mom bowed her head. "You're right."

Madison closed her eyes as her dad leaned forward and kissed her forehead. "Love you."

"Love you too, Dad," she said with a sigh.

Her mom pulled her into a tight hug. "No more wine tonight," she whispered.

"Sure, Mom."

"I mean it."

Madison rolled her eyes and nodded. "Have a safe trip home."

"We will," her mother answered, pulling away. "Give Cato lots of love from us."

Madison nodded again. "I will." Her dad pushed open the door to the dining room and held it open for his wife. Madison didn't follow immediately; she let the door swing shut, sealing her in quiet, peaceful solitude.

With a heavy sigh, she picked up her glass and swirled the liquid into a whirlpool. She held it over the sink, ready to pour the wine down the drain, but then she changed her mind and drained it in one gulp.

Wine, she knew, wouldn't change what had happened tonight. It wouldn't fix any of her problems. But it did help numb her disappointment.

— Chapter Eighteen —

Amnesia

I draped my arm over my face as Vivian circled the room, gathering glasses and plates that had been left behind.

"I thought tonight went pretty well," she said brightly. "Kit definitely won over Uncle Segan. Your lab-family is officially part of our family now."

"Yeah," I muttered despondently.

She paused and perched on the arm of the sofa, setting her pile down on the floor at her feet. "You okay?"

"I'm frustrated," I admitted.

"No one blames you."

"I know," I snapped, but my tone was sharper than I'd intended. "Sorry."

"It's okay. Don't be frustrated. It isn't your fault."

"Hey, Cato. Vivian." My blood-sister turned, and I moved my arm to find my grandparents standing in the foyer. "We're heading out now. Just wanted to say goodbye."

Vivian immediately hopped up and walked over to embrace them. "Thanks for coming to see us," she said. "I've really missed you."

"Oh, I know, darling," our grandmother said, sweeping Vivian's hair behind her ear and planting a kiss on her forehead. "Believe me, we worried about you and prayed for you every day."

"Cato," my grandfather began. He set his free hand on top of the one holding the cane and cleared his throat, apparently at a loss for words. "I, uh . . . I want you to be good for your mother. She looks like she's under a lot of stress."

"Okay."

"And take care of yourself, too. I know you're in a major adjustment period still, but know that we love you and support you. If you ever want us to come back, or if you want to visit us for a change in scenery and a break from all this chaos, you just let us know, and we'll make it happen."

"We love you so much, sweetheart," my grandmother added, smiling warmly at me.

I nodded and tried to force a return smile, but I barely managed to move my lips. Vivian pulled a coat out of the closet and held it up so our grandmother could slip her arms through the sleeves. "Take care of your mom and little brother."

"I will. Love you."

Our grandfather opened the door to the sound of steady rain. With one last look back at me, they stepped outside into the wet night.

Vivian stayed at the door to watch them leave, but I covered my face with my arm again and closed my eyes. The stress of the last few hours had left me completely drained, and a faint but persistent headache was starting to pound behind my eyeballs.

Vivian closed the door and plopped into the nearest armchair. "Whew, I'm beat. Looks like you are, too."

"Mmm," I grunted without opening my eyes.

"I'm so glad we got to see everybody, though. I love catching up with Terra, but sometimes she can be a bit . . . much, you know? Everything is just *so* dramatic. I can tolerate her in small doses. I guess I'm going to have to respectfully relinquish the title of 'favorite cousin' to you."

"Hey," a new voice interrupted. Viv and I both turned toward Madison leaning against the doorframe. She tried to smile at us but failed miserably. "We need to talk."

My initial assumption was that I was in trouble for the confrontation in the kitchen. I dropped my arm, already defensive and prepared to justify what I'd said to my aunt, but something about the drawn look on our mother's face told me this was about something else.

Uh-oh. I sat up, my stomach churning with unease. "What's up?" I asked, trying to play casual, but my success was equivalent to Madison's smile.

She took a few steps into the room but didn't come too close. Was she afraid of me? The way she maintained her distance made me suspect so.

"Cato," she began, then hesitated. Something was wrong with her voice—it was too deep, too solemn. "Did you recognize any of the family tonight?"

My lungs seemed to shrivel in my chest. Bloody Scout, why was the air so thick all of a sudden? I couldn't breathe. I rubbed my right arm, momentarily startled to touch skin instead of metal around my biceps. "I, uh . . . Why are you asking me that?"

"I need you to answer the question."

"Is this because I didn't want to hug them? Because that's not—"

"Cato, stop. I need a yes or no."

I swallowed, but my gaze danced away from her when I said, "Of course I did."

"Please don't lie to me."

"I-I did, I just . . . it's been a while, and at first I . . . they . . . I'm sorry."

Gently, Madison inquired, "Sorry for what?"

I ground my knuckles against my forehead, feeling the ports in my skull. "I don't know. I'm sorry."

"You're sorry for being sorry?"

"Yes. No. I mean, I'm glad I got to see Gram and Pop-Pop and Terra and Uncle Segan and Aunt Kara."

"Aunt Mara," Madison corrected quietly.

I stared at her, aghast. *Mara.* Kara was the first human we'd encountered Outside—the little girl in an orange dress who had shared a bucket of water with us on the dirt floor of a barn. *Damn it.*

"I knew that. I swear I knew that. I don't know why the wrong name came out."

Madison hung her head as if I'd just confirmed a hypothesis. "I should have known," she said softly, her voice cracking with pain. "Jay didn't know how old he was, or even his real name, so I should have known that you . . ."

She trailed off, but Vivian finally registered her train of thought. "Oh my gosh. They erased your memory."

"That's not true!" I cried, my voice rising in panic.

"Cato." Vivian stepped in front of me. She looked me in the eye and asked, "How old am I?"

"What's with the stupid questions?"

"Stupid or not, I want you to answer it. How old am I?"

I shook my head and stared at her, trying to will the answer into my mind. "S-seventeen."

Her face fell as she realized that I had indeed lost my memory. "No. *You're* seventeen. I'm three years older than you."

"Seventeen," I echoed in shock. "I'm seventeen? How old was I when I left?"

"Fifteen."

I swallowed. "So . . . it's only been two years? That's all?"

Madison shielded her face with one hand. I felt as if they'd just discovered that I had a terminal illness, and I backed away from them. "Don't look at me like that," I pleaded. "I'm okay. There's nothing wrong with me. I just . . . forgot some things, that's all."

My mother seemed to have lost the power of speech. Vivian approached me, holding her hands out to close the gap, but she was giving me a look of pity that I detested. "It's all right, Cato," she soothed. "It's not your fault. The Agents had to break you down somehow, and they did it by erasing your memories."

"No," I whispered, shaking my head as I continued to back away. I pressed the heels of my palms against my forehead, remembering the breathtaking pain of the NMS, the white lights of Quarantine, my metal cage, the Arena, the electroshock tests, the unempathetic eyes watching from behind surgical masks . . .

The memories of my time at that place were so much clearer than the broken, scattered remnants of those from my life Before. I remembered every single detail of every single experiment, and those sickening memories had replaced my childhood ones. I started trembling. "You don't . . . understand. *They* didn't erase my memories to break me down. That's not what happened."

"Okay—"

"*They* didn't have to!" When I squeezed my eyes shut, the tears broke free. Vivian was so wrong that she didn't even realize how wrong she was. "*They* made me do terrible things that I didn't want to do, but my memories were just collateral damage."

"I understand that, but—"

"*Don't* do that! Don't tell me you understand!"

"Cato, I'm sorry."

I pressed my hands over my ears to block out her voice. Prickling heat flared inside me. To my horror, I felt a frustrated scream clutch my lungs. My eyes flew open in panic at the familiar power infecting me again. If I let it out, I might not be able to reel it back.

Vivian hesitated, as if suddenly afraid to approach me. "Cay? Your eyes are glowing green. Are you angry with me?"

I had to suffocate the scream before it could escape. I had to run. My mother, frozen and mute in sorrow, simply watched me leave, but Vivian called me back.

Ignoring her cries, I took off at a mad sprint, desperate to get away. I wrenched open the front door and dashed into the rain, vaguely aware that Vivian was following me. I heard her continue to shout my name, and her footsteps splashed through puddles in my wake.

The cold, fat raindrops on my face countered the dangerous heat that had blossomed in my core, washing it back into the vault. Vivian lagged farther and farther behind as I ran as fast as my body could carry me. I wove through alleys, ducked around corners, and leapt over low hedges until I'd lost my pursuer, and even then, I kept running.

The early night deepened around me, bringing with it a cool breeze. This was the best time—when the birds were quiet in their roosts and the world was settling down to sleep, when the empty streets were aglow under streetlights reflected in the rippling puddles. I was free to run as fast and far as I could without crowds or curious eyes.

When I circled back to the park behind Saros Manor, I slowed to a stop, gasping for breath. I was surrounded by trees and grass and fresh air now, not the constricting buildings that leered down on me. The steady rain had become a faint drizzle. Still panting, I locked my fingers together and put my hands on top of my head as I walked.

My memorial, and also apparently my grave, loomed in the clearing before me. I approached and stood in front of Phantom, gazing at myself in a past life.

I remembered standing here once before, years ago . . .

The statue was gone, and the shadows were long in the late autumn afternoon. I was wearing dark clothes with a neoprene mask over my nose and mouth. I tore it off to inhale the fresh, crisp air.

Footsteps rustled the grass as someone approached from behind. Without turning to face my visitor, I said, "I'm done. I can't keep doing this."

Trey said, "You can't quit now. You're a real-life superhero!"

"This isn't a movie, Trey!" I snapped. "I'm failing my classes, Mom is literally hunting me, and if anyone finds out what I am, I'll either become my mom's own personal lab rat, or I'll be carted off to some secret government facility and never heard from again, assuming Mom doesn't shoot me dead the next time Phantom crosses her path."

"But look at all the people you saved already. Everyone's talking about you!"

"That doesn't make this any easier. Mom saw the new bruises today and thought I've been getting into fights at school. She said she's going to call Principal Solwitz."

Trey crossed his arms. "You just need more practice, that's all. You and me, we'll train together. Think about it—someday, you'll be a great hero, and I'll be a great ghost hunter, and we'll be an unstoppable team."

I sighed. Even when life had been complicated back then, it had somehow been simpler Before than it was now.

Chapter Nineteen

The Spy

As the second lunch bell rang across the schoolyard, Vivian smacked her tray down on the table. "Please tell me boys are as stupid as girls."

Trey lifted an eyebrow and smirked. "Hmm. Well, as much as I would love to score a point for the guys in the gender debate, A: I sense a trap in agreeing with your initial premise that girls are stupid, and B: as the son of a talented website developer and the apprentice of a bad-ass ghost hunter, both of whom are incredibly strong and intelligent women, I have nothing but respect for the fairer sex."

"All right, smart ass, then I'll ask you this—do guys turn into giddy, giggling fanboys and completely lose their minds?"

"What do you mean?" Trey asked with a curious but puzzled frown.

"I mean, the girls at this school have gone insane. Do you know how many times I've been stopped in the hall by mobs of girls who want to ask me stupid questions about Cato? Apparently, there are different factions of fangirls arguing about which Alpha ghost is the cutest."

"Ah," Trey said, the teasing smile returning. "So, which team are you on?"

"That's not funny."

"Not Cato, obviously, because that would be weird, although I bet he's got a hell of a following since he's half-human and, you know, formerly Phantom. Are you on Team Jay? Or do you have a thing for RC being the serious, quiet type? Oh wait, don't tell me you like bad boys and—"

"You're *not* funny. Seriously, do guys pull this crap too, or is it just girls going crazy?"

"I hate to disappoint you, but yep. Guys can be just as bad. Thing is, though, Ash is running uncontested in the competition. I promise you, if Kit were closer to our age, guys would be fighting over which girl was prettier."

Vivian rolled her eyes. "Good to know idiocy isn't gender specific, I guess. Except girls are shriller. I don't know if my ears can take the shrieking."

"Haven't heard the neighborhood dogs howling yet."

"Give it time."

Trey chuckled, but the smile faded quickly. He folded his arms on the table and leaned his chin on his arm.

"Not eating today?"

He shrugged. "I'm on a diet."

"What? That's ridiculous. No you're not."

Trey stared across the schoolyard for a moment, then reluctantly admitted, "I lost my lunch money."

"Again?"

"No," he said, frowning and sitting up straight. "I *swear* I remember grabbing it off my dresser this morning and putting it in my pocket. I'm telling you, Viv, this school is haunted or something."

She gave him a skeptical look. "Because you lost your lunch money? Maybe you have a hole in your pocket."

"I don't. Haven't you noticed that things seem to go missing a lot more than they used to?"

"No. I haven't lost anything."

"But you must have noticed. It seems like every day, at least one person is wandering around looking for a lost wallet. Amber has been upset because she still can't find her class ring and her parents won't buy her a new one. Chase lost a watch yesterday. Shannon's missing a charm bracelet. And I'm definitely not the only one whose lunch money keeps vanishing."

Vivian frowned. "You know, when you list it out like that . . . yeah. It does seem like people have been losing things left and right."

"I'm telling you—the school's haunted."

She smirked and retorted, "Well, then that seems like the perfect sleuthing job for a ghost hunter's apprentice, don't you think?"

"I hunt kálos, not moorlins."

"What would a moorlin want with your lunch money?" she teased as she slid her tray into the middle of the table. "Share with me. I'm not really hungry anyway, so that way my lunch won't go to waste."

"Are you sure?"

"Yeah. I haven't had much appetite lately."

"Thanks, Viv." He dunked a few French fries into a pool of ketchup and shoved them into his mouth. "So, how're things going?"

"Fine."

"Just . . . fine?" She stared at the food on her tray, but nothing looked appetizing. Trey said, "I thought that since, you know, Cato was back and everything, things would be better than fine. Great, maybe."

"You would think," she muttered.

"Come on, Viv. What's up?"

She heaved a big sigh. "The family came to visit a few days ago. It seemed like a good idea—they really wanted to see him, and we thought Cato would be happy to see them, too. But he acted like he didn't know who they were. When Mom confronted him about it, he got defensive and ran away. And now, it seems like he's always busy out on patrol or training, so we barely see him. He's pretty obsessive about it. I think he's been avoiding us ever since we found out that he lost most of his memory."

"How much is gone?"

She shook her head. "No idea. Enough that he didn't recognize his own grandparents, aunt, uncle, and cousin."

"You don't think he's forgotten me . . . do you?"

"I don't know," she admitted. "I knew he wasn't acting right, but it was just little things, you know? He was confused when I asked him if he wanted pop to drink, and he said the wrong thing when he tried to order a BLT, but . . . that all seemed so minor. I didn't realize how extensive the damage was." She blinked a few times to clear her eyes.

"But the family came to visit every Thanksgiving and Christmas, so we saw them only twice a year. He saw you just about every day. I think your chances are pretty good."

Trey munched thoughtfully on a fry. "What does your mom think about him spending so much time scouting?"

"She isn't happy about it. She doesn't want him or the others to fight anymore."

"But why? Cato fought ghosts before when he was Phantom. She knows that."

"Yeah, but back then she didn't. She never would have let him fight if she'd known. You know how overprotective she can be."

Trey studied her carefully. "What's really on your mind?"

"I don't know. Cato is completely different. He's not my little brother anymore. He's . . . I don't know. He's scared of us, Trey, and we're his family. All he does is fight ghosts and train. He doesn't talk to me, and I hear Mom cry at night when she thinks I'm asleep because she's frustrated that he doesn't talk to her, either." Vivian closed her eyes. "Cato's back, but at the same time, he isn't. Part of him never left that lab."

"What did you expect? After everything the Agents did to him, there's no way he could be the same Cato we knew from before. That was practically another lifetime. But I bet our Cato is still in there somewhere. We just have to find him."

Vivian nodded slowly. She swiped at a tear. "I know. I . . . I know. They tortured him. They tortured my little brother, and . . . I want to help, but . . . I don't know how." She scowled. "Why haven't you talked to him yet?"

"Huh? Oh . . . I, ah, well . . ." Trey sputtered nervously, lowering his gaze. "I don't know. I guess I figured I'd give Cato some space and let him spend time with his family first."

"You're his best friend."

"I used to be." Trey scratched the back of his head, tousling his blond hair. "What if we have nothing in common anymore? I mean, you're his sister, but me . . ."

Vivian set her hand on top of Trey's. "You guys were inseparable. I think you should spend some time with him. Maybe you can help trigger some of his memories, bring the old Cato back to the surface."

Trey stared at their hands. "He won't even talk to you. Why would he talk to me?"

Vivian exhaled, but before she could answer, a girl seated herself beside her. "Hello," Shannon chimed.

Clearly upset, Trey turned his head. Vivian glared at Shannon, furious that she'd so rudely interrupted their conversation. "Speaking of obnoxious fangirls," Vivian muttered.

Shannon smiled coyly. "Oh, that's not fair. You can't put me in the same category as the rest of the wannabes who are drooling over Cato but don't have a shot with him. So, where is he? I've been dying to talk to him."

"Don't know," Vivian snapped.

Shannon cocked an eyebrow. "You don't know where he is? But you're his sister."

"Yeah, his sister, not his babysitter," Vivian shot back irritably. "Why do you want to know where he is, anyway?"

Shannon shrugged. "I just want to talk to him, that's all."

"Why? You never gave a damn about Cato until after you found out he was Phantom."

Shannon narrowed her eyes and set her elbow on the table, resting her chin in her hand. "It's no secret that you don't like me. But Cato always did."

"Hate to break it to you, but you missed your chance."

Shannon smiled at the challenge. "We'll see, won't we?" she retorted, standing up.

Vivian rose from the bench. "Leave my brother alone."

Shannon regarded her with a cold, smug glare. "You weren't the only one in Cato's life, you know."

"You rejected him. Multiple times."

"That was before I knew who he really was."

"That's bullshit, and you know it! You never even noticed Cato.

Phantom is the one you fell for. You're no different than any of the other girls making fools of themselves by forming fan clubs and acting like idiots."

Shannon's eyes narrowed. "Okay, I'll admit, I had a stupid crush on Phantom. But it's not the same—not even close. Why would Cato pay any attention to the fan club fawning over him when he can finally have the one girl he's wanted to date since the seventh grade? He likes *me*."

"I'm warning you, Shannon, Cato doesn't need you messing with his life right now. He's got more than enough going on without you complicating everything with your stupid games. Leave. Him. Alone."

"I think that's Cato's decision to make, not yours." She tossed her long hair over her shoulder, turned on her heel, and strode across the schoolyard without a look back.

"I never did understand what he saw in her," Vivian muttered coldly.

"Other than she's pretty enough to make Aphrodite jealous?" Trey asked.

"And shallower than my shower," Vivian spat. "She always tempted Cato and then shot him down. And like an idiot, he kept falling for it."

"Men have done stupider things for love," Trey said, plucking a grape from the tray and popping it into his mouth.

"What would you know about that?" she teased as she sat down. Serious again, she leaned close and whispered, "You don't think Cato could possibly still have feelings for her, do you?"

Trey shrugged. "Dunno. Doesn't seem like he's as easy to read as he used to be."

"No, he isn't." Vivian leaned back. "I really do want you two to spend some time together."

"I will, Viv." At her dubious look, he added, "I promise. Just . . . not quite yet. I want to give him a little more time to readjust. Besides, I need to think about what I'm going to say to him."

"Just don't wait too long. He needs you."

Trey nodded.

Vivian frowned and turned at the sound of loud laughter. Shannon and her friend Amber were surrounded by a small group of students. The girls were giggling at something one of the boys had said. Vivian muttered, "Cay always did pick out the prettiest girl to fall for."

"And now he's got Ash," Trey said. "Looks like Shannon finally met her match."

Vivian's eyes widened. "Ash? You think they're dating?"

"They're almost always together, aren't they?"

"Oh, Cato," she groaned. "Why do you always fall for those kinds of girls?"

"That's not fair. You don't really know Ash."

"I don't need to. You've seen the way she dresses—she knows she's beautiful and isn't shy about flaunting her body in public."

"You know, a lot of people think . . . you're pretty, too." Vivian blushed, and so did Trey. "B-but, um, maybe Ash is different."

"In which case, she wouldn't be Cato's type," Vivian grumbled, folding her arms.

"You don't like Cato's new family, do you?"

"His *family*." She glowered at Casper napping on the sunny dumpster lid. "He's known them for what, two years? Cato isn't really their brother."

"Wow. Jealousy is an ugly color on you."

Vivian redirected her glare onto Trey. "I'm not jealous."

"Come on, Viv, would you rather Cato have sat all alone in a cage with no one to talk to? They helped him through a really tough time and . . . What's that?"

Vivian twisted around and craned her neck back to look up at a golden light arching through the sky over the school. It cut across the blue canvas like a falling star that flickered and went out before touching the roof. Casper leapt onto the dumpster and began pacing and mewling frantically.

Vivian stared at him. Why was she getting this sinking feeling of déjà vu? Hadn't Casper just been on top of the dumpster a minute ago?

The kitten's cries rose in pitch and volume. Students quieted and turned, their attention drawn to the wailing cat. Chase called, "Geez, what's gotten into that flea-bitten pest?"

"Where's your brother?" a voice whispered in Vivian's ear.

She turned slowly, taking a breath to tell Shannon to get lost, but then gasped and rose to step away from the stranger. The woman with glowing green eyes was completely hairless—not just bald, but without eyebrows, too—and she lashed out, backhanding Vivian across the face.

Vivian staggered back, stumbling into a table. The ghost was on top of her already, her hands twisted into the fabric of Vivian's jacket, pressing her spine into the edge. Their noses were almost touching. "Where is the Demikan?"

Vivian, too stunned to speak, stared into the woman's gleaming eyes. Trey appeared over the assailant's shoulder. "Hey! Let her go!" he cried, swinging. The butt of his ectogun struck the ghost's skull with a sickening *crack!*

She whirled, throwing Vivian to the side. Viv's shoulder struck the bench. She rolled off, then landed with a quiet *oomph* in the grass.

As if a spell had been broken, students scattered to take cover. Trey braced himself, both hands on the gun, finger curled over the trigger, barrel aimed at the ghost. The apprentice grinned. "About time I got some action," he said. "The Alpha ghosts steal all the good fights."

"You're not even worth my time. I want the Demikan."

"Well, you got me instead. And I—"

His eyes widened just before he had the sense to duck the ecto-plasm orb pitched at his head. "Maggot," the woman snarled. "You're annoying me."

Casper threw his head back and let out a pitiful wail. The ghost glanced at him, giving Trey a brief window to fire. Glowing green ec-toplasm illuminated the schoolyard.

Vivian dove under the table as a blast exploded on the tabletop. Another body crawled beside her. She turned, too high on adrenaline to experience her usual distaste for such proximity to Shannon. The girls peered between the table legs. Vivian wanted to help Trey, but what could she do without getting in his way? Her ectogun was in her back-pack, which was under a table right in the battle zone. Where were Cato and the other Alpha ghosts?

The hairless ghost, now thoroughly irritated with the apprentice, raised her hand. Vivian held her breath. This was it—the critical turning point of any fight with a ghost—the moment it revealed its Divinity. Trey knew it, too. He tried to fire one more shot, but as his finger pulled the trigger, it curled around air instead.

His gun was now in the hand of the woman. She leveled it at him. "You humans and your toys." Between Casper's yowls, Vivian heard the charging whine followed by the *shoom* of ectoplasm erupting from the barrel. Trey, shot with his own ectogun, was thrown backward from the impact.

"What just happened?" Shannon whispered.

"She must be an Apportator," Vivian said. "Instead of teleporting herself from place to place like Jay does, she can teleport objects and other people."

Another shot came from off to the side; the ghost raised an ecto-plasm shield just in time to block it. One of the teachers stood braced in the doorway to the school, both hands wrapped around an ectogun. The ghost held out her other hand, and the gun was teleported out of the teacher's grasp and into hers.

"Thanks for the toy!" she called. Giggling, the ghost approached Trey, who had pulled himself up onto his elbows but was still trying to catch his breath after taking a shot to the chest. She gazed down with wicked pleasure at her victim. "Maybe parading your head mounted on a stick will draw the Demikan out of hiding."

Trey glared at her defiantly.

A ball of fur streaked across the grass, and then little Casper crouched protectively in front of him, hackles raised, growling and spit-ting bravely at the ghost.

The Apportator paused and laughed. "Is this your guard kitty?" she taunted. "Adorable." She aimed both ectoguns at Casper, who crouched low as his growling increased in volume.

Before she could fire, the kitten gathered himself and leapt at the woman. Vivian caught her breath in disbelief as black smoke engulfed Casper's growing body. By the time his teeth reached the woman's outstretched arm, he had transformed into a little girl with long black hair and cat ears.

The ghost gasped in surprise and pain as the fangs pierced her skin. "Let go!" she cried, spinning wildly. Kit sank her teeth in deeper and squeezed her eyes shut, digging in and hanging on.

Trey pulled himself up into a sitting position. Vivian stared with wide eyes, not believing what she was seeing. Beside her, Shannon whispered, "Casper is . . . Kit?"

The Apportator flung her arm out, finally wrenching Kit loose and sending the Amínyte flying. Her small body hit the dumpster hard, sending a resounding *clang* ringing throughout the schoolyard. The girl crumpled on her side and didn't move.

The ghost advanced on Kit, blood streaming down her arm. "Damn Amínyte," she snarled.

Vivian started to crawl out from under the table, but Shannon grabbed her shirt to stop her. "What are you doing?" Shannon demanded.

Vivian opened her mouth to announce that she was going to save Kit, but before she could speak, a cloaked figure appeared between Kit and the Apportator. Silver eyes flashed beneath the hood as the ghost lunged forward, punching the woman in the stomach. She gasped and doubled over, giving Jay the opportunity to seize her shoulders and use her own downward momentum to drive her face into his raised knee.

Stunned, she fell to the ground, moaning as blood flowed from her nose. Jay hurried to Kit, who had opened her eyes. He knelt next to her and brushed the hair away from her face. Her brow furrowed as she sucked in a deep sob, tears pooling in her golden eyes. "Hey, now," Jay cooed, scooping the little girl up in his arms. She whimpered and started to cry, burying her face into his chest as he cradled her close.

Vivian watched silently. She had never seen Jay act so compassionately, nor had she witnessed such ferocity a few moments before.

Two strikes. That was it. Two intense, precise strikes executed with strength, fury, and deadly accuracy, incapacitating his opponent in a matter of seconds. Vivian felt goose bumps raise the hairs on her arms. She hadn't realized just how dangerous Jay could be even though he had a passive Divinity.

He murmured to Kit as he rocked her in his arms. "You were very brave. I'm so sorry, Kit-Kat. I should have been here sooner."

"I . . . don't understand," Trey said, stumbling unsteadily to his feet. "Casper was standing in front of me, and then . . . he turned into smoke . . . and then . . . Kit?"

"We've always guarded the school," Jay told him, wiping a tear from the girl's cheek with his thumb. He rose and carried Kit to the Apportator still moaning on the ground. Without another word, he set his boot on the ghost's chest, and then all three of them vanished into thin air.

Vivian stared at the spot where he had been standing, still trying to process what happened. Trey's face twisted into a grimace as he clutched his ribs.

A teacher approached and gripped his elbow. "You need to see the nurse."

"I'm fine," Trey insisted, but she pointed to the door, and Trey hung his head in submission with a quiet, "Yes, Mrs. Dermody." She steered him inside.

Students began crawling out from their hiding places. Teachers patrolled the schoolyard, checking for injuries and sending kids with minor cuts and bruises to wait outside the nurse's office.

"I thought Casper seemed awful smart," Shannon said.

Vivian was still turning the new information around in her head. "All this time," she muttered, more to herself than to Shannon, "there's been an Alpha ghost just a few yards away."

Apparently, Trey had been right—the school was haunted after all.

— Chapter Twenty —

Name

I took my seat at the dinner table.

Everyone was already eating except Axel, who was sitting with his arms folded and his head tilted back to stare up at the ceiling, and my mother, who was finishing setting the table.

"We can thank Wes for grilling the steaks tonight," she said. "And I baked potatoes, onions, and mushrooms to go with them, plus a green bean casserole. I hope you're all hungry."

I noticed that Madison had cut our steaks into small pieces already, as if we were little kids, but I didn't mind. Her extra preparation allowed me to shovel food into my mouth without wasting time trying to saw at the meat. I swallowed a mouthful of steak, potato, mushroom, and onion, then scooped up a forkful of the casserole and took a bite.

My chewing slowed. I savored the taste, which caused faint memories to stir just barely out of reach. "Is something wrong, Cato?" Madison asked in concern as she set salt and pepper shakers on the table.

I chewed a few more times, swallowed, then scooped another bite onto my fork and studied it. "This tastes really familiar."

She smiled. "It should. I made it every Easter, Thanksgiving, and Christmas." She casually walked around the table, dropped a plate down in front of Axel, and then strolled to her seat without a word.

I craned my head to look at Axel's plate, then wrinkled my nose in disgust. My mother was using a knife to cut her steak as if nothing were out of the ordinary. Without lifting her gaze, she said, "Wes thinks you're a carnivore, and I agree. So, if you won't eat the food I prepare for everyone else, will you eat that?"

Axel smirked and nudged the raw meat. The sight of the bloody steak turned my stomach. Although he seemed amused, he apparently wasn't hungry, or thirsty, or whatever it was that he felt. He picked up the meat with his thumb and forefinger; blood dripped from the steak onto the plate.

Axel studied the meat for a moment, and then his gaze flitted to my mother. He dropped the steak back onto the plate with a wet slapping sound. "You left out the good part," he said quietly. He shoved the plate away.

Wes set down his silverware to give Axel his undivided attention. "What's the good part?" he inquired. "The brain? Heart? Bones? Come on, one animal to another."

Axel scoffed. He crossed his arms and rested his head on the back of the chair to stare at the ceiling again.

Madison heaved a sigh and stood up. "Fine. If you won't eat it, we don't have to leave it on the table."

Although Axel didn't move, his crimson eyes shifted to follow her as she marched over and seized the plate again, then carried it into the kitchen.

Wes's gaze hadn't left Axel. He picked up his fork, speared a piece of rare steak, and took a bite. "The moon is getting bigger. Can you feel it?"

Axel shrugged, either genuinely nonchalant or a superb actor. "Guess so."

The door swung open, and Madison returned to her chair in defeat.

Between chews, Wes said, "In a few days it'll be full, and I'll leave Phantom Heights to go hunting. I don't know what you are exactly, but I know you're part animal, and you're a predator like me." Axel narrowed his eyes. "I was wondering if you might like to join me on my hunt. I avoid humans at the full moon because I become a little, shall we say, aggressive. But you can handle me, I'm sure."

"Oh yeah, I can handle you," Axel replied softly, and Wes grinned, assuming that Axel was accepting the invitation. "But you can't handle me."

Wes's eyebrows shot up in curiosity as he swallowed. "The full moon affects you?"

"No. The hunt does. I might accidentally kill you."

Wes scoffed. "I'm a two-thousand-pound wolf."

Axel replied coldly, "Believe me, I turn into something deadlier than an overgrown puppy. Thanks, but no thanks."

Wes looked Axel up and down. "What are you?" he asked quietly. "You don't smell like any animal I've ever encountered."

"Of course I don't. If you'd ever encountered a pureblood, you wouldn't be alive to tell anyone about it. Creatures like that are found in the deepest parts of the Ghost Realm where even the most powerful kálos fear to travel."

"Are you part fay?"

Axel reached up and pulled the hood over his head. "Enjoy your hunt."

Wes growled. "Come on, Axel. I thought you loved to rebel against the Agents. They don't want anyone to know what you are. Why won't you tell me the Agents' dirty little secret?"

His only response was a dry chuckle.

We dined in silence for a few minutes, only the sounds of silverware clinking above the faint ticks of the grandfather clock in the foyer.

"So . . ." Wes said, breaking the silence again. "I heard it was an interesting day at school today." He gave Kit a meaningful look.

"Why, what happened?" Madison asked as she sprinkled pepper on her food.

"Ah, Vivian didn't tell you? Apparently your apprentice took on a kálos by himself during lunch, and he was rescued by a stray kitten that's been hanging around the school." Kit squirmed in her chair. "Rumor has it the cat transformed into a little girl."

She leaned forward and seized her glass of milk in both hands, drinking deeply to avoid answering.

"Jay!" my mother cried, rounding on our leader. "What was Kit doing fighting?"

"She wasn't supposed to be," he said. "Her job is to watch the school and send a warning if there's trouble. I wasn't able to Blink to the school immediately."

"Why didn't you tell me?" Madison demanded. "Are you okay? Is Trey?"

Vivian briefly rolled her eyes. "Yes, Mom, everyone's fine. I was going to tell you."

"What happened?"

She shrugged. "A ghost showed up and wanted me to tell her where Cato was. Trey protected me—"

"Time out. *You* were the target?"

"It's not a big deal."

"Yes, it is," Madison said sternly. "That's exactly why I wanted you to be armed, so you could defend yourself."

"Students aren't supposed to be armed at school," Vivian shot back.

"You and Trey are exceptions."

Vivian slammed her fork down. "I don't *want* to be an exception! I'm not a ghost hunter, and I'm tired of always being labeled as the daughter of one!"

The silence in the wake of Vivian's outcry was tense. Madison's arguments with Axel were uncomfortable but predictable; the sparks now flying between her and Vivian made me want to crawl under the table to escape. I wasn't used to hearing them fight with each other, and this argument seemed like an old one that had been resuscitated.

The rest of my lab-family looked as uncomfortable in the tension as I felt, except Axel, whose smirk told me that he was enjoying sitting back and watching a fight for once instead of instigating it.

Madison's piercing stare was enough to make anyone want to shrivel up and disappear, but Vivian maintained a firm and angry glare of her own. Her voice level and dangerous with supreme authority, Madison said, "Sacrificing your safety just to fit in and not draw attention to yourself is a juvenile and foolish thing to do. You aren't just the daughter of a ghost hunter—you're also Phantom's sister. That puts an even bigger target on your back than before."

I bowed my head. She wasn't wrong. Vivian shook her head in anger and pointedly turned away from our mother to look at Kit across the table. "Hey Kit, you hit that dumpster pretty hard. Did you get hurt?"

Madison exhaled through her nose but opted not to acknowledge the less-than-subtle change in topic. Kit rubbed the side of her head, frowning. She nodded. "I have a headache," she whined.

Madison turned her admonishment back to Jay and reprimanded, "What were you thinking, leaving her alone to defend the school?"

"Kit isn't a helpless little girl," said Jay. "She lived on the streets Before. She knows how to handle herself."

"And was that before or after she was sold on the Black Market?" Wes asked.

Everyone froze. I glanced between Wes and Kit, whose golden eyes welled up with tears. Clearly uncomfortable under Wes's expectant gaze, she shifted miserably in her chair. "After," she whispered, twisting a strand of her long black hair around her finger.

"How did you know she was on the Market?" RC demanded.

One side of Wes's mouth twitched up into a satisfied smirk. "I didn't. But I do now. How'd you end up on the streets?"

"I ran away," she said, her voice barely above a whisper.

Ero said, "You must have been very brave."

Wes speared a potato chunk onto his fork and popped it into his mouth. "And lucky. I can't believe your master didn't come after you."

"Don't talk with your mouth full," Madison scolded. "You're setting a bad example."

Wes rolled his eyes. Kit, seeking comfort, slid out of her chair and crawled into RC's lap. "I found a Tear," she said, her voice muffled as she cradled her Name and buried her face against his chest. RC put his arm around her and held her close. "He would have punished me. But he never found me."

Wes nodded. "I figured you had some experience with the Black Market. You'd be worth a fortune in the Ghost Realm."

Kit's face crumpled as she began to cry.

"Enough," Jay snapped.

Madison rose. "Kit," she called gently. She circled the table and knelt down beside my lab-sister, who continued to sob and smear snot and tears into RC's shirt. "Honey, you're okay. Hey. Kit, sweetheart, please look at me," she beseeched.

Kit turned her head, her ears swiveling toward the sound of my mother's voice. "I'm sorry we upset you. Everything's okay. You know you're safe here, right?" Kit batted her wet eyelashes and dropped her head to study the pendant in her grasp. Madison peered down at it. "That's a pretty necklace. May I see it?" She reached for Kit's Name.

"Maddie, wait!" Wes warned.

Kit pinned her ears and hissed. Her eyes flared as she summoned golden ectoplasm into her small hand and blasted Madison, who couldn't dodge the close-range strike even if she'd had time to register it was coming.

The energy struck my mother in the shoulder, spinning her to the side as she went down. Kit was so young and her power level was so low that the blast should have been relatively weak. At most, my mother would have a bruise, but the hostility of Kit's actions was perfectly clear.

Realizing that she'd just attacked a human and was sure to be punished, the little girl transformed in swirling black smoke that slipped through RC's grasp. The kitten leapt from his lap, causing him to suck in a sharp breath when her claws pricked his thighs. I stood but hesitated in indecision, unsure who to approach—my upset lab-sister or my dazed mother.

Madison scrambled to her feet and took a step after Kit, but Wes intervened. "Whoa, wait a minute, Maddie," he said, seizing her arm. "Don't take it so personally."

I hurriedly added, "She didn't mean to hurt you."

"I did nothing to provoke her!" Madison exclaimed.

"But you did," Ero replied, his calmness a sharp contrast to the universal tension. "One thing to know about Amínytes—their Names are their most prized possession."

Wes nodded and explained, "They're unreasonably protective about those pendants they wear. I've even heard of Amínytes going feral and killing their master if their Name is taken away. That necklace around

Kit's neck is not something you want to be grabbing."

My mother's bewildered expression melted into remorse. "Oh."

"I'll go find Kit," Jay announced.

I said, "No, I'll talk to her." He raised his eyebrows. I returned the meaningful look. Kit had a dispute with my mother; this was my issue to mediate. He lowered himself back into the chair, wordlessly conceding.

The trouble with cats, of course, was their talent for hiding. Luckily, Ero hinted, "I recommend checking my room."

I strode out into the foyer and across the great room toward the row of French doors leading to the backyard. Ero's room was at the end of the hallway on the right, next to the sunroom. His door was halfway open.

I pushed it farther and paused in the doorway, listening to the sounds of soft sobs coming from under the bed. When I knelt down and lifted the edge of the covers, I found Kit curled up in a ball. Between sobs, she whimpered, "Mrs. Tarrow . . . hates . . . me."

"No, she doesn't," I soothed.

"She hates me now."

"Why do you think that?" I asked, folding my legs beneath me.

Kit swiped at her tears. "I hurt her." She clutched her pendant in her small fist and succumbed to a fresh wave of sobs.

"Hey, come here," I requested gently.

Still crying and sniffling, Kit crawled out from under the bed and curled up in my lap. "I'm sorry, Cato. Jay said to be nice to Madison, and I wasn't."

"I'm sure she'll forgive you. She didn't know that you don't like Outsiders touching your Name. She didn't mean to upset you, just like you didn't mean to hurt her." I stroked her hair and cuddled her for a minute, then stood up and set Kit down on the bed. I held out my hand as an open invitation. "Come on. We can go apologize and make this all better."

"I don't want to."

I stretched my hand closer. "If you tell her you're sorry, she'll forgive you. But you have to apologize first."

Two tears slowly rolled down my lab-sister's cheeks. "What if Mrs. Tarrow hits me?"

"She's not going to hit you. She promised, remember? And I'm right here to protect you."

"You promise?"

"Arena's Honor."

She wiped her nose with the edge of her cloak and reluctantly slipped her small hand inside mine. I pulled her up off the bed and turned toward the door. "We'll do this together, okay?"

— Chapter Twenty-One —
Like Old Times

My mother was cleaning the table after dinner while Wes read the local newspaper. They both looked up when we entered.

"Kit has something she wants to say," I announced, giving my lab-sister's hand a reassuring squeeze.

She stared at her toes and mumbled, "I'm sorry, Mrs. Tarrow."

My mother approached us and knelt in front of Kit so she could be at eye level. "I'm sorry, too. I didn't know that you don't like people touching your Name. That was my mistake."

Wes was watching from the corner of his eye. A knock at the front door prompted him to fold the paper and rise to greet the visitor.

Kit held her Name in her hand, gazing lovingly at it. For a moment, I thought she was going to offer it to Madison, but then she clenched it tightly and held it close to her chest, staring at my mother with her golden eyes. Madison smiled and compromised, "I won't be mad at you if you won't be mad at me. Deal?"

Kit nodded, becoming shy again in my mother's presence. "And," Madison continued, "if you want it, there's a bowl of ice cream waiting for you in the kitchen."

Kit's ears perked up. "Really?" she whispered.

"Uh-huh. You deserve it for protecting Trey and Vivian today. But you better eat it fast before it melts."

"What do you say?" I whispered, squeezing her hand again.

"Thank you, Mrs. Tarrow."

"You're welcome," Madison said, still smiling. Kit slipped her hand out of mine and ran across the dining room on silent bare feet. She hit the swinging door with both palms to push the door open.

My mother rose. "She is such a sweetheart," she crooned. I suspected that she missed having little kids to take care of. Viv and I were more or less independent now, and Kit could benefit from a mother's love—something she'd never had before.

"Thank you for doing that," I said.

"Well, it was my fault," she admitted. "Now I know."

My throat clenched. I sighed and leaned my forearms across the back of a dining room chair, bowing my head. Madison asked, "Are you mad at me, too? I'm sorry I—"

"No," I interrupted, shaking my head. "I'm not mad. I'm . . . I don't know." I pinched the bridge of my nose. "Kit thought you were going to hit her."

"What? Cato, you know I'd never lay a hand on her."

"Yes, I know that." I turned my head to look at my mother as a deep, cold sadness filled me. "I'm just upset that somebody must have in the past for her to react like that."

Her shoulders slumped as the weight of my words settled on her.

The front door opened, and Wes stepped into the foyer. "Cato? You have a visitor."

Surprised, I approached to discover a gangly blond teenager leaning against the railing beneath the porch light in the deepening dusk. I closed the door behind me, and for a moment, we just stared at each other in silence.

"Hey," Trey said quietly, lowering his gaze as he scuffed the toe of his sneaker on the baluster.

"Hi."

An awkward tension settled, thickening the air with each passing second of silence. Whether it really was or not, I couldn't shake the feeling that the discomfort was my fault.

Trey fiddled with the zipper on his jacket, then shoved his hands deep in his pockets. Suddenly, he broke into a grin and tossed something at me. I caught a hard cube. He said, "You owe me twenty bucks."

I was beyond confused. I stared down at the cube. Each side was a solid color made of nine squares. When I looked up at him again, he was beaming, as if he'd just told a hilarious joke and was waiting for me to laugh. "What?"

The stupid grin was still prevalent for a few more uncomfortable seconds before it wavered. "Don't you remember?" he asked. "When you gave that to me for my birthday, you bet me twenty dollars I'd never solve it. Well . . . it's solved." He forced the smile again and added, "Don't think you get to weasel out of our bet."

I shivered just as the air dipped with an unearthly charge, and then a cloaked figure with red eyes phased through the front door. Trey, unable to sense ghosts like me, jumped in fright when he saw Axel, who stalked past us and muttered, "Finn and Reese solved your stupid puzzle." Just before he went down the stairs, he rolled his eyes and added under his breath, "Moron."

He strode away. I stared after him, then at the cube in my hand, then at Trey, who chuckled nervously. "Okay, you caught me," he said with a shrug.

I'd pieced together enough to understand that I was holding a puzzle, one I had given him as a gift, and apparently, we'd made a wager. It took me half a second to weigh my options and decide my best course of action was to play along. "Then, you cheated," I ventured.

He laughed. That was what he wanted—for things between us to pick up as if nothing had changed. That was a tall order, but maybe I could fake it enough to satisfy him. He reclaimed the puzzle cube from me. "Okay, fine, I cheated, but I still have time. I've got until one of us drops dead to solve it myself, and *then* you'll owe me twenty bucks, although after we factor in the inflation . . ."

He trailed off. I wasted a few precious seconds in confusion before I realized that was a joke, and then I rushed to deliver an unconvincing chuckle in response. Trey's strained smile faded with my humorless laugh.

Trey studied me. "You don't try to hide your glowing eyes anymore," he noticed.

Yes, and right now, I cursed that choice because he could see every time I glanced away, every time I closed my eyes in a subconscious grimace, and I was going to have to be very careful not to roll them. "Why should I hide them? I don't have any reason to keep my ghost half a secret."

"I know," he replied quickly. "It's just . . . weird, seeing your eyes glowing when you aren't dressed like Phantom, that's all. We went through so much trying to keep that a secret." He stared down at his feet again and bashfully admitted, "I really missed you. It hasn't been the same since you left."

"Since I left," I echoed, the words tainted with bitterness. "That makes it sound like I went willingly."

"Sorry." He turned one of the rows on his puzzle cube, but he couldn't seem to force himself to ruin its solved perfection, and he turned the same row back to align the colored squares. "So, Axel, um, he seems . . ." Again, he didn't finish, but this time, I didn't think there was a hidden joke. He tapped one finger against the cube's surface and asked, "He's your brother?"

"Yes."

Even I could hear the hostility in my tone, but in my defense, there was some seriously acidic jealousy tingeing Trey's question. I couldn't blame him for feeling that way. I'd known Trey for what, most of my lifetime, and yet I called Axel, whom I'd known less than three years, a brother.

"So . . ." Trey muttered in an attempt to revive the dead conversation. "They're all . . . I mean, Ash in particular . . . she's very pretty. But then, I was wondering, what about Shannon?"

I blinked, caught off guard by his vague question and unsure how to proceed. "Huh?"

Noticing my discomfort, Trey quickly explained, "Well, it's just that you always said she was the one and only girl you were interested in dating. You wanted to take her to prom. She's interested in you, so, you know . . . you probably could, even if you aren't a student anymore. I don't think Principal Solwitz would say no."

I considered how trivial my life had been Before. "I've got a lot more to worry about."

"Right, sure, I understand, it's just that you and Ash, I mean, you're always together, so I wasn't sure if . . . ?"

I stared at him. Was that a question? I was unsure if I was supposed to answer or not because I didn't really know what he'd asked, if he had asked anything at all. He fidgeted, his discomfort actually painful to witness, and started anew: "Hey, Cay, ah, while we're here, I, um, I have something to confess." I watched him, waiting, puzzled by his obvious anxiety as he fiddled with his weapons and shifted his weight from foot to foot as if he had to pee. He took a deep breath and blurted, "I like Vivian."

I waited for more, but it didn't come. He was staring hopefully at me, awaiting a verdict. Still confused, I said, "Okay."

Immediately, his face brightened. "Yeah? You're cool with that?"

"Sure," I answered slowly, drawing out the word. "I'm glad you like her."

He nodded, smiling, but then his face fell. He sighed. "We're not on the same page, are we? I mean I *like* her. I . . . I'd like to ask her out on a date. Sometime. Maybe. I know she's your sister, and I don't want anything to come between us if you think it's too weird, but you left, and I kept thinking about, you know, if you were here, would you be okay with it, so I spent all that time wondering, and . . . and now I need to know what you think before . . ."

His ramblings trailed off, and I tilted my head. "Before I disappear again?"

He shook his head. "I didn't say that."

I gripped my arms and stared up at the warm porch light high above us, head bobbing in thought. I could practically feel the tension radiating off him; he was suffocating in my silence. "Trey—" he tensed at his name "—you were my best friend. If you like Vivian, I'm glad to know she has someone else to keep her safe when I'm not around."

Trey made an odd laugh-sob, as if he was choking on his relief. "You have no idea how much your approval means to me."

We both stiffened at the sound of the door opening. Vivian slipped outside, grinning. "It is *so* good to see you two together again," she said, shutting the door behind her. "Wes said you were here."

Trey had a look of silent horror etched on his face. He stared at me with comically wide eyes, wordlessly begging me not to mention our discussion. I couldn't stop the crooked grin from denting my cheek at his expression, but I reassured him with a wink.

"Hey," said Vivian, "you know what we should do? Let's go out tonight, like we used to." She shot me an accusatory look and added moodily, "Unless you have to go train with your *family*."

She and Trey were both staring at me, waiting. I rubbed my hand down my face with a sigh. Although Jay had given me his blessing to spend time with my blood-family, he'd been working me extra hard to make up for any training I'd missed, which meant tomorrow morning was going to be brutal. "Where do you want to go?" I asked heavily.

She beamed, opened one of the double doors, and shouted, "Mom, I'm going out with Cato and Trey! We'll be back in a while!" She closed the door before I even heard Madison's answer. "Anywhere," she said in response to my question. "Let's just start walking."

"Just like old times, right?" Trey said lightly as he trotted down the steps of the flared staircase.

I followed along behind, joining him on the circle of pavers at the foot of the stairs. "What do you mean?" I asked as we strode down the walkway lined with small trees on either side.

Trey's grin vanished, and he looked to Vivian for guidance. She said, "You and Trey used to sneak out all the time. Remember, Cay? I tagged along sometimes too, but I was usually at home covering for you so Mom didn't find out."

"Oh. What were we doing?"

Trey rolled his shoulders and said, "Oh, just out looking for trouble. We were pretty good at finding it. Think we'll cross paths with any gho—um, *kálos* tonight?"

We reached the sidewalk and turned right. "Doubt it. There hasn't been much activity since . . ." *Since word got out that we'd decimated an entire branch of Azar's military.*

"Hmm, too bad," Trey lamented. He drew an ectogun. "The dynamic duo is back on patrol tonight! With a lovely escort," he teased with a wink. Vivian rolled her eyes, but she seemed more playful than annoyed. Trey's grin broke a little too soon, and he holstered the weapon again. "By the way," he told me, "I'm really digging that cloak. I always did think Phantom should wear a cape, but you were never open to the idea."

I touched the charcoal-gray cloak Ero had given me. Trey continued, "I've been training really hard with your mom, you know. I've learned a lot. Maybe, ah . . . maybe I could come on patrol with you sometime."

"Maybe," I answered noncommittally.

He misconstrued that to mean *no* and added, "I can hold my own. Really. I'm not just, you know, a sidekick or something."

"If Ash doesn't mind."

Vivian demanded, "Do you *always* scout with Ash?"

"Usually."

In my peripheral, I was pretty sure I saw Vivian roll her eyes again, but before I could call her out, Trey said quickly, "That's cool. I'd love to get to know her better."

He shot my blood-sister a stern look until she said, "Sure. Me too."

I replied, "All right, but Ash is kind of shy."

Vivian scoffed and muttered, "I wouldn't have guessed based on the way she dresses."

"What's wrong with the way she dresses?"

"Come on, Cato. Strutting around in a bra takes a ridiculous level of self-confidence and shamelessness."

Her bitterness puzzled me. "What do you mean? Ash dresses that way because she's hot."

Vivian threw her hands up in exasperation and snapped, "Yeah, I get it. She's pretty and she knows it. You know it. I know it. But don't try to tell me that she's shy."

Now I was beyond lost. "Who said anything about being pretty?"

"You did!"

"I said she was hot."

"Exactly!"

I stepped in front of Vivian and halted so I could directly face her. "Ash is a Pyro. She's *literally* hot—her body temperature is higher than yours. Ash likes comfortable clothing that helps her stay cool but still offers enough support for combat. What she wears has nothing to do with her looks or self-confidence."

Vivian's mouth hung open like a broken hinge. I lifted my arm up from under the cloak so she could see my bare upper arm. "She wasn't the only one with a modified Arena uniform. My shirt was different from the ones Jay and RC wore—lighter fabric, less protective padding, no sleeves. I'm a Cryo, so I have to keep cool too, but my Divinity lets me cool down internally. Ash's doesn't."

Slowly, she closed her mouth. "I . . . I'm sorry."

I tilted my head and calmly inquired, "Why don't you like Ash?"

Vivian's gaze dropped to the side. "I never said I didn't."

We started walking again, but I pressed, "You just . . . what? Are you offended by the sight of people's skin? Would you be offended if I took my shirt off right now?"

"No."

"Then I don't understand the double standard."

She kicked a stone down the sidewalk. "I guess I'm just . . . Okay, I'm jealous. Ash is very pretty, and I thought she liked to wear clothes that show off her body. I didn't make the connection to her divine power."

"Viv . . ." I tipped my head back and stared up at the night sky as I walked. "We had no control over our bodies. We didn't get to choose when or what we ate, and we didn't get to pick out our own clothes, if we were allowed to wear any at all. Ash could have had her head shaved and been force-fed until she was so obese that she couldn't walk, if that was what *They* wanted. You wouldn't be jealous of her then."

Vivian hunched her shoulders and continued to stare at her feet. I went on, "Her physical appearance is a product of *Their* design, no different than mine or any of the others'. I'm strong because *They* wanted me to be strong so I could fight in the Arena. Finn and Reese are weak because *They* wanted them to be submissive. It's not fair to judge any of us for being molded into what we are now since it wasn't our choice. But regardless of what Ash looks like, she'd still wear the same type of clothing because it's about comfort, not appearance. Vanity meant nothing when we were locked in cages with no control over our lives or our bodies. We couldn't even look at ourselves in a mirror. What we wore or how we looked didn't matter."

Vivian nodded. "I get it. I'm sorry for being judgmental."

We lapsed into a silence so uncomfortable I actually wished we might be attacked just for the sake of breaking it. As we approached LeahRae Harris High, Trey asked, "So, Cato . . . are you going to come back to school?"

Wouldn't that be a disaster? I didn't want to reveal how slowly I read, and I was sure my writing abilities would be downright pathetic compared to those of my peers. I might as well return to elementary school. "I don't see much point. I'm way behind. Besides, it's not like I can go to college now."

"Oh. Yeah, I guess you're right."

Vivian smiled and reminisced, "We must have walked this route a thousand times."

I made the mistake of saying, "Really?" which caused her to close her eyes in a grimace.

"You don't remember." She sighed, so unbearably sad that we no longer shared memories she apparently treasured.

"I'm sorry."

Trey stopped suddenly. "Maybe the school will jog your memory." Vivian and I paused. He was already marching toward the two-story brick building with the confidence that we'd follow, and we did.

Vivian warned, "There are probably security cameras."

"They won't work," I said without thinking. At their confused stares, I added, "Finn and Reese created a program that erases any footage of us."

"No way!" Trey exclaimed. "But you know what? That makes sense. I tried to catch you guys on tape back when we were stuck in City Hall, but the data was always corrupted, and I could never recover a single image."

He suddenly gasped. "Cato, you gotta get Finn and Reese to talk to me! I would love to pick their brains about computers. Do you think they'd let me see their supercomputer?"

"ECANI? I don't know. They won't talk to you, though. You're human."

"Can you try?" he begged.

I rolled my shoulders. "I guess," I answered, knowing full well that I wouldn't be able to convince them to break a Rule. The only way they'd talk to him would be if he issued the right command and they were obligated to provide an answer.

Vivian pulled on the handle. "It's locked," she announced.

"Maybe a janitor could let us in?" Trey suggested.

Vivian cupped her hands around her eyes and peered through the window. "There aren't any lights on inside."

I glanced between Vivian and Trey, puzzled by the disappointment in their voices from the simple inconvenience of a locked door. I didn't understand what was so important about exploring the school, but they both wanted in, so I reached out and grabbed Vivian's hand. She flinched at my touch before she realized it was my hand that had brushed hers. I seized Trey, exhaled, and reached for my center, letting the warm power wash over me, spill over, and affect the humans I was holding. I stepped forward, pulling them with me. We passed through the doors.

Sometimes I forgot how much power it took to become intangible. It was one of the most taxing basic powers, and I felt the effects immediately. Normally I could walk through a door no problem, but I'd just used three times as much power by bringing Vivian and Trey with me. As soon as we were inside, I released their hands and stopped the flow of power. I swayed on my feet, momentarily light-headed.

"You phased us through the door!" Trey exclaimed. "Like it wasn't even there!"

Vivian gazed around the dark hallway, smiling. Depleting my power reserves was worth the strain to impress my friend and blood-sister. It seemed all I ever did anymore was disappoint people, so this was a pleasant change. Still grinning, Vivian twirled back to face me, her hair swishing through the air.

"Will we get in trouble for being here?" I asked.

"Probably," she replied lightly. "But you're practically a celebrity, so I think Principal Solwitz would forgive us."

"So," said Trey, "anything look familiar now?"

"Not really," I admitted.

"It's dark and empty, that's why," Vivian quickly dismissed. "Come on."

We roamed the halls until Trey stopped in front of a closed door and tried the handle. "Damn. Locked. Any chance you could phase through the door and open it from the inside?"

Without a word in response, I summoned intangibility and passed through the locked door, releasing the power as soon as I was clear so I could conserve as much of my reserves as possible. Something about this place felt familiar. I could barely see in the dark—it was more like the feeling of the space. This room didn't exactly give me comforting vibes. I could almost hear the faint chatter of people talking and the chimes of a bell echoing through the halls . . .

A knock made me jump and whirl to face the door. *Oh, right.* I turned the lock and opened the door to let Trey and Vivian step inside.

"So, what do you think, Cay?" Trey asked with a broad smile. "Feel familiar yet?"

Vivian flicked a switch on the wall, and I squinted as the fluorescent lights flickered to life above us. I held my hand above my eyes as my vision slowly adjusted to find rows of battered desks, a clock over the whiteboard on the wall, and windows overlooking the schoolyard. "Actually, yeah. It does. Was this my old classroom?"

Trey said, "First-period algebra. Pretty much the bane of your high-school existence."

"I was tutoring you to help you get your math grade up," Vivian said gently. "Do you remember which desk was your assigned seat?"

I stared at the rows of desks, but they all looked identical, none particularly significant. I frowned, trying to imagine myself walking through the door and sitting down.

Noticing my frustrated expression, Trey strolled into the room and said, "Maybe knowing where I sat will jog your memory?" He seated himself in the desk third from the front in the row closest to us.

Vivian walked toward the whiteboard. "Ms. Tighe stood up here to teach."

I meandered along the rows of desks, my eyes fixed on Vivian. My perspective was all wrong in the back; my seat wasn't there. But I knew I hadn't been in the front row, either. Viv's gaze followed me as I worked my way across the room, my hand brushing the backs of the chairs. "It's okay if you don't remember, Cato," she told me gently. "We don't want to put too much pressure on you."

"Right," Trey quickly agreed.

I froze—here, the angle between Vivian and me felt right. I sat down.

No. This chair was wrong; the perspective was slightly off. But I was close.

Trey opened his mouth to offer a hint, but Vivian shook her head warningly. I wanted to figure this out by myself, anyway. I rose and advanced to the next chair. *So close!* I stood again, then took a step to the right. No. I moved to the desk on my left and sat down in the seat.

I wasn't alone in an empty school anymore; every seat was filled with a student. Sunlight poured in through the windows, taunting us with the promise of a beautiful spring day. "All right, pencils out. We have a pop quiz today!" Ms. Tighe announced cheerily. The class groaned. I glanced across the room at Trey, rolling my eyes. He shrugged one shoulder in answer.

"This was my seat," I stated with conviction. I had sat here almost every day of the last semester I'd spent in school. I had watched the clock here, and doodled instead of taking notes here, and daydreamed as I stared out the window from here, and fell asleep during a lecture after a long night of ghost hunting here.

Trey nodded in affirmation. Vivian beamed, thrilled that I had remembered.

After turning off the lights and locking the door, they guided me to my locker next. I couldn't remember the combination to open it, but I pretended that I did remember meeting Trey in front of it before walking home after school every day, and that little lie seemed to be enough to satisfy them. I drank from the water fountain in the hallway before I dipped a little too deep into my reserves again to phase Vivian and Trey through the front doors one more time.

They were both in high spirits from our forbidden adventure, although Vivian's smile instantly vanished when she squinted at me in the dark. "Cato, you're bleeding."

I felt a tickle beneath my nose and quickly backhanded the blood away. "It's fine."

"Are you sure?"

"Yeah. Intangibility just takes a lot out of me, especially when I have passengers."

They still wanted to explore the town. I didn't complain, but my hands were shaking, and their voices echoed strangely in my ringing ears, so I trailed after them and kept quiet. Really, I just wanted to go Home and rest.

But I didn't have the heart to tell them that and put an end to the reunion.

— Chapter Twenty-Two —

Cure

The electrocardiograph screen flatlined.

"No, no, *no!*" Dr. Anders cried, pounding on the machine with his fist. The constant beeping had become one long note, and no matter how many times he struck the device, the results would not change. The naked man strapped to the metal table was dead.

"Damn it!" Anders snapped, throwing his clipboard across the room.

Agent Byrn stood in the doorway. "Lost another one?"

Anders stormed to his desk, plopped down in his chair, and then doubled over to snatch the clipboard from the floor. "The Origin dies when the ghost does. There's no getting around it." He shook his head. "Tell me you and Kovak have a lead."

"Possibly. Nothing concrete."

The doctor angrily tossed his clipboard onto the counter. "I never thought I'd say this, but I need the runts back. I'm not getting anywhere with the data."

"I know," Byrn sympathized. "That was a five-year investment we lost. Didn't they give you enough of a jump start on the research to continue without them?"

"It's not like they left detailed notes. They did all the calculations in their heads."

Agent Byrn picked at a piece of corn stuck in his teeth from dinner. "Look, I get it. Definitely a setback. A1 and A2 accelerated our timetable, but now we have to keep pushing ahead without them. Don't lose focus."

Dr. Anders leaned over to spit a wad of gum into the trash can, then took a deep drink of water from a glass sitting on the counter. "Easier said than done," he grumbled as he wiped his sleeve across his mouth. "I don't have ECANI. It's taking the system forever to process the data."

"Maybe you should call it a night. It's getting late."

"How can you even tell in this godforsaken underground bunker?"

"It's called a watch. Just because the sun isn't visible doesn't mean you should be pulling all-nighters. How long has it been since you took leave aboveground?"

Dr. Anders thought for a moment, then shrugged. "Our trip to Phantom Heights."

"Jesus. You need a vacation. Staying underground so long is going to start messing with your head."

"I can't," he muttered. "I feel like I'm so close to a breakthrough."

"Well, whenever you need a break, put in the paperwork, and I'll sign off on your request. You at least ate dinner, right?" At the doctor's silence, Agent Byrn rolled his eyes and said, "I'll send that new intern—Kate, Cassy, whatever her name is—to the cafeteria to bring you something."

"It's Kim," Anders corrected.

"Whatever. That's why I prefer numbers over names. She's next to useless, anyway. Lazy, incompetent . . ."

A tiny smirk dented the doctor's cheek. "No, she's human. You're used to having Mind-Readers at your beck and call. A1 and A2 spoiled you by tuning into your thoughts and waiting on you hand and foot before you even had to give them a command. You can't blame the intern for failing to match that level of efficiency."

Byrn complained, "Well, she's still slow."

Anders nodded sympathetically, although to be truthful, he didn't actually feel much empathy for his superior's plight. He'd always felt that Kovak and Byrn had wasted the twins' potential by turning them into personal servants, thereby splitting their focus away from ECANI and Project Alpha's ultimate objective. The weapon probably could have been finished by now if A1 and A2 had been utilized correctly.

Dr. Anders yawned, then said, "I'm sure the threat of being fired doesn't have nearly the same effect as the threats you used on the runts. Human rights, and all. No cruel and unusual punishment allowed."

"Slaves are so much better than interns," Agent Byrn grumbled. He turned away. "I'll send Kim down to get your order. Can't have you burning out on us before we reach the finish line."

He paused. "Have a little faith, Doc," he said over his shoulder. "History will remember you favorably for all of your hard work when we win the war."

The doors slid shut, leaving the doctor alone in the room with the body of the expired test subject. It had been terminal, anyway, destined for Project Omega. Anders heaved a deep sigh and slid a packet of gum from his lab coat pocket. What he really craved, even after all these years, was a cigarette, but the gum would have to suffice. He stared at the expired subject while he worked the fresh stick into a malleable lump between his molars.

Despite his failures, he couldn't completely fight the grin as he considered the fanciful daydream of helping to shape a new world. He could figure this problem out—after all, if two ten-year-olds could develop such advanced computer software, he could harness the power of the Origin, couldn't he?

***

"This better not kill him."

"It won't. I've been testing different doses in Omega, and I'm confident with the final combination."

"You're sure the venom isn't going to interact with the sedative? I can't risk him being conscious."

"Positive. Stop worrying; you're stressing me out. Only one of my Omega subjects was unable to be revived. The odds are good."

"What? You lost one?"

"We're operating on a tight time frame. The risk is low, and she's already on her way. Either we do this now, or you come up with a new idea."

"So help me, Doc, if he doesn't wake up, I'm going to destroy your career, you understand?"

Dr. Anders leaned over me and smiled. "Ready for a nap? A nice, peaceful, dreamless nap. I'm going to take you to the brink of death, my friend. But not to worry . . . I promise I'll bring you back . . ."

I jerked awake with a gasp. A dark figure was looming over me.

I reacted without thinking, propelling myself toward the human and taking her down with me as I rolled off whatever I'd been sleeping on. She let out a startled cry as I pinned her, my knees on her shoulders and my hands around her throat. I bared my teeth, my power thrumming. I was going to squeeze the breath out of Dr. Anders's assistant before she could hurt me.

"Cato!" she rasped, squirming feebly beneath me. "Cato, stop! I'm your mom! You aren't in the lab, remember? *Cato!*"

Her voice was scared. Familiar. Out of place in this setting. She didn't belong here in Quarantine with me. Wait . . . was I in Quarantine? This didn't feel right.

I blinked, finally focusing on her face in the darkness. I froze, staring at her for a few moments before I realized I was still choking her. I released my hold on her throat.

Horrified by what I'd done, I scrambled away as she sat up, coughing and rubbing her neck. "Wh-where am I?" I whispered.

She weakly held up a blanket. "You . . . fell asleep . . . on the sofa. I thought . . . you might be cold . . . and I was just . . . going to cover you with a blanket." She coughed again. "I'm sorry. I didn't mean to scare you."

My gaze roved across our dark surroundings. Windows. This room had windows. I definitely wasn't in Quarantine. I was . . . in Saros Manor, and it was Lightsout. No, nighttime. "Why did I fall asleep in the parlor?"

"I don't know, sweetheart. I found you here."

"Where's my lab-family?"

"I don't know," she said again. "Are they out training? Were you waiting for them?"

I sank down on the cushion as I dragged my shaking hand through my hair. Was I? What happened? My thoughts felt disjointed from the rude awakening. I remembered being out with Trey and Vivian . . . I must have gone upstairs, realized that my lab-siblings weren't Home yet, and come back down to sit on the sofa in the parlor and wait for them to return.

I swallowed, my heart racing. "I'm sorry," I whispered, still horrified by how I'd blanked out and mistaken my mother for one of *Them*.

Madison coughed again, then pulled herself up and sat down next to me on the sofa. I stiffened at her proximity, but she didn't try to touch me. We sat together in silence for several minutes, staring into the darkness while she caught her breath. Guilt filled me, and my thoughts revolved around what Madison must be thinking. Her silence bewildered me. Was she angry? Upset? Was she preparing to scold me? I could have killed her . . . How much trouble was I in?

"Cato." I cringed, but to my surprise, her voice remained gentle. "When you sleep, why do you curl your body into such a tight little ball? Back when Finn and Reese were sick and we cared for them, I noticed they do that, too. I didn't really think too much of it until I noticed that you sleep in the exact same position."

I paused, startled and rather perplexed by the question. Not only had I not been expecting it, but I also didn't realize I slept in that position. I shrugged and rubbed my right biceps. "Habit, I guess. I'm used to sleeping in a small space."

"Were you having a nightmare?"

I nodded, then realized that she couldn't see me clearly in the darkness and answered, "Yes."

"About the AGC?" she pressed.

"I don't want to talk about it."

"Okay. That's fine. You don't have to." I rubbed my hands down my face, trying to wash away the remnants of the memory that had taken over my dreams. She shifted and continued, "You know, Cato, if you ever need to talk . . . about anything . . . you can come to me. I'll always be here to listen."

I nodded even though I had no intention of telling her any more about that hellish place than I had to. "Madison?" I ventured.

"Mom."

"Right . . . Mom, um . . . what were you thinking when you found out I wasn't human?"

She was quiet for a moment. The sofa cushion shifted as she leaned away and turned on a lamp, then faced me. Apparently, my question had caught her off guard.

"Well," she began, "honestly, I'm still trying to figure that out myself. I suppose I was in shock at first. Then . . . hurt that you never felt like you could confide in me. Confused, certainly. I didn't have time to process what was happening. But I was ready to fight on your behalf and go to war with the AGC, even if I didn't have any answers or truly understand what happened."

She studied me closely. "What about you? What were you thinking after they took you away?"

"I was scared. And sorry for lying to you. I thought, if I could just get the chance to apologize to you, everything would be okay. And then you would come take me home. But when you never came, I thought you were mad at me. I thought you hated me and were so humiliated that you didn't want to claim me as your son anymore."

"You really thought I was embarrassed by you?"

"A half-ghost secretly living in the same house as a ghost hunter for almost a year without her knowing? I think it's safe to say I ruined your reputation, right? I guess I was thinking about myself and never considered what kind of consequences you'd have to deal with. I'm sorry."

Madison scoffed at her own ignorance. "Oh, Cato. That's on me, not you. In hindsight, a lot of things made sense after I finally put the pieces together—the cuts and bruises, the slipping grades, the evasiveness and irritability, the exhaustion. And you were always dropping things."

I nodded. "Intangibility. That was hard to learn how to control."

"I'm pretty sure I saw your eyes flash a few times when you were angry, too. But when I looked closer, you seemed normal." She shook her head. "I should have been more attentive. I think maybe I didn't notice anything too far out of the ordinary because I chose not to see it and I was so preoccupied with my research that I didn't give you the time and attention both you and Vivian deserved. I promise I am *not* ashamed of you at all. I couldn't be prouder of you."

"Proud?" I repeated, certain I'd heard wrong.

"Absolutely. Most teenagers with the abilities you have would have used their powers irresponsibly. You could have chosen to steal and vandalize and cause all sorts of mischief, but instead, you chose to protect people. I am so proud to say that Phantom is my son."

I felt a faint smile tug at my lips. I should have been happier to hear her say that. And yet, my grin faded. "But you said that Phantom was a mistake."

"When did I say that?"

"In town square. The day Wes brought Phantom's uniform from the museum."

Madison exhaled and leaned her head back against the sofa. "Okay, yes, you're right. I did say that. But I didn't mean it the way it sounded. Causing the accident that turned you into Phantom was the mistake, and it was my fault. I thought I had lost you, and I wouldn't have if I hadn't changed you in the first place."

"Oh."

"Cato," Madison said, turning her head to look at me again, "given everything that's happened . . . if you could go back in time and change anything, would you?"

"You mean, would I tell you about my powers?" She nodded. I considered the scenario. "No."

She frowned. "Really? Even knowing how events would play out, you still wouldn't tell me?"

"No. You would have run tests on me."

"But nothing like what the Agents did to you. I could have protected you from them. And I might have found a cure."

I gazed at her, horror-stricken. "Cure?"

She closed her eyes in a grimace. "That didn't come out right—"

"I'm not sick, and there's nothing wrong with me."

"I know."

"You just said you were proud of me."

"I am."

"But you want me to be 'cured.'"

She sighed, trying to collect her thoughts. "All I'm saying is . . . I might have been able to give you the choice to be human again. If that was what you wanted."

"I should go to bed," I said curtly as I stood up.

"Right," she said in weary disappointment. "Good night, Cato. I love you."

I hesitated between the parlor and foyer. "Good night, Madison," I replied.

— Chapter Twenty-Three —

Deterioration

Ash and I were scouting the second circle during Jay's ten o'clock shift to check on the twins when, to our surprise, he appeared in front of us and said, "Cato, you need to talk to your mother. *Now*, before she gets herself killed."

"What?"

"She's not listening to me." As he held his hand out to me, he looked at Ash and said, "RC is by the library if you want to meet up with him."

Ash and I exchanged puzzled looks, but I set my hand in Jay's and closed my eyes, braced for the uncomfortable sensation of Blinking. The pressure compressed my body as the wind roared in my ears, and then I opened my eyes and found myself on the large patio behind Saros Manor.

The sets of French doors leading to the great room formed a glass backdrop behind us. To my left, a vine-laden wood structure covered a pathway made of giant rectangular stones in the grass, leading to a smaller patio behind the garage with an empty pool, hot tub, and small building. Next to me, in the center of the rounded portion of the main patio, was a firepit contained within a circular wall of pavers. A pair of stone seating walls edging the patio partially enclosed the firepit section.

Across the vast lawn beyond the stone walls, Axel was pacing near the tree line of Alvarez Park. I immediately recognized the warning signs of his body language and knew not to approach him.

Usually, Axel's cycle took about a week for him to wane from a semi-healthy state to an irritable, pallid wreck until he'd leave us to go get his medicine, wherever it was. Whatever it was. I was still afraid to ask what he did outside Phantom Heights.

But this time, his normal cycle had taken twice as long. The slaughter of the Shadow Guards seemed to have renewed him to an almost glowing state immediately after the battle—his eyes were bright, skin radiant, hair glossy, overall physical health better than I'd seen in a long time.

On day eleven, I had noticed the dark circles under his eyes.

On day twelve, his pupils were dilated, and his mood plummeted.

And now, thirteen days after the battle, he'd become more unstable than ever. I watched him pace back and forth across the yard, his fingers twisted into his hair, growling and muttering under his breath and occasionally wincing as if in pain. Mostly he paced on two feet, but sometimes he crouched down to four. He would likely leave Phantom Heights this evening.

I pitied Axel, although I'd never admit that to him because he loathed being pitied. He'd been so careful to keep his nydæa half in check, but that one mistake in battle had ruined all those months of hard work to maintain control. Now, the urge to kill again was driving him insane. It didn't help that his senses were so sharp, that he could hear, see, feel, smell, *sense* all the potential prey in Phantom Heights.

But other than Axel, Jay was my only company. "I thought you wanted me to talk to Madison," I said in confusion.

No sooner were the words out of my mouth than one of the French doors opened behind me. "Oh, hi, Cato," she said cheerily. I turned to face her as she closed the door. "I didn't expect to see you back so soon. Didn't you just check on the twins a little while ago?"

Jay crossed his arms and glared at Madison, who was holding a steaming bowl in her hand. "What . . . are you doing?" I asked.

"Jay said Axel is sick. So, I made him some chicken noodle soup."

Jay gave me an exasperated look. Still trying to process the situation, I said, "Why in the world would you think that would be a good idea? Axel has rejected every single meal you've offered him."

"Well, I know," she admitted, cradling the bowl in both hands.

"But he still won't tell me what he wants to eat, so I thought I could offer this. I used to make chicken noodle soup for you when you were sick. Remember?"

No, I didn't, but before I had a chance to answer, she added, "If he doesn't want soup, maybe he'll finally be willing to tell me what he does want instead. This is a symbolic gesture. I want to let him know that I care and I'll make him whatever he wants. Even if it's . . . you know. Unconventional."

"I really don't think this is a good idea."

"Then tell me what I should offer him as an alternative."

I just stared at her, speechless. She lifted her chin and strode across the patio with purpose.

Jay and I trotted after her. "Axel isn't stable right now," Jay warned as we rounded the firepit.

"It's safer to give him space and let him be," I said.

"Bloody Scout," Jay muttered under his breath. We passed through the opening between the seating walls, stepping off the patio and onto the lawn. "Mrs. Tarrow, please listen to us. Axel goes through this cycle all the time, and soup isn't going to make him feel better."

"Well, I can't help him if I don't talk to him and find out what he needs," she said.

I told her, "Axel doesn't want to talk." *He wants to hunt*, I added silently, but I wasn't sure if I should admit that. Phantom Heights was already on edge after the Shadow Guard incident. They didn't need an extra reason to fear Axel.

"And he definitely doesn't want your help," Jay added.

I jogged in front of Madison and halted with my arm out to make her stop. "Okay. This is close enough. Don't crowd him; let him come to you if he chooses."

She wavered in indecision, glancing over my shoulder at Axel still pacing. I was nervous about turning my back on him, which made me easy prey, but at least Jay had the whistle. Madison heeded my suggestion and stayed in place when she called out, "Axel, I made you some homemade chicken noodle soup," and held the bowl up.

I turned to see his reaction, but he didn't acknowledge our presence.

Undeterred, she continued, "Trust me—it's the perfect remedy when you aren't feeling well. Why don't you give it a try?"

Axel shot her a quick glare and then dropped his head with a growl as he continued his restless pace in the grass.

"I think you should leave him alone," I told her nervously.

She disregarded my warning and took a few steps closer to my lab-brother. "Axel, I want to help you. Will you please tell me what you need?"

He stopped in his tracks and whirled to face her. "I need you to stay the *fuck* away from me!" His pallid skin shone with perspiration, his hair stringy and bedraggled, his dilated eyes haunted, shadowed by dark circles.

Jay and I both held up our hands as Axel crouched down to all fours, his rabid snarls raising goose bumps across every inch of my skin. "Back away slowly," Jay whispered. "Do not turn your back on him. Do not run."

I kept my movements slow as I reached out, gripped Madison's shirt, and stepped back, pulling her with me. She finally yielded and shuffled back. Axel had a wild, feral look in his eyes—one I'd seen many times before—and it put me on edge. At least I could still see a ring of red around his pupils. If the pupils dilated much more, they would completely eclipse his irises, and then we'd be in serious trouble.

"He isn't going to hurt us . . . is he?" Madison whispered.

"Not if we give him space," I muttered as we continued to retreat.

Axel bared his teeth at us with a ferocious snarl, but then he lifted his hands and pulled at his hair with his head bowed. He slammed his fists to the ground hard enough for me to feel the earth tremble beneath my boots before he stood abruptly. His cloak whirled through the air behind him as he turned his back and stormed away from us toward the park.

I let go of Madison's shirt and set my hand over my racing heart. "I don't think I've ever seen him that bad before."

"I know," Jay said, betraying a hint of worry.

"What's wrong with him?" Madison asked, her voice barely above a whisper. She was still staring at his receding form before he was lost in the trees.

I hesitated and glanced at Jay before I answered, "These phases are normal. But when Axel doesn't feel well, his temper gets shorter and he has a harder time reining in his animal instincts. It's best to leave him alone. I promise he'll be fine as long as we don't interfere."

"This doesn't feel right. If Axel's sick, he should be resting. I could take care of him, if he'd let me."

She stared at the bowl of chicken noodle soup in her hands. "So . . . what did you say causes him to go through these phases?"

"It's complicated," Jay said curtly. "The best way to help Axel is to give him space so he isn't tempted to harm you, either accidentally or on purpose."

My mother was frowning in thought. "Is there an external factor that dictates these phases? Like how Wes's form is tied to the moon?"

Again, Jay and I looked at each other, unsure how to answer without revealing too much about Axel's non-kálos half. "No," I said at the same time Jay replied, "Sort of."

"It's complicated," I repeated, turning away. "I need to get back to Ash. Please don't approach Axel if you see him again."

Jay vanished, likely to return to Finn and Reese. I left my mother standing confused and uncertain in the middle of the backyard, the bowl of untouched soup still cradled in her hands.

On the one hand, the voice in the back of my mind insisted that I should warn Madison. If she knew what Axel really was, caution might finally convince her to back off. Then again, it wasn't my place to reveal Axel's secret and potentially incite even more prejudice and fear against him. I'd managed to avoid the topic this time, but eight hours later, just as I was seating myself at the table for dinner, Vivian noticed, "Axel isn't joining us? Is he still sick?"

Madison frowned. "I'm really worried about him," she said. "He looked terrible this morning. I want Doc to check him out."

I almost choked on the water I was drinking. "That's not necessary," Jay replied coolly.

"Well, I already asked her to come by later tonight. I do think she can help Axel, and he can feel safe opening up to her. Anything he tells her is protected by doctor-patient confidentiality. He can be honest about his condition so they can work out a treatment plan. Axel clearly needs help managing his symptoms. Where is he now?"

"Not here," said Jay.

"I can see that," Madison snapped.

"Actually," Ero intervened, "Jay meant that Axel is no longer in Phantom Heights."

"What do you mean?" my mother asked, turning to me for an answer. "Where is he?"

I shrugged one shoulder. "Axel . . . uh . . ."

"Is getting his medicine," Jay finished for me.

I glanced at Ero, wondering if he'd comment on our loose definition of *medicine*. The Telepath remained silent, although he passed a subtle wink to me.

"He can't get the medicine from Doc?" Wes asked.

"No," Jay said. "Axel has to go get it himself. He should be back later tonight."

"A rare medicine . . ." Madison murmured thoughtfully. "He isn't doing anything illegal, is he?" she pressed, her tone hardening.

"No," I said in surprise. At least, I hoped not. Honestly, I wasn't sure.

Jay said, "Axel deals with his condition on his own, and it's best if no one interferes. It's no different than Wes leaving during the full moon."

Madison's stern yet inquisitive gaze was fixed on me again, and I felt obligated to elaborate: "Axel is a half-breed like me, but his two halves can't coexist the way mine can. What you saw today was the scale tipping and Axel's other half starting to surface. The, uh, 'medicine' revitalizes him so he's strong enough to keep his other half under control."

Wes leaned forward, eyes glinting yellow with eagerness. "What is Axel's other half?"

I picked up my fork and answered coldly, "He can tell you if he wants to."

Wes grudgingly dropped the topic. Madison muttered, "I guess I'll call Doc after dinner and tell her not to bother coming over since Axel isn't here. But . . . you're sure he'll be all right?"

We all nodded, and Madison had no choice but to accept our reassurances. She turned her attention to her meal, but I noticed how her brow was furrowed ever so slightly, and I knew she was still concerned about Axel.

I was worried about my lab-brother too, but not for the same reasons.

<hr>

Holly knocked on the doorframe of Shannon's room and said, "Dinner is ready. Sorry it's so late tonight."

Although she couldn't see her daughter, she heard a muffled voice call from the closet, "That's okay. Oh, hey, Mom?" Shannon emerged with a sky-blue blouse in one hand and a sea-green halter top in the other. "Which one do you like better?"

Holly stepped into her daughter's room to study the options. "They're both nice, but I personally think the blue one is more flattering on you. Why?"

Shannon laid the chosen shirt on the bed and ducked back into her closet to replace the other. "Just in case Cato is at school tomorrow." She migrated to her jewelry box and started riffling through it. "I know he probably isn't ever going to come back for classes, but I figure there's a good chance I'll see him at some point if he ever meets Trey and Vivian after school or stops by to join them for lunch or something. I want to look nice when I get a chance to talk to him."

Holly felt her lips immediately purse in disapproval. "I see. And what do you think you'd want to talk to Cato about?"

Shannon shrugged, but her cheeks were turning pink. "I don't know. Just, you know, see how he's doing. See if he might . . . I don't know."

Holly shook her head. She caught herself chewing on a fingernail and started sorting the coins scattered on Shannon's dresser to keep her hands busy. "I'd hoped you were over that silly phase."

Shannon draped an aquamarine necklace with matching earrings on the bed and smoothed out the wrinkles in the blouse, her cheeks now burning red. "It wasn't just a phase, Mom. And I wish you wouldn't dismiss my feelings like that. I really do care about Cato."

"No, you don't. You had a little crush on Phantom, that's all. It's understandable, but it's not rational." She glanced up into the mirror to see Shannon roll her eyes. "Shan, he's not human. Ghosts are dangerous, and I want you to stay away from him."

"Oh please, Mom. Cato isn't like other ghosts, and he would never hurt me. If anything, you should be happy that I want to be with someone who can protect me."

"Protect you? He's a magnet for danger, and besides that, he's half-ghost. Do you remember what ghosts did to me? And to your little brother?"

Shannon's body stiffened, but she retorted, "If Cato had been here, he would have saved Greyson. I know he would have."

Holly ground her teeth. "If Cato ever was one of us, he isn't anymore. Not after what the Agents put him through. That isn't the same boy you went to school with. Kovak himself said that Cato's powers have grown and they're unstable. Cato is dangerous."

Shannon froze. "When did Agent Kovak say that?"

Holly separated the pennies and nickels into two stacks. "Hmm? Oh, it was a while ago." When she looked up again, Shannon's reflection was staring back. Her face was pale, her expression slowly transforming from confusion to horror.

"Mom," Shannon whispered, "did you know?"

"Know what?"

"Did you know that Cato was alive?"

Holly arranged the dimes into a neat stack. "How could I have known that?"

Shannon took a step back. "That's not a real answer. You knew, didn't you?" Her voice rose. "Mom, answer me! Tell me the truth for once."

"Does it really matter at this point?"

"It does to me. Did you know Seph was really Cato from the beginning?"

Holly was silent for several long seconds. Finally, she replied, "Yes."

Shannon's chest heaved, as if she couldn't catch her breath. "Then . . . you knew Cato was alive all this time. How long have you known?"

Holly sighed. She took her time sliding the tower of dimes next to the other two stacks before she admitted, "Agent Kovak told me right before the funeral."

"Oh my god." Shannon sank weakly onto the bed. "Why didn't you say something? Mrs. Tarrow could have rescued him."

"I doubt that."

Shannon pressed her hands against her head and curled her fingers through her sleek black hair. "How could you? I can't believe . . . Cato was left there all alone to be tortured! Didn't you care about him?"

"Him?" Holly spun to face her daughter directly. "I care about Phantom Heights. It wouldn't have mattered, Shannon. Agent Kovak made it very clear that he wasn't going to let Cato go. There was no point in wasting time, effort, and resources trying."

"Mrs. Tarrow could have tried. How could you stand there at his funeral and not say anything? You held me while I cried! You let Mrs. Tarrow and Vivian and Trey and me and everyone else believe that Cato was dead! Do you understand just how sick and twisted that is?"

"It was a difficult but necessary sacrifice," Holly retorted. "Do you know why we lost Greyson? Because Madison was so preoccupied trying to rescue Cato that she stopped doing her job. So no, I wasn't thinking about Cato. I was thinking about Greyson, and the other kids that were at risk of suffering his fate, and all the mothers who would be crying over their missing children. I was thinking about the humans who were being killed for sport or captured for slavery. I was thinking about our survival."

"But—"

"I realize this is difficult for you to understand, but you have to look at the big picture. I had an obligation to all of Phantom Heights, not one little half-breed mutant in the AGC's custody. We needed Madison, but she was on a hopeless crusade to get her son back, and we were suffering for it. Kovak gave me the opening, and then I guided her onto the correct path to serve Phantom Heights in the face of an imminent crisis."

Shannon was trembling with rage. "You lied, all these years. Somebody could have saved Cato, but *you* didn't let that happen!"

"You don't get it, Shannon. That wasn't an option. If I had told Madison that Cato was still alive, she wouldn't have finished her entoplasm shield to protect us, and then Phantom Heights would have been wiped off the map. You can't tell *anyone*, do you understand? You have to swear to secrecy."

Tears of betrayal were pooling in Shannon's eyes. "How can you live with yourself?"

"I made my peace with God."

"*God*? What about all the people you actually hurt? Including me?"

"I'm sorry I hurt you, but God's forgiveness is the only one that matters in the end. I don't regret my choices."

Shannon stormed past her mother. Holly snatched her wrist, but Shannon jerked free. "Don't touch me!"

She tried to escape through the doorway, but Holly seized a handful of her hair and pulled her back. Shannon squealed in pain. Holly seethed in her ear, "This isn't a game, Shannon. Part of being an adult means understanding that sometimes the truth needs to stay buried at the risk of dire consequences that will cost human lives. Promise me you won't tell a soul."

Shannon was crying, but Holly wouldn't let go until her daughter squeezed her eyes shut and nodded. Only then did Holly release her hold.

Shannon glared at her mom, tears streaming down her face. "I hate you," she snarled as she rushed from her room.

Holly didn't pursue her. She sighed and faced the mirror again. She calmly adjusted her shirt collar, then used her thumb to wipe away a smudge of eyeliner beneath her eye.

There was no need to get upset. Shannon's anger would pass, just like her ridiculous and delusional lovestruck crush on an unstable mongrel. This was nothing more than teenage drama at its core; she knew the harder she pushed, the harder Shannon would push back.

"I'll assume I'm dining alone tonight," Holly murmured to her reflection. Her gaze fell to the dresser, and she arranged the quarters into a perfect stack beside the others.

— Chapter Twenty-Four —
Underdog

Few students were in the school cafeteria; most were on the lawn, enjoying their lunch on the warm, sunny day.

Vivian found Trey sitting at the end of a table on the far side of the schoolyard. "Hey. Have you seen Kit anywhere?" she asked.

Trey swallowed his mouthful. "Nope. I haven't seen her around here since we found out she was Casper."

Vivian turned in a slow circle, scanning the school grounds for the black-and-white kitten. "Yeah, me either. You don't think Jay reassigned her since her cover was blown, do you?"

"Dunno," Trey replied with a shrug. "He might have. Or she's still here somewhere keeping a lower profile."

Vivian absently tapped her lunch box in consideration. She left Trey and roamed about, checking around and under the dumpsters, beneath the tables, and in the shrubs, but there was no sign of the Amínyte.

Finally, she admitted defeat and took her lunch to the big tree so she could sit in the shade. She leaned her back against the trunk, then sighed and tipped her head back until it rested against the bark. Vivian stared up at the branches. Her eyes widened. She sat up straighter, gazing at the small, furry face peering back at her in the leaves. "Hey," she said softly. The kitten's ears pricked forward at the sound of her voice. "I've been looking for you."

Kit twitched her tail as Vivian stood and held up her lunch box. "I thought maybe we could share a sandwich. Why don't you come down?"

The kitten didn't move. "If you won't come down, I'll have to come up." After a few moments of a resolute standoff, Vivian said, "Fine, have it your way." She slung the strap of the lunch box over her shoulder and reached for the closest branch. "I can't even remember the last time I climbed a tree," she muttered as she hauled herself up and reached for the next branch.

Kit's ears fell back as she watched Vivian ascend. When Viv finally pulled herself onto the branch Kit was on, the kitten scampered farther along the limb. Slightly out of breath, Vivian looked down as her feet dangled above the leaves. She smiled at Kit and unzipped the lunch box. "I hope you like peanut butter and jelly," she said cheerily, setting half a sandwich on the limb.

Kit stared at the food, hesitating. She took a step forward, gazing at Vivian as her tail twitched to keep her balance, and then her body transmuted in a swirl of black smoke. Kit seized the sandwich, then scooted away from Viv and sat down before she sank her sharp teeth into her meal.

Vivian smiled and leaned against the tree trunk at her side. The sunlight streamed through the canopy to cast dappled shadows and brighten the hue of the leaves. "We're pretty high up, huh?" she said brightly. Kit silently devoured her sandwich, never taking her eyes from Vivian, who glanced at her and asked, "Do you like it?"

Kit blinked and nodded just before she shoved the last piece into her mouth. "Oh, I almost forgot," Vivian muttered, reaching into the lunch box again and bringing out two small bottles. "Milk always goes great with PB&J." She kept one bottle for herself and offered the other to Kit. The Amínyte's ears pricked forward as she crept closer to take the bottle. This time, she didn't retreat after accepting the gift.

Vivian's heart hammered with excitement at how close Kit was now, but she didn't want to scare the little girl away. She took great care to make no sudden movements. Slowly, she twisted the lid of her plastic bottle, uncapped it, and raised it to her lips. Kit was already gulping the milk from her own bottle.

"Kit," she said slowly, "you know if you ever need anything, you can come find me, right?" The ghost lowered her bottle to gaze at Vivian, who continued, "You're Cato's lab-sister, and I'm Cato's blood-sister . . . so I guess that sort of makes us sisters, too." Using their terminology was awkward, but she wanted to be sure Kit understood.

The Amínyte lowered her gaze to the leaves below. She didn't say a word. Vivian scrutinized her, trying to read her expression, but Kit was strangely composed. "Are you feeling shy? Won't you talk to me?"

Kit's ears slowly fell back as a frown settled into place. Her eyes narrowed. "Cato is *my* brother," she finally growled so quietly Vivian wasn't even sure she'd heard correctly. Kit gripped the bottle hard and stared straight at Vivian, her eyes blazing behind a glistening film of tears. "I know you had him first, but he's mine now, and you can't take him back. I'm a good sister. He said so."

Vivian donned what she hoped was a comforting smile. "I don't want to take him away from you. I want to share him with you. I can see that Cato loves you very much, and since he's a brother to both of us, I thought you could be my sister too, if you want."

Kit turned the bottle as she pondered. "Ash is my big sister."

"Can't you have two big sisters?"

The Amínyte absently twisted the lid on, off, on again, deliberating. Vivian compromised, "Why don't we start by being friends?" She held out her hand. Kit's ears drifted forward as she studied Vivian's palm. After another moment's hesitation, she reached across the gap.

Kit set the empty bottle in her open hand. Vivian, who had been hoping for a truce handshake, was frozen in surprise. Kit seemed more relaxed now, and she gripped the branch as she leaned back—too far. Vivian let out a cry and reached out to grab her as she fell backward, but Kit was now contentedly hanging upside down with her long hair cascading over her head. "Do you hunt ghosts? Like Mrs. Tarrow?"

Vivian exhaled, her heart pounding at the false alarm. "No, I don't. Not since I was on the raid team."

"Mmm." Suddenly quite serious, Kit righted herself and stared intently down at the schoolyard. Before Vivian could speak, the little girl vanished in smoke and transformed into a kitten, then deftly scampered higher into the tree.

"Kit?" Vivian called. "What's wrong?" Much clumsier, she scooted toward the trunk and followed. She called out for the Amínyte again, but Kit's only acknowledgment was to flick an ear back at Vivian as she scaled the tree.

Vivian lost sight of the kitten in the leaves. She was too busy concentrating on placing her left foot, right hand, right foot, left hand on sturdy boughs. The higher she climbed, the thinner the branches became in her sweaty hands. The breeze suddenly felt more like a gale that would topple the whole tree.

She froze. Through the screen of green leaves, a golden orb of ectoplasm arched from the top of the tree and fell toward the ground, dissipating well above the heads of the students. "Kit?" Vivian called again. Slower, she resumed her climb. She could see the Amínyte now, but Kit was too high. Those thin branches weren't strong enough to hold Vivian's weight.

The breeze rustled the leaves again; she gripped the trunk and squeezed her eyes shut. "Hey, uh, Kit, why don't we go down, okay?"

No answer. Vivian cracked open one eye to peer up at Kit, who was gazing down below with laser-focused intensity. Vivian tightened her grip and looked down. There was a commotion on the ground. In her limited views between the leaves, she saw students scattering to take cover. "What's happening?" she asked in alarm.

The kitten descended from branch to branch until she was just below Vivian, and then she turned back into a little girl crouching in the leaves as she craned her neck to observe the scene.

"Is it another ghost attack?" Vivian asked.

"It's okay," Kit announced merrily. "Jay and RC are here. They scared the ghost out of hiding."

"What do you mean?"

She shrugged. "I never saw the ghost. I just sensed it." Without any further explanation, she transmuted back into a kitten.

"Kit, wait!" Vivian called, but the black-and-white feline nimbly descended the tree, leaving Vivian stranded near the top. "Damn it," she muttered. She could feel the whole maple swaying beneath her in the breeze, and the faint motion of the tree caused her body to lock into place as she clung to the thin trunk.

Vivian looked down. Kit had landed on the ground and resumed her ghost form again, but she was dizzyingly far below, causing Vivian's stomach to drop and her arms to tighten. A minuscule figure in a dark cloak approached Kit and knelt to greet her.

"Jay?" Vivian called helplessly. He tilted his head back to look up at her, and then he was right there, just a few branches below her. She bit her lower lip. "Um . . . this is embarrassing."

He smiled good-naturedly. "Climb too high?" She nodded, and he held out his hand. "I'll Blink you down. It's your first time, so it'll be disorienting. I suggest you close your eyes."

Vivian had started to lean toward his open hand, but she recoiled. "Wait, is it going to hurt?"

"Not at all," he promised, extending his hand farther. "Do you trust me?"

"Yes." And yet, her fingers wouldn't unlock from the branch they were clutching in a death grip. Another gust of wind made the tree sway. "B-but, um, is there another option?"

Jay considered, then replied, "You can jump and trust RC to catch you with telekinesis before you hit the ground. Or you can climb down yourself. Those are your three options."

Vivian sucked in a deep breath and forced her hand to unclench. It found Jay's. His grip was strong and comforting.

"Are you ready?"

"No, but I'm as ready as I'll ever be."

"Close your eyes and take a big breath."

She nodded and did as he requested. The second her lungs expanded with air, an immense pressure collapsed on her from all sides as a deafening roar of wind filled her ears. She was suspended in a space of nothingness, and then the ground was underfoot. Her weight was too much; her knees buckled.

She gasped and let go of Jay, arms flailing, and her hands found another body that caught her and lifted her up. Her face was buried in someone's chest. Strong arms wrapped around her, pressing her against his body. "I got you, Viv," Trey murmured.

"I'm gonna be sick," she said with a groan, pushing away from him. She twisted as she fell onto her hands and knees so she didn't vomit on his sneakers.

"That's okay," came Jay's voice. "Cato threw up the first time I Blinked him, too. It takes a while to get used to Blinking."

She wiped her mouth with the back of her hand before she sat up. The schoolyard was still buzzing with energy after the commotion. Students migrated closer from all directions. RC was sitting on a hovering trash can lid, one leg bent with his knee raised and his foot resting on the lid, the other leg dangling over the side. He seemed relaxed considering only a few feet away stood a woman with glowing red eyes, her arms held up in surrender, RC's wicked bladed disks orbiting her in warning. Several teachers had also surrounded the ghost with ectoplasm guns aimed at her.

Despite the weapons, there didn't seem to be any immediate danger. Most of the ghosts Vivian had encountered were hostile, the spite and loathing written all over their faces when they looked down on humans with scorn. But this woman just looked devastatingly sad. She was trembling, tears streaming down her face, her shoulders shaking with quiet sobs. "P-p-lease," she begged. "I told you, I didn't mean any harm. I swear on King's soul—I seek asylum in this Realm. Please have mercy."

RC rolled his head toward Jay and said in a bored voice, "What do you want to do?"

Jay shrugged with one shoulder since his other arm was occupied with Kit cuddling lovingly against him. "Mrs. Tarrow can decide."

He gently detached Kit, who said, "Can I come with you?"

Jay glanced around at the awestruck students pressing closer and closer. Girls immediately started giggling, blushing, and murmuring when his gaze passed over them. "It's all clear here, so sure. You can come."

Kit beamed as she crouched and leapt up in an impressive vertical jump, veiled in smoke and shrinking in size until the petite kitten land-ed on Jay's shoulder and settled onto its perch. Suddenly stern, Jay strode toward the captive and warned, "No tricks, or it'll be the last thing you do."

"I understand," she croaked in a strained whisper. Before she or anyone else had time to react, Jay seized a fistful of the ghost's cloak, and all three of them vanished into thin air.

The teachers lowered their weapons. RC held out his hand to sheathe his blades in their shells, which glided back to their wielder and settled in his waiting palm. He pocketed the silver disks, then gripped the edge of the lid as he drew his leg back up and crouched in place. Without a word of farewell, he rocketed straight up into the air, the wind in his wake sweeping Vivian's hair back from her face.

A girl squealed and exclaimed, "He is *so* amazing!"

The spell over the schoolyard broke. A rush of noise swelled as students chattered in frenzied excitement.

Trey held out his hand, and Vivian shakily set hers inside of his. He'd barely pulled her to her feet when a mob of bodies surrounded her. Girls from every direction were all talking at once: "Oh my god, Jay teleported with you! What did it feel like? What did he say to you up there? Are you like totally embarrassed that you puked right in front of him? Did he hold you in his arms? How strong is he? I can't believe you got to teleport with Jay! I'm so jealous! Are you—?"

"Hey, hey, hey!" Trey interrupted, firmly pushing people back. "Jeez, give her space to breathe."

"Well, then let's hear the details," Shannon said coolly. She was standing farther back with her arms folded. Vivian wasn't surprised that she hadn't pushed her way to the front; Jay and RC weren't even on Shannon's radar. Cato was still the one in her crosshairs.

Vivian crossed her arms over her churning stomach. "It felt . . . re-ally weird. Like . . . I was inside a pitch-black vacuum for a second. There was this pressure pushing against me from every direction, and a really loud roar of wind, and then I was suddenly on the ground."

A girl said dreamily, "So, it was just the two of you together in that dark, secluded place, all alone? So romantic."

Over the instant wave of renewed chatter, Vivian said, "No. He wasn't there. I mean, he was, I guess, but I didn't feel him even though he was holding my hand."

Her answer didn't seem to satisfy anyone; they moved in again, their voices rising into an indiscernible cacophony as the girls jostled her, vying for attention with an endless stream of questions. "That's it!" Vivian cried. "That's all that happened! I already told you everything!"

Finally, to her relief, a teacher pushed her way through the mob. "Okay, that's enough. Back off. Leave her alone."

Reluctantly, the girls dispersed into small groups, still talking, giggling, and fawning over the unexpected arrival of Jay and RC.

"Thank you," Vivian said with a weary but grateful smile.

The teacher inclined her head. "Do you need to go to the nurse?"

She shook her head. "No, I'm getting better. Just a little lightheaded, but I think if I sit down, I'll be fine."

Trey and the teacher guided Vivian to the nearest lunch table. She sank down on the hard bench, relieved to have her feet back on the ground even though her head was still spinning as if gravity hadn't quite realigned everything back into its proper place yet.

The teacher brought her a glass of water and then left them in peace. Trey was excitedly drumming his fingers on the table. Vivian took a few sips, then sighed and said, "I already told you what it felt like to teleport. I don't have anything else to add about the experience."

"I know. It's just . . . really, *really* cool that you got to do it. So, yeah. I'm jealous."

"You sound like you're in Jay's fan club," Vivian teased.

"Not a chance," he disputed. "I'm interested in the scientific study of supernatural phenomena. Jay's fan club is interested in . . . uh, something very different."

Vivian smirked. "Just go get yourself stuck in a tree like a total idiot, and I'm sure he'd be willing to teleport you, too."

She took another drink. Sitting down and sipping water did seem to be helping her queasy stomach settle. "I can't believe I missed all the real excitement. What happened?"

He shrugged. "I can't even say for sure—it all happened really fast. I saw Kit's signal, and then Jay was here before I even had a chance to draw a weapon. RC must have been nearby because he showed up less than a minute later. But as soon as they cornered the ghost, she surrendered. There wasn't even a fight."

"That's weird."

"I don't know," Trey said with a shrug. "Maybe she really did want asylum. She didn't seem to have any interest in harming us or fighting with the Alpha ghosts."

"Speaking of the Alpha ghosts," said a masculine voice. Vivian turned to find Chase Johnson standing behind her with a nauseatingly cocky smirk on his face. He was two grades below Vivian, one above Trey, and the only reason she knew him on speaking terms was due to his past service as a raider. Another boy was lingering like a lackey just behind him. They were both wearing matching letter jackets.

"What about the Alpha ghosts?" Trey snapped, bristling at the unwelcome company.

Chase ignored him and stared directly at Vivian. "You're close with them, right?"

"So what?" Vivian asked coldly.

"I have a request. I mean, not *me* exactly—more of a general request I'm just passing along."

"What?"

"See, here's the thing—I hear a lot of guys talking, and . . . uh, they wonder if Ash might be open to some fashion input. Maybe she could be persuaded to upgrade her athletic look for something a little more . . . like . . . you know."

The boy behind him thrust a comic book over Chase's shoulder and said, "Like this."

The cover depicted a woman drawn with an inhumanly thin waist. She wore a mask over her eyes, a skimpy bikini costume that barely covered her massive breasts and cheeks, high-heeled boots with fur lining the tops, a dagger in a sheath strapped around her upper thigh, wrist gauntlets, absolutely useless plates of armor on her shoulders, and a necklace made of long, sharp teeth.

Vivian folded her arms in disgust. "You mean swapping the combat boots, pants, and sports bra for high heels and a string bikini instead?"

Chase snapped his fingers and pointed at her as if she'd just had an epiphany. "Exactly. You know, like a sexy superhero outfit. For her fans."

The boy behind him sniggered and added, "Or, I wouldn't complain if she wanted to swap her whole outfit for a leotard." He swept his hand in an arc across his chest and added, "Something low cut."

"Or strapless," Chase said.

"You're pigs," Vivian snapped.

"What?" Chase snatched the comic book out of his friend's grip and held it up. "Come on, this is an empowered woman. Strong, fearless, confident, sexy. What's wrong with that?"

"I realize this is a difficult concept for your testosterone-filled pea brains to grasp, but Ash is a real warrior who has to be able to move and fight and kick ass without worrying about popping out of her top or breaking an ankle trying to run in high heels. She's not a comic-book character to prance around for your perverted fantasies, and you're way out of line if you think you're entitled to give her any fashion advice or notes about her body, creep."

The other boy chortled and reclaimed his comic book while Chase smirked but held his hands up innocently. "Hey, I'm just relaying what I've heard other guys saying, that's all."

Trey muttered, "Bullshit," under his breath.

Chase seized the back of his neck and smashed his head down, pinning him to the table. "Something you wanted to say, sidekick?"

"I'm not a sidekick," Trey seethed.

"No? You are from where I'm standing. First you were Phantom's sidekick, and now you're Madison's, but either way—" he leaned down to quietly murmur "—a sidekick is nothing by himself without a real hero around to protect him."

Trey swung without warning, clocking Chase in the head with his elbow and breaking free. Before Chase could recover, Trey twisted and launched himself from his seat, tackling the athlete to the ground and getting in two more solid punches before Chase's friend wrenched Trey away.

"Hey!" Vivian cried as Chase scrambled up and jumped back into the tussle with his teeth bared in rage. "Stop it!"

Like sharks drawn to blood in the water, students converged and surrounded the three wrestling on the ground. "Fight! Fight! Fight! Fight! Fight!" most of them chanted, while some shouted, "Show 'em who's boss, Chase!" or "Hit him back, Trey! Knock his teeth out!"

"*Stop!*" Vivian screamed, her voice lost in the pandemonium.

Even against Chase by himself, Trey was the underdog, but with the two-on-one odds, he didn't stand a chance. He was pinned within seconds, covering his head as the blows rained down on him.

One of the English teachers shoved his way through the crowd. "Hey! That's enough! Break it up!" he commanded, seizing Chase's jacket and pulling him back. The other boy stood up but made sure to get one final kick in before he retreated. "Principal's office, now!"

Mr. Hartwick grabbed both boys' arms and hauled them toward the school as another teacher knelt next to Trey. Now that the action was over, the students dispersed to avoid the risk of being punished as an accessory to the event.

"Are you all right?" Mrs. Dermody asked.

Trey pulled his arm away from his face. "Fine," he muttered, sitting up. His lower lip was split and dripping blood onto his shirt.

Mrs. Dermody helped him rise. "Nurse Renn's office first, then the principal," she said sternly.

Trey touched his lip with a wince, then stared at the blood on his fingers. He shot Vivian a downtrodden look as the history teacher gently but firmly steered him toward the doors.

Vivian didn't see Trey for the rest of the day, and when he didn't show up at his locker after school, she had to assume that he'd been sent home or was still sitting in the principal's office. She lingered by his locker for a few extra minutes just to be sure, then joined the stragglers trailing after the throng of students.

Vivian trotted down the front steps and strolled down the sidewalk at a slow, thoughtful pace. She wasn't used to walking home alone. Trey's absence made her miss the old days when she used to have both Cato and Trey for company. She wondered where Cato was right now.

With Ash, no doubt. Vivian couldn't smother the hot ember of jealousy burning in her chest. After school was supposed to be her time with him, not Ash's. This was supposed to be their walk, just like it used to be.

She shook her head and slowly exhaled through her teeth. *I have to stop thinking like that*, she reminded herself. It wasn't fair, and she knew it. Ash had no idea she was encroaching on a meaningless routine that Vivian considered sacred. And for that matter, neither did Cato. Not with most of his memories obliterated.

Vivian's spirits sank even lower. She sighed and let her gaze wander the residential street. To her surprise, a teenager was walking farther ahead, a black cloak clasped around his neck. For a split second, she thought it was Cato, and her heart soared. She opened her mouth to call out to him, then hesitated.

He was walking alone—without Ash. And he hadn't approached her. And, now that she looked closer, his black hair was too long. His relaxed stride didn't match her brother's usual cautious gait, and he seemed to have a dangerous, repulsive aura that evaporated her joyful salutation before it even left her throat.

Vivian had to do a double take to confirm it really was Axel. Yesterday when she had seen him, he was half-mad, muttering to himself, pacing, and keeping a wide berth from people. He'd looked deathly ill with pale, sweaty skin that hung from his bones and dark circles shadowing his crazed eyes. Now, he was alert and healthy, the dark circles gone, the hollows in his body filled out, and his eyes bright red again.

She jogged across the street, determined to connect somehow with Cato's moody lab-brother. She'd made progress with Kit today, after all. Why stop there?

"Hey, Axel," she greeted warmly, drawing nearer and stopping on the sidewalk. "Wow, you look so much better today! We missed you at dinner last night."

The half-breed rolled his eyes. "I doubt that. And the answer is no," he snapped, never breaking stride.

Vivian frowned and jogged after him, matching his pace. "No what? I haven't asked you for anything."

"You know, most humans stay away when they see me walking down the street. You're the only idiot stupid enough to follow and annoy the hell out of me. I'm not interested in bonding with you."

"Who says I wanted to bond? Maybe I just wanted to chat."

Axel arched an eyebrow, watching her from the corner of his eye as they walked. His transformation from yesterday was truly astounding. "Vivian," he said with mockingly overabundant patience, "the best liar in the Realm can't fool me, and you're a terrible liar to begin with."

She huffed indignantly. "I'm not lying! I really would like to get to know you better."

He sneered. "I'm not as easy to win over as Kit. A piece of advice—try a few intermediate steps and work your way up the list. Go bother Jay; seems like he's able to tolerate you."

"C'mon, Axel. You're Cato's lab-brother, I'm Cato's blood-sister, and I think we should make an effort to get to know each other better. If you won't do it for me, will you do it for Cato?"

Axel chuckled, but the sound wasn't of amusement. It was bitter and scornful. "Is that really the best you could come up with?"

Unfortunately, yes, Vivian thought glumly, her fists clenching.

"Uh-oh, I'm making you mad," Axel mused.

"What are you, a Mind-Reader?"

"No."

Vivian's eyes widened. "Are you an Empath? Is that your divine power?"

"Bloody Scout, how many times do I have to tell you I don't have a Divinity before it sinks into your empty head? I don't need the power to read your emotions because they're written all over your face for any-one who knows how to read it."

Vivian stepped in front of him and halted. She'd expected him to stop or turn—any of the other Alpha ghosts would have avoided direct contact—but he didn't deviate from his course, forcing her to put out her hands.

She'd never expected to touch him; she gasped when her palms met his chest. A strange current of energy made goose bumps rise on her skin. He was solid muscle. She pushed, hoping to make him stop walk-ing, but she might as well have been pushing a brick wall because Axel never even faltered. "Talk to me, Axel," she pleaded, walking back-ward.

"You're wasting your time," Axel snapped, eyes flashing. For a brief second, red ectoplasm crackled around him—raw and uncon-trolled. Vivian let go, stumbling away from him in surprise. He hadn't hurt her, just startled her.

Axel narrowed his eyes, finally halting and crossing his arms. "I scare you."

Vivian swallowed. "No, you don't," she denied, although she real-ized too late that her chin dipped and her gaze fell to the side when she spoke.

"You liked me better when you thought I was blind and helpless, right?" He tauntingly mimicked, "Listen, Axel, if you're lost and you can't find the other Alpha ghosts, I can help you. I can lead you back to Wes's house."

She mutely shook her head in denial, but Axel continued in a dark, serious voice, "Now, you don't know what I am exactly, but it doesn't matter because we both know I could rip you into bloody pieces in less than a second and it would be too easy. You don't really want to get close to me; you're trying to convince Cato that you accept us even though the truth is that I terrify you."

"Okay," Vivian whispered. "Yes, sometimes, you scare me. But . . . I trust Cato's judgment, and he trusts you."

Axel cocked his head, studying her. "Cato used to talk about you."

She straightened. "Really?"

"Sure . . . when he first came to Alpha. It killed him that you never made contact. Literally. He almost succeeded in taking his own life. It was hard to watch, and I didn't even like him back then."

She winced. "It wasn't my fault."

"Of course it wasn't," Axel snapped. "It never is, right? It amazes me how quick humans are to shuffle the blame onto somebody else."

Vivian squeezed her eyes shut. His words stung. He had a talent for that, she was quickly realizing. He seemed to know exactly which words to choose that would nettle the most, and then he could read body language to gauge how effective his statement had been and alter his approach if it didn't have the desired effect. She whispered, "What should I have done? I thought my little brother was dead."

"Don't start crying."

"Why are you such a jerk? I'm going out of my way to be nice to you."

"Then maybe you should just leave me alone."

"Like it or not, you aren't Cato's only family. I was his sister long before you were his brother."

Axel's glare was cold and steady. "Oh, I get it. You feel threatened because Cato has a whole new life now and you haven't been a part of it."

"Or maybe *you* feel threatened because you've had Cato all to yourself for the last few years, and now you have to share him with people who loved him way before you ever met him."

Axel smirked. "Give me a break."

"Did I hit a nerve?" Vivian challenged.

"Nope. Unlike you, I got no problem sharing Cato."

"Me either."

"Oh yeah? You're awful defensive. You want Cato? You can have him. I don't care."

Vivian scowled. "Do you care about anybody other than yourself?"

"Mmm . . . not really, no."

Sensing he was about to leave her, she begged, "Axel, please. I'm trying to be your friend."

The half-breed's eyebrows shot up as he appraised her standing in front of him. She'd caught him off guard for only a second, and then the sneer reappeared. "You remember when Jay sacrificed himself to save you?"

Her body turned cold when she remembered the feeling of a blade to her throat. Vivian nodded. "Yeah. I owe him my life."

Axel leaned closer and whispered, "If it were up to me, I would have let you die."

Before she had time to answer, he was gone. Vivian stood where she was, although she felt as if Axel had taken the ground with him and now she was falling into the black abyss where Jay had taken her when they Blinked.

***

Madison knocked assertively on the door. "Come in," said a woman's voice.

She twisted the knob and opened the door to the principal's office. Trey was sitting in a chair looking rather forlorn and wretched. His parents were seated on either side of him.

Principal Solwitz stood up from behind her desk. "Madison," she greeted monotonously. "So glad you could join us."

"I wish it were under better circumstances," Madison replied. She glowered at her apprentice, who practically withered under her stern glare.

Trey's mom said, "We thought you should be here for this conversation."

Kaitlyn Selman was a soft-spoken woman. She had long, straight blonde hair and petite features, but her eyes glinted with an intelligent stare that seemed to analyze everyone and everything. Tom Selman was an average man who spoke very little but whose words carried great weight when he chose to use them. He wore thick rectangular glasses and had wavy light-brown hair, and Trey's facial structure bore a striking resemblance to his father's.

The Selmans had never been overly thrilled about their son's apprenticeship, but they held the unwavering belief that children should have the right to choose their own path, make their own mistakes, and find their own success without parental dictatorship interfering. They generally preferred to stay out of the ghost-hunting part of Trey's life even though it was such an important piece.

Madison folded her arms. "This is a first, Trey," she said crossly. "I didn't expect to be summoned to the principal's office to deal with trouble from my apprentice instead of my kids. I'm so disappointed in you."

Trey hung his head. "Chase started it," he muttered under his breath.

Principal Solwitz sat down again and laced her fingers together on top of the desk. "I wanted your input because I have concerns about Trey's exemption to carry weapons at school. I want to hear your thoughts on whether or not you still think he's responsible enough to remain armed at all times."

"But I didn't draw a weapon!" Trey protested. "I would never use any of my ghost-hunting weapons against a human."

"Mr. Johnson claims otherwise."

"He's lying—"

The principal held up her hand. "I know. Dozens of students and two teachers at the scene testified that at no point did they ever see you draw a weapon."

"Then what's the problem?" Trey grumbled.

Tom replied in a cutting voice, "The problem is your clear lapse in judgment."

"Exactly," said Principal Solwitz. "If you couldn't demonstrate enough self-control to stop yourself from getting into a fistfight with another student, how can you convince me that you'll be able to restrain yourself from using a weapon the next time someone antagonizes you? It was with great reluctance that I agreed to let you be armed at school as an extra defensive measure to protect your fellow students. But now I'm not sure if you're responsible enough to handle this trust."

Kaitlyn turned slightly in her chair and softly inquired, "As his trainer and supervisor, what do you think, Madison?"

Trey complained, "Don't I get a chance to plead my case?"

"No," said Tom. "Your actions have already spoken for you."

Madison tapped her finger on her biceps, staring at her apprentice as she considered. "I agree that he demonstrated poor judgment today. Getting into a fight with a student was beyond stupid, Trey. You're going to run laps for it during your next training session."

She exhaled, still contemplating. "But I do think it's noteworthy that he didn't draw a weapon during the fight even though he was outmatched. He easily could have. Considering that the school has already had threats from ghosts and Trey has actively defended his peers, my recommendation would be to continue the arrangement and let him remain armed with nonlethal weapons under a probation period. Any more fights with students, and that's it. No more second chances."

Principal Solwitz leaned back in her chair. "You agree?" she asked his parents.

Kaitlyn replied, "I don't think we're in any position to make that judgment call. As far as punishment for fighting at school goes, we'll certainly be handling that at home, but this issue at hand comes down to the school's weapon policy and Madison's recommendation as Trey's ghost-hunting master."

"Mr. Selman," Principal Solwitz said as she leaned forward again, "I want to make sure that you understand the effects of your actions. I did not come to the decision to let you carry weapons at school lightly. I didn't want students to be armed because teenagers aren't exactly renowned for making the most rational decisions, as evidenced today. But I thought your extra training and discipline would justify making you an exception, and Madison vouched for you. So did your parents. All three of them signed a waiver granting their permission and assurance that you, as a ghost hunter's apprentice, would act responsibly and help to protect this school. Your poor judgment reflects back on them for vouching on your behalf. Do you understand?"

"Yes, ma'am," Trey murmured, hanging his head in shame.

The principal opened one of her desk drawers, pulled a paper out of a folder, and set it down on the desk. "And it looks like they're going to vouch for you again even though I'm not completely convinced you deserve it. You don't get three strikes, Mr. Selman. You get one, and you've already used it. You're on probation. The next time you turn your aggression on a human, whether that human is a student, a faculty member, or any other citizen, I'm revoking your exception to the weapon policy. I don't care if you draw your weapon during the conflict or not. Have I made myself clear?"

"Yes, ma'am."

"Good. I don't want to see you back in this office again." She set a pen on top of the paper and slid them across the desk to Trey's mom.

Kaitlyn picked up the pen and stared at the document for a moment, then turned her head to gaze solemnly at Trey. "Do you understand that there are consequences for your actions?"

He nodded.

"This is an enormous responsibility we're granting you. Do I have your word that I can trust you?"

"Yes, Mom. I promise. I'll be responsible."

She stared at him for several more uncomfortable seconds. "I certainly hope so," she muttered, turning back toward the desk and scooting forward in her chair so she could sign her name with swooping pen strokes. Kaitlyn passed the paper down to her husband, who signed without a word and threw the pen back down on the desk to make his anger clear.

Madison stepped forward and picked up the pen. She pressed the tip to the paper, poised to sign, and yet she didn't move. Her eyes shifted to glance sidelong at Trey. "I'm really sorry," he murmured, peering up at her with his head bowed. "I won't let you down again."

Madison shook her head. "We'll see, won't we?" She scrawled her name and slid the paper and pen back to the principal, who also signed and dated the document.

Principal Solwitz filed the paper back in her desk drawer, then gave Trey a wintery smile and said, "I'll be seeing you in detention after school for the next couple of weeks, starting Monday."

Trey sighed, his shoulders slumping. "Yes, ma'am."

She stood up, as did his parents. Trey remained seated while they shook hands with the principal, and then he meekly rose and trailed after Madison and his parents into the hall. He was a solemn and silent shadow in their wake.

"Not how you were planning to spend your afternoon, I'm sure," said Kaitlyn. "I know you have your hands full with your own kids. But we did feel that it was important to have you be a part of this."

"No, I understand," Madison said quickly. "I chose to take Trey on as an apprentice; I agreed to be responsible for him."

Tom said, "Well, don't go too easy on him. You have our permission to punish him as you see fit. Feel free to make him run laps until he pukes or passes out." Madison smirked and nodded.

"You know," said Kaitlyn, "I'm surprised that Cato hasn't dropped by yet. I know the boys were usually at your house rather than ours, but still, Cato was so close with Trey that he was almost like a second son. I keep expecting him to pop in and say hi."

"He's having a hard time readjusting," Madison admitted.

"Well, he's always welcome in our home. As are you and Vivian. We'd be happy to have your family over for dinner sometime."

"Thank you. I appreciate the invitation."

Kaitlyn tenderly touched Madison's arm. "I can tell you're under a lot of stress. If you ever need any help, please let us know. You've given Trey so much support over the last few years—it's the least we can do."

A rush of emotion swelled inside Madison's chest and threatened to manifest in the form of tears. She nodded and blinked to keep them at bay. "Thank you," she said again.

— Chapter Twenty-Five —

Kin

Ash swung her staff at me with a quick, precise cutting motion, but when I blocked it with my ice blades, the impact wasn't as hard as I was expecting.

"You're holding back," I accused.

"Well, I don't get why you want to spar anyway."

I went on the offensive, slashing out and forcing her to back up as she blocked my attacks. "Because I've missed a lot of training, and Jay's kicking my ass for it," I said through gritted teeth. "I need the extra practice."

She ducked my last blow and swung; I had overreached with my strike and wasn't in a position to block. In a last-ditch defensive move, I formed ice on the left side of my head a split second before her metal staff made contact and shattered my impromptu armor.

The impact sent me to my knees and made my ears ring. I stared at the chunks of ice in the grass as my vision swam in and out of focus.

"Oh, yes, I see your point," Ash teased.

"Yeah. Funny," I muttered, rubbing the throbbing point of contact across the side of my head. *I should have used intangibility, not ice.*

"Hey, you're the one who told me to stop holding back, remember?"

"I know." I cupped my hands together, summoned my Divinity to form ice, and then melted it as I lifted my hands to my mouth and drank.

Ash twirled her staff in one hand and then smoothly slipped it into her harness. "You've been distracted these last couple of weeks."

"No kidding." I fell back into the gravel and dry grass and stared up at the clouds. We were in an empty lot in the outskirts where we wouldn't disturb anyone with our fight . . . and where we wouldn't be disturbed, either. "Please don't tell me that you're here to listen if I want to talk about it. I'm getting really tired of people saying that."

"Okay." She knelt next to me. "We don't have to talk. We can sit here in silence and enjoy the Outside, or we can keep sparring, or we can go to the park and walk around the lake. Whatever you want."

"You don't like being near the lake."

"But you do."

I studied my lab-sister out of the corner of my eye. The laced edges of her pants showed off wide swathes of pale skin all the way from the tops of her outer thighs, along the sides of her legs, and down to her boots. Her muscular abdomen was rising and falling with heavy breaths after our workout.

I still couldn't understand why the sight of Ash's bare stomach and legs seemed to have offended my blood-sister. Was I missing something because I was used to seeing Ash in sweatpants and a sports bra? "Hey. Have you had a chance to talk with Viv yet? Get to know her?"

Ash shot me a funny look. "No. Why?"

I shook my head and directed my gaze skyward. "No reason, really. I just want you two to get along."

"Why? Did she say something? Does she not like me?"

"No. It's just that . . . I see you both as my sisters, and it would mean a lot to me if you were on friendly terms with each other. That's all."

"We're not on unfriendly terms with each other. Isn't that enough?" At my silence, Ash let out a sigh. "Look, Cato . . . you may be my lab-brother, but Vivian being your blood-sister doesn't mean that she's a part of our family by default."

"No, I know that," I said quickly. "I don't expect you to embrace her as a sister. I was just hoping that maybe you could see her as a friend. And she could see you as one."

She folded her arms. "I can't promise that. But I don't have any issues with Vivian. As long as she's on good terms with you, I respect her."

I closed my eyes. *I wish Vivian could reciprocate that sentiment.* "Thank you."

In the distance, City Hall's bell tower announced the top of the hour. My shift. I stood up with a groan, my head still pounding from the rude introduction to the wrong end of Ash's staff.

"I'll come with you," Ash said as she rose. "I need a drink after that match."

"All right. Race you back!" I challenged with a grin. I took off before Ash could react.

In my wake, she called, "Seriously?" But even without looking back, I knew she was pursuing me.

I couldn't help but laugh. It felt so good to run, to let my body stretch itself out at full speed with nothing in my way and nothing holding me back. There wasn't room to run in the Arena—not like this. This was what freedom felt like.

Ash kept pace on my heels the whole way. We dashed down streets, leapt over hedges, and skirted confused people, occasionally making eye contact with each other and smiling when one of us pulled slightly ahead.

By the time we reached the homestretch and were propelling ourselves neck and neck up the front lawn toward Saros Manor, we were both gasping for breath. Ash broke away to skirt the landscape bed of weeds edging the pavers, but I maintained course and leapt over it.

Madison was standing on the wide porch with a precariously balanced stack of boxes and bags in her arms. She turned when she heard us approach. Ash and I both reached out for the railing at the base of the stairs as we charged forward, and— "I win!" I crowed triumphantly when my hand made contact half a second before hers.

Ash doubled over with her hands on her knees as I collapsed on the porch steps. "You . . . cheated . . . with that . . . head . . . start," she said between gasps, but she was still grinning.

I didn't have enough oxygen left in my brain to think of a comeback even if I'd been able to force any words out. Madison smiled and said, "That was a close one. She gave you a run for your money, Cato."

She awkwardly tried to shift the boxes into one arm so she could seize the handle on the door, only to jump with a startled gasp when a figure phased through and stepped onto the porch. "Oh! Axel, you startled me. Would you mind opening the door for me? I would really appreciate it."

Axel froze in his tracks. He glanced back at the double doors, then at Madison holding the teetering armful of boxes and bags, and then his face hardened. "I'm not your servant."

"Axel!" Madison cried in disbelief, but he strode past and proceeded down the walkway without a look back.

Ash scrambled up the stairs and said, "I got it, Mrs. Tarrow," as I labored to my feet and relieved the top two boxes from my mother's stack so her load was lighter.

"Thank you," Madison said. She entered the foyer with me trailing behind. Ash closed the door behind us.

"What is all this stuff?" I asked, peering curiously into the box on top.

"Groceries," she replied, turning left into the dining room. Ash and I followed. "I definitely wouldn't be able to afford feeding so many people every day, so we can thank Wes for the generous meal budget. It takes a lot of food to make these big dinners."

She turned around so she could back through the swinging door. Ash followed and held the door open behind my mother so it didn't swing back and hit me.

Madison dropped her load of groceries down on the island with more force than necessary. "I swear," she muttered, "that boy is testing my patience on purpose. I've been trying really hard to get along with Axel."

Ash ducked her head and skirted my mother to grab a couple of glasses out of the cabinet and avoid the conversation. I set my groceries down on the counter. "He has a bad habit of lashing out when he's frustrated or uncomfortable," I said. "Don't take it personally."

"All I did was ask him to open a door," Madison fired back over the sound of running water. "Excuse me for inconveniencing him." She started unpacking a box and slamming packages of food down on the countertop with a little more force than necessary.

I gave her a stern look to let her know that I didn't appreciate the sarcastic tone. "I understand your frustration. But you need to remember that Axel went from being a normal kid to suddenly being so strong that he could knock down a building with his bare hands. I know that was half a lifetime ago for him, but he never had the opportunity to master that strength when he was locked in a cage. He has a hard time opening doors without ripping them off their hinges, which is why he usually phases through instead."

Madison paused to give me a somber look over her shoulder as Ash handed me a full glass of water. I paused to take a drink, then finished, "Axel's pride was at risk. He'd rather let you be angry with him than face the embarrassment of letting you see his lapse of control."

"Maybe," she reluctantly conceded. "But he still hates me."

I drained my glass to avoid answering because she was correct—Axel did indeed loathe my mother. Everything about her, from her profession as a ghost hunter to the human blood flowing through her veins.

Madison was no fool to my evasive tactic. "Okay," she said forcefully, "then tell me how to earn Axel's respect."

Ash scoffed, then immediately blushed under my mother's attention. "I'm sorry. I didn't mean to sound disrespectful. It's just . . . there's not exactly a secret to earning Axel's respect. Either he thinks you're worthy, or he doesn't. He didn't like Cato when he first met him, either."

She held out her hand, and I passed her my empty glass for a refill. "Axel and I have a complicated relationship because I'm a hybrid," I admitted. "If you're ever going to earn his respect, you'll have to stop being human first."

Madison frowned. "Stop being . . . ? Oh. I see. You're saying nothing I do is going to change the fact that I'm human."

I nodded. "Axel will always hold that against you. There's just no getting around it."

"But I don't understand why he seems to blame me personally."

"We don't know what happened to Axel in Project Delta. All we know is that he survived hell at the hands of humankind. *They* really messed him up."

"What can I do to stay on his good side?"

Ash handed me a second glass of water. I stared at it for a moment of consideration before I answered, "I guess just give him space. And never give him orders."

Madison shook her head. "That's what I've been doing, and he still hates me."

"I know. I wish I could give you better advice. It takes a while to learn how to read Axel, and the harder you push him, the more likely he is to rebel. I think the best you can hope for is mutual coexistence."

Officer Jana let her miserable gaze wander the stone walls. No windows—only veins of iridescent lumenite crystals casting an eerily beautiful blue light on the interrogation room. A large cluster of crystals glowed on either side of the metal door.

Lieutenant Cisco set a steaming cup of herbal tea before her. She glanced at it but made no move to take it. "No thank you."

He pulled out the chair across from her and took a seat. "I must insist."

"I'm not thirsty."

"As your commander, I'm ordering you to drink it."

Her gaze snapped to the wooden cup, then lifted angrily to Cisco. "This is humiliating," she seethed. "I'm a loyal Shadow Guard. I have nothing to hide." She snatched the cup and lifted it to her lips. As she'd suspected, she tasted the bitter undertones of veritas root in the blend—an ingredient that had a tendency to scramble a liar's thoughts but leave the drinker clearheaded if telling the truth.

She drained the cup and slammed it down on the tabletop.

Cisco, as laid-back as ever, leaned back in his chair and set his boots on the table as he folded his arms behind his head. "It's protocol.

Nothing personal. I know you're a good officer."

"Then why am I locked in an interrogation room? Is Veto on his way to torture me?"

"No, of course not," said Cisco, the furrows in his brow indicating genuine surprise at the question. "We're having a private, one-on-one chat between a lieutenant and an officer. You're not in trouble. I just need to ask you some questions."

Jana slumped in her chair. "About my sister?"

"About her son."

She clenched her fists and scowled at the empty wooden cup. "That *thing* you confronted in Cröendor was not my kin."

"And you're absolutely certain, beyond the shadow of a doubt?"

"Yes."

Cisco was silent while he pondered. Finally, he asked, "What was Axel's Divinity?"

"It hadn't developed yet. He was a late bloomer. But that's normal with Remotes; it's a unique power that requires intense focus and meditation—not something a child can master or even tap into until the mind has had several years to develop. I didn't get my Divinity until I had seven years. Vera had eight when she found hers."

"The creature I Sensed was very powerful but didn't have a Divinity. You don't think it's possible the Agents took Axel and manipulated his body to make him stronger? Whatever they did to corrupt him likely prevented his Divinity from manifesting if it was still dormant."

When Jana didn't answer, Cisco added, "The age seemed to match the years Axel would have by now. That seems like an incredible coincidence."

Jana glowered at Cisco for several loud heartbeats in the otherwise-silent room before she bent down and opened a satchel at her feet. She pulled out a child-sized cloak and set it on the table. "I bought this for Axel in his fifth year. It was his favorite cloak. After Azar told me that he suspected Axel was alive, I tried to find him remotely by focusing on this. I found nothing. Only the same blackness and emptiness I saw when I searched for Vera with *this*."

She snapped a gold locket off her neck and tossed it carelessly onto the table. It slid past the cup and settled to a stop near Cisco, who swung his feet to the floor and leaned forward to pick it up. The lieutenant pinched the thin chain between his fingers and lifted the locket so it spun slowly in front of his face.

"Is it possible," he said, "that your Divinity isn't working on Axel because he's changed so much from the person you remember?"

Jana shrugged and stared at the small cloak. Her throat clenched in sorrow when she remembered how Axel's face had lit up with joy the first time he'd held it. *"Will you please fasten it for me?"* he'd asked, holding it up and smiling at her.

She reached out and stroked the forest-green fabric between her thumb and forefinger. "I didn't look for them when they fled," she said hoarsely. "I didn't want to know where they were."

That's the veritas root talking, she realized. That little truth had slipped out. She gripped the cloak tighter and added, "But if I'd been given the order, I would have found them and brought them to justice."

"I know." Cisco set the locket down on the table and leveled an impassive stare at Jana. "That's why I didn't give you the order."

Jana frowned, puzzled. "Sir?"

"I knew you had the potential to be a good officer, but you would have lost your rank if your sister was convicted of a crime, even a minor one. Promoting you to the rank of officer reaped higher benefits than chasing your sister and her family into Cröendor for a relatively insignificant transgression."

Cisco sighed and rubbed his neatly trimmed beard. "Well, this conversation has been inconclusive."

Jana reached out to reclaim the locket. "What happens to me now?"

He set his hands on the table and stood up with a quiet sigh. "You're free to go. Your assignments will likely be constrained to Szion for now, though. This isn't a punishment, simply a precaution."

He opened the door. "If I may offer a little friendly advice? I suggest you do your best to keep a low profile. I suspect Rayven will have eyes on you."

— Chapter Twenty-Six —
Ear for an Eye

Jay's nightmare-induced thrashing woke me in the early hours of dawn.

I yawned, but before I had a chance to wake him, he bolted upright with a quiet cry that roused Ash, RC, and Kit.

Jay was still shivering from his nightmare. He yanked his shirt off, his hands roving across his bare skin as if searching for something. "Do I have scars on my back?" he asked hoarsely.

I squinted in the faint gray light. "I don't see any."

"A-are you sure?" Jay's fingers kept moving as he tried to find scars that didn't exist. Kit rose and stood behind Jay. She gently pressed both hands on his back. "No scars," she said.

Ash asked, "Are you okay?"

He wasn't feeling his back anymore, but he kept his arms wrapped around his body as if hugging himself. "Weird dream. I was falling out of the sky."

Kit knelt and rested her cheek against Jay's back to comfort him. He wiped his brow, then patted Kit's knee and reached for his shirt. "Let's train," he said.

A gentle rain had fallen throughout the night, ushering in a cloudy, humid morning. The temperature was warmer than I would have preferred, but I appreciated the moisture in the air—plenty of my sister element to work with. The dew soaked my boots and the bottom of my cloak.

Jay kept our training light, which was a welcome relief after a brutal game of All-On-One last night that had left us all lying bruised, sore, and exhausted on the ground with Jay standing mostly untouched and barely out of breath. My muscles were still tight until the morning exercises loosened them up.

The teams separated to scout Phantom Heights, and the morning passed without any notable incidents. As noon approached, Jay found Ash and me scouting the abandoned outskirts near our old Home. "I'd like the two of you to come to town square," he requested. "RC's already there."

"Why?" I asked, my stomach immediately dropping with dread. "Is something wrong? Is Phantom Heights under attack?"

"No, it's nothing like that," Jay said with a dismissive wave of his hand. "Ero wants to bring Finn and Reese downtown for their lesson today so they can practice singling out individual minds from a crowd."

"Okay," Ash said slowly, dragging out the word. "But why do you need us?"

Jay shrugged and rubbed the back of his neck. "Because I'm being overprotective. I trust Ero to keep Finn and Reese safe, but Azar made it very clear that he wants them. They know a lot of classified information. I'd just feel better if we're all nearby to keep watch and make sure they're safe."

I nodded. "I don't think that's unreasonable. We'll head downtown and meet you there."

"Thanks," he said, inclining his head just before he vanished.

Ash twirled her staff in one hand as we started walking in the direction of City Hall. "You don't actually think Azar would launch an attack just to kidnap Finn and Reese, do you?" she said.

"I don't know. I do understand why Jay's nervous, though. Better to be safe than sorry. If any Shadow Guards do try to attack the twins, they'll have to get past Ero and Axel, plus the rest of us. Not great odds, and I'm betting Azar knows that."

Ash was quiet for another block before she said, "I've had a bad feeling ever since the battle. Phantom Heights seems a little . . . I don't know. Too quiet. You know what I mean?"

"Yeah. I've noticed, too."

"Remember how many ghosts were here when we first arrived? Trying to sneak around without being detected was almost impossible. Now, it almost feels like that tense, foreboding calm right before a severe storm hits."

"I know. I can't help but wonder what Azar's planning. There's no way he gave up just because we killed some of his Shadow Guards." I clenched my fists and stared straight ahead. "We just have to train and stay on guard for his next move so we can be ready."

Ash fell into a grim silence. We kept a casual pace all the way to town square, where we found the rest of our lab-family. Finn and Reese, both wearing face masks in public as an extra measure of protection for their compromised immune systems, were seated on the bottom step of City Hall with Ero. Their lesson had already begun; Ero was pointing to one of many humans milling around town square to indicate which mind he wanted his students to focus on.

At the top of the stairs, Jay was leaning against one of the stone columns, RC was sitting on the steps, and Axel was lying on his back with his arms folded behind his head. Kit was the only one missing, likely keeping watch over the school.

Ash and I trotted up the steps. Jay watched us approach, but RC frowned and turned his head away, as if irritated by our arrival. Without looking at us, Axel grumbled, "Prepare to be bored out of your mind for a few hours."

Jay replied, "It won't be that long. I think this is a strenuous exercise for them."

"Besides," RC shot back, "how is this different from how you usually spend your days?"

I sat down on the step next to him as Ash seated herself a step below us. Our presence here hadn't gone unnoticed; just about every human in town square was either directly staring at us or practicing a little more subtlety by giving us sidelong glances.

I watched Ero speak to his students, waving his arms and gesturing at different people as he talked. Finn and Reese nodded occasionally.

"Hey, Ax," I said quietly to make sure my voice didn't carry.

"Have you sensed any changes in Finn and Reese since they started training with Ero? Are they getting any more powerful?"

He rolled his head to the side so he could study them. "Nope. Bot's at the same power level as before. As far as I can tell, they haven't tapped into any new telepathic abilities."

Jay snapped, "Axel, don't call them Bot. You know I don't like that nickname."

"Why? It's accurate, and they don't seem to mind."

"I still don't like it."

Axel rolled his eyes and then closed them. "Whatever. Ero was wrong. They're not Telepaths, and these lessons are a waste of time."

"I disagree," Jay said, balancing a dagger on the tip of his finger and spinning it. "Ero was upfront in the beginning and said he didn't know if their Divinities would ever evolve, but that doesn't mean these lessons aren't worthwhile. He can still help them hone their mind-reading skills so they have more control. And besides that, I think he's a good mentor for them."

I raised an eyebrow and said, "Hey, isn't that Kit's dagger?"

"It is," Jay said with a smirk as he tossed the dagger up and caught the handle. "I traded with her to get it. Kit-Kat drives a hard bargain, let me tell you. Pretty sure she made out a lot better than I did."

Axel's eyes flew open. "Ah, things are finally getting more interesting," he said as he sat up, his attention on the fence surrounding the Rip.

Jay sheathed the dagger in his boot, fully alert. "What is it? The Shadow Guard?"

"Nah, not that interesting."

I shivered; a ghost was in range. Ash, RC, and I scrambled to our feet. Jay Blinked to the foot of the steps in front of Finn, Reese, and Ero to protect them.

Ash and RC were already armed. I formed a pair of ice daggers in my hands as I descended the stairs with my lab-siblings to join Jay. The ghost had to be close for us to sense it. Axel had been looking at the Rip, so that was where my attention was even though he stayed in place at the top of the stairs.

The humans noticed our defensive formation around the twins and hastened to clear the square in anticipation of trouble. The officers on patrol shifted into their own formation with weapons drawn and aimed at the Rip, but they seemed to be waiting for us to take the lead since the threat hadn't revealed itself yet.

I tightened my grip on my ice weapons. It would've been helpful if Axel had been a little more illuminative. Was one ghost coming, or a whole group? It wasn't the Shadow Guard, but that didn't mean the threat wasn't real, and I wasn't sure what to prepare for.

I detected movement within the faint shimmer where the Realms were connected. At first, I couldn't tell if the dark smudge was really there or if my eyes were playing paranoid tricks. But it seemed to be growing darker, and then it materialized into a strange form as something emerged into the Human Realm.

I held my breath, staring at the visitor in bewilderment for several long seconds before I finally understood why the figure seemed to walk on two legs but didn't appear to be humanoid. It was hunkered behind a tall black shield with a silver carving of a tree on the surface. Apparently, the ghost had anticipated a confrontation with the patrol guarding the Rip.

When no shots rang out, he slowly lowered the shield enough for his glowing red eyes to peer over the edge.

Jay strode assertively across the square, holding up one hand to signal the patrol not to open fire. I stepped into his place so I was in front of the twins with Ash and RC flanking me.

"Turn around and go back," Jay said as he halted a short distance from the stranger. "This is your only chance for a peaceful retreat."

The ghost, seeming to realize that he wasn't under immediate attack and had the opportunity to partake in a civilized conversation, lowered his shield to the side.

I narrowed my eyes. Something seemed eerily familiar about the young man standing inside the fence. He was tan and lanky with the stubble of an immature beard emerging. His dark hair had natural loose curls that blew across his red eyes in the summer breeze. Why did he look so familiar? Had I met this man before?

The stranger looked Jay up and down. "I didn't come here to fight you, and you aren't the one I want," he said. His gaze wandered beyond Jay to survey the rest of us. "I'm looking for RC."

Beside me, my lab-brother stiffened with a faint gasp. I frowned and looked at him in confusion as he gazed at the newcomer with wide, disbelieving eyes. "Emmett?" he said uncertainly.

The ghost shook his head in apparent disappointment and became intangible as he stepped through the metal links. His shield had disappeared somehow. It wasn't on the ground, and it wasn't on his arm or his back, and it wasn't leaning against the fence. I was so confused. Who was this guy? Despite intentionally seeking RC out, he didn't seem thrilled or relieved to have found my lab-brother. Was he an ally or an enemy?

Jay teleported back to us as Emmett strode toward our group. "So, still alive, are you?" said the newcomer. "Nice scar, by the way."

RC, normally calm and focused when facing an opponent, seemed to wilt into a smaller and meeker version of himself as Emmett approached. My lab-brother glanced around nervously and demanded, "What are you doing here?"

"What am *I* doing here? What are *you* doing here?"

RC lowered his voice with embarrassment as he muttered, "Let's, uh . . . let's go somewhere else and talk."

Emmett halted in front of us and crossed his arms. "There's nothing to talk about. I came to take you home."

"I'm not going home."

Emmett's eyes narrowed into a spiteful glare. "And I'm not going back without you."

"RC," Axel interrupted from above with an uncharacteristically sweet tone to indicate his annoyance at being excluded. "Who the fuck is this?"

RC hung his head in shame. Emmett redirected his icy glower onto Axel. "His brother, if that's any of your business. Who the fuck are *you?*"

Axel smirked at Emmett and coolly replied, "His brother."

Emmett laughed, as if Axel had just told a joke.

I felt as if someone had yanked the ground out from under me. No wonder Emmett looked so familiar. Now I saw it—the shape of his face was so similar to RC's, and his tan skin was almost the same tone, and even his posture and the way he carried himself was reminiscent. Erase RC's scar and change his eyes from violet to red, and Emmett could have been a glimpse at RC's future self. We all turned to stare in shell shock at our lab-brother, who refused to look at any of us.

Jay finally forced out, "You have a blood-brother?"

Emmett taunted, "What's the matter, RC? You never talked about me? I'm insulted."

RC stepped down onto the cobblestones and said urgently, "Emmett, please. Go home and pretend you never saw me, okay?"

"Not a chance. Father knows you're here. He sent me to get you."

RC turned a sickly ashen shade. He shook his head and pleaded, "I can't go home."

Emmett took a hostile step forward. "What am I supposed to do, leave you on your own to continue embarrassing our family?"

He took another step, and RC retreated from his blood-brother as he stammered, "Father . . . h-he never has to know that you found me."

"You know what your problem is? You were always so weak, *little* brother."

"No—"

"You're a coward."

"I'm not!"

"You ran away."

"But it wasn't my—"

"Stop whining and making excuses! Father and I were glad to be rid of you until a few days ago when a Shadow Guard knocked on our door. You're a *fugitive*, RC! Azar has a price on your head! Do you have any idea how humiliated Father was? He sent me here to find out if it was really you, and I gotta say, we were both hoping that Shadow

Guard was wrong."

"RC," Jay began.

He waved his hand and snapped, "Stay out of this." Louder, he proclaimed, "Emmett, you need to leave. Right now. I mean it."

"Not without you," Emmett said. "If I have to drag you back with me, I will."

RC had a disk clenched in his hand. He turned slightly and backed away from his blood-brother, parallel to City Hall's steps. He was putting distance between us in case this confrontation turned violent. "Please. I don't want to fight you."

Emmett laughed. "Because you'll lose, like always?"

RC flung his disk in a quick streak of silver. The blades embedded with a *thud* into Emmett's black shield, which I'd assumed from a distance to be metal but was definitely some other kind of material that had caught the disk instead of deflecting it. The large kite shield was at least three feet in height, maybe more. It seemed to have materialized out of nowhere in time to block RC's warning shot, which, based on where it landed, would have just missed Emmett if he hadn't stopped it.

Emmett remained calm and collected as he lowered his arm to study the disk. With a smirk, he rested the shield on the ground and plucked RC's disk from its surface. "Neat toy, little brother." He dropped it onto the cobblestones. Without warning, he threw four small blades I never even saw him draw.

RC seemed to have expected a retaliatory attack; he was quick to hold up his hands and redirect the course of the knives back toward Emmett, who blocked with his shield again. As soon as the blades made impact, the shield was gone and Emmett was throwing an ectoplasm orb from his right hand.

RC, his focus on the red energy whizzing toward his face, managed to dodge it, but only at the last possible moment did he realize that Emmett had also fired a bolt from a crossbow he was clutching in his left hand; RC's telekinesis froze the weapon midair less than an inch from his leg.

I was pretty sure I'd finally figured out what Emmett was. He might resemble an older version of RC, but he didn't share my lab-brother's power of telekinesis. Emmett, I was fairly confident in identifying, was an Arsenal. He had access to his own metarealm where he could store objects and swap them at will, which explained how such a large shield and other weapons could appear and vanish without a trace. There was no telling what Emmett's cache might be.

Already, Emmett had replaced the bow with a flail, but RC made the next move before his blood-brother could use it. He sent his remaining two disks at Emmett and telekinetically retrieved his third off the ground, but I could tell he was holding back.

Emmett knew it, too. A smaller and more maneuverable metal shield appeared on his arm to block the disks. Even though they were coming at him from different directions, he seemed to have a talent for deflecting them. He was no stranger to a battlefield.

Emmett knocked the last disk away and charged RC, the flail swinging through the air. My lab-brother waved his arm, and the deadly spiked ball at the end of the chain swung back toward Emmett, who was forced to use his shield to block his own weapon.

"Stop!" RC begged. "Emmett, please stop! I don't want to hurt you!"

His blood-brother answered by slamming his shield full-force into RC, who grunted and careened backward. "You couldn't hit me even if you wanted to," Emmett growled. His shield was now a sword driving toward RC's stomach.

RC leapt back, his arm cutting through the air to direct one of his disks in front of the blade. The point glanced off RC's weapon with a *clang* and a brief burst of sparks.

Enraged, Emmett howled and turned his flail into a second sword. He rushed at RC, both swords swinging, and RC backed up, deflecting each strike with a disk. Sparks flew amid the echoing rings of metal striking metal.

I turned to Ero and said, "Can't you stop this?"

He watched the battle with a solemn expression for a few seconds before his gaze lifted to meet mine. "How would you have reacted if I had stopped your battle with Madison here in this very square?"

"That was different."

"How so?"

"They're—" I helplessly swept my hand in the direction of RC and Emmett. "They're going to kill each other."

Ero raised his eyebrows, silently reminding me that I had been on the brink of ending my mother's life when we had squared off with one another on the bloody battlefield.

Ash asked, "What should we do, Jay? Should we help RC?"

Axel jumped the full flight of stairs and landed nimbly next to Ash, at the ready. I turned to Jay for his answer. I was ready to jump into the battle and aid my lab-brother. But to my surprise and disappointment, Jay shook his head and replied, "Ero's right. This is a family feud. RC told us to stay out of it."

"He's holding back," I muttered.

"Wouldn't you, if you were fighting Vivian?"

I solemnly turned back to watch. Emmett was seething now that RC was his equal on the battlefield. His little blood-brother had been turned into a warrior in the Arena, and their fighting styles were drastically different. Emmett relied on strength and speed and power, but his moves were unrefined. RC was just as quick, but his movements were smaller and more precise to consume less energy, and he was more efficient with each strike and block . . . At least, he would be if he'd actually fight back. Emmett was bigger and stronger; RC's technique was cleaner.

"Please, Emmett," RC begged. "We don't have to fight!"

"I've never lost to you, and I'm not about to start now," Emmett snarled. He took a wild swing, and this time, RC didn't deflect it with a disk; he ducked beneath the blade and let it slice through the air above him. As he rose, he threw out both hands, telekinetically yanking the swords out of Emmett's grip and into RC's waiting hands.

"That's enough!" RC shouted, pointing the swords away from his body as he lunged forward.

The sound of his forehead cracking Emmett's nose made me wince.

Emmett staggered back, his hands flying to his face to catch the river of blood. "Argh, you little bastard!"

A deep shiver traveled down my spine. I whirled, gaze dancing as I sought the new ghost that had just entered my range. If I couldn't help RC against his blood-brother, the least I could do was stop anyone else from interfering.

I immediately located the ghost—a tall, burly man with a thick beard and violet eyes—leaning against the fence by the Rip with his arms crossed and a deep scowl etched into his face. Before I could act, RC and Emmett both noticed the man. RC gasped and dropped the swords. In the echoes of the metallic *clang*s on the cobblestones, I heard him whisper, "Father?"

I straightened. *Father?*

I had no idea how to react, and my lab-brother wasn't giving me any clues. I knew absolutely nothing about RC's father. Or RC really, for that matter. I'd suspected that maybe RC had run away from home after his mother's death because he and his father weren't getting along. But his dad was here now. Maybe he was sorry, and he'd actually been searching for RC all this time.

If that were the case, this certainly wasn't the warm reunion I would have expected. RC's father was still scowling, and my lab-brother seemed to be petrified in place.

"What a surprise. Both of my sons are disappointments."

Emmett skulked over to him and muttered, "Father, I—"

"Shut up. I'll handle your brother." Emmett backed away as the man held out his hand. "RC, come here."

RC didn't move. His father's hand fell to his side, and his face reddened. Short fuse on his temper—no wonder RC wasn't getting along with him. He seethed, "What in King's name is wrong with you? I said *come here.*"

RC shook his head and stepped back.

His father's frown deepened. "What do you mean *no*? I didn't give you a choice."

"I'm not going with you."

"Damn it, RC. Get your ass over here *now*!"

"No!" RC flung out his hand, shooting a silver disk at his father. The weapon stopped a few inches in front of the ghost, whose violet eyes were also glowing even though he hadn't moved. Unlike his son, he didn't need his hands to guide objects.

RC was lifted into the air, clutching his throat and kicking his legs as if an invisible hand had wrapped around his neck. His disk clattered uselessly to the ground now that his concentration was broken. A great force smashed him down onto the cobblestones, causing him to grunt upon impact as the air rushed out of his lungs, and then he was hoisted back up off his feet and pulled toward his father.

"Don't you *dare* use your Divinity on me!" the man thundered. "It's a gift that *I* gave to you, and you have the nerve to turn it against me?"

RC's face was turning red. I stared at him flailing in the air as I struggled to process the situation. Axel crouched on all fours, snarling ferociously.

Seeing the panic in RC's expression and hearing Axel's growls finally made me realize that my lab-brother was in serious trouble. This wasn't a sibling skirmish anymore. My grip on the icicles tightened even as I felt the green rage burn brighter and hotter in my core as my sonokinesis stirred. RC would forgive me for hurting his father.

But Jay put a firm hand on Axel's shoulder to hold him back. Axel turned, snarling in confusion and fury. Jay calmly said, "This isn't our fight."

Ash clutched her staff in distress as she glanced at the leader. "But RC needs us," she said.

Jay gazed past us and stared at RC still clutching at his throat as he weakly struggled against his father's telekinetic hold. "If RC loses, then we'll step in. But we didn't interfere when Cato confronted Madison. RC needs to fight this battle on his own."

I slowly straightened, realizing that Jay was right. I would have been livid if any of my lab-siblings had stepped in when I was dueling Madison because I never would have gotten the closure I needed. As much as I wanted to help RC, I understood that he had to face his father and blood-brother on his own, and we couldn't interfere unless he truly needed us. As difficult as it was to be a helpless bystander, all I could do was watch.

RC, his face a deep purple now, jerked one hand away from his neck. The silver disk lying beneath his feet quivered, then shakily rose a few inches off the ground and started spinning. He flung his arm out in a final act of desperation even as his kicks slowed to a stop and his eyes started to roll back in his head. The disk rocketed toward his father, who cursed as the blades sliced his thigh open.

The telekinetic hold seemed to snap. RC fell to the ground, coughing and heaving as he tried to suck in great lungfuls of air. His father was holding his leg as a red stain spread outward from his fingers. "You always were worthless. Just a disrespectful nuisance eating my food and getting in my way."

"And you," RC panted hoarsely, "always were . . . a drunk . . . bastard."

"You watch your goddamn mouth! I've got half a mind to cut out your tongue next. Apparently, you didn't learn after your eye. Maybe a few more scars will finally make the lessons sink in."

My jaw dropped. The power of speech had been stripped from me; all I could do was stare in dumbfounded shock at my lab-brother. When RC finally found the strength to scramble to his feet, I could see just how violently he was trembling. I took a step forward, but Jay seized my shoulder. "Not our fight," he reminded me.

RC stood up straight and proclaimed, "I have a new family now, and you aren't a part of it."

His father laughed coldly, glancing at us for the first time since his arrival. "Is that so? You and that little ragtag gang of misfits? That's cute, RC. Real cute. But if you think I'm going to sit back and let my son drag my reputation through the mud while you continue to be Azar's fugitive, you're even more of an idiot than I took you for. If I have to drag you to Szion, I will."

"Szion?" RC repeated, visibly confused. Apparently, that wasn't his home. Then the puzzlement dawned to enlightenment, immediately eclipsed by wide-eyed horror. "You . . . conscripted me?"

I didn't know what that meant, but Ero bowed his head with a sympathetic sigh.

Emmett, who seemingly hadn't been informed of this development, blinked in surprise, and then he grinned devilishly as their father roared at RC, "You're damn right I conscripted you! What did you expect?"

"I'm not going!"

"The paperwork's already been signed. YTP is waiting for you."

"In which case," RC growled, his voice now level and dangerous, "you have no control over me anymore."

"This is your last chance. I am ordering you to come here *right now* before I change my mind and decide to send you to a grave next to your bitch of a mother. At least then I wouldn't have to worry about you destroying the family's reputation."

RC's eye flared as he clenched his fists. Faint tremors beneath my boots preceded a deep and terrifying rumble that seemed to come from every direction. I gazed around in unease as everything began rattling as if a minor earthquake was rocking Phantom Heights. RC was always so collected; I'd only ever witnessed him truly lose control of his power once before, and it had been nothing like this. His father was pushing him over the edge.

"Don't talk about Mom like that!"

Glass started to fracture. Long splits ripped through the ground as the cobblestones were pulled apart.

RC's father, seeing that he'd struck a nerve, pulled his lips back in a cold, cruel smile. "You know, it's your fault. If it weren't for you, Nimia would still be here."

His teeth clenched to trap an angry scream, RC reached out, made a fist, and then jerked his arm in toward his body. The silver disk that had been lying on the ground a few feet away from his father shot upward and zipped toward RC. It whizzed past his father's face as it cut through the air and halted in front of its wielder.

The ghost roared in pain and clapped his hand to the side of his head, his eyes wild. Blood was gushing between his fingers and dripping onto his shoulder. He limped away, still favoring his cut leg and glaring at his son with a soul-shaking look of pure, uncensored hatred. "You rotten little bastard! Damned be King—you're going to pay for that! Mark my words, RC, I swear on your mother's grave—if Azar doesn't get his hands on you first, I am going to *kill* you before I let you walk away!"

The silver disk hovering in front of RC propelled forward without warning. My lab-brother, as if expecting his father to strike, became intangible at the last second, and that was all that spared him from having his own blades slice into his stomach when his father's telekinesis overpowered his own. The disk passed harmlessly through his insubstantial body and struck the steps a few yards away from us.

RC's father phased through the fence and retreated through the Rip.

Emmett, still cradling his broken nose, moved his hands enough to spit a mouthful of blood onto the cobblestones and growl, "Next time, little brother." He turned and stormed after their father.

RC didn't move. The rumbling receded like thunder rolling into the distance, but even though the world had stilled, RC was frozen in place, unresponsive, staring blankly at a small object lying a few feet from where his father had been standing. He seemed to be in a state of total shock. Jay followed our lab-brother's gaze and approached the object.

He studied it passively, then knelt and seized the bloody object between two fingers. He held it up but away from his face in revulsion. "An ear for an eye," he said quietly.

RC fell to his hands and knees, vomiting violently. Ash rushed forward and knelt down beside him, then awkwardly patted his back as he retched. Axel, I realized, was gone. I hadn't noticed him leave.

Poor RC was shivering and sobbing. He shakily brushed Ash away and staggered to his feet again. "I need to be alone," he croaked. He turned away from us and took off in a mad sprint without looking back, leaving his bloody disks behind.

— Chapter Twenty-Seven —
Shifting Alliances

Dinner that night, as if it hadn't already been doomed to be tense, was off to a bad start before it even began.

Axel was fidgety and couldn't stop bouncing his foot while drumming his fingers on the tabletop. RC, who had been staring despondently down into his lap, grimaced and dragged his hands down his face in irritation.

Vivian noticed and said, "Please stop doing that. You're upsetting RC."

Axel snapped back, "You think you know him well enough to say what's upsetting him? Fuck off, Vivian. You don't know shit."

"Axel!" I cried at the same time Jay said, "Enough."

RC closed his eyes and leaned forward until his forehead rested on the table. Vivian retorted, "You just say whatever you want because you think nobody's going to stand up to you. It's easy to pick a fight when you're the strongest person, isn't it? You're nothing more than a bully."

Jay, seeming to realize the skirmish was beyond remediation by this point, simply shook his head. The door to the kitchen swung open, and Madison cheerily announced, "I hope everyone's hungry!"

Axel stood up and snarled, "Call me whatever the fuck you want. I don't have to sit here and take it." He stormed out of the dining room and phased through the front door.

My mother frowned as she set a plate topped with spaghetti and meatballs in front of Kit, whose ears pricked forward. She eagerly reached for the pasta. "Fork," Madison reminded sternly.

Kit froze, her hand a few inches above the plate, fingers splayed apart and ready to seize a handful of the saucy noodles. Her ears fell back, but she retracted her hand and picked up the fork beside her plate.

"Thank you," said Madison. "What was that all about? Is Axel not feeling well again?"

"Sort of," I muttered, angry enough with my lab-brother to feel the current of hot, potent energy that had probably caused my eyes to glow green. Tonight of all nights, couldn't he make an effort to not cause trouble? I swore he had instigated that spat on purpose just for an excuse to leave.

Madison surmised, "Then I take it he isn't joining us for dinner tonight." I shook my head. Vivian rose and stormed into the kitchen to help serve the meal.

Ero set his napkin down on the table and followed suit, kindly offering, "Allow me to assist you." He followed Madison back into the kitchen.

No one said a word as the three of them worked in sync to serve everyone at the table. Vivian set my plate down in front of me with a loud clatter and more force than necessary. "Thank you," I whispered. She locked her jaw and returned to the kitchen without answering.

I picked up the piece of garlic bread on the side of my plate and took a bite.

Wow. I closed my eyes. That intense flavor took me back to a dark alley when Jay and I were crouched over a garbage bag, eating our first meal Outside. I sat still for a moment, not chewing, just appreciating the taste and remembering the first time I had sampled this food. Back then, it had been cold, stale, and soggy from sitting in pasta and sauce in the trash. Madison's was warm and soft on the inside with a pleasant crisp on top. It was perfect. This whole meal was—it felt like a testament to how far we'd come. When I had been ravenously devouring garbage as my first meal Outside, I never could have imagined I would someday be eating a fresh version of it at this fancy dining room table in Saros Manor with my blood-family and my lab-family sitting side by side in comradery.

Madison and Vivian returned and set their own plates down as they took their seats. Ero followed with two plates, one of which he handed to Wes before he strolled to the other end of the table and settled back into his chair.

The room was uncomfortably silent except for the clinking of silverware. Even without Axel here, the tension was like invisible smoke suffocating us all.

Finally, Madison was brave enough to break it. "RC, do you want to talk about what happened today?"

He was slumped back in his chair, glaring at his plate and pushing the food around with his fork. I hadn't seen him take a single bite yet. "There's nothing to talk about."

For a moment so brief I wasn't entirely convinced it happened, every plate, glass, and piece of silverware jerked away from RC as his left eye flared. The table was still in perfect arrangement, just shifted slightly out of place. All that affirmed the event really did occur was the quiet tinkling of the chandelier above us.

RC stabbed his fork into a meatball and pushed his chair back from the table. "I'm not hungry."

Nobody, not even Madison, said a word as he left the room. Instead of phasing through the front door as Axel had, he yanked it open and slammed it shut behind him.

Madison surveyed the rest of my lab-family. "I don't want any more surprise visits. I need to know whose parents are still alive."

I kept my head down but subtly watched my lab-siblings. They hesitated, glancing uncertainly at one another. Finn and Reese raised their hands. Kit pondered for a moment, then raised hers as well.

"Only the three of you?" my mother said dubiously.

Wes narrowed his eyes, his attention on Kit. "Do you know for a fact that yours are alive?" he asked. Her ears fell. She lowered her hand and shook her head. "That's what I thought. Did you ever meet them?" Kit caught her lip with her short fangs, then shook her head again.

"Axel?" Madison asked.

"No," I answered in his absence. "His parents were both killed."

"Then only Finn and Reese have living family besides RC? I find that hard to believe. Ash?" My lab-sister shook her head. "Jay?"

He exhaled slowly. "I'm not sure," he admitted. "My mom is gone. It's possible that my father might be alive, but I can promise he isn't looking for me. I don't think he knows I exist."

I frowned and turned to Wes. "I don't understand what happened between RC and his father. What is YTP?"

"The Youth Training Program," Wes muttered, a new bitterness edging his tone. Ero shook his head in sorrow as Wes continued, "Orphans and abandoned children in Avilésor end up in YTP to be trained as Shadow Guards or serve the military in other capacities if they're unfit for combat. Parents who don't want their kids anymore can surrender them to YTP. They call it conscription."

"Wow." I leaned back, my stomach sinking. "So, RC's father sold him out to Azar."

Wes nodded solemnly. "If the paperwork has been signed, RC is now a ward of YTP until he turns twenty, and then he'd be drafted into the Shadow Guard until his hundredth birthday. After that, he has the choice to continue serving or quit. But until then, he can be charged with desertion, which would constitute a lifetime Prison sentence. The military has custody of him now, and since Azar oversees the military, he basically owns RC."

Jay said, "I don't see how it matters. We're all fugitives anyway."

"That's true," Wes acknowledged with a roll of his shoulders. "But . . . technically all of you except Cato and Kit would be considered abandoned youths, automatically enrolled in YTP unless a guardian came forward to claim you."

Madison asked, "Why not Kit?"

"Amínytes are slaves, not soldiers," Wes said simply. "Rather than YTP, Kit would . . ."

He realized just in time what he was about to say and trailed off. I didn't need to read his mind to finish his train of thought: *Kit would be sold into slavery.*

My stomach churned, threatening to upheave the nostalgic meal.

RC skipped training for the first time ever that night. The rest of us didn't have the heart for an intense workout, so we ran laps around the lake.

I skimmed the dark water for Chelvistin, but the surface was quiet. To my knowledge, she hadn't revealed herself to anyone except Ash, Ero, and me, so I suspected I wouldn't see her while the others were with us. Axel stood watch over the twins, who were sitting on the pier gazing at the placid lake.

"You didn't know?" I asked Jay. My voice was the first to break the steady footfalls in the mulch. Ash turned her head to hear his answer.

"Not a clue," Jay admitted. "He never wanted to talk about his past, so I didn't push. I suspected that his father was alive . . . but I had no idea about Emmett. RC never mentioned any blood-siblings."

Crickets filled the void of our voices. RC had always been a mystery, an integral part of the lab-family but also secluded behind invisible barriers that prevented him from fully opening himself up to us. I was still struggling to wrap my mind around today's events. I wasn't upset that he kept secrets. On the contrary, his vulnerability had been revealed like an open wound, and now I wanted to protect him.

It didn't matter that Emmett was related to him by blood. As far as I was concerned, we were RC's real family now. I was his brother, and I'd prove it if Emmett ever tried to hurt him again.

Next time, RC's father and blood-brother would have to face his lab-family.

Agent Kovak leaned back in his office chair, his heels propped up on the desk, the phone cradled against his shoulder. He listened to it ring as he studied the clipboard in his lap. When a woman's voice issued a tentative, "Hello?" on the other end, he smiled.

"Hello, Maddie."

He narrowed his eyes, certain that he heard a faint gasp on the other end of the line. Before she could return the greeting, he said, "How are you?"

"I-I'm fine," she answered weakly.

Kovak rocked the chair back and forth. He knew his former colleague well enough to notice the uneasy tremor in her voice. "Good, good," he murmured. "I've heard rumors that your entoplasm shield has been down for a while now. I've been meaning to pay you another visit, but my schedule has been so busy. You know how it is. I have to say, my curiosity has been eating away at me. However did you manage to rid the infestation and reclaim your quaint little town?"

Madison cleared her throat. "A lot of work, strategic strikes by the raid team, extra training. Your enhanced ectoguns helped."

"Is that so? I don't suppose you've had a chance to tinker with them, have you?"

"Sorry, I've also been very busy."

Kovak skimmed over the sheet on the clipboard for the hundredth time. "Yes, of course. I assume you know why I'm calling?"

Silence. He could practically taste the ghost hunter's sheer terror through the phone. "Um, no, sorry, I-I don't."

"No?" Kovak smiled, purposely drawing out his pause to make her sweat a little more. "Do the words 'Project Alpha' ring any bells?"

She didn't answer. Kovak counted to ten before breaking the silence with, "I was wondering if you have any news to report about my fugitives."

"I don't."

"Are you sure?" Kovak pressed, giving her one last chance to change her answer.

"I am. Either they already passed through the Rip, or they never came this way. Sorry. I wish I could have been more help."

He sighed, drawing out another lengthy pause. "Well, that's too bad. If anything changes, I trust you'll do the right thing. I really do need those test subjects back if we're going to have any hope of defeating the army from the Ghost Realm. You're right in the line of fire. I would hate to see Phantom Heights obliterated if their army invades before ours is ready to face them."

"Yes. I understand. I will."

"Mm-hmm. And Maddie, I do hope you remember what I told you earlier. I really want the twins. If you happen to find them, I'm ready to bargain. Just name your price."

Another pause, then she abruptly said, "I'll keep that in mind. Goodbye."

The call ended. He drummed his fingers on the desk, then dialed another number. On the third ring, a woman curtly answered, "Councilwoman Jennings speaking."

"Holly."

"Agent Kovak." She was much less surprised than Madison had been. "What do you want?"

He smiled and leaned back again. "Just checking in. Anything of interest to report from Phantom Heights?"

This time there was a hesitation, and that was unusual for her. "Besides S-O-S failing to pass, no."

That wasn't what he'd expected to hear. Her answer made him sit up straighter. "We never gave you the green light to implement Shoot-On-Sight. We weren't ready."

"Phantom Heights was. Or so I thought. I miscalculated."

Kovak rested his forehead against his palm and gripped his temples as he closed his eyes. "You can't act on your own like that. You have to wait until we're ready to back new laws with military power."

"Well, you're taking your sweet time, and I got tired of waiting. We all did. These people want action taken, and if I don't deliver, I lose my authority."

"I sponsored your election so you could pass legislation that *I* approve. Phantom Heights is supposed to be the testing ground, and if the anti-kálos laws are successful there, then we can scale them up to a federal level. That requires your cooperation. I can easily replace you with someone more reliable."

"That won't be necessary. I apologize for pushing the timetable before you were ready. But I'm getting a lot of pressure here. You don't have many supporters."

"I can't say I care much about a popularity contest. When I stop traffic through the Rip and people can finally feel safe in their own homes, any past transgressions will be forgiven and forgotten. We still want the same results, correct?"

"Yes." Holly took a deep breath. "Agent Kovak, I wanted to ask you—"

"And I wanted to ask *you* if there's been any sign of my missing test subjects."

Silence. Then, "You know how I hate to be interrupted."

Kovak raised his eyebrows; it was such a rarity for anyone to rebuke him. He smiled. "I apologize."

Holly let her breath out slowly, then continued, "I wanted to ask you about Greyson." Kovak rolled his eyes and slumped lower in the chair, but he didn't interrupt again. "We've done a massive cleanup in Phantom Heights, but nobody has found his body. He could still be alive. Madison won't look for him, but you—"

"Maddie's right," he said, risking the interruption. "Greyson is long dead by now. You'll be wasting your time and sanity if you embark on a manhunt for him."

Silence on the other end.

Kovak continued, "Listen, I just got off the phone with Maddie, and she told me she doesn't have any news of my fugitives. Thing is, I'm not sure I believe her."

Holly didn't speak at first, and when she finally did, her voice was frigid. "You won't help me look for Greyson?"

Kovak closed his eyes briefly in irritation. "I need you to focus on the issue at hand. Do you know anything about my fugitives from Project Alpha?"

Again, Holly took her time to answer, fueling his impatience. "I'm sorry, Agent Kovak. To my knowledge, they never passed this way."

"Really? You don't think it's possible Maddie might be protecting her son?"

"I know everything that goes on in this town. There's no way Tarrow could keep something like that a secret from me."

He shook his head as he stared at the clipboard in his lap. "Are you absolutely sure?"

"Yes."

"I see. Well, I hope you remember where your loyalties lie."

"I do."

She ended the call. He waited another few seconds, then slowly took his feet off the desk and leaned forward to hang up the phone. He set the clipboard on the desktop. Beneath the metal clip was a seismograph reading that showed unusual spikes of energy waves over the last few weeks. Phantom Heights was the epicenter of the surges. Kovak lifted the sheet to compare the readings with A7's electroshock test underneath. The patterns were almost identical.

He dragged his hands down his face, then snatched the phone again and pressed a button to make an internal call. While he waited, he twisted the top off a medication bottle and popped a small pill into his mouth. On the second ring, a tired female voice answered, "Zelkowitz."

"Agent Zelkowitz, where are we on that satellite imagery of Phantom Heights?"

She sighed. "We're nowhere, sir. Exactly where we've been."

"That's unacceptable."

"I wish I could give you a better answer. I've thrown every idea and resource at the problem, but I haven't been able to override ECANI and take control back. The satellites and security cameras are still unreachable."

"Goddamn it." Kovak slammed his fist down on top of the clipboard. "What's the problem? ECANI isn't an AI; it's just a very powerful tool wielded by two smart runts who are going to be in so much trouble when I finally get my hands on them. Why can't you override it?"

Agent Zelkowitz yawned before she replied, "ECANI may not be an artificial intelligence, but its programming is so sophisticated that it behaves like one. It has a broad range of adaptive parameters that allow it to continue evolving its code every time I find a weak point and make even the slightest bit of progress. It's impregnable."

"I need to see what's going on in Phantom Heights. I can't afford to lose another drone as soon as it gets close to the city limits. You need to get those satellites back."

"Sir? Can't you just send in a strike team? I know they'd be going in blind, but—"

"Can't risk it." Kovak leaned back in his chair. "I don't want to spook my test subjects. Not with the Rip so close. If the extraction attempt were to fail, we're not in any position to go into the Ghost Realm after them. We'll have one shot. When I make my move, I have to make sure there's no room for error."

He leaned forward. "I don't care what regulations, laws, or constitutional rights you have to break. I'll deal with those consequences. Find a way to get me eyes on Phantom Heights."

A nightmare woke me in the dead of night.

I lay perfectly still on the mattress, my chest heaving. Usually, my nightmares took me back to that underground hellhole, but tonight was different. Tonight, I had dreamed that I was Phantom, and I was standing under a streetlight at night. Downtown was deserted. Madison was standing in front of me with her gun trained between my eyes.

"Mom, it's me. I'm Cato," I had said behind my mask.

"I know," she'd replied.

And then she had pulled the trigger.

I swiped at my wet eyelashes and sat up. My audible cry when I'd jerked awake in the reverberations of the gunshot in my head hadn't woken my lab-siblings, who were still slumbering. In fact, Kit and Jay seemed to be in the middle of their own nightmares. No sign of Axel. No RC, either.

I didn't want to close my eyes and risk seeing my mother shoot me in the face again. Gently, I slipped my arm free from Ash's limp grasp, then rose and backed away. Wes had a weight room on the second floor, and I was tempted to spar with the punching bag since none of my lab-siblings were available. But I felt sick to my stomach. I wanted fresh air to clear my head.

I crept from the sleeping quarters into the living room, each foot carefully placed before shifting my weight to keep my passage as silent as possible. My lab-siblings were more likely to be disturbed by my sneaking around than by my predictable nightmare-induced thrashing. That had been conditioned into us. We were used to hearing each other suffer from nightmares or moan in pain. It was the handlers quietly entering the room who were the real threat.

Rather than risk the sound of the door opening and closing, I phased through and stepped onto the balcony. The cool nighttime breeze swept over me, tousling my hair and carrying a faint but sweet floral scent from the overgrown gardens far below.

I leaned against the railing and spent a few minutes staring at Alvarez Park in the distance, sure that I could see the faint glimmer of Chelvistin's lake in the moonlight through the dark trees. I yawned, then hopped onto the railing to reach the rooftop, where I sat down on the rough shingles with my knees drawn up to my chest.

The night was clear and calm. I lay down to admire the breathtaking tapestry of stars that was just as magnificent as it had been the first night Outside. Hard to believe I'd needed to ask Kit what they were called. How could I forget about the stars? I never wanted to forget them again.

A deep shiver racked my body, and I stiffened in sudden alarm.

"Must be nice to have a blood-family that loves you."

I exhaled in relief and turned my head. A dark figure with a single glowing violet eye was standing on the far side of the roof. Slowly, I sat up and forced a smile. "Hey. We were wondering where you'd gone."

"I needed some time to think." RC shifted in hesitation, then approached and sat down next to me. "You mad?"

"What? No, of course not. Why would I be mad?"

He shrugged. "I don't know. I mean, you were always so transparent about Vivian and Madison. You guys were blindsided today. I'm sorry."

"Don't worry about it. I mean, seriously, we don't even know Jay's real name," I joked. "Compared to that, your father and blood-brother showing up is nothing."

I managed to draw a dead grin from him, although it was gone in an instant. He stared off into the moonlit distance. "Is Jay mad, do you think?"

"No. None of us are mad. I promise. Although, I think Axel did say something about kicking Emmett's ass if he ever comes back . . ."

This time, his lips twitched with genuine amusement. "So . . . I had wanted to talk to Jay, actually, but . . . then I thought maybe . . . you might understand better, since you're the only one who knows your blood-family."

Whoa. My brief elation that he'd chosen to confide in me was almost immediately smothered in silent panic. *Me?* Bloody Scout, I didn't know what to say to him. He and Jay had been the unbreakable pair. The four of them—Jay, RC, Finn, and Reese—were a family before I was even a half-breed. I felt as if I barely knew RC—a feeling that had only been exacerbated in light of the day's events.

"Sure." I wanted to say more, but that was all I could muster.

RC continued to stare out into the night. I wasn't sure if I should start the conversation or wait for him to. The silence expanded between us.

"Do me a favor, Cato," he finally said. "Don't ever take your blood-family for granted."

I tried to say "okay," but I choked on the word and bobbed my head instead. "So," I said, the discomfort painfully obvious in my voice. "Emmett . . . were you guys ever close?"

RC shrugged. "I don't think so. But I guess I don't actually remember."

"Do you have any other blood-siblings?"

He shook his head.

"You really don't remember Before? Not even pieces?"

His gaze turned skyward. "I wish I could completely forget. I see

Mom die again and again and again in my nightmares." He paused, but I sensed he wasn't finished yet, so I waited. Sure enough, he released a long breath. "It's weird though, you know? The memories are still partially there, but the faces are gone. Just . . . I don't know, entities. I know them but can't see them anymore."

I did understand, actually. Madison and Vivian had remained sharp in my mind only because I'd had my photograph to keep the memories alive. Everybody else, even Trey, became, as RC had described, a faceless entity, only their essence left.

He continued, "But the moment I saw Emmett, it's like it just clicked into place. I knew who he was. Father, too. I just wish . . . I mean . . . I hate that Mom is the only one I can't see now. I have no idea what she looked like. Emmett got her Divinity, so I assume she had red eyes like his, but that's all I have to go on. The thing is, though, I can't trust my memories. I don't know which parts are real and which parts were blanks that my mind filled in. Sometimes in my dreams when Father's beating her to death, Emmett is standing there, watching. Other times, he's not there at all. And when he is there, sometimes he's laughing, sometimes he's cheering Father on, sometimes he's begging Father to stop, and sometimes he's crying. I don't know, Cato. I don't know which version is the truth, if any of them are."

"That's okay," I said. "As long as you know Emmett and your father are lying when they say it's your fault she died."

RC slowly shook his head, his jaw clenched. "She was protecting me," he choked out in a hoarse whisper. "I do know that. I got between her and Father in one of his rages. If I had just stayed out of the way like she told me to . . ."

"Stop," I told him sternly. "Don't give your blood-family the satisfaction of making you feel guilty for something that wasn't your fault. You just wanted your father to stop hurting your mom. That's perfectly normal. I mean . . . is that when it happened? When your father cut your face?"

Ever so slightly, he nodded. "I tried to protect her," he whispered. "But she sacrificed herself to protect me instead. I had to run away. He was going to kill me, too."

RC drew his legs up and wrapped his arms around them. His emotional shields had been down when he'd first approached me, but I could sense them rising again. Not good—he was shutting down. I redirected, "Your mom was an Arsenal?"

"Yeah." A phantom of a smile made another appearance, and then it was gone again. "But she didn't really live up to the reputation. I don't think she kept a single weapon in her metarealm. She called it . . . Oh, what did she call it?"

He squeezed his eyes shut. "Damn it, I know this," he muttered as he pulled at his hair. "She called it a . . . called it . . ." He straightened at the illumination of a memory. "A treasure chest. Yeah. I think that was it. She used it to store her favorite things, like books and jewelry and drawings that I made for her. Her treasure chest was a safe place Father couldn't reach."

It was as if a great weight was finally sloughing off his shoulders, but a shadow of sorrow passed over his face again. "Emmett started collecting weapons in his metarealm as soon as he was old enough. Everything from slingshots to swords and bows."

"How much older than you is he?" I inquired.

RC shook his head. *That was a tough question*, I realized. I hadn't known how old I was, or Vivian until she told me, so it really wasn't fair to ask that of RC. He replied, "I'm not sure, but I don't think he's reached his second coming of age yet."

He stood abruptly and turned away. "I'm not tired. Tell Jay I'll be back for training tomorrow."

"Why don't you just tell me what's been bothering you?"

"What do you mean?"

I rose and folded my arms. "I mean, even now, you can't look at me."

RC didn't move. I said to his back, "You haven't been able to look me in the eye ever since we learned the truth about my blood-family. And I want to know why. Are you upset with me? Did I do something wrong?"

He turned and tried to prove me wrong by meeting my eyes, but his gaze immediately fell to his feet again. "I don't have anything to say, Cato."

"That's not true. You don't like my blood-family, do you?"

"I don't really know them," he mumbled.

"Then what's your problem?"

He shrugged.

"Just tell me. Let me have it. Tell me what's bothering you."

RC finally raised his head to glare at me. "This is your dream come true, isn't it? To have your real family back. That's all you've ever wanted."

I studied him for a long moment, the root of his anger finally starting to make sense. "That's what this is about?" An inappropriate laugh escaped as I finally understood. "You think I'm going to abandon our lab-family."

RC's eye burned with resentment. "We were always just your temporary replacement family, right? If you're going to choose Madison and Vivian, I wish you'd just do it already and stop drawing this out."

"RC, I'm not Emmett."

"What is that supposed to mean?"

"I get it, okay? You could never really trust your blood-brother. You're afraid of getting too attached in case the lab-family falls apart, too."

"That's not true," he denied, shaking his head.

Right. Jay was the only one RC really trusted, simply because Jay so passionately held this mismatched family of ours together with every fiber of his being. RC never had faith the rest of us were that loyal because his only blood-brother never was.

I clapped my hand on his shoulder, and he flinched. "I promise you're not just a temporary replacement. What we went through together bonded us in ways our blood-families can never understand. As far as I'm concerned, we might as well be blood-brothers." I squeezed his shoulder and gave him a light, playful shake. "Okay? You are my brother, and that's not going to change just because Madison and Vivian are back in my life. I didn't think I needed to say that out loud."

RC bowed his head, but I was fairly certain I saw a smile. I let go and finished, "If Emmett doesn't want to be your brother, that's his loss. He doesn't know what he's missing. And tough luck—you won't be able to run away from us like you did him. Jay will sic Axel on your scent faster than you can say, 'Arena's Honor.'"

He nodded, now definitely smiling as he turned away. In a husky voice, he said, "Thanks. Good night, Cato. I'll see you for training in the morning. I promise."

— Chapter Twenty-Eight —

Kiss

The afternoon breeze carried voices and laughter across the schoolyard in the echoes of the final bell.

I curled my fingers through the chain-link fence, my gaze skimming the groups of students dispersing from the school.

"Trey is stuck in detention for the week," Madison had told me this morning. "Do you think you might be able to meet Viv after school? I bet she'd be ecstatic if you walked home with her."

I sighed. The crowd was thinning, and there was no sign of Vivian. I must have been too late.

I flinched when a girl leaned against the fence post next to me. "Hello, Cato," she chimed, flashing her perfect white teeth as she smiled widely at me. At first glance, I thought Vivian had found me, but no. This girl had long black hair that trailed over one shoulder and fell all the way to her waist, and her body was slender with daintier features than my blood-sister's. She seemed vaguely familiar.

"Um . . . hi." I turned my head and continued scoping the schoolyard in case Vivian was one of the stragglers trickling away from the building.

Resentful that I wasn't paying attention to her, the girl leaned closer so her face was in my line of vision again. "You remember me, right, Cato? We went to school together. I'm Shannon." She smiled uncertainly, as if waiting for me to acknowledge that I did know her. "Shannon Jennings," she said after a few uncomfortable seconds of silence.

I pulled away from the fence. "Have you seen Vivian?"

She pursed her lips and frowned. "Vivian," she repeated slowly, as if the name were unfamiliar. "I think she already left."

"Are you sure?"

She nodded. "She usually waits around for Trey, but since he's in detention, I'm pretty sure she went straight home."

"Oh," I said, turning away.

"Cato, wait. I-I'm afraid to walk home by myself."

I paused and reluctantly glanced back at her. "What?"

"It's silly," she said, twisting a lock of hair around one finger. "But my brother was taken by a ghost a couple of years ago. We never found his body. Could you please walk with me? I'd feel so much safer with Phantom protecting me."

I hesitated, finally giving her my full attention. "I don't think—"

"Please? It's not too far. It's actually just a couple of blocks away from your house. Your old house, I mean."

I rubbed my right arm with an indecisive sigh. Ash was scouting with RC and Jay since I'd planned to walk home with Vivian anyway, so I wasn't on a strict time limit to return. With great reluctance, I inclined my head.

Shannon's face lit up with a broad smile. "Thank you!" she said, spinning on her heel with an elegant flourish as if she expected me to follow. I traipsed after her, and she slowed her pace so we could walk side by side.

"I owe you, Cato. Really. I feel so safe when I'm with you. I'll have to find some way to repay you."

"It's fine," I dismissed.

"Hmm." She wasn't discreet about staring at me, which was making me squirm. I wished she'd look at something else. "We should have done this before now."

"What do you mean?" I monotonously inquired, keeping my steadfast gaze forward to avoid eye contact.

"I mean, you know. Before you left. I don't feel like we ever got the chance to talk—I mean, really, truly *talk* before. And that was my fault. You were always kind of quiet but still a nice guy, and I'm an idiot for not noticing until after you were gone. But you should know that I fought like hell on your behalf. I organized protests and rallies after the Agents took you away."

"Oh. Um, thanks."

"And do you remember Project Safe Haven? With the ribbons? That was my idea. I wanted to bring people together and offer you a support system since you were risking your lives to protect us. See?" She hooked her thumb under her shirt collar to stretch the fabric toward me and indicate a small black-and-silver ribbon pinned in a loop. "If there's any other way I can help you, please don't hesitate to ask. Seriously. I want to help. I want to be there for you, Cato. Whatever you need."

"Thanks," I mumbled again.

We were in a quiet part of town now. "Here's a shortcut," Shannon said, turning down an alley. I noticed a calico cat slinking between a couple of garbage cans, but the cat paid us no heed, which meant no danger in the vicinity.

Shannon twisted a strand of hair so tightly around her finger that her skin was starting to turn white between the black coils. "Cato, I . . . I wanted to say I'm sorry. About everything that happened to you. I swear I didn't know."

"Nobody did," I said, gracing her with a quick glance. To my surprise, a spasm of pain made her brow twitch as sadness briefly swept over her features.

She blinked rapidly and nodded, her gaze falling to her feet.

"Right," she whispered. "But if I did, I never would have given up on you. I would have continued to fight."

I didn't answer; I was tired of vocalizing empty gratitude. "How far is your house?"

"Not too far," she replied. I could feel her intense gaze boring into me again, and I subtly put an extra step between us. "You know, I was always grateful for what Phantom did. What *you* did. Cato . . . you were my hero." She freed her bound finger from the hair coil.

Without warning, she stepped in front of me, seized my cloak, and pressed her lips against mine before I had time to react. Startled, I became intangible and backpedaled away from her, eyes wide and brain locking into a standstill.

"W-what are you doing?" I stammered.

"Kissing you," she said bluntly. "I . . . thought that was obvious."

"But . . . why?"

Shannon smiled and stepped toward me again. I backed away. "What do you mean *why*? I'll admit I always had a silly crush on Phantom, even when I thought he was a ghost. Then when I learned that you were Phantom, I guess I finally realized what I hadn't noticed before—how sweet and heroic and strong you are."

I swallowed, painfully uncomfortable. I had no idea how to respond. She giggled. "What's with that confused look, Cato? It's no secret you had a crush on me. You didn't hide it well. It's like a fairy tale, isn't it? The invisible superhero nobody ever noticed makes a grand return and gets the girl he always wanted. It's a happy ending. It's what you deserve."

My mouth was suddenly cotton dry. I continued to back away. I didn't remember this girl. There was something familiar about her, but she might as well have been a complete stranger. Her kiss had caused my power to flare up in my core, but I couldn't decide if it was in excitement or pleasure or fear. She obviously wanted to kiss me again, but I didn't know how to kiss her back, and I didn't want to. She was too close. She kept coming forward, and I kept retreating.

"What's the matter?" Shannon teased. "Don't tell me the all-powerful Phantom is afraid of a defenseless human girl."

"I . . . I don't . . . uh . . . Y-you're almost home. You should be able to make it the rest of the way by yourself."

Shannon's face fell. "Cato . . . I thought . . . I thought you liked me." She blinked back tears and wrapped her arms around herself. "I'm too late, aren't I? You chose Ash instead of me."

"I don't know you."

"What?" She smiled at me even though tears were cutting trails down her cheeks. "Of course you do."

"I have to go," I said, turning away from her.

"Cato!" she cried as I ran. I tapped into my power supply, using the energy to become invisible. I was so confused and flustered that the only relief was the pounding rhythm of my soles on the pavement and the push and pull of my muscles as I sprinted down the street.

As my power weakened, I released it before I burned out. I wanted to leave Shannon and the confusing emotions she'd forced upon me far behind as I dashed through Phantom Heights.

Saros Manor was visible up ahead, at the top of the hill. I raced up the front walk and wrenched open the door. Faintly, I could hear my mother's muffled voice in the kitchen.

I tried to steady my breathing as I crossed through the dining room and pushed open the door. "Madis—?"

I stopped dead in my tracks, staring at my mother's visitor.

"Hello, Cato," said Doc.

My whole body turned cold in an instant.

Madison was setting a steaming mug down on the small table in the breakfast nook. "Oh, Cato," she greeted as she straightened. "I just made some tea. Would you like some?"

"No." I remained rigid, glaring at the doctor with distrust.

Doc smiled warmly at me. "You have my sincerest apologies for frightening you the last time we met."

I wasn't in the mood to deal with this right now. Blood was still pounding in my ears from the sprint, my heart throbbing against my ribs, my breathing barely under control. The doctor wasn't wearing her lab coat anymore—just slacks and a flower-printed blouse. But I didn't trust her, regardless of her clothes.

She seemed to sense this, and she glanced uncertainly at my mother, who tried to alleviate the tension by gesturing toward the table. "Why don't you sit down?"

Doc nodded and seated herself, setting a folder—my medical file, I presumed—on the table. Madison crossed the kitchen and stood at the sink as if nothing were out of the ordinary. "Anything else I can get you?" she asked over the sound of water running from the faucet.

"No, thank you. The tea is fine," said Doc.

"Cato? Are you hungry?"

"I'm leaving," I announced, shuffling toward the door without turning my back on the unwelcome enemy sipping tea.

"I wish you would stay." Madison turned off the water and leaned her hip against the cabinet as she dried her hands with a towel. "Doc is here for a friendly visit. Will you please join us? No surprises this time. We both promise."

Doc laced her fingers together and offered me another pleasant smile. "I was hoping we could talk," she said, nodding at the empty chair across from her.

I narrowed my eyes. She was an older woman, probably in her sixties if I had to guess, no match for me in a physical fight even if my powers were neutralized. The nurses weren't here to try and hold me down again, and Doc's relaxed, seated position indicated that she had no intention of directly confronting me. But I wasn't going to give her the chance by positioning myself so close to her. I remained where I was.

"Okay," she relented, opening the folder and setting a pair of reading glasses on the bridge of her nose. "You see, Cato, my job is to make sure people are healthy."

"I feel fine."

She frowned ever so slightly at my response. Madison clutched a mug in both hands, observing our interaction through the steam.

"You look tired," Doc noted in a sympathetic tone.

When she didn't continue, I snapped, "Is that a question?"

"Just an observation. How many hours of sleep did you get last night?"

I shrugged.

"Can you give me a guess?" she asked, tilting her head slightly to the side.

"I don't know. Three, four hours."

"I see. And did you sleep the whole night through?"

I hunched my shoulders, wishing I could turn invisible and then, upon remembering that I could, seriously contemplating it. "Not exactly. I woke up several times. Nightmares."

For a moment, the only sound in the silent kitchen was the scratch of Doc's pen as she wrote in my file. "Would you say that's a normal night for you? Three to four hours of sleep interrupted by nightmares waking you up?"

I nodded. Doc paused to take a dainty sip of her tea before she said, "Would you mind if I ask you some questions about your time at the AGC?" Without waiting for a reply, she continued, "Did the Agents inject you with anabolic steroids?"

I swallowed and glanced at my mother. She nodded and said, "Please answer her questions truthfully."

"You have my file from that place," I replied. "Isn't everything you need to know in there?"

Madison gently reminded me, "The file contained data from only the first month. You were there for two years. During that time, did the Agents inject you with steroids?"

"I don't know," I admitted. "I have no idea what *They* injected into my body. There were probably steroids in the mix."

"May I ask for what purpose?" Doc inquired.

I shrugged again. "Probably to see if muscle mass affected my power level."

My mother eagerly asked, "Did it?"

I redirected my dark scowl onto her. I found her less-than-subtle curiosity about the results of the experiments disturbing.

"I don't know."

Doc jotted down notes. "Did all eight of you in Project Alpha receive steroid injections?"

"Just me, Jay, RC, and Ash."

"Not the four youngest?"

I rubbed my temples, struggling to remember what I'd tried to forget. "I'm not sure about Kit. Definitely not Axel or the twins."

"Hmm." Her pen scratched across the paper, her expression thoughtful. "How often were you fed?"

"It depended."

"On what?"

I hung my head. "Usually twice in one Lightson span, which might have been a day. I'm not sure. But *They* wanted us to be hungry and thirsty when we went into the Arena, so we wouldn't get anything to eat or drink in advance."

"And your diet consisted of water and a paste that was high in carbohydrates and proteins, correct?"

"How did you know that?"

My mother solemnly reminded me, "Trey's visit to Project Alpha."

Doc didn't wait for my confirmation. "Were you exposed to any radiation?"

I shifted and muttered, "Just scans."

"No intentionally high amounts?"

"Not to my knowledge."

I watched the pen travel across the paper for a minute until she set it down. "Madison, does Wes have a scale in the house?"

"Yes, there's one in the upstairs bathroom," my mother answered.

"Could you please bring it here?"

Madison hesitated. She set her tea down on the counter and looked straight at me. "I'll be right back. Please wait here. Okay?"

I stepped aside to let her pass, but I made no promises, because my willingness to stay was contingent upon Doc's actions.

As soon as the kitchen door swung shut behind her, I tensed again. One hostile move, and I was ready to fight or flee.

Doc, however, remained seated, sipping her tea and watching out the window. I glared at her, silently daring her to give me an excuse to bolt. She didn't look at me or say a word until my mother returned with a device in her hand, and then Doc explained, "I'd like to know how much you weigh, Cato."

Madison set the scale on the floor. I eyed it warily. Doc added, "It doesn't hurt a bit. All you have to do is stand on the scale for a few seconds until a number appears. Easy, right? I just need that number."

My mother smiled in reassurance and stepped onto the scale to demonstrate. Without budging my feet, I craned my neck to watch a digital number appear in the tiny screen. Madison stepped off. "Your turn."

I took a few tentative steps forward and paused, then stepped onto the scale. I held my breath, braced for the worst as I watched the small screen. As soon as the number lit up, I retreated. "One-nineteen," I reported.

Doc frowned at my answer. "Are you sure that's what it said?" she asked.

My mother said, "Yes, that's right. Is that bad?"

The doctor shook her head in clear dissatisfaction and wrote the number in my file. "Last time he had a physical, he was five feet, six inches tall and weighed a hundred and forty-two pounds. Perfectly normal for his age. But now, he must have grown at least two inches and lost more than twenty pounds. That concerns me, especially because he actually lost more than that."

I glanced at my mother in confusion, and she said, "I don't understand. What makes you say he lost more than what the scale shows?"

"Muscle weighs more than fat. Cato was healthy with very little excess fat to burn; if anything, his weight should have gone *up* when he gained muscle mass."

My mother was staring at me with a pitiful expression that made me uncomfortable. "What do we need to do?" she asked softly.

Doc was scribbling again. "Keep him on a balanced diet. He'll gain some of the weight back, but don't start feeding him junk food to put it on quickly. I'd estimate he's probably around five-eight, five-nine now. Ideally, he should weigh about a hundred and fifty pounds. A healthy minimum for someone his age and size would be one-thirty-five. I'd like to see him hit that number at the very least."

Madison nodded. "I think we're already on the right track as far as consistent meals go."

"That's good. Would you mind handing me my bag? I left it over there."

My mother fetched Doc's bag beside the island and brought it to the kitchen table. The doctor reached inside and pulled out a black coil. "I'd like to listen to your heart and lungs now, Cato, if you'll let me."

I backed away, shaking my head. "This doesn't hurt either," Madison promised. "She's just going to set this end on your chest and put the other end in her ears so she can hear your heart beating."

"I know how a stethoscope works," I snapped. Both Madison and Doc looked frustrated by my lack of cooperation, but I didn't care. That doctor was not coming near me, especially with any instruments in her hand. No way was I letting her get close enough for a sneak attack with a syringe.

Doc gave me a compassionate smile as she rose. "Cato," she said soothingly, "I know at the lab, the Agents hurt you. And they did those things only for the sake of their cruel experiments. But everything I do is for *your* benefit to keep you healthy."

"I told you I feel fine. I'm not sick."

"I want to prevent you from becoming sick," Doc explained patiently.

"Then give me what you're giving the twins."

"I can give you supplements to strengthen your immune system, but I need to evaluate you and see what else you might need. Not every person can be on the same regimen."

I backed up another step, giving a clear indication that I was not going to let her approach me. Madison soothed, "Cato, you never used to be afraid of Doc. She's a very nice lady, and she'll be gentle with you. I promise we won't hurt you. No needles this time. Nothing that's going to cause you any pain."

I shook my head. I didn't believe her. I'd seen the hospital where Doc worked, and it reminded me of that place. Nothing but pain came from that place, so why should I assume the hospital was any different? If Doc worked there, she might as well be one of *Them*.

This time, my mother tried to bribe me, her voice unnaturally sweet: "If you do this for me, Cay, we can go get some ice cream afterward as a treat. And I'll make you whatever you want for dinner tonight. How does that sound?"

"No," I said firmly. I was aware that my back was close to the wall and I had only a few steps left if I needed to retreat. I judged the distance and calculated that any more than three steps backward and I'd have to become intangible to escape.

My mother and the doctor seemed determined not to chase me away this time; they both stepped back to prove they weren't going to force me. Doc set her stethoscope down on the table to further ease me. To my surprise, I realized I had started trembling. "I want to leave," I said.

"Please don't," Madison urged. "We're willing to compromise with you, but I need you to stay here and try really hard to compromise with us. Can you do that?"

Doc held up her hands. "See?" she said. "No tricks. No stethoscope, no needle. Okay?"

"Okay," I said weakly.

"I'd like you to do some simple exercises. Can you walk a straight line for me?" I took a few steps, enough to satisfy the doctor but not enough to put myself in close proximity to her. As she jotted another note into my file, she said, "Now, can you bend over and try to touch your toes?"

I did this too, and she seemed surprised when my fingertips easily brushed the ground. "You're quite flexible," she said, writing again. "That's good." She then had me stand on one foot to test my balance, then the other, and then I read letters off a paper she taped to the far wall. I passed all of her tests.

My mother seemed pleased that I was cooperating again. I wanted to please her, but I would only go so far to make her happy, so her frown returned when Doc suggested we try the stethoscope again and I refused. "But I haven't hurt you," the doctor tried to persuade. "And I'm not going to hurt you now."

"No."

"I need to make sure your heart and lungs are healthy."

"No."

My mother sighed. "Cato . . ."

I backed away, shaking my head. "I want to leave," I told her again.

"This new fear of yours is irrational," Madison said. "You're afraid of the Agents, and I completely understand that. But Doc is not an Agent. She's never worked for the AGC, and she just wants you to be healthy. I think you should give her a chance."

I narrowed my eyes and took another step back. "I think I've had enough, and I'm leaving, and you can't stop me," I challenged.

Madison's eyes widened in surprise at first, and then they narrowed. "Watch it, young man. I acknowledge that you're scared, but I don't like that tone. Let's stay civil."

A newfound boldness made me stand up straighter now that she seemed to be done coddling me. "I'm sixteen—I'm not a little kid you can order around anymore."

My mother briefly closed her eyes in a wince. "You're seventeen."

Damn it. My mistake only made me more irritable. I proclaimed, "I can freeze you in a block of ice, or eclipse you, or shoot you with ectoplasm, or scream and bring this whole house down. You can't stop me from leaving."

I was really testing Madison's limits now; I'd never threatened her in such a way before. If she were a ghost, her eyes would have been blazing. "Cato Jaxon Tarrow! That is where I draw the line. You can *not* threaten to use your powers to hurt people, including me."

Doc was glancing between the two of us, growing increasingly uncomfortable in the middle of the feud. "Stop me," I dared, backing away and letting my power rise up and consume me. I became intangible, and there was nothing Madison could do as I stepped backward and disappeared into the wall, emerging in the next room.

I heard running footsteps, and I knew she was coming after me. I took off toward the foyer. By the time she skidded to a stop at the foot of the staircase, I was already on the second floor. "Cato!" she yelled, giving chase.

I was too fast and had too much of a head start for her to even hope of catching me. I passed the second floor and charged up the steps to the third level before phasing through the door to my room. Madison pounded on the wood, calling my name, but I turned away. She could break the damn door down for all I cared because I was now protected by Proto.

The room was empty—even the twins were gone, probably with Ero for a lesson. My heart was flying, the deadly green Divinity scratching at my lungs to escape. I really wanted to scream.

I clenched my teeth to keep it contained, then dragged my hand through my hair and strode into the living room to stand at the French doors. Across the lawn, a strong wind had kicked up, causing the distant trees to wave and bow.

Madison had stopped hammering on the door, and she was calmer now as she apologized and gently asked me to come out so we could talk.

I ignored her and opened the balcony door, then stepped outside.

The wind took my breath away, extinguishing the scream of frustration still festering in my lungs.

I clenched the railing in both hands. Being trapped up here on the third floor brought a creeping feeling of claustrophobia tightening around my lungs like invisible hands squeezing the remaining breath out of me. It felt frighteningly reminiscent of my cage—a place of safety, but also confinement and powerlessness.

A gust of wind swept my cloak over my shoulder. I peered down far below, seriously considering jumping to the deceptively soft-looking blanket of grass at the bottom, but from the third story, I would surely break a leg. Then I'd have no choice but to see Doc.

Although . . . the second-story balcony jutting out over the sunroom didn't seem so far away.

I stared at it in contemplation. That drop was feasible. However, that balcony connected with the guest bedroom where Madison and Vivian stayed sometimes, and I didn't want to risk getting cornered on the balcony if Madison went into her room.

I held up my right hand and stared at my fingerless glove, an idea taking shape. The black material began to crust with a layer of frost.

I might be trapped up here, but I was *not* powerless.

My heart rate accelerated at the stupid stunt I was about to attempt. I knelt down and set my hand on the balcony, fingers curled over the edge. The blue Divinity came to life in my core, manifesting in a flow of ice that spilled over the balcony and stretched downward, reaching for the ground until I stopped the flow of power and ended its journey just above the patio.

The giant icicle was nestled in the corner of the manor, flanked by the sunroom but bypassing the second-story balcony. I had a straight shot down to the patio directly below.

Satisfied with my creation, I rose and gripped the railing in both hands again, then jumped over it and twisted so I landed on the other side facing the French doors, my heels hanging over the edge. I craned my neck to peer down at the massive icicle receding toward the ground. It was going to be a fast, slippery ride.

The height was making my hands feel clammy inside the gloves. I shifted my grip from the railing to the balusters and worked my way down into a low crouch before letting my feet slip off the edge. I trusted the strength in my arms as I lowered myself even farther until I was hanging off the balcony.

With a single exhale to steel my nerves, I hooked my ankles around the ice. Then, before I could think about it too much and lose my courage, I let go and wrapped my arms around the slick surface.

The wind whooshed around me, my cloak billowing over my head. I used the insides of my boots to grip the ice and slow my descent. The ride lasted only a few seconds before I dropped to the ground, and although I landed on my feet, I fell backward onto my ass with a startled grunt, off balance from the abrupt stop. An adrenaline-filled laugh bubbled to the surface as I flopped onto my back to let my heart catch up with the rest of my body while I lay on the stone patio.

The monstrous icicle towered above me. From here on the ground, the distance between the patio and the balcony seemed much greater than it had from above.

Slowly, I sat up—ears ringing, limbs numb, heart thrumming. I scrambled to my feet and turned away from the manor, and then I crossed the patio and took off running across the open, grassy backyard.

This exhilaration was familiar—the thrill of escape. I felt exposed and panicky on the lawn, much as I had when we'd trekked into the open fields and had nowhere to hide when the helicopter bore down on us.

Once I reached the safety of the trees, I stopped with my back pressed to a thick trunk so I was safely out of sight from Saros Manor. I leaned my head against the bark and closed my eyes, sucking in gulps of air and focusing on steadying my breathing to decelerate my heartbeat.

I peered around the tree. No sign of Madison pursuing me. No sign of anyone. Just the forlorn manor on the hill, looking rather small from this vantage point.

I pushed off from the trunk and wandered into the park, instinctively drawn to the water. I craved the peace of the secluded lake. Upon arriving at the shore, however, I was disappointed to see a young couple standing on the pier. I crouched behind a tree and waited, watching them for a few minutes until they walked hand in hand to the bank and strolled away down an overgrown mulch path.

Still, I waited, just to be sure no unwanted company was nearby. Only when I was certain that I was truly alone did I navigate to the pier and roam to the end, where I sat down cross-legged and inhaled the fragrance of the lake and woods.

Birds were twittering in a frenzy nearby, and I watched a battle erupt over the treetops as several small birds swooped and attacked in a coordinated mob to drive away a crow that must have drifted too close to a nest. The crow flapped away in retreat.

As the ruckus settled, a serene quiet enveloped the park, just faint birdsongs in the trees and the gentle, almost imperceptible lapping of water beneath the pier.

I stared across the surface in search of Chelvistin. Despite the wind at Saros Manor, all was quiet here, as if the hill and trees had buffered the roar down to a nearly insignificant breeze. The lake was an almost perfect mirror of the sky, unbroken with even a single ripple, which meant the sirien was likely far below in her cool, dark, underwater world. I could only imagine how peaceful it must be down there with the soothing lull of currents and muted quiet in the depths. Uninterrupted solitude.

I realized I was leaning over the edge of the pier, closer and closer to the smooth surface. My reflection stared back at me. Perhaps it was my cryokinesis pulling me toward the lake like a magnet—my Divinity did have deep ties to the element of water, after all, its pull even stronger than the Rip's.

The surface of the lake was not unlike the invisible barrier between the Realms. I yearned to break through that barrier and discover what was below—to feel the pressure of the water all around me, dampening my senses—to experience that blissful quiet while the aboveworld and all its troubles continued on without me.

An unexplainable thrill of excitement made me jittery; I felt like an addict craving a high that was within my grasp. I stripped off all of my clothes. The faint breeze swept across my bare skin, tossing my hair out of my eyes.

I curled my bare toes over the edge of the pier. Did I know how to swim? I couldn't remember, but the urge to jump was stronger than the fear. If my instincts didn't kick in, I could create an ice float.

I took a deep breath, bent my knees, and dove in headfirst.

A rush of bubbles tickled my skin in a pleasant tingle as they swarmed around my body and retreated back to the surface. My descent slowed, and I cracked open my eyes. As the bubbles cleared, I squinted through the murky water. My vision was limited, but I could see a field of underwater plants sprouting up from the bottom of the lake. I kicked deeper, close enough to sweep my open hand across the tops and feel the leaves brush my palm.

Whether I'd been a swimmer Before or not, the motion came naturally to me. My body seemed to know exactly what to do in the water. I maneuvered onto my back so I could stare up at the mesmerizing surface from below. What a different view than it had been from above. The ripples and bubbles from my dive had turned the blue sky and clouds into a kaleidoscope.

I let out a burst of bubbles from my mouth, then watched them climb toward the sky and break the surface. With a grin, I swam after them.

I erupted from the lake with a sputter before I inhaled sweet air. The water probably would have been frigid for a human, but to a Cryo like me, it felt tepid. I treaded in place, marveling at how natural it felt to be in the water. I took a deep breath, kicked off the piling, and dove again, swimming deeper into the lake.

Small fish darted between the plants, scattering out of my path and vanishing like tiny shadows. I caught occasional glimpses of lost objects half-buried in the pebbles and plant matter on the lake floor—sunglasses, beach toys, fishing lures, glass bottles. As I swam toward the center of the lake, I noticed the plants were thinning out.

I surfaced again and treaded water for a minute to catch my breath before the next dive. Not only was I a natural-born swimmer, but my lungs seemed to have a great capacity for holding air. I could swim much deeper and farther between breaths than I'd expected. The water, I noticed, felt cooler this far out, although I was still comfortable. My body seemed to have connected with its ancestral roots and acclimated instantly.

The plants were gone now, just a rocky bottom that had a steep drop-off into the dark depths. I hovered at the verge, gazing into the blackness of the underwater pit. That must be where Chelvistin lived.

I wondered what her house looked like, if she lived in a house. Or maybe it was an underwater cave. Or, perhaps, a sunken boat. It was possible Chel didn't have a house at all and simply slept in the open water.

An unearthly sound made my movements slow. I strained to listen. A faint but high-pitched wail echoed above a series of quick, sharp clicks and clacks. The synchronized sounds cut through the water with surprising clarity while every other noise seemed to be muted.

I paddled at the water to turn my body and seek the source. Visibility was low this deep. A quick flash of green, like that of a fish's scales briefly catching the light, made me jump.

I became aware that something was circling me just out of sight.

My first thought was that Chel had discovered me, but then my body turned cold with fear when I wondered . . . was she the only creature from the Ghost Realm that lived in this lake? She'd mentioned that a Tear had occurred here centuries ago, long before the Rip appeared. What if Chelvistin wasn't the only one who had come through? She might be the only sirien, but there could be something else not of this Realm lurking in the water. Something with an appetite for humans— the real lake monster from the scary stories I'd heard when I was a kid.

I was starting to panic. I twisted, desperate to find and identify the creature. I saw a silhouette, a flash of indigo this time, and then it was gone. My hand warmed as I summoned ectoplasm in my open palm. An eerie green light permeated the water, revealing bubbles and floating particles. I squinted, straining to see beyond the light's short range.

When I heard the unearthly call again, I went rigid with fear. Something brushed my shoulder from behind.

In my other hand, I conjured a long, sharp icicle from the water around me and whirled as I stabbed at the creature.

Webbed fingers seized my weapon and held it fast. I was staring into the face of a slim woman with large eyes, her wild hair fanning out in all directions. Green, blue, and violet scales sheathed her breasts and torso, tapering into a powerful tail. I stared at the spiny ridge along her forearm as she let go of my fist.

Chelvistin opened her mouth and made the odd wailing, chittering noise again. It was an eerie sound, and yet, even though I couldn't understand it, I was certain it was a language. A complex, intelligent language probably never heard by human ears before. Not in this Realm, at least.

"Hi," I tried to say, but the word was lost in a rush of bubbles. No wonder the siriens had their own language for underwater.

Chel tilted her head, unable to understand me. She pointed up toward the surface. I frowned and shook my head, pointing toward the center of the lake. My lungs were still full, and I wanted to explore.

She smiled and swam in a graceful arch above me, then dove down toward where I had pointed. I melted my ice weapon into the watery abyss and swam after her.

As much as I wanted to see her home in the center of the lake, I knew I wouldn't be able to travel that deep. The water pressure was already hurting my eardrums and compressing my diaphragm to the point of discomfort, and it was too dark down there to see, anyway.

Chel's sleek, slender body was designed to cut through the water with effortless grace. I kicked and paddled after her, so slow and clumsy in comparison that the sirien was literally swimming circles around me. She vanished out of my sight and then reappeared from a different direction.

I treaded in place and watched her pass in front of me, feeling envious of her ability to slip through the lake with movements as fluid as the very water we were swimming in. I held my hand up in front of my face, fingers splayed apart. My human hand was not designed to swim with the speed and agility of a sirien, but what if it could be? I sought my cold power and channeled it to my open hand. Ice formed in the gaps between my fingers until I had solid webbing of my own. I experimentally pushed my hand through the water, pleased with the resistance I met. I performed the same procedure to my other hand, then crafted ice fins on my feet.

Now when I swam forward, I propelled myself faster with less exertion. Chel drifted close to inspect my handiwork and then beamed at my ingenuity.

We traveled along the edge of the ridge, circling the pit. I'd thought that I wanted solitude, but I was enjoying Chel's company. She gestured and talked as she swam, probably telling me about her home as we toured it even though I couldn't understand. That didn't seem to bother her, and I liked the sound of her sirien voice. Somehow, her vocal cords produced at least two distinct yet simultaneous sound layers— the long, undulating waves of an almost ghostly feminine wail below the short clacking notes. I could feel faint vibrations in the water and suspected that echolocation was involved.

My lungs started to ache with a new, intense pain I'd never experienced. I needed air.

I looked up, judged the distance to the surface, and knew immediately that I was in trouble. We were too deep. There was no way I could make it in time before I had to breathe.

I made a desperate noise in my throat and kicked toward the surface even though I knew it was hopeless. Chel circled me in concern as I ascended. She pointed to her mouth and chittered at me, but I ignored her and kept paddling. A foreboding burn prickled my muscles as I pushed them to work in overdrive without oxygen. My lungs felt as if they were going to explode.

I'm going to drown. Bloody Scout . . . all the battles I've been in, and this is how I die? It's all my fault. Stupid! My last words to Madison were in anger. I didn't tell anyone goodbye. I'm so sorry. Jay, please forgive me. I didn't mean to leave the family like this.

My progress was slowing, and the surface was still high above me. Panic seized my body as my final oxygen reserves were depleted. I released my final breath in a rush of bubbles, then closed my eyes and gasped, knowing that I was going to drown but unable to subdue the instinct to inhale. I felt pressure on both sides of my head as something pushed against my mouth. As I breathed in, my lungs expanded with air.

Stunned, I opened my eyes. Chelvistin was in front of me, her hands on my cheeks, her head tilted with her cold lips pressed over mine to form a seal.

This was nothing like Shannon's kiss. Shannon had left me in a state of confusion with a mixture of pleasure and guilt and fear all tumbling inside me at once. With Chel, I felt none of that. We weren't kissing—we were breathing. She was breathing for me.

I trapped the air in my lungs as she pulled away. She solemnly pointed up toward the surface again, and this time, I nodded. Chel stayed close to me as I swam toward the light.

When I finally broke the surface, I coughed and sputtered, sucking up deep lungfuls of air. I called upon my Divinity and formed a crude ice raft that I could cling to. I didn't have the strength to tread water anymore.

"Just breathe," a soft, feminine voice soothed. "In and out. You're all right."

I rested my cheek on the ice. "Thank you," I croaked.

Chel was watching me, her head and shoulders above the waterline. She was so still, it was as if she were standing in place on a solid surface rather than treading water. "Cut that a little too close, huh?" she said with a faint smirk and a tilt of her head.

I wanted to tell her that she'd saved my life, that I wasn't going to make it, that if it weren't for her, I would have drowned. But all I could force out was another "Thank you."

I had a feeling she understood.

— Chapter Twenty-Nine —

Farewell

After a half hour of pleading to the door, Madison finally had no choice but to accept that Cato wasn't going to answer.

She rubbed her temples as she entered the kitchen, then paused, surprised to find Ero seated in Doc's place at the table, scrawling in a notebook. Doc must have admitted defeat and left.

"Hello," Madison greeted warmly, her voice a glaring contradiction to how she was actually feeling. He inclined his head in acknowledgment. "What are you doing?"

"Writing notes," Ero answered absently.

"About your last lesson?" she pressed.

"Yes. And the answer to your question is no."

"I haven't asked you anything yet."

Ero paused in his writing to raise one eyebrow and fix her with a meaningful look. Madison sighed as the Telepath returned to his work. "But it's important."

"I will not risk betraying the trust of my students and their siblings so Dr. Crawford can poke and prod them all to her liking."

"But they *need* a doctor, Ero."

"My concern is with their studies."

Madison folded her arms. "Okay, then what happens if one of them gets sick? They could die. How do you think that will affect the twins' studies?"

Ero stopped writing and sighed, although his gaze remained fixed on the notebook. Finally, he raised his head to meet Madison's gaze as he set the pen down and folded his hands in front of him.

"Their trust is fragile. If you push even slightly, it will shatter, and you can never earn it back."

"But if you use your telepathy to put them all to sleep, then Doc can do what she needs to, and they'll never know. You can erase their memories. It would just be one time."

"First of all, that violates my ethics. Second, it may sound easy in theory, but my students make the situation more complicated than you realize. You would feel guilty for manipulating them, and you would not be able to stop thinking about how you—and I, as an accomplice—betrayed their trust. I would be continuously erasing their memories, which could cause permanent damage."

Madison raked her fingers through her hair. "I don't know what to do. I'll never forgive myself if anything happens to them because they didn't get a vaccine or they had an underlying health condition that Doc could have diagnosed and treated."

"I cannot make the decision for you, but I can give you some advice. I believe the best way to handle this is to be patient. Either they will eventually trust you enough to allow Dr. Crawford to give them medical attention, or an opportunity will arise that may play to your advantage. But as I said, if you break their trust now by forcing the issue, you can never repair it."

Madison turned away, but then she pivoted to face him again. "Listen, Ero, about Cato's memory . . . what's wrong with him? Can you fix it?"

The Telepath didn't answer immediately. When he did speak, his voice was heavy with sadness: "Cato suffers from the same issue as the others. His memory is not gone, per se. It is just . . . inaccessible. Unfortunately, repairing his memory is not as simple as unlocking a door. Neural pathways have been damaged. Some of the pieces can be recalled at will, some are triggered by familiarity, and some, unfortunately, can never be recovered. The most I can do is help him connect some of the accessible fragments when he has difficulty."

She bobbed her head to indicate that she understood when words failed. Her eyes filled with tears, and she buried her face in her hands.

"You know," she said hoarsely, her voice muffled in her palms, "I thought I pretty much had this whole motherhood thing figured out, more or less." She dragged her hands down her face and stared at the floor. "But I feel like I did twenty years ago when I was a mom for the first time and had no idea what I was doing."

"You do not give yourself enough credit," Ero soothed. His words were kind but hollow, and they brought her no peace.

After a few long moments of silence, Ero said, "May I ask you a question?" She nodded, and he gestured toward the bay window. "What is the purpose of the loud machine outside?"

Madison didn't even need to look; she could hear the rattling drone of a lawn mower. "To cut the grass so it doesn't get too tall."

Ero tilted his head in puzzlement. "How strange. Would it not make more sense to simply plant foliage that does not grow tall?"

She stared open-mouthed at him for several seconds. "Uh . . . yeah. That would be a more rational solution. Is that what you do in the Ghost Realm?"

"Correct, but our lawns are moss, not grass."

"Really?"

"Mm-hmm. They do not require cutting, and they bloom with tiny, delicate blossoms in late summer. It seems like a much more practical solution than planting grass that needs to be cut and is never allowed to bloom."

Madison muttered, "Humans aren't known for being the most practical creatures. So, kálos don't use lawn mowers. Do they rely on much technology in the Ghost Realm?"

"No, not particularly. Technology much more advanced than yours does exist, but it is rarely utilized."

"Why?"

"Two reasons, I suppose," Ero said, leaning back in his chair. "First, Technopaths control our technology, but they are notoriously untrustworthy. When their inventions break, they are the only ones capable of making repairs, so their services are costly. Not to mention the potential for widespread hacking and critical malfunctions if Avilésor were to become as reliant on technology as Cröendor is. A single Technopath could, in theory, destroy your modern civilization with the right access. Azar would not be willing to leave such vulnerabilities in his defenses. For that reason, it is in his best interest to keep technology in check."

"And the second reason?"

"Is more of a personal bias because technology is associated with humankind. Our Divinities can often accomplish what you compensate for with technology. For example, you require machines and vehicles to construct houses; our builders are Telekinetics and Elementals who can manipulate the materials with their Divinities. Most of the kálos population views technology as a crutch that humans use in the absence of true power. Leaning on that same crutch is generally seen as a sign of weakness and an insult to our gifts."

"I see. Thank you for explaining. Your people, your abilities, your culture . . . I find it all so fascinating. I'd love to pick your brain more later."

"Pick my brain," Ero repeated. "Interesting turn of phrase."

"Yes, I guess it is." She opened the door leading to the library and collided with a body that was entering the kitchen. She said, "Sorry," at the same time Wes said, "Oops."

"Maddie, what's going on?" he demanded.

"What do you mean?" she said with a sigh, not in the mood to deal with anything else that might go wrong today.

"There's a giant icicle hanging off my roof even though it's seventy-six degrees outside."

Madison blinked in surprise, then scowled and muttered, "That means I've been talking to a door for thirty minutes."

"What?"

"Never mind," she said, walking past him.

Invisible, I slipped through the back door to find Ero seated at the kitchen table. "Cato," he greeted without turning around. "No need to waste your power; I am the only one here. You just missed Wes and your mother."

I released my invisibility but remained where I was, and after a moment, Ero's pen stopped moving. He set it down on the table. "But you were not looking for Madison, were you?" he asked.

"We had another fight," I told him hollowly. But of course, he already knew that.

Ero kindly gestured to the chair across from him and asked, "Would you like to talk about it?"

I lingered in hesitation. Chel had guided me back to the shore so I could lay on the pier and muster the strength to walk here. I was exhausted, and I reeked of lake water. All I wanted to do was take a bath and go to sleep, but I sighed and shuffled over to join Ero at the kitchen table.

I said, "Do you remember during the twins' first lesson when you promised you wouldn't share any personal information about us with anybody, including Madison and Wes?"

"Yes," Ero answered patiently, his full attention focused on me.

"So, I can talk to you about anything and you'll keep it a whisper?"

"Anything you say will remain between you and me," he assured.

I nodded and stared at the tabletop. "I don't feel like I belong here anymore."

Ero leaned back in his chair. "Did you really expect to jump back into your old life and pick up where you left off?"

I shrugged.

"Cato, the damage done in two years cannot be undone in two weeks. Have patience. There are some major adjustments to make, both on your part and on the part of your friends and family. They will never be able to understand what you have been through. Even I, with the ability to access your mind, cannot fully appreciate your suffering. A rocky transition back to normalcy is to be expected."

I rubbed both hands across my face, pressing my fingertips into my closed eyes. Ero's answer hadn't satisfied me at all. He waited, and when I didn't reply, he said, "Is there something else you would like to discuss?"

I massaged my eyelids, trying to find words. Ero offered, "Azar is on your mind now."

My fingers moved toward my temples, squinting my eyes into slits until I pulled my hands away and met Ero's cool blue gaze. "I want to protect both of my families, but I don't feel prepared to face Azar again. I don't know how to fight somebody who can turn into a shadow."

Ero's eyebrows climbed higher. "Azar does not have that ability."

"Yes, he does. I fought him. Well, tried. He stabbed my shadow with a sword. He was the darkness. He was everywhere, all around me, and I couldn't touch him."

"Hmm, all right. Let us examine your theory with logic. True or false? Azar is an Elemental."

"True. I think. Maybe." I scratched my head. "Well, wait, is darkness an element? I mean, you can't touch it like earth or water. It's not tangible."

"Nor is air, but that is not the focus of this lesson. According to Avilésian culture, light and dark are indeed considered elements. Let us move on. True or false? You are an Elemental."

"True."

"And you can turn into your element of ice."

"False." I hesitated. "Right?"

Ero smiled. "Correct. You cannot turn into ice, just as a Hydrokinetic could not melt into a puddle of water."

"But Azar *did*," I insisted.

"Light and dark can play tricks on your eyes, and darkness is arguably the most unique element. Azar's divine power evolved from photokinesis. Consider this carefully: what is darkness?"

"The absence of light?"

Ero inclined his head. "So, when Azar summons darkness, he is not really *summoning* anything, is he? He is banishing the light. Would you agree?"

I pondered, then nodded.

"Now, bear with me here. A long time ago, there were only six elemental Divinities. Those six have since evolved into a total of fifteen. Yours, for example, evolved from water. You can freeze steam and water, but you cannot turn ice back into steam, can you?"

"No."

"And you also cannot manipulate water once the ice has melted. Just as your control over water in liquid form degraded with the evolution of your elemental Divinity, so has Azar's control over the light. He can bend the negative spaces of shadows to a form easier for him to control, but he cannot bend the light like a Photokinetic can."

I thought back to the night I'd confronted Azar in the street. I'd become aware of his presence not by sensing him, but by realizing that my shadow was on the wall even though the streetlight was directly above me. It must have been easier for Azar to grab me when the shadow had my shape instead of being a round blob at my feet.

"Okay, so Azar controls the spaces where light is absent. That doesn't explain how he stabbed my shadow with a sword and I felt real pain. He grabbed me, Ero. But not *me*—he grabbed my shadow, and I felt his hand gripping my arm."

Ero explained, "Netherkinesis is different from all the other elemental Divinities. Azar's control slips beyond the element of darkness and into another Realm. Have you ever heard of an interrealm?"

"You mean like Emmett's Divinity?"

He blinked in surprise. "Ah, that is a perceptive observation, but not quite where I was going. RC's blood-brother has access to a meta-realm, which is different. Let me try to explain."

"Okay," I said weakly, already feeling the early signs of a budding headache.

"Think of the Realms as rooms in a house. The kitchen we are sitting in represents Cröendor." He pointed across the room. "Avilésor is the library, and the door separating the two rooms is a Tear. Usually, that door is locked, but when it is unlocked, we can easily pass from one room to the other. Are you with me so far?"

"Yes."

"Now, imagine interrealms as the space between the walls of those two rooms. Present, but generally not accessible, never connected by any door."

"Okay," I said, nodding to show I was still following.

"These interrealms are reflections of the Realms. There is the positive reflection—Rodeledor, the Mirror Realm. And the negative—Grimwħa'r, the Nether Realm, also known as the Realm of Shadows. Without a door, only those with particular Divinities have access to those interrealms. A Mirror-Blinker like Lieutenant Inalli can traverse the positive interrealm and affect the people's reflections. Azar is not quite as diverse. He cannot enter the Nether Realm himself because Grimwħa'r, as far as we know, lacks something Rodeledor has—access points."

Ero paused to let me think for a few seconds. "Mirrors," I realized, although I wasn't sure if I'd come to the conclusion myself or if Ero had given me a telepathic hint to help me get there.

"Correct. We can cross between the Realms through Tears, and Mirror-Blinkers can access Rodeledor through mirrors, but there does not seem to be a clearly defined access point into Grimwħa'r. However, just as Inalli can affect a person's reflection, Azar's Divinity does allow him to affect a person's shadow in Grimwħa'r, therefore impacting the person who casts that shadow."

I digested Ero's explanation. "Azar stabbed my shadow, and I felt the pain but had no wound. Are you saying Lieutenant Inalli could do the same, but with my reflection in the mirror instead of my shadow?"

"Yes. Hurt, but never kill," said Ero. "We are linked to our shadows and reflections, but the copy cannot die first."

"Is that why Azar chose Inalli to be his lieutenant? So between the two of them, both interrealms are under their control?"

"Likely one of many reasons. Mirror-Blinking is not quite as rare as Blinking, but as of now, it is constrained to Inalli's bloodline. Her family is the last, and it has a proud history of serving during King's reign."

"I've encountered Lieutenant Cisco and Captain Hassing, but not Inalli."

Ero stroked his beard. "If you are lucky, you never will. She rarely leaves the Prison."

"Will Azar someday be able to go into the Realm of Shadows if his Divinity keeps evolving?"

"Your time frame is a little off. Think about evolution here in your own Realm. It takes thousands, even millions of years. If a Netherkinetic is ever able to step foot into Grimwha'r, it will likely be many generations in the future, long after Azar is gone. Does that ease your mind a little?"

I reached under my shirt and touched the place where Azar's shadow had stabbed mine. I still remembered that pain, but my fingertips found no scar, no trace of any physical injury. Did it ease my mind to know that Azar could only manipulate the shadows and not become one himself or slip into the Nether Realm? Not really. However he'd done it, I had been defenseless when he'd grabbed my shadow under that streetlight.

"How is a metarealm different from an interrealm?" I asked.

"Ah, yes. Hmm, how best to explain . . . In our original example with the Realms as rooms in a house, think of Emmett's metarealm as a locked box under the floorboards. Only Emmett knows exactly where it is, and only he can phase through the box to retrieve what is inside."

I crossed my arms and set them on the table. All this talk about evolving Divinities had steered my train of thought in a different direction. "Axel and I, we're supposedly the only half-breeds. How can that be?"

"You are most certainly not."

I gaped at him. "W-what?"

"Well, not technically. You are not the only ones with mixed blood. In fact, Avilésian blood is present, though ancient and diluted, in many humans here in Cröendor. You can see it in certain traits, if you look hard enough. The blood of a selkie in a swimmer who is so at home in the water she seems to command it to move around her. The blood of a sirien in an opera singer who can hit notes that seem impossible. The blood of the weir in people who like to stay awake until dawn, or in a hiker who never gets lost in the woods. The blood of a Shifter in an actor who can effortlessly adopt a new role. There are many, many more examples."

Ero appraised me. "And there are numerous half-bloods in Avilé-sor. But supernatural abilities cannot cross races. Any pairing outside one's own race—like a kálos and a weir, for example—results in a child with no powers, no form-shifting abilities. A human, as far as our definition is concerned. These children may not seem completely nor-mal to you. They may have unusually colored eyes by your standards, and they would likely have certain traits and talents that could be traced back to their supernatural bloodlines. So no, you and Axel are not the first half-breeds. But you are the first *true* hybrids of mixed blood to possess supernatural abilities. That is the difference."

"Huh. Okay, I understand," I said, bobbing my head in thought as I mulled over this new knowledge.

Ero smiled. "Is there anything else on your mind that you would like to discuss while we have this privacy?"

I shook my head as I rose. "I really need a bath."

"Well, I enjoyed this impromptu lesson. I will see you at dinner."

I hesitated. "Actually . . . I'm not hungry tonight. I don't think I'll be at dinner."

He gave me a knowing look and said quietly, "You cannot avoid your mother forever."

With a shrug of reluctant acknowledgment, I left Ero to continue writing in his notebook, my ears strained for Madison as I snuck through the manor and up the stairs to my room.

In the bathroom, I plugged the tub and turned on the cold water, then stripped my clothes off as the tub filled. I had dried myself off us-ing cryokinesis before returning Home, but even though the fabric wasn't wet, it was still saturated with the smell of lake water.

I shut off the water and lowered myself into the tub with a long sigh that morphed into bubbles as I completely submerged myself. For a few minutes, I stayed underwater with my eyes closed, replaying my lake exploration. The near-death experience should have made me appre-hensive about going under again, but the water was still soothing to me.

It was my sister element, after all, and according to Ero, the founding element from which my Divinity had originally evolved. No wonder I felt so connected to the rain and the lake.

I sought my center, focusing on the blue point of light I envisioned in my core. All around me, the water started to solidify into hard, cold pieces so by the time I surfaced, I was sitting in an ice bath. I leaned my head against the tub and closed my eyes.

I must have dozed for a while because Ash's gentle knock and muffled voice calling, "Cato? It's six o'clock," made me jump to attention.

"Erm, yeah. Okay. You can start without me," I said. "I'll be down in a bit."

And yet, I took my time washing myself and getting out of the tub. Dread was inflating inside of me, making it harder to catch my breath. I really didn't want to go downstairs and face my mother. Would dodging her tonight make our next encounter more or less awkward? *It'll probably make things worse. I should just get it over with.*

I dressed myself and then walked downstairs. To my surprise, the dining room was empty. Everyone was on the patio, where a fire burned in the firepit and Wes hovered over a grill. As soon as I opened the door, the mouthwatering smell and sizzling sound of cooking meat made my stomach rumble.

"About time," Wes greeted with a smile as he offered me a stick skewered with grilled meat and vegetables. "Careful, it's hot."

"What is it?" I asked.

"A shish kebob."

"Are you drunk already?"

Wes laughed. "No, that's really what it's called. Go on, give it a try."

Kit popped up beside me and brandished her stick at Wes. "Can I have another one? Please?"

"Sure," he said with a smile.

"No veggies this time," she requested. "And could you please not cook the meat so much?"

"Ah, a carnivore. My kinda girl."

Ero chimed in from his seat next to Finn, Reese, and Ash on the pavers around the firepit: "I must say, Wes, the pack life seems to be suiting you well."

Wes scowled and opened his mouth for a retort, but Kit blurted, "What's a pack?" before he could speak.

"A very close family," Ero said.

Her ears perked up, and she gazed around the patio. "We're a pack?"

"No. We are not a pack," Wes said irritably. Her ears fell. "This is . . ." He waved his hand in an attempt to draw out the right word. "This is just a convenient and beneficial living arrangement. Nothing more."

"Oh," Kit said softly, her shoulders slumping.

Madison set a pitcher of water down next to the grill. "I think we've sort of become a pack." She gave Kit a wink even as Wes rolled his eyes. Kit's ears lifted a little.

"A pack of misfits living under one roof," Wes grumbled.

My mother's gaze was drilling into me. I turned my back to avoid eye contact with her. I wasn't keen on being so close to the fire, so I approached Jay and RC sitting on the low seat wall edging the patio.

I plopped down and started devouring my stick of food. I hadn't realized just how hungry I was.

Jay's attention was trained on Kit bouncing on the balls of her feet next to Wes as she eagerly accepted her stick of partially cooked meat. Subtly, keeping his voice low, he inquired, "You all right?"

I should have answered "yes." I thought the word as I chewed on a charred shrimp. But I couldn't seem to force the word out of my brain and into my mouth.

Jay glanced at me sidelong. I stared between Reese and Ash into the dancing flames, still chewing. Finally, I shrugged one shoulder.

Madison blocked my view. She smiled hesitantly, laced her fingers together, and said, "Would you mind if I had a private word with Cato?"

RC immediately rose to his feet, but Jay didn't move. He watched me, waiting for my reaction. If I wanted him to stay, I knew he would. I swallowed the shrimp and used my teeth to slide a small potato off the skewer.

Slowly, Jay stood, giving me plenty of time to vocalize a request. Madison waited patiently. Maybe she was grateful that Jay cared about me. Or maybe she was masking her irritation. Either way, her faint grin never wavered, and she didn't move a muscle.

Jay and RC reluctantly left me alone with my mother. I watched them so I didn't have to look at her as she sat down next to me and awkwardly greeted, "Hey."

I swallowed but didn't answer. I knew what was coming—the stern voice, the layer of disappointment beneath the anger, the reprimand for my actions this afternoon.

Yet her voice was surprisingly soft when she asked, "Why are you wearing that?"

I blinked and stared down at my tattered Alpha uniform. "Because my clothes were dirty and these were clean." I lifted my head with a scowl. "Why? Am I forbidden from wearing this?"

"Of course not," she said, her tone gentle to contradict my challenge. "You can wear whatever makes you comfortable. I just . . . would have thought that you wouldn't want to be reminded of the AGC. I don't understand your attachment to the uniform, that's all."

I bowed my head and reached up to clench my cloak in my fist. No, she didn't understand. I didn't fully understand it myself. This little piece of that hell shouldn't bring me comfort, but for some reason, it did.

"I can wash your clothes for you tonight, if you want."

I pulled a piece of marinated chicken off the skewer. A full minute of silence passed between us while I ate my dinner and Madison watched my lab-family gathered by the firepit. Ash seemed to be mesmerized by the flames. She held her hand toward the fire. The flames curled around her, as if they were sentient, trained beings that knew not to harm their master. But Ash had an air of sadness when they obeyed her, not pleasure.

"Doc really scares you, doesn't she?" Madison finally asked.

I clenched my jaw, keeping my gaze trained on the fire. My nod was so slight it was almost imperceptible.

Madison sighed and rubbed her eyes with her thumb and forefinger. "I'm sorry I lost patience with you today. I didn't mean to raise my voice at you."

I mumbled resentfully, "Yelling at me won't make me any less afraid of the doctor."

"I know that."

"Will you make me see her again?" I asked, wondering if this was yet another ruse.

But to my surprise, she answered, "No."

I frowned and raised my head. "Really?"

"Really."

"Are you mad at me?"

Madison seemed surprised by my blunt question. "No, Cato. I'm not mad. I'm just . . . incredibly frustrated, that's all, and then I lose my temper, and I'm sorry. I know it isn't your fault."

". . . I'm sorry I threatened to use my powers on you," I muttered.

"I just want us to get along. I hate fighting with you."

When I didn't answer, she added, "I wish you would talk to me more."

I rubbed my arm where the neutralizer band used to be attached like a leech. "I'm trying. It's just . . ."

"What?"

I shrugged. "It's hard. To find the words, sometimes. Especially when I'm back there, like a flashback, in pieces, and I can't think straight." I shook my head. "That doesn't make sense. I don't know how to describe it."

"No, it does." She reached for my hand, which I instinctively snapped back out of reach. A hurt expression shadowed her face, and she slowly drew her hand back into her lap in sorrow. "I think I understand what you're saying. It's hard to explain exactly what's frightening or upsetting you in the moment. That's why we both need to work on our communication."

Madison picked at a hangnail on her finger. "Cato, Doc suggested . . . we try talking to the school counselor. Do you think maybe—?"

"No."

She sighed, as if my response had been anticipated. "I think a professional might be able to help you work through your trauma better than I can."

"I don't want to talk to *you* about what happened to me in that place," I seethed. "I'm sure as hell not going to sit down in a stuffy office and talk to a stranger about it."

Madison forced her weak smile back into place. "Let's not fight again. It was only a suggestion. I'd like you to think about it, that's all. Keep an open mind."

I seized the last steak cube between my thumb and finger, slid it off the skewer, then announced, "I'm still hungry." I popped the meat into my mouth, stood up, and strode away from my mother, who remained seated as she watched me march across the patio to Wes.

She emanated sadness, her body slightly bowed as if yielding to an immense pressure, but she didn't pursue me. We'd reconciled in the most minimal terms, and she seemed to accept that any more progress was unlikely to happen tonight.

"Can I please have another?" I asked, offering my stick to Wes.

He pointed at a platter beside the grill. "I already have some cooked up. Take whatever you want."

I set my skewer down on top of the used pile stacked on a plate, then selected a new . . . what was it called? Something ridiculous. Sheesh-ka-pop. *Whatever.* I bit down on the grilled shrimp, slid it off the stick with my teeth, chewed, swallowed, and then bit into some sort of green vegetable next in line.

Whatever it was had a revolting flavor. Startled by the rude jolt, I spat the vegetable out onto the patio, but the taste lingered in my mouth.

"Something wrong?" Wes asked.

Everyone was staring at me. I shook my head in disgust and spat again, then wiped my mouth with the back of my glove. "What the hell is that?"

"A bell pepper. Sorry, I didn't realize you didn't like them. Here, I'll trade you." Wes offered me a new stick. "No peppers on this one."

I reluctantly accepted the skewer from Wes and handed over the one with grilled peppers, although I made sure to inspect my new stick for any sign of the vile vegetable before I dared to take a bite.

Ero stood up from his seat by the fire, carried his plate to the grill, and set it on a stack of dirty dishes. "It was delicious. Thank you," he said with a smile and a nod at Wes. He turned back to face everyone on the patio. "I am afraid this will be my last dinner with you for a while."

Axel folded his arms with a suspicious glare. Otherwise, Ero's announcement was met with blank looks. Jay said, "What do you mean? Are you going somewhere?"

Ero inclined his head. "Unfortunately, an urgent matter has arisen, and I must return to Avilésor. One of my former students has been struggling to control her telepathy in the wake of a personal trauma, and her family has written asking me to come for a short visit. I hope to return in a week or two."

"But what about Finn and Reese?" I demanded. "You can't just leave them."

"I have given them some simple exercises to practice in my absence. I do apologize for the abrupt departure, but I have to go where I am needed most."

I looked at the twins, who were staring blankly across the wide backyard. They didn't look particularly happy, but they weren't surprised, either, so I assumed that Ero had already broken the news to them before dinner.

"A few weeks, you said?" Madison asked.

"If all goes well," Ero replied.

Kit's silky ears fell back against her head. "But . . . I'll miss you," she whimpered, her lower lip trembling.

Ero smiled and knelt onto one knee. "I will miss you as well." He opened his arms. Kit threw herself into Ero's warm, strong hug and buried her face in his cloak. "We will meet again very soon," he promised as he let her go.

Kit sniffled and wiped away a tear with the heel of her palm. Ero stood up. "I must take my leave now. I promise to return as soon as I am able to."

He retreated to the French doors. Every step he took carved an empty void deeper and deeper into my chest. The pain surprised me—I hadn't realized how attached I'd become to the amiable Telepath living with us in Saros Manor.

Ash gently rubbed Reese's back in sympathy, but he didn't react. The twins must be upset, and yet, as usual, they were masters of their emotions, completely unreadable to the untrained eye. The vacancy in their stares and the subtle downward tilt of their heads gave them away, though.

I set my skewer on the platter and followed Ero. His room was down the short hallway, past the den on my right and the sunroom on my left. I folded my arms and leaned my shoulder against the doorway, watching him pack his few belongings into a satchel. I knew he was aware of my presence, but he didn't acknowledge me. "I wish you didn't have to go."

"It cannot be helped," the Telepath replied heavily.

"You know Finn and Reese think of you as a father figure."

Ero froze in the middle of putting a book into his bag. His head was turned just enough that I could see his frown soften into an almost pained expression. "I never intended to replace their father."

"I know. But they never met theirs, and you're the closest they've ever had. They're upset that you're leaving, even if they don't show it."

"I know how upset they are, Cato. But I have a duty that I cannot ignore."

I turned so my back was pressed against the doorframe now. "This sucks."

"I agree. The situation does, as you put it, suck. Right now, Finn and Reese are stable. My other student is not. Therefore, she is the one who needs my attention. But if their telepathic powers begin to manifest in my absence, Axel should be able to track my scent. I have no doubt that he can find me no matter what remote part of either Realm I am in."

"It's not their powers I'm worried about."

Ero took a deep breath and exhaled slowly. "I cannot take them with me, and they would be unhappy if I did." He turned to face me. "Cato, they admire me. But you and the others are their family, and they love you more than anything in this world. You understand that, right? Our relationship is nothing like the one they have with you."

"Finn and Reese don't know how to love," I muttered.

"Not in the traditional sense, no. But between their lab-family and me, I am the one they could live without."

I picked at a splinter pulling away from the edge of the doorframe. "When do you leave?"

"Now," he said, straightening and slinging the satchel over one shoulder.

He walked past me. I pivoted and followed, calling in protest, "Now? Aren't you going to tell Finn and Reese goodbye?"

"We already bid our farewells." I slowed to a halt and stood in the middle of the hallway, watching the back of his cloak sway with each step. He paused to give me a sad but friendly smile. "Our goodbye is only temporary. I will see you again soon enough."

And then he strode out of sight around the corner.

Just like that, the first true ally we ever had in the Outside, the first adult who cared about us and acted as a trusted guardian and advisor, was gone. I swore I felt an unnatural draft sweep through the mansion, as if it had just lost a vital organ and was exhaling in sadness.

— Chapter Thirty —
Tracking a Predator

That night, Wes woke with a start.

He sat up in his bed. Something, although he couldn't pinpoint *what* exactly, had disturbed his slumber, and he knew better than to disregard his instincts.

He stared at the dark window. "Seriously?" He threw the covers back and touched his bare feet to the cool floor, muttering, "I'll be damned if an intruder thinks they can break into *my* house."

He was already shirtless, so he stripped off his pants and crouched to the floor, willing the transformation to start. The change came easily. His bones shifted smoothly into place with barely any pain or crunching, tail sprouting out behind him, thick gray fur sweeping across his naked skin in waves, as if unfurling in a nonexistent wind.

Wes growled as he fumbled with the lock to the French doors that led into the neglected private garden outside the master bedroom. By the time he pushed down on the door handle, his fingers were gone, replaced by a massive paw.

Wes nosed the door open and dashed into the garden, then gathered himself and cleared the fence with room to spare. He landed in a wide stance, lips pulled back over his sharp teeth, nose wrinkled under the force of the low snarl.

A shadow rounded the corner of the manor.

Wes trotted after it, his padded paws quiet on the lawn. He slowed when he reached the steps on the side of the long porch. Belly brushing the dewy grass, he crept forward and peered around the corner to find a creature in a black cloak slipping through the night toward Phantom Heights. It paused and glanced back over its shoulder, its eerie red irises glowing beneath the hood.

Wes narrowed his eyes. *Axel.*

The werewolf didn't move. Axel didn't seem to have noticed him crouched beside the stairs. He turned his back and dashed nimbly into town, so silent that not even the wolf's sharp ears could detect Axel's footsteps.

Wes rested his chin on his paws. That was almost disappointing— Agent Kovak's "perfect hunter" certainly hadn't lived up to his reputation. Maybe the great A6 wasn't as in tune with his surroundings as Kovak thought. Wes watched the half-breed reach the street at the edge of the front lawn.

It's after 3 a.m. . . . What is he doing?

After a brief hesitation, Wes rose and followed, keeping his distance. He trailed the elusive shadow that slipped around the pools of light cast down from the streetlights lining the empty roads.

Axel was fast, but Wes was able to keep him in sight. He was panting softly as he tried his utmost to escape Axel's sharp hearing and sense of smell. He meticulously made sure to stay downwind so he could smell Axel but Axel couldn't smell him, and he had to place every paw carefully to keep quiet while at the same time covering ground quickly.

Axel's cloak vanished around a corner several blocks ahead. The wolf lengthened his stride and jogged around the corner to find . . . nothing. Silver ribbons tied to doorknobs caught the breeze and reflected the moonlight with faint flashes. A discarded newspaper blew across the otherwise-deserted street. Axel was gone.

The wolf stiffened and shivered. "C'mon, Wes. You didn't think you were actually being stealthy, did you?" a cold voice said from behind.

Wes turned to find the creature from Project Delta standing behind him, arms folded, glaring at him with red eyes that glowed with piercing intensity in the darkness.

A deep, primitive instinct stirred in Wes, causing the hackles along his back to rise. He didn't know what Axel was, and yet he was con-

sumed by an ancient fear passed down from his ancestors who had encountered creatures like Axel before.

His primal desire to survive made Wes want to flee—he sensed that
Axel was a dangerous predator to avoid at all costs. He was startled to
hear a sound vibrating in his own vocal cords, even more surprised
when he realized it was a petrified whimper.

Wes swallowed his terror, forcing himself to hold his ground. He
faced Axel, tilting his head with a quiet whine of inquiry. Axel studied
him. "You want to know how long I knew you were following me," he
translated.

Dumbstruck that he'd been understood, Wes just stood there like an
idiot as Axel narrowed his eyes and answered, "Since I left the mansion. I heard you get out of bed, and I smelled you as soon as you
changed forms. You reek like a wet dog, especially in the dew, and
your breathing is so loud I could find you without my eyes or nose. I've
been leading you around town to see how long it would take you to
give up and turn back. You're a stubborn bastard, but I got bored. This
game isn't fun anymore, so you might as well go home."

Wes growled softly, unnerved by how precise Axel's senses were.
Even in wolf form, Wes couldn't compete. What was worse, he wasn't
even good enough to be a player. He leaned back on his hind legs, allowing his body to shift into limbo form so he could speak. The paralyzing fear weakened slightly as his human senses dulled his wolf instincts.

"Why aren't you asleep?" he asked. The words were jumbled in his
distorted mouth, his sharp wolf teeth in the way of his tongue. A warm
summer breeze ruffled his fur.

Axel didn't answer at first, but then he replied, "Do you realize
how much of your life is wasted in sleep?"

"You don't sleep," Wes realized aloud. "And you don't eat or
drink, either. How can you function without any energy?"

"There are other sources of energy," Axel answered vaguely.

"Are you a Dynamo? Do you draw energy from your own power
supply?"

Axel heaved a deep sigh. "I don't know how I can make it any clearer that I don't have a Divinity, and I'm getting really tired of repeating myself."

"What are you?" Wes whispered, burning with curiosity now.

"It's driving you insane not knowing, isn't it?" Axel said with a twisted smirk. His short fangs were illuminated in the white smile gleaming in the dark.

Wes hesitated, but he knew Axel could sense a lie, so he admitted, "Yes."

Axel turned away and stared up at the swollen moon. "I'm an abomination. Two creatures that were never meant to be combined in one body." He redirected his red eyes onto the wolf-man. "And I won't tell you. So stop following me, because you can't keep up in your wildest dreams."

In a rush of wind and a blur, Axel was gone again, so far away that Wes couldn't even detect his presence.

He stood still in the middle of the sidewalk. His body abhorred being bound in limbo; it preferred to be wolf or human, one or the other, so he sank to all fours and allowed the power to wash over him again.

Axel's scent was still light on the air, and Wes shivered again. The scent made him want to run away with his tail between his legs until he couldn't smell it anymore.

He was irreparably torn between his human curiosity that wondered what terrible creature Axel was and his wolf instincts that warned him to avoid Axel at all costs if he wanted to survive.

— Chapter Thirty-One —
An Unusual Request

I couldn't find Finn and Reese.

Dizzy with panic, I descended the steps two at a time. At five o'clock in the afternoon, there was no reason the twins shouldn't be in our room.

I bypassed the whole second floor—I couldn't imagine what Finn and Reese would possibly be doing on that level—and landed lightly on both feet in the foyer.

It took every ounce of self-control not to sprint toward the archway of the library. *Maybe Finn and Reese got bored in our room. Maybe they were upset about Ero leaving and wanted to get lost in books as a distraction. They must be in the library. I don't know where else they would be.*

Someone was sitting in one of the armchairs. My racing heart took a microsecond roller-coaster ride in relief, then disappointment, then renewed panic when I identified the reader as Wes, which meant my lab-brothers were still missing.

Wes peered up from his book and smiled when he saw me. "Hey, Cato. I—"

"Have you seen Finn and Reese?" I blurted.

He blinked, taken aback by my breathless interruption. His nonchalance while I was on the verge of mind-numbing panic caused irritability to prickle inside my chest, stirring my green Divinity.

"Yeah," he said, still way too slow and calm. "They're in the kitchen with your mom. They're fine."

I set my hand over my heart as I expelled a colossal sigh of relief, then stormed through the library toward the swinging door that led into the kitchen. Wes called, "Hey, wait. What do you think of this?" He set an open book on the tabletop and slid it toward me.

Half-curious, half-annoyed, and very self-conscious about my rusty reading skills, I glanced once more at the kitchen door, then approached the table and leaned over the book. My brain didn't have enough oxygen to focus on the blurry words and make sense of them after the panic attack, but the drawing of a strange creature with abnormally long arms and fingers, legs that were bent and distorted into haunches, a rough mane, claws, and what looked like wounds or sores on its skin captured my attention.

"A wendigo?" I read from the title above the drawing.

Wes set his elbows on the tabletop, laced his fingers together, and rested his chin on his hands. "One of the legendary five fiends. Neat creatures. Very strong, very fast. If you're bitten by a wendigo, an intense craving for flesh will drive you to madness. Resist the temptation, and you'll eventually make a full recovery. But if you give in and partake in an act of cannibalism, you'll become a wendigo yourself."

I had an inkling as to where he was going with this topic, but I chose to ignore the foreboding pit in my stomach and play the ignorant card instead. I pushed the book back at him and asked, "Have you ever met a wendigo?"

"I'm not sure," he replied cryptically. He tried to meet my gaze, but I wouldn't humor him. "Have *you*?"

"Am I in this book?"

His eyebrows twitched up in surprise. Now that I'd taken the upper hand, I felt confident enough to look him in the eye. "I mean, I'm the Demikan, right? If this is a book of creatures, shouldn't I be in it?"

Wes smirked. "This is an old book, and you haven't been around very long."

"Okay, well, have fun with your reading," I said lightly, turning on my heel and walking away.

"Is Axel part wendigo?" Wes blurted out.

I shrugged one shoulder. "You should ask Axel."

"Come on, Cato. That's not fair." The armchair made a muffled *fwoop* sound as he slumped back against his seat with disappointment. "I think I deserve to know."

"I disagree," I replied without looking back.

I hit the swinging door with both palms and left Wes sulking in the library, listlessly turning the pages of his book.

Finn and Reese were seated on the countertop. Axel was hanging upside down from the counter's edge, eyes closed, cloak falling behind his head and pooling on the floor. Kit stood on her tiptoes to watch my mother pour baking soda into a measuring spoon and then add it into a large bowl.

"*There* you are!" I exclaimed.

Finn, Reese, Kit, and Madison turned at the sound of my voice. My mother said, "Oh, hi, Cato," but my gaze was on the twins.

"Do you know how worried I was when I couldn't find you?"

Finn and Reese bowed their heads, but that didn't appease me.

"I know you're sorry, but if you're going to leave the room, next time leave a note so I know where you are, okay?"

Axel yawned and said, "Don't piss yourself—I was watching them."

"Yeah, that's reassuring."

He opened one eye to glower at me. Kit happily sang, "We're baking cookies!"

"Are you?" I said, lightening my tone for her.

Madison smiled uneasily. "I'm sorry for worrying you, Cato. I thought it would be a fun activity to help get their minds off of . . . you know. Here, Kit, could you stir this for me? Please be very careful to keep it inside the bowl." My lab-sister beamed at being tasked with such an important responsibility. She hopped onto a stool.

Axel heaved a dramatic sigh of boredom and flipped over as he let go of the counter. He landed silently and effortlessly on both feet, then stretched his arms over his head. "Well, now you can babysit. I got better things to do."

He headed for the swinging door that led to the library.

Madison said, "Oh, come on, Axel. Not even you can turn down homemade chocolate chip cookies. Don't you want to stick around and try one?"

Her only answer was a disgusted grunt and an utterance of "I hate cookies" as he stormed away.

Madison reclaimed the wooden spoon from Kit and called, "Just a second, Axel. That book right next to you there on the counter—how many cups of flour does it say we need?"

Axel hesitated, glanced at the cookbook, then shook his head and phased through the swinging door without a word. Finn solemnly slid off his perch and walked over to peer at the page. He held up three fingers.

"Thank you," Madison said. "Reese, could you please measure that out and add it to the bowl?"

As my lab-brother took painstaking care to level off an exact cup, she snapped at me, "I've been trying to get along with Axel. He still goes out of his way to spite me."

Finn lifted the cookbook and tapped on the page.

"What?" I asked. "You want me to read something?"

He shook his head and set the book down, then held up six fingers. He tapped his temple with his index finger, then planted it on the open page.

"Oh," I said in surprise.

He nodded that my interpretation was correct.

"What?" Madison demanded.

"Axel doesn't know how to read."

Just like that, the irritated wrinkles in her brow vanished. "Oh." She stared down into the bowl as she continued to mash the dough. "I wish he would just say that instead of acting the way he does."

Kit's ears perked up, and she hopped off the stool. "Axel can learn to read with me. We can learn together!"

"No, Kit. Um . . ." I knelt on one knee to meet her at eye level and lowered my voice to a whisper even though Axel could still probably hear me. "I don't think Axel wants us to know that he can't read."

She tilted her head. "Why?"

"It would hurt his pride. Let's promise not to say anything. Deal?"

"Deal!" she chimed, throwing her arms around my neck in an embrace.

I stood up and set Kit down on the edge of the counter. "Okay, I think Madison still needs your help with these cookies. What's next?"

Kit donned her fur in a swirl of black smoke, padded along the countertop, and transformed back into her skin when she reached my mother.

I leaned back against the counter to watch. Kit was radiating pure joy as she dumped the bag of chocolate chips into the mixture. Under Madison's supervision and instruction, she balled fistfuls of cookie dough and gingerly placed them on the baking sheet. Finn and Reese were more subdued, and yet they were attentive and focused, which was a good indicator that they were enjoying the activity. Food had always been handed to them, already prepared, so making it themselves and seeing all the ingredients mixed together must be an intriguing learning experience for them.

I couldn't fight the grin tugging at the corners of my mouth, although it slowly faded as heartache moved in like a thunderstorm clouding up a clear day. The four of them looked like a real family. A mom baking cookies with three little kids.

For a moment—just a glimmer of recollection—I remembered when Vivian and I were in their place. That was me in another life, baking cookies with Mom and Vivi in our small sunlit kitchen with white cabinets. I missed those days.

The twins paused. Madison and Kit continued, oblivious to them staring at me. I forced a smile at them and thought, *No, it's okay. You weren't supposed to hear any of that.*

Despite my reassurance, they were still hesitant, and their gazes wavered uncertainly between Madison and me as if the twins were now feeling guilty that they'd stolen something from me.

It's not mine—not anymore, I thought at them. *I grew up. I don't mind sharing Madison with you.*

Yes, I did—I swore I felt a heartstring break.

This was stupid. If Madison had asked me to bake cookies with her, I would have refused. I had no reason to be jealous of my lab-siblings.

Unfortunately, I couldn't make my heart agree with that logic.

"What's the matter?" Madison asked, peering down at Finn and Reese. "You stopped helping. Are you bored?"

I crossed my arms. *A human wants your help. What are you going to do?*

That wasn't fair, but it was effective. Finn and Reese reached into the bowl to ball up the dough for cookies, but they were much more solemn now, focused on the duty of obeying a human's request rather than enjoying the task. And it was all my fault.

Please don't be so melancholy, I silently begged. *I feel bad. You deserve to have fun with Madison and Kit—really. I mean it. I don't understand why I feel jealous, but it's not your fault. I wish you couldn't read my mind and know all of my private thoughts and feelings.*

I bowed my head and squeezed my eyes shut in a grimace. *Damn it. You weren't supposed to hear that, either. I'm sorry.*

They weren't looking at me, but I could feel a rift expanding between us. I couldn't hide my unbidden thoughts, nor could I stop them from coming.

"I need some air," I announced, turning on my heel and striding toward the dining room.

"Are you okay?" Madison asked in concern. "You're not feeling sick, are you?"

"Nope. Fine. Great. I'll be on the porch."

I pushed through the swinging door. Rather than cross the length of the dining room to reach the front doors, I phased through the outer wall and emerged in the shade of the porch.

"What is wrong with me?" I muttered as I leaned against the railing.

I wanted Finn and Reese to be happy—I really did. So why was I jealous? And how was I supposed to hide those feelings from two Mind-Readers? I'd always felt that good people were allowed to have bad thoughts, as long as they didn't act on them. But I felt lower than low. My private thoughts might as well have been actions since I couldn't hide them, and really, that wasn't fair. My mind should be a sanctuary where I could harbor whatever nasty thoughts I wanted and they couldn't hurt anybody.

"Cato!" a woman called from a distance.

The interruption made me jump. I looked up to find one of the last people I wanted to see—Councilwoman Jennings marching up the front walk with short, quick steps.

I smothered the instinctive groan and reluctantly shuffled across the porch to meet her by the front door.

She halted just in front of the bottom step, chest heaving, cheeks flushed, untamed strands of hair pulled free of her usually impeccably tight bun. She was clutching the handle of her briefcase so hard that her knuckles were white and a blue vein was raised across the back of her hand. I'd never seen her look so flustered before.

The councilwoman forced an unnatural smile that made me cringe. "This is . . . such a fortunate happpenstance."

"Is it?" I muttered under my breath.

"As a matter of fact, I came here to ask Wes or Madison . . . if they knew where I might find you." Holly eyed the railing, as if considering reaching out and using it as a brace while she caught her breath. Instead, she opted to remain standing by her own strength to preserve her dignity. "There's something I wanted to ask you. I . . . think you might be able to help me."

I folded my arms, immediately defensive. "With what?" I asked suspiciously. This better not involve another public spectacle, because I was *not* going to dance on command like her puppet again.

She took a steadying breath, flattened her hair, and wiped her palm on her skirt. "It's about my son, Greyson. Have you . . . I mean, are you aware of the situation?"

I nodded, unsure where this was going. "I'm sorry for your loss," I recited uncomfortably.

Although Holly tried her best to remain composed, I noticed the way her hands trembled despite the death grip on her briefcase. "He was taken, but his body was never recovered. I know I don't have any right to ask you for a favor, but I want you to find him for me."

I gawked at her. Did I hear that correctly?

She was waiting, the anxiety making her fidgety. I said, "Uh . . . Mrs. Jennings, my Divinities are cryokinesis and sonokinesis. I'm not sure how I can help."

"No, no—not *you*—I mean . . . I was actually hoping you would facilitate the effort, because . . . I heard Axel has a nose that's better than any bloodhound's, if Agent Kovak was telling the truth."

She fumbled with the clasp on her briefcase before it popped open, and then Holly withdrew a crumpled T-shirt. "I'm not under any disillusions. I know Greyson is probably dead, but I can't have closure until I know for sure. I want to lay him to rest. Do you think Axel could find his body after all this time?"

I stared at the small shirt, struggling to process her request.

"Um . . ." I scratched my head, feeling rather helpless and overwhelmed. "I don't know. Maybe. But he's not likely to do either of us any favors. Especially not one that would require so much effort."

When Holly's features hardened, her expression returned to a much more normal, oddly less alarming state than the wild-eyed, desperate demeanor she'd possessed a moment ago. She closed the briefcase with a tense *click*. "Then convince him."

"But—"

"I just want to bury my little boy. Your mom won't help me because she thinks it's a lost cause. If you can't help, my only other option is Agent Kovak. Would you rather I owe a favor to you, or him?"

I rubbed the back of my neck. "I can't speak for Axel."

"I know that. But you can convey the seriousness of the situation and ask him on my behalf. And if you can't convince him, then I hope you can convince Jay to give Axel the order and force him to comply."

"Axel doesn't take orders from Jay," I replied with a cold edge to my tone. "He respects Jay as our leader, but that's not the same as admitting fealty."

Holly set her foot on the bottom step and extended the T-shirt toward me. "Please, Cato. I just want to bury my son's remains. Nobody else will help me."

I sighed. Her pleading voice and pathetic expression were making me squirm with discomfort. I reluctantly reached out and accepted the shirt. "I'll talk to Axel. But I can't make any promises."

"That's all I ask," she said, stepping back with a tearful smile. "Thank you. I won't forget this—I promise. If Axel can find Greyson, dead or alive, I'll be in his debt."

"Don't let him hear you say that," I muttered. "I guarantee you'll regret it."

She nodded with an unnatural laugh that sounded more like a sob. "Yes, I suppose you're right." Holly blinked rapidly and bowed her head to hide the tears. "Please let me know what Axel says after you've had a chance to ask him."

I nodded. She stood there, staring at me, the uncomfortable tension dialing up to a miserable level. I took an awkward step back. "I, uh, guess I'd better take this up to our room."

"Oh. Right." The councilwoman clenched her briefcase handle in both hands. "I hope to hear from you soon."

I backed away, then fumbled for the door handle and let myself back inside, leaving Holly standing there at the bottom of the porch steps, still watching me.

Once the door was closed, I exhaled and stared at the navy T-shirt in my hands. Convincing Axel to help Councilwoman Jennings was going to be an impossible task. I'd have to think carefully about exactly what to say, and I'd also have to time my opportunity just right if I were to have any hope of catching him in a good mood.

I crumpled the shirt in my fist and strode through the foyer, then took the steps two at a time until I reached our room on the third story and tucked the T-shirt into an empty dresser drawer.

My descent back down the grand staircase was slower. The whole mansion was filling with the sweet and tantalizing fragrance of baking cookies. I paused on the second floor.

I don't mind sharing Madison with my lab-siblings, I told myself in an attempt to corral my thoughts in the right direction before facing Finn and Reese again. *I'm not jealous. Kit and the twins deserve this quality time with a mom.*

The sound of breaking glass made me jump. I hurried down the staircase and rushed into the library to find Kit standing over a shattered plate and cookie bits on the floor. Her ears were pinned back, her eyes flooded with tears, and she stared in heartbroken shock at the mess, on the verge of crying.

Madison, looking rather pale, was standing behind her. "Kit?" she inquired gently, stepping forward and holding out her hand in an offering of condolence. Wes was sitting in the armchair, his mouth open in disbelief.

"What happened?" I demanded.

Kit's lower lip trembled. She looked at Madison's hand, then whimpered and spun into my mother's embrace with a sob. "Shh," Madison soothed, stroking her hair.

Kit's voice was muffled in Madison's stomach: "I . . . thought he might . . . like one, just to try. Just one."

"I know, honey," Madison consoled. Her expression hardened when she raised her head to look at me. "Axel," she said, and that was the only explanation I needed.

I looked around the library, but Axel was gone. Madison continued to stare at me, clearly waiting for an explanation as to what set him off this time, as if I were now the designated expert on Axel's mood swings. He'd already made it clear that he didn't like cookies, and they should have just left it at that, but I never would have imagined he would go so far as to knock a plate out of Kit's hands.

I knelt next to the mess on the floor and selected the biggest piece of a cookie. After an experimental sniff, I took a bite. It was shockingly sweet—too sweet for me while I was still adapting to the extremes of the flavor palate Outside. "Mmm," I said. "Wow, that's really good."

Kit, who had no doubt wiped plenty of snot onto Madison's shirt by now, sniffled again and turned her head to look at me with bloodshot eyes, her cheeks glistening. I smiled at her and took another bite. "You did a great job," I praised.

She pulled away from Madison to face me. "You really like it?" She wiped her nose with her sleeve.

"Best cookie I've ever eaten," I said.

Wes closed his book, set it on the table, and then sat down beside me on the floor. He followed my lead and selected part of a cookie to sample. "Delicious," he affirmed.

Kit smiled through her tears. Slowly, her grin faded, and her ears fell again. "Axel wouldn't even try one," she croaked in a hoarse whisper.

I said, "Kit, you know how Ax can be when he's in a bad mood. He doesn't know what he's missing."

Madison shook her head in disapproval. Kit gazed sadly at the mess on the floor. "That was going to be dessert for tonight," she lamented. "We made enough cookies for everybody."

Madison set her hand on Kit's shoulder and said, "We can make some more. If we start now, they'll be baking while I make dinner, and they should be ready to eat for dessert."

Kit's ears perked up. "Okay," she said, although she wasn't nearly as enthusiastic as she had been before.

Madison nudged her toward the kitchen door. "Why don't you go get the ingredients out? Finn and Reese can help you. I'll be there in a minute."

Kit swiped at her drying tears and padded into the kitchen. As soon as the door swung shut, Madison snapped, "Axel—"

I interrupted by holding up my hand. "I'll try to talk to him."

She scoffed and started picking up the larger pieces of glass. "You say that like talking to him will actually make a difference."

Wes set his hands on his knees and rose. "I guess this was my fault. I was pushing Axel for answers. I didn't think he'd take it out on Kit, though."

"Something must have triggered him," I said.

"That's no excuse," Madison snapped. "Do you know what he said to her? He said, 'Didn't I tell you I don't want any of your fucking cookies?' Then he knocked the plate right out of her hands. How can he treat her like that?"

"I don't know," I muttered as I stood up. *Great, Axel's already pissed. So much for asking him to find a missing kid. Even if I can find Axel, now is definitely not a good time to ask him for a favor.*

Wes waved his hand and said, "You go bake another batch with the kids. I'll clean this up." He pointed at my mother and sternly added, "But I don't want to hear a single joke about dogs cleaning up food spilled on the floor."

I turned away from them. "I'm going to look for Axel."

"Dinner's in less than an hour," Madison called from behind.

"I know," I said as I strode away.

— Chapter Thirty-Two —
Brother's Betrayal

If Axel didn't want to be found, I had no expectation of crossing paths with him. The only place I could think to look was our old Home.

I dropped down from the window in the abandoned office and straightened. This place still looked exactly the same as when we'd lived here, and I found that inexplicably comforting.

The door creaked when I pushed it open and emerged into the cavernous warehouse. Beams of late-afternoon sunlight were streaming in at a slant through the holes in the ceiling. The industrial drums we'd left underneath to collect rainwater had overflowed, leaving puddles that reflected the light and ceiling like an incomplete mirror puzzle that was missing pieces where the floor was still dry.

But, except for a fat gray rat that scampered along the edge of the wall and vanished into a hole, I was alone.

I wandered inside, then stopped beside one of the rain barrels. I peered down at my reflection for a moment before I dipped my cupped hands into the water and scooped a handful for a drink.

Before the water touched my lips, I paused. Insect larva twitched and wriggled in the stagnant rainwater. Disgusted, I spread my fingers apart and let the water spill back into the full container, then froze the moisture out of my gloves and whisked the ice away. I hadn't heard the clock tower chime six yet, but I might as well return to Saros Manor before Madison's anger extended to me, too. There was no point in continuing the hunt.

Although I felt guilty for thinking it, I almost hoped Axel would skip dinner with us tonight for the sake of peace. I shook my head as I returned to the broken window in the office. Why did my lab-brother have to be so damn stubborn and argumentative? I was getting tired of apologizing on his behalf, and I was going to tell him that the next time I saw him. As if he'd care.

I leapt onto the windowsill and hopped down into the alley. A shiver instantly traveled down my spine and erected goose bumps across my skin.

Uh-oh.

I whirled, icicles already clenched in both fists. A cloaked silhouette was standing at the mouth of the alley, eyes glowing red, a coiled rope clasped in one hand. For a moment, I thought it was Axel, but no. The form was too tall and bulky.

I shivered again and turned my head to find two more ghosts at the other end of the alley. All three started to move in.

Not good. This wasn't an ideal place to fight multiple opponents—too restrictive, and if others phased through the walls in these close quarters, I wouldn't have enough time to see them and react.

I reached for my center and summoned intangibility, then darted through the wall and reemerged back in the warehouse, already in a sprint. Footsteps pounded right behind me. I cursed to myself; I didn't have enough time to stop, get my bearings, and face my opponents. Not when they were right on top of me with unknown Divinities.

I chanced a quick look over my shoulder as I ran. Three ghosts in pursuit, and although I couldn't get a good look, they seemed to be armed with weapons. They weren't dressed in Shadow Guard uniforms, which meant they were likely Traders.

A broad, barrel-chested man with blazing green eyes appeared through the wall in front of me. I veered left, never breaking stride, and leapt through the wall. An ominous chill swept over my body again. Another ghost was right there, bearing down on me as soon as I solidified. I deflected his blow with an ectoplasm shield and ducked away from him, turning toward the street. The big guy appeared through the wall up ahead and charged toward us, blocking my way.

Damn it! There were too many, and they were coming at me too fast. I had to keep moving—the three who had been chasing me through the warehouse would be on top of us any second.

With both ways to an open street blocked, I had no choice but to become intangible again and phase through the wall of the next building.

I appeared in an office cubicle. Immediately, I took stock of my surroundings and rushed toward the doorway, only to find yet another Trader blocking my path. I cursed and darted through the wall on my left instead.

This floor was a frustrating maze of cubicles and offices. Every time I emerged in a new room and tried to reach the doorway, a Trader had already beaten me there to block me in. The only escape route available was through the walls. I understood their coordinated tactics—they were forcing me to use intangibility, trying to make me burn out. And if this chase continued, they'd succeed.

Another office, and this time, the doorway wasn't blocked yet. I dashed through.

A pair of Traders charged down the hallway toward me. I threw out my arms, freezing ice needles and sending the storm of sharp shards toward my opponents. They became intangible, never even breaking stride as they bore down upon me.

I pivoted and sprinted down the hall in the opposite direction. A foreboding tickle under my nose alerted me that I was bleeding. My reserves were running dangerously low. No way I'd last long in a fight now, but if I could get outside again, I could send a distress call to my lab-siblings.

There was an exit ahead of me, but as I drew near, another Trader appeared from a door up ahead. My only option was to phase through the wall on my right and escape into the next office.

This one had an outside window! I phased through the last wall. I was using my last reserves now, and I could feel it—the drain on my strength was immediate and alarming. When I stumbled outside, my vision was dark at the edges and starting to spin. I labored to draw rattling breaths into my burning lungs.

I was in another alley. At each end, a Trader stood guard to block me from reaching the street. I raised my hand straight up to send an ectoplasmic distress call into the sky.

A hot blast of red ectoplasm hit me from the side before I could release my own. I went down, sprawled out on the alley floor, but I scrambled to my feet immediately. *No time!* The other Traders would be charging through the wall any second.

Trapped yet again, I had no choice but to force my body to become intangible and make a desperate leap for the brick wall of the next building.

My power failed.

The warmth in my core went out like a candle, and instead of running through the solid barrier, I collided hard and rebounded. I lay on the alley floor and gazed up in a daze at the puffy white clouds so dizzyingly high above me. My ears rang. I could feel the stream of blood trickling from my nose and down my cheek.

I scrambled to get my limbs back under control as I rolled over and stood up to assume a defensive position, but I was too slow; I'd barely risen to my feet when a rope caught my right wrist and went taut, pulling my arm. I scowled and heaved back with my remaining strength.

Even though I was weakened from the burnout, the Trader's boots slid as I dragged him after me. I took a sudden step toward him, slackening the rope. Startled and off-balance, he flailed as he fell back.

I reached for the rope with my free hand to remove it, but before I could hook my fingers under the tight loop, another rope was thrown from behind me to catch my left arm. It tightened, yanking my other hand back.

I whirled to face my next opponent, but the first Trader pulled his rope tight again. My arms were being pulled in opposite directions. I gritted my teeth and flexed my arms inward with all my strength, overpowering my captors for a moment.

Just a moment.

Then another rope looped around my neck. Two more found my left arm, another my right, and these weren't lassos—they were ribbed with metal barbs that bit into my skin. The other Traders were closing in. Once hooking me, they pulled in opposite directions so no matter how much I struggled, I was trapped in the middle of a painful game of tug-of-war.

I opened my mouth to scream for help just as another Trader stepped up behind me and looped a strip of cloth between my teeth to gag me. Panting like a wild animal, I continued to squirm. My heart pounded against my ribs. Restraints left me helpless; they took me back to a dark place in my memories where anyone could hurt me and there was nothing I could do to defend myself.

More Traders approached, ropes in hand. I counted a total of twelve, but there might have been more behind me, out of my field of vision. The ghosts stepped aside to let a man—I assumed the leader—approach. His deep voice echoed down the alley: "Good job. Hold 'im steady. Ha, got 'im now, eh?"

I glared at the leader, who halted and observed me with a satisfied smirk that turned my stomach. When his hand drifted toward my face, I flinched and tried to back away, but the ropes held me firm, trapped in a web of cords. The soles of my boots slid on the asphalt in my vain attempt to retreat.

I scowled and took advantage of my taut restraints, seizing ropes in each fist and using the leverage to push off the ground and kick out with both feet. The leader calmly stepped back out of range. I'd made a mistake; as if prepared for this move, more Traders threw ropes around my ankles before I landed on the ground again. They shuffled back, tightening their ropes and completely subduing me so I couldn't kick anymore. I squirmed, a frustrated scream muffled behind my gag.

"Easy, boy," the leader murmured as he drew closer again. "No need t' fight so hard. You're a-right; I wantcha in one piece." Despite his gentle voice, he seized my hair with a hard grip that reminded me of *Them*. I shuddered, grinding my teeth against the disgusting cloth in my mouth while he tilted my head back to inspect his catch. "What's a-matter?" he teased. "Ya look a bit tired. All burnt out?"

All I could do was glower at him as he released my hair and reached for my wrist instead. He phased away my gauntlet so he could study my Mark. "A7, huh? Where's yer strong friend? I gotta score t' settle with 'im."

Axel? What could he possibly want with Axel?

He turned just enough for me to notice an anomaly that made my heart sink. This man had only one arm. The other ended at his elbow, and the fresh scars marring his skin partway up the stump possessed the curious texture of cracks, as if the piece of his arm that was missing had crumbled away like broken stone . . . which was exactly what had happened. I was pretty sure I was now a captive of the Talon Gang that used to guard the Rip and demand a toll for crossings. The leader was a Morphis, and the last time I'd seen him, Axel had shattered his arm.

The woman next to the leader casually picked dirt from under her long fingernails. "So, whatcha wanna do, Ryland? Use this one as bait to grab the one who messed you up?"

"Nah, this one'll do for now." He smiled at me. "We'll get Mateo outta Prison first, then come back t' settle the score with the rat I really want."

I started struggling again, but it was no use. My joints ached as the tension pulled at my sockets. The woman tying the gag behind my head muttered, "An' how come Teo gets the pardon?"

The others murmured in quiet dissent. Ryland grinned and answered, "Nobody else has been able t' catch an Alpha. Trust me— Azar'll give the whole gang pardons for life."

A seedy-looking man with yellow eyes pulled out a parchment from his pocket. "But it says that a pardon will be given to whoever turns in an Alpha. *A* pardon. We can split the money, but we can't split one pardon."

The leader waved his hand in dismissal. "Naw. Look, the way I see it, we c'n demand whatever we want an' Azar'll have no choice but to pay up. If he wants this fugitive as bad as I think he does, we'll have no problem. We c'n demand triple payment an' pardons fer everyone."

"No," said the woman behind me. "Azar don't negotiate, an' ya know it. If you piss him off demanding extra payment, he'll jus' arrest us all an' take what he wants, and then we're finished."

"Yeah," another chimed in. "If there's only one pardon per capture, then how come it gets t' go t' yer brother?"

"Cuz I'm the leader an' I say so!" said Ryland.

My gaze shifted between each speaker. I was still now, silent, obedient. Resting. Waiting.

The group was distracted, and I had recuperated enough to summon intangibility for one second, maybe two if I pushed myself. That wasn't much, but it was all I needed to free myself from these ropes. I closed my eyes and concentrated, searching for my center. The power was unusually difficult to find, even harder to summon, but I forced it up from the deep well. A rush of warmth bloomed for one heartbeat.

I expected the tight ropes to fall away as my body passed through them . . . but they didn't. My power died again, and I was still trapped.

I frowned, bewildered, doubting that I'd actually summoned enough power and then reassuring myself that I had. I'd been intangible. I'd felt it. And yet, I hadn't been able to phase through the ropes.

I jumped at the uncomfortable tickle of hot breath in my ear. "Nice try, kid. Can't phase through these ropes; they're made from vidon fibers."

I swallowed. With the failure of my last resort, my power was completely gone, leaving me helpless in my human state. I bowed my head in defeat. I couldn't raise my arms or summon enough ectoplasm for a distress call to signal my lab-family. I couldn't shout. I couldn't maneuver. *Okay, think. How would Trey get out of this situation? He's human. He doesn't rely on any powers. What would Trey do?*

The gang was still arguing. I opened my hand and rotated my wrist until I could close my fingers into a fist around the rope in my right hand, and then I closed my eyes, let out a sigh, and went completely limp. The ropes kept me suspended for a few seconds before my captors realized something was wrong, and then they went slack.

I fell in a heap and kept perfectly still. Ryland nudged me with the toe of his boot. When I didn't respond, he kicked me, *hard*, and it was all I could do to keep the grunt trapped between my teeth while maintaining a neutral facial expression even though he'd probably fractured at least one rib.

Ryland muttered, "Stupid kid burned out. Ah well, it'll make 'im easier t' transport. Truss 'im up and let's get a move on."

Hands were on my body. They were removing the ropes around my ankles, neck, and left hand—I'd intentionally landed with my right hand beneath my body.

"Wait a minute, Ry. We ain't goin' anywhere 'til we figure out this whole ransom business."

"Nothin' t' figure out," Ryland snarled back. "We're usin' the pardon on Mateo."

"Teo don't deserve the pardon!" a woman said.

"Yeah!" a man agreed. "We all worked hard t' catch this slippery rat while Mateo sat on his fat ass in Prison!"

A hand seized my cloak possessively. "This was *my* idea!" Ryland shouted back at his gang. He knelt over me like a wolf guarding its kill. "I call th' shots, remember?" He grabbed my left hand and moved it into position over my spine, then started to work my right arm out from under my deadweight so he could bind my wrists behind my back.

I made my move. Ryland didn't have time to react when I rolled away, rose up to my knees behind him, and looped the rope around his neck. I crossed the ends and pulled, tightening until Ryland gasped and scrabbled at it. With one finger, I pulled my gag down and let it hang around my neck. "Stop struggling," I growled in his ear. "And don't move."

A Morphis had to be touching a material in order to use their Divinity and change forms. As long as I kept Ryland from leaning to the side to touch the brick walls or bending down to touch the asphalt, I'd have the upper hand. He'd managed to work his fingers under the rope, but my leverage prevented him from loosening it, so he stilled. His gang was before us, stunned and waiting for an order. Ryland, panting as his face deepened to vermillion, rasped, "Where d'ya think yer gonna go?"

Good question; I hadn't thought that far ahead.

Ryland choked when I inadvertently tightened the rope as I rose, bringing him up with me. We faced the Talon Gang, which, despite the disagreement a few moments ago, looked downright pissed that I was now holding their leader hostage. My vision was swimming, and I had to partially lean on Ryland just to keep my balance as the world tilted too far to one side. "I'll kill him," I threatened.

Ryland started, "Don't listen t—" but I cut him off by jerking the rope tighter.

"Back up," I ordered. He didn't want to give in to me, but when I shuffled backward, the rope pulled him, and he complied.

"Yer gonna regret this," he whispered hoarsely. "Azar wants y' alive . . . but he never specified in how many pieces."

We were maneuvering around the corner. The moment we were out of sight, I slammed Ryland's head into the brick wall, removed the rope from my wrist, and took off. It wasn't enough to knock him out as I'd hoped, but I had stunned him enough to send him to his knees. He made a rasping noise in his throat, and I knew without turning around to look that he had pointed after me to wordlessly order his gang into pursuit.

Not good—*really* not good. I was operating on pure adrenaline. We were still in the industrial district of the outskirts, and the Traders would outrun me before I could reach the second circle where I might be able to find some help. My only chance was to outmaneuver them and hide. At least they wouldn't be able to sense me in my human state if I could get away.

I ducked through the first open door on my right. The ground level of this building seemed to be a series of storefronts that were connected to each other by open doorways. My stride wasn't steady anymore; I kept stumbling, and I felt as if I were running in slow motion.

A *crash* from behind urged me onward. I started to weave back and forth as I ran, which ended up being a wise tactical move when a crackling orb of ectoplasm clipped my left ear and struck a dusty book display. Had I been running in a straight line, I would have taken the blow in the back of the head.

Ahead of me, the door leading back to the street flew open. A cloaked creature with blazing violet eyes stepped in my path and braced himself, prepared to flatten me with a tackle. I pivoted left, running deeper into the store. The Traders were closing in. There was nowhere to hide. The inevitability of capture was driving me into a panic attack, and as I approached the back wall, my heart sank when I realized there was no door. Only a small window.

I made a wild leap for the glass, curling my body into a ball and covering my head and neck with my arms. The impact vaguely reminded me of diving into the lake—a rather surreal shattering through a barrier between spaces.

I landed on the pavement with a grunt as the air was knocked out of my lungs.

Weakly, I stirred. Glass tinkled around me. My whole body hurt far beyond a summation of words. I unfolded my arms to find dozens of shards embedded in my bare skin. The glittering glass was already stained rusty red from my blood.

With a groan, I pushed myself up onto my elbows. I shivered and raised my head to find a figure dressed in black standing across the street. His red eyes were trained intently on me.

"Axel," I whispered in relief. "Ax, help me." I reached out to him, the sea of sharp glass slicing my bare arm as I extended my hand toward my lab-brother. "Please. I need you."

He stared at me. Despite my plea, his expression was hard. He narrowed his eyes.

"Axel," I called again.

He backed away, vanishing from sight. I was on my own.

My pursuers phased through the wall behind me, ropes at the ready, faces twisted into scowls and sneers.

Helplessness washed over me.

I was all alone against the gang, injured and bleeding and powerless. In the wake of Axel's abandonment came hopeless acceptance. I was too weak to be scared anymore. The effort needed just to reach for Axel had cost me the last of my strength, and my arm went limp, my heavy head resting on top of it.

I closed my eyes as my enemies closed in.

— Chapter Thirty-Three —
The Ghost Hunter

Jules Pilecki crouched beside a dumpster, her ectogun firmly clasped in both hands, finger curled over the trigger.

She'd been tracking the ghost for two days, first in a small farm community about fifteen miles south of Phantom Heights, then into the town of Foxdale a few miles east.

Her prey was an anomaly. Usually when a ghost was confronted, it would fight back. Kálos were violent, war-ready creatures with no regard for human life.

This one, though, had chosen to flee rather than fight. She was crafty and particularly skilled at darting out of sight, then vanishing without a trace, not even leaving a heat signature, making herself impossible to track until she reappeared in a different location.

Jules suspected her quarry was either a Waymaker or a Jumper. Or a Blinker, if those were still around, but Blinking was an extinct Divinity, so she'd ruled that possibility out. Waymakers had the power to create portals in doorways so the kálos could simply open a door and step into a new location. Jumpers could create Tears at will and "jump" between the Realms.

The ghost Jules was hunting hadn't fled the area despite all the bouncing around, which was perplexing. The only logical explanation behind the odd behavior was that the ghost wasn't familiar with much of the Human Realm yet. If she was making portals, she had to know where the other side would be, so she was hopping from place to place based on her past travels. She must have come via the Rip, which meant she was limited to creating portals along her route in Phantom Heights, the rural farm town, and now Foxdale.

Between the two Divinity options, Jules suspected she was probably dealing with a Waymaker. Either that, or a Jumper who was using the Ghost Realm as a brief landing point to create another portal back into the Human Realm almost immediately, but in that case, why wouldn't the ghost just stay in its own Realm?

Either way, the behavior was bizarre.

Slowly, Jules bent forward, peering around the edge of the dumpster. The ghost woman was wearing a green skirt with a long-sleeved white shirt and a brown belt that matched her boots. At a glance, one could easily mistake her for a human. No cloak, no Tolkienesque outfit to give her away. She was even smart enough to wear sunglasses over her glowing red eyes.

But Jules knew what she really was.

The creature was crouched on the balls of her feet, staring intently at a map spread out on the alley floor. A small brass object was cupped in her hands.

Jules took a deep, slow breath through her nose, then exhaled through her mouth. Time to gamble.

She stepped out from behind the dumpster and fired.

The ghost was quick to react; she raised an ectoplasm shield in defense, blocking the ghost hunter's shot. In an instant, she lowered her barrier and threw an orb of ectoplasm, forcing Jules behind the dumpster again.

By the time the ghost hunter stepped out for another shot, her target had already snatched the map and was running.

"Turn left," Jules whispered. "Come on." She fired again, this time purposely aiming just to the right of her prey so the ectoplasm missed its mark.

The ghost covered her head with a yelp and veered left into another alley.

Jules pounded after her. "Lady Luck, have mercy," she muttered. If the ghost was a Jumper, she was already gone. But if Jules was right and she was a Waymaker, she would have headed straight for the first door in sight—the door Jules had purposely left unlocked.

She rounded the corner and jabbed her fist through the air with a whoop of success when she spotted the door ajar and glimpsed a figure thrashing in a synthetic vidon net just inside.

Still elated from the thrill of the hunt, Jules laughed as she strolled into the alley. "Finally gotcha, bitch," she said as she stepped inside the back room of a store and closed the door behind her. "Ah-ah—hold still, unless you want a bullet in your head."

The ghost quieted, although her chest rose and fell with rapid breaths. "Interesting," Jules mused as she surveyed the room, which wasn't the same as the room where she'd rigged the net in the doorway. She opened the door and peered out. Instead of staring down a narrow alley, she was gazing across a derelict parking lot in front of a corn-field. "I guessed right. You're a Waymaker."

"I don't want any trouble," the ghost said. Her voice was meek, timid. Almost squeaky in comparison to Jules's deep rasp. "Please. I meant no harm."

Jules closed the door and returned to her victim, who, in her rush to escape, had charged right into the vidon net strung in the doorway and was now entangled. The ghost's sunglasses had fallen off, and she stared up at Jules with terrified, tear-filled eyes.

"No harm, huh? And I'm supposed to believe that?" She crouched down, her ectogun pointed at the concrete floor but her finger still on the trigger. "You seem to be on a mission. Scouting our Realm so your race of heathens can invade soon?"

"No. I'm not affiliated with the Shadow Guard. I swear."

Jules slipped two fingers through the net, seized the ghost's map, and pulled it free. She studied the map of the county, which wasn't marked with a location to offer any insight into the visitor's intended destination. "Then where were you going?"

The ghost squeezed her eyes shut, setting a tear free. "I had to es-cape from Avilésor."

"That didn't answer my question." Jules noticed a round object ly-ing just outside the net. She reached for it, surprised to find a normal-looking brass compass. But as she held it in her palm, the needle spun and spun in an endless circle. "Your compass is broken. No wonder you got lost."

Jules pitched the compass at the wall. To her amazement, a burst of sparks erupted when it broke against the cinderblocks. The ghost winced as the pieces fell to the floor and a faint curl of smoke rose into the air before dissipating, as if the compass had been a vessel for a spirit that was now free.

"I'll ask again. Where were you going?"

"I . . . was looking for someone."

"A human?"

The ghost hesitated. "Not exactly."

"I know you can't possibly be alluding to a nonhuman community living here. Right?"

The ghost bit her lower lip, as if conflicted. "Not all of us want war," she said softly. "Some of us came here in peace to escape the Shadow Guard."

Jules waved her ectogun at the prisoner. "Sit up. Come on, up. Let's talk face-to-face."

The woman shifted, her limbs still tangled in the netting as she labored to sit up on her knees.

"So," Jules continued, "what was the plan? To live among humans here in this Realm? C'mon, did you think you'd blend in with those glowing eyes of yours?"

The ghost's gaze dropped to the floor. "I'm looking for a Charmer who helps assimilate kálos." Her hand drifted up to a pendant shaped like a crescent moon around her neck. "I was going to pay her to turn my mother's amulet into a Charm that would create an illusion so my eyes would look human."

"Huh. I see. You're looking for a secret kálos network that's been integrated into human life here like a terrorist cell waiting to be called to action."

The woman's eyebrows drew together, creasing wrinkles into her forehead as if she were about to break down and start sobbing at any moment. "No, it's not like that. The community I'm seeking is peaceful. We just wanted to escape the wars and violence in Avilésor. Please. The other ghost hunter believed me."

"Oh? And who would that be?"

"Her name was Madison, I think."

Jules graced her victim with a humorless smile as she tilted her head. "I'm not as nice as Madison. You'll have to do a better job of convincing me."

"I'm not your enemy. I swear on my soul. If the Shadow Guard ever invades from Avilésor, I'll use my Divinity to aid humans, not harm them. I can help them evacuate to a safe location. I can be an ally, like the Demikan."

"The Demikan? I don't know what that means." Jules pressed the muzzle under the ghost's chin. "You'll have to enlighten me."

"The half-breed. H-he used to go by Phantom."

"You're mistaken. Phantom died a few years ago."

"What?" the woman whispered. "N-no. The Demikan isn't dead. He's in Phantom Heights."

Jules slowly lowered the ectogun, then leaned back on her heels. "Is that so?" She barked out a humorless laugh. "Oh-ho-ho, Kovak, you sly bastard!"

The ghost smiled uncertainly. "I was helpful to you . . . right? You'll let me go? I won't cause any trouble—you have my word. All I want is asylum so I can live in peace."

"Asylum," Jules repeated, studying her ectogun. She sheathed it at her hip and rose. "Well, you're only Level 2. Not even worth the time and fuel it would take to turn you in to the AGC." Her hand shifted to another holster.

The ghost bowed her head in relief. "Thank you. I'm in your debt."

Jules drew her Glock and fired.

The ghost's body flopped lifelessly on the floor in a spray of blood. Jules sighed and pointed the pistol at her heart, firing one more shot just in case.

She holstered the weapon, then wandered to the window and stared outside at the green corn stalks waving gently in the breeze. The new information about kálos living in secret communities, undetected, in the human world was perturbing, but Jules was too distracted now to think about it in light of even bigger news:

The half-human mutt wasn't dead after all.

She shook her head and laughed out loud. That secret by itself was worth a small fortune—Kovak definitely wouldn't want that news to leak out to the public, and he'd surely pay through the nose to keep it quiet. No wonder the press releases and network listings for the Alpha lab rats had been so frustratingly vague.

Every day, she'd been watching the network, waiting for an update on the Alpha fugitives. They were the ultimate payday, much more valuable than that worthless Level 2 Waymaker who had led Jules on a wild-goose chase for days.

Her head was spinning. Which course of action would result in a fatter bank deposit? Should she tell Kovak that his test subjects were in Phantom Heights and collect a reward for the tip-off, plus charge an extra fee for her silence about his dirty little secret?

No . . . capturing the Alpha ghosts herself and negotiating the final price tag would be more profitable. She'd been so sure they were out of reach in the Ghost Realm when in fact, they'd been ripe for the picking in Phantom Heights. Tarrow had been harboring the fugitives all along.

Jules pulled out a pack of cigarettes and tapped it on the windowsill while she dug into her pocket for the lighter. Her hand shook as she drew out a cigarette.

She took a slow, steadying breath. *No rush*, she reminded herself. This kind of mission required patience and reconnaissance.

And yet, her heart was already racing at the thought of the upcoming hunt.

I rose from the blackness of unconsciousness slowly.

The acute awareness of pain and fatigue came first.

Then, taste. My mouth had a bitter aftertaste, as if I'd been sleeping for a long time.

Then, I discerned sounds. The steady *tick-tick-tick* of a clock. I was no longer lying in an alley of broken glass—that much I could tell. The ground beneath me wasn't asphalt. It was soft now.

Finally, my eyelids peeled apart.

I was lying on my back, staring up at a ceiling. Someone had removed most of my clothes and bandaged my wounds. I stirred, expecting to find restraints tying me down to the bed. To my surprise, my movements were unrestricted. *Maybe Azar isn't completely cruel. But I bet the door is locked.*

The bed was strange, although it took me a few minutes to realize why. On my right side, it rose up like a padded wall. I needed a few more slow seconds to process before I comprehended that it wasn't a bed at all. It was a couch.

I turned my head at a quiet noise that sounded like a page turning, and it dawned on my sluggish brain that I wasn't alone. I twisted my head farther to find a woman sitting in a chair, illuminated in the glow of a lamp. At my movement, she closed her book and stood. "Thank goodness you're awake."

"Madison?" I croaked.

"Mom," she corrected, kneeling beside me.

Two more figures entered my field of vision and stood on either side of her—Jay and Wes. The werewolf held out a glass of water and ordered, "Drink."

"I'm not thirsty."

"You burned out. You're a Cryokinetic; you need to rehydrate. You'll recover faster if you do."

Jay added, "Just drink it, Cay."

I sighed and shifted my aching body. Jay helped me sit up while my mother tucked an extra pillow behind my shoulders and then pressed the glass into my hands. "Drink up," she repeated.

I did. As soon as the water touched my lips, I realized that Wes was right and I wasn't just thirsty; I was parched. I gulped down the water without reservation.

"Where am I?" I inquired as Wes reclaimed the empty glass.

"In Saros Manor," my mother said gently. "I was so worried. You really need to see Doc, but Jay won't let her in."

I surveyed the armchairs and couches around the room and realized that I was in the den on the ground floor. My stony gaze found Jay. "How'd you find me?"

"Axel."

I closed my eyes, reliving the cold, unempathetic look on Axel's face when I'd begged him to help me. He had looked me straight in the eye and left me there alone and defenseless in the broken glass. I hadn't seen even a glimpse of regret.

I took a deep breath and winced.

"What's wrong?" Madison asked. "What hurts?"

"Nothing," I said in a strained voice, knowing she'd insist on a doctor visit if I admitted that I might have fractured bones.

"Cato. Don't lie to me."

"Nothing," I repeated. "I'm just . . . I'm sore. Everywhere."

"You have a hell of a bruise on your torso." Her fingers trailed lightly across my skin, but even the faint touch caused an intense wave of pain that made me flinch and suck a sharp gasp through my teeth. "Sorry," she murmured.

I arched my neck to study the mottled purple bruise turning a sickly yellow at the edges. My arms and torso were covered with too many bandages to count, and the familiar ridge of scar tissue trailed down the center of my chest. I was wearing a pair of long, loose shorts and nothing else.

Madison said, "I can bring you some pills to help with the pain."

I shook my head. I didn't want to be drugged.

Jay knelt beside me. "Do you want me to Blink you to our room?"

"*No,*" Madison said before I could answer, and the irritated tone indicated this had been an ongoing argument. "You aren't taking him upstairs where I can't see him. Not unless you lower that shield around your room and let me in."

Tears jarred my vision unexpectedly. I blinked, and one rolled free to trickle down my cheek and drip onto the cushion. Madison noticed and asked again, "What's wrong?"

I forced a rather miserable, wavering grin. "I was really scared."

My mother's expression softened. "Oh, Cato." Her hand came down gently on my head. Even though I squeezed my eyes shut and tensed at her touch, she stroked my hair with loving caresses. "I was scared, too. Jay brought you back all bloody and unconscious, and . . ."

She trailed off. Or did I doze off? I was lingering on the cusp of unconsciousness again. Now that I'd had some water and I knew I was safe, the fatigue was dragging me back down.

"Cato?" drifted her voice.

"Hmm?"

A pause, then: "Rest now. You're safe."

"Hmm."

As I floated into the welcoming black waves lapping at my consciousness, Jay's voice brought the promise, "We'll protect you."

My name is Cato, I remembered on the verge before I passed into the realm of slumber.

— Chapter Thirty-Four —
Sisterhood

By the time Vivian reached the mansion with a vase of flowers in hand, she was out of breath.

She closed the front door and crossed the foyer to find her mom pacing in front of the French doors leading to the backyard patio, her phone pressed to her ear. Madison inclined her head and gave Vivian a little wave in acknowledgment.

"I'm just concerned, that's all," she was saying into the phone. "He's burned out twice in a few weeks. I don't know what damage he's doing to his body every time he pushes himself past his limit like that."

Vivian paused to listen as Madison reached the end of the great room and pivoted to pace in the other direction. "No. As much as I want you to come, that can't happen. Yeah, I know. I know. I just want some advice is all. Hold on a second."

Madison lowered the phone and asked, "How was school?"

"Fine. Can I see Cato?"

"Yes, but be quiet. He's sleeping."

Vivian nodded and turned toward the den. Behind her, Madison's soft voice continued, "No, he did wake up once and talk for a few minutes. He drank a glass of water before he went back to sleep. I don't know, Doc. I think he might have fractured ribs, but if you so much as step foot in this house, they'll take him up to the third floor, and then I won't be able to see him, either."

Vivian was careful as she turned the knob and quietly swung the door open. Cato was fast asleep on the couch, his chest rising and falling with deep, even, peaceful breaths. A ball of fur was snuggled on his lap, and Ash was sitting cross-legged on the floor, polishing her metal staff.

Vivian's spirits plummeted at the unexpected company. She hesitated in the doorway, then slipped inside and closed the door, sealing her mom's faint voice outside.

Kit lifted her head, then rose, arched her back, and opened her mouth in a wide yawn that showed off her sharp fangs and curled tongue. She leapt from Cato's lap. By the time her feet touched the floor, she'd assumed her ghost form. "Cato has all three sisters watching over him now," she said with a smile.

Vivian and Ash regarded each other coldly across the room. "How long have you been here?" Vivian asked.

"A few hours."

"Well, I would have been here earlier, but I was at school."

"Okay," Ash dismissed coolly.

Vivian wandered forward to set the vase of flowers on the table. She turned her back to Ash and gazed down on Cato. "I'm worried about him."

"Just a burnout," Ash said, resuming the rhythmic motion of wiping her staff. "He's going to be okay."

"Then why are you here?" Vivian challenged.

Ash didn't answer.

Vivian looked away, her eyes burning with tears. The stress and worry of thinking about her brother all day at school had been overwhelming enough as it was, but she'd been expecting some solitude with him. And yet here she was, face-to-face with Ash of all people, and Vivian felt the same level of disdain building in her chest as when she was talking to Shannon Jennings.

"Shouldn't you be out scouting or something?"

"No. It's my turn to stay with Cato."

"Well, I'm here now. So you can leave if you want to."

Ash raised her burning gaze to glower at Vivian. "It's my turn to stay with Cato," she said again. "I'm not leaving."

"Okay, look. I need to know . . . are you in love with him?" Vivian blurted.

Ash tilted her head slightly. "I don't understand your question."

"It's not hard. Do you love Cato?"

"Yes."

"And he loves you?"

"Yes."

"So, you're dating?"

Ash blinked. "What? No. He's my lab-brother. I thought you knew that."

"But you aren't related by blood."

Ash dropped her attention to the staff in her lap. "He's basically my brother. I love Cato the same way you do."

Vivian stiffened. It was hard enough hearing Ash call him her lab-brother, but without that prefix, she'd lifted him up to the same pedestal Vivian kept him on. A sudden realization made her eyes widen. "Oh. Are you . . . gay?"

"What?"

"You know, attracted to women."

Ash shot her a perplexed and irritated look. "No. Why is my romance status suddenly so important to you?"

"I'm just looking out for my little brother. Cato always falls for the same type of girl, and I want to make sure . . . I mean, you . . ."

Ash narrowed her eyes. "What 'type' do you think I am, exactly?"

"I don't know. I can't quite figure you out. But Cato always seems to be attracted to pretty, shallow girls who take sick pleasure in toying with him and leading him on with no intention of reciprocating his affection."

Faint fingers of steam curled up into the air from Ash's skin. So quietly Vivian almost couldn't hear, Ash muttered under her breath, "Sorry for not fitting into your narrow stereotype. I don't know why you think I'm pretty, anyway."

Vivian snapped, "Oh, please. False modesty doesn't flatter you."

Ash wasn't just steaming now—she was smoking. "You really think I'm pretty? *Why?*"

"Have you even looked in a mirror? I mean, you're . . . you know.

Basically perfect. Thin but strong with the right curves and proportions. Your hair is the color of a dark apple and has this gorgeous natural wave that wouldn't last five minutes in my hair no matter how many products I used. Your skin is practically flawless even though you don't wear any makeup, and I wish I had a body like yours."

Heat burned her cheeks. She hadn't meant for that last part to spill out, but it had, and there was no taking it back. "And I'm an idiot for falling for that act. You just enjoy hearing me praise you, right?"

Ash glared down at her staff, which burst into flames at the same time the flowers ignited. Vivian instinctively jumped back with a gasp, then seized the vase and turned it upside down to pour the flowers onto the table and drench them. An acrid, burnt smell filled the room.

The fire continued to dance in Ash's lap. Although the initial spark had been an accident, she appeared to have the small blaze under control. Ash gripped the fire staff in both fists and let her eyes lose focus in the flames. "No," she seethed quietly. "I hate being obligated to say 'thank you' for an unsolicited compliment I know isn't true. It makes me feel sick."

"Are you kidding me?" Vivian couldn't tell if the buzz making her head spin stemmed from anger or envy. How unfair that such a blessing had fallen upon someone who didn't even appreciate it. Even now, the light of the fire cast a warm glow on Ash's skin and drew out the varying tones of deep red in her hair, accentuating her natural beauty. "Tell me one thing that's wrong with you. One flaw."

Kit, her ears pinned, meekly intervened, "She doesn't have one. She's perfect."

Ash winced at that proclamation, as if the adoration were a physical blow. "Kit, please don't say that."

Vivian pressed, "The shape of your nose. A mole or scar. Your smile. I could give you a whole list of my imperfections I wish I could change. You don't think you're pretty? *Why*? What do you think is wrong with you?"

Kit watched her older lab-sister intently, waiting for Ash to respond to the challenge.

Slowly, Ash released a long sigh. The flames in her hands died down, although the staff still glowed like a white-hot ember. "I don't know exactly." Vivian arched her eyebrows in an I-told-you-so look, but Ash finished, "The reflection I saw for the first time Outside wasn't what I thought it would be."

The tightness of Vivian's scowl unwound. In Ash's hands, the hot metal staff darkened as it cooled. She continued, "I spent so long in a cage. There aren't any mirrors in that place. Beauty doesn't mean much when you don't even know what your own face looks like anymore. Someone there told me I was beautiful almost every night, and each time he said those words, I felt . . ." Her gaze danced to Kit, and she lowered her voice.

"Disgusting. It wasn't a compliment or a privilege. If I really was beautiful, then my beauty was a curse, and it belonged to him, not me. I wanted to light myself on fire to get rid of his stink and burn off the parts of me his hands had touched."

Vivian felt her stomach drop.

"Ash . . . did someone at the AGC—?"

"Everything's fine," Ash interrupted, forcing a pained smile and glancing meaningfully at Kit, whose ears fell back again.

"Are you talking about the bad man?" Kit inquired, her voice barely above a whisper.

"Everything's fine," Ash repeated. "He's far away, so there's no reason to talk about him, right?"

Kit nodded, but her shoulders hunched and her head dipped lower. She seemed to shrink in size.

Ash turned her head to gaze fondly at Cato still fast asleep on the couch. "Cato thought I was pretty when we first met. He could barely get his words out in a complete sentence."

Vivian's lips twitched to contain a grin—yeah, that sounded like the brother she remembered. Always tripping over himself like a tongue-tied idiot when he tried to talk to an attractive girl.

Ash solemnly continued, "If you can't see your own face but everybody tells you how pretty you are, then you have no choice but to take their word for it even if you feel like a ruined, tainted creature that could never be anything beautiful. Then we escaped, and I saw my reflection for the first time since I was a kid, and I stared at it, and stared, and I realized the reflection I see must be different from what you see. Because the face staring back at me is a total stranger, and she's not beautiful. I can't see what you see."

Ash's face was flaming red. She focused intently on her task of cleaning the staff in her lap.

Vivian said, "I'm really sorry about what happened to you." She sidled over to the nearest armchair and sat down. "Cato's your lab-brother—I get it. I don't want to compete with you, okay? Let me tell you what Cato means to me. I've always tried to protect him. When we were kids, I took care of him because Mom was busy with her research and Dad was gone. I cooked dinner most nights. When Cato was failing algebra, I tutored him. When he snuck out to be Phantom, I made excuses so Mom wouldn't find out what he was doing. We walked to and from school together almost every day. Cato and I were very close. He wasn't just a brother—he was actually one of my best friends. We got really close after Dad died."

Ash kept moving the cloth back and forth, her gaze fixed on the weapon in her hands. Vivian waited, her frustration festering, until she finally snapped, "Do you have anything to say?"

Ash's hand stilled. "All right. Let me tell you what *I* mean to Cato."

She raised her head, and Vivian gasped. Ash's eyes were smoldering like hot coals that burned right through her. "His cage was next to mine at the end of the row. When he woke up in that place for the first time, my face was the first one he saw. I answered his questions. I tried my best to comfort him when he was upset because *you* never came. We fell asleep every Lightsout holding onto each other's fingers until Kit arrived, and then we slept back-to-back so he could reach through the bars and pet her to help her fall asleep. You seem to think there has to be some kind of competition, but I don't need to compete with you, Vivian. My relationship with Cato isn't the same as yours, and it isn't going to change just because you're in his life again."

Vivian's head fell, her dark hair forming a curtain to conceal her tears from Ash's scorching gaze. She didn't speak until she heard the sound of the cloth rubbing the metal staff again. "Thank you for taking care of my little brother. You were there for him when I couldn't be."

Once again, Ash's rhythmic motion stilled. Although Vivian chanced a peek at her, Ash wasn't looking at her. She had turned her head to watch Cato sleep.

Vivian swallowed her pride and mumbled, "I'm sorry, Ash. I made incorrect presumptions about you, but I'd like to get to know the real you. Maybe we could hang out sometime? No offense to the guys, but I bet you could use some girl time."

Kit excitedly bounced on the balls of her feet. "Me too?"

"Sure," Vivian said with a warm smile. "Girls' day out. What do you say?"

"Girls' day out!" Kit cried gleefully. "Right, Ash? Please?"

Ash resumed polishing her staff. Back and forth . . . no answer . . . back and forth . . .

"I don't know," she finally mumbled.

"It'll be fun," Vivian promised. Ash rolled her lips together, silent again, prompting Vivian to add, "Come on, Cato's out of commission while he recovers, so you don't even have the excuse that you'll be busy scouting with him."

Ash shrugged. "I guess," she relented.

Vivian forced a smile. A soft knock on the door preceded Madison, who entered with a glass and a pitcher of water. "Still out?" she whispered.

Ash was immediately on her feet. Vivian nodded.

Madison hesitated in the doorway, her nose wrinkling at the offensive odor as she noticed the spilled vase and the soaked, blackened flowers strewn across the table. "What happened?"

"Nothing," Vivian said quickly. "Really."

Her mom gave her a doubtful look but seemed to understand the unspoken plea to let it go. She closed the door and approached the couch, then set the pitcher and glass down amid the scorched flowers.

She knelt next to Cato and tenderly took his wrist in her fingers as she looked down at her watch.

Ash took a stiff step forward. "What are you doing?"

Madison glanced at her for a brief moment before her gaze traveled down to the watch face again. "I'm checking his pulse."

Kit's ears fell back again. Madison and Ash were both statues—Madison silently mouthed the heartbeat count, and Ash looked as if she was ready to pounce forward and swing her staff at any second.

Vivian folded her arms and sank back into the cushion. Finally, her mom let go of his wrist, although Ash remained taut and wary. "Seems normal," Madison said, touching the back of her hand to Cato's forehead. "He feels cold, though. I'll get him a blanket."

"He doesn't need a blanket," Ash said, her tone devoid of emotion. "He's a Cryo. He's supposed to be cold."

Madison stroked Cato's face. "Okay." She was silent for a full minute, then said, "Ash? Could you . . . tell me about this scar on his chest? And this weird mark on his arm where it looks like his veins turned black?"

Ash shook her head with a stiff, jerky motion.

Madison didn't push. She gently lifted Cato's head so she could settle onto the couch and let him rest in her lap. At the slight readjustment, Cato grimaced and released a pained groan from the back of his throat, although he didn't wake.

Ash shifted, her knuckles straining the fabric of her fingerless glove as she tightened her one-handed grip on the staff.

Vivian leaned forward, causing the chair to creak. "Ash, don't get me wrong—I'm really glad Cato has someone like you that he trusts to protect him. But I wish you could acknowledge that we're his family and we aren't going to hurt him. You act like Mom's going to start dissecting him the second you turn your back."

Ash's gaze flicked briefly to Vivian and then back to Madison again. "It's nothing personal."

"But we—"

"It's all right, Viv," Madison interrupted. She traced aimless patterns across Cato's face and swept her fingers lovingly through his hair. "But I think Cato is hurt worse than he wants us to know. I just hope it's nothing serious." She lifted her head to make eye contact with Ash. "If I think he's declining, I *am* going to take him to Doc."

Ash snapped her staff into her open palm so she was now holding it in both hands. It was a subtle but clear challenge, and she certainly looked as if she knew how to wield her weapon with deadly skill. "I'm not afraid to fight you, Mrs. Tarrow," Ash said in a low voice. "I don't want to, but I will if I have to. Cato trusts me to keep him safe. He's not going anywhere, and the doctor isn't allowed in this room. Not on my watch."

Despite the threat, Madison regarded her with a calm, weary expression. "Hopefully, it won't come to that. I just want to make it clear that Cato's well-being is the priority, and if I think he's at risk, I'm going to do what I think is best for him. You can relax for now."

Ash's stance eased marginally, but she made no indication of sitting again—she was still on full alert. Vivian settled deeper into the cushions and drew her knees to her chest. "Did Cato ever talk about us at the AGC?"

"Only in the very beginning," Ash said.

Kit transformed in a swirl of black smoke and trotted back to the couch. She leapt onto his lap and curled into a little ball of fur safely out of Madison's reach.

"What did he say about us?" Vivian asked.

Ash's shoulders sagged. She gave Vivian a sad, sidelong stare. "He said you'd come to take him home. We told him that was a delusional fantasy, but he wouldn't listen. He promised you'd come, and you'd free all of us if he asked you to."

Madison sat perfectly still with her jaw locked. She didn't say a word. Vivian shifted with guilt. "Sorry for letting you down."

"You didn't." Ash sheathed her staff and folded her arms, although she was still plenty lethal without the weapon in hand. "The rest of us knew you weren't coming. Cato was the only one holding onto that hope."

— Chapter Thirty-Five —
Purest of Demons

I lingered on the shore of consciousness, eyes closed, listening to the steady *tick* of the clock on the wall.

I knew where I was, and I knew I was safe. But the burnout and long sleep had left me weak, and my body was slow in crawling back to wakefulness.

I stirred. The sharp pain in my rib cage hadn't dulled much. When I clenched my fingers, my grip strength was so feeble that I couldn't make a tight fist. I opened my eyes.

On the table sat a pitcher of water and an empty glass. I'd expected someone—anyone—to be here and greet me, but I was alone in the room. My solitude was disheartening, although I tried to tell myself that it was selfish to expect people to be waiting around for me to wake up.

When I glanced at the clock, my disappointment faded into relief. I knew where everyone was.

I hauled myself up with what little strength I could muster. My mouth was so cotton dry that I didn't think my rusty vocal cords would even work. I ignored the glass, instead opting to drink straight from the pitcher. Once it was drained, I set it down with a quenched sigh, then took a deep breath and winced, my inhale cut short. *Note to self: avoid deep breaths for a while.*

I sat on the couch for another minute before I felt clearheaded enough to stand and stagger to the dining room, where everyone was just settling down for dinner.

"Cato!" Kit greeted with a fanged smile. I grinned back at her and shuffled to my chair amid warm greetings. Madison stood up, likely to hug me, but I held up a hand and sat down with a quiet groan before she had a chance to suffocate me in an embrace.

"I figured you'd be waking up soon," she said. "Hang tight—I have a plate ready for you in the kitchen." She pushed through the swinging door and returned a moment later with a plate of food and a glass of ice water.

"How do you feel?" she asked as she set my dinner in front of me.

"Sore and groggy, but better," I replied.

Madison took her place again. Ero's empty chair was a depressing reminder of his absence, but there was also another vacant chair at the table.

"No Axel tonight?" Vivian noticed. "Is he sick already?"

Jay said, "He isn't feeling well, but he's still in town."

"Then why isn't he here?"

I stared down at my plate. I'd thought I was starving, but my stomach felt queasy now. "Because he's avoiding me."

Vivian frowned. "Why? Did you guys have a fight?"

"No."

"Then why would he be avoiding you?"

I sloughed off the question with a shrug and downed my glass of water in a matter of seconds. Madison stood again to refill it for me, but I said, "I can get it."

My body disagreed. As I struggled to stand, Madison ordered, "Sit. You still need to rest." RC casually flicked his hand, and the glass flew out of my hand and into Madison's. She turned back toward the kitchen with a pleasant, "Thank you."

Vivian said, "Hey, Ash, could you please pass the salt?" Jay and Wes were engaged in a conversation about the different types of weir. When Madison returned with my water, I sipped it slower this time, observing the dining room over the rim. Without Axel driving a wedge of tension into conversations, my families actually seemed to be interacting on a compatible level.

That was the superficial impression, anyway. I suspected this pleasant atmosphere had less to do with appreciating Axel's absence and more to do with forcing a sense of calm before the storm, as if everyone knew the fuse was burning on the fireworks and they were try-ing to make the peace last as long as possible.

Madison wanted me to give my account of the events that had led to my burnout and capture. Reluctantly, I told my story, although I skipped the part when Ryland kicked me in the ribs. I should have also omitted the end, because Madison was instantly livid when she learned that Axel had left me to face the Traders on my own.

I kept quiet during the rest of dinner, although I was sure no one read too much into my silence since I was still recuperating. Beneath their chatter, I replayed the last time I saw Axel. He was healthy. His eyes were still bright red when they had locked with mine. That was my lab-brother, conscious and coherent, staring at me while I bled on the asphalt in front of him. All he had to do was pick me up out of the glass and carry me away. Or he could have guarded me against the Talon Gang. He'd stood up to Ryland once without fear—why couldn't he do it again when I needed him?

Instead, he'd left me there alone as my enemies closed in. Even though I tried to rationalize Axel's behavior—there was almost always some underlying issue making him tick, even if it wasn't obvious—the betrayal still stung.

I turned in for bed early that night, replaying the memory over and over again. Even when my lab-siblings' return from training roused me—even when a nightmare jolted me awake just before dawn—the red eyes I was so accustomed to finding in the shadows weren't there.

Axel was not guarding us this night, and I knew it was because of me.

He was still absent the next morning, which didn't surprise me. I slept through training, but when the others returned, Jay handed me a note that had been taped to our door. Madison wanted to speak to the two of us.

We found her brewing coffee in the kitchen. "Good morning!" she greeted merrily.

"What did you want to talk about?" Jay asked, holding up the note.

"Straight to the point," Madison said, turning away from the coffee pot and leaning against the counter. "All right. I wanted to chat about Finn and Reese."

Jay crossed his arms and tilted his head with a slight frown. "What about them?"

"I think they're feeling a bit depressed with Ero gone, so . . . I had an idea and wanted to get your opinion. But first, I want to be clear that my intention is *not* to take advantage of them."

She paused, as if waiting for us to acknowledge her statement. "Okay," I said.

"You said they're inventors, right? They enjoy working with computers and learning how things work? Well . . . I thought, maybe, if you're okay with it and they're willing . . . I could bring them with me to City Hall today and show them how the entoplasm shield works, then give them free rein to make any upgrades they think might improve efficiency. It would get them out of the house for a breath of fresh air and a change of scenery, plus give them something to focus on."

"And you would benefit, too," Jay noted.

"I said I didn't—"

"I know," he replied, raising one hand to interrupt. "I don't think it's a bad idea. What do you think, Cay?"

I shrugged. "It would probably be a good distraction for them . . . if you're comfortable letting them be so close to the Rip without Ero as an extra source of protection."

He pondered for a moment, then said, "What if they brought ECA-NI with them? That way they could activate Proto if there's an emergency. And we'll all be there to guard them. I was going to ask you and Ash to scout with us today anyway since you're still recovering."

"What about Axel?" I muttered under my breath.

Jay rolled his shoulders rather nonchalantly. "I'm sure he'll be close by if we need him. He usually is."

Madison grumbled, "I'm not counting on Axel for anything. But I bet Wes wouldn't mind keeping a lookout. I can ask him to join us."

"All right," Jay said, probably because it was easier to relent than try to defend Axel while Madison was still furious with him.

"So . . . you're on board?" she asked with a hopeful smile. We nodded, and she clapped her hands together. "Great! Would you be opposed to letting Trey tag along? I've been meaning to teach him how the generator works so he can help me with maintenance and repairs. He might have some upgrade ideas, too."

"That's fine," Jay said.

"Thank you. I hope Finn and Reese see this as a fun project rather than a chore. I thought maybe it would be better if you asked them instead of me since, you know, I'm human. I want it to be their choice."

Jay and I exchanged looks. Neither of us wanted to break it to Madison that no matter who asked the twins, they would say yes because the request had come from a human.

An hour later, I was standing at the bottom of City Hall's stone steps with Jay, RC, Ash, Finn, Reese, and Kit.

Madison, who had been speaking to the police officers on patrol, glanced at her watch as she returned to us. "Wes and Trey should be here any minute."

The masked twins were seated on the stairs, and they surveyed the humans in town square with solemn, emotionless expressions. I couldn't tell if they were pleased or disappointed to be tasked with this job. Reese was wearing ECANI's sensor gloves, and Finn had the device pressed against his chest with his arms crossed, as if afraid someone was going to steal it.

My mother sat down on the step next to them and cleared her throat to ensnare their attention. "I really want this to be a fun activity for you," she said with a kind smile. "We can stay as long as you want. If you get tired or bored and you want to go home, we'll leave whenever you're ready. But if you're having fun and want to stay, we can get sandwiches from C-Sully's for lunch and keep working. It's your call—you just let me know what you want to do."

They blinked at her, otherwise giving no response. While I appreciated Madison's intent, she was wasting her time. Finn and Reese were trained to see a job through to the end. It didn't matter how hungry, tired, or bored they were—they'd stay until their task was finished to the satisfaction of their overseer, even if it took days to complete.

"Hey!" called a voice in the distance. On the far side of town square, two figures approached City Hall. Trey was waving one arm in the air to greet us as Wes strolled beside him with his hands thrust in his pockets. The werewolf maintained his casual pace when Trey broke into a run to reach us first.

"Thanks for inviting me! This is so exciting!" he said with a breathless smile now directed at the twins. "I can't wait to learn about the shield and brainstorm new ideas with you!"

Finn and Reese regarded him with cold impassiveness, polar opposites to his overflowing enthusiasm.

Wes sauntered up to Madison, who set her hands on her knees and rose. "So, we're on guard duty?" he said. "What's the game plan?"

Jay said, "Cato and I will be inside with Finn and Reese. I'd like Ash to be positioned at the door leading to the basement, RC to stay out here and watch the Rip with Wes, and Kit to scout the area. If you're okay with that."

I inclined my head. Jay's strategy was smart—he as the leader and I as a half-human were the most likely candidates to be successful mediators between Madison, Trey, and the twins. Ash's preferred close-combat fighting style made her ideal to guard the entrance, while RC's long-distance skills better equipped him to aid Wes and defend City Hall before potential enemies could even reach the steps. And Kit's spy network should detect any unexpected intruders in the vicinity.

"Works for me," Wes said with a shrug.

A shiver traveled down my spine. "Where do you want me?" came a quiet voice. We all turned to find Axel above us, leaning against one of City Hall's pillars with his arms folded.

His presence ushered a tense, uncomfortable quiet across the square. I shuddered with an inexplicable chill that had nothing to do with sensing ghosts.

Madison set her hands on her hips and called up, "You've got a lot of nerve showing up here."

Axel's crimson gaze shifted marginally to lock onto her. "I wasn't talking to you," he said.

"Excuse me?"

"I. Wasn't. Talking to you," Axel enunciated louder.

"Don't take that tone with me," Madison snapped. She marched partway up the stairs before halting in a wide stance with her arms akimbo. "I'm mad at you, and you know exactly why. Cato was hurt. He needed your help, and you turned your back on him."

"Please," I begged in embarrassment. People in town square were pausing to watch the argument. "Just let it go."

"I will not. You could have been killed or captured, and it would have been Axel's fault."

I cringed, expecting my lab-brother to retaliate with his infamous temper. Instead, he glowered at my mother in silence. Not guilt. Just judgmental silence.

That pissed Madison off even more. "Aren't you going to apologize?"

"No."

I shifted and glanced over my shoulder at the onlookers. "He doesn't have to apologize."

Madison twisted to peer at me over her shoulder. "Why are you okay with what he did?" She turned back and jabbed her finger at Axel, who continued to glare at her. "You and I, we have a problem."

Axel said, "You can't blame me for Cato's weakness."

I winced, shame instantly warming my cheeks. He was right—I was the one who screwed up. It wasn't his fault I'd pushed myself into a burnout with a flawed escape strategy.

My mother retorted, "He was outnumbered, and he was hurt. You should have protected him. You have no right to call yourself a brother."

"Isn't it a *mother's* job to protect her children?" Axel shot back. He peeled away from the pillar and descended a few steps. "Where were you when Cato was in trouble? *Again.*"

"Okay," I interrupted, burning with humiliation. "Please stop—"

Wes drawled, "You know, actually, I don't think you're all that powerful, Axel." His deep, calm yet mocking voice disrupted the tension like a stone plunking into a pond and sending ripples across the surface. Madison turned to stare at him. Although Axel didn't move, his red eyes shifted so he could deliver a sidelong look of daggers.

Wes shrugged with a little smirk now that he'd captured the spotlight. "You ran to Jay with your tail between your legs and begged him to face that gang of Traders when Cato went down. Why is that, Axel? You couldn't handle it yourself?"

"You're an idiot, and it's none of your fucking business, *mongrel*," Axel snarled, turning on his heel and walking away from us along the step. Jay didn't correct Axel's language this time; he sensed the tension and knew better than to push. Wes, on the other hand, didn't.

"Running away again? I didn't peg you for a coward. I guess Agent Kovak was wrong about you."

Axel wordlessly held up his fist and displayed his middle finger, otherwise refusing the bait.

"Why do you hate everyone?" Wes demanded to Axel's back. "Is it because you think you're better than us?"

Axel stopped cold. Realizing that he'd succeeded in striking a nerve, Wes grinned maliciously.

Axel's fists were clenched, his entire body as rigid as a trigger spring ready to be released. Wisps of ectoplasm swarmed around his hands.

"That's a really bad idea," I warned.

Jay added, "Axel, just walk away. It's not worth it."

Wes continued, "You know what I think? You don't deserve all that power. Level 9, and you don't even use it. I would kill to have the kind of power you supposedly have, and you just let it all go to waste."

The energy crackling around Axel's fists was growing stronger and brighter. A low growl vibrated in his throat.

"Ax?" Jay asked softly, backing up and stepping in front of the twins as if to shield them. That, more than anything, frightened me. Jay was always in control, and Axel usually listened to him. If Jay was uneasy, that meant this situation was taking a nosedive into danger.

Wes still seemed to be oblivious to the impending hazard. "Humans gave you this great gift, and what do you do? You spit in their faces. I think you should be grateful. You should *thank* humankind for what they've given you."

Axel whirled with a ferocious snarl.

I gasped. Something was most definitely wrong.

Axel's eyes were now glowing red in a way I'd never seen before. Only a ghost's irises ever glowed, but now, there was no distinction between the pupils, irises, and whites of his eyes—they were all glowing solid red. Tendrils of ectoplasm coursed along not only his arms, but also his torso and legs.

Wes, finally realizing that he'd stepped out of line, stumbled backward.

But he'd reached this conclusion too late—Axel's awesome power was officially out of control.

Raw energy crackled like red lightning around his body, revolving around him as if he were the central point in a bizarre solar system of pure power. The energy was densest closer to his core, lashing out in stray tendrils farther away from his body. The displaced ectoplasm created a strong wind, whipping his hair and cloak in a frenzy. His fangs had lengthened—they seemed to have grown in his fury.

"*Shut UP!*" Axel screamed, bleeding even more power that was so bright it hurt to look directly at him. Some of the people in town square were smart enough to bolt; others backed away in awe. Madison retreated down the steps, her right hand resting on the gun at her hip.

Thank a bloody Scout he isn't a Sonic, I couldn't help but think as I lifted my hand and squinted through the blinding light. Phantom Heights would have been smithereens.

He roared, "You stupid, mangy dog—you have no *fucking* idea what you're talking about! You power-hungry monsters *ruined* me!

And you want me to *thank* you?"

"Axel, please," Jay intervened, taking a timid step forward. The rest of us backed down the stairs, leaving the leader alone against the raging half-breed. "You're out of control."

But Axel was too absorbed in his fury and hatred to listen.

"I lost *everything*!" Axel screamed. "You think it's so great having all this power? Then why don't you *take* it! Because I don't want it! *I! NEVER! WANTED! IT!*" Ectoplasm surged outward from his body. People screamed and threw themselves to the ground, covering their heads with their arms. Wes stumbled backward, tripping over his own feet and landing hard on his ass.

Axel's ectoplasm had degraded to Grade G, its rawest form, making it act almost like electricity. The lights strung across cables over town square popped in brilliant mini fireworks that traveled down the wires in procession before triggering an explosion with a *boom!* when the current reached the nearest electrical pole.

Axel was no more than a black silhouette with glowing eyes in the middle of blinding red light. Kit hid behind me, gripping the fabric of my cloak.

I knew how powerful Axel was, how effortlessly he could counter any attack, but we had never actually seen him exert his full power. *They* hadn't even seen him at full power because he caused too much damage.

The hot, charged wind whipped at my cloak. Jay's fingers were clenched around the whistle, but he didn't raise it to his lips. No doubt blowing it would make matters worse and send Axel completely over the edge. Instead, Jay cupped his hands around his mouth and yelled, "Axel! This has to stop! Somebody's going to get hurt!"

At the sound of his voice, Axel turned toward Jay, snarling, still emanating raw demergy. I tensed, afraid that Axel didn't recognize Jay and he was about to attack him.

The blinding light dimmed ever so slightly as the half-breed focused on his lab-brother. He clutched his arms and seemed to fold in on himself, his body trembling as he tried and failed to draw his power back in.

It was no good—he'd crossed the point of no return. That ectoplasm had to go somewhere now. He fell to his knees, head bowed, teeth bared, fighting to keep the power contained.

"Let go!" Jay cried. "Axel, you have to let it go!"

Axel threw his head back and screamed. I shielded my eyes with my forearm as the light flared even brighter, engulfing Axel's figure.

I squinted below my arm to see a massive column of ectoplasm rushing skyward with my lab-brother's dark silhouette kneeling in the center. My cloak snapped around me in the wild wind that kicked up dust and debris.

I tilted my head up in wonder as Axel's ectoplasm met the low cloud cover, causing the gray clouds to roil and glow and swirl around the column. The sky rumbled like a colossal beast, alight with crackling streaks of red lightning that shot through the clouds with terrifying intensity.

Finally, the column diminished in size and intensity until it vanished completely. The red lightning continued to streak through the churning clouds, but it became less concentrated as it dispersed.

Awestruck, I lowered my gaze to ground level again. Even after that impressive exertion, ectoplasm still flickered around Axel's figure in an eerie red halo. He had his palms pressed to his temples and his fingers intertwined in his hair, teeth gritted as he tried to seal the remaining power away. I knew Axel would deny it, but I swore I could see glistening trails of tears on his cheeks. His eyes were still wrong, still glowing solid red. But as I watched, they faded until the irises were visible again—blazing in rage, but normal.

I realized I was trembling. I hadn't realized that much power could exist within one person. Such an exertion should have completely drained Axel, and yet he was still leaking more power than I had in my entire body.

The last of the lightning finally dissipated, and a suffocating calm was left in the wake of the final rumble.

Wes stood up slowly, looking shaken as he stared up at the sky.

"Unbelievable," he whispered.

Axel, finally succeeding in locking away the rest of his power, lowered his hands and scowled at the werewolf. "You think humans gave me a gift?" he whispered hoarsely. "If you had even the slightest idea what I lost to get this curse . . ."

The werewolf blinked, then smiled. "Don't take it so personally, Axel. I just wanted to see how powerful you are. Powers are affected by emotions, so I figured if I made you angry enough . . ."

The blood drained from Axel's already-pale face. His irises flared again as his face twisted into a snarl. "You sick bastard!"

"Are you crazy?" Madison cried. "You could have gotten all of us killed!"

"What?" he asked innocently. "You started the fight. I just pushed a few extra buttons."

Before he could say any more, Wes was flung down onto the steps, then pinned on his back by an unseen force. The werewolf squirmed, snarling, eyes glowing yellow with power that seemed weak and pathetic compared to Axel's.

I turned my head to see RC standing with his hand outstretched before him, violet eye glowing, focused on Wes. A spinning disk, blades unsheathed, hovered on either side of the Telekinetic, the third one rotating above his head.

Jay stepped forward, his eyes also glowing in his anger. "You took that way too far."

Realizing now who was attacking him, Wes stopped struggling against RC's telekinetic hold. "I'm sure I'm not the only one sick and tired of Axel acting like he's better than everyone."

Axel seethed, "I'ma kill that motherfucker."

"Don't," Jay warned as the half-breed stormed down the steps toward the pinned werewolf. Jay Blinked in front of Axel to intercept, but Axel phased right through him without breaking stride. "Axel, think this through," Jay pleaded as he seized the half-breed's cloak. "You know what will happen. Use your head, Axel!"

"I'll rip his heart out and bleed him dry."

That wasn't his voice.

It was that of a stranger—darker, deeper, just barely above an animal's growl—and it turned me cold with terror. It possessed no emotion, no mercy, no compassion.

Jay begged, "Ax, listen to me. Listen! You're letting your other half dominate your thoughts. You're not a killer. You don't want to kill. Right? Axel!"

Finally, Axel halted. Absentmindedly, he raised his hand and pressed his thumb against his fangs as if they were causing him pain.

Jay exhaled in relief and let go of Axel's cloak. "You need to clear your head before you do something you'll regret."

Axel stared at the few remaining steps between Wes and him, his eyes dancing. He sighed, and some of the tension finally seeped out of his muscles.

"Ah, Bloody Scout," RC muttered, and then he landed on his knees, hard. The Spasm brought him all the way down. His control over the hovering disks broke, and they fell with a clatter on the cobblestones as he screamed and thrashed, his fists digging into his temples, fingers pulling his hair, anything to alleviate the agony. Wes scrambled to his feet now that he was free.

Axel rubbed his temples, although I couldn't say for sure if it was because RC's screaming was giving him a headache or because he was still struggling to tether his rage and temptation to kill.

As the Spasm receded, Trey bent over to pick up RC's disk that had landed by his foot. He lifted it, only to utter a quiet curse and drop it again.

"You okay?" Madison asked.

"Yeah." Trey studied his hand. "Shit. It was sharper than I thought it'd be." Blood was already streaming down his hand and dripping onto the stone step.

Madison marched over and seized his wrist to study the injury. "You probably need stitches." She pulled her jacket off. "Here, grip this, nice and tight," she instructed, holding out the sleeve and then wrapping the jacket around his fist once he'd taken hold.

I glanced up at Jay and Axel . . . and froze.

"Jay?" I called. My serious tone must have caught his attention, because he turned to me and frowned in a silent inquiry. "When was the last time that Axel had his . . . medicine?"

"Five days ago. Why?"

Jay's gaze shifted from Trey to our lab-brother. Axel had gone unnaturally rigid, staring straight ahead, head cocked stiffly to one side, brow drawn. His lips were parted, as if he was suffering a great agony in silence. He inhaled with a peculiar strangled sound.

"Ax?" Jay said.

"Get away from me," he whispered. He let out a long moan, his face twisting in agony as the groan evolved into a snarl.

"No, don't do this. Not now. Stay with me," Jay pleaded, putting his hand on Axel's shoulder. "Axel, don't give in. Listen to my voice. I need you to focus. You have to fight your instincts."

Madison drew her ectogun and took a few steps toward Jay and Axel. "What's wrong with him?"

Axel closed his eyes, his whole body shuddering, fists clenched, face white with pain, teeth bared in a grimace. The dark circles under his eyes deepened like lengthening afternoon shadows. His snarls became more intense, more vicious, and I watched in horror as his inner pairs of fangs extended from his gums. He gnashed his teeth.

"Oh no," Ash whispered.

"Jay, Blink him out of here!" I cried.

Too late.

The half-breed threw his head back, screaming at the sky as his terrible transformation finished.

Physically, the change wasn't drastic. His body had always been a lethal weapon—what had changed was the consciousness that controlled it.

He swung his arm with a snarl. Jay tried to leap back as he reached for the whistle, but he was too slow; Axel clipped him, sending Jay flying up the steps. My lab-brother crashed into the stairs. His skull smacked the stone with a sickening sound, and he went limp, out cold.

"Jay!" I shouted.

But it wasn't Jay I needed to worry about.

Axel crouched on all fours, his gaze fixed on Trey.

And I knew that Axel was not Axel anymore—his eyes no longer glowed at all because his dilated pupils had completely overtaken the irises, erasing the ring of red that indicated his ghost half was in control.

He was now A6.

And he was going to kill my friend.

— Chapter Thirty-Six —

Bloodlust

Axel rushed at Trey so fast his body was a blur of motion.

Trey squeezed his eyes shut and turned away. He had no time to react, and neither did I; all I could do was stare, expecting to see his mutilated body on the ground by the time I blinked.

To my complete shock as well as Trey's, Axel's lethal trajectory was stopped short by a transparent blue dome of ectoplasm that enshrouded the apprentice. The unlikeliest of saviors were standing in front of Trey to protect him.

Finn and Reese must have realized that Axel's descent into a bloodlust was inevitable before the rest of us did. While we had all hesitated in shock and horror, they had reacted, and their quick response had spared Trey from certain death.

Reese dropped to his knees, frantically activating ECANI while Finn stood with his arms out to maintain the ectoplasm shield around the three of them.

Axel stopped short at the edge of the barrier with a vicious snarl. He raised his hands over his head and slammed his fists down on the ectoplasm dome. Finn was only a Level 2—his shield couldn't withstand Axel's brute strength. Hell, I wasn't even sure if my shield was strong enough. The ectoplasm barrier broke apart into dissipating tendrils of energy as its creator reeled backward, falling to the ground at Trey's feet.

Reese instantly took his place, making a shield of his own to replace his blood-brother's.

"ECANI, voice control on," Finn muttered now that Reese was occupied and couldn't operate the holograms. "Alpha One. Activate—"

I couldn't hear the words over Axel's roar as he directed his fury against Reese's shield. He hit it once—twice—the barrier failed.

A bladed disk struck Axel in the back, but the half-breed didn't even flinch when the weapon embedded in his body. His full attention was on the wounded human saturating my mother's jacket with blood.

He lunged for Trey again. Finn seized Trey's jacket, and the two became intangible—Axel leapt right through them. Mind-reading gave the twins the slightest edge over Axel's speed, but there was no room for error.

I finally had the sense to react, dashing in front of them and sweeping my arm to create an ice wall. This was a stupid, *stupid* move, getting between Axel and his prey when I was absolutely no match for a nydæa in a bloodlust, but it was the only idea I could think of.

"Stop it, Axel!" I shouted, hoping my voice would distract him.

He snarled and smashed my ice shield as I retreated, creating another wall and leading him away from Trey. Axel took the bait and advanced, growling with wrath, his dilated eyes fixed on me. He could probably sense that I was also wounded even though my injuries weren't as fresh.

"C'mon, Ax," I begged as I continued to back away from him. "It's me—it's Cato!" He shattered my wall into slivers again. I swept my left arm out to form another. Wrong move—that was the side where my ribs were either bruised or fractured, and the movement elevated the persistent pain to a breathtakingly sharp jolt that forced me to stop short.

Axel obliterated my ice before I'd finished conjuring it. "I'm your lab-brother! Please, stop! I know you're in there! You don't want to hurt me!"

Axel either couldn't hear me or didn't understand. There was no recognition in his crazed black eyes.

"Cato!" Madison cried. In my peripheral, I could see her on the steps, aiming the gun at Axel.

"Don't!" I shouted. At least with my powers, I had a slim chance. Axel would cut my human mother down in an instant if she became his next target.

I'd barely created another wall when he smashed it with so much force that I stumbled backward, tripping and falling hard on my ass in a storm of ice splinters. I gritted my teeth as the pain almost made me black out. Axel reached over his shoulder, plucked the blades out of his back, and dropped the disk, then seized the front of my shirt in his iron-strong hands.

He hauled me up so high my feet dangled above the ground. Teeth bared, he let out a deep, meaningful snarl, as if taking a moment to reprimand me for interfering before proceeding to drive his fangs into my neck and rip me apart.

This was it. I knew the end was coming, but I couldn't process that Axel was going to be the one to kill me. My only consolation was that it would be an instant death, so fast that I probably wouldn't have a chance to feel much pain.

I gasped as a massive furry head lunged into my field of vision and locked its jaws around Axel's arm.

Axel snarled in pain and fury, but he didn't let go of me. I became intangible and slipped through his grasp as I fell to the ground and crawled backward with my hand pressed against my ribs, watching in a numb stupor as he wrenched his arm loose even though Wes's sharp teeth shredded his skin and muscles down to the bone.

The werewolf charged at him again, but Axel swatted away the two-thousand-pound wolf as if it were a ten-pound puppy.

Wes hit the ground with a yelp. He struggled to get back up, whining and scrabbling at the cobblestones, but Axel must have broken a few bones. The giant wolf gave up with a quiet whimper of pain and defeat.

Axel crouched onto all fours, his head turning back to locate his original prey. He was moving all wrong. Every motion was jerky and disjointed. With his pupils completely dilated, he must not be able to discern more than shapes and shadows in the daylight, so when he turned his head, his eyes weren't guiding the rotation. It was his ears, I thought, and his nose. That was what he was relying on in lieu of his eyesight.

He charged Trey again. "No!" I cried.

Something—I couldn't tell what—made Axel stop short of his quarry once again. He let out a guttural roar and attacked an invisible barrier that was blocking his passage.

I stared, completely brain-locked in shock and confusion. Finally, I noticed ECANI in Reese's arms and the answer dawned on me—the twins had activated Proto and adapted the program to form an invisible shield around Trey. Since it was now blocking Axel's DNA from passing through the barrier, there was no way he could break his way through.

We'll all be safe inside Proto, I thought in relief, then realized I was wrong. If Axel couldn't get to Trey, he'd go on a killing spree in Phantom Heights. We had to deal with him right here, right now, before he took someone's life.

A wall of fire sprang up from the cobblestones, separating Axel from Trey and the twins. The half-breed stumbled back, hissing and growling in displeasure before he was jerked off his feet. RC sent him flying through the air until he crashed into City Hall at the top of the stairs.

Axel hit the ground with a furious yelp, but he was on his feet again in a fraction of a second.

We'd been lucky so far, but our good fortune was overdue to run out. Axel was too fast and too strong. He wouldn't stop, not while the smell of Trey's blood was driving him insane. Even if we could get Trey out of here, Axel was too far gone.

All we had going in our favor was that in this state, Axel wasn't using his ghost powers, and his obsession with Trey had him distracted, which meant he wasn't detecting and dodging attacks as he normally would. Wes had dealt some damage but not enough—Axel didn't seem to be favoring his injured arm at all. My sonokinesis might be effective against him, but I couldn't risk the damage it would do to Phantom Heights.

The grim truth was, if Axel were to give up on Trey and turn his full predatory attention onto the rest of us, we'd be done. Right now, we were obstacles, not prey. That wouldn't last much longer.

A series of gunshots made me flinch and cower. I whirled—the patrol was firing at Axel now that he'd been separated from us. "Don't shoot!" I yelled. "Please, don't shoot him!"

They ignored me and kept firing. I screamed, "Madison, *do* something!"

She hesitated—her own gun was trained on Axel too—but then she turned away from him and sprinted down the steps toward the officers, waving her arms and crying, "Cease fire! Stop! Cease fire!"

Ash shouted, "The whistle!"

I turned, my gaze settling on Jay still lying unconscious on the stairs. Around his neck, the silver whistle dangled on its black cord.

Ash was holding Axel off with a volley of fireballs. The half-breed had his face protected behind his forearm, teeth bared and head down as he braced himself against the flaming attacks. I couldn't tell if he'd been hit with any bullets, but at least the patrol had listened to my mother and the gunshots had stopped.

RC and I both had our attention on Jay's whistle. RC raised his arm—the cord snapped off its host as the whistle shot through the air toward his hand.

But Axel, whose growls had been growing angrier and angrier with Ash's attack, finally lost it. With a ferocious snarl, he charged down the steps, teeth bared for her throat.

RC pushed both hands out, palms extended, body strained forward as if he were shoving against an invisible wall with all his might. His intervention managed to stop Axel on the stairs, but the half-breed resisted RC's attempt to push him back. He held his ground. The sheer telekinetic force bearing down on him was so strong that the marble steps were cracking under Axel's boots.

With RC's concentration redirected, the whistle clattered onto the stairs with a light tinkling sound, rolled down the last few steps, and settled to a stop between the cobblestones.

I dashed for it, my tunnel vision seeing nothing but that whistle lying on the stones. It was Axel's one weakness and our only chance to stop him from killing someone.

RC fell to his knees. His arms were trembling, and the lines of blood from his right nostril and the left corner of his mouth warned that he was close to burning out as he clenched his teeth under the strain.

Axel, sensing that RC's power was failing, smiled through his growls and pushed forward, advancing to the next step. It was taking everything RC had just to slow Axel down.

In a desperate final act before he burned out, RC cut the telekinetic pressure and flung his three disks at Axel.

The half-breed swatted each one away with his forearms. The spinning blades struck the metal in his gauntlets with a dull *clink!* and ricocheted in different directions.

A streak of silver in the edge of my vision was the only warning I had. I dove to the ground, hitting the cobblestones on my stomach with a sharp grunt of pain as one of the lethal disks whizzed right over me. I pushed myself up onto my elbows and opened my eyes to focus on the whistle an arm's length in front of me.

I reached out, snatched the hollow object in my fist, and drew it back, the cord trailing across the cobblestones. It was hard to imagine this little whistle could stop a force like A6.

I turned my head to look at Axel, hoping to see some glimmer of consciousness or recognition in his eyes. But the pupils were still dilated, his eyes black, blank, and soulless.

"I'm sorry, Ax," I whispered. I rose to my knees, raised the whistle to my lips, and blew as hard as I could.

No sound came out.

My heart sank in despair—it was broken?

Axel shrieked in agony and clapped his hands over his ears, shaking his head and staggering backward before he collapsed and fell down the last few stairs.

I'd never heard him make such a sound before. It wasn't the guttural roar of a wounded animal—it was human. It was my lab-brother screaming, not a monster. He writhed on the ground, palms over his ears, pounding his face against the cobblestones until it was bloody while he wailed as if being ripped apart fiber by fiber.

My breath died. I felt sick.

As soon as I stopped blowing the silent whistle, Axel was on all fours, snarling, somehow even more ferocious than before. I'd hoped the pain might jar him out of the episode, but no. His black eyes were still empty when they settled on the source of his pain—me. I hadn't stopped him. All I'd done was delay him and piss him off.

"Take him down!" I cried before I blew again. The pain ripping through my torso prevented me from taking deep breaths, so these short bursts were the best I could do. Axel's screams broke my heart as he fell to his knees once more.

Ash swung her staff at his head with all her might. The metal smashing into Axel's temple made a sickening *crack*, but he didn't flinch. Only the whistle seemed to have any effect on him. He fell onto his back and thrashed at Ash's feet, howling in agony that must make a Spasm feel like a minor headache.

I had to pause for another breath. I was running out of ideas. The whistle was damaging Axel's ears, and it was only a matter of time before the damage was severe enough to make him deaf. Then, the whistle would be useless.

Somehow, we had to take him down before that happened.

Axel sprang to his feet, his black eyes locked on me again. I inhaled and blew.

He threw his head back with a yowl, then interlaced his fingers through his coal-black hair, shaking his head with his eyes squeezed shut.

Time was running out. In one last act of desperation, RC threw out his hand. The half-nydæa was yanked off his feet and flung through the air until he smashed into the stairs, where he continued to scream and writhe. Nothing we did was strong enough to knock him out.

Axel suddenly went still, even though I was still blowing the whistle. My breath shriveled in my lungs as I noticed the blood trickling from his ears.

Slowly, I rose. Ash and RC backed away from City Hall in horror.

Time was up. I had destroyed Axel's ears. He was now immune to the whistle.

And I was dead.

He leapt up and charged at me in a blur. I stumbled backward, eyes frozen open, each microsecond dragging on as though time itself had slowed.

I'm going to die. This time, I'm really going to die.

I closed my eyes.

Something pushed me, hard, and I went flying. I landed on my back with a harsh grunt as the air was knocked out of my lungs and my injured ribs sent a sharp pain zinging through my nerves.

My eyes fluttered open. I stared up at the gray clouds, struggling to suck in short gasps of air to refill my lungs. In a daze, I labored to sit up.

The impact had somehow cast a green tint over my vision. Axel was standing a short distance away from City Hall's steps, snarling and pounding his fists as if beating against something solid that was blocking his passage. I slowly comprehended that it wasn't the fall that had shifted my color perception. It was the Dome. Axel was trapped inside.

I stared at him, my sluggish brain taking way too long to put the pieces together. Who had activated the Dome?

Trey, Finn, and Reese were trapped inside with Axel, but at least they were safe within Proto. A fourth figure appeared right next to them, and then they all vanished, only to appear beside me a split second later.

Finn and Reese were clutching Jay's cloak, and the leader was gripping Trey's upper arm. The moment he let go, Trey fell to his knees.

I staggered to my feet. I'd never seen Axel so pissed before. With feral brutality, he slammed into the shield with all his strength, but it held firm. Like Proto, it wasn't a solid object for him to break; it repelled the ectoplasm in his body. A pureblood nydæa could pass through it, but not Axel. He couldn't suppress his ghost half the way I could.

Now, his screams were not of pain, but of frustration that all of his prey was out of reach. I could see glimpses of bone in his shredded arm where Wes had bitten him, and the skin on his forehead was a sticky, bloody mess from when he'd slammed it repeatedly against the stones in agony from the whistle. A few holes in his black clothes made me suspect he'd met a few bullets as well. He paid no attention to his wounds, as if he didn't even feel them. I was the only one who had been able to hurt him.

My stomach twisted when I realized what I'd done. *It was necessary*, I told myself. I didn't have a choice. Axel wanted us to stop him from killing at all costs, even if that cost was his own life. Yes, I had hurt him, but nobody died, and that was what mattered right now.

I looked around in a numb state of shock. My mother was holding Trey, whose face was sheet white. Finn and Reese sat beside them, looking exhausted and relieved. Ash was still frozen in a fighting stance. RC was on his knees. Wes had reverted to his human form and was sitting, naked, hunched over nearby.

A loud *crack!* made me automatically duck and cower before I was even conscious there was more danger. Axel flinched as a hole was pulverized into the marble step near his head.

"No!" Jay screamed. "Don't shoot! He can't hurt anyone now!"

I was moving, running with a stiff, uneven gait as if autopilot had taken over, and then I found myself standing in front of Axel with my arms spread wide as I faced the dark barrel of Chief Emerton's gun. He ordered, "Get out of the way. I'm putting that animal down."

"He's contained," I said breathlessly. "He's no longer a threat."

Axel threw his body against the shield so hard that he rebounded back in a daze. He closed his eyes and screamed at us in a terrifying, haunting wail of hunger and rage, then sank to all fours and began to pace along the edge of the shield like a caged animal.

RC made a quick movement with his hand, and Emerton's gun was yanked away. It landed by my feet. I bent down, picked it up. Stared at it.

"Cato," Emerton warned, holding up his hands and retreating a step. "Put that down."

My gaze lifted toward his voice, and so did the gun. My finger wasn't on the trigger—I didn't trust my shaking hand not to accidentally fire. The fear in Emerton's voice puzzled me. I could scream and level this whole town, or skewer everyone with a storm of ice shards, and yet, he seemed to be more afraid of the human weapon in my hand than of my own power.

The patrol took aim at me. RC relieved them all of their weapons, levitating them out of reach. A few officers jumped and swiped at the air in a futile attempt to reclaim their arms.

Jay heaved a deep sigh and approached the Dome, then set his palm flat against the surface of entoplasm. Immediately, Axel tried to attack. "He's gone," the leader proclaimed.

Humans were still eyeing me, wary of the gun. I let my arm fall so the barrel pointed harmlessly at the ground. "Get Trey out of here." My voice sounded dead, alien, as though it didn't even belong to me.

Madison didn't move. "The shield will hold him . . . right?" she asked.

Jay's grim response was, "I hope so. Axel could smash your generator or short-circuit it with his ectoplasm. The only benefit of his current condition is that he isn't coherent enough to strategize or even think, really. He's acting on pure instinct, so he won't use any of his powers. Honestly . . . I don't think he knows he has them."

I said, "He needs his medicine."

"I know."

"So, give it to him."

"It's not that simple. And besides, if I Blink inside the Dome, he'll rip me apart." He shook his head, watching Axel pace.

Ash asked, "Will he snap out of it on his own?"

"I don't know," Jay admitted. "Back up and give him space. Hopefully, he'll come around."

As the rest of us retreated, a tiny black-and-white kitten slunk forward and transformed in a swirl of smoke. "Axel," Kit whimpered in sorrow. Ash picked her up and held her tight.

Madison's voice started in a whisper that rose to a stressed pitch as she said, "What . . . the *hell* was that? Cato?"

I tore my attention away from Axel to stare blankly at my mother for a few long seconds before my vacant gaze returned to him. "This is A6," I said, my voice hollow.

"I don't understand."

I swallowed, trying to make my hands stop trembling. I stared down at the silver whistle, realizing it was still clenched in my fist. "Thank a bloody Scout this worked," I whispered.

She turned away. "Wes? What is he?"

The werewolf still hadn't risen, but he was studying Axel with a peculiar expression of pain and intrigue etched into his brow. I held my breath. Now that Axel's other half was in control, would Wes be able to recognize him for what he was?

I studied every detail of Wes's face, searching for the subtlest indication of what he might be thinking. Despite his interest, his eyes didn't light up with recognition. I still wasn't sure of the human translation for the word *nydœa*, but I felt confident enough to decide that Wes had never crossed one before.

He said, "Honestly, Maddie, I'm not sure. He almost seems like he could be . . ." He trailed off and glanced up at the sun shining through a break in the clouds. "No, scratch that. Hmm." He rubbed his chin while he continued to study the half-breed monster. "I wonder . . . if maybe Axel's physical appearance isn't accurate."

I swallowed and glanced at Jay, whose lips were drawn together. When he met my gaze, his mouth pressed into an even tighter line.

Wes explained, "I can fully shift between two different forms, but I think Axel's transition is more subtle, like Cato's. I can't tell what his other half is while he still has the form of a kálos."

"Madison?" Trey asked in a weak voice. He was still deathly pale. "I don't feel good. I think I'm gonna pass out."

"We need to get you to the hospital," she said. And yet she hesitated, glancing uncertainly between Trey sitting on the ground, Axel pacing the edge of the Dome, and me still holding the gun. She was visibly torn between the multiple crises all demanding attention at once.

One of the patrol officers volunteered, "I can take him."

"I can Blink you both there," Jay added.

Madison inclined her head. "Are you okay with that? I want to go with you, but . . ."

"I'm okay," Trey whispered. "You can stay here."

"Thank you." She gave him a quick embrace, then rose and stepped back.

Wes grumpily called, "And I'm just fine and dandy over here, thanks."

"You're a fast healer," Madison snapped.

"Yes, and if Doc doesn't set these broken bones quickly, they're going to heal wrong," he retorted.

Jay said, "You need to be touching one another in order for me to Blink you all at once."

Madison and the police officer helped Trey to his feet. He leaned against the officer for support as he guided him over to Wes.

Without a word, Jay set one hand on Wes's shoulder and the other on Trey's, and then they all vanished. Jay reappeared again in his original spot by the Dome a few seconds later.

Madison gently called my name. She started to approach. I automatically stiffened and backed up half a step before I stood my ground. She reached for the weapon clenched in my hand. "Cato, please give me the gun."

She was calm, not angry, and she gently wrapped her hand around the weapon, waiting for me to relinquish it rather than trying to rip it away from me. I tightened my grip. "Why, so you can shoot Axel?"

"I'm not going to shoot him. I promise. Please let go."

I gazed into her emerald eyes for a long moment, and then I released my hold. She immediately holstered the gun in her own belt so no one could use it. "Thank you for trusting me. What's your plan, Jay?"

He had his back to us, arms crossed, attention solely focused on

Axel. "We wait," he replied. "Hopefully, Axel will snap out of it and come to his senses."

"And if he doesn't?"

"Plan B."

"What's plan B?"

Jay was silent for a moment. "I'll let you know when I figure it out."

Madison rubbed her temples with her thumb and forefinger, then let her hand fall with a weary sigh. "Okay. Is anyone hurt? Jay, you hit your head really hard."

"I'm fine," he dismissed.

"But you were unconscious for—"

"I'm fine. Just a headache."

She pursed her lips and shook her head in disapproval. "You okay?" she asked me in her gentle mom voice.

I nodded and refrained from pressing my hand against my rib cage.

Madison went to Finn and Reese and knelt down in front of them. "You were *so* brave. Did you get hurt?" They stared down at their feet and shook their heads. Madison threw her arms around them and pulled them into a tight embrace. "You saved Trey's life. I'm so proud of you."

Finn and Reese stared over her shoulders, eyes wide in shock at receiving such high praise from a human.

The weapons that had been levitating above town square fell on top of the officers, who cursed and covered their heads too late to avoid bumps and bruises.

"Burned out," RC muttered, staring at his shaking hands. "I hit my limit." He swiped at the blood still trickling from his nose and mouth.

Madison let go of the twins and stood. She ran her hand across the top of her head to smooth down her ponytail, looking rather overwhelmed. "Okay. Sit down and rest. All of you. Let me talk to Emerton, and then we'll figure out our next steps."

The next hour passed in a blur of numb exhaustion. The police officers had reluctantly listened to my mother and agreed to close off town square. Word had already spread throughout Phantom Heights, though, and the officers had their hands full keeping curious spectators away.

Madison brought us food and water, but we were all so upset that we barely ate. She told Jay that he absolutely could not fall asleep in case he had a concussion. RC, weakened from his burnout, dozed on and off while the rest of us sat in front of the Dome to keep a vigilant watch over the officers and ensure no one else attempted to execute our lab-brother. I hadn't fully recovered from my own burnout, and I felt my eyes getting heavier and heavier.

"Is he sleeping now?" came Kit's timid voice.

I turned. Axel had finally stopped pacing and was lying on his side with his eyes closed. His chest rose and fell with rapid, shallow pants interspersed with faint whimpers.

Jay tilted his head, studying the half-breed before concluding, "No. I think he's going through withdrawal."

The lines in Madison's brow deepened. "Withdrawal from what?"

Jay ignored her and approached the shield, then knelt down. "Axel," he called.

I held my breath, watching. Axel didn't respond. He just lay there, panting. Then, his eyes flickered open.

The pupils were still fully dilated. He snarled and lunged at Jay, stopped once again by the transparent shield.

Axel tried to break through for a few minutes while Jay sat on his knees, watching our lab-brother in mournful silence. Finally, Axel gave up and leaned his head against the shield. He was trembling now, his skin wet with beads of perspiration. He let out a single snarl and spun away.

Axel paced for a while, then fell to his knees. He wrapped his arms around his stomach and wilted inward upon himself, rocking back and forth as if suffering a psychotic break. Despite the grim appearance, I hoped this was a good sign that meant our lab-brother was clawing his way free from the throes of the demon within.

He alternated between pacing, rocking, licking his wounded arm, pulling at his hair, and squirming on the ground. His animalistic growls were steadily becoming more humanlike moans.

Axel rolled onto his back. "Somebody, help me," he whispered, voice cracked and hoarse. "I'm dying . . . somebody . . . help me . . ."

"You're not dying," Jay said.

Ash muttered, "He can't hear you."

"I know. But I think he can feel the vibrations of my words."

Axel's semicoherent whispers degraded into an agonizing moan. Despite the language progress, he hadn't fully returned. One second, he'd be bawling like a baby, and then he was laughing manically, then throwing a temper tantrum and screaming as he pounded his fists against the shield or the ground, and then just like that, he was sobbing again.

I'd seen Axel go from placid to pissed in half a second, but these were violent extremes even for him.

Kit didn't budge from her place beside the Dome. She sat on her knees, completely still, gaze trained on Axel as if she was afraid to break contact even long enough to blink. Jay lingered behind her.

"You hate me," Axel sobbed, as if he somehow knew Jay was there. "You like watching me suffer. You've always hated me."

"That's not true," the leader said patiently.

"Yes, it is. You want me to die."

"Axel, you know I don't think that."

The half-breed's face suddenly twisted from miserable to livid. "You're lying! You're a fucking *liar*! I'ma kill you—I'ma rip you to pieces, you motherfucking bastard—I hear your heart beating—I smell your blood—I'm going to *kill* you . . ."

Jay didn't even blink at the violent threats. "Axel, what's my name?"

Axel, now rocking back and forth again, started muttering a stream of profanity. Jay nodded, as if unsurprised. "When we can have a civil conversation, then I can help you."

Hours later, I couldn't tell if Axel was better or worse.

He'd been quiet for a while, curled on his side with his eyes squeezed shut. The light was hurting him, I suspected, with his pupils so dilated. When the sun had pushed the shadows back so the warmth could touch his face, he'd whined and crawled partway up the stairs to return to the shadows.

His skin was pallid and slick, his hair soaked from perspiration, his body shuddering with painful tremors, his teeth chattering. No words— just agonizing groans and whimpers. Tears had been slipping down his cheeks for so long I was amazed he wasn't dehydrated. Every few minutes, he'd tense and moan, as if his muscles were having spasms. He really did look as if he were dying.

Kit remained poised in the exact same place she'd been.

Jay knelt next to her at the edge of the Dome. "Axel," he called.

No response.

"Axel," Jay called again, and Axel shuddered but still wouldn't answer. Jay pushed, "I can't help you if you won't talk to me."

Axel's diaphragm convulsed with a hard sob. He raked his hand through his drenched hair and shook his head with his eyes squeezed shut. Jay asked, "What's my name?"

Axel must have forgotten that his fangs were still longer than normal because he bit down on his lower lip, drawing blood from the sharpened tips.

"*Axel*," Jay said sternly. "What's my name?"

"Jay," Axel whispered.

"Good. You know who I am?"

". . . Yes."

"And do you still want to kill me?"

Axel opened his eyes but stayed silent. He took a long time to ponder his answer. That was a good sign, I hoped. It meant he was thinking. It was hard to tell for sure, but I thought I could see a thin ring of red around his dilated pupils.

Quietly, he admitted, "Yes." Over Jay's disappointed sigh, he added, "But I know it's wrong."

Jay perked up. "Good, Axel. That's good."

The half-breed's arms circled his abdomen as he whined, "It hurts."

"I know," Jay soothed.

"Are . . . we still brothers?"

"Of course."

Axel rolled his head toward Jay. "A real brother wouldn't leave me to suffer. Please kill me," he whispered monotonously. His eyes were bloodshot. "Make it stop. I want to die."

"It's almost over."

"You promised. You have to keep your promise. I want you to kill me."

Jay set his open hand on the surface of the Dome. "Sorry, Ax. I promised I'd stop you by any means necessary, but I'm not losing you if I can help it. That means you'll have to suffer a bit longer."

Axel sobbed and weakly reached out toward his oldest lab-brother. "Jay, please—it hurts so bad. I can't take it anymore. If you had a heart, you'd put me out of my misery. It's a mercy kill. I want you to do it. Please end my pain."

Kit set her little hand on top of Jay's on the Dome. He replied, "You're going through withdrawal, but you're getting better."

"It hurts . . . I just want it to stop . . . I just wanna die . . ."

Jay pulled his hand off the Dome and leaned back, considering. "Maybe I can take you to get your medicine now. If you tell me where to go."

"No."

"Ax, I can't Blink you there if you don't tell me."

Axel covered his ears and shook his head in refusal. Over my shoulder, Madison whispered, "You don't know where Axel goes every week?"

I shook my head. I thought Jay did, but apparently not. Realizing that Axel wasn't about to divulge this information, he compromised, "Okay. Then let me take you away from here, where there aren't any people to hurt. No more temptation."

Axel stared at Jay with the blank incomprehension of a dog listening to its master speak a new command. At first, I didn't think he understood, but then he croaked, "Okay."

"You have to come to me, though."

Axel squinted at him. "I can't. You come into the shadow."

"No. You have to come into the light if you want me to help you."

The hybrid worked his jaw in frustrated irritability. He stirred, testing the strength of his muscles, then squeezed his eyes shut and dragged his body down the steps. Axel was weak, but that was no reason to lower our guard. A6, if it were to reawaken—which was a likely possibility—would be just as strong as before and even more desperate after going through withdrawal.

Axel crawled to the edge of the Dome, collapsed in front of Jay, and pressed his forehead to the ground. "Let's go, let's go, right now," he whined into the cobblestones.

Jay rose. "Not yet. Will you let RC muzzle you?"

Axel peered up at Jay through the crook of his arm. He sighed and rolled onto his back, which I assumed must mean submission.

Jay asked, "Have you recovered enough to use a little telekinesis?"

RC inclined his head. He surveyed the nearby construction equipment for materials.

Jay said, "Open your mouth." Axel complied, and RC gagged him. "Bite down."

He did, then closed his eyes as RC contorted strips of metal over Axel's face, reminiscent of the three-strapped muzzle *They* had used when transporting our lab-brother. Axel didn't resist.

Solemn, Jay ordered, "Bind him."

RC used rebar to do it. Axel grunted when the rods circled his body too tightly and compressed all the air out of his lungs. His eyes fluttered open. He looked so wretched lying there, trussed up, muzzled, weak, and bloody. It seemed cruel.

But he's not really restrained, I had to remind myself. All he had to do was move, just a little, and those metal bars would bend like aluminum foil. He was restrained for the moment only because he was willingly holding still.

I handed Jay his whistle, both of us fully aware that it wouldn't work. "You know that won't hold him for more than a few seconds at most," I murmured.

"I just need one." Jay knelt again, and Axel watched him miserably. "When I count to three, okay, Ax?" The half-breed nodded and closed his eyes, bracing himself. "One . . ."

It was so fast I almost missed it. Maybe half a second. Jay disappeared, and then he was crouched beside Axel inside the Dome for a moment so brief I wasn't entirely convinced I actually saw it.

And then they were gone.

— Chapter Thirty-Seven —

Red Eyes

Hassing lingered behind one of the columns in the Prison's peristyle courtyard.

It was a creepy place, he'd always thought, but since this was the first part of the Prison incarcerated victims saw, the pillars of the colonnade were appropriate, even if they were disturbing. Each column had been masterfully sculpted into a naked figure of a Prisoner in chains standing on a stone base, laboring to hold up the heavy pillar. The talented artist had detailed the figures so perfectly that they were eerily lifelike, the agony palpable in every crease on their faces.

Hassing leaned his back against the calf of a stone woman contorted beneath her eternal burden. He waited, gaze skyward. A shadow glided across the columns, and then a black bird with a white-tipped wing drifted into sight.

The captain pursed his lips and let out a two-tone whistle, catching the Amínyte's attention. Rayven swiveled his head. His sharp eyes instantly locked onto Hassing, who gestured for him to approach. The bird obediently changed course and fluttered to the ground. Before its talons touched the courtyard, it was engulfed in black smoke.

Hassing was already on the move. By the time Rayven fully assumed his kálos form, the captain had seized a fistful of his long black hair and wrapped his other arm around the Amínyte's neck. Rayven clutched at Hassing's forearm in panic, but the captain had already dragged him behind the pillar, out of sight from Azar's office window.

Hassing slammed him against the sculpted column with enough force to draw a hefty grunt. "All right, you flea-bitten pest," the captain seethed, his nose inches from Rayven's. Over the scarback's resentful mutter of "I don't have fleas," Hassing demanded, "Tell me where Azar sent you."

Rayven blinked at him, then snickered. Hassing felt his Divinity stir in anger. The slave had the audacity to laugh at him?

"Master isn't patient. He got tired of waiting."

With that said, the Amínyte transformed in a swirl of smoke. Hassing lost his grip as the body morphed, becoming a bundle of feathers and wings that flapped into the air with a triumphant squawk.

The captain strode out from behind the pillar, his head tilted back to watch the bird climb higher until it flew through the open window on the top floor. Hassing stood in place for a long moment, processing Rayven's last words.

He ground his teeth. His gaze turned from the window to the front gate, and then he stormed away—his destination the Rip in the center of Szion.

* * *

I sat on the bed with my knees hugged against my chest.

This used to be my bed. This used to be my room. But I felt so small, so lonely, so out of place here. Shadows loomed on the walls, and I imagined they watched me with red eyes.

I rested my chin on my knees, replaying the catastrophe with Axel this morning. Somehow, we had prevented him from taking a single life, but it certainly didn't feel like a victory. Jay wouldn't say where he had taken Axel, only that it was someplace safe and far away from potential human casualties.

Councilwoman Jennings didn't believe him. She had demanded to speak with me and hadn't bothered to hide her aggravation when Madison insisted on being present. The best response I'd been able to give when Holly asked what Axel was, where he went, what he was doing, and why he'd completely lost his mind was silence. I had locked my teeth together and refused to speak a single word during the interrogation until finally, she'd switched topics and said, "We're having a public meeting in an hour. I have a speech written for you. This time, read what's on the card, got it? No improvising."

"Now wait just a minute—" Madison had started to protest, but I'd already cut in, "Why do I have to speak?"

"Because people are terrified that *thing* is going to kill them in their sleep tonight, that's why."

"I can't do it. I look at all those people watching me, and I—I just freeze. I can't answer that reporter's questions. Jay is a better speaker; have him do it."

"I need Phantom."

"Yeah, well, Phantom doesn't exist anymore! Don't you get it? That mask doesn't make me Phantom."

Holly had stared at me so long that I could feel my face turning red. Stoic, she'd said, "It doesn't matter. Phantom is an image—one that people trust."

"But there is no Phantom. Jay needs to be your new image. He's the leader."

"Mm-hmm, and that's also a problem. Jay isn't the *right* image. People aren't thrilled about their hero taking back seat to a pureblood ghost. You're half-human, so you're more relatable. And you're more powerful than Jay. You should be the leader."

"Jay is more qualified," I shot back. "He's earned the position."

"I don't care. Regardless of the true hierarchy of your little group, I need you to portray the role of leader in public."

That was it. I was done. After everything that had happened, I couldn't take any more. The green power had burned hot as the stress boiled over. "I realize this is a difficult concept for you to grasp, but there's more to leadership than just power. I'm not the leader, and I'm not speaking."

Madison, despite her initial frustration about being in the dark during this whole mess with Axel, had softened after I cracked under Holly's interrogation. She'd followed me and inquired, "Do you want to talk?"

"What do you think?" I'd shot back. Every time she asked me that question, I always gave her the same answer.

"Cato . . . would you consider spending the night with us at home?"

"What do you mean?" I'd asked suspiciously.

"Well, Viv and I have been staying at Wes's as often as we can. I'd like you to consider spending one night a week at home with us, and after what happened today, I think some peace, quiet, and normalcy would be good for you."

As if she'd read my mind and knew I was about to make excuses, she'd immediately added, "One night, that's all I'm asking. I think it'll do you a lot of good to sleep in your old room, in your old bed, and to walk Viv and Trey to school in the morning. Going through your routine might help you de-stress. It might even help bring some of your memories back."

But she was wrong. This room felt bigger than I remembered. Emptier. Flat people stared at me from posters on the walls. The ceiling was lower, and the room itself was much smaller than the one I shared with my lab-family at Saros Manor, which made me feel as if the walls were shrinking in on me. I was dressed in loose pajama pants and a T-shirt. Unable to bear the feeling of vulnerability, I threw my cloak over my shoulders.

A timid knock on the doorframe made me jump. Vivian poked her head inside. "Hey. Can I come in?"

I nodded, and she breezed into the room, tying the belt of a fleece robe around her waist before she sat on the edge of my bed. Although she eyed my cloak, she didn't acknowledge it. "Does it feel good to finally be back home?"

I knew the answer she wanted me to give, but I couldn't force myself to say it. I pulled the cloak over my nose and breathed in the familiar scent of it—the only familiar thing in this room.

"It'll get better," she promised.

I didn't believe her. This had been a long trial with poor results. I hadn't readjusted, and I didn't think I ever would despite everyone telling me otherwise.

"Viv, how did Dad die?"

She gave me a sad, crestfallen look. "Well, I was six, so you were only three when it happened. There was a snowstorm, and he was driving home when he hit a patch of black ice and lost control of the car. I barely remember him, so it's no surprise that you don't."

"Was he a good dad? I mean, did he love us?"

"Yes, very much."

I stared at my bare toes. "I don't know what he looked like."

Vivian rose and walked out of my room without a word. I waited, afraid that I'd somehow offended her and wondering if I should follow, but after a minute, she returned with a large book and sat down beside me. She set the album between us so when she opened it, I was holding one half in my lap and she had the other.

The pages were filled with pictures. Viv pointed to a photograph of a man and woman holding each other and smiling. "Here—this is Mom and Dad."

I leaned so close that my face was inches away from the page. I studied every detail of the man's features, from his tousled hair to his blue-gray eyes to the small mole by the corner of his mouth. My mother had said I was almost the spitting image of him. Although I'd inherited Madison's green eyes, I had his black hair, and I could see a pronounced resemblance between my facial features and his.

Vivian tapped her finger against another picture, redirecting my attention. In this vignette, the same man was on his knees with a little girl sitting atop his shoulders and a small toddler standing beside him, sucking his thumb. I pointed to the boy. "That's me?"

"Yup. That picture was taken shortly before Dad died."

Enthralled, I turned the page, absorbing the photos to fill some of the blanks in my memory. "It's like our entire lives are in this book," I said as I flipped to the next page, then frowned. "What about the Tarrow side of the family? I only see the Hays side in here."

"We lost touch after Dad died. They live far away, and without Dad here, I guess there wasn't much reason for them to visit." She turned a few pages and then pointed at a photograph of a stern-looking woman in glasses sitting beside a heavyset man with a salt-and-pepper beard. "Grandma and Grandpa. Dad didn't have any siblings."

"Do they know about me? I mean, what I am?"

"No, they don't."

I touched my father's face. "His name was Jaxon, right? Like my middle name."

"Yeah. It's kind of a silly tradition in our family. The firstborn daughter gets her mom's first name for her middle name, and the firstborn son gets the dad's."

I closed the album and said, "So . . . if you have a daughter, her middle name will be Vivian?"

"I haven't thought that far in the future. If I decide to have kids and keep up the tradition, then yes."

We both looked up when Madison appeared in the doorway. "Viv, it's a school night. Better get to bed."

"Okay. Have you heard from Trey?"

She nodded. "He's all right. He has fifteen stitches in his hand, but he says he still wants to go to school tomorrow. And Wes is back at Saros Manor, resting. It won't take him long to recover."

"I'm glad they're okay. I'll sleep better now." Vivian rose, then hesitated and turned back to me. "See you in the morning, Cay. You're walking with me to school, right?"

"If you want me to."

"I do. So . . . okay. See you tomorrow. You can keep the album, if you want."

"Thanks," I said. She gave me an awkward smile, but I couldn't muster one in return.

Madison said, "All settled in?"

I nodded. I didn't trust my voice not to crack. "Good. Your clothes are in the dryer. I'll have them folded and waiting for you in the morning." She shifted her weight, causing the floorboards to creak. I suspected that she wanted to come hug me and kiss me on the forehead like she used to, but she refrained. "Good night, Cato," she said. "It's really good to have you back. If you need anything, come wake me or Vivian up. Sleep well, okay?"

"Okay," I croaked, starting to panic. They were going to leave me all alone in this room that made me feel claustrophobic and insignificantly tiny at the same time. Was that even possible? To be claustrophobic in a room that was too big and empty and lonely? I didn't want to sleep, and I didn't want to be alone in the dark.

My lab-family would have noticed the nervous hitch in my voice, but my blood-family didn't. Madison smiled and blew me a kiss, then backed out the door and left. Vivian reached for the light switch, and I almost begged, "Wait! Don't turn out the light!"

But I didn't. Darkness cast its cloak over me, and Vivian was a silhouette in front of the lit hallway. She started to close the door, but I weakly called, "Viv? Please leave it open." *Don't lock me away in the dark.*

Her hand fell off the doorknob. "Okay. Good night, Cato."

She left.

And I was alone.

I set the heavy photo album on the nightstand, then drew my legs in and hugged them tightly against my chest. Alone. I hadn't slept alone since the last time I was in Quarantine. I hated that room with its padded table and restraints, the harsh white lights, the *beep* of machines. Needles, poking and pricking. Drugs that made my head fuzzy. The nauseatingly sharp scents of peppermint and disinfectant masking the odor of various bodily fluids.

I must have dozed off because a cry woke me. I gasped and sat straight up, even though the sudden movement sent a jolt of pain through my left side. My heart raced.

"Where am I?" I asked aloud. My voice startled me—was it my own cry that had roused me? This place wasn't familiar. There was enough faint light from the window to cast strange shadows, but not enough for me to distinguish the details of my surroundings. Blades whirred above me, creating a breeze that stirred my hair. *Helicopters.*

A spotlight turned on, blinding me, forcing me to squint and shield my eyes with one arm. *They* had found me!

"Cato, you're okay," a woman said. Two silhouettes in the doorway were coming toward me, cutting off the escape route.

450

I scooted away from them, alarmed and confused that the ground beneath me was soft and I was partially tangled in something. I couldn't get my footing to stand up.

"Stay away! Who are you? Where am I?"

A shiver down my spine was severe enough to make my entire body shudder.

"Cato."

I froze. I knew that voice. Once I located the speaker, all the fear and tension melted from my body.

The two women whirled. They were shocked that he was here, then furious, but before they could speak, my voice broke the tense silence. "Axel," I identified in relief.

He had tried to kill me today, and yet, I wasn't afraid of him. Not now. He was back to the lab-brother I knew—an invincible force of power and protection with a clairvoyant gaze that could see everything. Axel was not growling, which meant I was safe. That had always been true, even in that place.

Calmer now, I exhaled and surveyed the room. The last memories before closing my eyes returned—I knew where I was.

Sleep was weighing me down, and I settled back onto the mattress. The bed still felt too big and empty without the tangled nest of arms and legs I was used to, but at least one lab-sibling was with me now, and that put me at ease.

Madison asked, "Are you all right, Cay?"

"Yeah. I'm okay now."

She glowered at Axel, who scowled back, but her voice was still soft when she offered, "Would you like to come sleep in my bed? Like when you were little and you used to have nightmares?"

No, no, no, absolutely not, hell no. I restricted my answer to just one "no."

"Okay." She lingered in the doorway. "If you change your mind, or if you need me for anything, I'm right down the hall, okay? And Viv's room is across from yours. Good night, sweetheart."

Their departure was reluctant, but finally, they were gone. The light in the hall shut off, blanketing the room in darkness again.

I watched the fan blades turn above me as my eyes adjusted. Axel didn't say a word, and neither did I. Finally, I swallowed my pride and whispered, "Will you stay with me?"

He was a statue in the night. His red eyes didn't even blink. "Yeah. Go to sleep."

I lay still. "Hey, Ax? Um . . . how are you?"

No answer. Afraid that I'd driven him away, I propped myself up onto my elbows. He was standing in front of the window, red eyes glowing—a silent, perfect, tireless sentry.

Finally feeling safe under Axel's unwavering watch, I closed my eyes. "My name is Cato," I whispered to myself as I curled into a tight ball and let the black waves of sleep pull me down into the depths.

I heard Axel scoff in the darkness. "I know what your name is, moron. Don't worry; I ain't gonna let you forget it."

"Mom. Mom, wake up."

Madison stirred. Hands were shaking her shoulder, snapping the lingering tendrils of sleep. "What's wrong? Is Cato having another nightmare?" She bolted upright. "Did Axel hurt him?"

"No, he's okay. But you need to see this."

Madison rubbed her eyes and swung her legs over the side of the bed. She followed her daughter into the hallway, matching Vivian's stealthy footsteps.

Outside Cato's door, Viv pressed a finger to her lips. Madison peered inside, expecting to see her son sleeping safe and sound in his bed where he belonged. Instead, she found him on the floor. And he wasn't alone.

She counted seven bodies. Cato had one arm around Kit, who was snuggled against his side. RC and Ash were pressed together on his other side. Jay had an arm around each twin. Together, they formed a tangled heap on the floor that looked like a Twister game gone wrong.

Sitting cross-legged on the bed, glowing red eyes watching the humans, was the dark silhouette of a half-demon.

Madison asked quietly, "Aren't they uncomfortable on the floor?"

Her voice was barely a whisper, and yet it caused RC and Ash to stir, Cato to groan, Kit to sit up, and Jay's silver eyes to snap open as the leader lifted his head, disturbing the twins. Jay's gaze settled on Madison and Vivian in the doorway, and he stiffened immediately.

"Hey," came Axel's soft voice from the bed. Jay blinked and twisted to look at Axel, who added quietly, "It's okay."

To Madison's surprise, Jay instantly relaxed. Kit let out a big yawn and snuggled into Cato's side again as Jay settled back, pulling Finn and Reese close. Already, his eyes were closed and his breathing had evened out.

Axel glared at Vivian and Madison in stony silence, his message clear: *get out.* They backed away, and Madison pulled the door shut.

For a moment, she and Vivian stared at each other in the darkness before parting without a word. As Madison crawled back under the covers, she couldn't calm her rampant thoughts. Why, she wondered, was Axel's presence so soothing to Cato and the others? He was a monster, an experiment gone wrong, an animal that almost killed them all less than twenty-four hours ago.

The bitterness festered inside her. She resented Axel for many reasons, but now a new one had surfaced. He, not she, had the power to soothe her son from a nightmare. Why? *Why?* How could the unblinking watch of a carnivore lull Cato to such peace when Madison's very presence made him cower in a corner?

— Chapter Thirty-Eight —

Warning

Vivian shuffled into the kitchen with her shoulders slumped and a downtrodden expression on her face.

When she spotted me leaning against the counter, she immediately perked up. "Oh, you're still here! I was afraid you'd left. Where's everybody else?"

I stepped aside so she could reach the cupboard behind me. "Out," I said. "Finn and Reese are back at the manor, and the others are scouting."

"So early?" she asked as she poured cereal into two bowls.

I watched her add milk to one of the bowls. "Early? We've already spent a few hours training."

Vivian set the gallon of milk on the counter. "Are you hungry?" she asked, holding out the box of cereal. I shook my head. She accepted my reply with a shrug and opened a drawer to fetch two spoons.

I didn't know how I knew our mother was there—I didn't sense her as I'd sense a ghost—but somehow, I felt her gaze on me. Sure enough, when I turned, she was leaning against the doorframe, watching us with a teary smile. "Morning," she said. Her voice was husky, but not with sleep. "It's so good to have both of you here for breakfast."

Vivian added milk to the second bowl now that Madison had arrived. She set both bowls on the table, put the milk back in the fridge, and then sat down with Madison.

"Not going to eat with us, Cay?" my mother asked.

"Not hungry," I insisted.

We coexisted in the silence for several long minutes. "So," Madison said quietly. "Your lab-family spent the night."

I tensed. "Is that a problem?"

"Not at all," she said, her voice remaining calm and patient. "I could have put some extra blankets and pillows out for them if I'd known."

"They didn't plan on coming. That was just . . . the first night since . . ." I sighed. "Never mind."

Vivian spooned the last bite into her mouth and then glanced at her watch. "I have to finish getting ready. Cato? Will . . . you stick around and walk with me to school?"

I inclined my head, and Vivian exhaled as if she'd been holding her breath in anticipation. She set her bowl in the sink and strode out of the kitchen, leaving me alone with Madison.

The silence, broken only by Madison's muffled crunching, resumed. She swallowed and stirred the milky mixture in her bowl. "How is Axel?" she finally asked.

"Do you actually care?"

She gave me a measured stare. "Of course I do."

"I don't know," I admitted. "He didn't say. He was gone when we woke up."

"He looked like he was seriously injured yesterday."

"He's a fast healer. Like Wes."

She ate another spoonful, then asked, "And everyone else?"

I hesitated. "I think we're all still a little on edge."

She nodded. "I know I haven't earned their trust yet. But I do feel like I'm starting to connect with Finn and Reese."

I couldn't stop my right eyebrow from rising into an incredulous expression at her announcement. She chuckled and said, "Don't look at me like that. I mean it."

"Did they talk to you?"

"Well, no. And that's okay. I don't want to push them too hard if they're still not comfortable. But I think they enjoyed baking with me the other day. I let them pick what kind of cookies we made. Also, I know their favorite color is purple."

I frowned and tilted my head, still dubious. "How do you know that if they won't talk to you?"

"I asked them," she said with a smile. "I put swatches on the counter and asked them to point to their favorite color. They picked the prettiest deep purple. I want to buy them some new shirts in that color. Maybe a blanket, something to add a little color to their—well, *your*—room in the manor."

I let my breath slowly escape through my teeth. I didn't want to puncture Madison's elation since she seemed so proud, but . . .

"What?" she asked, sensing my doubt.

"I don't think they have a favorite color. A favorite anything, really."

"They barely hesitated when I asked."

"Did they happen to point to *your* favorite color?"

She stared at me, considering. I nodded, interpreting her silence to mean "yes."

I explained, "Finn and Reese were taught that human desire supersedes all of their opinions. They read your mind and pointed to the answer that would satisfy you the most. They're very . . . what's the word? Pragmatic, I guess? I think the concept of having a favorite color is lost on them. They wouldn't understand why one color would be preferred over another."

"Okay . . . I see what you're saying. But I gave them three options for cookies, and they picked chocolate chip. I wanted the choice to be theirs."

"They've never eaten cookies, so they wouldn't have known the difference between the options. Which of the three was your favorite?"

Madison sighed, her shoulders slouching. "Chocolate chip," she muttered, shaking her head. "Shoot. I thought we were actually connecting, but they just picked the one I would have picked."

"They don't have free will when humans are around," I told her gently. "I know you're trying. It's not your fault. If you give them a direct order, they'll obey. If you ask them to make a decision, they'll gauge your preference and respond in the way that's going to make you the happiest. That's just how they were trained."

"Do they do that with you, too?"

"Huh," I muttered in surprise as I pondered. "I hadn't thought about it. Yeah, they probably do. But your preferences outrank mine in the hierarchy since you're a pureblood human and I'm only half."

She shook her head. "I can't believe how much damage Agent Kovak did to them. I don't know how to undo it."

"I'm not sure it can be undone," I said solemnly. "If it's possible, it'll be a slow process." I folded my arms and tilted my head back to stare at the ceiling. "Finn and Reese didn't want to come with us. After the accident, I mean. Jay and I had to pull them out of their cages and force them to leave. They tried to run away from us more than once."

"How did you convince them to stay with you?"

"We didn't. Not really. I think once we got some distance from the humans hunting us, Finn and Reese were too scared to run off and be completely alone and lost in the Outside. It was a big, terrifying new world, and everything was alien to them. Everything except us."

Madison leaned back in her chair, her breakfast abandoned. "I guess Agent Kovak wasn't totally off base when he said the twins would have Stockholm syndrome."

"What's that?" I asked.

"A captive bonding with their captors to survive. But I suppose that goes both ways—they also bonded with the Agents in a twisted way despite the abuse. Finn and Reese are a psychological puzzle I don't know how to solve."

"Ero might be able to."

As if sensing the unbidden longing that manifested in my tone, Madison said, "I'm sure he'll be back any day now."

An uncomfortable silence settled over the kitchen. I blurted, "I don't want to spend the night here again."

My outburst was met with more silence. I watched my mother, waiting for her reaction, but she just stared blankly at the tabletop. Slowly, she nodded. "Okay." She swallowed and lifted her head. "Thank you for at least trying. I appreciate you spending a night with us before making your decision."

Vivian's footsteps descended the staircase and crossed the living room before she appeared in the doorway. "I'm ready, Cay. Are you?"

"Sure." I pulled away from the counter, grateful to escape.

Madison said, "Weapon belt?"

Vivian rolled her eyes and gave me an annoyed look. "I have e-zaps in my pocket and an ectogun in my backpack."

"It takes a lot more time to get your gun out of your backpack in an emergency than it would if you had it holstered in your belt and easily accessible."

"See you after school," Vivian dismissed as she opened the door.

Madison made sure her exasperated sigh was audible from the kitchen. "Have a great day," she said wearily.

"Thanks, love you," Viv called over her shoulder.

"Love you, too. Both of you," she made a point to add.

"You too," I muttered with a nod, although I grimaced with my back to her. Why did I still have such a hard time properly returning the sentiment?

I closed the door behind me and trotted down the porch steps after Vivian. "Why are you so resistant to being fully armed?" I asked as I caught up to her.

"C'mon, Cay, not you too."

"I just think Madison has a good point is all. You've already been targeted twice."

"Three times if you count when you kidnapped me to blackmail Mom."

I smirked. "You're only making my case stronger."

"Cato," Vivian said, tipping her head back to stare at the clouds as we walked, "it's not like I walk around defenseless. But when I'm in full gear, people don't really see me as *me*—they just see the ghost hunter's daughter. And I'm really tired of that stigma."

"Hey! Wait up!" called a voice from behind.

Vivian and I both turned to see Trey sprinting from a block away, waving one hand in the air. We paused and waited for him to catch up and then double over with his hands on his knees, gasping for breath even though he was grinning. "Hey, Cato," he said between pants. "Didn't . . . expect . . . to see you."

I gestured at him. "Trey doesn't seem to have a problem displaying his weapons in public."

She folded her arms. "Trey chose to be an apprentice. I didn't."

"Uh-oh," he said as he straightened. "This argument again?"

"Nope, because we're not talking about it anymore," she said, turning on her heel and marching down the sidewalk. We exchanged glances and followed in her wake.

"She's stubborn," Trey muttered with a wink.

"It runs in the family," she snapped without looking at us.

"Oh, I'm very well aware of that," he teased. "So, Cato, are you actually going to school today? Will you be in class? We're mostly still reviewing old material, so it's not like you missed too much—"

"No," I interrupted. "I'm just walking you to school."

"Mom thought it would be good for him to go through his old routine," Vivian said.

"Yeah?" he replied. "Did it help?"

Before I could answer, Vivian said, "Considering he didn't actually go through his usual morning routine, I'm guessing no."

"Why?" I snapped. "Because I woke up early to train?"

"*Yes*, Cato," she said in exasperation. "You completely missed the point. Mom wanted you to feel a sense of normalcy in your old routine."

"That *was* normal for me, Viv. I train with my lab-family every morning. Are you upset about that?"

She shifted her backpack higher up on her shoulders and continued to stare straight ahead. "Old normal, Cato. Just one morning. I think Mom was onto something—I think it would have been beneficial for you to seriously give it a try."

Irritation was starting to heat my core and cause my power to stir. Trey glanced at me and then averted his gaze. My eyes were probably glowing green.

"Old normal can't account for a lot of changes, Viv," I said. "I'm sorry I can't be who you remember and easily step back into that routine. I can't change the fact that I'm still being hunted and I have another family that needs me just as much as you do, if not more."

She cast me a sorrowful look. "Cay, I—"

"I'm sorry I don't feel comfortable wearing human clothes anymore. And that I can't sleep without my lab-family because their presence was the only tiny bit of solace I had in the pitch black when I was locked in a cage, so now I can't stand the loneliness if I can't hear the sound of them breathing. And I'm sorry that the nightmares are so bad, and that training so early helps me forget them. If that new routine doesn't work for you, I'm sorry. But I can't change it."

Tears flooded her eyes. "I'm the one who's sorry." She turned to me and opened her arms for an embrace, but I held my arm up and stiffly pushed past her.

"Hugs make *you* feel better," I snapped. "I tolerate them for you, and I can't do that right now."

Her arms fell. She stood in the middle of the sidewalk, tears rolling down her face.

I kept walking.

Trey followed, hesitated to look back at Vivian, then took a few more steps and paused. "Okay, wait," he called. "C'mon, Cato, please? You guys shouldn't be fighting. Please stop."

I halted and partially turned to glare at them with my arms folded. The anger was still boiling, so I had no doubt my eyes were still blazing green.

Vivian wiped her eyes. "You don't have to walk me the rest of the way to school," she said hoarsely. "You can go scout with Ash. I know you'd rather be with her, anyway." Her expression crumpled. "She knows you better than I do." She buried her face in her hands and started sobbing.

Trey returned to her side and draped one arm over her shoulders, and she leaned into his embrace.

I felt my frown relax as the anger cooled. I shifted, glancing around in guilt. A few people across the street were watching. They didn't even pretend to turn away when I looked at them.

"I'm sorry, Viv," I said. "You know I hate seeing you cry. Especially when I'm the cause."

She sniffled and pulled away from Trey. "It's my fault," she croaked, wiping her bloodshot eyes again. She lifted her teary gaze to look at me. "I keep trying to turn you back into the little brother I remember from before. And that's not fair. It's not—I know that. I'm not the same person I used to be, either. Mourning your death, watching this town fall apart, surviving in City Hall, scavenging for food and supplies with the raid team . . . I'm sure I'm not the same as you remember."

Her face suddenly spasmed with grief, and I knew why—she'd just reminded herself that I *didn't* remember. Not really. I knew who she was, and I'd retained essences of experiences, but I couldn't try to constrain her in the same parameters like she wanted to do to me because I didn't have a clear picture of Vivian Before versus Vivian now. To me, this was just who she was. There wasn't an ideal version of her that I wanted her to convert back into.

Seeming to realize this, she squeezed her eyes shut and hung her head. Trey didn't move, giving her the option to embrace him again if she wanted. I shifted awkwardly. "You can have a hug if you want," I muttered.

She sniffed again and shook her head. "I don't want to make you uncomfortable."

A little late for that, I couldn't help but think bitterly. I took a few steps toward my blood-sister, and Trey backed up to give us space.

I cleared my throat. "You know . . . the first time Ash and I were together in the Arena, she clobbered me in the head with her staff. Knocked me out cold."

Vivian's body jerked with a sound that was somewhere between a sob and a humorless chuckle. "What?"

I nodded. "We were supposed to fight each other. But I refused."

"And she didn't?"

I shook my head with sadness. "I didn't blame her. When you're hungry and thirsty enough, you get desperate. There were times when I hurt her, too. But . . . I guess I'm trying to say that I never saw Ash as a replacement for you. I just want to make sure you know that."

Vivian nodded slowly. "Do you ever hug Ash?" she asked weakly. She twitched her lips with a faint, apologetic grin and added, "I realize that's a shallow thing to—"

"No," I replied. "I've never hugged Ash. I think the only one I've ever hugged is Kit. The rest of us, um . . ." I shrugged. "I don't know. I mean, you can't really hug someone when you're separated by bars, and the only time we were all together was in the Arena when we had to fight, so . . . our relationship was always a bit distanced, I guess."

She wiped her wet eyelashes on her sleeve. "I really am sorry, Cato," she mumbled. "I promise I'll try to be better about respecting that things are different and they're not going to return to normal."

Trey awkwardly rocked back and forth in place, swinging his arms and making a point to stare up at the nearest tree instead of watching us. "So . . . looks like good weather today," he said.

Vivian laughed. "That's how you choose to break the tension?"

"Did it work?" he asked, shooting us a look from the corner of his eye and grinning.

Viv and I glanced at each other, then turned to Trey and said, "No," in unison. We started walking.

"Okay, fine, so that's how it's going to be," Trey teased as he followed. "The Tarrows ganging up on me again. Jeez, some things never change."

The ghost of a smile tugged at the corners of my mouth. The Tarrows. It felt strange to be included in that category again.

I asked, "How's your hand?"

"Check it out!" he said with a broad smile. "I think I'm going to have my first battle scar!"

Surprised by his joyful attitude, I glanced at the row of dark sutures and felt a chill wash over me when I thought about the needle stitching his torn flesh back together. "Does it count as a battle scar if you got hurt picking up RC's disk and not actually fighting?"

"Hey, don't take this away from me. If anyone asks, I'm telling them it's a battle wound."

LeahRae Harris High School was up ahead. "Oh look, there's a cat," Vivian said. "Hey, Cato, when Kit is in her feline form, is she able to talk to—?"

"Something's wrong," I announced, seizing Vivian's backpack to stop her.

"What?"

Trey drew an ectogun. "Did you sense a ghost?"

I shook my head, staring at the tabby cat sitting in the middle of the sidewalk half a block ahead. "Not yet," I muttered. "But that's a warning."

Vivian swung her backpack off one shoulder to unzip it and draw her ectogun. "Are you sure?"

I nodded. "I'm going on ahead. If Kit's at the school already, she might have some information. You two can stay behind if you want."

"I'm going," Trey asserted. "I've got your back, Cay."

"Me too," said Vivian.

I crept toward the cat, ears strained for the slightest noise out of the ordinary. Trey whispered, "Do you think the school's under attack?"

I surveyed the scene in front of us and shook my head. "I don't hear any screaming," I murmured. "And Kit hasn't sent a distress call, which means she hasn't spotted or sensed a ghost at the school."

"But neither have you," Vivian whispered. "How do you know there is one?"

"I don't know for sure that it's a ghost," I muttered. "Just that there's danger. It could be anything." Contrary to my warning, everything seemed perfectly ordinary. Birds were chirping in the trees that lined the street. I could hear students talking and laughing up ahead in the schoolyard. If it weren't for the cat sitting resolutely on the sidewalk, watching us approach, I'd have no reason to be suspicious.

I could sense that Trey and Vivian were doubting me as we drew nearer to the school. I halted in front of the tabby, who gazed up at me with big green eyes. An ominous shiver traveled up my spine. I gasped and spun around, eyes darting, searching for the ghost as icicles formed in my hands.

"Was it the fleabag that gave me away?" asked the deep voice of a man.

I whirled to locate the speaker just as he materialized in the shadowy alcove of a boarded-up shop. Vivian and Trey aimed their ecto-guns at him, but he seemed perfectly relaxed with his arms folded as he leaned casually against the brick doorway. The cat trotted away.

His glowing green eyes shifted as his gaze followed the tabby's retreat. "Shoulda killed the damn stray," he muttered with a subtle and disappointed shake of the head. "I forgot about your pet Amínyte's spies."

"Captain Hassing," I stiffly acknowledged. "Haven't seen you since Axel made Titon bolt. Sorry we missed you in the battle."

Hassing smirked at me. "I received a full report. And what an interesting report it was."

"Where's your army?"

"Mmm, just me today. Sorry to disappoint you."

"And what do you want?"

He yawned and inspected his glove, as if bored. "If I'm being honest, I wanted to incapacitate you with a sneak attack before you sensed me, then bring you to Azar as a gift. But now, since I'm presuming you won't come quietly, things are about to get more fun. Do you want your human bodyguards to be collateral damage, or are you going to have them give us some room?"

— Chapter Thirty-Nine —

Weakness

I ground my teeth, assessing our soon-to-be battleground.

Adrenaline had my heart humming, but I was clearheaded. We were close to the school—so close that any altercation was guaranteed to attract onlookers who might be injured, killed, or used as hostages.

Barely moving my lips, I muttered, "I've got this. Go to the school."

"But Cato—" Trey started to protest.

"Viv, find Kit," I interrupted. "She might be in danger. Trey, you gotta make sure people stay out of the way. I don't want anyone to get hurt."

Vivian lowered her weapon and took a couple of hesitant steps toward the school, then paused. Trey hadn't budged. His ectogun was still trained on Captain Hassing.

"I can fight," he insisted. "I can. I'm not a sidekick or messenger who runs away."

Hassing chuckled. "If he's ready to die at such a young age, that's fine by me. You can't hold that against me; I gave him a fair chance to live."

I melted one of my icicles and seized Trey's shoulder. "Listen to me—Hassing is an Ectokinetic, which means your ectogun is useless here. He needs me alive, but you're expendable. I need you to get out of the way. If I'm in trouble, I'll need you to call for help."

Trey's hands were shaking. He blinked rapidly, glaring at Hassing, then let his breath out in a sharp exhale and turned away. "Go," I said. He and Vivian took off toward the high school.

"Good choice," Hassing said as he peeled away from the doorframe and stepped onto the sidewalk. He lifted his hand and tugged on his glove, flexing and bending his fingers to secure the fit. "So, the infamous Phantom, in the flesh. You were one of the more interesting details of the report, considering you were supposed to be dead."

"So I've heard," I said, re-forming my second ice blade.

Hassing flicked his hand, sending a charge of ectoplasm in my direction. I leapt sideways to avoid it, but it curved to follow my movement. *Shit, I forgot he could do that.* I was already airborne and couldn't alter my course; the ectoplasm struck me in the shoulder and spun me around as my foot landed on the curb. I fell, sprawling into the street. Intense waves of needle-sharp pain cutting through my rib cage reminded me that I still wasn't healed from my encounter with the Talon Gang.

"Not off to a great start," Hassing taunted as he advanced, flicking small bursts of ectoplasm at me. I scrambled backward, barely dodging the attacks and unable to get to my feet under the onslaught. "You're an abomination, you know that? The very idea of a lowly human, the spawn of a ghost hunter, no less, being graced with divine kálos power. If it were up to me, you'd be executed. Put down like the unholy mutt you are."

I ducked a shot aimed for my head, then threw my hand out, sending a dozen ice needles back at Hassing. He became intangible to avoid them, buying me the precious second I needed to regain my footing.

He snapped his fist downward, conjuring a glowing green ectoplasm whip that cracked down on the asphalt, forcing me to leap backward out of the way. My injury was definitely slowing me down.

Hassing stepped off the curb, continuing his advance. I took brief stock of my surroundings and realized that despite my best efforts to hold my ground, he was driving me toward the school, where the casualties would be high.

The whip was coming down on me again; I poured more power into my left hand, transforming the ice blade into a shield and raising it to meet the blow. Hassing drew his ectoplasm back and lashed out again—again—again, his movements fluid and his stride never breaking. I had to back up every time I braced myself for the impact.

I chanced a brief glance at the schoolyard, where a crowd of enthusiastic students had gathered to watch. Several adults armed with ecto-guns—teachers, I assumed—stood guard in front of the fence, their weapons trained on Hassing and me battling in the street, ready to protect their young wards if Hassing's attention shifted from me to the onlookers. Trey, his mission fulfilled, was creeping away from the group to take a more strategic position down the street where he could hit Hassing from behind if an opportunity arose. I couldn't see Vivian or Kit.

"Come on, Phantom! I deserve your full attention," Hassing called.

I turned back toward him, but too late—it wasn't the whip coming down on me this time, but a bright orb of potent ectoplasm instead. I had a single second to align my shield in front of my chest before the blast struck me dead-on.

The impact sent me flying. I landed on my back and slid, my head thwacking the asphalt. Sharp pain zinged through my torso and stole my breath. Faintly, through the ringing buzz in my ears, I could hear shouts from the spectators. I forced a few short, painful gasps and rolled over, my head spinning.

"Uh-oh, you're disappointing your fans," Hassing teased. As I labored up onto my knees, he swung his whip, which struck me in the neck and wrapped around. I clutched at it, but Hassing jerked it tight, choking me. We made eye contact. He smiled coldly, his irises glowing. My eyes widened as he released excess power, which coursed along the whip and sent a current of energy through my body. I cried out, my muscles spasming with pain.

"Has-sing," I begged. Was this what he wanted? An audience? He'd toyed with me, backing me up while a crowd gathered, and for what? So they could watch their hero fail?

I detected movement coming up fast behind Hassing. Through the green haze of ectoplasm, I focused on the form of Trey charging the Captain of the Guard from behind. Rather than strike with force, he smacked Hassing in the neck and darted away before the captain could retaliate.

The e-zap's effects were immediate; it drew out Hassing's own ectoplasm from his body and reduced it to a painful Grade G. Wild tendrils of uncontained energy snapped around his head and upper torso, highly concentrated at the connection point on his neck. Hassing bellowed in pain and tried to pry the e-zap off, unconsciously ceasing the extra voltage traveling through his whip.

I clutched at the ectoplasm, but it was firmly wrapped around my neck. New tactic—I seized the whip and yanked it out of Hassing's hand while he was distracted. The ectoplasm dissipated when it left his grasp, finally freeing me.

Hassing screamed like a barbarian and ripped the e-zap off. He shouldn't have been able to remove it yet; the current of ectoplasm was supposed to bind the e-zap to him until the gadget burned out. Bright green light leaked through his fist as he overloaded the tiny device with more ectoplasm than it could handle.

"How *dare* you," Hassing seethed, throwing the blackened e-zap onto the pavement, where it lay smoking. His gaze locked onto Trey. "I command ectoplasm! How *dare you* try to turn my own power against me, you filthy human!"

I conjured ectoplasm in my right hand and fired at Hassing before he could harm Trey. The captain turned his head. He saw it coming, but he didn't try to dodge the glowing green ball of energy. Instead . . . he smirked.

I gasped, realizing too late that I'd just made a thoughtless error. My ectoplasm orbited Hassing and then rocketed back toward me.

Bloody Scout.

That was all I had time to think before my own attack struck me in the gut and sent me flying. The air was forced from my lungs when I crashed hard onto my back, the pain resounding throughout my entire body as if I'd just been socked with a baseball. I tried to suck a breath into my shriveled lungs.

"Grade B, Level 4," Hassing murmured. "Impressive for someone your age, especially considering the tainted blood in your veins. But apparently you weren't listening. What did I just say?"

"Cato?" Vivian called from somewhere in the crowd. "Are you all right?"

I coughed once and dragged in a few frail breaths. I hadn't realized how powerful I'd become. *Note to self: remember not to use ectoplasm against an Ectokinetic. Duh.*

Trey said, "Cato? I can't shoot him. What do I do?" I was still too stunned and breathless to answer. "Ah, C-Cato, now would be a good time to get up."

I groaned as I rolled over. Hassing was bearing down on Trey, who backed away from him. I hauled myself up onto my hands and knees. "Hey! This is between you and me, Hassing!"

I flung out my hand, freezing water molecules in the air and propelling them forward. Hassing leaned back, his gaze settling on the icicle that embedded into a tree trunk mere inches in front of his nose. I stood up, fists clenched at my sides.

Captain Hassing turned to face me with a smile. "Very well." I slid my right foot back, shifting into a fighting position. Hassing held out his hand, palm toward me, and I braced myself for an offensive strike. But instead of a targeted attack, loose tendrils of ectoplasm started to materialize all around me.

"What . . . ?" I backed up a step. The ectoplasm grew denser and started swirling, trapping me in a vortex of green energy. I reached out, only to snap my hand back with a yelp at the painful shock that followed when the ectoplasm touched my fingers.

"Oops, careful now," Hassing said with a chuckle. "I think you'll find my ectoplasm packs a bit more of a punch than yours." I gritted my teeth at him in a silent snarl. His fingers curled inward, and I gasped when I realized the vortex was shrinking. I stood up straighter and crossed my arms over my chest, sucking in my breath to make my body as small as possible. The ectoplasm gave off heat that prickled my skin.

Hassing taunted, "This is going to hurt."

The hot green power flared in my core. "*ENOUGH!*" I screamed.

The glass in every door and window shattered. Students shrieked, hitting the ground and cowering while teachers fell back against the chain-link fence. Hassing's ectoplasm vortex dispersed under the force of the shock wave.

With a battle cry, I launched myself at the captain, an ice dagger clenched in each hand. I'd hoped to catch Hassing by surprise with the blitz attack after the blast, but he smiled as if he'd anticipated that strategy. Four glowing green tentacles erupted from his back. I tried to stop short—too late. One of the ectoplasm appendages encircled my wrist and yanked me off course.

Damn it! I threw the other icicle, guiding it forward with my Divinity. Hassing calmly became intangible and let the projectile pass right through his chest.

Damn it, damn it, damn it . . . This is bad! Hassing was pulling me toward him. I clutched at the warm tentacle gripping my wrist. Like his whip, this was Grade A, so condensed that it was basically a solid, and yet it still acted like energy in some ways. There was no end to the tentacle; it had merged with itself, forming a continuous loop around my wrist, too tight to pry off.

My soles slid across the asphalt as Hassing drew me closer. "Was that your final trick, Phantom?" he asked. A second tentacle lashed out and seized my other wrist. My arms were yanked apart, and I was hoisted off the ground. The ectoplasm crept inward, coiling around my arms like a pair of pythons for a more secure hold.

I kicked and squirmed, but I was held firmly in place with my arms bound almost perpendicular to my body, which meant I couldn't fire a distress call up into the sky. The tentacles continued to wind their way up my arms until they encircled my neck and tightened.

Hassing clasped his hands behind his back and strolled toward me, the other two tentacles sweeping back and forth around him to prevent Trey or anyone else from getting close again with another e-zap. "I have to say, I'm rather disappointed by your performance. Apparently, the real Phantom doesn't live up to the legend."

"Trey," I choked out.

Hassing taunted, "What was that? Did you have final words you wanted to say before you pass out?"

"Shoot up," I croaked, hoping he could hear me and understand what I wanted.

"What?" he asked in confusion.

"Up," I wheezed. "Straight up. Call for help."

Trey hesitantly pointed his ectogun toward the sky.

Yes, I thought, but darkness was disintegrating the edges of my vision, and I couldn't speak. He pulled the trigger. I heard the charging whine followed by the telltale *shoom* of ectoplasm being fired from a gun.

A moment later, Jay appeared in my fading peripheral. The tentacles retreated from my neck and dropped me to my knees. My wrists were still bound, arms held away from my body, but at least I could breathe, and I was on solid ground again.

Captain Hassing was smiling. "About time you showed up. I was starting to worry that Phantom was going to let me capture him before he had a chance to call you."

My eyes were watering; I gazed helplessly at Jay through a film of tears. Hassing *wanted* me to send the distress signal? Had I just led Jay into a trap?

"Jay—" I rasped.

"Ah-ah, hold that thought," Hassing said. "It's not your turn." The two tentacles snapped together with my wrists, merging into one solid binding. With a wave of the captain's hand, the other end of the tentacle detached and flung itself away from Hassing to loop around a tree.

It all happened so fast I was still trying to process my new predicament. I lifted my bound hands and stared at the flow of ectoplasm tethering me to the trunk a few yards away.

Jay Blinked and appeared next to Hassing, already in motion to strike. He landed a solid punch in the captain's abdomen and Blinked away before the lashing tentacle could catch him. He was quick, there and gone again, striking and retreating, no more than an afterimage. Jay was a master at this strategy. It was the reason we couldn't beat him at All-On-One, and I felt confident that Hassing wouldn't be able to counter Jay's attacks, either.

Now that my wits had returned, I pulled on my bonds. I had to get loose in case Jay needed help. The ectoplasm tether was taut, but it wouldn't break, and there were no weak spots or ends to untie. I wriggled and pulled and cursed. "You have *got* to be kidding me," I muttered. Being tied to a tree to await collection was beyond humiliating.

Trey fell to his knees next to me with a pocketknife in his hand. "Hold on, Cay."

I continued to squirm like a fish at the end of a line. "It's energy," I said through clenched teeth as I struggled. "I don't think you can cut it."

"But you can't phase through it."

"I *know*."

"Can you slip your hands free?"

"Too tight." My fingers were already tingling from the lack of circulation.

"What do I do?"

"I don't know."

The pocketknife fell with a clatter. His hands were shaking too badly to hold it; he was panicking. "Tell me what to do!"

"I'll figure something out. Leave me. Go protect the students."

Trey stared at me with wide, uncomprehending eyes. "What?"

"Hassing might make a desperate move if he realizes he could lose the fight. Make sure he can't take a hostage again."

He bobbed his head. "Okay. Okay, I got this." He scrambled to his feet and dashed away.

I paused in my struggles and craned my neck to see how my lab-brother was faring. Hassing looked winded and frustrated, but Jay hadn't been able to get a critical strike in yet.

My lab-brother Blinked into range for another hit, but a crackling web of ectoplasm around Hassing's body forced him to teleport away in retreat before he could land the blow. The second he reappeared outside the captain's immediate range, Hassing flicked a tiny burst of ectoplasm in Jay's direction.

It exploded halfway between them in a flash of blinding green light, seemingly falling short of its target. But something seemed off. Hassing was in complete control of his ectoplasm; he wouldn't have detonated early by accident. And the blast didn't seem to have caused much damage. It was just bright.

Hassing grinned. One of the tentacles lashed out toward his victim.

Something's wrong with Jay, I realized in horror. He wasn't moving out of the way. He seemed to be in a total daze, eyes unfocused, his battle stance relaxed. He wasn't responsive.

"Jay!" I shouted, hoping to break him out of the trance.

No good—the tentacle wrapped around his neck and yanked him toward Hassing, who caught Jay's shirt in both fists so they were face-to-face as Jay clutched at the ectoplasm choking him. "Not so fast now, are you?" Hassing seethed, Grade G ectoplasm crackling around his hands.

"No!" I cried, thrashing wildly again in a desperate attempt to break free and aid my lab-brother. Raw energy attacked Jay's body. He squeezed his eyes shut in pain, fighting to contain a scream behind his bared teeth. His back arched as his whole body seized up.

A sudden idea struck me. I couldn't break this ectoplasm, and like the neutralizer, it seemed to tighten with my struggles so there was no way to slip free. But what if I could stretch it wider?

I reached for my center and called upon the cold Divinity that turned my eyes blue. A ring of ice formed around my wrists inside of the restraints. Although the heat from the ectoplasm hindered my progress, I poured more power into the ice formation, thickening the ring and pushing the ectoplasm outward with it.

Once the layer of ice was thick enough, I became intangible and phased through it, slipping my hands free. Hassing's ectoplasmic tether was still intact, but it was now holding a ring of ice to the tree instead of me.

I leapt to my feet just as Hassing cut off the electrifying Grade G ectoplasm that was swarming Jay. My lab-brother was barely conscious. With a twitch of Hassing's hand, the tentacle holding Jay shot upward, carrying him with it and then driving him straight into the ground where he lay helplessly on his back, gasping, his fingers still hooked around the solid ectoplasm cutting off his air supply.

I sprinted back toward the battle, forging bands of ice around my wrist gauntlets as a precaution. If Hassing snagged me again, I'd have a way to phase through—at least the first time. He'd probably adapt, and then I'd have to as well.

Hassing loomed over Jay. "Looks like Cisco was right about your weakness," he gloated, then glanced in my direction. "And Phantom, it seems congratulations are in order. Apparently, I did underestimate you after all."

A dozen new ectoplasm tentacles sprang from the center of Hassing's back. He was now standing in a swirling mass of writhing appendages. Dread made me falter.

I delved deeper into my own power and forged a shield of ice in each hand, then found my stride again and continued the charge. Jay needed me. Hassing must have used up a lot of power making so many ectoplasm tentacles, which meant he might not have enough reserves to rely on intangibility. If I could get close enough, maybe I could take him down.

I leapt over the first strike, which was a low sweep targeting my ankles to trip me. The second was coming from the right—I lifted the shield and braced for the blow while moving my left shield in front of my chest to protect against the oncoming direct strike.

The attacks were coming too fast. I managed to block some, but the blows rained down on me from every direction. Within seconds, I was crouched on the ground, cowering behind my shields, trying to form a protective dome of ice so I could buy a little time and reevaluate my strategy.

A tentacle slithered through and encircled my boot. As soon as I realized it had me, I tried to form ice around my ankle, but I was too late—the ectoplasm yanked my foot out from under me and hauled me out of my incomplete shelter, dragging me across the ground.

Above, I caught a brief glimpse of a silver flash in the sky. I almost laughed in relief despite the peril I was in. A moment later, a bladed disk embedded itself in Hassing's arm.

He let out a howl cut short when he was thrown backward with telekinesis. Unfortunately, the tentacles didn't let go; Jay and I were pulled along with him. I gritted my teeth and continued to focus my power on my boot as the rough asphalt scraped my skin raw. RC must have realized we were at risk because he redirected his power downward to smash Hassing against the pavement instead.

My ankle was entirely encased in ice. I phased through, freeing myself from the ectoplasm, and then I crawled toward Jay.

RC was hovering above us on a trash can lid. He spun one of the disks around his finger and called down, "The only reason I aimed for your arm instead of your neck is because Azar probably won't be happy if we kill his Captain of the Guard. But the next one might land in a more critical spot."

Hassing cursed at him and stretched his tentacles into the sky, trying to pluck RC out of the air even though he was still pinned on his back with telekinesis. RC rose higher, easily maneuvering out of reach and forcing Hassing to merge some of the ectoplasmic appendages so they could stretch farther.

"Hang on, Jay," I whispered when I reached him. "I'll get you free. But you're going to be cold." His eyes were halfway open. I wasn't sure he'd heard or understood me.

I directed my cryokinesis at his neck, forming a solid ring of ice just as I'd done with my wrists and ankle. Once it was wide enough, I seized the ice in both hands and started to slide the band over Jay's head to free him from the ectoplasm.

I realized he was being pulled away from me. As soon as he was free, I dropped the ice collar and whirled, ready to ward off another tentacle, but instead, I found Ash holding onto Jay's ankles. She'd been pulling him to help get him loose. "Is he okay?" she asked.

"I think he's just dazed," I said.

"Are there other ghosts?"

"Just Hassing. Get Jay out of range."

She nodded and hooked her arms under Jay's armpits, then dragged him away from the fight. I turned back toward Hassing and discovered that he was on his feet again. He must have driven RC far enough away to escape his telekinetic range.

Captain Hassing looked much less confident now than he had a few minutes ago. He backed away, eyeing the battlefield, his gaze darting between Ash and me, then up at RC hovering above us. His ectoplasm tentacles had all dissipated, and I suspected that he'd depleted too much power. The tide had turned out of his favor.

With a quiet curse, Hassing held up his hands with his palms facing each other, fingers curled to cage a small, bright point of green light forming between his hands. I created an ice shield and ducked behind it, then braced for the blast as RC dove toward the ground, landed next to Ash and Jay, and held up the trash lid as a shield.

A blinding green light washed over the scene, but rather than the sound of an explosion, I heard a sizzling crackle that sounded like a firework. The shock wave never came.

I raised my head, blinking in confusion and panic when I realized that I couldn't see. Bright spots in my eyes minimized my vision, which was likely the purpose of the blast. Hassing wasn't trying to detonate an ectoplasm explosion; he wanted to blind us so he could make his getaway.

"Damn it," I said, rising and rubbing my eyes. "Where did he go?"

"I don't know," RC called. "I can't see."

I could hear confused and panicked murmurs from the direction of LeahRae Harris High—apparently, we weren't the only ones blinded. I kept blinking, my vision recovering at a painfully sluggish rate. Shapes and shadows were starting to take form.

I stumbled toward where I thought my lab-siblings were. As I drew closer, I was able to make out their familiar forms, and I knelt beside them. "Anyone hurt?" I asked.

"Just Jay," Ash replied. "What about you?"

"I'm fine. I think." My eyes were finally starting to refocus. Sure enough, when I scanned the street, Hassing was gone.

RC rose. "I'll meet up with Axel. He'll be able to track Hassing down."

"Is that a good idea?" I asked.

"Track, not engage," RC said, as if reading my mind. After Axel's episode yesterday, we'd decided that it was best for him to avoid any fights unless absolutely necessary.

RC added, "I'll feel better when I'm sure Hassing is back in the Ghost Realm." He tossed the lid up and held out his hand to make it hover in the air, then jumped aboard.

Ash said, "We'll take care of Jay."

"Send a signal if you run into trouble," I said before RC took off. He inclined his head in acknowledgment and levitated straight up, then disappeared over a building.

— Chapter Forty —
Playing with Fire

I flopped onto my back with a long groan.

Everything hurt. My ribs. My muscles. Especially the headache throbbing behind my skull with every heartbeat. I knew I should get up. I should be with RC, tracking down Hassing. But my body didn't want to move.

"Cato!"

I turned my head. Trey was sprinting headlong toward us. Ash drew her staff and leapt to her feet, then stepped protectively in front of Jay and me.

Trey stopped short outside of her swinging radius. "Cato," he said breathlessly, "are you okay? Are you hurt? How's Jay?"

"Fine, more or less," Jay murmured, watching with his eyes half-open and his mouth curled into a faint, crooked grin. "Thanks for asking."

I rubbed my eyes, still seeing residual spots in my vision. "I'm sorry, Jay. Hassing baited me into calling for help so he could get to you. Something didn't feel right about the way he was toying with me, but I didn't figure it out until it was too late. I played right into his plan."

"You have nothing to apologize for," Jay assured.

Trey was still holding his ectogun in one hand. He dragged his other hand through his hair, laughed in disbelief, then held up his hand and stared at it. "Oh man . . . I'm still shaking. That was seriously intense!"

I labored to sit up. "You did a good job."

"Yeah?" he said, his face splitting with a wide grin.

I nodded. "That was quick thinking with the e-zap."

"Cato," Jay said wearily, "you're bleeding."

"I am?" I touched the back of my head and discovered that my hair was matted and sticky, and there was a smear on the sidewalk where my head had been resting. "Oh," I said dazedly, staring at my red fingers. "That's not good."

"The school nurse can check you out," said Trey.

"No, I'm fine." I set my hand on the back of my head and froze the blood to stop the bleeding.

A streak of black-and-white fur was barreling toward us. When the kitten reached me, it expanded into black smoke. A pair of arms wrapped around my middle as a small body struck me. I grunted on impact and said, "Easy, Kit. I'm sore."

She nuzzled in tighter until I put my arms around her. Vivian, who was jogging toward us, slowed to a walk as she neared Trey.

"That was scary," Kit said into my chest, her voice muffled. She pulled back to look me in the eye. "But I tried to be brave, like you. I protected Vivian."

"You did? Thank you." She cuddled into me again. I glanced at Viv, who winked.

Two women, each holding an ectogun, had detached from the chaos in the schoolyard and were approaching. Ash braced herself in a battle stance again, ready to defend us. Kit resumed her fur and leapt up onto my shoulder. She pinned her ears and hissed at the intruders.

"Whoa, hold on," Vivian intervened, holding up her hands. "It's okay. That's Principal Solwitz and Ms. Tighe. They're not enemies."

They came to a halt, although the tall, thin lady stayed a step behind the shorter woman with long white-gray hair braided over one shoulder. Somehow, whether it was from an out-of-reach memory or just intuition, I felt confident that the woman in the back was my former algebra teacher, Ms. Tighe, which meant the one in front must be Principal Solwitz.

"What's the damage?" the principal asked, all business. "Any serious injuries?"

"Cato's bleeding," Trey blurted.

I shot him a severe look. "I'm fine," I muttered.

Jay managed to pull himself up into a sitting position. "We just need a little time to recuperate," he said.

Principal Solwitz asked, "Do you believe all threats have been neutralized? Is it safe for the students to be in school?"

Jay bobbed his head wearily. "I think so, yes."

Ms. Tighe leaned forward and spoke into the principal's ear. Principal Solwitz nodded, muttered something back, and then waved the teacher away to relay instructions to the other faculty. She turned back to us and asked, "Can you make it to the school? We can get you water, ice, first aid, let you rest. Nurse Renn can give you medical attention and arrange for transport to the hospital if needed."

"No," I said at the same time Vivian said, "Yes, please." She held up her hand in my direction, silently telling me to be quiet, then added, "Yes to the water, ice, and first-aid kit. We'll ask for Nurse Renn if we need her." Quieter, she said, "I don't think they'll let her examine them."

The principal nodded. "Come with me and get whatever supplies you think are necessary."

Vivian glanced at us. "I'll meet you in the schoolyard, okay?" She followed the principal back to the school.

Kit leapt off my shoulder and sat down on the sidewalk. Ash waited until she was satisfied that the principal was far enough away before she turned back to face us. She wordlessly offered me her hand, and I accepted.

I couldn't help but groan as Ash pulled me onto my feet. My muscles were stiff and sore after being electrocuted with Grade G ectoplasm, and my head was still throbbing.

"Can you walk?" Ash asked, peering down at Jay still sitting on the ground. Kit stood, arched her back in a dramatic stretch, and then padded over to Jay and rubbed her furry little body lovingly against his knee.

He ran his hand down her back and admitted, "Not on my own."

I stepped toward him, but Ash pushed her staff into my arms instead. "I got him."

"You sure?"

She shot me an exasperated look. "I don't need to be scraping both of you up off the ground."

I couldn't help but grin. "Fair enough." Ash knelt beside Jay and let him put his arm over her shoulders. Kit transformed, then held out her hands for Jay to set his free hand in. As Ash pushed herself up, bearing most of Jay's weight with her, Kit leaned back with all her might to help, although I doubted she actually contributed much assistance.

Jay staggered to his feet, and I grasped his arm to help keep him balanced. We slowly shuffled toward the school after Trey. Kit resumed her fur again and lapped us in circles as if on patrol as our personal bodyguard.

I had hoped that classes would start so we could have some privacy, but the schoolyard was still packed. Teachers urged students to back up and give us space, clearing a path for us. "Let's rest under the tree," I suggested.

Trey dropped back to guard us from behind as we maneuvered in that direction. Once we were safely in the shade, Jay sank into the grass and leaned against the trunk in exhaustion. He stared at his hand as he opened and closed his fingers to regain feeling. "Remind me not to underestimate Hassing again," he muttered. "His ectoplasm is no joke."

"Tell me about it," I sympathized. Unfortunately, today hadn't been my first experience taking a direct blast of Captain Hassing's Grade G ectoplasm.

Ash reclaimed her staff with an authoritative twirl, snapping it into place and glaring at the starstruck students inching closer and closer to us. One of the boys whistled at Ash while groups of giggling and blushing girls attempted to make eye contact with Jay and me. I tried to tune them out, but I heard several call my name, and I caught snippets of sentences. "So brave" and "the cutest" were uttered more than once. I couldn't stop my eyes from rolling.

"Excuse me, coming through!" Vivian called, pushing her way between the bodies. "This isn't a freak show, so you can all stop staring. Move it." She finally broke free and knelt down next to me with bottles of water, ice packs, and a first-aid kit. "Morons," she muttered under her breath.

"Break it up!" shouted Principal Solwitz. She clapped her hands and marched through the throng in Vivian's wake. While students hadn't paid any heed to my blood-sister, they immediately scattered as the principal bore down on them. "Let's go, move along. Give them some space." She stopped when she drew near. "Sorry about that. Do you have everything you need?"

"I think so," said Vivian as she passed water bottles to us.

"Are you sure you don't want the nurse to come?"

"We're sure," I snapped, glaring at the principal as I untwisted the cap.

She met my hostile look with a neutral expression. "Renn knows you're here, so if you change your mind, her office is through those doors, left down the hallway, second door on the right. Vivian and Trey know where it is."

I started guzzling water. "I think we're fine," Vivian said. "Thank you."

Trey shifted and said, "Um, Principal Solwitz? Do . . . we need passes? You know, if the bell rings and we're still out here helping them."

She gave him a restrained but amused grin. "No, Mr. Selman. Your teachers are aware of the situation." She turned back to us and said, "We're doing a security sweep of the school before we let students inside, just in case. Please reach out to me or any of the faculty if you need anything."

"Thank you," Viv said again.

"Thank you," Ash, Jay, and I meekly echoed.

I downed the rest of my water as she strode away. The drink definitely perked me up; I already felt more alert.

Vivian exchanged my empty bottle for a full one. "How's your head?"

I touched the back of my head and winced. The ice had mostly melted, leaving the raw wound exposed again. "It hurts. I think I just scraped it, though." She passed me a pad of gauze and an ice pack. "You know I can make my own ice, right?"

"I know. But there's no need for you to waste your energy." I set the gauze on top of the ice pack and then pressed it to the back of my head. Vivian closed the first-aid kit, but she was frowning. "Cato, head injuries can be very serious."

"I'm fine."

"But I would feel a lot better if you'd let—"

"I said I'm fine."

She settled back in the grass. "We should probably call Mom."

"Why, so she can worry and make a big fuss and lecture me about going to a doctor?" I set the ice pack down so I could pop the lid off the water bottle. "No thanks. Besides, the bleeding's slowed," I added, nodding at the blood on the gauze.

"She's going to find out anyway."

I took a deep drink, glancing at Vivian and shrugging one shoulder to reiterate my earlier reply. I pressed the ice pack on my head again.

Jay set his empty water bottle down. His silver eyes looked brighter and more alert, and he was sitting up on his own without needing to lean against the tree. He started doing basic stretches to loosen up his muscles, much to the delight of the girls watching from a distance. Ash had wandered closer to the edge of the canopy, and her gaze magnetically scanned the sky.

"No distress calls?" Jay asked.

She shook her head. "Nope. It'd be nice to know that RC is okay and Captain Hassing returned to the Ghost Realm."

Despite the teachers on patrol, students were drifting toward us again, although they made sure to stay just far enough away to avoid being reprimanded. A girl called, "Jay, you were *amazing*!"

"So was Phantom!" another girl said, stepping forward rather aggressively as if she were ready to fight for my honor. She beamed at me and said in a rush, "When you made those shields on your arms and charged back into battle . . . that was so brave! You didn't even hesitate to put your life on the line and protect us."

"And I *love* your eyes," another girl said dreamily, pressing in next to her friend and practically hanging off her shoulder. "They're *so* unique."

"Yes, they are," said a familiar voice. Shannon had sidled her way to the front of the group. She flashed me a dazzling smile and crept closer than anyone else before she knelt in the grass so we were on the same level. "Don't scare me like that, Cato. I would be devastated if anything happened to you."

Before I could even think of a response, a mocking male voice taunted, "Look who's finally slumming it here at school. I thought you were too good to grace us with your presence."

Trey snapped, "Leave him alone, Chase."

I surveyed the boy Trey had identified as Chase. He was standing in front of a group of boys with his arms folded, but despite Chase's scowl, his followers looked much more awestruck as they stole glances between Ash and me. All of the boys were wearing matching jackets, so I assumed they must be athletes on the same sports team.

Chase sneered at me and said, "Would you like us all to bow down and kiss the mighty Phantom's feet? Looks like Shannon's already started."

"I'm sorry, do I know you?" I snapped.

Chase's eyes widened in shock. Trey burst into uproarious laughter and doubled over, clutching his sides. Several students let out a low *oooooooh*, creating an eerie undertone below the giggles and murmurs.

Beet-red, Chase ground his teeth and glowered at his peers, then redirected his glare toward me again. "You're not serious."

Still laughing, Trey taunted, "How does it feel, Chase? You think you're so tough and important, but apparently not if he can't even remember your name."

"He knows who I am," Chase said defensively, although there was a layer of uncertainty under his angry tone. "He's just messing with me."

I tipped my head back to finish the rest of the water bottle, then said, "Sorry. You don't look familiar. I'm assuming we weren't friends, though."

Chase was so red now that he looked as if he were about to spontaneously combust. Before he could respond, a teacher strolled between the students. "Everything all right over here?" he asked in a warning tone.

"Fine," Chase seethed, whirling and shoving his way between two of his buddies. The teacher ushered the students back again, then continued his rounds. Shannon sent a little wave in my direction as she reluctantly retreated.

Trey sprawled out in the grass to catch his breath. "That . . . was . . . *so* worth it," he said, still grinning. "I've been waiting *years* to see that look on Chase's face."

"I have no idea what you're talking about," I said. "I really didn't know who that was."

Trey rolled onto his side to face me. "That prick has been bullying you and me since the fifth grade. He constantly shoved us around every time he crossed our path. It's about time karma came back to bite him in the ass."

"I'm not sure my amnesia counts as karma." I glanced over at Jay, who was struggling to stand up. "What are you doing?"

Ash rushed to his side and helped him rise. "Thanks," he said. "Let me find my balance."

Reluctantly, she let go and stepped back. "You should go Home and rest."

"I'm sore and tired, but I'm still functional." He started stretching again. "And I won't be able to rest until I know Hassing isn't in Phantom Heights anymore. I'll rendezvous with RC and Axel and get an update on the situation."

"We'll come with you," I said, standing up as well. The ground plane tilted with the sudden change in perspective, and I sidestepped to keep my balance. Vivian reached out to catch me, but the dizzy spell passed, and I righted myself on my own. "I'm all right," I muttered. "I just stood up too fast."

Jay slowly bent down to touch his toes, then straightened. "You three stay behind," he said, setting his hands on his hips and arching his back until it cracked. "I can Blink, but I don't think it's a good idea to take any passengers with me yet. Let me find out what's going on, and then I'll come back and we can strategize accordingly."

"I don't like this," Ash muttered, shaking her head.

"Well, our options are limited," he said. "And besides, I'll have RC and Axel to keep an eye on me. Cato . . . I'm not sure it's a good idea to have you near Axel with an open wound, anyway."

I pulled the ice pack away and looked at the smeared blood on the gauze pad. "Yeah, okay. Just hurry back. Don't get mixed up in another fight with Hassing."

He inclined his head and shuffled away from the tree. Although he was slow, he did seem to have his balance back under control. Jay cupped his hands around his mouth and called, "Ax, what's your location?"

A red streak of ectoplasm arched over the rooftops to our right. "Be back soon," Jay promised, and then he vanished.

Kit's ears fell. Vivian handed a first-aid kit to Ash, speaking quietly to my lab-sister. Ash accepted the kit and then turned to face me. "Let me look at your head."

"Bloody Scout, how many times do I have to say I'm—"

She pointed her staff at me. "Let me look at your injury, or I'll give you another lump to complain about."

Vivian folded her arms with a smug look. "Maybe you can knock a little sense into him while you're at it."

"I've tried," Ash said. "It didn't work."

"Hilarious," I said dryly as Ash circled around behind me. "I wish the two of you could bond over something that isn't at my expense."

"Mm-hmm," Ash muttered, setting her warm hand on the back of my neck and tilting my head down to get a better view.

Vivian said, "How many fingers am I holding up?"

"Four," I replied, to her immediate look of panic. "I'm kidding! Lighten up, Viv—it was a joke. Two."

Ash said, "I don't think it's serious. But there's dirt and debris mixed with the blood. I'm going to flush it with water, okay?"

"Yeah, fine, whatever. If it'll make everyone stop pestering me."

Vivian tossed her the last water bottle, and I suspected Ash took pleasure in dumping the water unceremoniously over my head. My blood-sister added, "I'd feel better if you used the disinfectant spray."

Ash plucked a small spray bottle from the kit. "What's it do?" she asked uncertainly.

"Kills any bacteria that might have gotten into the wound. It'll help to prevent an infection."

I waited, hunched over, water dripping from my hair. Ash took a few more seconds to study the bottle and read the tiny print to verify that Vivian was telling the truth, and then I heard the spritz.

Immediately, a freezing, burning pain spread across the back of my head. I recoiled, driving my elbow back into Ash's gut to make her release her hold on my neck. "*Bloody* Scout," I seethed through bared teeth, ducking away and pressing my hand against my soaked head. "That stings."

"Serves you right for that move," Ash snapped, clutching her stomach. She tossed the spray bottle back into the kit.

"Thank you," Vivian said. I shot her a sour look.

A series of bells chimed across the schoolyard, calling my attention to the building. The sound was chillingly familiar; it echoed through my head long after the last chime faded. "Does that mean school is starting now?" I asked, noticing that only a handful of students had moved in the direction of the doors. I didn't see any teachers left in the schoolyard.

"It's the warning bell," Trey said. "It means classes will start in ten minutes."

Ash said worriedly, "Jay's taking longer than I thought for a simple report."

"We didn't miss a distress call, did we?" I asked.

Kit said, "I'll be lookout!" She transmuted in a swirl of black smoke and scaled the tree.

Ash wandered farther away so she was free of the canopy, her gaze skimming the skyline in the direction of Axel's earlier signal.

Vivian gathered the empty water bottles. "What do you want me to do?" she asked. "Should I call Mom? Someone probably did already, but if not, she needs to know if there's a threat so she can alert the police and activate the raid team."

"Let me touch base with Jay first," I said. "We don't have anything to report yet."

"Except that the Captain of the Guard attacked you and may still be lurking around waiting to do it again."

"I want to know what Jay found out first. If Hassing's already returned to the Ghost Realm, there's no need to make Madison worry."

"If Hassing's in the Ghost Realm," Vivian rationalized, "Jay would probably be back here telling you that, don't you think?"

She jumped rather suddenly, then pulled her vibrating phone out of her pocket. After a quick glance at the screen, she shot me an I-told-you-so look and answered, "Hi, Mom. Actually, I was about to call you. Yeah. No, he's okay. Everyone's okay. Trey and I are with Cato, Ash, and Kit. Yeah, here."

Vivian held the phone out to me, but I shook my head.

"Talk to her," Vivian pleaded. After a few more seconds, she sighed and brought the phone back to her ear. "Sorry, he's resting and doesn't want to talk right now. I promise he's okay. A little bruised, but nothing serious. Yeah. Okay. All right. We'll be here."

She ended the call and slid her phone back into her pocket. "Mom's on her way. She wants us to wait for her here."

I grumbled, "Don't tell her I hit my head."

"I think *you* should tell her that."

"Uh, C-Cato?" Ash called. Her voice sounded wrong. Frightened.

I turned, expecting to see the foreboding light of an ectoplasm distress call in the sky. Instead, I realized that several boys had crowded around my lab-sister. Wide-eyed, she backed away from them.

Although a couple of the boys held up their hands and retreated after she called out to me, Chase brazenly moved in closer. "Hey, c'mon, I'm just giving you a compliment," he said, his voice deep and quiet in a way that was probably intended to be seductive but instead made the hairs rise on the back of my neck. Ash visibly shivered. "The least you can do is give me a smile in return. Don't I deserve that? I bet you have a prettier smile than any other girl in this school." He murmured something in her ear as he slid his arm around her waist.

"Hey! Leave her alone," I snapped, striding toward the group. Hot rage made my blood boil, coaxing up my sonokinesis and most certainly changing my eyes to blazing green.

Ash spun away to break free of his grasp. Chase started to reach after her, but then he recoiled. When I saw why, I gasped. A hungry flame was devouring his jacket sleeve.

For a few seconds of total shock, nobody reacted beyond the initial disbelief of trying to process what they were seeing. Ash took off, her long legs carrying her across the schoolyard. She didn't look back.

"Ash!" I called after her.

Like a spell breaking, chaos erupted. Chase hollered and flailed, screaming, "I'm on fire! Oh, god! Help! I'm on fire!"

Boys openly pointed and laughed at his misfortune. A girl shouted, "Pigs deserve to get roasted!" amid a chorus of concurring cheers.

I took a step in Ash's direction, my gaze fixed on her cloak as she receded in the distance. Then I glanced at Chase in frustrated hesitation. I wanted to go after my lab-sister, but the fire was still burning, and he was fanning the flames by leaping around like an idiot. Students were shouting, "Stop, drop, and roll!" but he was in too much of a panic to heed them.

I exhaled with one more look at Ash before I turned to Chase. "I'll help you. Just hold still." I had to sidestep as he spun my way, swinging his burning arm. "Stop moving!" I reached for the flames, but he was still twirling and flapping. I couldn't grab him.

Fed up and tired of wasting precious time, I crouched and dove forward, hitting him in the stomach and tackling him hard to the ground. "I said *hold still*!"

Finally, I was able to press both hands to the flames. I summoned my blue power and moved my hand down the length of his arm, putting out the fire with a thin sheet of ice that melted on contact with a popping, hissing sound and a release of steam. The flames had eaten away much of his sleeve and left angry red burns across his skin.

Chase was sobbing as the last spark went out, although I doubted the pain had fully set in yet through the shock. I veered back and punched him in the face. "Don't *ever* touch her again," I snarled as I rose. Blubbering, he curled up and rolled onto his side, covering his head with his other arm.

I sprinted in the direction Ash had gone. In my wake, I heard a boy suggest I should try out for the football team after that impressive tackle.

"Ash!" I called. My burning muscles were stiff, but adrenaline forced them to move, and my choppy gait smoothed out a little more with each stride. I dragged quick, ragged breaths through my teeth to avoid the deep inhales that made me double over in pain. "Ash!"

"Cato, wait!" Vivian shouted from behind. She and Trey were pounding across the lawn after me.

"Kit, stay!" I shouted over my shoulder, ignoring my pursuers. The chain-link fence was approaching, but it didn't slow me down as I became intangible and leapt through it. "Ash, wait up!" I caught a glimpse of her green cloak disappearing around a corner.

Vivian and Trey hit the fence with open hands, coming to an abrupt halt with their fingers curled through the links. "Cato!" Vivian called again. "We're supposed to stay here and wait for Mom!"

Determined to close the gap with Ash, I lengthened my stride. But by the time I reached the street corner, she was gone.

I stood on the sidewalk and turned in a circle, breathing in short, choppy pants. My gaze roved across the streets, alleys, windows, doorways, and alcoves. No sign of her.

"Damn it!" I shouted, then—keeping a tight lid on my power—tipped my head back, cupped my hands around my mouth, and called one more time, "*Ash*! Where are you?"

I was answered not with a verbal reply, but with a bright red-orange ball of light rising over the buildings and plummeting like a piece of falling sun. Judging by the distance, she was only one street over. I dashed for the firing point.

As her ectoplasm dissipated above the rooftop, I rounded the corner and collided face-first with a wall of green ectoplasm so solid it might as well have been made of brick. I rebounded and was introduced rudely to the ground.

With a groan, I propped myself up on my elbows. The transparent green barrier reminded me of the Dome, except this was pure ectoplasm, which meant I couldn't bypass it by suppressing my powers. I scrambled to my feet. On the other side, Ash was throwing fireballs at Hassing while RC stood farther down the street, manipulating his lethal silver disks.

"Hey!" I shouted, pounding my fists on the wall. Whether the intent was to pen my lab-siblings in or keep me out, I couldn't reach them. I considered how much time it would take to circle the block, but then I noticed that the street on the other side was also walled off with ectoplasm. And my lab-siblings weren't alone—there were humans trapped inside as well. They cowered behind trees, mailboxes, trash cans—whatever hiding places they could find.

Despite the onslaught, Hassing seemed rather carefree and relaxed as he used a pair of ectoplasm tentacles to deflect the attacks. He threw out his hand, materializing a net of ectoplasm before him. It flew straight at Ash, who had no defense against ectoplasm and couldn't dodge such a broad attack; the net wrapped around and entangled her before she had time to react. She fell to the ground, then screamed and convulsed as Hassing degraded the energy to shock her. The net disintegrated, leaving her lying limp, dazed, and hurt.

Without missing a beat, Hassing launched another net at RC. The Telekinetic extended both hands, freezing Hassing's net in midair. My lab-brother, surprised by his own feat, triumphantly shouted, "Ha!"

Hassing smirked. He curled his fingers into a fist, and his net collapsed into a tiny, blinding point of energy that exploded in a burst of green light. RC was thrown backward in the shock wave of the blast.

The captain's glowing green eyes flicked in my direction to give me a knowing sidelong glance. In an instant, the solid wall of Grade A ectoplasm degraded to a raw, electrified form that swarmed me as the barrier collapsed. I didn't register hitting the ground; I writhed in stiff, jerky thrashes and cried out in pain as my body was electrocuted with Grade G ectoplasm yet again.

The energy dissipated, and something—a tentacle, no doubt—seized my ankle and dragged me toward the Captain of the Guard. I was hoisted upside down and found myself face-to-face with my adversary, my arms dangling limply toward the ground with my cloak. "Nice to see you again, Phantom. Did you miss me?"

"I can't say that I did," I muttered.

"Ah, still talking? I guess I didn't give you a strong enough zap."

Despite my comeback, I was in no position to do anything except squeeze my eyes shut and brace myself for the next wave of pain I knew was about to come. Instead of the burning agony, I felt my body swinging through the air. A thudding impact in my ribs preceded a breathtakingly sharp pain. My eyes snapped open as I gasped.

A bladed silver disk was embedded in my ribs. Hassing had used me as a shield against the incoming attack.

"Cato?" RC called in alarm.

The captain laughed. "Careful!" He lowered me a bit to inspect the weapon protruding from my body. "A little higher, and that might have been a fatal shot."

Hassing suddenly flinched and grunted in pain. The tentacle let me go. I fell in a heap at the captain's feet, just in time to see Jay on the ground, holding onto the handle of an ornate dagger embedded in Hassing's calf. My lab-brother vanished. An instant later, an ectoplasmic tentacle lashed out, striking the road right where Jay had been.

Hassing limped backward, his eyes darting. "Curse King, you miserable lab rat!" He bent over, seized the dagger, and pulled it out, clutching the weapon in preparation to stab Jay the second he reappeared. "I'm going to make you pay for that!"

A powerful telekinetic push sent Hassing flying away from me until he came to a hard stop against a wall and crumpled to the ground. RC fell onto his knees next to me. "I'm so sorry!"

"Get it out," I said through gritted teeth.

"I'm not sure that's a good idea."

"Get it out," I repeated. "I'll freeze the blood, but I need you to pull the blades out."

RC hesitated, then nodded. With a flick of his hand, the disk wrenched itself out of my body. I cried out in pain, then pressed my palm over the wound and called upon my cryokinesis to stop the bleeding.

A few yards away, Ash seemed to have recovered, at least partially. She'd risen to her feet and was holding her staff in a defensive position, ready to fight again as dozens of ectoplasm orbs started to manifest in the air in front of Hassing. "Gotta move," RC warned urgently, leaping to his feet. "Cato, if you can't fight, you have to get out of the way."

Too late—Hassing launched all the blasts toward us at once, and we faced a wall of incoming projectiles. RC held out both hands to stop the ectoplasm with his telekinesis. As if on cue, the orbs exploded, sending all three of us sprawling in the street. Hassing shambled toward us through the smoke. Even as I watched, two more ectoplasm tentacles sprouted from his back, making four in total. One for each of us.

"Shit," RC muttered, flinging the bloody disk he'd plucked out of my body. One of the tentacles swatted the spinning disk away. It ricocheted off a *No Parking* sign and careened toward Ash, who didn't react fast enough to become intangible. The blades struck her arm with a *clang* and a burst of sparks, connecting with her neutralizer. The metal band had protected her from what would have been a severe slice.

Ash pressed her hand over the neutralizer, her face turning deathly white. "It's not working," she whispered in terror.

The mailbox next to me exploded.

I yelped, throwing up my arm as sparks and pieces of hot metal rained down on me. Ash squealed in a wild panic; what had originally been a miracle had suddenly become a curse of bad luck. Jay called her name and ran toward her. Waves of flames whipped like sidewinders slithering up and down the street, hindering his progress. I scrambled to get my feet underneath me and force my injured body back into motion.

I stumbled out of the way but not fast enough to save my cloak, which caught fire. I yanked the edge out of the flames and doused them in ice. Ash's fire was indiscriminately starving for fuel—no one was spared. The burning tree overhead dropped leaves that drifted like fiery rain mixed with black snow. RC was telekinetically trying to keep the flames contained in the street and minimize the damage.

Hassing was closer to me than I'd expected, but he wasn't paying attention to us anymore—he was too busy trying to stamp out the flames licking his cloak.

I took advantage of the chaos and lunged toward him, driving an icicle straight toward his neck. I'd expected him to see me coming and turn intangible. To my absolute shock as well as his, my ice blade made contact. He staggered to the side, his hand rising to press against the wound. Blood spurted in a powerful stream; I'd hit his carotid artery.

Hassing fell to his knees, his eyes wide in horror as he felt his life-blood draining through his fingers. I stared at the dying man, struggling to process what I'd done. He would bleed out in a matter of minutes.

The acrid breeze blew a billow of smoke over us and temporarily obscured my surroundings. *I can't let him die*, I realized. That would be an unforgivable sin in Azar's eyes. Despite all the crimes we'd committed, killing the Captain of the Guard would be indefensible. It would set Azar on the warpath for sure.

I seized Hassing's arm and pulled it away from his neck, then clapped my palm over the wound and called upon my blue Divinity. Hassing was too stunned to resist. I froze his blood to temporarily clot the injury, then thickened a layer of ice on his neck to prolong his time.

"You have until that melts to find a Healer," I said coldly as I removed my hand. His blank eyes rolled to find me since the solid ice on his neck minimized his mobility. "After that, you bleed out. Better not waste a second."

He blinked twice as my words registered. The smoke was getting thicker. I turned my back on the captain—he wasn't a threat anymore. If he chose to stay here and continue fighting, he'd die, and that wouldn't be my problem. I gave him a chance to survive.

Ash was standing in the middle of the street with her fists pressed against her temples, eyes squeezed shut, face crumpled in panic. "Somebody *help me*!" she screamed.

Jay finally reached her and seized her shoulders. "Ash, you have to calm down," he said. He leapt back with a cry as flames swirled around her.

"I can't!" she sobbed, triggering more fiery explosions.

I'd never seen Ash at full power before. She suffered from a crippling lack of control, which was why even in the Arena, her powers were kept partially neutralized at all times. Now I saw why.

"Cato!" Jay shouted, stumbling backward as a ring of fire sprang outward from Ash.

I sprinted toward my lab-sister. My core grew warm as I summoned my power, but the rest of my body temperature dropped as I ran through the flames and threw my arms around Ash.

Steam erupted when our bodies collided. My ice quenched her fire; her fire melted my ice. We canceled each other out. Ash was trembling as I held her close. "If you calm down, you can control your Divinity," I told her.

"No," she cried, burying her face against my shoulder. "I can't! Not again. It's going to burn you. It's going to burn everything!" She was hyperventilating in the grips of panic.

"No, it's not. Don't worry about me; you can't burn ice." The steam enveloped us in fog that obliterated the world around us. We were an island.

She tightened her arms around me and cried, "Don't let me go!"

"I won't," I promised. "Arena's Honor. No bars, right? It's just you and me."

"I'm so sorry!"

"It's okay. I'm here with you. I need you to breathe, Ash. Focus on your breathing. Your Divinity is tied to your emotions. The more you panic, the more out of control your fire is."

I squeezed my eyes shut and held her tightly as I concentrated on maintaining my ice. Despite my assurances to her, I wasn't fireproof. If her flames burned hotter than my ice could withstand, I was going to be in serious trouble.

"I'm so sorry . . . Please don't let me go . . . I'm so sorry," she whispered over and over.

"I won't," I whispered back. I kept my arms firmly around her torso as we slowly sank to our knees. I had to be careful with the placement of my hands, so I kept a tight grasp on her cloak to ensure my grip didn't slide. Chase had already rattled her by slipping his arm around her waist and trying to pull her against his body by force; I didn't want to accidentally trigger any further trauma. In a rational state, Ash knew I would never harm her that way, but a wrong touch could cause her to lash out in panic if, even for a brief instant, her mind took her back to the night guard's groping fingers as he yanked her out of her cage by her hair and dragged her into the closet in the hall. My ice probably wouldn't be able to withstand a full-power flare-up if she felt threatened.

"I'm so sorry . . ."

"Ash, will you count with me? Something to concentrate on. One thousand. Nine hundred ninety-three. Nine hundred eighty-six. Come on. Nine hundred . . ."

"Seventy-nine," she croaked.

"Right. Good. Nine hundred seventy-two . . ."

As we quietly continued the incremental countdown, I noticed that the heat seemed to be losing its intensity. "Nine hundred fifty-eight. Nine hundred fifty-one."

I detected movement in the fog. Jay knelt next to us and held up an intact neutralizer.

"Hey," I said gently above her hoarse voice as she continued to count. "Jay's here. He brought a neutralizer for you. Everything's going to be okay now."

Ash lifted her head, then held her trembling hand out toward our lab-brother. Gently, with her unspoken permission, he pried off the damaged neutralizer, then took her wrist and slipped the new silver band up her arm. He grasped the neutralizer in both hands and twisted in opposite directions to activate it.

She went completely limp in exhaustion or relief, or both. I couldn't support her deadweight, and we both collapsed on our backs, her head lying on my arm.

I closed my eyes. Slowly, I moved my free hand to the wound in my rib cage. The heat had melted my ice, and I was bleeding again. I refroze my blood and lay still on the pavement, my thoughts drifting on the edge of unconsciousness.

I just needed to rest . . . just for a minute . . .

— Chapter Forty-One —
The Witch & the Healer

I hear sirens.

They sounded so far away.

My eyes fluttered open. Above me, the tree was still burning through the wispy fog, sending plumes of smoke and flame into the sky in a mesmerizing kaleidoscope of swirling patterns.

Jay's face leaned into my vision, blocking the beautiful sight. "How bad are you hurt?"

"I can still fight," I whispered, although my body felt as if it had turned to stone.

"The fight's over. How bad are you hurt?"

The sirens were getting louder. Along the edges of my vision, I could see a flurry of movement—lights flashing, people wearing uniforms and dragging hoses, streams of water turning the fires to smoke, civilians coughing and running away. The images didn't seem to be in real time; they lagged, leaving a trail of afterimages.

"Not too bad," I murmured. "I'm just catching my breath."

Jay raised an eyebrow. "You know you look off to the side when you lie, right? Just like Vivian."

I twitched my lips in a rather pathetic grin. "You know you were supposed to come back and give us a status report instead of taking Hassing on yourself, right?"

"Things got messy fast. Can the two of you stand up?"

Ash's grip on my cloak tightened. I turned my head toward her and asked, "Are you okay if I let you go now?"

She sniffed and nodded, her bloodshot eyes finally opening to meet my gaze. Jay offered a hand, and she reached up to accept. He pulled her to her feet, then extended his hand back down to me.

I didn't move. My hand was still pressed against the frozen gash on my left side. "Don't pull me," I said. "I think . . . I need you to push me up from behind."

Jay nodded and knelt by my head, sliding his hands behind my shoulders. He gently but firmly lifted me, and I labored to push myself up with my left hand so my right could keep applying pressure on the wound.

At least I was sitting up now. I gazed around at the organized chaos. Police and firefighters were on the scene, directing people to safety and diminishing the remaining blazes.

"Cato!"

I turned my head toward the sound of my mother's voice. She sprinted toward us from across the street, ectogun in hand. "Oh my god, what happened? Are you hurt?"

I pulled the edge of my cloak over my wound to conceal it from her. Raw emotion suddenly swelled in my chest, and I had to clench my jaw to keep from breaking down. "We're . . . having a really bad day," I croaked, blinking back tears as I forced a wavering smile.

Ash bowed her head in sorrow and shame, gripping her arms and crying. Madison surveyed the three of us, then glanced around at the surrounding mayhem, still trying to process the scene.

"Okay," she said gently, holstering her ectogun. "Okay, everything's all right now. One step at a time. Is there still danger?"

I swiped my fist across my eye. "I don't think so. Not anymore."

"Is anyone seriously hurt?"

Jay solemnly replied, "I think Cato's in the worst shape. The rest of us . . . aren't great," he admitted, "but it's nothing serious."

I kept my right hand in place to cover the wound. I still didn't actually know how bad it was other than Hassing's less-than-trustworthy assessment that it would have been fatal if the blades had struck me lower in the abdomen and pierced my organs. I stared blankly at the ground and monotonously said, "I just need a first-aid kit to patch myself up." My gaze wandered up to Jay. "Are you able to get me Home?"

He nodded.

Madison looked torn, as if she didn't fully believe me but was too distracted by the pandemonium around us to press the issue. "Okay," she said again. "You can get back to the manor, then? You'll be okay for a little while so I can coordinate with Chief Emerton?"

My "yeah" was barely audible.

She nodded. "I'll call raiders and arrange for extra patrols so you can recuperate. Go home, clean yourselves up, and rest. I'll be there as soon as I can." My mother strode toward a group of police officers.

Jay set his hand on my shoulder. "You ready?"

I bowed my head and closed my eyes in preparation. Darkness compressed the space around me in a roar of wind that swept away the noise of people and sirens and water hissing into steam, and the smell of smoke, and the warmth of sunshine on my face. I opened my eyes and found myself sitting in the middle of our living quarters on the third floor of Saros Manor.

Jay gently instructed, "Get the first-aid kit from the bathroom, please."

Reese stood up immediately to comply. Although he probably shouldn't have pushed himself, Jay had Blinked Ash with us as well. She sank into a chair, buried her face in her hands, and started sobbing.

Jay turned to Finn and said, "Can you please get some food and plenty of water?"

"I'm not hungry," I muttered.

Jay gave him a meaningful look, and Finn walked away to complete the request. I lowered myself onto my back with a strained groan. The room was spinning. I closed my eyes and let the dizziness sweep me away into a restless doze that wavered on the razor-thin edge of consciousness.

***

The Rip opened onto a granite platform beneath a stone archway.

It had been a place of execution for war criminals during King's reign and the following Red Years after his assassination. If one believed the myths, it was the accumulation of spilt blood and the cursed last words of the fallen amassed over thousands of years here on this very platform that made this a powerful spiritual place—powerful enough for the vengeful spirits to grow stronger over the centuries and tear apart the fabric of the living Realms.

Hassing landed hard on his knees beneath the stone arch. The frozen blood was melting fast—he could feel it trickling between his fingers. Keeping his hand pressed over the wound was no doubt making the ice melt faster, but he couldn't help it.

"Captain?"

He kept his head down but lifted his gaze to find the two Shadow Guards stationed on either side of the archway peering down at him in concern. "Rank. Divinity," Hassing croaked.

They both straightened and performed the Guard's salute with their right fists on their chests and left fists swinging behind to rest on their lower backs.

The man with thick horns curving behind his head and black markings trailing down his face from the inner corners of his eyes answered, "Ensign Cassel. I'm a Chimæra."

"Ensign Amaya," said the woman with silvery, blue-white hair. "Electrokinetic."

Hassing clenched his teeth. *Useless.* Those Divinities didn't do him any good. Cassel could transform parts of his body into animal appendages, and Amaya was an Elemental who controlled lightning and electricity.

"Titon," Hassing said. He staggered to his feet, his attention on the jet-black valdenar that was still standing right where Hassing had left him, obediently waiting for his master to return. "Help me get to Titon. I have to find Leah."

Amaya seized the captain's elbow to help him regain his balance as he lurched forward and stumbled off the platform, but as Hassing drew near, the steed pinned his ears and balked, throwing his head back.

Hassing pulled free of Amaya's grasp and made a wild grab for the reins. Somehow, he managed to seize one and pull it taut.

Titon reared and whinnied, his cloven hooves striking out as his great feathered wings unfurled. Amaya dove out of the way, covering her head with her arms as Titon landed, bucked, and then reared again. He gathered himself into a takeoff position, and the captain had no choice but to let go lest he be dragged off the ground in a dangerous flight over Szion.

Titon launched into the air with a graceful but deadly leap, coming down directly on his master. Hassing called upon his intangibility just in time to escape Titon's sharp hooves as they passed through the captain's body and struck the cobblestones before he pushed off again, this time taking flight.

In the street, the passing unicorns and bilocorns pranced, whinnied, and reared in response to Titon's ruckus. Riders and drivers cracked their whips as they shouted for obedience above the clatter of hooves and the creaking of wagons and chariots being wheeled off course.

Hassing lay in a daze of fury as he watched his mount fly under a sky bridge, heading back to the Prison without a rider.

"What happened?" Amaya asked, slowly rising with her eyes trained on Titon's receding form against the lavender sky. "I've never seen Titon act like that."

Hassing coldly replied, "Titon does not tolerate weakness. I'm not worthy to command him or sit on his back." He grimaced, hand still plastered over his neck, afraid to turn his head at the risk of breaking the ice seal and bleeding out. "I need a Healer. I won't make it to Leah in time without Titon."

Amaya cupped her hands around her mouth and called out to the onlookers subtly observing from windows, alleys, and doorways lining the street: "Are there any Healers here?"

People ducked their heads and proceeded with their tasks. Cassel solemnly offered his hand. After a moment of reluctant consideration, Hassing reached up to clasp the ensign's hand, allowing the Chimæra to pull him up into a sitting position.

"We need a Healer!" Amaya shouted. "Please!"

The only reply was the clatter of hooves and wheels on cobblestones as traffic returned to a normal flow.

"I'm familiar with this area," said Cassel. "There's a shop not too far from here called the Three Sisters. One of the sisters is a Healer."

Hassing leaned forward, set his free hand flat on the cobblestones, shifted onto his knees, and then staggered to his feet like an old drunkard. "Take me there. I'm running out of time."

"Yes, Captain," the ensigns chorused.

Amaya positioned herself next to him and said, "You can use me as a support. If you need to," she added to avoid insulting him.

Hassing shuffled after Ensign Cassel for a few steps, then clenched his teeth and swallowed his ego down deep enough to seize Amaya's shoulder for balance, although he tried his best not to lean too heavily on her. The captain made a point to glare at any onlooker he caught watching, although he couldn't blame the civilians for not coming forward. He knew he was in bad shape; if he didn't survive, nobody would want to be caught with his blood on their hands.

Szion's tall architecture with cloud-stabbing spires, flying buttresses, sky bridges, and arches was creating a dizzying effect in conjunction with Hassing's blood loss. He felt so very small, so very mortal and vulnerable as he shuffled along with his two subordinates, every heartbeat bringing him closer to death's icy grasp. Hassing spotted a gargoyle perched on a ledge and glared at the stationary beast, alert for any signs of movement in case the wretched creature was enticed by the scent of his blood.

Cassel glanced back, and the alarm in his expression was proof that Hassing must look as cadaverous as he felt. The ensign forced an unconvincing smile that revealed his pointed teeth. "It's just up ahead, Captain. If you need to stop and rest, please tell us."

Hassing locked his jaw and didn't answer. He couldn't afford to waste the energy, and he didn't have time to rest. If he did, it would be the end. He likely wouldn't be able to rise.

"Who did this to you?" Amaya asked. "Was it a human from Cröendor?"

"Don't insult me," Hassing growled. He shouldn't talk more than necessary, but he couldn't let the slight go unchallenged. "It was one of the Alpha rats. The Demikan did this."

"Oh," Amaya murmured, her voice like an echo of wind between the buildings. "So, he's real, then? The Demikan truly does exist?"

Hassing grunted in affirmation. He bowed his head and focused on putting one foot in front of the other with Ensign Amaya remaining a steady support.

"Almost there," Cassel promised.

Hassing grunted again. The frightened, judgmental stares of on-lookers made his skin crawl. The captain glowered at anyone who dared to make eye contact with him, although his expression softened when he caught the gaze of a woman whose belly was swollen with pregnancy. For her, he bowed his head in respect. Even if he was on death's doorstep, he had enough dignity left to observe revered customs. There was nothing more sacred than choosing to harbor a new life within one's own body.

"Here," Cassel said breathlessly, pushing open a door. A bell above the door rang to announce their arrival.

Hassing lifted his head to sweep his gaze around the shop. Bundles of fragrant dried herbs hung from the ceiling. One wall was filled with glistening crystals, jars, and vials—Witch's brews and raw materials, if he had to guess at a glance. The rest of the shop was filled with junk—jewelry, baskets, chalices, clothing, and an assortment of knickknacks. A black cat with vibrant yellow eyes watched them from its perch on a high shelf, tail twitching.

As the door closed behind the trio of Shadow Guards, a heavy, muted quiet settled over the shop like a thick blanket, sealing out the noise from outside.

Through a doorway covered by an orange, red, and gold tapestry depicting an ornamental sun, a faint voice called, "I'll be with you in a moment!"

Hassing swayed and leaned into Amaya to stay upright. "What . . . kind of shop did you say this was?"

"It's called the Three Sisters," Cassel replied. "One sister is a Healer, one is a Charmer, and one is a Witch."

The tapestry shifted, and a heavyset woman emerged with her hands fumbling behind her back to untie a stained apron. "Hello, welcome to our . . ." She stopped short when she realized that her customers were Shadow Guards. "Shop," she finished in a whisper.

"I need a Healer," Hassing said, lifting his hand to show the melting blood. "Now."

"I'm sorry, but you have the wrong sister." She slipped the apron over her head and draped it on the counter. "Both of my sisters are at the market. Here, sit," she said, pulling out a stool.

Amaya guided Hassing forward and steadied him as he lowered himself onto the seat. "Are they . . . on their way back?" he labored to ask.

"Not for a while. They—"

He seized her wrist. "I don't have time to wait. I can't imagine having the Captain of the Guard die on the floor of your shop would be good for business. Whatever you have—a Charm, a brew—I don't care what it costs. I don't care if it's legal. Do something. Help me."

She phased her hand free. "We run a respectable shop here, Captain. Even if we were involved with the Black Market, I don't have access to the ingredients for a healing brew. Not unless you happen to have alicorn and the blood of a fiend with you."

Cassel and Amaya exchanged bewildered looks. The woman turned away without waiting for an answer. That had been a rhetorical request—one of those ingredients was illegal, the other nearly impossible to obtain. She strode to the shelves of jars and vials with short, quick steps, then riffled through the brews. Vials clinked as she sifted through her inventory until finally snatching the one she was looking for and returning.

"Drink that," she ordered, pushing the vial into Hassing's hand.

He passed it to Cassel and said, "Uncork it for me." Once the ensign complied and returned it, Hassing sniffed the brew and wrinkled his nose. "What does it do?"

"It'll help to stabilize you." The Witch pulled his hand away from his neck and shook her head as she studied the stab wound. "But it's not going to be enough."

She exhaled and straightened, setting her hands on her wide hips and turning in a circle to catalog available resources. Hassing downed the brew in one swallow, then coughed and wiped his mouth. "Is it really so difficult to make a brew that tastes good? Or do you Witches just enjoy making people suffer?"

"The ingredients have to be precise," she murmured. "Additives to improve the taste would reduce the brew's effectiveness." She stared at the black cat watching from the top shelf. Her shoulders straightened, and she spun back to face Hassing. "I have an idea. It's not an ideal solution, but it's your best chance. I'll be right back. Here, drink." She seized a chalice and handed it to him as she headed for the doorway to the back of the shop.

Hassing stared into the chalice. "It's empty," he said dryly.

She paused in the doorway with the sun tapestry draped over her arm. "It's a Charm," she said. "Focus on water." She pushed through the tapestry and disappeared.

Cassel wandered along the shelves, skimming the merchandise for sale. "There has to be something else here that will help," he muttered.

The Witch's brew was leeching all of the strength out of Hassing's body. He bowed his head, his eyelids weighted with drowsiness. Faintly, he heard the sound of footsteps ascending a wooden staircase in the back of the shop.

"Get me onto the floor," he mumbled, his words slurred. "Before I fall off this damn stool."

Cassel returned to his side. The Guards guided their captain down until he gracelessly thumped onto the wooden floor, then leaned back against the wall. He stared into the empty chalice and whispered, "I'm thirsty." The cup immediately filled with water that was clean and cold as he gulped it down. Hassing drank and drank well beyond what the vessel should have been able to hold. When his thirst was quenched, he set the empty chalice down on the floor. "How do you feel, Captain?" Amaya softly inquired.

Such a ridiculous question didn't warrant a response. He stared up at the bundles of herbs hanging from the ceiling with the curious thought that he felt as if he were upside down, staring at plants growing out of the soil.

The footsteps were returning, but he was too tired to lift his head when the Witch entered and said, "My sister's daughter has been blessed with the healing hands of her mother's Divinity. However, she's only just started her training."

"Fine, she'll be fine," Hassing murmured. *Stupid Witch. There was a Healer here all along, and you only just now thought to bring her down?*

"Come here, Katiria." The Witch gestured for the young Healer to approach. "Here, right here. This man needs your help."

To Hassing's surprise and dismay, a tiny twig of a girl with flowers braided into her hair timidly shuffled around the Witch's side and blinked at him with wide, doe-like eyes. At most, she had five years. Maybe four. A faceless doll was cradled in her arms.

"This is a joke," Hassing said, his voice barely above a whisper.

"I'm afraid not," said the Witch. "Like I said, it's not an ideal solution, but Katiria is your best chance."

She knelt down and set her hands on the girl's small shoulders, then steered her into position. "All right, Ria. Do you think you can try to heal him, like Mama showed you?"

Hassing scowled at the child, silently warning her not to make a fatal mistake. Cassel shifted with uncertainty. Amaya protested, "Wait. This isn't as simple as healing a flesh wound. If she doesn't heal the artery first, he'll die of internal bleeding."

The Witch leaned back on her heels. "Do you have a better idea? Katiria's mother won't be back until midday. Will your captain survive that long?"

Barely moving his jaw, Hassing said, "It has to be done." He looked the little girl in the eye and said, "My life is in your hands."

The black cat—a familiar, no doubt—leapt down from the shelf and, with a swish of its tail, trotted over to the little Healer. It rubbed its sleek body against her ankles as if giving her silent encouragement.

The Witch nudged Katiria closer. "Come here, Ria. Don't be shy. See the blood flowing out of his neck? I need you to heal him and make him feel better. Think you can do that? Like Mama would?"

Katiria tilted her head to one side, gazing at the stream of blood that was growing stronger with every passing minute. She bent down, lovingly arranged her doll next to Hassing on the floor, then straightened again. The mute brat was so short that she was at eye level standing up while Hassing was seated on the floor.

The Witch pointed to Hassing's neck. "You've seen Mama heal people. I need you to be a big girl and do it just like Mama does. But do you see where all this blood is coming from on the inside? You need to heal that first. Okay? Do you see where I'm pointing? Do you understand?"

I'm as good as dead, Hassing thought dismally.

Katiria tilted her head the other way but otherwise didn't move. The Witch gently took the little girl's hands and pulled them toward the wound. "Come on, Ria. I'm going to melt the ice now. Once I do that, I need you to make the blood stop coming out of the man."

Hassing winced when the small fingers made contact. Despite Katiria's hesitancy, she seemed to be more afraid of his strangeness than of his blood, which didn't appear to bother her in the slightest.

The Witch splashed a bitter-smelling brew onto the wound, which seared with heat as a billow of steam rose like a cloud into the air.

"Heal the inside first," the Witch reminded the tiny Healer. "Where the blood is coming from."

Katiria's fingers slipped into the wound, causing Hassing to gasp. The girl's glowing blue eyes were trained intently on her work under the close scrutiny of the Witch. Hassing held perfectly still, afraid to even breathe. His neck throbbed with unnatural warmth, which he hoped was a good sign, but his vision was fading in and out as he wavered between consciousness and oblivion.

Katiria withdrew, leaned back, and stared at her bloody hands. "Is it done?" Hassing whispered. "Am I healed?"

"Not completely, sir," Cassel answered.

"But healed enough," the Witch decreed. "At least, enough to rest here until my sister can heal you the rest of the way." She kissed the top of Katiria's head and praised, "You did a wonderful job. I'm so proud of you, and your mama will be, too. Go back upstairs and wash your hands until they're clean. Don't touch anything on your way up."

Katiria tore her gaze away from her hands to stare longingly at her doll. "I'll bring it up to you," the Witch promised.

As the child started to shuffle away, Hassing weakly called, "Hey. Kid." She paused to look back at him. He wanted to smile at her, but the Witch's brew and blood loss had stolen his strength. "Thank you. I'm in your debt."

Katiria blinked at him, then vanished behind the tapestry without a sound.

The Witch hooked her thumb into a jar of paste and spread the thick salve onto a leaf that was bigger than Hassing's hand. She plastered the leaf over the wound and held it in place for a few seconds to make sure it was secure. Hassing breathed in an intense fragrance of earth and herbs. A cold tingle replaced the heat in his neck.

The Witch rose and pulled a cloak off a hanger, then wrapped it in a bundle and set it beside Hassing. "Lie down and rest. You're stable. When my sisters return, we can properly heal you."

Amaya and Cassel helped Hassing reposition himself and cradle his head on the cloak. The Witch, who must have noticed the blood staining Hassing's breeches, had already pulled off his boot and was rolling up his pant leg so she could treat the stab wound in his calf.

Consciousness was slipping out of his grasp. "You," he whispered, pointing to Cassel. "Return to your post." His hand fell, but his half-opened eyes shifted to Amaya. "You, stay here to serve me."

"Yes, Captain," they replied in unison.

As Ensign Cassel headed for the door, the Witch said, "I hope this good deed won't be forgotten by the Shadow Guard."

Cassel hesitated and glanced back at Hassing, who had only enough strength left to make a noise of affirmation in his throat. Cassel inclined his head, performed the Guard's salute, and replied, "You and Katiria served honorably. Consider yourselves and the Three Sisters in the Guard's favor."

As Hassing's eyes closed, the last image he saw was Cassel turning on his heel. His body was a receding silhouette as he strode away.

"Cato."

Hands were shaking me.

"Cato."

"Mmm?" I opened my eyes and stared in disoriented confusion at RC kneeling over me.

"You're bleeding," he told me.

"What?"

"Your ice melted, and you started bleeding through the bandages. I can't get it to stop."

I blinked, and then my gaze wandered down to the red-stained towel he was pressing against my body. Groggy, I let out a half-moan, half-sigh and reached up. He moved the soaked towel out of the way so I could press my palm against the gash and freeze my blood again.

RC leaned back and shook his head, casting a worried glance at Jay and Ash both fast asleep nearby. "This isn't working, Cay. You can't stay awake forever to keep freezing the blood. Your wound isn't going to heal like that."

I stared up at the ceiling. I didn't want to admit that he was right, but he was. "Is Madison home yet?"

"I think so. I had to get more towels, and I thought I heard her downstairs talking on the phone."

I licked my dry lips and took a breath, then winced. I had to remember to take shorter, shallower breaths. "Can you help me up?"

He held his hands up, palms facing the ceiling, and I felt a telekinetic pressure beneath my body gently lifting me to my feet. A dizzy spell made the room spin. I swayed, my knees almost buckling. If it weren't for telekinesis making my body feel much lighter, I would have fallen back down. "I need to get downstairs," I mumbled.

"I'll go with you."

I secretly felt relieved that he'd volunteered and I hadn't been forced to admit that I needed help making it down two flights of stairs. RC walked beside me, matching my slow, shuffling pace, and although he didn't physically hold onto me, I knew he was lending telekinetic assistance. Finn and Reese watched us leave.

RC didn't say a word as we took the stairs one slow step at a time. I wondered if he was feeling guilty since his weapon had caused my injury. As we descended the second staircase, my mother's faint voice came into range.

"Mm-hmm. Uh-huh. Yes, I understand," she was saying. "No, I haven't had a chance yet." I stepped into the foyer, and my stomach started to sink with dread. We headed toward the library, where Madison's voice was. I had to lean against the arched doorway to keep my balance. RC lingered behind to lend support if needed while staying out of the way.

My mother was slowly pacing in front of the bookshelves, her back to us. She paused by the table in the far corner and picked up a glass of water, then took a short sip while listening to whoever was on the other end of the phone. She set the glass down again. "No, not yet."

She turned and noticed me in the doorway. "Okay. All right. Look, something just came up. I'll call you back."

She ended the call and slipped her phone into her pocket. "Hey there," she greeted, her voice immediately adopting a gentler tone. "I thought you were still resting."

I bobbed my head wearily. "I was."

"Are you hungry?" she asked, pointing her thumb over her shoulder toward the kitchen door. "I can make you something to eat."

My head was too heavy to hold up, and I had to rest it against the doorway. "I think I need your help with something," I admitted.

"Sure, anything." She frowned, finally noticing my posture and expression. "What's wrong? You look pale. Are you all right?"

I gripped my shirt with trembling fingers and pulled it up.

"Oh my god," she whispered, rushing toward me.

"Don't touch it," I said as she drew near. "Just . . . look at it and tell me what I need to do to stop the bleeding."

She bent down for a better angle, then straightened again and marched into the great room. "Here, come here, come into the light so I can see."

I pulled away from the doorframe and shuffled after her. RC sat down on one of the barstools by the fireplace to observe and intervene if needed. Madison guided me toward the row of French doors, where ample afternoon sunlight was still streaming in. "Wait there," she ordered before jogging back into the library and returning with a chair.

I waited for her to situate it the way she wanted in the light, and then I sank into the chair with a groan. Madison knelt to study the wound. "Oh, Cato," she murmured, shaking her head. "Why does it look like that?"

"I froze my blood to stop the bleeding."

"Is it deep?"

"I don't think so. I'm pretty sure my rib stopped the blade. But the blood won't stop."

"Are you having any difficulty breathing?"

"No. It just hurts if I take deep breaths."

"But you're not winded or struggling to get enough oxygen?"

I shook my head. She reached out, and I sternly reminded, "I said don't touch it."

Madison sighed and looked up at my face. "What do you want me to do? How can I help you if I'm not allowed to touch it?"

"I don't know," I said miserably.

She dragged her hands down her face with a sigh. "Cato . . . you're probably going to need stitches. I'm sorry, but there's no getting around it if the bleeding won't stop."

I stared out the windows in silent panic as I processed her diagnosis. "Is, uh . . . is that something you know how to do?" I whispered hoarsely.

She shook her head. "No. I'd have to take you to the hospital so

Doc could stitch you up."

"No."

"Cato—"

"No."

"What if Doc came here to do it instead?"

"*No.*"

Madison leaned back, visibly frustrated by my stubbornness. I knew I was being irrational, but I didn't care.

She rubbed her forehead. "Okay. Let me . . . let me call the hospital and talk to Doc. Just to see if there are any other options." She stood up, pulled her phone out again, and walked into the den as she dialed the number. She closed the door behind her so I couldn't hear the conversation.

I glanced over my shoulder at RC. "Any chance you could bring a glass of water?"

He leapt down without a word and headed for the kitchen. A trickle of liquid rolling down my abdomen made my skin itch; the frozen blood was thawing again. I resolidified it.

RC returned and handed me a glass of water with five ice cubes floating on the surface. "Thank you," I murmured before gulping it down. I melted the ice cubes and drank those too, then handed him the glass. We both jumped when the door opened and my mother strode out, looking grim as she returned the phone to her pocket.

"You have two options," she said sternly. "Doc is on her way here. You can either let me clean your wound and seal it with a medical glue that she's bringing, or you can let her sedate you and stitch the wound shut. It's your choice."

I felt sick with dread. I glanced at RC, but I already knew which option I'd prefer. "I'll take the choice that doesn't involve any needles," I muttered.

"You have to promise that you aren't going to hurt me when I try to clean it. I'm not going to hold you down or fight with you, Cato. If you can't stay still and let me do what I need to do, Doc will sedate you."

"Good luck with that," RC threatened.

"I won't fight you," I promised. "But I don't want Doc near me."

Madison rubbed her mouth in deliberation and glanced down the length of the great hall toward the front doors. "She agreed to supervise and give me instructions. But she'll keep her distance, if that's what you want."

"That's what I want."

She nodded. "All right, then. I'm going to get some towels and pillows so we can get you down on the floor in a more comfortable position."

I didn't answer. I locked my jaw and blinked back tears while my stomach churned with anxiety. "You okay?" RC murmured.

I shook my head, setting a single tear free to roll down my cheek. I swallowed the lump in my throat and hoarsely said, "Please don't let her stick a needle in me."

"I won't."

"And . . . I might need you to help keep me still." I took a shuddering breath and winced. *Damn it—short breaths.*

"If that's what you want me to do."

I nodded in quick, jerky movements. "It's the better alternative."

We fell silent as my mother returned with an armful of towels and a pillow. She knelt and started to arrange the makeshift bedding on the floor. "I need you to lie down here," she said as she set the pillow in place.

A knock on the front door sent my heart into my throat. Madison let out a shaky exhale, then placed her hands on her knees and rose. "Breathe," she reminded me. "We'll get through this, and then you'll be able to rest."

I couldn't twist my body, but I craned my neck as far as I could to watch Madison glide toward the front doors with long, confident strides. She opened the door, said a few inaudible words in greeting, and then gestured to invite our unwelcome visitor inside.

My whole body turned icy cold in dread as I watched Doc approach with a medical bag in her hand. "Hi, Cato," she greeted in a voice that was a little too cheerful considering how much I *really* didn't want to see her. "I heard you're a little worse for wear after that fight earlier today. How are you feeling?"

My voice was gone; I couldn't have answered even if I'd wanted to. I just stared at her in mind-numbing panic. It helped that she wasn't wearing her lab coat, but that didn't lessen the terror that filled me in her presence. She and Madison stopped several yards away, giving me space for now. "What did he decide?" Doc asked.

"He'd like me to do the procedure and use the glue. Can you talk me through it?"

Doc nodded, although she looked at me and said, "If I may offer my professional opinion, the other option would be less stressful and painful for you, and stitches would be a more secure hold. With the glue, there's a risk of the wound reopening if you do any strenuous activities before you've had a chance to heal."

I shook my head. "No needles, no drugs," I managed to squeak out.

Doc inclined her head. "Although I advise against this option, I have to respect your decision." She knelt on the floor and opened her bag. "I thought it might be beneficial to look at what we're going to use before we try to do anything." She set a plastic tray on the floor, then laid out a bottle of saline, a pair of latex gloves, gauze pads, adhesive strips, and medical glue.

She spread her hands to indicate the assortment. "See? No needles. Madison, please put these gloves on. Cato, are you having any difficulty breathing?" I shook my head, which made her nod. "Okay, that's good. It means your pleural cavity hasn't been penetrated."

As Madison worked her fingers into the second glove, Doc said, "Here's what I'll need you to do. After Cato melts the ice, you're going to flush the wound with saline. The saline itself isn't going to burn, but the pressure from the stream is probably going to feel a bit uncomfortable. After that, Madison, you'll need to pat the area as dry as you can with gauze. Then comes the tricky part. You'll have to pinch the wound to hold the edges together as you apply the glue."

I grimaced at the prospect of the upcoming pain, and another tear leaked free. It rolled down my cheek and plopped onto the pillow, leaving a cool streak behind on my skin.

Madison said, "RC? Do you think maybe you could help with that part? If you can hold the wound together with telekinesis while I glue, I think we can do it."

"I can try," he said.

Doc said, "Once that hard part is done, we'll reinforce the seal with these adhesive strips and cover it with a bandage."

Madison nodded, but she was as white as a sheet and looked as if she might throw up. "Ready, Cato?" she asked weakly.

My breaths were coming in short, shallow gasps. I was on the verge of hyperventilating—the panic attack was creeping over me like an ominous black supercell roaring in. I whispered, "I, uh . . . I-I'm kinda freaking out."

"You have to hold still," Madison warned. "You know the alternative."

I blinked rapidly to keep the flood of tears from spilling, then jerked my head to indicate that I understood. "RC? I think I need you."

He stepped into position just behind Madison and stared at me with a grim, resolute expression. "Here we go," he said, holding one hand over me with his palm facing the ground. I groaned as telekinetic pressure blanketed my body and pushed me down, as if gravity were steadily increasing.

"Melt the blood, Cato," Madison said. "I'll do this as quickly as I can."

I closed my eyes, stole a few more precious seconds to prepare myself, and then focused on my Divinity. As the ice melted, my wound became warm with blood.

I flinched and sucked a breath in through gritted teeth when I felt the cool stream of saline hit the gash, jolting my pain receptors. The liquid didn't burn, but the pressure of it being squirted into my open wound hurt.

Madison's gentle yet firm touch followed as she frantically tried to pat the area dry. She pressed the gauze against my side for a few seconds. "We're going to glue it now, Cato. Bear with me."

"Don't tell me what you're doing," I seethed with a locked jaw. "Just do it."

Her hand pulled away, and then pain ripped through my side. I moaned and squirmed, but I could barely move under RC's hold.

Madison must have been gluing the wound, but I could barely discern the pressure of her fingers amid the dizzying and nauseating pain. More than once, I drifted over the verge of unconsciousness, only to have the pain pull me back. My sense of time was useless—I had no idea how long it took Madison to finish.

I faded out again. In and out . . . I heard Madison's voice talking to me . . . pressure on my side as the adhesives were stuck to my skin to help pin it in place . . . a cool cloth on my forehead . . . someone carrying me . . . I groaned as I was laid down on a cushion . . . everything faded to darkness and silence.

— Chapter Forty-Two —

Embrace

"Hey, sweetheart."

A gentle touch swept across my cheek. "How are you feeling?"

I frowned and forced my eyes open. My mother's face filled my vision. "I brought you some water. Do you think you can sit up?"

My heavy eyelids fell shut again as I mentally cataloged my body. There was a deep, burning pain in my torso where the wound had been sealed. My joints ached, and my head was pounding with a headache that wasn't really a headache, more like a throbbing pressure inside my skull. "I don't feel good," I whispered.

She set the back of her hand against my cheek, then draped her cool palm across my forehead. "You feel hot," she said worriedly. "You're running a fever."

Wes's voice said from farther in the room, "That's not good, Maddie. You need to break that fever immediately."

"You think it's serious?"

"He's a Cryokinetic. I don't need to explain to you that heat and ice don't mix, do I?"

My eyes fluttered open again at the sound of the door opening. Wes said, "I have something that'll help. Have him drink some water and use his cryokinesis. That will help lower his body temperature. I'll be back."

Wes walked out into the hallway, quietly closing the door behind him. RC's voice said, "I can help you prop him up."

I wasn't sure where in the room RC was, but Madison nodded and said, "Thank you. If you can lift him just a little, I can set an extra pillow behind his head."

Telekinetic pressure lifted me from below, pulling out a groan as the movement shifted my sealed wound. Madison slipped a pillow behind me. The pressure eased, and I sank back into the pillows. She stroked my hair out of my eyes and then lifted a glass to my lips. "Here, Cay, drink up."

I rolled my lips together, turning my head away. "Is it . . . just plain water?" I asked, barely moving my mouth to prevent giving her an opening to force anything down my throat.

"It is," she promised.

RC added, "I brought it from the kitchen."

I weakly raised my hand and cupped it around the glass, although Madison was still supporting it for me. The first few swallows were small and slow, and then I drank deeper. Madison tipped the glass as I finished, then pulled it away and set it down on the table. "That probably tasted good, huh? Do you think you can make some ice for me now?"

I closed my eyes, letting my head fall back against the pillow with a long sigh. "I want to sleep."

"You can sleep," she said, slipping her hand inside mine and giving a squeeze, "in a little bit. I really need you to make some ice for me. Wes thinks it'll help cool you down. Come on, Cato. Can you make a ball of ice? Let's say about the size of a baseball. Could you please do that for me?"

I made a noise in my throat to acknowledge that I'd heard. I frowned, focusing inward, searching for the point of light in my center. Why was it so hard to find? Cold. I needed to find the cold blue Divinity.

Finally, I felt the faint stirring of power deep in my core. Now that I had it, I concentrated on that point, on reawakening the light and dredging it up from the depths. I directed the flow to my right hand—the one Madison wasn't holding. A hard ball of ice started to form. I kept up the current to engorge the ice ball inside my fist until it was large enough to satisfy my mother's specifications, and then I wordlessly opened my eyes, reached out, and offered it to her.

Madison smiled and let go of my hand to claim it. "Thank you." She glanced over her shoulder at the sound of the door opening and closing again.

Wes came up behind her. "Eyes look a little brighter already," he commented. "That's a good sign."

I closed my eyes as Madison draped her hand across my forehead again. "Still warm, though," she said.

"I've got just the remedy." I peered up at Wes as she removed her hand. He was holding a glass vial containing green sludge that turned my stomach just looking at it.

"What is that?" Madison asked with a curious but suspicious frown.

"Witch's brew," I identified.

She glanced at me. "How do you know that?"

Wes said, "Because it's the same brew I offered to Jay when he was shot with a crossbow. Tastes like piss, let me tell you, but it'll stabilize your condition and help your body heal. Should also take care of the fever. It will make you sleepy, though."

"Yeah, I know." I remembered how groggy Jay had been after taking it. But it had seemed to eliminate his pain and accelerate his recovery. I held out my hand, and Wes set the vial in my weak grasp.

"Whoa, wait a minute," Madison protested. "Do you even know what's in it? What about side effects?"

Wes snapped, "I wouldn't have given it to him if it wasn't safe."

"Cato, are you absolutely sure you want to drink that? Doc prescribed you painkillers and antibiotics. We can—"

"Trust me, Maddie," Wes interrupted. "This is better than anything Doc could have prescribed."

I uncorked the vial and almost threw up when I caught a whiff of the stench, which smelled like swamp muck mixed with rancid meat. "I recommend holding your breath," Wes advised. "And chase it with this. That'll make it slightly more bearable." He handed me a shot glass of yellowish liquid I identified by smell as pickle juice.

I stared at the Witch's brew. "So . . . what's in it?"

"Believe me, you really don't want to know."

I held my breath and tried to gulp down the sludge before I could think too much about it. But as I brought my head back down, I gagged, and the brew came right back up in all of its unpleasantness.

"Hold it in," Wes warned. I clapped my palm over my mouth. Teary-eyed, I forced myself to swallow again, then downed the shot of pickle juice and leaned back against the pillows to keep everything down.

As revolting as it had tasted, the brew took effect almost immediately; the pain melted away from my wound, and the persistent ache left my head and joints. Barely moving my lips at the risk of having to swallow my own vomit again, I muttered, "You lied. Piss would have been a major improvement."

Wes chuckled as he reclaimed the vial and shot glass from me. "True, but that extra shot helped, didn't it?"

Actually . . . it had. Something about the acidity of the pickle juice seemed to have countered whatever was in the Witch's brew, neutralizing any residual aftertaste.

My body was already shutting down for a restful sleep. My breathing had evened out into a slow and steady rhythm, and my muscles had completely relaxed. I felt as if I were melting into the cushions.

Far off in the distance, the deep undulations of his voice echoing as if at the end of a long, empty tunnel, Wes said, "I also brought this salve. I know Doc wanted to keep the wound taped to make sure it stays closed, but Cato's not going to be moving for a while. I promise this will also help to speed up the healing. I recommend removing the adhesive strips, putting this paste on the wound, and covering it with a bandage . . ."

His voice drifted out of range. A softer, female voice answered. They went back and forth. I could hear the tones and vibrations of the voices, but not the words. My shirt was lifted up, and something sticky was peeled off my skin. Then, I felt a cold, creamy wetness that smelled like herbs and had a surprisingly pleasant icy tingle that warmed into a buzzing heat, as if my molecules were pulsating in response.

A hand on my forehead again. "He feels cooler already."

"Good."

The pressure of the hand was replaced with the light touch of a damp cloth. "Are you still awake, Cato?" came my mother's voice.

"Mm-hmm."

Her fingers trailed across my cheek. "How are you feeling now?"

"Mmm. Sleepy," I managed to force out, the word slurring.

"I think you're going to feel a lot better when you wake up." She started humming that eerily familiar tune I remembered from childhood, the lilt of her voice carrying me away to a state of calm and peace. Her fingers continued to trace soothing patterns across my cheek. She paused from the lullaby to whisper, "Thank you for trusting me to help you. I really missed taking care of you."

The song resumed, and I was lost in the land of slumber.

I drifted in and out of an eternal place that might have been between Realms. The time I spent there could have been hours or years— I had no concept of time's passage.

I did remember waking up for a few intervals. Once, when someone lifted me up and pressed the rim of a glass to my lips, then the cool trickle of water filling my mouth. My body instinctively knew to swallow. I drank for as long as the person holding me allowed before laying me back down on the soft pillow.

Another time, it was dark. I was aware enough to open my eyes and study mysterious mounds nearby that drew air in and out, causing the lumps to rise and fall with deep, even motions. I finally pieced together that my lab-family was with me. They had pushed sofas and armchairs up against the couch where I was sleeping so we could all be together, cradled inside a makeshift nest with the backs of the furniture penning us in.

Sometimes, I drifted close enough to the surface of my hibernation to hear voices. Sometimes, I could even make out a few words. But my eyes were too heavy to open. I felt as if I were underwater in Chel's lake, but when I reached for the surface, my hand couldn't break through. Inevitably, I sank back into the silent, dark depths where I could float in timeless existence.

"Cato . . . Hey, sweetheart. Can you drink some water for me? Come on, Cay . . ."

The liquid hit the back of my throat. I gasped and sputtered, coughing it back up.

"No, wait," I croaked, reaching for the retreating glass. I grasped it with a weak grip and pulled it back to my mouth. The hand holding the glass kept it steady for me as I guzzled the cool water. I settled back against a woman's chest with a sigh.

"You seem more alert," came Madison's voice. My gaze followed her hand as it set the empty glass down on the table and then returned to blanket my forehead. "No fever. How do you feel?"

I pondered the question for a moment. How *did* I feel? Tired, groggy, and stiff, but the pain I remembered seemed to have left me. "I feel like I slept for a year."

I turned my head. Finn and Reese were dozing in the armchair. By my feet, Ash was perched on the arm of the couch. She smiled when we made eye contact. "Welcome back," she greeted.

My hand crept to the wound. "How bad is it?" I asked, afraid to look. "I don't have to see Doc again, do I?"

Madison replied, "Not unless you act reckless and get yourself hurt again. Doc's procedure stopped the bleeding, and Wes's remedies from the Ghost Realm sped up the healing process. You're almost as good as new."

I tried to grip my shirt, but my body was still waking up. My fingers were numb, clumsy, and next to useless as I shakily lifted my shirt and craned my neck to look. I expected to see a gash glued and taped together. Instead, the wound looked as though it was in its final stages of healing. The new skin was pink and tender beneath a flaking scab. Even the cuts from jumping through the window had healed.

"How long was I out?"

"About two and a half days," Ash said.

I struggled to sit up, and Madison gently helped me from behind. "Don't push yourself too hard, Cay."

"What about Hassing?"

Ash shrugged. "No sign of him."

I wanted to feel relieved, but a pit settled in my stomach. Hopefully, no sign was good news. Azar probably would have retaliated with full force if his captain was dead, so that must mean Hassing had survived my fatal blow.

I ran my tongue over my dry lips. "I'm still thirsty."

"I'll get you some more water," said Madison. She picked up the empty glass and rose now that I was sitting up on my own.

I labored to haul my legs over the side of the couch. "I'll come."

"You need to take it slow—"

"I need to get my blood flowing," I countered as I scooted to the edge of the cushion and tested a little weight on my feet. "I feel like a statue." My joints cracked when I stood and swayed in place as my body recalibrated to find its balance.

Ash hopped to her feet, but I said, "Maybe you should stay. Finn and Reese might freak out if they wake up and everyone is gone." As she glanced between the twins and me in clear indecision, I added, "I'm just going to the kitchen. You're both treating me like I'm made of glass. I think I can handle a short walk."

She folded her arms and reluctantly lowered herself back onto the couch.

Madison let me set the pace. As much as I wanted to prove that I was fine, my slow, unsteady shuffle into the great room wasn't convincing anyone that I was back to normal yet. My mother's unwavering stare made my skin crawl.

"Did I miss anything important while I was sleeping?" I asked to break the tense silence.

Her unexpected hesitation tied my stomach into a knot. "Nothing you need to concern yourself with right now," she finally replied with an absent airiness in her tone as we entered the library.

"What does that mean?"

"Exactly what I said."

"Madison—"

"Mom."

"I'm serious. Did something happen?"

She stepped in front of me and pushed open the swinging door to the kitchen, then held it for me to follow. "Your classmate was admitted to the hospital a couple of days ago."

"What classmate?" I seized the edge of the counter for balance. "Did Hassing hurt someone? I thought I kept everyone safe."

Madison pressed her lips together as she crossed the kitchen, turned the faucet on, filled the glass, and returned to me. She set the glass on the granite countertop. "Chase had to be treated for a broken nose, frostbite, and second-degree burns on his arm."

I wrapped my hand around the glass but didn't lift it. My sluggish mind was struggling to replay the events from the schoolyard. Without a word, I raised the glass to my lips and downed the water in a few deep gulps.

"That's too bad," I finally said as I set the glass down.

"You don't sound very upset."

My gaze flitted up to find her while I kept my head tilted down. "Could I please have some more?"

She sighed, seized the glass, and returned to the sink. "Cato, I need to make sure you understand that hurting humans is unacceptable. You and Ash are both in trouble."

I felt the heat of my Divinity stir as I glared at her back. "If you want me to say I'm sorry, I'm not. He shouldn't have touched Ash the way he did, and if he ever does it to her again, or if he ever touches Vivian against her wishes like that, I'll do a lot worse than break his nose. Punish me if you want, but I don't regret my actions."

The sound of running water shut off. Madison turned and stared at me as if having a hard time comprehending my words. "Are you saying he touched Ash inappropriately?"

"Yes. He deserved to get burned, and he deserved to get punched in the face. The frostbite was collateral damage—I was trying to put out the fire. The rest of it was his own fault."

Madison nodded. "Okay." She returned and set the glass of water in front of me. "That puts the situation in a new perspective. I'll talk to the principal and his parents, but I do still need to talk to Ash."

"Why?" I demanded before downing the water and finally quenching my insatiable thirst.

"Because setting students on fire is still not acceptable," she replied, keeping her voice calm and steady. "As her acting guardian, I do have to address that."

"But it was an accident."

"A boy ended up in the hospital with second-degree burns. Regardless of the circumstances that led up to it—"

"That's not fair. You're defending him?"

"Absolutely not. What he did was wrong. But so is lighting people on fire, Cato. I just want to talk to her and hear her side of the story—"

"And punish her, right?" I snapped.

Madison exhaled to stay calm. "I don't know yet. Chase's parents are demanding some sort of punishment, but according to his testimony, all he did was invite Ash to come watch the basketball team practice after school, and then she set him on fire without provocation. He conveniently left out the part about inappropriately touching her."

"There were a lot of witnesses, including Vivian and Trey," I said. "If he says he didn't touch her, he's lying."

"I still need to talk to Ash."

"Please don't bury her in the ground."

"I'm not going t— Wait, what? You mean ground her?"

"Yeah, that's what I said. You're going to yell at her, aren't you?"

"This doesn't concern you."

Madison headed for the door, but I sidestepped so I was in front of her, blocking her path. "Please," I begged. "It wasn't her fault."

My mother folded her arms. I could tell by her tight lips, rigid body stance, and deepening frown that she was losing patience. "Cato, move.

Now."

I swallowed but held my ground. "It wasn't her fault," I repeated. "It really wasn't. Ash reacted the way she did because . . ."

"Because what?"

I shifted. It wasn't my whisper to tell. But I had to make my mother understand. "Because . . . she was . . . abused when we were at that place."

I'd caught Madison off guard—she stood frozen for a moment, and her impatient frown changed to one of confusion and suspicion. "What exactly are you saying?"

I pressed my fingertips into my temples and hung my head. My lab-sister's extra suffering still made me sick, especially because I'd been helpless to stop it. I stared blankly at my feet. "The night guard . . . he liked to . . ." I squirmed; I could feel my cheeks reddening. "He took Ash into a closet where there weren't any cameras. Almost every night. If she resisted, he beat her. They'd be gone for a while. When they came back, she was always crying."

I glanced up to see that Madison had turned ashen at my disturbing story. Although she said nothing, I continued, "There was one night when he brought two of his friends who patrol other Projects. They were gone for hours. Ash cried the whole rest of the night."

In a hoarse voice, she asked, "Did Agent Kovak know what was going on?"

"*He* knew. There are security cameras everywhere, and Ash had bruises when the guard was too rough. *He* didn't care as long as *His* test subject wasn't too damaged for the experiments."

Madison seemed to be struggling to collect her thoughts. "Did, ah, did the guard do anything like that to the rest of you?"

I shook my head. "But I knew when Kit got old enough . . ." I hung my head again, the shame engulfing me. My eyes were burning, and I angrily swiped at a tear about to spill over the edge. "I couldn't save her. I was locked in my cage, and all I could do was sit there and watch him take Ash away night after night, and I knew the horrible things he was going to do to her, but I was so helpless. I wanted to protect her, but . . . I couldn't."

"You aren't to blame, Cato. You have to understand that. Okay?"

"Okay," I echoed in a whisper, but I only partially believed that. The terrified look on Ash's face every time those doors slid open after Lightsout would haunt me forever. The sound of her crying—the fearful whimpers and quiet pleas when the night guard yanked her out of the cage by her hair—the utter defeat and broken spirit every time he brought her back. Ash was my lab-sister. I should have been able to protect her.

I took a breath and exhaled to clear my head. "That's why she panicked when Chase put his arm around her waist and tried to pull her closer. Her mind went back to those nights. So . . . Ash isn't in trouble, right? Please don't yell at her."

"I won't. Thank you for telling me. I still want to talk to her, though."

She shifted forward half a step, but I still didn't budge to let her pass. "You promise?"

"I promise."

Finally, I stepped aside. Madison approached the door, then paused to glance back at me. "Thank you for trusting me." I nodded. My throat felt swollen, so I couldn't speak.

Madison pushed the swinging door open. I trailed after her, the guilt suffocating me. I shouldn't have betrayed Ash's trust. That whisper wasn't supposed to leave the confidence of our lab-family, and now I was certain that Ash would hate me.

When Madison reached the den, she twisted the doorknob and gently pushed the door open. "Hey, Ash," she greeted with a wavering smile.

Madison's overly saccharine tone immediately put me on edge, so I wasn't surprised when Ash leapt to her feet in alarm, one arm instantly raised over her shoulder to clutch her staff. Finn and Reese stirred—restless, but still asleep.

My mother held up both hands. "It's okay," she said. "I just want to talk to you." Her hands fell to the clasp of her weapon belt, which she removed and handed to me.

Ash's anxious gaze shifted to find me. "I'm right here, right outside the door," I promised. "You can call if you need me."

Ash drew her weapon as Madison slowly entered the room and closed the door behind her, although she left it open a few inches so they could have privacy but not be completely shut in. I peered through the crack to monitor their conversation.

Madison gestured to the couch. "Would you like to sit?"

Ash shook her head. Her right foot shifted back while the staff remained held at a diagonal in front of her body. That was a defensive move; all she had to do was bend her knees to be in a true fighting stance. My mother no doubt recognized that.

As she crossed the room at a leisurely pace, she said, "I'm going to sit, if that's okay. You're welcome to join me at any time, but you don't have to if you don't want to." She seated herself delicately, crossing her legs and folding her hands in her lap to strike an unassuming pose that wouldn't come across as threatening. Although some of the tension left Ash's shoulders and she lowered her staff a bit, her feet stayed planted.

Madison started talking in a low voice, but now that she was on the other side of the room with her back to me, I couldn't make out the words.

I watched Ash. Her expression remained stony for a few minutes while my mother spoke, and then she seemed to lose the strength to hold her staff—she lowered her arms until one end of the weapon rested on the floor. Her teeth caught her lower lip; she nodded and started to speak, but then her face crumpled and her shoulders began to shake with sobs.

Madison leaned forward as she spoke, and Ash bowed her head as if in pain. One hand rose to cup her mouth in an attempt to contain the sobs. She fell to her knees, her hand sliding down the staff until she was kneeling with it held erect in front of her.

My grip tightened on the doorknob. Should I go in? Ash hadn't called for me . . . Did she need me to read her body language and come to her aid?

Madison slid off the couch so she was kneeling on the floor, too. She scooted forward—but not too close—and held out her arms in an open invitation.

Ash sobbed, then dropped her staff and crawled toward her. She threw her arms around Madison, who returned the embrace and held my lab-sister's shaking body.

Ash buried her face into Madison's shoulder, her raw cries carrying across the room. Madison stroked Ash's hair and held her close while my lab-sister released the sorrow she'd been harboring all alone for so long.

I relaxed, leaning my temple against the doorframe. I'd give anything to my lab-sister. My support, my loyalty, my protection. But this was a role I couldn't fulfill for her.

When was the last time, I wondered, she could feel safe wrapped in a mom's arms? What had happened at that place was deplorable and sickening, and although I sympathized with Ash, her trauma was something I could never fully understand. She needed a woman.

She needed a mom.

So, since I couldn't be what she needed right now, I'd give her mine.

— Chapter Forty-Three —

Tempest

Unfortunately, my mother decided that we weren't eating enough to meet Doc's minimum weight quota. Her solution—decreeing a daily breakfast mandate on top of our dinner requirement.

Poor Finn and Reese had to be woken up for the 7:00 a.m. breakfast call, and they couldn't stop yawning. Kit was the only one who seemed happy about breakfast. She hummed and swung her bare feet as she merrily stuffed scrambled eggs in her mouth. Two chairs were vacant at the table—Ero's and Wes's.

I nudged my full glass of orange juice, wishing it was water instead. The dining room was too quiet. Just the *tick* of the grandfather clock in the foyer, the clink of silverware, and Kit's muffled, atonal humming.

Madison cleared her throat, accidentally triggering the twins to sit up straight. "Cato. Ash," she said solemnly. "I thought you should know that I talked to Principal Solwitz and the Johnsons yesterday. Chase's father is still insisting on some type of punishment for what happened to his son."

Ash bowed her head. "I understand," she said in resignation as I snapped, "This isn't fair. Are we grounded?"

"No."

We both stared at her in shock. I said, "Really?"

"Really. Since the incident, several more girls have come forward to report Chase for inappropriate comments and unwanted physical contact. I think Mr. Johnson is going to have his hands full dealing with his son's conduct. That being said, Wes agreed to pay the medical bills as a little extra incentive to drop any further complaints."

Madison set her fork down and leaned forward as she swept her gaze around the table. "I want to make sure I'm crystal clear. You can *not* use your powers to harm humans, either purposefully or accidentally. No exceptions. We got lucky this time. I know we've become more familiar and comfortable with each other over these past weeks, but city council still expects me to keep you in check as your guardian. Are we on the same page?"

Kit shrank into her chair, squirming under the weight of the warning. Finn and Reese solemnly inclined their heads even though their conditioning prevented them from so much as thinking about harming a human. Jay, RC, and Ash nodded.

My mother had ended her little speech with her gaze fixed on Axel, and I knew that wasn't an accident. He narrowed his eyes, returning Madison's stern look with a defiant glare.

Vivian forced a smile in the suffocating tension and said, "Way to go, Ash. You put that misogynistic jerk in his place, and now other girls are brave enough to stand up for themselves, too."

Despite the praise, Ash clenched her jaw. Her eyes flared, and steam rose from her body with waves of radiating heat.

Vivian's smile faded. "What's wrong? You've sort of become a feminist icon at school. Aren't you proud?"

"No." Ash sniffed and swiped the back of her fist across her nose. "I'm sick of undeserved praise, and that's all I ever seem to get. What I did to Chase was an accident."

The steam was darkening into smoke. "I didn't stand up for myself. I should have been assertive and told him to stop or pushed him away. Instead, I panicked and lost control of my Divinity, then ran away like a coward. I don't deserve praise for that. I'm so tired of saying thank you for empty compliments. Just once, I wish I could get credit for something I actually worked for, like training hard or taking down a strong opponent or being brave. But nobody ever seems to notice those accomplishments. All they care about is how I look or what I'm wearing."

The crisp, cringe-inducing pitch of the interrupting smoke detector made us all wince. RC waved his hand in annoyance, and the gadget was yanked out of its dock in the ceiling. It smashed to the wood floor and broke into pieces, effectively silenced.

Ash took a deep, steadying breath. The smoke dissipated, and she raised her head to reveal a placid, expressionless face, as if she'd put on a mask. "I apologize for being petty. I should just shut up and be grateful for the compliment."

Vivian seemed rather diminished in the wake of Ash's outburst. She pushed the eggs around her plate and said, "Actually, I don't think you're being petty at all. You're right. You put your life at risk every day, and you train just as hard as Cato and Jay and RC. You deserve way more credit than people give you."

Wes appeared in the open doorway, his pajamas wrapped in a silk robe and a newspaper tucked under one arm. "Ah, I thought I smelled something good," he said with a smile.

The tension snapped like a rubber band breaking. Ash subtly thumbed away lingering tears as Axel muttered, "Leave it to a dog to come begging when it smells food."

"Well, good morning to you too," Wes replied cheerily. Axel glowered at him. The werewolf casually stepped over the broken smoke detector on the floor and said, "Ope, guess I'll need to replace that."

Madison greeted, "Morning, Wes. Eggs are on the stove, and I just made a fresh pot of coffee." He grunted in acknowledgment as he set the newspaper down on his chair and pushed through the swinging door into the kitchen.

The tense silence crept in around us again. Madison awkwardly said, "I hope everything tastes good."

She received a few nods and *mm-hmms* in response. "Finn? Reese? Have you ever eaten scrambled eggs before?" They kept their gazes on their plates and shook their heads. "Do you like them?" They nodded.

Wes pushed the door open with his foot and returned with a plate of eggs and toast in one hand and a mug of coffee in the other. He stopped short, as if instinctively, when a butter knife shot through the air and embedded in the wall, barely missing him. Wes gave RC a steely stare. "I take it you're not a morning person."

RC slouched lower in his chair. "I saw a spider."

"Hmm." Wes calmly plucked the knife out of the wall and set the plate, mug, and butter knife on the table. As he picked up the newspaper to take his seat, he grumbled, "Just once, I would love to have a meal together without my house or possessions being damaged."

"Sorry," RC mumbled.

Madison leaned forward, her attention still on the twins. "You know, I don't even know what your voices sound like."

The twins raised their heads just enough to blink at her, expressionless and silent as usual.

"Give it a rest, Maddie," Wes muttered through his mouthful of eggs as he skimmed the paper. "They aren't going to talk."

She leaned back in her chair. "Ero says you respond best to logic and reasoning. You know I've never punished your lab-siblings for speaking. That sets a lot of precedents, right? If they're allowed to speak, so are you."

Although they were watching her, the twins made no indication of breaking their vow of silence.

Madison waited for a few seconds to give them time to respond, then said, "Okay. Consider this: Vivian follows two sets of rules. Here, she can say whatever she wants whenever she wants. But when she's in class at school, she isn't allowed to speak unless she raises her hand and receives permission from the teacher. Let's apply this logic to your situation. At the AGC, Agent Kovak expected you to obey his rules. But here, you need to learn a new set of rules."

The twins cocked their heads, studying Madison keenly as they digested her argument. I nibbled on a corner of toast, curious to see if my mother might actually achieve the impossible and convince Finn and Reese to speak. Her argument was based in logic, but she was contradicting years of harsh lessons taught through shock collars, beatings, and forfeited meals.

"How about it?" she pressured with a kind smile. "I'd love to have a real conversation with you. Why don't we try implementing school rules to start? You can raise your hand if you have something to say, and then when a human acknowledges you, you'll know it's okay to speak because you have permission."

They glanced uncertainly at each other. Reese scratched at his neck, as if his skin hadn't forgotten the pain of electricity from a training collar. Finn took a breath and opened his mouth, but then he froze, immediately looking guilty about the Rule he was about to break.

"I give you my permission," said Madison. "You're free to speak."

Finn lowered his gaze. "Okay," he whispered.

"We understand the new rule," said Reese.

"Yes, great!" Madison cried, clapping her hands together. "I'm so proud of you!"

She was beaming, but Finn and Reese looked absolutely miserable, their gazes darting around the room as though they expected an assailant to pop up and punish them.

Axel sneered and said, "You know, Bot, you don't need permission. You're free. You don't have to give a shit what humans want anymore."

"Axel!" Jay and Madison scolded. Surprised by the unified reprimand, they stared at each other across the table. The twins shook their heads in silent condemnation of Axel's disrespect toward humans.

"Mrs. Tarrow?" Kit inquired, her voice like bells as she kicked her feet in the air while happily chewing. "Where's Mr. Tarrow? How come we've never seen him?"

Her face suddenly pallid, Madison stared down at her plate with a haunted, vacant expression. Vivian's brow twitched in pain, and she hung her head. "He died, Kit," my blood-sister said. "In a car accident a long time ago."

Wes glanced up from his newspaper to look questioningly at Madison, who choked out, "That's right."

Finn and Reese frowned as they glanced between Madison, Vivian, and Wes in apparent confusion. "Oh," Kit sighed in sympathy, her feet stilling.

Axel leaned forward with sudden interest. A devilish smile made a foreboding appearance as he stared my mother down. "Oh-ho-ho, I love family secrets," he said. "And this feels like a big one."

Madison dropped her fork with a loud clatter. Puzzled, Vivian and I turned to face her. I asked, "What are you talking about, Ax?" while still staring at Madison.

"I don't know yet. Why don't you ask your mommy? Those two little words she just said weren't the truth, were they, Maddie? And now you're nervous." He had an ornery gleam in his eyes while Madison's expression was a cross between livid and horrified.

"I'm not. I have no idea what you're talking about," she snapped.

"No? Then why is your heart beating faster? You're perspiring. Your blood pressure is rising. I can smell the hormones being released into your body. It doesn't matter what you say—I can read your physical changes like a polygraph. You're *lying*."

"Mom?" Vivian said slowly. "What's he saying? Dad died in a car accident . . . didn't he?"

Axel mimicked, "Didn't he?"

Madison glowered at him in silent rage. "No," she finally whispered.

I processed the revelation without emotion. I had only recently learned of my father's demise—the specifics were minor, inconsequential details. It didn't matter to me how he died. Either way, he was gone. But Vivian's eyes widened as if she'd been betrayed in the worst possible way.

Our mother swallowed hard and tried to explain, "You were both so young—"

"So you lied to us for fourteen years?" Vivian demanded.

"I was going to tell you when you were older, but . . ."

Calmer than my blood-sister, I asked, "How did he actually die?"

She pushed scrambled eggs across her plate without taking a bite. "Jaxon was a scientist. I hunted ghosts, and he studied ectoplasm. We were a great team, until . . . a kálos killed him during a field experiment."

Vivian said, "Why didn't you just tell us that? Why did you lie?"

"Because you were both little kids. Maybe I was wrong to lie, but I didn't want you to be afraid of a monster coming to get you like it got your daddy. I hope you can forgive me." She shot Axel a look of daggers. "Are you happy now?"

"Ecstatic," he said dryly. Now that he'd effectively ruined a fourteen-year-old secret and fabricated enough friction in the room to create an electrical storm with one more spark, he propped his feet on the table in boredom.

Madison sighed in defeat and pressed her fingers into her temples, leaving Jay to say, "Axel, feet off." The half-breed made a point to roll his eyes before obeying.

My mother pushed her chair out. She rose without a word and drifted out of the dining room, leaving her half-empty plate on the table. The kitchen door swung shut behind her.

Silent tears dripped down Vivian's cheeks and landed on her plate. I glared at Axel and said, "Did you have to do that?"

"What?" he retorted with a shrug. "I'm not the one who lied."

I stood up. "Bloody Scout, why is it so hard for you to get along with anybody?"

He stood, too. "Because this is stupid—eating meals together, pretending we're one big family. We're not. Madison can try to play mommy all she wants, but I *had* a mom, and she was ten times the mom yours can ever be. I don't want a replacement. It's just a *game*." He pointed at Vivian. "That's *your* sister, but she ain't ever gonna be mine, and Madison can just go to hell, and Wes, I don't know why you're even here."

"It's *my* house," Wes muttered indignantly.

Axel shook his head. "Why am I wasting my time with all of this?" He stormed out, leaving a suffocating silence in his wake. Slowly, I lowered myself back into my chair.

Wes was the only one with an appetite left. He kept eating as if nothing had happened. Vivian's red-rimmed eyes were about to overflow again.

"You okay?" I asked. She squeezed the tears free and shook her head.

Kit flattened her ears and tilted her chin down. "Vivian?" she inquired shyly. Viv blinked, and a single tear spilled as she turned to face Kit. "You can still be my sister, if you want."

Vivian smiled and brushed the tear away with her thumb. "Thank you, Kit."

Ash frowned at her plate, her fingers balling into fists. RC, his mind no doubt on his blood-family, locked his jaw. Nobody else spoke. Finn and Reese couldn't look more uncomfortable from the surge of unpleasant thoughts.

Vivian pushed her chair back and rose. "I have a meeting with my teacher before class, so I have to get there early. I'll see you after school." She wiped her eyes again as she strode toward the front doors, careful not to smear her eyeliner. In one smooth move, she scooped up her backpack and walked out the door.

His gaze still trained on the newspaper, Wes said, "Well, that was an eventful way to start the morning." He seized his mug and took a sip, then added under his breath, "Can't wait to do it again at dinner."

Jay said, "Are you going to make us stay, or can we go?"

The werewolf peered at him over the top of the paper. "I don't care what you do." His gaze fell back to the print. "Maddie's the one who insisted on breakfast, and she's not here. Do whatever you want."

With his blessing, we all stood up in sync. Finn and Reese departed for the grand staircase. Kit left to scope out the school while the rest of us lingered in the foyer. Jay asked, "Are you sure you're up for patrol, Cato?"

"Don't coddle me," I snapped. "I'm healed and ready to go."

"You're not completely back to full strength. I want us to scout as one unit today."

"But—"

"Prove to me that you've fully recovered, and then tomorrow we can break into the usual teams."

Ash touched my arm. "It's all right. I think it's for the best."

RC waved his hand, and the front door swung open. As soon as I stepped outside, I knew something was wrong. It was *hot*. A miserable, sweltering heat that instantly snatched my breath away and drained my strength. The heavy moisture made me feel as if I were sweating even though my body cooled itself internally.

Jay looked up at the hazy sky as he stepped onto the porch. "I bet we have an Atmokinetic in town."

We headed down the front walk toward the street. As much as I wanted to prove that I'd regained my strength, I had to admit that scouting together as a group was ideal under these conditions. Atmokinetics could be great allies or deadly enemies to Cryokinetics. They could give me all the moisture and cold I needed to use my Divinity at maximum efficiency, or they could just as easily disempower me with dry desert air. Based on our track record of ghosts in Phantom Heights, this one probably wouldn't be friendly if we crossed paths.

"Hey, Cato."

We all turned at the unexpected voice. Trey was lingering on the sidewalk, a backpack slung over one shoulder, his dripping blond hair plastered to his head. He smiled uneasily. "Is Viv coming? Are you walking us to school today?"

"No, she already left. Said she had to be there early today."

"Oh. Okay. So, are you guys going on patrol?"

"Yeah," I muttered, tugging at the neckline of my shirt. *Damn, this heat is going to be the death of me.*

"Can . . . can I come?"

"Don't you have to go to school?"

"I can skip." He lowered his voice. "But don't tell my parents. Or your mom."

"Um . . ." I instinctively looked at Jay. Trey followed my gaze and redirected his pleading, puppy-dog stare onto the leader.

Jay didn't look particularly thrilled about the request. He possessed an air of weariness, as if he was already exhausted by the thought of having a ward to watch.

"I can fight," Trey blurted in Jay's hesitation. "Really. I've trained with Madison, and I can hold my own. I swear I won't get in your way."

Jay said sternly, "Only if you can keep up and you promise to do what I say if there's any trouble."

"Absolutely," said Trey as he bobbed his head. "Your word is my command."

Jay started walking. "We'll see."

Trey gleefully fell into step beside me. "Cato and I used to scout Phantom Heights together all the time. Right, Cay?"

I humored him with a faint smile but kept my attention forward. "This'll be a little different."

Ash wiped her hand across her forehead. Two blocks later, she and I shed our cloaks. "Hey," I said, "any room in your backpack for these?"

"Yeah, sure," Trey replied, instantly dropping to his knees. "It's just notebooks in here anyway." He stuffed Ash's cloak inside but then hesitated when I passed mine to him. "Uh, Cato . . . this is kind of a weird question, but . . . could I . . . ?"

"What?" I stared blankly at him. His pink face was deepening into a scorching red, but I couldn't tell if the cause was embarrassment or the stifling heat. "You want to wear my cloak?"

"Can I?" he asked, perking up. "Just to try it on?"

"Sure, I don't care," I muttered with a shrug. While he threw the gray cloak over his shoulders, I peeled off my shirt, although I opted to keep the gauntlets and gloves on.

Trey hesitated at the sight of my bare chest. "Whoa. Some scar you got, Cay."

I glanced down at the long pink line of scar tissue that started at my collarbone and trailed down the center of my torso. "Yeah."

"What happened?"

I tossed my shirt to him. Understanding that I had no intention of answering, he shoved it into the backpack and then held out his arms, beaming. "So? Do I look like a kálos?"

I didn't have the heart to tell him that he looked like a nerd playing dress-up. The gray cloak was an odd addition to his blue jeans and T-shirt, and the backpack underneath the Avilésian garment gave him a lumpy, hunchbacked form.

"No," RC said, turning away and resuming the walk. Ash fought a grin and followed.

Unabashed, Trey shrugged and marched along with us, although I was sure he must be sweltering beneath my cloak.

Axel could have sniffed the intruder out in a matter of seconds, but he was nowhere to be found after the morning's outburst. Trey wiped his brow and said, "I don't remember this heat advisory in the forecast."

"Jay thinks there's an Atmokinetic affecting the weather," I said.

"Oh, that makes sense! So, how do we find him? Or her. The ghost. Kálos."

Without turning around, Jay replied in a measured tone, "We patrol as usual until we sense the intruder or find something out of the ordinary."

"Right. Got it." Trey was quiet for a minute, then said, "Hey, uh, I was wondering if . . . maybe . . . I could train with you guys sometimes. I want to be a better fighter. The way you took on Captain Hassing— that was amazing. I want to learn to fight ghosts in hand-to-hand combat."

I said, "I thought Madison was training you."

"Well, yeah. Don't get me wrong—she's great. But there's no way her training will ever get me to the level you're at."

Jay snapped, "I don't mean to sound harsh, but you won't be able to keep up. We can't afford to waste our training time teaching you the basics."

"I'm a fast learner. Can't you train me like you trained Cato?"

Jay shot him a glare over his shoulder. "I didn't train Cato."

Trey turned to me. "Then how'd you learn to fight like that? I know you weren't that skilled before you went to the AGC."

"You sort of trained me," I said quietly, my gaze on Jay's back. "You gave me tips and corrected me when I made errors."

Jay shook his head. "You want to know how Cato learned to fight? He faced us in the Arena and lost, over and over and over again until he learned from his mistakes. We beat him until he was unconscious. We were all starved before the matches so we were fighting for food as a reward. Last one standing got to eat while the others went hungry. I don't think that's the kind of training regimen you had in mind."

Trey dropped his gaze and stared at his feet as we walked. The tense silence was somehow even more suffocating than the overwhelming heat. I wouldn't have blamed Trey if he buckled under the hostility and chose to go to school instead of continuing the patrol.

Finally, he said, "I can't even begin to imagine what you've been through. But I stood in the Arena when I went to the AGC. And I sat in your cage. And I know what the texture of that tasteless paste feels like in my mouth. I know, better than anyone else in Phantom Heights, what kind of hellhole you escaped from. I'd still like to train with you, if you'll let me. I'm ready to take the bruises and push my body to its limits."

Jay didn't answer. I said, "He could always start with laps and basic exercises to get stronger while we train."

"We'll see how today goes and if he can follow orders," Jay replied.

"I won't let you down," Trey promised.

The day passed without any sign of the unwelcome weather-changer or a chance for Trey to prove his worth to Jay. The stifling air seemed to leech away our energy, even dampening Trey's optimistic attitude until we were all trudging along in silence.

Ash and I both downed water as often as we could to stay hydrated. The only slight relief for me was that it was a humid heat, which made the others miserable but gave me plenty of moisture in the air to freeze and then melt in our cupped hands when we needed to drink.

Phantom Heights was abnormally and ominously quiet. The weather seemed to infect the town's inhabitants with chronic laziness, and apparently it made the Ghost Realm more appealing because we didn't encounter a single ghost all day.

Trey glanced at his watch as the scorching sun dipped below the buildings. The shade brought no relief. "School's over," he announced. "Hopefully I didn't miss anything too important."

Jay suddenly halted, and Trey plowed into him from behind. "Sorry—" he said as he backpedaled, but Jay held up his hand for silence.

"There," said Jay, pointing.

We all tilted our heads to follow his indication. Up above, a lone figure stood on the edge of a rooftop, arms crossed, cloak shifting in a weak breeze that felt like a dragon's hot breath.

Trey drew an ectogun, but the ghost didn't seem to be aware of us. "Why isn't he attacking?" Trey whispered.

Jay shook his head. "I don't know. But I don't like it." He held out his hand. "I'll Blink us up there."

Ash set her hand in his while I placed mine on his shoulder and extended my other to Trey. My friend started to reach for me, then drew back. "Blinking makes me sick and disoriented," he said. "I won't be in a state to fight."

"I'll take him," said RC. He held out both hands. A manhole cover rose from the street as a sidewalk sign of restaurant specials levitated away from a storefront and drifted toward him. "We'll meet you there."

Jay inclined his head. Ash and I braced ourselves for the uncomfortable vacuum of Blinking between spaces. When we opened our eyes, we were on the rooftop. I shivered. Behind us was a single metal door that likely led to a staircase. Before us was the ghostly stranger.

He didn't acknowledge us. The old man continued to stare off into the distance, as if lost in thought.

Admittedly, he didn't look intimidating. Now that we were closer, I could see that he was ancient. His snow-white beard, intricately braided with carved wooden beads, fell to his waist. His stormy gray eyes were buried beneath thick eyebrows, but his weathered gaze never shifted in our direction. The stiffness of his body indicated that he was agitated, and now that we were closer, I noticed that his lips were moving, as if mouthing a silent rant beneath his wispy mustache.

RC and Trey joined us—RC standing cool and calm on the manhole cover and Trey sitting on the sign while desperately clutching the sides like a petrified cat trying to stay afloat on a piece of debris in a flood.

Trey shakily scrambled off his ride once the sign was safely over the roof. RC stepped down and released his hold over the objects so gravity could reclaim them. Ash, RC, and Trey drew their weapons.

Still, the ghost ignored us.

Jay held out his hand as he stepped forward, silently instructing us to stay back. "Excuse me," he called as he approached.

The stranger jerked his head slightly to deliver a withering glare. "The proper greeting is 'eh-lai.' And I don't want company."

Jay ceased his advance. "Are you an Atmokinetic?"

"What's it to you?"

"You're affecting the weather, and I have to escort you back to the Ghost Realm. You can't be here."

The ghost turned marginally toward Jay. I slid my foot back and sank into a defensive position, eyes skyward. The humidity seemed to boil the air as low, dark clouds formed in rolling waves over Phantom Heights.

The ghost finally pivoted to face us, and any misconception about this old guy being frail vanished. A hot wind kicked up around him, whipping his cloak. "The *Ghost Realm*?" he repeated, practically spitting the words from his braided beard. "Who in King's name do you think you are, insulting your own race by using scarback terminology for our home? And what right do you have telling me where I can or can't be?"

Ash ignited her staff; the flames sputtered in the wind. Jay held up his hands and said, "I—"

Too late. The Atmokinetic's temper had a shorter fuse than Axel's. I stepped back and threw my arm over my face as a dust storm pelted my skin with enough force to convince me that my epidermis was being sandblasted off. He demanded, "How dare you disrespect me? What's your name?"

"Jay—"

"*Jay*," the Atmo mimicked before my lab-brother could continue. "Do you not know who I am?"

"N-no—"

"*No?*" he roared, the word booming above a foreboding rumble of thunder that vibrated through my boots. "Haven't you heard the name Tempest?"

The Atmokinetic seemed to be growing in size while Jay shrank beneath his wrath. "I'm sorry. I haven't."

"Listen here, you miserable, human-serving worm. I'm a high-ranking Guild member and close ally to Azar, not some low-level scum who takes orders or feels intimidated by the likes of *you*." He took a threatening step toward Jay, who was nearly blown off his feet.

RC threw a disk, but the wind around Tempest was so strong that even with telekinesis, it was swept off course and away from its target. Trey shielded his eyes with his arm. Ash's weak flames were barely able to survive in this storm.

I clenched my fists, focusing on Tempest. Rather than try to form ice splinters to shoot through the vortex surrounding him, I formed them inside the cyclone. I held my hand out, ready to drive them into Tempest's body, but he emitted a heat wave so strong that it melted my ice and ripped the breath from my lungs. *Damn it, he knows my Divinity now. Not good.*

He singled me out easily. Ero had told me once that almost all Cryokinetics had blue eyes—a dead giveaway. Tempest locked me in his sights and said, "A traitor to Osias. How disappointing."

Osias. I've heard that name before.

While Tempest's attention was on smothering me in unbearable heat, Jay Blinked inside the windstorm. He was too fast for Tempest; the old man didn't even know what hit him when silver-white light separated him from Jay and he was thrown onto his back. Jay could have knocked Tempest off the roof, but instead, he'd blasted the old Atmokinetic away from the edge in an act of mercy so Tempest landed between the leader and us.

The wind died the instant the air was knocked out of Tempest's lungs. Jay said, "My first request was polite. I don't care who you are—I said you have to leave."

Without the wind, RC had control over all three disks again, and they orbited Tempest to add emphasis to Jay's threat. Tempest's age was evident in the slow, halting way he picked himself up from the rooftop and regained his footing to rise.

He turned his back on us to face Jay, his fury manifesting in red ectoplasm that sparked across his knuckles. Above him, the sky flickered. Lightning crackled in the black clouds, moving inward, as if converging into a single point above Jay.

A blinding flash erupted so close I could hear the air sizzle and feel the electric heat on my skin.

I saw Jay's silhouette illuminated in the white light. The figure was rigid in pain as electricity coursed through his body. He stayed suspended for a moment that expanded into an eternity, hair and cloak whipping about in the wind, and then the light vanished and he fell over the edge.

"*No!*" I cried. Thunder crashed, drowning my scream with a *boom* so deep it reverberated through my whole body and left my ears ringing.

— Chapter Forty-Four —
Lichtenberg Figures

I stumbled forward, my muscles moving on autopilot. The sickening smell of burnt hair, flesh, and fabric filled my nose and turned my stomach.

At the edge of the roof, I fell to my knees and peered down at the smoking, charred body lying lifeless on the sidewalk far below. Ash came to an abrupt halt beside me. "Jay!" she screamed, as if he might miraculously sit up at the sound of her voice.

To my bewilderment, we were answered with a soft groan nearby. Slowly, I turned toward the sound, too afraid to dare being hopeful.

Someone was lying on the rooftop a few yards away. He pushed himself up onto his hands and knees, his gaze wandering across the scene as if he was dazed and confused.

I stared at him, unable to process what I was seeing. The boy on the roof was definitely Jay. His gray hair was disheveled, but other than a scrape on his chin, he seemed to be unhurt. But then . . . who had been standing in his place and was now lying dead on the ground?

I looked down again and squinted at the body dressed in dark clothes and obscured in smoke. Ash whispered, "It's Axel."

My brain was working in overdrive to make sense of what had happened. Axel, whose eyes were so sharp that he saw everything in slow motion, whose reflexes were so fast that he was no more than a blur when he moved at full speed, must have shoved Jay out of the way at the last possible moment, taking the full force of the blast himself.

Time froze for several long heartbeats. A hot breeze swept across my bare skin from behind and stirred my hair as I remained a watchful statue, waiting. Hoping. Praying to a god I didn't really believe in. Refusing to accept a truth I knew was inevitable.

Get up, Axel, I silently pleaded. *Come on. Like you always do.*

He didn't.

Jay let out a cry of anguish and vanished from the rooftop, reappearing instantly with our fallen lab-brother down below. Ash and I stared at them, brain-locked, struggling to process and react.

RC's half-growl, half-scream of rage finally jolted me out of the trance. I turned just in time to witness the broadside of the heavy manhole cover smash into Tempest with a pulverizing force that catapulted him away.

The smug sneer on the Atmokinetic's face transformed into shock and pain. He grunted on impact, too surprised to turn intangible, and now it was too late—he was already over the edge. Intangibility wouldn't save him from falling.

RC didn't linger to witness Tempest's fate. The restaurant sign was already levitating, and he jumped aboard before rocketing down to Jay and Axel.

I rose as the arid breeze cooled. Tempest must be injured, unconscious, or dead, or he'd burned out. His Divinity over the weather had broken.

Without a word, I reached for my center and let the numbness swell inside of me in the form of intangibility. I dropped through the roof and landed on the floor below, then dropped through that floor, then another, each time landing in a crouch to absorb the impact. I landed on the ground level of the building and dashed for the door. Ash was right behind me.

We burst outside, where a crowd of humans had already gathered around three figures. In a mutual trance, Ash and I drifted forward to join RC.

Jay was kneeling over Axel, who had landed in a crumpled heap. A pool of dark blood had formed a glistening, amorphous pillow around his head.

Hands trembling, Jay carefully rolled Axel onto his back. The half-breed's eyes were closed, mouth agape, skin swollen and burnt. Eerie red-and-purple marks that reminded me of tree branches had formed a strange pattern across the side of Axel's face and down his neck, disappearing under his shirt. The other half of his face was stained with blood.

Nobody came forward to offer assistance. The solemn crowd surrounding us was there to slake their curiosity and mourn, not try to save Axel. They knew he was already gone.

"Cato?" My mother pushed her way to the front, flanked by a pair of police officers. "Oh, no. Is he . . . ?"

I turned to her, tears jarring my vision and blurring her face. I wished she could magically make everything all right even though I knew she couldn't.

"Axel," Jay choked. Tears slid down his cheeks. He shook Axel hard enough that I wanted to intervene and say, "Stop! You're hurting him!"

But my voice was gone, and I couldn't move.

Jay shouted, "Axel! Wake up! Come on, this isn't funny, you hear me?" He let go. Axel's bloody head smacked the concrete.

Jay leaned over him and clutched his body, sobbing. "No, Axel, you can't do this. You can't leave us. Damn it, Axel, wake up. Wake up, wake up . . . wake . . ." His pleas were muffled in Axel's charred shoulder.

Jay fell silent and turned his head so it rested on our lab-brother's chest. The cool breeze ruffled my hair, carrying away the heat and humidity.

This couldn't be happening. Axel couldn't be dead. Not him. He was supposed to be invincible.

My heart sank even lower when I remembered my last words to him at breakfast. How was I supposed to live with that?

I let my vacant gaze drift across the wall of human faces. They were probably secretly thrilled that the beast they couldn't control was finally dead. Whether or not that was really what they were thinking, I felt the creeping disease of hatred heat my green Divinity.

Madison holstered her gun as she approached the leader cradling the half-breed. "Jay, I'm so sorry—"

She stopped short, her way blocked by a silvery, transparent ecto-plasm dome surrounding Jay and Axel. The leader's blank gaze lifted to deliver a cold, emotionless stare, as if he were looking right through her. "Shhh."

His eyes danced with rapid movements, unseeing. He seemed to be listening for something. With a sigh, the tension in his body melted, and he shut his eyes as his mouth formed a faint grin. "His heart's beating."

Ash gasped and seized my arm in an iron-strong grip that was def-initely going to leave bruises, but I didn't care. Madison said, "Are you sure?"

Jay shifted Axel's limp body into his lap, then set both hands on ei-ther side of his face and used his thumb to push Axel's eyelid up. He peered into Axel's sightless gaze as if awestruck and perplexed. He nodded.

"I need paramedics! Make room—we need to get a stretcher over here."

Jay absently traced the strange red marks across Axel's face. "It's a miracle, isn't it?"

Her voice level with forced patience, Madison answered, "Yes, it is. But if we don't get him to the hospital, he's not going to make it. I need you to lower your shield."

He clutched Axel's body with fierce protectiveness. "No."

"We can help him. You have to put him down, Jay. Holding him like that might be causing more damage with the broken bones and in-ternal bleeding."

Jay shook his head. "Axel's body is stronger than yours or mine. It would take a lot more force to break his bones. I think the lightning caused more harm than the fall."

"The only way we can accurately assess the internal damage is if we let Doc examine him. It's his best chance."

"Don't." He raised his steely gaze to glare at her. "Don't pretend like you suddenly care about Axel."

"That's not fair. Just because Axel and I argue doesn't mean I don't care. Please let me help."

Jay firmly shook his head. "You can't help Axel. The doctors can't help him, either."

"Damn it, Jay, I don't want to fight you. But if you won't lower your shield, I'll break my way through." Madison set her left hand—the one wearing a glove—onto Jay's ectoplasm dome, which partially disintegrated with a bright flash of light and a muffled *pop.*

As soon as the hole appeared, Jay fired an orb of ectoplasm through the opening, striking my mother with enough force to make her stumble a few steps backward. The protective dome resealed itself.

He murmured, "This was my fault. Axel could have easily dodged a lightning strike, but he didn't. Because of me. He had to concentrate on pushing me out of the way without accidentally flinging me off the roof. He'll never forgive me for letting you take him."

"You'd rather let him die in your arms than get treatment?"

He didn't answer.

She drew her ectogun and aimed it at Jay. "I hope you'll be able to forgive me for this."

I was frozen in dumb confusion, watching the standoff. My mother was about to fight my lab-brother over Axel's half-dead body, and I had no idea what to do.

Jay's silver eyes blazed. "I won't let you take him," he repeated, bravely staring into the barrel of my mother's gun and clutching Axel even tighter.

Trey, out of breath from his dash down the stairs, dutifully took his place beside Madison. He pointed his ectogun at Jay. My mother said, "You know how this is going to end. You're a Level 2 with a passive Divinity. Your shield won't hold for long."

Jay set his jaw and didn't answer. His stubborn glare was one I was familiar with; he wasn't going to yield. "I'm taking him Home."

"Don't!" she cried. "Cato, please talk some sense into him. We might be able to save Axel if we act right now."

Jay's unwavering glare shifted to lock with mine. He pleaded with me in silence, and I wished now more than ever that I had the Divinity to read minds. I stepped forward. His shield vanished so I could approach.

Madison started to rush in, but I held out my hand to stop her. "Not yet."

She reluctantly halted to let me approach Jay without interference. "Fine. But hurry. Axel doesn't have time to wait."

I reached my lab-brothers and let my shaking knees finally give out so I was kneeling beside them. My brain still couldn't process that Axel was the one lying unconscious in Jay's arms. Axel didn't get hurt. He was too fast and in tune with his surroundings to let anything harm him.

Which meant he had willingly sacrificed himself this time.

When Jay had been shot with a crossbow bolt, I'd blamed Axel. It wasn't really Axel's fault because he couldn't have predicted the outcome, but I'd told him that he was a bad brother and he needed to get his priorities straight. Had my words driven him to save Jay at the cost of his own life this time?

I studied his face. Something was different. Not the swelling, not the angry red streaks across his skin. It was . . . his teeth, I finally realized. His canines—the "fighter" fangs—weren't quite as long as when he went into the bloodlust, but still elongated, as if they'd been pushed farther out of his gums.

"He's in bad shape," I said quietly. "Maybe you should let Doc try to help—"

"Look at his eyes."

My trembling fingers navigated toward Axel's face. I was afraid to touch his skin; it was swollen and burnt, and I didn't want to hurt him. He didn't react when I hesitantly pushed up his eyelid.

Eerie. I'd seen his eyes so dilated that the pupils had completely overtaken his red irises, but this time was the exact opposite. The pupil was gone. His iris was a blank red drop, like blood on snow, as if he'd closed the window into his soul and locked himself away from the whole world.

Madison craned her neck as she demanded, "Any reaction? Are his pupils responsive?"

I stared into his weird, pupilless eye and shook my head. To Jay, I whispered, "Have you ever seen that before?"

"No, but I think it's a good sign," Jay murmured. "Something is happening. I don't know what exactly, but we shouldn't interfere."

"Is it safe to Blink him?"

His brow furrowed. "I don't know," he admitted.

I let Axel's eyelid fall over the blank red iris. "If Madison is right and there's internal damage, the pressure on his body when you Blink could make things worse." I set my hand on Axel's forehead. "Keep him safe. Let me handle her."

Jay nodded. I took a deep breath. Set my hands on my knees. Rose.

Okay. It's going to be okay. Axel might be bloody and brain-dead in Jay's arms, but he was still alive. And he wasn't just fast enough to avoid getting hurt; he was a fast healer, too.

But humans had a tendency to think in terms of their own bodily limitations. Convincing my mother to stand down and let Axel recover or perish on his own was going to be a challenge.

I reached for my center, seeking my blue Divinity. With ice daggers in my hands, I turned to face her. "I'm sorry, but I agree with Jay's decision."

RC and Ash flanked either side of me, eyes glowing, bodies braced in defensive positions with weapons drawn. Even without confirmation beyond Jay's assessment and mine, they were ready to defend our fallen lab-brother.

Madison swallowed, her gun aimed at my chest, but it shook in her unsteady hand. With the cool breeze chasing away the sticky heat, I suddenly felt naked and vulnerable without a shirt—not that it would have protected me from an ectoplasm blast anyway.

She said, "Why? Axel will die if we don't get him on an operating table. His head is bleeding, Cato. He fell from a four-story building— he has to be bleeding internally, too. Why can't you understand that?"

Memories of Quarantine sent a chill through my whole body. I remembered the machines Dr. Anders had used to keep me alive when all I wanted to do was die—the needles, the electrodes, the tube in my throat—humans in white coats and paper masks—the harsh medley of smells—latex and cleaning solutions, bleach and peppermint.

"I do understand. But Axel is a fast healer," I explained. "Like Wes. I think you'll do more harm than good if you interfere with his natural healing process."

"You *think*. But you don't know for sure. Neither do I. That's why we need a doctor."

I didn't answer.

"Stand down," Madison said. "Right now. That's an order."

"No. Axel isn't human. You can't treat him like one."

"Doc is a hell of a lot more qualified to make that judgment call than you or I am. We've already wasted too much time. You're letting your own irrational fear of doctors override your logic, and that's going to cost Axel his life." Her finger curled over the trigger.

Bloody Scout, she's actually going to shoot me! I tightened my grip on my ice weapons and focused on forming a hardened crust on my skin. Armor would be my best defense against my mother's ectogun if I wasn't quick enough to form a shield in time.

"Cato?"

Vivian's soft voice pulled my gaze past Madison to my blood-sister's solemn but familiar face in the crowd. Her red-rimmed eyes were filled with tears. She shifted the backpack on her shoulder and said, "I think you should trust Mom."

I snapped, "Maybe she should try trusting me for once."

"*Please*, Cato," Madison begged. "Please don't make me shoot you. I really don't want to."

"Then don't."

She took a step forward. "You trusted me to help you when you were hurt. Let me help Axel now."

"That was different. Axel doesn't trust you, and he would expect me to protect him."

"I won't be able to forgive myself if he dies here on the street when Doc could have saved him."

"You still aren't *listening* to me! Axel isn't like you, and he's not like me, and he's not like any other ghost or human. I'm sure you'd love to get him on an examination table while he's unconscious, but that's not going to happen."

"Don't twist my intentions. You know I'm not interested in experimenting on him."

"Do I? If you want to get to him, you're going to have to shoot me. There's no way around it."

She clenched her jaw, hand trembling, but her finger didn't leave the trigger. Rather than pull it, she took another step forward.

RC pushed one hand toward her; she slid backward several feet across the asphalt. Her initially startled expression turned livid in an instant. "You—"

A weak moan caused her to break off in a gasp. My eyes widened, and so did my mother's. Slowly, I turned back toward Axel.

The burns, the blisters, the red streaks—they were all gone. His eyes fluttered open. They were still wrong, still without pupils, and the blank red irises wandered blindly for a few seconds. Even as we watched, pinpricks of black in the center of each eye expanded as his pupils dilated.

Axel's gloved fingers drifted up to touch his lips. He groaned again and whined, "Ow, my teeth."

His teeth? Lightning had electrocuted his whole body and his *teeth* were what hurt?

He retracted his hand and raised his head, teeth now bared in a grimace that turned into a manic smile as his dark eyes fixated on Jay. His moan transformed into a deep, starving growl. Axel's pupils, gone a minute ago, were now so dilated that they'd almost completely overtaken the red irises while his inner fangs—the feeder fangs, which contained his venom—were now elongated just like his fighter fangs.

"Axel," Jay warned in his sternest voice.

The half-breed blinked when he registered his name. The grin vanished as he stared, wide-eyed in horror, at Jay. He clapped both hands over his mouth and leapt to his feet in a blur of motion. "I'm sorry," he whispered behind his palms.

Jay stood too, but he was clutching the whistle, and his face was pale. That was closer than we should ever admit to anyone. The on-lookers, confused and nervous from Axel's miraculous recovery, backed away from him, and they had no idea just how smart that was.

Although my mother's gun was still drawn, it hung limply at her side now, aimed at the ground. "Axel?"

His gaze skipped over the humans as he turned toward the sound of her voice, and yet he barely graced her with a glance. Vivian made a strange laugh-sob and stepped forward with her arms open as though to embrace him. "You're okay!"

Axel growled and backed away as if repulsed. "Stay away from me."

Vivian halted. "I'm just glad you're alive."

"I don't know why you'd waste your tears on me. I don't even like you."

My blood-sister gaped at him, her mouth hanging slack. I couldn't find any words to erase the shock from her face because I was equally stunned by his harsh dismissal while still trying to process the miracle.

He flinched in pain, raising his fingers to his mouth again. "Ah, shit," he said with a groan, squeezing his eyes shut. "I need my medi-cine."

Jay said, "Okay—"

"*NOW*!"

"*O-kay*," Jay enunciated. He held out his hand. "Tell me where to go, and I'll take you there."

Axel shook his head and retreated from Jay's proffered hand.

"Axel, I'm trying to help you."

"I didn't ask for your help." Axel backed away, his mouth covered by his palms. He cringed again as his fangs drove through the gums. "Damn it," he uttered, and then he was gone.

An eerie quiet swelled in the wake of his departure, further ampli-fied by the absence of the pulsing energy Axel's body emitted.

Madison said, "We need to talk. Now."

"Later," I dismissed.

"No, Cato. *Now*."

She tried to grab my arm, but I stepped back out of reach. The stress finally boiled over. "I'm tired and dehydrated. I don't want to talk."

She pointed in the direction of Saros Manor. "Home. Right now. You need to get some water and rest before you pass out."

"We have to find Tempest. He could have survived."

"Absolutely not. Emerton's team will handle it."

I glared at her in continued defiance, but now that our standoff was over, I could feel my energy draining. The heat had definitely taken a toll on my body today. I was weak and light-headed, and keeping a tight grip on the icicles was the only way to stop my hands from shaking.

Without a word, I started walking. The crowd parted to let us pass, and Madison fell into step beside me. Jay, RC, Ash, and Vivian trailed after us in a somber procession. Trey stayed behind—apparently, he'd determined that was the safest course of action, and he was probably right.

A refreshing natural breeze was blowing away the stifling remnants of Tempest's heat wave. I lifted my face to greet it. Madison, I noticed, still had the ectogun clenched in her hand, as if she expected to be attacked on the way home.

She flinched, then snatched her phone and lifted it to her ear. "Talk to me. Uh-huh. You sure? Okay, thanks. Yeah, double the patrol at the Rip, just in case. I'll touch base with you later."

She replaced the phone. After a moment, she said, "Tempest is gone. The police found where he landed and followed his trail of blood to the Rip. There was a lot of wind damage in the area; Emerton thinks he used it to break his fall."

Nobody said a word in the aftermath of her announcement.

I searched for relief to ease the sick knot in my stomach, but it was nowhere to be found. Tempest should have died. He'd come dangerously close to killing Axel while trying to murder Jay, and I wanted him to pay for that transgression with his life. It was a vile desire, and I realized that, but I couldn't stop myself from surrendering to the dark thoughts as I imagined him crawling into the Ghost Realm on his hands and knees—a bloody, broken mess—and then collapsing as the last breath was forced out of his blood-filled lungs. That was the fate he deserved. If he ever returned to Phantom Heights, that was the fate he would get.

Not another word was spoken as we walked through town. When we reached the manor, my lab-family lingered in the foyer while I followed my mother through the dining room and into the kitchen. Vivian trailed behind.

As soon as the door swung shut behind us, Madison demanded, "What the hell happened out there?"

I ignored her as I walked to the sink, turned on the faucet, removed my gloves, and cupped the cold water in my hands to slurp.

"Cato. I have a right to know."

"Know what?" I muttered as my hands refilled.

"*Don't,*" she warned. "You know what."

"No, I don't. Axel was hurt, and now he's not. I told you he would recover on his own. Maybe you should have listened to me."

Before she could answer, the door swung open. Kit skipped in and announced, "I'm hungry." She tilted her head, her gaze trained on the gun still in Madison's hand. She glanced between the two of us. "Were you gonna shoot Cato?"

My mother hurriedly holstered the weapon and flashed Kit a reassuring smile. "Of course not. I guess it is getting close to dinnertime, isn't it? What do you want to eat?"

"Scrambled eggs!" Kit chirped.

"For dinner? We just had that for breakfast." Kit masterfully dipped her chin and peered up while batting her big golden eyes. "Okay," Madison relented. She started pulling plates out of cupboards.

Kit beamed in victory and returned to the dining room.

Vivian leaned against the counter, her downcast gaze fixated on the bracelet tied around her wrist. "Did Axel mean what he said?" she asked quietly.

She wanted me to make excuses and tell her no, of course not, my lab-brother didn't really hate her. But the truth was, I didn't know. She raised her emerald eyes to gaze mournfully at me. "I tried, Cato. Really hard. You know that, right?"

A voice said, "He's good at that, isn't he?"

Jay was leaning against the doorframe. At our apparent confusion, he straightened and added, "Pushing people away, I mean." My lab-brother sauntered into the kitchen and selected an apple from the basket of fruit on the counter. His silver eyes found me. Quietly, he said, "You know, I've never asked Axel this, but I don't think he ever meant to stay with us."

"What are you talking about?" I said. "We left Axel behind. He found *us* in the woods, remember?"

Jay inspected his apple for blemishes that weren't there. "Yeah." He rubbed an invisible bruise in the red skin. "But I wonder if he just wanted to make sure we escaped. I think he meant to guard us from a distance and then leave once he was sure we'd be safe, but then he decided to say goodbye, and he realized it wouldn't be as easy to walk away as he thought. It's just a theory." Jay held up the apple and said, "This is all I want for dinner, Mrs. Tarrow." He walked away.

My mother pulled a carton of eggs and a gallon of milk out of the fridge. She didn't say a word.

Viv and I watched her in silence. I felt as though I should speak to ease the tension, but I didn't know what to say, so it dragged on, broken only by the sounds of cabinet doors closing. Finally, she slammed the skillet onto the stove with unnecessary force. "I don't understand him."

"I've already told you all that I can."

She set her hands on the stove and leaned over it, hanging her head. "This medicine Axel gets every week . . . it suppresses his other half?"

"Sort of, I guess, yeah." She gave me a measured look at my less-than-helpful answer as she turned on the stove. "Yes," I said clearly after another moment.

"And his other half is that demon that attacked Trey?"

"Yes."

"What kind of medicine could possibly suppress something like that?"

I stared down at my feet.

Madison didn't seem surprised by my renewed silence. She cracked an egg with too much force and sent pieces of eggshell into the skillet with the yolk.

"Damn it," she said under her breath. "So, Axel leaves you injured and powerless to face Traders on your own, but he sacrifices himself to save Jay? Explain *that* to me."

"Those were completely different circumstances."

She whirled to glare at me. "They were not."

"The Traders weren't going to kill me."

"Oh, I see, so Axel doesn't want you to die, but he's okay with letting bounty hunters drag you into the Ghost Realm so Azar can torture you."

The acidity burned her words and made me wince. I almost told her not to take it so personally—it wasn't the first time Axel had sent Jay to deal with a ghost problem instead of handling it himself. But then I remembered that Jay had ended up with a crossbow bolt in his arm last time, so I kept my mouth shut.

I said, "I trust Axel. If you don't trust him, then I guess you don't trust me."

"I trust you. It's just that for reasons I cannot fathom, Axel has manipulated you."

Vivian added, "He doesn't care about you."

I shot her a sour look and snapped, "And you know him well enough to decide that?"

"He told me so," she said, wounded, as if she'd been keeping this bottled up inside for a while.

"You misunderstood."

"Cato," she said patiently, "he couldn't have been any clearer."

"Well, I don't believe you."

"Why would I make that up?"

"Look," I said, turning my back on them both, "you probably took his words out of context. I already forgave him, and I wish you would, too."

"Jeez, what could he have possibly done to make you so blind?"

I seethed, "Well, to start with, he was there for me when neither of you were."

Ouch. That was a low blow—lower than I'd meant to go—and I could see the hurt shining in their eyes. Madison said, "Cato, that's not fair."

"But it's still true. Whether you like him or not, he's my lab-brother, and you're going to have to deal with that."

Vivian demanded, "Are you saying you choose that unstable demon over us?"

I raised my head. Vivian, comprehending the depth of my anger by the green glow that had no doubt manifested in my irises, took a step back. "That right there is the difference," I said. "Axel never asked me to choose."

I was hitting every exposed nerve, and yet I didn't feel guilty. Vivian's face fell. "But—"

"And you know what else? We're more similar than you'd like to believe."

Her expression morphed from crestfallen to bitter. "You think you're alike? You're nothing alike! You were born human, and Axel, he was born a ghost, an *enemy.* Mom turned you into a hero while Agent Kovak turned Axel into a monster. Look at your Divinities. You have two, and Axel doesn't have any. Yeah, you're both different, but you deviate from the norm in completely opposite directions. You're a good person, Cato. Axel is everything you're not."

I was shivering in rage, vaguely conscious that my lungs were stretching with compressed power that burned with green light. Even Madison was speechless.

I couldn't keep arguing. I was going to scream. I couldn't—not again.

Lips quivering under the strain of sealing the devastating power inside, I stormed out. "I'm not hungry," I snapped over my shoulder. Still spiteful, I paused at the door and added, "Please try not to kill my lab-family by letting them choke on eggshells."

My resentment continued to fester, and I went out of my way to avoid Madison and Vivian for the rest of the evening. I didn't even want to look at them.

I needed a solid night's sleep for the anger to fully cool, but to do that, I first needed to clear my head, and even a game of All-On-One wasn't enough. I lay on the mattress afterward with Jay and RC on either side and Kit tangled between my feet, but I just stared at the ceiling, still replaying the standoff and ensuing argument. Did Axel really tell Vivian that he didn't care about me, or did she take his words out of context?

I wasn't sure how I knew he was near, just that he was. Perhaps on some level, I perceived that unearthly energy pulsing from him, and I instinctively knew where to find him.

I sat up and carefully detached Kit, who groaned, rolled over, and snuggled up against Ash's stomach. Barefoot, I crossed the moonlit floor and became intangible to step through the wall and onto the second-story roof.

I climbed up to the top, where I found Axel pacing along the edge of the roof. His movements were jerky and restless, prompting me to ask, "You didn't leave Phantom Heights for your medicine, did you?"

"No," he said, refusing to look at me. "The bloodlust passed. I just needed to get away from people." His voice was unusually husky.

"Are you crying?"

Axel whirled on me, eyes burning in the dark. "Don't be a fucking moron." He turned away again, swiping the back of his fist across his nose.

Sometimes, I forgot he was only fourteen. I shifted and cleared my throat. "It's okay to cry, you know. I'm not judging."

"Fuck off, Cato. I'm not in the mood for a speech."

I nodded, my left hand rising to rub my right arm. I didn't answer, but I didn't leave, either.

Axel released a hiss of breath and snarled, "What the hell do you want?"

"I wanted to say I'm sorry—"

"About what?" he interrupted.

Barely maintaining my patience, I said, "About what I told you after Jay was injured. I said you weren't a good lab-brother. But that's not true, Ax. I was just mad. I didn't really mean that. I'm sorry."

Axel glowered at me and folded his arms. Any tears I'd seen (or thought I'd seen) were long gone. "Bloody Scout. You really piss me off sometimes, you know that?"

Completely bewildered by his reaction to my apology, I gawked at him. "Huh?"

"Quit acting like such a spineless human." At my insistent blank look, he said, "You spoke your mind and didn't hold back. If you're going to say something, mean what you say and stand by your words. I was wrong, you told me I was wrong, and that's that. Got it?"

I nodded with a weak smile. "Got it."

"Good."

I rubbed my arm again. I still, after all this time, expected to press my fingertips into the metal neutralizer band, not flesh. "I, uh . . . I'm glad you're all right. You really scared us today." When he didn't answer, I added, "I didn't know you could heal yourself that quickly."

Axel grunted as if annoyed by his amazing ability. "My healing coma is efficient but inconvenient. It leaves me completely vulnerable. But if my injuries are critical, I don't have a choice. My mind and body shut down so all of my energy can be directed to healing."

"I get it. But you know . . . you can trust us to protect you. Like you always protect us."

Axel turned to walk away, but I called, "Wait. I need to ask you a favor."

"I don't do favors."

"If you care at all about protecting this family from *Them*, you might."

His back was to me, and although he didn't respond or turn to face me, at least he held still.

"Just . . . wait there, okay?" I became intangible and landed in our room below, bending my knees to absorb the impact. Rather than risk waking my lab-siblings by trying to open the dresser drawer, I thrust my intangible hand through the wood and seized Greyson's shirt.

To my relief, Axel was still waiting when I returned to the roof. I offered him the clothing and explained, "The owner of this shirt went missing more than two years ago. Can you find him? Or at least find out what happened to him?"

Axel scoffed. "Two years? Seriously? You expect me to track down a scent that's *two years* old? Do you even realize what you're asking?"

"Look, if you can't do it, just say so."

He growled indignantly and snatched the shirt. "I never said I *can't* do it." He stormed away.

I took a breath and blurted, "Did you sacrifice yourself to save Jay because of what I said to you that day when he got shot with a cross-bow?"

Axel paused. He turned his head to look over his shoulder at me with one glowing red eye. "No. I woulda saved Jay anyways. So you can stop feeling guilty."

"Then why didn't you save me when I needed you?"

His eye narrowed. No answer.

I was suffocating in the tense silence. "I think I know. I just need to hear you say it."

He turned forward again so I was facing the back of his head. "If you already know the answer, then why are you asking stupid questions? Go to sleep—you look like shit."

And then he was gone, and I was alone on the rooftop.

— Chapter Forty-Five —

The Unicorn Hunter

Azar strode down the long hallway with Lieutenant Inalli at his heels.

The short, thin woman barely reached his rib cage. Cloaked in her hood, she drifted in his shadow, her sandals quietly slapping the stone floor.

The corridor was narrow. Natural veins of lumenite in the stone walls glowed with a faint, iridescent blue light. To Azar's left, recessed mirrors lined the wall in an evenly spaced, infinite row of rectangles that shrank into the receding focal point of the seemingly endless hallway. A large lumenite crystal mounted on the wall between each mirror offered brighter intervals of blue light to fully illuminate the walkways of the vast Prison.

"He's in Cell Block D," the lieutenant informed him.

Azar gave no answer, but he knew that Inalli expected none. They walked in silence while turning down a spiraling staircase and descending one, two, three levels lower, then striding down yet another corridor.

Ahead, a rickety chair was positioned against the wall, unoccupied. But when Azar turned to face the mirror directly across from it, a man was sitting in the chair in the reflection. "Hello, Sandt," he greeted.

The Prisoner looked up at the arrival of the Warden and lieutenant. Sandt set his hands on his knees, rose, and approached in the mirror. His mouth formed words, but his voice was muted. When he tried to grab the shoulder of Azar's reflection, his hand passed through it.

Azar kept his composure even though an eerie chill rippled across his skin where Sandt's fingers had phased through his reflection. "So," he said, earning Sandt's attention, "how does it feel to be a moorlin in

Rodeledor?"

Sandt, realizing that he couldn't interact with the reflections, redirected his attention to the real people watching through the window of the mirror. He stepped in front of Azar's reflection and raised his fist threateningly.

Inalli didn't react. Azar held up his hand and calmly said, "Ah-ah. Break that, and you'll be trapped forever." Sandt's spiteful green eyes locked onto Azar, but he resentfully folded his arms across his chest in defeat. "Inalli."

The lieutenant stepped forward and reached for the mirror. The cloak fell away from her pale arm to reveal a decorative black leather band around her biceps and a matching wrist gauntlet laced over her forearm. She wore thin black gloves that covered only her index and middle fingers.

When her fingertips touched the smooth surface, they slipped through as if the mirror weren't even there. Inalli moved forward, merging with her reflection until she was inside the room in the mirror with Sandt. She cordially offered her hand. He glowered at her partial glove for a few moments out of spite before he grudgingly set his hand in hers.

Inalli backed through the mirror, pulling him through the reflective prison until they were standing in the hallway.

Sandt jerked his hand free from Inalli's grip. He twisted to stare at his reflection in the rectangular portal from which he'd just emerged. Now, without him inside, it looked like a normal mirror showing the bleak hallway, three kálos, and the empty chair.

Sandt scowled and backed away. "I've committed no crime."

"Is that a fact?" The Warden held out his hand. Sandt flinched, but Lieutenant Inalli simply handed Azar a file. He made a grand show of skimming through it while Sandt shifted uneasily. "Hmm, interesting. According to reports from multiple informants I have in the Black Market, you're the man to see when it comes to buying high-grade alicorn."

Sandt nervously wiped his palms on the sides of his pants. Azar continued, "Now, granted, it's been almost two hundred years since I wrote the Law, so maybe my memory needs refreshed. Inalli, wasn't there a section explicitly stating that harvesting horns from live unicorns was illegal?"

"But—" Sandt started.

"*And*," Azar continued, holding his hand up for silence, "didn't the Law also make it very clear that slaughtering any creature for alicorn was also illegal?"

"That would be correct," Inalli answered.

Sandt was an imposing man, tall and strong in stature with deep green eyes and a weathered appearance. *Ruffian* was the word that came to Azar's mind. Sandt certainly looked strong enough to saw off a dense unicorn horn by himself. But sneaking up on the skittish creatures? He looked about as sneaky as a hydrilia dragon crashing through the forest.

And yet, Azar's informants were never wrong, and Sandt didn't deny the accusations. He chuckled nervously and said, "Okay, you got me. But my crime is worth a fine at most, which I'll gladly pay. Prison is a bit harsh, don't you think?"

"Is that your best argument to convince me?" Azar asked.

"What do you want?"

Azar's lips peeled apart in a smile. "Ah, now that's the question, isn't it?" He closed the folder and leaned casually against the wall. "Frankly, what you do is appalling, but here's what impresses me—you harvest alicorn from wild unicorns. Higher quality, higher profit, right? But the wild ones are so fast, so intelligent, so shy, most people never even see one in their lifetime, let alone catch one. And yet, they just lie at your feet, don't they? Tell me, do you kill them before you saw off their horns, or do you leave them to die a slow, painful death afterward?"

Sandt's eyes remained downcast. He muttered, "They don't suffer. It's an enviable way to die, really. Easy, quick, painless. They go right to sleep. Never feel a thing."

"How do you trap them?"

Sandt shrugged. "I'm patient. I wait for them to come to me."

Azar nodded slowly as he returned the file to Inalli. "I think I have need of your skills."

Sandt narrowed his eyes. "I know how you operate. I either ruin my reputation by doing your bidding to pay off my debt, or I rot in here, right?"

"Most people would be honored to do me a favor. It's in your best interest to be on my good side. If you're on my bad side, I can keep you locked up here for as long as I see fit, even if you're innocent. Although I think we both know you aren't."

Sandt's brow creased as his frown deepened. "A bribe and a threat at the same time," he muttered. "What exactly does this favor of yours entail?"

Azar made eye contact with his own reflection in the mirror. "I have a problem that requires a quiet resolution. If I employ you for the job, can you guarantee success?"

Sandt smirked. "Captain Hassing can't do your usual bidding?"

"Hassing lacks the . . . *finesse* needed for such a task."

"What do you need me to do?"

Azar smiled. "You've heard of the escaped prisoners from Project Alpha, yes?"

"I have."

"I want them."

Sandt laughed. Although he stood at least six feet tall, even he had to tilt his head back to look up at the Warden. "You're insane. I heard they wiped out the First Branch. I'm not going on a suicide mission, even for *you*."

Azar signaled Inalli, who solemnly handed Sandt a wanted poster. "That reward?" Azar said softly. "I'll double it. I'll wipe your slate clean. No crimes on your record, no fines to pay, no Prison time."

"Yeah?" Sandt murmured. He rubbed the stubble on his chin as he read the parchment.

Azar knew the clean record didn't appeal to the Trader nearly as much as the tantalizing monetary reward. He pressed, "If you complete this job, I just might consider hiring you again. I like to have a handful of resources outside the Guard."

"And if I fail? I suppose you'll hunt me down and drag me back here, right?"

"I have confidence in your abilities. The targets are all children."

This caused Sandt to jerk his head up and stare dubiously at Azar. "Children? That's not what I heard."

"I've met them in person."

"Really? Huh. How old?"

"None of them have reached their first coming of age."

Sandt scratched his neck. "I also heard there was a Telepath protecting them."

"Not at the moment. I've removed him from the picture, at least for the time being."

"Yeah? How'd you manage that?"

Azar shrugged and flashed a nonchalant smile. "One of Ero's former students had a little accident. Young Telepaths can be so touchy when they're distressed. I don't know how long he'll be occupied in this Realm, though, so I suggest you don't squander your chance. The clock is ticking."

"Why didn't you just have him killed? Then he wouldn't be a factor."

The Warden chuckled. "While I appreciate your preference for a simpler, permanent solution, do you have any idea how many generations of students Ero has trained? I guarantee eliminating him would not be worth the consequences of igniting a small army of vengeful Telepaths and Mind-Readers against me. Besides, while Ero and I do have our differences, I don't hate him enough to end his life. He may still prove to be useful in this war."

Sandt stared down at the parchment in his hands. Seeing that he was still hesitant about the assignment, Azar added, "I'll send my Amínyte with you, and a handful of elite Shadow Guards to see this job through."

"That's it? After all I've heard about these fugitives, I'd prefer to have an army behind me."

"I told you, I want a quiet extraction. With your Divinity, you shouldn't need any more reinforcements than what I've offered."

"So . . . what exactly do you want me to do with these fugitives?"

"I want you to go into Cröendor and subdue them, then bring them to me. All eight of them."

Sandt raised his head and looked up at Azar. He nodded slowly in acceptance of the task he'd been charged with.

Azar held out his hand, and Inalli handed him a bundle of fabric. "I have a present for you," said Azar as he unfolded the burgundy cloak. "This is a Charm that will completely mask your scent and prevent anyone from sensing you. It may give you a slight edge to set your trap."

As Sandt accepted the Charmed garment, Azar added, "If I may make a recommendation? Based on the past failure of the First Branch, I highly suggest you take down the boy with red eyes before targeting the others."

He turned, then paused. "Oh, and one more thing—I want all of them alive and relatively undamaged when you deliver them."

Holly opened the bathroom door and released clouds of steam into her bedroom. She'd just twisted a towel around her wet hair and was tying the belt of her bathrobe when she froze in her tracks.

An intruder was in her room. The cloaked figure was a silhouette in front of her window. A pair of red eyes glowed in the darkness.

She was too petrified to move. Her worst nightmare had finally come to life—a Trader had returned to take her back into Avilésor and sell her into slavery again.

The ghost stepped forward into the light spilling from the moist bathroom. He was holding something, and when the light illuminated the body in his arms, Holly's knees almost gave out.

"Greyson," she whispered. She reached out, tears filling her eyes, but she couldn't make her feet move. She'd expected a decomposing corpse or even a skeleton, but . . . "He looks like he just died yesterday."

At the sound of her voice, Greyson stirred. His eyelids fluttered. Axel knelt to lower him onto the carpet, and Holly fell forward with a cry.

"I found him in the Ghost Realm," Axel said dryly.

Holly scooped her emaciated, filthy son into her arms and rocked him back and forth, his head cradled against her bosom. "Thank you, thank you, thank you, Axel. I can't thank you enough."

He folded his arms. "I want something in return."

She nodded vigorously. "Yes, yes, I promise I'll use every resource and connection I have to protect you from the Agents."

"Good, but that wasn't what I was going to say."

"What, then? I'm in your debt. Anything you want, it's yours."

Axel took a moment to choose his words before he said, "You won't tell anyone what I did."

Holly blinked through the flood in her eyes. She lifted her head to look at him. "What?"

"Your son ran away from his master and found his way back to the Rip by himself. I had nothing to do with it. Got it?"

She stroked Greyson's hair, which had faded from the lovely honey brown she remembered to a lackluster mousy hue.

She shook her head in confusion. "But . . . I don't understand. If people knew, they wouldn't be afraid of you."

"They need to be afraid." He turned his head. "It's better that way."

"But—"

"You promised me anything I wanted. That's what I want."

"But Axel, you could be a hero."

He let out a low, mocking chuckle. "You actually think I give a damn what people think of me?"

"Mom?" rasped Greyson.

"Shh," Holly soothed, pulling him closer and resting her cheek on top of his head. "You're okay now. You're safe. I've got you."

She squeezed her eyes shut in indecision. Axel had saved her son. He, the monster she'd been so afraid would be the downfall of them all, had somehow managed to repair her crumbling world, and she wanted to share his greatness with everyone. And yet, he insisted on being a hated outcast when he had the opportunity to claim the title of a hero.

"I don't understand," she whispered again.

"I don't expect you to."

Although it broke her heart to do this, she nodded. "Okay. If that's really what you want, this will be our secret."

No answer.

She lifted her head again. The intruder was gone.

Dawn was quiet.

Axel led the way down the stairs with Kit and RC at his heels. Ash and I trailed behind. The twins stumbled along at the back of the group, yawning and rubbing their eyes. Although they usually accompanied us for our nightly training exercises, they were rarely awake when we left in the early morning hours. Today, however, they had woken up as we were leaving and insisted they couldn't go back to sleep, so they wanted to come with us.

Ash yawned. "Rough night?" I asked.

"I barely slept. Just one night, I wish I could close my eyes and not feel his hands on me or see children on fire."

Her words possessed a chilling bite. There was no condolence for her suffering, so I stayed quiet as we made our way down to the ground floor and out the back door. In my night terrors, Madison had been hunting Phantom while *He* whispered over our heads, "She doesn't want you. You're going to grow up to be a monster, and she knows it. She doesn't want you . . ."

I drew in a deep breath as I stepped outside. The crisp morning air cleared the residue of the nightmares like a cool breeze sweeping away the humidity in the wake of a summer thunderstorm. I loved the smell of mornings. Everything was so fresh, quiet, and calm while the world was in the final stage of sleep. The birds hadn't even roused yet. Dew soaked my boots as I strode through the faint wisps of fog hovering above the lawn. To the east, the sky was just starting to lighten across the horizon.

Kit cartwheeled across the grass, giggling. She ended her routine with an effortless backflip and an airborne backward somersault, landed on her bare feet, and then challenged, "Race you to the junkyard!" She took off with her cloak flapping behind her.

Axel rolled his eyes and maintained his stride. I grinned and sprinted after the Amínyte even though I knew I couldn't catch her. Ash joined the race. RC hung back with Finn and Reese.

The three of us dashed through backyards and alleys, over fences and hedges, and down the empty streets of the outskirts. Kit was well ahead of us when she wriggled through a broken section of chain-link fence. I became intangible and walked through the fence before halting at the edge of a field of debris.

Jay was standing in the middle of the junkyard next to Axel, waiting for us. From above, RC drifted down on a large piece of plywood with Finn and Reese sitting at his feet.

"I didn't expect to see you two up this early," said Jay.

They seemed a little more alert as they dismounted, although Jay sternly told them, "You have to stay out of the way so you don't get hurt."

I crossed my right arm over my body and hooked it in the crook of my left arm, then increased the pressure to stretch out my muscles in preparation for the morning training. Only after the twins had seated themselves safely against the perimeter fence to watch did Jay face the rest of us and ask, "Ready?"

Ash, RC, Kit, and I converged toward Jay and Axel in the junkyard. Mounds of rusty car parts, construction debris, trash, and scrap metal formed small mountains around us. Kit was the only one who looked excited—she bounced eagerly in place, ecstatic that she was allowed to participate in this exercise.

RC stretched his arms high above his head with a quiet groan. His left eye glowed bright violet as he lowered his hands, keeping them extended outward to guide his telekinetic power.

All around us, pieces of debris rose into the air and hovered at varying heights. I tilted my head back to study our training field as the debris slowly began to circulate in various orbits interweaving between each other. It was a complex rotation pattern that required total concentration and mastery on RC's part to prevent the pieces from colliding.

To my right, Ash muttered, "Come what may," as she drew her staff, twirled it once, crouched, and then leapt onto a car door as it floated past her.

Kit remained in her skin as she stooped to all fours, then pounced onto a cooler and leapt from obstacle to obstacle as she advanced high up into the moving maze of debris. In front of me, Axel vaulted straight up nearly thirty feet to the highest piece of metal orbiting the junkyard. Jay and I were the last ones to enter the levitating arena.

I wobbled to find my balance as the tire bobbed in the air when my weight settled on it. This piece was moving up at a diagonal, rising higher above the ground. Debris drifted all around me, moving at different speeds, directions, and heights.

At the sound of an object swishing through the air, I turned my head to find Ash bearing down on me with her staff, a fierce expression on her face. I spun and leapt back, throwing up my arms as I fell over the edge. My gloved hands gripped the side of the tire as her metal weapon struck the rubber right where I'd been standing.

I glanced down and timed my release to drop onto a car hood that had glided below. Above, Jay and Ash exchanged blows.

Crash! Something hit me hard and fast from beneath. The hood flipped over and dumped me onto the ground. I lay on my back in a daze, staring up at the bizarre sight of floating parts. Axel peered over the edge of the hood with a cocky smirk.

Kit was high above all of us now. For her, this exercise was more about gymnastics, balance, and strength than combat. I watched her raise her hands and perform a daring but graceful dive. She tucked into a somersault as she landed on a metal slab far below, then did a back handspring and landed on a bicycle—one foot on the seat, the other raised, knee bent, arms out in a perfect pose. Her stunts always scared me, even if she did have the nimble sure-footedness of a cat.

Way up in the sky, a black bird with a white-tipped wing glided above our training arena.

I sat up and glanced to the side where RC was staring up at the moving parts, his eyes narrowed in intense concentration. The task of levitating and moving all this debris in sync was a challenge in and of itself, but compensating for our maneuvers changing the weight of certain pieces made it even more difficult. Even though he wasn't sparring, this exercise was probably harder on him than it was on us.

Axel pushed off the hood with his gaze set on Jay and Ash. The leader ducked Ash's swing and then vanished in the instant Axel landed on the door.

Off-balance with Jay's sudden departure and Axel's intentionally heavy landing, Ash pinwheeled her arms in a futile attempt to get her footing as she fell over the side. She managed to regain control in the air and execute a graceful landing on an old dishwasher below, crouching to absorb the impact.

Annoyed that Axel had knocked me out of the battlefield so soon, I stood and dashed toward the lowest object near me—a rusted, partially disintegrated metal locker. I jumped, landed, and jumped again, easily advancing skyward until I was high above the ground.

This time, I saw Axel coming. No time to think—I had a microsecond to react. I leapt sideways and landed on a passing table as he settled on the dresser drawer I had been standing on just a moment before. He smirked and muttered, "Good reflexes," as he jumped away.

Jay was close by, strategically positioned with his body turned so he could keep both Ash and me in his sights.

I pitched an orb of ectoplasm at him. He flung out his hand, conjuring a silvery streak of ectoplasm to deflect my attack. I hadn't expected my weak and obvious attack to actually hit him, but I *had* distracted him enough for Ash to make a move. She took a flying leap, staff cocked, ready to complete the swing once Jay was in range.

This wasn't All-On-One, and our target wasn't specifically Jay, but we were so used to working together against the leader that habit drove us to single him out as a team.

Before Ash could strike, he leapt backward and landed on the edge of the rim he was standing on, using his weight to flip it over. He was holding onto the bottom when Ash landed on the top. I fired more ectoplasm at Jay while he was stuck in the vulnerable position, forcing him to block with another shield.

As a toolbox drifted within reach, Jay planted both feet on it and then kicked off, flipping the rim over again. Ash had no choice but to bail as it tipped. Her off-balance leap wasn't planned, and her timing was off—there were no pieces of debris within easy reach.

She tried to grab a broken windshield but fell short. Ash caught the edge one-handed with her fingertips, gritting her teeth as the windshield dipped under her weight. With the staff in her other hand, she had no choice but to dangle there until something drifted below her and she could let go.

Jay jumped after her. It was an offensive move—he wasn't going to help her. His goal was to land on top of the windshield and make her fall.

I held out my hand, concentrating on the window. Ice crystals formed on the cracked glass and spread until the surface of the windshield was a solid, slippery sheet of ice by the time Jay's boots made contact. His feet went out from under him; he crashed onto his back, hard. Ash braced herself as he went over the edge, falling over her.

Jay seized her ankle. They were both dangling in the air now, completely at my mercy. Grinning, I formed a curved piece of ice in each hand and flung the weapons in opposite directions. They whirled through the field of floating debris, curving through the air to come at Jay from the left and Ash from the right.

Ash swung her staff, connecting with the ice and knocking it away. Jay Blinked—the ice sliced through air and struck an empty metal tank with a hollow *clang*.

I sensed Jay behind me, but before I could turn my head, I felt his arms encircle my abdomen as he tackled me and we both fell forward over the edge, the ground rising up fast to meet us. Jay winked at me and kicked away, and then he was gone again. I was flailing through the air alone, gravity pulling me down to what was going to be a painful stop.

I glimpsed an object in my peripheral and reached out in desperation. My fingers found a metal pole and latched on with a death grip to stop my free fall. I tipped my head back to see what I was holding. To my surprise, it was Ash's staff. She was clutching the other end, straining to hold my weight.

I teased, "We're supposed to be fighting, not helping each other."

"I know," she answered with a sly grin. Steam erupted from my hand; the metal staff was scalding hot. Shocked, I let go with a yelp and landed in the dirt.

Ash waited a few more seconds until a basketball hoop drifted below her. She landed on it with the grace of a bird alighting on a perch. I rose to reenter the game.

The morning was a blissful blur of movement, strategy, balance, and strength. I needed this. Not just the physical challenge, but also the mental focus.

Usually, this training exercise was a short one because it was so difficult, but we all seemed to enjoy the release. The sun had cleared the horizon when we finally stopped, and we did so only because our floating battlefield was slowly sinking lower and lower to the ground and RC's eye was bleeding.

I glanced up at the clear sky. "Guess we lost track of time."

Ash sheathed her staff and said, "I hope Madison isn't mad that we missed breakfast."

I shrugged. I was still peeved at my blood-family for yesterday's clash—yet another in a long procession that seemed to be piling up quickly. Who cared if Madison was mad that we didn't conform to her decreed schedule?

Kit skipped ahead of us to lead the way. Phantom Heights was stirring, but Kit was almost as masterful as Axel at maneuvering through the backways to avoid as many humans as possible. She guided us to Alvarez Park so we could approach Saros Manor from the back. As we passed the townhouses lining the northern edge, she said, "If we missed breakfast, do you think Mrs. Tarrow still saved some for us?"

"Maybe," Jay said.

Kit proclaimed, "Even if it's cold, that's okay. I hope she made scrambled eggs again!"

The twins seemed to be more interested in the surrounding trees than Kit's breakfast hopes. Reese tilted his head and quietly said, "That's a red maple. *Acer rubrum.*"

"And that one is a tulip tree," Finn identified. "*Liriodendron tulipifera.*"

They seemed to be talking to themselves, not us.

"Honey locust. *Gleditsia triacanthos*, inermis variety."

"And that's—"

Axel interrupted, "Did Ero give you a tree book before he left?"

"Yes," they chorused.

He grunted in annoyance, but I smiled. *How far Finn and Reese have come since that first day Outside when they thought humankind had built trees.* So much had changed since then . . . It almost felt like a dream. This moment right now didn't even feel real.

I gazed around Alvarez Park in a dopey trance, surprised to realize that we weren't moving. I hadn't even noticed that we'd slowed to a stop. My body felt drained and exhausted, as if I'd just experienced a severe adrenaline crash. The invigoration from our bout in the junkyard had evaporated. I shivered.

RC yawned and dragged his hand down his face. "That training exercise took more out of me than I realized," he said.

"You okay?" Ash asked.

He stared at his steady hands as if expecting them to be shaking, but they weren't. "I don't know. I'm low on power, but this doesn't feel like a burnout. I'm just really tired."

Jay turned in a slow circle to make sure we were alone. "I guess we can rest for a minute," he said. "We're already late for breakfast—doesn't matter if we're a few minutes later."

Ash plopped down in the grass. "It's a beautiful day, huh?"

I heard her voice, but the words were far away. It really was a beautiful day. The sun was warm, but a gentle breeze kept the temperature cool and comfortable. The birds sang clear, sharp songs to greet the morning above the soothing white noise of rustling leaves.

Kit crawled into Ash's lap and stuck her thumb in her mouth with a contented sigh. I succumbed to a yawn and sat down in the grass, then lay down on my back to stare up at the cottony clouds against the backdrop of blue sky framed by trees. Crows circled high above me—six by my count, but my eyes struggled to focus on the moving black specks.

This is wrong.

The thought tickled my foggy brain like a feather. I felt . . . drugged. It was an alarmingly familiar sensation. Black waves nibbled at the edge of my consciousness, creeping inward like a rising tide crawling across the sand.

Reese leaned against a multi-stemmed tree and stared up at the leaves. "Eastern redbud. *Cercis* . . . something." He slid down the trunk and slumped forward when he hit the ground.

"*Canadensis*," his blood-brother mumbled, slurring the word. He swayed, dangerously off balance, eyes already closed when he collapsed.

"Axel?" I whispered. My voice was thick, or was it my tongue? I wanted to ask him if he sensed any danger, but the connection between my brain and my body seemed to be out of alignment. I turned my head to discover Axel lying next to me. He was on his side, his eyes closed, his breathing deep, even though I'd never seen him sleep unless he'd been sedated . . .

I couldn't think anymore. It was too hard.

Something was wrong, but I couldn't remember what. Too tired to try. My body was shutting down, sinking into the grass, into the darkness, and I felt detached from it as my mind drifted on the summer breeze like a kite tethered by a frail string about to snap.

Wrong.

Something was wrong, but I was too sleepy to pinpoint what it was.

I just need a quick nap, and then I'll be able to think clearly. I'll just close my eyes, and when I wake up . . .

— Chapter Forty-Seven —

Missing

Madison looked up when Vivian hurried into the dining room.

"Sorry I'm . . . late?" Vivian hesitated in confusion, staring at the table filled with full plates of food but empty chairs. Wes was the only one keeping Madison company. "Where is everybody?"

Madison scowled. "None of them showed up for breakfast."

"They might still be training," Vivian reasoned. "Maybe they're running late, too."

"Or they're avoiding me because I raised a gun on Jay and Cato yesterday," Madison muttered. She stood and started to clear the untouched plates of food from the table. "Fine. They can heat up their leftovers and eat them later if that's what they want."

Vivian frowned as she took her place. "They must be really upset. I mean, Cato has been angry with us before, but he's always come back."

Wes shrugged with indifference. "They just need some time to cool off, that's all. No need to make a big deal."

Vivian stood. "I'm going out to look for Cato."

Madison remained motionless as she watched her daughter stride across the dining room, enter the foyer, and leave out the front door. She sighed and hung her head.

"Sit down, Maddie," Wes advised. "Enjoy your breakfast. Cato and the others will probably be back for dinner, and then you can make up and things will go back to normal."

Slowly, she lowered herself back into her chair, but her stomach felt sick. "I'm not so sure. This fight was worse than the others. I threatened to shoot Jay and Cato."

"To save Axel's life. Your heart was in the right place. I think they'll realize that in time."

Madison stared at all the empty chairs lining the long table. The loneliness expanded into a gnawing void that felt cold and bottomless in her chest. Without a word, she set her hands on the table and rose, then strode out of the dining room.

Her footsteps made hollow echoes in the foyer. Madison ascended the staircase and stopped at the third-story door, then rapped her knuckles on the wood. "Finn? Reese? I want to talk to Cato. Will you please tell me where he is?" She waited, straining to hear a noise on the other side of the door, but she was met with silence.

Madison knocked again, louder this time to rouse the boys if they were sleeping. "Hey! Come on, open the door. That's an order."

Her hand fell to her side. Finn and Reese wouldn't disobey a direct order from a human. They either weren't in the room, or the others were preventing them from answering.

She spun away from the door and marched back down the stairs, irritation raising her blood pressure. It wasn't her fault! Axel had been in critical condition, and she'd made a judgment call. Cato should be grateful that she cared enough to try and save the dangerous half-breed after all the unnecessary fights he'd caused over the last few weeks.

"I'm going out," she called when she reached the foyer. Madison stormed out the front door before Wes had a chance to protest about being stuck with breakfast cleanup.

Madison spent the rest of the morning and afternoon in her lab to keep her mind off the Alpha ghosts. Wes was right—they needed time to cool down, and so did she. Staying angry wasn't going to make reconciliations any easier.

She was so absorbed in her work that she completely lost track of time until Vivian knocked on the door. "Come in," Madison said absently without looking away from the microscope.

The hinges made a faint creak as the door swung open. "Have you been down here all day?"

"Hmm? Maybe. I don't know. What time is it?"

"Almost five. School's over, and I've been out looking for Cato for the past two hours. Why didn't you go out and look for him?"

Madison finally pulled away and rubbed her tired eyes. "If he's still avoiding me, it's a waste of time to go looking. Cato can come home whenever he's ready. I'm not going to play hide-and-seek with him."

Vivian crossed her arms in clear disapproval of her mom's answer. "What happened to your finger?"

Madison glanced at the bandage on her index finger. "I needed a control sample."

"For what?"

She hesitated, then reluctantly said, "To compare against the blood samples I have from Cato, Axel, and Tempest."

Vivian glared at her in stony silence for several long seconds. "How did you get their blood?"

Madison shrugged. "Doc and I retrieved Cato's sample from the bloody towels when I glued his wound. I had Emerton collect what he could off the street when Axel and Tempest were injured."

"And they have no idea that you're testing their blood?"

"I assume not. I won't deny it if they ask, but I wasn't planning on telling them."

Vivian shook her head. "Seriously? You don't think this will cause another fight when they find out that you took blood samples and are running tests without their permission?"

Madison chewed on her thumbnail as she spun her chair and surveyed the equipment on the counter. "Was Kit at school today?" she deflected.

"No. I'm really worried, Mom. This doesn't feel right. Trey went home to grab a quick snack, and then we're going back out to keep looking."

Madison nodded, the familiar pit of worry settling back into her stomach. "Okay. You get some food and go rendezvous with Trey. Check any places you think Cato might go. I'll talk to Chief Emerton and coordinate search parties with the raid team."

Vivian blinked back tears in her shining eyes, spinning away with a *swish* of her long hair before any could fall. She hurried up the steps without a look back.

Madison returned the samples to storage and put away her equipment. By the time she locked the lab and went upstairs, Vivian was gone.

Madison pulled out her phone and called the chief of police. "Hey, Em," she said when he answered. "I need to meet with you."

"Can it wait?" he said. "I'm just about to have dinner with my family."

"No, it's important. Cato and the Alpha ghosts are missing. Nobody has seen them since yesterday evening. I need you to help me coordinate search parties."

"Where are you now?"

"At my house."

"How long have you been there?"

"I don't know. Most of the day. I'm just getting ready to leave."

"Are you absolutely positive they're not back at Saros Manor?"

"Well . . . no."

"That's the most logical place they'd be, right? Especially so close to dinnertime?"

Madison snatched her keys off the counter. "I'm heading there right now. If they're still missing, I'll see if Wes can track them, but I still want to send out search parties." She slammed the kitchen door shut behind her and fumbled to jam the key into the lock.

"All right, keep me posted. Let me know as soon as you confirm they're not at the mansion, and then we can gather the raid team at City Hall and split off into groups to cover more ground."

"Got it." Madison hung up and tossed her phone into the passenger seat as she started her SUV.

She was grateful that she was one of the few citizens still allowed to drive in the city limits, but the ride was anything but pleasant. Even if the roads weren't a treacherous obstacle course of potholes, she had to drive at a frustratingly low speed and honk her horn multiple times to prompt pedestrians out of the way. People had gotten into the annoying habit of walking in the streets since police cruisers and the occasional ambulance or fire truck were the only sources of sparse traffic these days. Since Wes's house was in the outskirts, beyond the edge of reconstruction progress, many of the streets were still blocked with debris, so she had to take an indirect route.

By the time Madison navigated up the circular drive to Saros Manor and pulled into the three-car garage, her hands were shaking. *Please be here*, she thought in numb desperation. *I won't forgive myself if you needed me and I selfishly chose not to look for you because I was mad.*

She shut the car door, but although her mind screamed that she needed to hurry, her body didn't move. Her gaze slipped out of focus as she thought for a moment. Instead of going straight into the mudroom to enter Saros Manor, Madison strode onto the driveway made of stone pavers encircling a landscape bed. She cupped her hands around her mouth. "Axel!"

She turned in a slow circle. "I know you can hear me! Come on, I need to talk to you! Right now!"

Her only reply was a warm breeze. "Don't play games! At least have the audacity to give me an answer! *Axel*!"

"Fighting again?" a familiar voice asked.

Madison whirled. She stared at the man standing on the front porch in a two-fold midnight-blue cloak, a satchel slung over one shoulder, his sapphire eyes glinting in the late-afternoon sunlight. "Ero!" She beamed and trotted toward him. "You're back!"

"I am," he said, descending the steps to meet her.

"I'm so happy to see you!" Madison wanted to hug him, but she stopped short. Ero smiled and held out his arms in an invitation. She laughed to keep herself from crying as she embraced him.

Ero chuckled. "I did not expect such a warm welcome."

"Do kálos hug each other in the Ghost Realm?" she asked as she let go and stepped back.

"A forearm clasp would have been the standard greeting," he replied, although he looked amused by the experience. "But we are in your Realm, not mine, and I am happy to honor your customs. I brought you a present." He riffled through his satchel in search of something.

"Really? You didn't have to bring me . . . Oh. A rock," she said as he placed a crystal in her hand. "Uh . . . thank you."

"Not just a rock," Ero said with a smile. He reclaimed it and held it up. His eyes glowed, and the crystal was illuminated with a beautiful internal blue light. "It is the Avilésian equivalent of your light bulb. The crystal's luminescence is activated by an energy current. Right now, I am powering it with my ectoplasm."

He handed the crystal back to her. Madison lifted it in wonder to watch the brilliant light diminish. "It reminds me of labradorite," she murmured.

"It is called lumenite. We use it all over Avilésor. You seemed so interested in our culture that I thought you would appreciate seeing how it works. I brought one for Finn and Reese, too."

Madison's grip tightened over the crystal as the last bit of light faded away. She blinked rapidly to contain the rush of tears as panic resurged in place of jubilation. "About that . . . I can't find any of the Alpha ghosts. I-I'm sure it's nothing—we had a bit of a fight yesterday, so they're probably just avoiding me. But . . ."

"I see. You are concerned, and rightfully so."

She nodded. "It's not like them to be absent all day like this, especially Finn and Reese. I was hoping maybe they came home while I was gone."

Ero turned and studied the mansion with grim concentration, his blue eyes aglow with the power of his Divinity. "They are not here."

The words felt like a physical blow that nearly made Madison's knees give out. She raised her trembling hand to cover her mouth. *Okay. I can't panic. That's not going to solve anything. Focus on the next step. I need to call Emerton. No, wait. I need to talk to Wes. Get him to start tracking before the trail goes cold.*

"Where's Wes? Is he here?"

"Yes. In the kitchen."

Madison hurried up the porch steps and burst through the front door, then took an immediate left and marched through the dining room. Wes had, amazingly enough, actually had the decency to clean up after breakfast and reset the table for dinner.

When Madison shoved open the door to the kitchen, she found the werewolf skillfully managing multiple sizzling skillets and bubbling pots on the stove. If she hadn't been on the verge of panic, she would have been impressed.

"Hey," he greeted as he wiped his hand on his apron. "I thought I'd surprise you with— Oh!" His smile widened when he caught sight of Ero behind Madison. "Looks like you managed to surprise me instead. Welcome back!"

"I wish my return were under better circumstances," Ero said solemnly.

Madison blurted, "They're still missing, Wes."

"What?"

"Cato. Kit. All of them. Nobody's seen them all day."

Wes just stood there in an infuriating daze, completely unresponsive as he processed the news. Losing patience, Madison strode over to the stove and started turning off the burners. "Dinner will have to wait. I hope your nose is good, because I need you to track them down. I'm going to coordinate search parties with the raid team, but you're the best hope of finding them quickly. You can find their scent and follow the trail, right?"

Wes reached behind his back to untie the apron. He was still moving at a slow pace that made Madison want to scream. "I'll do my best," he said. "But I'm telling you now—if I catch even the faintest whiff of the Agents, I'm done. I am *not* going to risk ending up in a cage at the AGC."

"You really think Agent Kovak could have snuck into Phantom Heights and taken the Alpha ghosts without anyone knowing? He doesn't even know they're here."

Wes shrugged as he draped the apron on the counter. "As far as we know. There's one likely candidate I can think of who might have helped Kovak collect his lab rats under the radar."

"Who? Holly?"

He raised his eyebrows.

"Oh, come on," Madison said. "Holly can be a manipulative bitch sometimes, but she wouldn't sink that low."

"You don't think so? Who was adamantly against our deal with the Alpha ghosts from the very beginning? Who repeatedly threatened to report them to the AGC the second they made a mistake or failed to do their job? Whose political career was funded almost entirely by Agent Kovak? I'm not accusing her, just asking—have you talked to Holly yet? Do you know for sure that she didn't go behind your back and call Kovak?"

Madison ran her hand over the top of her head to smooth back rogue strands of hair. "Damn it. All right, I'll deal with Holly. You start tracking."

"I will join you shortly," Ero promised.

Madison was already calling Emerton as she strode out of the kitchen. "They're not here. Assemble the raid team and start the search. I have to meet with someone before I can join you."

She hung up before he could reply.

Madison's mind was whirring at light speed while her body acted on autopilot. So many variables could have gone wrong. Were the Alpha ghosts trapped somewhere? Injured? Kidnapped? They had a long list of enemies. But if they'd been involved in a fight, how did nobody notice? Axel wouldn't have gone down easily or quietly. Somebody had to have seen or heard something.

The thought of Cato and his lab-family locked in a transport truck on the way back to the AGC brought a wave of nausea that came dangerously close to vomit.

Madison realized that she was at Holly's front door even though she didn't remember the journey. She pounded on the door hard enough to send pain ringing through her hand with every strike, but she didn't let up until she saw a silhouette moving on the other side of the frosted glass window in the center of the door.

The moment Holly opened the door, mouth already open to reprimand her rude visitor, Madison caught the councilwoman's shirt in both hands and hauled her out, then slammed her against the doorframe. "What have you done?" she snarled.

Affronted and perplexed, Holly was helpless to do anything more than blink at her assailant before she came to her senses. "I beg your pardon?" she finally asked, her voice as smooth and controlled as always.

Madison pulled her forward and slammed her again to draw a grunt from her victim. "Cato! Where is he?"

"I suggest you take your hands off me before I call the police and file an assault charge," seethed Holly as she shoved Madison back a step. "I haven't seen your precious son. Maybe he ran away, did you consider that? He—"

Madison drew an ectogun. "Does Kovak have him?"

"How should I know?" Holly cried. Wide-eyed, she stumbled away, only to be followed with the barrel. "Look, Madison, I understand you're upset, but I didn't call Kovak! Come on, what good would that do me? Turning him over to the Agents wouldn't make me a favorable mayoral candidate, would it? Goddamn it, put that *away*!" she shrieked.

"Mom?"

Madison froze. A gaunt boy lingered timidly by the staircase inside the house, watching. He was dressed in sweatpants and a T-shirt, his brown hair still damp from a shower but already starting to stick out in every direction as it dried. Madison's jaw dropped. "Is that . . . ?"

Holly leaned forward to whisper in the ghost hunter's ear, "Yes. Axel tracked him down and brought him home to me last night. I owe him, Cato, all of them. I wouldn't betray them to Kovak, not after what they did for my family. You have to believe me."

Madison's gun fell to her side. "Axel found Greyson? Why didn't I know about this?"

"Because he insisted that I keep it a secret."

"They're missing," Madison said. "I can't find them anywhere."

Holly was staring over Madison's shoulder. Softly, she said, "I think we have a problem."

"I know. I just told you—"

"No. Behind you."

Madison started to turn, but Holly gripped her shoulders. "Not too fast. Don't act alarmed. But look at the woman across the street."

She let go, and Madison drew a shuddering breath to calm down. Slowly, she turned. A slim woman with short, red-tipped blonde hair was leaning against one of the maple trees lining the street, arms folded, subtly observing the confrontation. Upon noticing that she'd caught their attention, she casually pulled away from the tree and walked down the street.

"Tell me that's not who I think it is," Madison muttered.

"What are you going to do?"

"Beat the answers out of her, if I have to."

"Don't do anything rash—"

"Jules Pilecki is here, and the Alpha ghosts are missing. That's not a coincidence."

"But if she already has them, why would she stick around?"

"I'll be sure to ask that while I'm interrogating her."

"Madison!" Holly called, but the ghost hunter was already sprinting away in pursuit.

Jules glanced over her shoulder, then burst into a run. Madison gritted her teeth and pumped her arms harder. Jules might be younger, but she was a heavy smoker, and the habit had taken a toll on her speed. Even if her quarry had been healthy, Madison was operating on pure adrenaline. She was closing the gap.

Realizing that she was losing ground in a flat-out race, Jules veered to the side. She shoved open a door and barreled into a restaurant.

Madison blasted into the building a few seconds behind. Jules was weaving between tables of startled guests. A server dropped a tray of glasses and tried to scramble out of the ghost hunter's path, but not fast enough—Jules shouldered her aside, sending the poor girl sprawling across a tabletop.

"Stop!" Madison shouted. She bolted after her as Jules pushed through the swinging door that led to the kitchen.

Madison caught the door on the backswing and shoved her way forward. A wave of strong aromas hit her with the mouthwatering, multilayered fragrances of fresh garlic and onions, baking bread, cooking meat, and simmering soups. The kitchen staff was at a standstill—everyone was staring at the back door, where Madison caught a fleeting glimpse of Jules escaping into the alley. She drew her ectogun and continued her pursuit past the stovetops beneath yawning ventilation hoods, the rows of stainless-steel cabinets and shiny countertops, the white door of a walk-in cooler, the service window holding steaming plates of food waiting to be delivered to tables, and the dishwashing station filled with stacks of dirty cookware.

Madison threw open the back door, braced herself, and fired a single shot down the narrow alley before her prey had a chance to round the corner. The ectoplasm struck Jules in the shoulder, knocking her off balance and sending her sprawling. Madison took off again before Jules had even hit the ground.

As the intruding ghost hunter scrambled back up, Madison swung her ectogun. The butt of the gun connected with the back of her victim's head, and Jules went down again with a hoarse squeal.

Panting like a madwoman, Madison fumbled for zip ties in her weapon belt as she pinned Jules to the ground. By the time Jules regained her wits and started squirming in resistance, Madison had already secured the zip ties around her wrists.

"Have you . . . completely lost . . . your goddamn mind?" Jules demanded between deep, raspy breaths.

Madison dug her knee into Jules's back and pressed the muzzle of the ectogun to her head. "Where are they?"

"Who?"

"You know who. Why did you come back to Phantom Heights?"

Jules relaxed and rested her cheek on the asphalt, her diaphragm still rising and falling with labored breaths. "Just visiting. You have such a lovely town."

"I don't believe you."

"What are you going to do? Lock me up? Announcing my presence to a fellow ghost hunter is a courtesy, but being here without your blessing isn't a crime."

Madison ground her teeth. She didn't have time to play this game. Cato could be locked in Jules's trunk, or maybe she was holding him somewhere, waiting for Agent Kovak to arrive for the pickup. Madison removed her knee from the ghost hunter's back. "Get up," she ordered. "We're going to visit a friend."

Jules took her time rising to her knees. "I hope your friend is a police officer, because I have a few complaints about my constitutional rights."

"Not exactly," Madison said, seizing the ghost hunter's jacket and hauling her onto her feet. Madison dug the muzzle into Jules's back to guide her forward.

They walked slowly, both women trying to catch their breath, although Madison had regained hers after the first block while Jules was still drawing in ragged gasps. "I'm not a ghost, you know," said Jules. "I have human rights. You have no authority to detain me."

"If you aren't going to answer my questions, then shut up until we reach our destination."

"And where would that be? Do you have a secret torture chamber?"

Madison didn't answer.

"What happens if I start screaming for help?" Jules taunted. "How long do you think it'll take someone to call the police?"

"Try it, and I'll knock your ass out with a stun gun and drag you the rest of the way. And the police will help me carry you there."

Jules must have found the threat credible, because she didn't say another word. Madison maintained a firm grip on her captive's jacket with one hand while keeping the muzzle of the ectogun jammed into the center of her back to make sure Jules could feel it.

Saros Manor loomed ahead. Jules faltered when they reached the base of the hill, but Madison gave her a shove to walk up the dogwood-lined allée to the front entrance.

"Some friend you must have," Jules muttered as they ascended the porch steps. Madison opened the front door. Jules stepped into the grand foyer and let out a low whistle of appreciation. "Nice place. Don't tell me you live here. Does ghost hunting really pay that well in a small town like this?"

"Keep moving," Madison snapped, digging the gun into Jules's spine. Their footsteps echoed in the great room. Madison steered Jules past the bar and the dark fireplace, then turned right and guided her down the hallway, past the den and sunroom, until they finally halted in the doorway of the guest bedroom that had been depressingly empty for too long.

To her relief, it wasn't empty anymore.

Ero observed his visitors with a troubled frown. Jules, noticing his odd clothing and glowing eyes, instantly went stiff. "That's . . . a ghost," she said, her voice wavering. She balked, trying to back away, but Madison shoved her into the room and slammed the door shut behind them.

"You fucking *bitch*!" Jules screeched. "You're a traitor to humanity!"

Madison gripped Jules's leather jacket and forced the ghost hunter to her knees. "Find out where she's keeping Cato and the others."

Ero rubbed his chin, studying the two ghost hunters. "She does not have them."

"What?"

"Make no mistake—they are the reason she is here. But they are not in her custody."

Madison demanded, "Does Kovak know? Did you tell him?"

Jules glared at her in defiant silence. Ero said, "She did not contact him. Her intent was to capture them herself and claim the full reward."

Jules seethed, "Agent Kovak is going to lock your psycho ass in prison when he finds out what you've done."

Madison let go of the jacket and seized a fistful of Jules's hair, evoking a strained groan. "He's not going to find out. And you aren't going to tell him. Not after Ero wipes your mind clean."

Jules clenched her teeth, chest heaving as she glared at Ero, who appraised her with a stern expression.

"Obliterating memories is not something I am ethically comfortable doing," he said. "Unfortunately, I see no other alternative, given the circumstances."

He knelt in front of Jules, who shied away from him despite Madison's hold. "Stay the fuck away from me, demon," she snarled. Madison tightened her grip.

"I promise you will not feel any pain," Ero soothed, his sapphire eyes glowing bright. "Just a brief moment of discomfort."

Jules stiffened with a gasp, and then the tension seeped out of her body as her irises glowed blue to match the Telepath's.

"There we go," he said with a remorseful smile. Madison tentatively released her as Ero reached out with both hands and pressed his fingertips into Jules's temples. They stared into each other's eyes. "Let us begin."

Madison blinked back tears and retreated until her back met the closed door. Jules didn't have Cato. She'd come here to take him away, but someone else had beaten her to it.

Madison slid down the door, then drew her knees up to her chest and buried her face in her hands. Quiet sobs shook her body. Once again, she'd failed as a mother.

— Chapter Forty-Eight —
Chains & Shadows

Slowly, I pulled myself up from the depths of blackness.

My first conscious thought—*ouch*.

My veins felt as if they'd been flooded with cement. I cracked my eyes open, straining to focus on a bare stone floor. *Where am I?*

I remembered dozing off in the sunshine, but this definitely wasn't the park. I wasn't even sure I was in Phantom Heights anymore.

Pain shot through my stiff neck when I stirred. Apparently, I'd been in this position for a long time. As my consciousness returned, I became aware of increasing pain in my knees, shoulders, and wrists.

My vision wasn't working right, as if I were cross-eyed. The flat, shadowy floor prevented me from picking out a specific detail to focus on, and my neck ached so much I didn't want to raise my head. I let my gaze wander, skimming blank grayness until fixating on black smudges I slowly identified as a pair of boots.

I grimaced as I lifted my head. Up the pair of boots framed by a long black cloak, up the long legs clothed in dark breeches, up the lean torso, until I finally focused on a pair of red eyes leering down from a shadowed face high above. "Oh good, you're finally awake," said Azar.

I should have been petrified, and yet, I was so drowsy that all I wanted to do was lie down and go back to sleep. But something was holding me up. I stirred again, puzzled by the way my leaden arms wouldn't fall.

When I moved, a clinking rattle held me in place. I realized that my wrists hurt because manacles encircled them. I'd been forced to my knees—which explained the pain there—in the middle of the room with my arms held out to either side, connected by chains that bound me to the walls.

"You may leave now," Azar commanded, and I noticed another ghost—not one of Azar's usual uniformed Guards—in the room. "I'll call if your services are needed."

The ghost left without a word, slamming the cell door behind him. I winced at the *bang* so loud it rattled inside my skull and made me nauseous.

My skin crawled under Azar's gaze. He murmured, "Well, well. Look at you. The infamous Phantom—the great Demikan in the flesh. I have to say, I've been looking forward to meeting you. You've earned yourself quite the reputation, Cato."

"Have I?"

"Certainly. And I'm sure my reputation precedes me as well. I must apologize for our very first meeting in Cröendor. Hopefully, you understand that I instructed Hassing to hold Madison Tarrow's daughter as a hostage because I needed to neutralize the threat of the ghost hunter. I couldn't have known that girl was your sister. My sincerest apologies for that little misunderstanding. It wasn't a good first impression, was it?"

His words possessed an echoing ring in my ears. My hollow stomach was a dull, persistent ache that felt like an abyss. It hurt. Everything hurt. My whole body was as weak as it had been when I'd tried to end my life with a hunger strike. "I don't feel good," I rasped.

"No, I don't suspect you do," Azar responded in a light, casual tone. "You've been asleep for a couple of days with nothing to eat or drink."

I licked my lips, but my dry tongue wasn't moist enough to wet them. I couldn't even swallow.

Azar held a crystal-clear glass of water in front of my eyes.

I locked my gaze obsessively on it. As much as I didn't want him to see any weakness, I couldn't help it. Was he waiting for me to beg? I tried to swallow again and said, "You're bribing me with water?" My lips cracked when I spoke. When I licked them again, I tasted the coppery tang of blood.

"Not a bribe," he replied, sinking to one knee. "I don't want you to die. If I change my mind and decide to execute you, it won't be here. It'll be a public spectacle so I can make an example of you. Take solace in that, if you wish."

He tilted the glass toward my mouth, but I pressed my lips together and turned away. "It's drugged, isn't it?" I said, barely moving my lips.

Azar chuckled. He lifted the glass and inclined his head, as if giving me a toast, then took a deep drink. I watched greedily, and when he lowered the glass with a satisfied *aaaah*, I didn't need any further convincing. This time when he offered the glass to me, I leaned forward to accept it, lips pursed and ready.

As I guzzled the cool, clean water, Azar explained, "The man who just left goes by the name Sandt. He's an Oneiro, and I employed him to bring you here. His Divinity seems harmless enough, doesn't it? But he can decide when and if a creature sleeps, not to mention total control over dreams. Sleep deprivation is an underestimated weapon." He tipped the glass up so I could swallow the last few drops, and then he set the empty vessel on the stone floor and rose. "So are nightmares."

The water had cleared my head, but only marginally. "Where am I?"

"Avilésor."

"I'm . . . in the Ghost Realm," I mumbled, as if stating it aloud might make this experience feel more real.

"That would be correct, if you insist on using the human name for this world. More specifically, you are in the Prison of Szion."

His words took longer to process than usual. "And what are my charges?"

"Where to begin? Primarily treason, I suppose. But just for fun, let's add in multiple counts of resisting arrest and assaulting the Shadow Guard, resulting in deaths. Not to mention all the offenses you managed to accumulate during your little crusade as Phantom."

"Oh, is that all?" I asked with what sarcasm I could muster.

"It doesn't matter. The charges are irrelevant. My Prison, my Realm, my rules. You may not be familiar with how things work around here, but my word is Law. Honestly, it doesn't even matter if you actually committed a crime or not."

Azar exhaled to calm himself. "This meeting should have been under much more pleasant circumstances. We could have been having a civilized conversation in my office. Drinking tea, eating delicacies, sitting in comfortable chairs, and talking as equals. Instead, here we are, Warden and Prisoner in the deepest, darkest bowels of the dungeon."

He knelt again so I didn't have to crane my sore neck so far to look up. "Such a pity. I hate wasting talent. Power. Youth. I don't sentence many children to life in my Prison because they're brimming with potential, and who am I to smother that? Most of the Prisoners here are the filth of Avilésor, the low-level scum who have nothing to contribute to society. The only powerful Prisoners are the ones who chose to become my enemy. You are young, talented, and powerful, Cato. I don't want to throw all that away by keeping you here."

"Then let me go," I offered.

Azar pretended to consider my suggestion. "Well, I'm afraid I can't do that. But believe it or not, I'm not here to interrogate you for information."

I frowned. "Really?"

"Really. I already have everything I need to know from Jay."

"You're a liar," I whispered. "Jay wouldn't tell you anything."

"But he did. I know all about the search for the Origin and the intent to artificially recreate it as the ultimate weapon."

I closed my eyes, hanging my head in defeat and hopelessness that caused time to stretch into endless infinities between each heartbeat. This couldn't be happening. How could Jay betray everything we'd sworn to keep secret?

Azar rose and began pacing slowly in front of me, hands clasped behind his back. "It's the ultimate sacrilege, worse than anything I'd imagined. I want to stop the Agents from committing this atrocity. I thought we wanted the same thing."

"You don't just want to stop *Them*," I mumbled. "You want all-out war."

Azar paused. "I don't think you understand. The war has already begun. Humans initiated it when they hunted our kind, locked them in cages underground, and experimented on them. I'm simply fighting back."

I scowled at the floor. "You're twisting words to fit your agenda."

"I get it, I really do—I'm telling you things you don't want to hear, so you want me to be the bad guy. But I'm not, Cato. I just want to protect my people. Is that so wrong?"

"Yes. The ends don't justify your means."

"I am the villain only because that's the role you have chosen to cast me in. There are much better words to describe me—liberator, leader, guardian, savior. Then there's your role in this mess, protecting the very enemy trying to destroy my people. What does that make *you*?"

"I'm not protecting *Them*. I'm protecting innocent humans."

"Is that what you think? I don't require an answer—just give this some serious thought for a moment. Imagine how differently our situation could have played out. Would you still see me as the bad guy if, instead of running, you had accepted Hassing's first invitation to meet with me? If my Healer had been the one to save Finn and Reese instead of the human doctor? If I had been the first one to offer you protection? Think about it—instead of hiding from your enemies, you could have been strategizing with me to eliminate them, to rescue the kálos still suffering in that cruel laboratory, to destroy the place you hate and fear the most. Would I still be your villain then?"

I stared at his boots. I didn't want to consider that alternative scenario, but Azar was probably right—we would be in a completely different situation right now if I had followed Captain Hassing that night and agreed to meet the Warden.

My captor studied me for a long moment before interrupting my thoughts: "For the sake of the argument, let's go along with the ridiculous human fallacy of good and evil. You want me to be the bad guy. Fine. Who represents my inverse? The truth is that my adversary, whether you agree or disagree, isn't you—it's the Agents who locked you away and tortured you. Are they the 'good guys,' Cato?"

"No. I mean . . . no. I-I don't know."

"You admit, then, that this is not a fairy tale and our situation is not so simple. This weapon is an insult to our natural Divinities, and it's doomed to bring about the destruction of both kálos and humans. Look at the wars humans have fought over the course of their short history. So much death and destruction, and they don't even have natural powers. Imagine the devastation that would ravage Cröendor if they successfully recreate our Origin and harness our Divinities for themselves. First they would obliterate us, then destroy themselves."

"You can't know that."

"But I do. Humans have destroyed their world already. They polluted the atmosphere, poisoned the water, burned the forests, ravaged the land, and slowly but surely, Cröendor is dying. It's no wonder the fay have all but abandoned that Realm for ours."

"The what?"

Azar shook his head in pity. "Fay. Spirits. Honestly, your ignorance is unacceptable considering you're half-kálos and don't seem to have any grasp on your heritage or this Realm at all. You actually think humankind would be responsible with our Divinities? The Five Cities of Avilésor fell to the very power the humans are trying to harness."

I considered his words. Humankind did have a tendency to bring about its own destruction. It was in our nature. "Why can't there be peace between the Realms?"

Azar scoffed. "I'm still trying to figure out if you're noble, naïve, or just a fool." He reached for my right hand, and for a moment, I thought he was going to unchain me.

Instead, he phased my wrist gauntlet away to study the Mark tattooed on my arm. "Seven," he murmured. His thumb passed over the ink. "I'll admit, you've been at the forefront of my mind for a while, Cato. Or do you prefer *Seph*?"

The old name was an unexpected jolt. I didn't answer Azar, but I didn't think he had expected one. His red eyes were fixated on my Mark. "You've been . . . a problem. One I haven't been sure how to deal with. I wasn't going to stand by quietly and watch you take what's rightfully mine."

I said, "I don't know what you're talking about," but he continued as if I hadn't spoken.

"I did consider killing you. It would have been so easy when Sandt laid you at my feet. You wouldn't have felt a thing. Just gone to sleep, nice and peaceful, and never woken up."

The words poured from my mouth before I weighed the consequences: "I haven't come of age. It's against the law to kill me."

His eyes flashed as he released me. "I *wrote* the Law," he seethed, throwing my gauntlet to the ground. "Don't you dare lecture me on it. What spared you had nothing to do with Law. You're too valuable to simply kill. And then I got to thinking . . ."

Azar bent at the waist, hands behind his back, his long cloak trailing across the floor with the shadows so I couldn't tell where the fabric ended and the shadows began. "Blood of the enemy. Not only half-human, but also the spawn of a ghost hunter. You're one of the Eight, so how could you possibly be the Seven, too?"

I was so confused that I couldn't even form the bewilderment into a question. All I could do was stare as he straightened and started his leisurely pace again. "That's the trouble with prophecies. They're cryptic. They drive people to madness. You think you've got it figured out, but all your certainty does is blind you to other possibilities. I no longer believe you are the foretold Seven. Just a coincidence."

"What prophecy?"

Azar stopped and looked at me. "Seven to bring the Seventh, but Eight are the key. Your Future has been prophesized by one of the greatest Seers of the Sixth Dynasty. So, back to my initial problem of how to deal with you. This war is about to change the Realms forever, and you can't keep dancing around in the middle. You're either an enemy or an ally, and if I can't have you on my side, I have to remove you from the battlefield. I have no qualms about locking you away for the rest of your life. Let's think carefully about this, shall we? You have seventeen years, if I'm correct. The rest of your life likely means hundreds upon hundreds of years, long after the humans you love have died and turned to dust. While you are rotting inside my Prison, the Prison will be rotting around *you*."

Azar grabbed my chin and held my head up, forcing me to meet his gaze and evoking a groan from my throat as my tight muscles stretched. His hand was cold against my skin, and yet his grip was surprisingly tender. "But that's such an unnecessary waste," he said, his voice softer. "Just as I have the power to take your freedom away, I also have the power to give it back. You wouldn't have to run anymore. No one would hunt you. I can give you anything you want."

"Your price is too steep," I said.

"What is the price of freedom to you?" Azar challenged as he released me. "Throughout history in every Realm, people have waged wars and killed each other for the sake of freedom. How is this any different?"

"That's easy to say when you're sitting on your throne, ordering your foot soldiers to fight your battle."

"On my *throne*?" he mused with a smile. "You seem to have a serious misconception about my role here in Avilésor. No throne—just a modest office at the top of the North Tower. Once we reconcile our differences, I'd be happy to give you a tour and show y—"

"We aren't interested in your offer."

"*We*?" Azar's deep, booming laugh reverberated off the cell walls. "No, actually, the rest of your lab-family has already allied with me. Like I said, Jay and I had a long conversation, and he told me everything. *You* are the last one who refuses."

I frowned. The hunger and thirst were making me slow, but surely he was lying. He had to be—the twins would never turn against humankind. Axel might, but not Finn and Reese.

"I want to talk to Jay," I announced, studying Azar's expression.

He tried to keep his expression neutral, but I detected a hint of frustration as his eyes flickered in the dim cell. "I'm afraid that's not possible right now," he replied.

"That's convenient."

What was I doing, kneeling here before Azar, completely at his mercy? I wasn't a helpless human. I reached for my center, searching for the reservoir of power in my core. My goal was to become intangible and phase through the manacles.

Instead, pain lanced through my body. I cried out and let go of my power. The pain dissipated, although it left a dull throb throughout my muscles.

"I'm sorry we aren't as humane as the Agents," Azar said. He caressed his fingers along a metal collar that I hadn't noticed around my neck. "We don't have the technology to neutralize power. I could commission a Technopath to recreate their equipment, but this is effective enough for my needs." He exhaled, trying one last attempt to convince me. "You've been granted a great gift. You're a kálos now, Cato."

"I'm a human, too."

"Then what exactly are you? The Demikan, they call you. Are you a human with the powers of a kálos, or a kálos who can expel his powers at will? Are you both, or neither? Are you the only one of an entirely new species? If that's the case, then perhaps you belong with neither the kálos nor the humans."

I bowed my head. Azar raised a point that had haunted my thoughts ever since I'd obtained my abilities more than three years ago. *The Demikan* was just a title given to something that didn't have a name. What was I? And I still had no answer.

Azar, however, did. "I know you've been trying to find your place in the world. You might have claimed to be the champion of humankind, but we both know Phantom wasn't really a hero."

"That's not true."

"Oh, come now, Cato, let's be honest with each other. Every hero of legend is noble and selfless. But you didn't become Phantom to save people, did you? Phantom was born because you refused to let go of your perfect human life. You couldn't bear the thought of being shunned as an outcast, so you tried to separate your halves by creating another identity. Cato the human, Phantom the kálos. Two identities, two lives. But we both know you're more kálos than human, don't we?"

"No. I was born and raised as a human."

"Admit it—Phantom was the one who felt right to you. Your human half was the one that really wore the mask when you suppressed your powers."

"You're wrong."

"And once your mask was finally torn away, how did the humans treat you? They sealed you away in a laboratory. Locked you in a cage. Tortured you. Would they have done that if they considered you to be one of them? Why do you torment yourself trying to decide what you are when they already decided for you?"

I stared at the stone floor.

"You wouldn't be treated like that here. You would be an equal to every kálos in Avilésor. More than that, even. Here, power is everything, and you are very powerful."

Azar knelt in front of me, but I kept my gaze trained on the floor. He reached out and set his icy fingers beneath my chin again, then tilted my head up so I was forced to look into his red eyes. "There's something interesting about you, Cato," he murmured. "And I don't think you've realized it yet."

He released his hold on me, but I kept my head up by my own strength, tentatively curious. Azar continued, "It's my turn to be honest with you. When you made your first appearance three years ago, I had no interest in you. You weren't in my Realm, and from all accounts of kálos who encountered you back then, you were Level 2 at most. I figured even if you were a new species, it didn't matter. Your blood was impure, and you were weak in power, half of what a normal Cryokinetic or Sonic is. You could barely freeze a pond or break a window. But that's changed, hasn't it? Surely you've sensed it. I've confirmed that you're now on the upper scale of Level 4 and still growing."

"So? Power grows with age. There's nothing unusual about that."

"You're right," he acknowledged. "But not the way yours has."

"I don't understand."

"I'll do my best to explain. Usually by the age of four or five, a child's powers will stabilize at a particular level. Age is factored into our categorizing system, so a child of five years categorized as a Level 2 will still be a Level 2 in five hundred years. He would be more powerful, certainly, but still in the same category compared to his peers."

He paused, giving me a chance to ask a question, but so far, I was following his explanation. He continued, "At seventeen, your powers should be stable by now. If you were a Level 2 just a few short years ago, you should still be a Level 2 now. Jumping two levels at your age is unheard of. I'm sure the reason for that is although you physically have seventeen years, your powers have only, what, three or four years? Your Origin is not the same age as your body. It's still maturing."

"What are you saying?" I whispered.

Azar revealed that soul-chilling smile he was famous for. "I'm saying you believe yourself to be half-human, when in fact, you're less of a human than you thought. The more powerful you become, the more of your humanity is lost. You will no doubt mature as a high Level 4 or even a Level 5, which is fascinating considering your human blood should have diluted your power. And yet, you have not one, but two powerful Divinities."

He had a greedy gleam in his eyes. "Something incredible happened to you. Three years ago, I couldn't have cared less about you, but now I believe you will grow up to be one of the most powerful kálos of the next Dynasty. I don't understand why you ally yourself with the powerless human race after their betrayal. You aren't one of them anymore, and I think you know that deep down, even if you haven't been able to admit it yet. Just look at you. You're wearing our clothes. You don't hide your glowing eyes. You've embraced your power and started slipping out of your human bonds, but there are a few pieces still holding you back. If you would finally let go, you could truly be free."

I couldn't breathe. Could he possibly be right? Was I losing my humanity as my power grew? I needed him to stop talking so I could think without his poisonous words seeping doubt into my thoughts, and yet he continued, "You truly are something special, you know that, Cato?"

"So, what, you want to dissect me, too?"

Azar chuckled humorlessly. "Why would I want to do that? I don't care *how* this happened. My interest is in the end result." He tapped one finger against my forehead. "Humans look at you and see a monster, or a mutant, or a force that needs to be contained and controlled. I look at you and see a great power coming of age."

He leaned forward. "Congratulations. You've not only earned your impressive reputation—you've also earned my attention. If you ally yourself with me, I can make you great. I can teach you how to hone your Divinities to their maximum potential. We can destroy the Agents together and prevent a bloody massacre that would end both Realms."

I let my head fall again. "You want to enslave the human race, and I won't take part in it," I answered in a monotone.

I could sense the heightening tension as Azar stared at me in silent fury. "I don't think you understand. There's nobody in Avilésor more powerful than me—"

"Axel."

He blinked. Apparently, he wasn't used to being interrupted. "I beg your pardon?"

I glared at the floor and said, "Axel is more powerful than you'll ever be."

Laughter echoed in the cell, and yet it was cold, empty. "That supercharged mutt? I'm not talking about power levels. I mean authority. Influence. I just offered you everything. Are you really going to refuse?"

I didn't answer. The room grew darker and darker with each passing second. Finally, he stood, turned his back on me, and opened the cell door. "I'll let you think about my generous offer. But remember that as long as you insist on being my enemy, you will be treated like one. I think it would be beneficial to remind you why the Agents are our mutual enemies."

He slammed the door shut, locking me in the dark cell with nothing but my confusing thoughts, an empty stomach, and the heavy chains that bound me in my prison.

I shifted, testing the pull of the chains.

They were tight on my wrists—no way I'd be able to slip my hands out. And unless I spontaneously obtained Axel's strength, I wasn't going to be breaking the links or yanking those bolts out of the walls, either.

No powers. No one was coming to rescue me. I was in the Ghost Realm, trapped in the heart of Azar's Prison, alone. All alone.

I shivered. My humanity made me feel so helpless, like when I was in Project Alpha at *Their* mercy. What a peculiar thought. I'd been incarcerated for *not* being human, and yet, I'd felt more like a human in my cage than a ghost.

I made a fist and pulled at the chain again. The feeling of restraints holding me in place was all too familiar, and had I not been dangerously dehydrated, I might have succumbed to tears. The panic condensed in my throat instead, cinching it tight.

My miserable thoughts wandered to my mother. What were the last words I'd said to her? I couldn't remember, but I knew they'd been said in anger. Even if she forgave me—even if she was looking for me— she'd never find me here. I closed my eyes, feeling as low and wretched as I did the day I saw her signature on the custody transfer.

No sooner had my eyes closed than I heard the door open again. I sighed. Azar couldn't give me a few minutes of peace? I thought he was going to give me some time to think.

But when I raised my head, it wasn't the Warden I found standing in the doorway. It was the green-eyed ghost named Sandt.

He shut the door with slow deliberateness, then folded his arms and leaned against it, watching me. "Before we begin," he said, "I just want to say this is nothing personal."

I barely managed to force a swallow. "What are you going to do to me?"

He didn't answer. Darkness began to close in around me. Was this Azar's doing, or Sandt's? My eyelids were getting heavy. The pain in my stomach and joints receded—that wasn't so bad. I should have been scared, and yet, in the moment, I was grateful.

The last image I saw was Sandt's glowing eyes burning green holes in the shadows before my vision went black and I succumbed to his power.

To be continued

ACKNOWLEDGMENTS

Although writing itself is a solitary craft, publishing a book takes a network of supporters to properly bring the story to life. My heartfelt thanks to:

My talented editors, Kayla M. Ware and Nikki Mentges, who spent so much time polishing this story to its full potential.

Jason Anderson for his time and attention to detail while formatting the ebook.

My awesome team of beta readers—Gordon Glanders, Lorraine Tighe, Andy Ryder, Tom MacLennan, and Kim Noë—for providing honest and thoughtful notes on the rough draft. Many of these beta readers also gave feedback on the maps as I was finalizing the concepts.

The supportive members of my Patreon community: Renn Parker, Kim Noë, Harmony Todd, Kaitlyn Summers, Lorraine Tighe, and Silhouette Nimiane.

My medical consultants, Lana Glanders and Melissa Rendlen, whose expertise ensured that any scenes containing physical injuries, doctors, and medical diagnoses were accurate and realistic.

Sue Spitler for being a continuous source of inspiration and lifelong mentor. I'd also like to thank Jo Pilecki, the Lubeznik Center for the Arts, and the Sandcastle Writers for providing a safe space to write.

Silhouette, who has opened so many doors for me and made it possible to reach new readers.

My friends, family, and fans—everyone who has found a place in the pages of my novels—who have offered endless encouragement in both dark times and success.

Sara A. Noë is an award-winning author, photographer, and artist. She lives in a little cottage in Indiana with her cat, Calypso. Sara's writings have appeared in various anthologies and literary journals since 2005, and her poetry is available in the Indiana Archives. Her photography has been exhibited in galleries and featured on the cover of a literary journal. Sara designs and creates her own book covers, maps, graphics, and artwork for her novels.

A Fallen Hero, Book I in the Chronicles of Avilésor: War of the Realms series, has been critically acclaimed by The Prairies Book Review, Literary Titan, and NAM Editorial, among others, since its 2018 release. The debut novel made reviewer Lauren Gantt's Top 10 Favorite Books of 2019 list and won Literary Titan's Gold Book Award in 2020.

Phantom's Mask and *Blood of the Enemy* followed in their predecessor's footsteps and received a Literary Titan Book Award soon after their respective releases.

The story will continue with
Book IV:

Lab Rat

www.ingramcontent.com/pod-product-compliance
Lightning Source LLC
Chambersburg PA
CBHW022008300726
48970CB00003B/790